# BIOSHIFTER

*Volume One*

Natalie Maher

# Contents

# 1

# TWO WORLDS

Once again, I wake up trying to figure out which of my limbs are actually real.

It's my own special little form of sleep paralysis, and the fact that it occurs nearly every single morning has not made it any less terrifying over the years. I dream every night, though I don't usually recall it beyond a few vague feelings. When I do remember, though, I know myself as something vastly different. A monster with ten hard, claw-like legs, scraping away at something rigid, yet soft. Digging. I'm trapped underneath somewhere impossibly deep and horribly suffocating, and I have to get out but I don't know *why*. Every night, I learn to move my horrid new body in order to burrow towards freedom, and by the time I wake I've forgotten my old one entirely.

So here I am. I try to twitch a muscle, move a leg, but I guess wrong. I expect to grab and pull my covers off, but all I flex is a phantom. Next, I move a leg instead of an arm. I cycle through every part of my body, twitching and gasping for breath as the ever-present fear of never figuring myself out again screams in the back of my mind.

But of course, less than a minute later, I remember how to be a human and everything is fine. If nothing else, I suppose I rarely struggle to stay awake after all this. I get up out of bed with my heartbeat still hammering, and walk across the room to silence my blaring alarm.

Today's a school day, so I'd better go take a shower.

I grab some clean clothes, head to the bathroom, and strip down. The girl in the mirror isn't what the still-waking part of me expects to see, but she's nonetheless the same as always. My straight black hair and slightly thin eyes hint at my half-Asian heritage, but it's not super noticeable unless someone goes looking for it. I'm still pretty pale thanks to my mom's side. My little brother got way more of the other end of things. I'm fine with that, as I've never even been to Asia and my dad never talks about where he was born much anyway. I'm thoroughly American, which is to say I've lived my whole life in the United States and not, y'know, the thirty-four other countries in the Americas that we've decided to completely steal the title of 'American' from like the arrogant pricks we are.

Anyway, after a quick check to ensure I'm still me, I take a quick shower (defined as merely forty-five minutes instead of an hour and a half) and emerge to dry off, get dressed, eat breakfast, and put on a light coating of makeup before covering most of it with a facemask and dragging my abusively heavy backpack to wait for the schoolbus. I don't run into my parents for the entirety of my morning routine, since my dad doesn't bother to get up at the ungodly hour I have to go to school and my mom is already gone by the time I get out of the shower. My brother and I manage to share a single grunt of communication, but that's about it. The agony of waking is almost entirely forgotten. I understand that my dreams are pretty darn weird, but I'm so used to them that I find them even more mundane than simply going to high school.

So here I am, waiting at the bus stop and doing little other than getting annoyed whenever one of my yawns forces me to readjust my N95. I have a driver's license, but even as a senior I don't have a car to call my own. It doesn't really bother me; I don't like driving anyway. The bus is fine, and it's not as though it lacks good company.

"Hannah!" a familiar voice calls out, and I turn to grin at its source. Speak of the devil.

"Hey, Brendan," I greet him as my excessively tall friend happily bounds up to me. And when I say excessively tall, let me assure you I mean truly, exceptionally, *stupidly* tall. Brendan is six foot *eight,* which means my piddly five foot two puts me at eye level with his armpits... if I look up. The poor guy has not taken his growth spurt gracefully, either: he's worryingly thin and knobby-limbed, a complete beanpole without much in the way of shoulder width or muscle. He's got blonde hair, big goofy glasses, and that special kind of pale skin that makes you wonder if vampires are real. (They probably aren't, but sunburns definitely are.) I met Brendan in elementary school when I walked up to him out of the blue and declared that he had the same name as my rival in *Pokémon Emerald,* and therefore he was my rival in real life. We've been best friends ever since.

"How's the morning treating you?" he asks, his voice a bit muffled under his own mask.

"Just another refreshing day in the plague-apocalypse," I grumble. "Plagocalypse? You know what I mean. It's cold and I'm tired and my body's sore from sleeping weird and the planet is dying and there's *still* COVID everywhere and yet half the people we go to class with aren't even vaccinated."

"So... grumpy?" Brendan interprets. "You sound grumpy."

I open my mouth to answer, then close it.

"Yeah, okay, I might be grumpy," I admit. "Take my mind off it?"

"Sure!" he says happily, and immediately launches into a story about a Pathfinder game he's been playing in which his character— a mermaid summoner that can't walk so she sits on top of giant magical servants and rides them into battle—helped the party's sorcerer successfully seduce a sapient house by enlarging him enough to polymorph into an awakened gazebo. Which, of course, forces me to ask questions like "why do you need this sort of leverage on a house?" and "did the sorcerer agree to this plan?" and "if you have access to eighth level spells, couldn't you have solved this with dozens of methods that *don't* imply the existence of house

3

sex?" This, of course, means the story gets rewound a ways back to give me 'important context,' and things only get sillier from there.

Brendan loves tabletop games. Once he starts talking about them he will absolutely never shut up, and it's *great*. I love hearing him ramble about the crazy nonsense he and his groups get up to. I don't play much myself, but I've played enough to know what he's talking about and that's all I really need. I enjoy tabletop games, but I simply don't have the time for them. Brendan plays three or more five-plus hour games a *week*. It's basically all he does outside of school. Between my classes, my job, and my sort-of-leisure-time-sort-of-other-job, I haven't been able to fit in time for a tabletop game in at least a year.

Inevitably, the bus ride is over long before Brendan's story. This is entirely expected; I suspect this particular one will last through lunch period and the ride home as well. He can seriously talk about this stuff forever, and I find myself with a delightfully goofy grin on my face throughout all of it. Unfortunately, we have to go to class eventually, and despite the pleasant start I spend the day antsy and exhausted for no discernable reason. My body keeps trying to pass out, which is unusual for me. I didn't stay up late last night or anything. Perhaps I'm simply tired of bullcrap.

Still, I push through my exhaustion, ignoring most of the lectures in my classes in favor of simply doing the assigned homework from the textbook. I learn the same things that way, and it's a much more efficient use of time. I'd rather read than listen anyway. The teachers let me do it, too, since I'm getting straight A's and not bothering anyone. Pretty much all of the teachers like me for those two very simple reasons, and I'm happy that way. I go to a public school but it's pretty upper-middle class; there isn't too much in the way of nasty bullying, at least not in terms of physical violence. It still doesn't hurt to be one of the kids the faculty will actually go to bat for, though. I don't have the energy to deal with high school bitchiness today.

When we finally get to lunchtime, I'm both exhausted and absolutely ravenous. I bribe another friend to drive Brendan and I out to eat, where I purchase and eat three different hamburgers, against my better judgment. I just feel worse and worse as the day goes on, though. When school ends my head is throbbing and I'm itchy all over so I'm *probably* getting sick, but I just down a bit more than the medically recommended amount of ibuprofen and power through. I'll be home soon, and then I'll have to go to work. and *then* I'll get to rest. Not before.

"Hey, Hannahgator," my dad greets me when I finally get home. Apparently I used to bite a lot as a kid, so he's been calling me that since I was around two years old. And yes, he worked today, despite getting out of bed after I left for school and getting home before me. He's a dentist, and he works from nine in the morning to three in the afternoon. What kind of hours even are those? It's infuriating.

"How was school?" he asks.

"Fine," I lie automatically. "Will we have time to grab food before my shift?"

"Uhhh... yeah, I think we can swing that if we head out in the next few minutes."

I thank him and rush upstairs to drop off my school things, double-check my makeup, and quickly throw on my work uniform. Then I run back downstairs and hop into my dad's already-running car, and we head out to grab a Little Caesar's pizza, which I eat nearly all of in one sitting. What the heck is up with you today, metabolism? Geez.

"Anything interesting happen today?" my dad asks.

"Nope," I answer truthfully. Me feeling like crap isn't particularly interesting.

"Could you... maybe try to give me even two sentences to work with here?" he presses to my mounting frustration.

"I'm tired," I grunt. "I have a headache."

"Did you take—"

"Yes, I took medication. I'll be fine."

The conversation thankfully doesn't continue after that. I'm dropped off at my job, which is of course in the food service industry and therefore terrible. Money is money, though, and I'll need to earn a lot of it if I expect to be able to afford college and not end up in a crippling, infinite debt spiral. I work at what the industry calls a 'fast casual' restaurant. You know, the kind where there's no drive through and everything costs three times as much as McDonald's but they still have the food ready less than five minutes after you order it? (Or at least we're *supposed* to have the food ready five minutes after you order it.) Yeah, it's one of those. I'm working at the register tonight (oh goodie) so it's time to turn on Customer Service Mode and pretend that I'm happy to see everyone. Which, to be fair, I'm actually pretty good at. People can be *very* annoying, but it only makes things worse to take it out on them. Self-control is the key to a good experience at work. Whatever the manager says to do, I find a way to get it done, no matter how ridiculous or inane. It is, after all, work. I don't come here and expect to do what *I* want to do.

At least my shift is boring and uneventful. I really needed that, today. There aren't many customers so I just focus on cleaning the whole time, which of course makes my boss very happy. I've got to keep her happy so that I can be the next shift manager. They make two more dollars an hour, after all.

I carpool home with a female coworker I barely know and I don't particularly like. Thanking them for the ride, I get out and trudge inside only to get ambushed by my mother, who scoops me up in a hug that I tolerate with dignity.

"Welcome home, honey!" she coos. "How was your day?"

"It was fine," I insist.

"Your father said you had a headache?"

"I probably just need sleep," I tell her, both to reassure her and to hope she takes the hint and lets me go do that.

She, of course, does not.

"Did you have a good time at work?" she asks.

"It was slow," I inform her.

"Oh, I'm sorry. Days like that are always so boring."

I mean, no, you're completely wrong, I like the slow days. But I'm not going to say that, lest I receive that disappointed *look*.

"I made it through," I say instead. "May I go?"

"We've barely even started a conversation!" she complains. "I'm your mother, don't I get to talk to you at least *sometimes?*"

I don't know what to say to that. I'm too tired to find the right answer. Customers are easy to talk to because all of them want things and I can just give those things to them. But I don't know the correct answer here, and I'm taking too long trying to think of one, so I just shrug. Which is, of course, a mistake. I get a *look*.

"I've picked out more colleges for you to apply to," she says, and *that* conversation starts. None of the things she shows me look appealing, so I try to guess which one *she* seems to like the most and pretend to express interest in it. I guess correctly, and I'm rewarded with a slightly faster end to the conversation. If I didn't pick her favorite, she'd have tried to convince me to change my mind until I did.

Finally, I'm free to head upstairs. I walk into my room, shut the door, glance longingly at my Switch before ultimately deciding that collapsing into bed is my only real option. Which sucks, because I hate going to bed almost as much as I hate waking up. When the dream starts, it's just as jarring as when it ends. I haven't seen a therapist in years, but I did talk to my old one about my dreams. They were a curiosity, a strange quirk noteworthy only because they caused me distress. Nothing we tried ever stopped them, though, not even sleeping medication. And ultimately, my therapist and I both decided the dreams weren't really worth the effort to try and stop. They're disruptive and unpleasant, but... well, only for

7

about five minutes of my day. They never change. I'll learn to deal with them.

I sit down on my bed, peeling layers of clothing off. I know that as soon as I lie down, I'm going to pass out. So I hesitate, just a bit. But ultimately, I know I need rest. So I get under the covers, go to sleep, and immediately wake up as something else.

New sensations pound at me with horrid lucidity. They are familiar, but until now it has only been in that dream-like way where many things you've never done or never been feel familiar. Tonight, I remember falling asleep. Tonight, I know I am dreaming. I try to scream as alien sensations attack my mind, but find that I *cannot breathe.* Blood pulses rapidly through my body. I have a heartbeat but no breath!? I'm going to die! My panic rises higher and higher, and with it I take my first clattering steps.

Two, then four, then six, then eight, then *ten* legs all step forwards in sequence, each extending from my body in a radial pattern from my orb-like core. I look like a spider without a head, and I know this because I *see myself,* my senses somehow ignoring the pitch darkness and showing everything in a wide radius around me. It's not sight, not really. I have no concept of color, by which I don't mean 'everything is black and white,' I mean that color as a concept does not *exist,* I merely understand the shape and texture and composition of everything around me with complete ignorance of how it reflects light. This sense has a limited range, but it goes in all directions and doesn't care if objects are in the way: I feel myself, I feel the walls around me, I even feel the inside of my own body. I see my chitinous exoskeleton, the mouth at the bottom of my circular core, the way my many-segmented legs move in undulating patterns as I walk. I also see my tube-like heart and the proof I will not suffocate: openings in my body lined with thin, page-like structures passively let air flow over them to collect oxygen. Book lungs, they're called. I remember feeling a need to learn how spiders breathe once, so I looked them up. I suppose this is why. The lack of breath is a sensation I'm not sure I will ever get used to.

8

The area around me is much less interesting. I am in a tunnel, a jaggedly-dug tube traveling in a single direction. Everything around it, for as far as I can sense, is solid matter. It's layered, fibrous, and rigid. It's wood. I'm trapped inside a giant chunk of wood?

It doesn't matter. I need to dig. I know that in my... er, exoskeleton. (Oh god, I don't have bones.) My legs are sharp, and with my front legs—defined as the legs pointing in the direction I want to go, since I'm radially symmetrical—I start scraping away at the inside of my prison, digging great gouges in the end of the tunnel in front of me, consuming the shaved wood, and making progress cut by cut. It's relaxing in a way, almost meditative. My panic falls for the first time since my dream started as I work away, putting all my attention into being productive, into *doing* something, so that I don't have to focus on the horrid nature of my circumstances. It is the best kind of distraction: the kind I feel good doing. Even though the tunnel seems endless, I keep making headway because that is all I know. My body is tough. I'm not getting tired, even after what must be countless hours of work. The wood tastes horrible, but something about it invigorates me, fills me with the power to keep going. I'll eventually suffer from fatigue of the mind, but my body will not falter.

So. This is the nature of my dream. Is this what I experience every night? Will I remember this when I wake up? I don't know. I don't have any way to know. Despite the trance-like state of my work, I feel strangely... awake. It feels new. It feels exciting. It makes me think I'm almost there. This tunnel is impossibly long, but even as I start to get sleepy, I carry on. Something urges me to.

That's when I feel it. The end. I have been digging this tunnel *my entire life,* and I'm finally at the end!

I have been digging diagonally upward, I note. At the edge of the seemingly infinite wood there is a relatively thin layer of soil, roots, and what I can only assume are plants. The roots burrow deep, many of them worming into the wood below and eating from it much like I do. And above it all is glorious empty space, glorious *freedom.* The closer I get to the surface, the more of it I feel. Rolling hills, broken boulders, shrubs and grass and moss. It's like the plateau on top of a mountain, where only the heartiest of plants survive the thin air. Smaller animals wander about as well, making the toothy, lamprey-like mouth at the bottom of my core start to masticate with anticipation. Something to eat besides all this ding dang wood! I'm going to be *free!*

I hurry through the layer of dirt, avoiding the many rocks along the way, until finally I burrow myself to the surface! I pop my body out of the hole I've been trapped in, attempting and of course failing to take a deep breath. Still, I feel the fresh air flow into my body and wriggle with delight. It's so open and flat here! I feel the warmth of the sun on my body! I wonder how far I can… see?

I can't see. My lack of vision wasn't due to the darkness of the tunnel, I simply don't have *eyes.* Even though there is nothing blocking me, nothing but open space, my sensory perception simply *stops* at the same edges it did before, only showing a radius of about fifty of my body lengths in every direction. And as that realization sinks in, as my instinct to dig dies away to nothing, I'm left with nothing to do but recognize the utter absurd horror of my situation.

I am a monster, and everything around me is wrong.

The animals and plants around me are nothing like anything I know from Earth. It all looks relatively benign until it *moves,* at which point even the smallest, most harmless-looking critters undulate into warped nightmares, their bodies stretching and twisting around strange patches of barren land where no plants grow. Hesitantly, I move towards a small creature next to me, and it scurries off in a disturbing zig-zag pattern without ever actually seeming to turn. It's avoiding the barren patches, and I don't know why but it can't be good.

I shudder nervously. I've played enough *Pokémon Mystery Dungeon* to know where this is going. I'm in another world, aren't I? This is too lucid, too real. And try as I might, I'm not waking up.

I scuttle along the ground, my movements instinctive and natural unless I try to think about them. The prey around me—and it's difficult not to think of the creatures as prey—all seem to be much faster than I am, much better-suited to the zigzagging paths required to avoid the seemingly-dangerous barren zones. If I want to eat them I... wait, wait wait! Why do I want to eat them? Could I please focus on the absurdity of the situation right now?

I spin in a tight circle, rotating like an office chair as my legs easily scuttle to pointlessly reorient. I don't *have* a forward or a backward, only an up and a down. I have even less need of rotating to zig-zag, even though I don't really understand how the other creatures are pulling that off. And while yes, this situation is absolutely impossible, I feel hungry and tired. On the off chance all this is real, I should focus on getting food and shelter. And if this is fake, well... why not get food and shelter anyway? It's not like I have anything better to do, and the dream is denying me any control over my surroundings despite my lucidity. Maybe I'll manage to think up something tastier than wood fiber if I have to work for it.

I spend a while chasing smaller, herbivorous-looking critters, and though I start getting better at controlling myself I ultimately fail to catch anything. I do manage to chase a tasty-looking morsel all the way back to its burrow, but unfortunately it's too small for me to crawl my way in. I can, of course, 'see' into the burrow without issue: there's a thin tunnel down and a cozy little room at the end of it, which *would* be plenty big for my body if the way in wasn't so thin. Although... hmm. As much as I'm not a fan of digging, it would be pretty trivial to widen this hole enough to enter, stab the occupants with my legs, and swallow them up. I find myself weirdly excited about this idea, considering that it involves eating raw meat. I'd be disturbed to even *consider* that while awake. Plus... you know. More digging.

I spin around some more as I think, an odd nervous tic that I suppose I'll have to live with if this all turns out to be real. In the end, I decide to go for it. Whether these are my new instincts or the

11

pull of some strange dream logic, it's not as though I have anything else to do. I stick a few of my legs down the hole, yank on the dirt, and start widening the tunnel.

The occupants, predictably, do not like this. The fuzzy little things remind me of chipmunks, and though they chirp and yip angrily at me, I do not find myself particularly intimidated by the display, not even with two of them ganging up on me. When I dig far enough to stick a leg into the burrow proper, one manages to bite me. ...Or at least they try. The critter's teeth gnaw uselessly on my carapace, and a simple application of force is all I need to push the leg through the rest of its head, killing it. A shudder of mixed revulsion and satisfaction fills me, but I don't hesitate to do the same to the other animal. My hunt is successful.

Now then. How do I, um... how do I eat them?

My mouth is on the underside of my body, which is of course raised up into the air by my legs. My legs are sharp and not the least bit prehensile, designed for digging and climbing and killing, not object manipulation. I could stand over the corpses and then... sit on them, basically? That would get them in my mouth, but it just seems gross. In the end, I enter the burrow and scuttle overtop my prize, balancing myself on five legs while the other five wrap underneath my meal. I bring it up to my mouth with all the precision and gripping strength of a carnival claw game. I drop the corpse a few times, but ultimately I am successful. The meat is juicy and bloody and far more satisfying than wood fibers, though after eating both my prizes I find myself feeling... bloated. I guess I did just swallow at least a quarter of my own body weight.

Scooting down onto a not-so bloody part of the dirt, I curl my legs up under me, causing me to roll slightly like a ball. It's comfortable, though, and I feel myself getting tired. Freedom, food, and shelter. Today was a good day. Quickly and easily, I nod off to sleep.

...And I immediately wake up, my alarm blaring in my ears. I try to jolt upright and ready my clawed limbs for an attack, but all it does is cause my fleshy body to spasm wildly as every instinct comes out

12

twisted and wrong. I'm *huge* and I'm *heavy* and I'm *soft* and everything is shaped wrong and I can't feel anything around me and *I'm not breathing I have to breathe now I have to BREATHE!*

Air comes in, air goes out. I open my eyes. Air comes in, air goes out. I'm Hannah, I'm human, and I have no idea what just happened. My dreams... aren't normally like that. I don't usually remember that much. There's never that much *to* remember because I never escape the tunnel. Everything feels so wrong. Slowly but surely, I flex my muscles, reminding myself which body parts go where and how they move. It takes me a lot longer than normal, but I still get up after about six minutes to finally turn off my alarm. Holy crap, that was all so disturbing. What a freaky frickin' dream.

Yawning, I stumble into the bathroom, wincing with every step. My toes all hurt, I must have kicked something in my sleep. I strip down and hop into the shower, doing my best to let the warm water wash away those disturbing memories. It's calming. I like water. There's a reason I get up early to take long showers, despite all my complaining about having such little time. This is how I center myself and get ready for the day. When I have a good job and my own place to live, the first thing I'm doing is buying a hot tub. That's my promise to myself.

Unfortunately, the calmness quickly ends as the water in the tub runs red. I start to panic immediately. It's way too early for my monthlies (and it's been years since they could sneak up on me in the first place) so I have to be injured somehow. But where? Agh, my toes, of course! The pain is more serious than I thought! I squat down, pinching my big toe ever so slightly. A shot of pain jolts down my foot, causing me to let out a hiss and a small squirt of blood. I get similar results from every toe, and the more I poke at them the more wrong they feel. I think... I think there's something wrong with the bone. When I press down hard enough, it almost feels like it's poking out of my toe from the inside. Which would explain the blood, but... that's impossible, right?

What's happening to me?

# 2

# UNRAVEL

A frustrated pounding on the outside of the bathroom door startles me so hard I nearly fall into the toilet.

"Hurry up, Hannah!" my brother shouts at me. "I have to shower, too!"

"S-sorry!" I call back. "I'll be out in a minute!"

Annoyingly, I don't think I've even spent as long as I usually do in the bathroom today. My shower is already done, and I'm currently busy bandaging my feet up. I don't really know what's going on but I do not have the time to deal with it right now. School. Job. Rest. Repeat. I realize this is definitely abnormal. My dream was weird and now my toes are all simultaneously screwed up in a way that can't be anything other than a physiological issue. But there's still a chance it will heal on its own, right? Right. Of course. I just gotta get through the day. The alternative is heading to the emergency room, getting poked at by strangers, freaking out my whole family and just... no. No thanks. No doctors, and *definitely* no getting my family involved. I'll figure this out on my own.

I finish wrapping up my feet, steal our gauze roll in case I have to change them out at school, and get to completing the rest of my morning routine. My brother yells at me two more times before I get out of the bathroom, but screw him. Today's one of the days I really have to pay attention to my makeup. Also, my toes might be mutating.

15

I manage to limp out to the bus, enjoy listening to Brendan's nonstop ramblings on our way to school, and do my best to keep my weight on my heels as I stagger into my first class. Brendan, unfortunately, notices that I'm in a lot of pain. He's usually very unobservant, but I guess as he would say 'everybody nat twenties sometimes.'

"Is there something wrong with your feet?" he asks with obvious concern.

"...Yes," I admit, because as much as I don't want to have this conversation there's no way I'm lying to Brendan. "My toes hurt like hell. I'm not sure what's wrong with them."

"You seem tired today, too," he notes. "Maybe you should take some sick days?"

"I'll be fine," I insist, reassuring both of us. "It's a little weird, but... um. I'll tell you after school?"

Brendan hesitates, giving me that confused squint he does which means 'I think I'm misreading something in this conversation but I'm not sure what.' Which is usually my cue to explain something, but I'm *really* not up for an in-depth conversation right now. I hope he at least picks up on that much. He hunches down a little when no explanation is forthcoming, retreating further into the recesses of a hoodie that's somehow simultaneously too baggy and too small.

"...If you're sure," he agrees to my relief. "Don't push yourself too hard, okay Hannah?"

"Don't worry about it," I tell him. "I don't have work today anyway."

"Which just means you're doing your 'other work,' doesn't it?"

"Well... yes," I admit. "But it's still basically relaxing. And I don't have to stand up for that, so it's fine. Anyway, I gotta go to class! Bye, Brendan!"

He sputters a few of his usual protests about overworking myself as I run (or I guess quickly stagger) to my first class. I gratefully plop down in my seat nearly ten minutes before the class is

16

scheduled to start, partly because punctuality is an important gesture of respect but mostly because my feet hurt. People start trickling in shortly after, including my friend Ida who approaches me with the sort of shit-eating grin that makes me mentally place a parenthetical question mark after the word 'friend.'

Ida is a tiny and incorrigible bundle of chaos. The first word that comes to mind when I think of her is 'gremlin.' She's one of the few people in the school even shorter than I am, with a blonde pixie cut, almost childishly thin body, and mischievous glint in her eye that all combine to make me wonder if she was replaced by a fae as a child. She approaches with one of her other friends, some curly-haired gossip girl who carries herself exactly like the kind of person I tend to avoid for the sake of my mental health.

"Hey Hannah," Ida greets me with a concerning air of smugness. "Are you taking your autistic boyfriend to the dance this year?"

I blink, utterly blindsided. That... how *dare* she? She knows better than that! What the... why!? There's only one response I can muster which properly expresses how I feel.

"Fuck. You," I hiss vitriolically.

Ida just grins brightly, turns to the girl next to her, and holds out her hand, palm-up. The curly-haired girl groans, pulls out ten dollars, and slaps it dramatically into Ida's hand. Then she walks away, leaving Ida to triumphantly beam at my furious glare. What the f— what the heck just happened!?

"Did... did you just win a bet?" I ask Ida disbelievingly.

"Yeah, sorry Hannah," Ida says, projecting token contrition. "We were talking about you and she said you were too much of a goodie-two-shoes to ever swear, so I bet her that I could make you cuss me out after only a single sentence. And then she bet against me, because she's a fool."

Wh—really? That's it? I know I don't swear much, but I don't get why *anyone* would swear much. If you swear too often then none of your swears have meaning. Using them constantly is just intellectual laziness. There are better ways to indicate more general disgruntledness. When I tell someone 'fuck you' I want them to know I'm getting dangerously close to punching them in the mouth. Speaking of…

"You *don't* get to talk about Brendan that way," I say, glowering at her. "You should know better."

"What way?" she asks. "The boyfriend way? Because like, he *is* autistic, right? It's pretty obvious."

"That is *his* business," I snap. "Not yours, especially not when you say it that way. And the boyfriend thing isn't your business either, but you already know we aren't!"

"Okay, okay!" Ida says, raising both hands placatingly. It's not very effective, since one of them is still holding the money she won by betting she could piss me off. "I can see that I owe you an apology! I'm sorry for implying you are anything other than an absolutely massive lesbian."

"Ida I swear to god—"

"Let me make it up to you!" she continues, barreling through my fury. "I'll buy you lunch. No tricks, just girl talk. After all, thanks to you I happen to be ten dollars richer."

I scowl at her. She's a smarmy bitch, but also I am quite hungry.

"…Not wanting to date my best friend doesn't make me gay, Ida," I protest lamely.

"Of course, of course, yeah," Ida agrees in that blithe manner that means she doesn't believe a word of it. "So. Free food?"

"…I'll be ordering more than your winnings will pay for," I tell her.

She shrugs.

"Sure, it's your waistline."

Gah! She never cared about the money, did she? I've definitely been played, but I don't know how!

"Just... please don't test my patience any more today, Ida," I grumble. "I'm in a lot of pain."

"Aw, I'm sorry Hannah," she replies genuinely (for once). "What happened? You okay?"

"I... think so," I hedge. "It's my feet. I'm fine as long as we sit down."

"Alright," she nods, quickly perking back up. "I'll see you at lunch, then!"

Class starts shortly after that, and I do my usual bit of largely ignoring the teacher since today's material is all review. It's fine. Unfortunately, the next period is gym class, which is absolutely not fine.

I fit solidly in the nerd/geek clique and so somewhat predictably, I'm not the biggest fan of gym class. I don't really *hate* it, though. I'm pretty firmly middle-of-the-pack in terms of athletic capability, under all the kids on actual sports teams (and the marching band, all of whom are secretly kinda jacked). But not being on a sports team means I'm still in that group of people the gym teacher doesn't really care about. It can be... frustrating. But today, of course, I have bigger problems.

I head into the locker room and take off my shoes in order to switch to gym shoes and find my socks stained red. I grimace and quickly put the shoe back on before anyone can see. Wonderful. I can't ignore this. Running around for an entire class period would be an absolutely horrible decision. But if I talk with the gym teacher, he's going to send me to the nurse's office. And then the nurse is going to look at my feet, and then she's going to freak out and tell my family, and then...!

An unexpected surge of panic hits me, but I swallow it down. I don't know what to do. This clearly isn't normal!

"You okay?" someone asks me. What's her name? Amanda or something?

"Just ducky," I respond, my voice cracking just a little bit.

"You sure?"

I flash her my best smile, remember I have a mask on, and give her a thumbs-up instead.

"I've repressed worse!" I reassure her. It does not seem to have the desired effect.

"Well, um... class is about to start, so you should get changed."

I put a bit of pressure on my foot and decide that, regardless of the consequences, I'm definitely going to mess myself up if I try to actually run around on my feet today. My choices are to request permission to go to the nurse's office or to just ditch, and I'll definitely get an earful at home if I'm ever caught ditching.

"I think I need to go to the nurse, actually," I admit. "I'll go talk with Mr. Attenborough."

"Autumn, Hannah, you're late!" the gym teacher barks when we emerge. (Ohhh, her name is Autumn. Eh, I was close.) "Five extra laps for both of you!"

"Sorry sir, she was helping me," I say, doing my best to take the blame for her. "My feet are bleeding."

"Like blood-blood?" he asks.

The heck does that mean? What other kind of blood would I be talking about?

"...Yes sir, I have open wounds. Autumn was just helping me. May I go to the nurse?"

He considers this imperiously for a moment before nodding, because thankfully my school is not a ridiculous fantasy land in which gym teachers wouldn't get fired so hard you'd hear gunshots if they made a student run around while actively wounded.

"Yeah, get out of here," Mr. Attenborough grunts. "Autumn, you still get five more laps."

Wow! I guess he's still a jerk though! I whisper 'sorry' at Autumn and put 'making it up to her' on my mental to-do list just under 'scream into a pillow for four hours.' She just groans and starts jogging, which I suppose is an entirely fair reaction under the circumstances. Time to limp to the nurse's office, I suppose.

I stagger on over to the front of the building and let myself into the medical room, earning a pleasant smile from the nurse sitting inside. She is not wearing a mask. Why is our *nurse* not wearing a *mask!?* Like I know it's no longer mandated but... seriously? Gahhh!

"Ms. Hiiragi!" she greets me. "Welcome! Do you need something?"

No, I'm limping into the nurse's office for a social visit, obviously. How does she even remember my name? We've talked like, maybe twice ever. In lieu of a verbal answer I just plop down in the nearest seat and take a shoe off, showing the blood on my socks.

"I need to change my bandages," I tell her.

On the way here, I developed a genius strategy: pretend this is entirely mundane and that I don't need or want help. That's my strategy for most things, really. The more in control of a situation you pretend to be, the less people try to help you. I pull out the bandages I brought myself and remove my sock, carefully refusing to wince at the sight of the bloody red rows of gauze over the front of my foot. Why is it bleeding so much? Shouldn't it have scabbed over by now? I'm being careful not to put much pressure on my toes!

I try to angle my body away to not show much to the nurse, but I am unfortunately the only other person in here so I have her full attention. That's fine, it's fine. Just keep pretending it's normal. I'm careful to block the nurse's view with an innocuous hand placement as I peel the bandages away from my big toe.

I almost vomit.

No. No no no no. That's bone. That's *definitely* bone. Even as stained with red as it is, it's impossible to mistake the curved white structure as anything but a claw. It's grown since this morning, the core of my foot straining to gouge its way free of my flesh.

"Do you need any help?" the nurse asks, noticing me freeze up.

I barely register her words. My *bones* are growing out of my *feet.* Hesitantly, a numb horror moving me, I pinch the protruding spear of bone between two fingers. It's sturdy. It's not broken. I'm growing claws. Fuck. What the fuck. No. No no no no.

"Ms. Hiiragi?" the nurse addresses me again, placing her hand lightly on my shoulder.

*"Don't touch me!"* I snap at her.

She pulls back immediately, schooling her face into a calm expression and putting her hands on her lap.

"Breathe slowly, Ms. Hiiragi," she suggests.

What? Oh. I... I'm hyperventilating. I feel cold.

"Look at me," the nurse says. "It's okay. Breathe in, breathe out."

Numbly, I try to follow her orders. Breathe in, breathe out. My breath is shaky. My chest is starting to hurt. Wait, my *chest hurts!?* Am I having a heart attack!?

"I... I..." I start to stutter, but the words don't come out. "I f-feel..."

Tears run down my cheeks. Am I dying? What's going on? I'm growing fucking talons out of my feet and I'm dying and everything is insane and I can't speak, I *can't fucking breathe...!*

"You're having a panic attack," the nurse says calmly. "This is perfectly normal. I promise you're going to be okay."

Panic attack? *Panic attack!?* I don't get panic attacks, I'm not... I never...! This is so much worse than that!

"M-my chest...!" I manage to choke out. I'm dying. I'm dying I'm dying I'm dying...!

"Does it feel like squeezing, or stabbing?"

"S-stabbing!"

"Do your arms hurt?"

What? My arms?

"No?"

"Tell me if your arms or hands start to tingle," she instructs, as calm as ever. "Would you like to lie down?"

I shake my head emphatically no. I still have one hand grasping my toe, blocking it from her view. I squeeze it slightly, verifying that *the claw is still there.* I can't let go. I can't let her see it!

"Would you like me to go farther away?" she asks.

I quickly nod yes, and she scoots her chair to the other side of the room. Oh god I just walked into her office with an unexplained injury and started acting like a PTSD victim when she touched my shoulder she's going to call fucking social services. I'm an idiot. I'm a freak. I'm the world's stupidest moron freak and everything is going insane.

Okay. No. Hold on a second, brain. Calm down.

So I might... I might actually be having a panic attack. The more I think about that the more signs seem to be pointing that way. That's, um... that's good, right? Better than a heart attack, haha.

Yeah, no, this doesn't feel good at all. This is hell. I must be going insane, I would never... I mean. Okay so panic attacks *are* normal. Intellectually, I know that. But I feel weak and pathetic anyway. This isn't something that should be happening to me. I should be *better* than this. I know that's a horrible thing to think but it still claws at my mind anyway.

I shudder. Ugh. 'Claws.' What a horrible choice of words.

It takes another couple minutes that feel like eternities, but my breathing starts to stabilize. My aching chest starts to dull down, and the tears running down my face start to dry. I did not, it would seem, have a heart attack. Oh boy!

I still have talons, though, so as soon as my hands stop shaking I bind my toe back up. The nurse waits patiently while I do so, likely not wanting to be the first to address me after I asked her to give me some space. Credit to her, she probably *has* dealt with this before. She seems in her element. I finally turn to face her once I finish my patch job.

23

"S-sorry," I manage to choke out, because 'thank you' feels foreign and wrong.

"You have nothing to apologize for," the nurse tells me firmly. "Have you ever had a panic attack before?"

"No," I admit. "Never."

"Well, like I said, it's normal," she assures me. "Downright common, really. Now if you're comfortable with it I'd really like to take a look at your f—"

"N-no!" I blurt immediately. "I... I don't consent."

She sighs slightly, but nods.

"Okay," she allows. "Well then, if nothing else you should definitely rest. I'm going to write you an attendance exemption. Feel free to take as long as you need in here. There are cots you can lie down on in the room next door. Are you comfortable walking?"

"Yes," I tell her, and stand up to prove it. "I... I'm fine."

I'm *fine.*

"Then rest well, Ms. Hiiragi."

"C-call me Hannah," I tell her. "Please."

"Hannah, then," she agrees, and I walk next door and collapse into a cot.

Immediately, I realize I've made a mistake. Because I'm *exhausted.* The cot isn't very comfortable, but my panic-addled body doesn't care and demands rest immediately. I'm very much the kind of fallen-log sleeper that can immediately pass out pretty much anywhere I lie down, so if I'm not careful I might end up... I might... I...

...

I shudder as I suddenly become aware of my surroundings without ever opening my eyes. I'm in an underground burrow, all ten of my legs curled up in a ball. My stomach growls at me, and I roll slightly as it causes me to flinch.

Dang it. I'm here again.

I have a mouth, but I still can't scream. I settle for uncurling my body and furiously clawing at the walls, trying to make my silent despair known through violence. I'm here again! *I'm here again!* It's all real, isn't it? It's either real or I'm sobbing somewhere in a padded cell! *What is happening to me!?*

Unfortunately, my silent tantrum is soon interrupted by strange, quiet noises that catch the edge of my attention. At least I can still hear things that are outside my weird sensory bubble. And if I'm not mistaken, what I hear sounds like... voices.

Not English-speaking voices, of course, it's all gibberish to me. But the sounds absolutely have the complexity and the back-and-forth between speakers that I associate with language. The voices themselves even sound pretty close to human, albeit not speaking any Earth language I know of. It sounds like there's two men and one woman, and their conversation seems to be entirely congenial. Of course, I'm recently coming down from a panic attack and I'm also currently shaped like a horrible little ball-spider monster, so I'm less than confident that a social interaction is going to go well for me. Not to mention that if this is some freaky fantasy world (and it certainly appears to be), this could just as easily be a terrifying voice-mimicry monster as it could be a person. Brendan has told me harrowing stories about those! As such, I opt to wait inside my burrow as the voices continue to approach.

They start to get quieter as they get closer, and eventually the voices stop. I don't find this particularly reassuring. And sure enough, when something finally steps into my range, I can't help but shudder with terror. I am clearly looking at a monster.

The three creatures that approach me are vaguely humanoid, in that they seem to have arms, legs, a torso, a head... you know, human stuff. But the closer I look, the more twisted and distorted it all becomes. What I thought was clothing on two of the figures is actually a thick coat of fur, and they have two extra arms, long and low-hanging. Though the third doesn't have any such alien features

25

(even, seemingly, on the inside of his body; it all looks like human anatomy to me) he walks in front, and as he does his visage warps horribly, shifting and stretching and twisting as he moves like he's a reflection in a funhouse mirror. The others suffer similar horrid twists of body, and the worst is when they pass over one of the barren zones. These creatures are far bigger than anything else around, so large that I could barely reach their knees if I stretch my body as tall as I can go. As such, they don't zig-zag around the smaller barren zones because they can't. They're too large. Instead, they just... unravel. Their bodies twist and warp like horrid flesh monsters as they split open their own foot so it lands evenly on either side of the barren zone.

The horrid creatures have stopped talking entirely, though sometimes they turn to look at each other and make what I can only assume would be facial expressions on a body not twisted into a Cronenberg horror creature. One of them points at my exact hiding spot.

For the second time today, I'm certain I'm about to die.

I watch as the mostly-human-looking one kneels down and holds out its hand. Not at me, though; it seems to be pointing at nothing in particular. Yet then I notice one of the small animals nearby halt and start slowly walking towards them. It seems hesitant and stiff, undulating around the barren spots of land as it approaches the monsters.

It stops right in front of the hand, leans forward, and nuzzles it. The monster pets it kindly. And then its partner stabs it in the brain with a spear that seemed to materialize out of nowhere.

Oh god.

I'm not moving. I am completely, utterly still, curled into my little hole as I pray to whatever horrid god brought me here to make this stop. I'm just a little spider-ball! Don't mind me! But my prayers, of course, go unanswered, as any god horrible enough to make this world clearly isn't interested in preventing my suffering. The corpse of the small animal is set gently outside my den. The smell of it is enticing. Then the monster stretches out its hand to me, and waits.

I... am being baited. I'm obviously being baited. There's no fucking way I'm going out there! In fact, maybe I can dig myself a different exit? Crap, I should have been doing that this entire time! I turn to face a wall before remembering that the concept of turning isn't really a thing for my body, and scrabble away at the back of the burrow. Just as I start, however, a nagging feeling starts to itch its way into my head.

*What if they're friendly?*

Haha, what? I just saw them murder a little creature, and I am currently a little creature! Nope, no way.

*They have food. They're friendly.*

That's... no. What? That is bait. That is a trap. No thanks. Except, y'know, what if it's not a trap? I *am* pretty hungry. They could be friends. Friendly friendly friends. They're nice and I should go to them. Yes, that makes sense. A refreshing breeze wafts over my body as I step out of the burrow, right in front of them. How nice of them to bring me a me... a... how nice of them to... to... to get me...

A freakish, twisted thing that looks like a hand run through a taffy machine reaches forward to pet the top of my carapace. This is wrong. It's wrong. No, it's fine. They're friends. *They're not friends, they just killed something by doing this!* But not me though. They only killed that animal to feed me. I'll be fine. It's fine. They're friends!

The hand touches me. I freak out and bolt.

I don't even think about it, I just sprint away. This seems to startle the monsters, and as a result I feel the fog on my mind disappear with a jolt. Holy crap, did I just get siren song'd? Does this world have *predators with mind magic?* Crap crap crap crap!

The monsters recover from their surprise quickly and give chase, which is *extremely bad* because I'm currently very small and their legs are very long. They are absolutely going to catch up to me in a footrace. Worse, a bunch of those barren patches are coming up, and I still don't know what sort of horrible thing happens if I step in them!

I swerve to avoid the first one, and my pursuers twist to do the same. What *are* they? How the heck do their bodies work? They look like they're being constantly warped by a weird instagram filter. There's no time to consider it, though, because they're still gaining on me! If I don't do something, they *will* catch me. In front of us is a particularly large patch of barren terrain. Going around it will require me to drastically change direction and move in a wide arc around it. Going through it, however... I mean, I have no idea what could possibly happen to me in that case. But surely, nothing lives in the barren patches for a reason?

Well, I suppose I should just stop running, then. The ones behind me are going to catch me no matter what, and they just want to be friends!

I almost start to slow down before I catch myself, a redoubling panic casting the foreign thoughts out of my mind. You know what? Better the unknown problem in front of me than the certain mortal danger behind me! When we reach the next barren patch, I don't swerve around it. I go straight.

My legs skitter across the empty space, no longer impeded by errant rocks or inconveniently-placed shrubs. Instead, I note there's only solid wood underneath me, the same kind of wood that I dug through before reaching the surface last night. Well, last Earth night. I don't have any idea if it's day or night here in this world, or if the concept of day and night even exists. Though I suppose I recall feeling the sun on my chitin when I first stepped outside. I think there was something that felt like sunlight while I was running away, too.

There isn't any sunlight anymore.

It's cold here, very cold. Not uncomfortably so, but the difference in temperature is immediate and stark. The monsters behind me skid to a stop as I pass into the barren patch, looking around with apparent confusion, as if they can no longer see me. Maybe they can't? Are these areas some kind of dark patch or something? That could explain why no plants grow here, but there's no *dirt* either. Just wood.

Either way, my pursuers have stopped. That's great news, but I'm going to keep on running! I dash to the other side of the barren patch, but the moment I step back out on normal ground the monsters seem to spot me and they start chasing me again! Gah!

I duck onto a different barren patch nearby and the monsters slow down, jogging up to the intersection between the normal ground and the barren ground and stopping to wait, once again with apparent confusion. I slow to a stop and wait. They begin to babble at each other as I watch. I scuttle in a terrified circle, realizing suddenly that my body is incredibly tired. Just that short little run really took it out of me, which does not bode well for my escape chances.

The monsters start to pace around the barren patch, sometimes in a normal circle but often in horrid, jittery warping movements where they seem to stretch along the outside of the barren zone like a shadow crawling up a wall. They're pinpointing me somehow, but they don't ever step inside. It seems like their bodies might be physically incapable of it. I can hide from them here. They can't come in. I'm safe. But I'm also hungry, and this area is barren. My singular valve of a heart beats rapidly as my panic starts to come out of fight-or-flight mode. I can rest and think a little, but I can't stay here forever.

What's my next move?

# 3

# PERSISTENCE

*They're friendly,* my mind insists. *Just go to them.*

Even in the chill of the barren zone, my body feels like it's burning from my recent death-defying sprint. I need water, food, and rest, but even though I'm hiding somewhere safe I don't think I'll be able to get any of them.

*Of course you're safe. They're friends.*

...Because the longer I stay here, the more insistent those voices become. The three horrific monsters know where I am. They've been stalking around the barren zone, and while they seem unable to enter they're certainly able to call out to me with that... I don't know what it is. A charm spell, I guess? Charm spells make someone your friend while Dominate spells directly and completely remove agency from someone, at least in *Dungeons and Dragons*. What's happening to me reminds me of the former, and by extension the few times I've seen it used in those games and the many times Brendan has described shenanigans involving them. Ultimately, when you think about it, there's not much point in using a charm spell on someone if you plan on killing them. So they probably *actually* just want to be friends, and I should—Gah! Not this again!

Okay, I need to get out of here. I need to move. Ignoring my painfully protesting body, I get back to my feet and start planning a route. They're faster than me, sure, but so far nothing bad has happened in this barren area, they can't seem to enter barren areas, and there are barren areas absolutely everywhere. As far as I can see (which is admittedly only like fifty feet or so, assuming the human-shaped monsters are human height) the barren areas are interspersed seemingly at random with the normal landscape. Most barren areas are very small, but some are huge and I bet I can take advantage of them to escape my pursuers. It'll be just like a stealth game: the bad guys can't see me as long as I'm in the darkness. I'll clown on these monsters like they're the stupid guards in *Metal Gear Solid*. Right? Right. Of course. Let's just ignore the fact that MGS guards are AI designed to provide the player a challenge and not actual intelligent creatures designed, presumably, to catch and eat me. I mean, they probably won't eat me. If they wanted food they could just catch more fantasy chipmunks. I bet they just want to be fr—

Agh, no no no! Running! It's running time!

I burst out of the barren zone, skittering as fast as I can to the next largest one close by. One of the monsters cries out and points at me, then all three give chase, rapidly gaining on me until I manage to enter the next barren zone. I keep sprinting straight while my pursuers have to zig-zag, putting a healthy amount of distance between us before I'm out the other side, rushing to the next zone. This is working. I can outpace them this way!

Or at least I could if it didn't hurt so much.

I'm definitely making distance, but the longer I run the worse I feel. I'm not the most athletic person in the world, but I've never struggled this much before. My muscles burn like I've just jogged a mile. I barely have any stamina. Terror is just about the only thing moving my legs at this point. I can't sprint for much longer. If I stop running they'll catch me and I'll die, but I have to stop, but I *can't* stop...!

I stagger into another barren zone, slowing down to a crawl but resisting the urge to collapse on the spot. I'm burning up. Why? Why am I so weak? I feel lightheaded, insofar as I can feel that way without a head. I'm so hot, I'm too hot. I have to rest. I... I can't breathe.

Wait. That's right. I can't breathe. My body is making a lot of heat when I run but I have no way to cool down. I can't sweat, I can't even pant for air. I'm cold-blooded, I can't thermoregulate without using my environment, and while it's nice and cool in these barren zones my mad sprint for my life is still overheating me. I'm not built for this.

Again, I desperately wish I could scream. If my brain is working well enough to analyze why I'm screwed, maybe it could think of a way to survive this!? Yet thinking too hard about my body only brings attention to how impossible my current situation is, mixes up my legs and makes me worse at running! How am I even moving this naturally? It feels like I've been a freaky ball spider for my entire life. Were those stupid dreams seriously all real? How? What the fuck *is* any of this!?

Maybe I should go ask my new friends.

I claw at the ground, a wave of panic pushing me to focus. No. Screw this. I just have to keep going. I'm not getting mindfucked by monsters! Again, I start to sprint. Pain wracks through my body, every part of me feeling sick. Skittering out of my safe zone, I'm immediately chased. Why do they keep following me!? Why won't this *end?* I suppose it can end easily. I could just turn around and be done with this. I could just make some new friends... No! Agh! Get out! Get out of my head! Get out get out get out *I need to get away!*

The ground grows steeper as I flee, the tundra slowly becoming less plateau and more mountain. This is awful, but it's an awful that works somewhat in my favor. My small size means that going uphill is less of an impediment to me than it is for my huge pursuers. It just doesn't really matter, because I'm dead on my feet. I don't really have a good grasp on what my body's limits are but I am being pushed well past them, every part of me screaming for mercy as my mind starts to get foggier and slower. How long has it been? Hours? More? I don't feel the sun on my carapace when I'm outside

33

a barren zone anymore, which means it's probably nighttime. Another thing that helps me out but doesn't seem to matter. The monsters behind me have slowed down a lot, not really bothering to exert themselves as they stalk me. I'm just forced to flee without rest or food, over and over, as their long legs and the permanent threat of mind magic inevitably catch up with me.

Maybe I'm dying. Wouldn't that be funny? Dying of exhaustion while trying to escape my death. I'm not even running anymore, just staggering painfully forwards. I think... I think I might be starting to pass out. But I can't sleep here. They'll find me. They'll worm their way into my brain while I rest. Or just stab me. Whichever is worse. I have to keep moving. Keep going until they give up. I have to move. I have to. Just... just another step. It hurts. I can't... I can't move.

They're gaining on me. I'm going to die. I'm going to—

*Bong. Bong. Bong. Bong.*

My eyes shoot open as the school bell rings, signifying the end of second period and the start of lunch. A cold sweat covers my body in a disgusting, sticky film. Wait, how am I sweating? Why am I so heavy? I'm in bed! But I'm at school? What...

Right. Right, right, right. Nurse's office. Human stuff. I'm Hannah and I'm human and as real as that horrible nightmare felt, I... hah. Yeah, no. As I twitch my muscles and get a handle on being me again, I can already tell that there's no way I'm convincing myself that what happened isn't real. There would be no way I could do that even if I *wasn't* growing claws out of my body, but that's *also* a thing that's happening. I shudder with stress and pull myself into a sitting position, grabbing my gauze roll and forcing myself to look at my feet again. Still bloody, though they don't feel as wet.

Last I was awake, I had a panic attack and thought I was dying. Then, when I fell asleep, I *actually* almost died. Perhaps I am dead in the other world. What happens to me if I die there? Do I die here, too? Do the dreams stop? Or do they just get replaced with something else? Perhaps I'll find out tonight.

34

Perhaps I'll die tonight. There... there really is a solid chance I will die the next time I fall asleep.

I can't keep my hands steady as I peel the bandages off my feet, though fortunately the shaking merely makes the task annoying rather than impossible. My feet are naturally still a bloody mess, but they don't ache as badly as they did when I passed out and the blood seems to be drying. The claws are obvious now, curved and prominent. Flexing my toes only elicits a dull ache, as does prodding at the base where they connect to my flesh.

The claws have entirely replaced my toenails, but they aren't mere extensions to the nails themselves. Thick and talon-like, they have grown to encompass most of the end of each toe, the sharp, thick bone protruding like a horn and curving down to claw at the ground. I take an experimental step, and a resounding click echoes in the room as my feet scrape at the porcelain flooring. I glance hesitantly out the small window in the door, seeing the nurse still buried in other work. I need to be careful. If anyone walks in here now, the freakish mutation will be obvious.

...Also the blood. I should really clean them. Keeping an eye on the nurse, I get up and rifle through the nearby cabinets, most of which are locked but one of which thankfully has some alcohol swabs. I shamelessly steal them and start to wipe my feet clean, yet another task made frustrating but not impossible by my shaking hands. There's only one way in or out of the room, and I'm positioned carefully on the bed so that the blankets are poised to block the view of anyone coming in through the door. My now-clean claws are both more and less horrifying to look at than my bloody ones, a pristine ivory white that contrasts even the relative paleness of my skin. They are undoubtedly real, undoubtedly talons, and if not for how much worse my recent experience as a radially symmetrical spider monster was, I'd undoubtedly be having a second panic attack right now. Instead, I only feel that classic full-bodied tension that borders on the edge of painful with how tight all my muscles are. Just thinking about my dream pumps my body full of adrenaline, making me feel jittery and frayed. I'm also *starving,* which no doubt compounds the issue significantly.

I guess I should probably go get some lunch.

My cleaning done, I bandage my feet back up in case the scabs break, put my bloody socks back on, and put my shoes on over them. They don't fit right anymore, thanks to the extra half inch or so of bone jutting out of the end of my toes. Even worse, putting any pressure on my foot causes the talons to poke through the bandages and socks, digging into the sole of the shoe. It's a horrifying, alien feeling that feels equal parts terrifyingly impossible and worryingly pleasant. Little tingles crawl up my toes as my claws dig into something soft. That's... you know what, I'm just not going to think about that.

I napped through the entirety of second *and* third period, so while I feel jumpy and stressed I am at least no longer exhausted. I politely thank the nurse, still angry at her for not wearing a mask during a pandemic but also undeniably thankful that she was around when I had that... panic attack. Even if it's painfully embarrassing to have been seen like that. She once again asks to look at my feet. I insist that they're no longer bleeding (which is true, at least for now) and that it's nowhere near as bad as it looked (which is true, because it's worse). I'm certainly not going to tell her or anyone else that my friggin' feet are growing dinosaur talons because that just seems like a one-way trip to being prodded at by strangers with less respect for consent than they have for science. Science is cool and all, but not if I'm the experiment. *Especially* since whatever's happening to me is obviously supernatural.

It's frustrating. I know some people that would squeal with delight if they started growing claws out of their feet. Being a huge nerd means that a big chunk of my social circle is firmly in the 'fantasy is way cooler than reality' camp, and I know a lot of them would think that this is cool as heck. And I get that, really, I do. I've wished to be whisked away on a magical adventure more than once in my life. I love fantasy stories, including urban fantasy. There's one particularly dangerous element of urban fantasy, though: *there's a reason normal people think the magic isn't real.*

In *World of Darkness,* werewolves literally drive humans insane whenever they transform, causing all witnesses to have a temporary psychotic episode they don't remember. And that's probably the kindest secret-keeping method. Vampires systematically slaughter any of their own kind that reveal their nature along with anyone that nature is revealed to. Mages friggin' *explode* if too many normal humans witness them breaking physical laws. And *World of Darkness* is obviously just one of many examples, because *every* urban fantasy has examples, because if something is real but most people think it's fake, it means the information is being actively suppressed. I am either entirely unique on Earth, the first of my kind in recorded history (which is statistically unlikely), or I'm part of a group so invested in keeping themselves secret that not even *I* know about them, and I can expect someone or some*thing* will be extremely miffed with me if I go public.

...I swear, if my dad has like, kitsune blood or some dumb crap like that I will blow a gasket. Now I'm imagining my parents throwing me a little private party celebrating my toe-hatching day, inducting me into their secret cult now that I've come of age or whatever. Except that 'parents don't tell their children that they might turn into monsters, even though this is a known possibility' is dumb tropey bullcrap that only makes it *more* likely that the secret will get out because the kid (i.e. me) will have *no idea* what to do when ding dang claws start growing out of their feet and will react badly, possibly publically. My parents aren't dumb enough to make that kind of mistake, so it's probably safe to assume they don't know anything.

And even if they do, I don't want to talk to them about this either way.

As I absentmindedly walk towards the lunch room, still limping to keep the pressure off my toes, I run into a rather impatient-looking Ida.

"There you are!" she grumbles at me. "Geez, I thought you were gonna ditch me. We're running out of time, you know."

I blink with confusion.

"H-huh?" I ask.

"Uh, you promised to go out to eat with me today?" Ida presses. "Remember? We're not gonna have time to drive somewhere if you keep dragging your feet, slowpoke."

Oh. Right. She ticked me off in order to win ten dollars. Man, that feels like days ago. Well, I'm absolutely freaking starving and she agreed to pay. That counts for a lot. A school lunch will *not* fill me up. On the other hand...

"I'm pretty sure I'm on the edge of a mental breakdown, Ida," I tell her. *Another* mental breakdown, technically, but she doesn't need to know that.

"So... like pretty much always?" she asks, grinning at me.

I glower back at her.

"No," I gumble. "Much worse than usual."

"Oh," she says, deflating a bit. "Alright, Hannah. I'll be gentle, promise. Just good food and good company, no shenanigans."

I glower harder.

"...No shenanigans directed at or nonconsensually involving you," she corrects herself.

Hmm. Much more believable.

"Swear on your true name, you little goblin," I grunt at her anyway, mostly for my own amusement.

She sighs dramatically, bringing a hand up to rest over her heart as she solemnly recites her oath.

"I, Ida Miranda Kelly, do solemnly swear on my name and my blood that I shall neither cause nor allow the occurrence of shenanigans, tomfoolery, goonishness, horseplay, trickeries, or deceptions which would target nor involve Hannah Banana Hiiragi, my stalwart friend and fruit, for the duration of today's lunchtime outing."

I continue to glare. She smiles innocently.

"Good enough," I say, and we depart for her car, an admittedly fancy-looking four-door... or at least fancy to me, as I pretty much think any car that looks new and clean is fancy and have zero understanding or interest in them beyond that. We exit the parking lot and rocket down the main road, Ida having no interest in pedestrian concepts such as 'speed limits,' 'safety,' or 'the law.' At least she wears a seatbelt. She's reckless, not moronic.

Though I wish she (along with 95% of my school) would wear her dang mask properly. She *has* one, but she doesn't usually have it on.

We don't speak as the car roars down the road. Ida sings along with the radio a little, which is almost as annoying as the radio itself, but overall it's not too bad. We eventually park and walk into Wendy's and Ida's eyes bulge comically when I order three baconators. She waits until we sit down before saying anything, though from the strange looks I'm getting I suspect I'm not about to like the conversation that's about to happen.

"So, uh," Ida says slowly. "I'm gonna have to do the good friend move here and ask if you have an eating disorder, I think?"

Oh. Well, that's awkward but not too bad. Honestly, this kind of thing is why I tolerate Ida's... abrasive nature. She's just as willing to plow headfirst into uncomfortable subjects whether they're for or against you. I manage a bit of a smile.

"Ah, no, I'm not binge eating," I tell her honestly. "Or... anything else like that. Thanks for checking. I'm just really, *really* hungry right now, and you're paying, so I figure if I have leftovers I'll just save them."

"Okay, but like, eating three burgers in one sitting cannot be healthy for you. Won't this eventually give you a heart attack?"

I stiffen, my mind suddenly flashing back to the panic attack. My chest hurt so much. I thought I was dying. My hands start shaking again.

"...Hannah?" Ida asks, leaning forward a little. "You okay?"

"I... I already told you that I'm not," I say, turning away from her intense gaze. "Just don't talk about heart attacks, okay?"

"Did something happen in your family?" she asks.

The question takes me by surprise. No, of course nothing happened to my family? Why would she... oh, I see the train of logic now. Heart attacks usually happen to older people.

"No, they're all fine," I insist, perhaps a bit forcefully. "Can we talk about something else?"

"Fiiiine," she sighs, leaning back. "I suppose I'll be your escapist fantasy for the day. What would *you* like to talk about, Hannah Banana?"

"How do you manage to be so abrasive while also trying to be kind?" I ask, narrowing my eyes a little.

"An intensive daily training regimen," she answers immediately. "And also, *wow,* I give you leave to talk about anything you want and you pick *me?* I'm so flattered! Are you sure you're not gay?"

I can't help it, the question prompts me to give her an instinctive once-over. Even as a tiny little evil pixie creature, I can't deny that Ida is attractive. Her skin is clear and soft, her makeup is flawless, and while she's not some kind of comically stacked short girl she has some very nice curves for her height; no one would mistake her for a child, even as short as she is. Years ago, back when puberty was first starting to hit us like an entire subway system with broken brakes, I stole a few regret-filled opportunities to peep on her like an absolute creep. Which *probably* should have been a pretty big hint that yes, I am extremely gay.

But I'm also extremely in the closet, and awful gross garbage I did when I was eleven that gives me an urge to scream if I so much as

40

think about it does not make me any more inclined to come out. *Especially* not to Ida, because she's an incorrigible gossip and, despite her attractiveness, I very firmly do not want to date her anymore. I'm quite certain that would go poorly for both of us.

"Lay off it, Ida," I growl.

"Aw, man!" she complains. "Does questioning your sexuality count as a shenanigan?"

*"Yes!"*

"Well, shoot. I guess I owe you another lunch, then."

Another point in the 'Ida is a fae creature' column: she keeps her promises, both in spirit and letter. Or at the very least, she takes them seriously and actually makes up for it when one is broken. It's another thing I like about her.

I guess, given recent events, it's not outside the realm of possibility that she *actually is* a fae creature. I don't think that's particularly likely; it's a common joke I make but there are plenty of counter-examples. I guess I'll keep an extra eye on it, though. I grew talons so all bets are off.

...Holy fucking *shit* I grew talons. My heart rate spikes just thinking about it. I want to vomit. Fortunately, my stomach loudly vetoes this idea, and when the food arrives I quickly devour all three burgers to Ida's clear discomfort. Just keep going, get through the day, and try not to think about it until there's something I can actually *do* about it.

"Don't look at me like that," I grumble as I start on the fries. "It's not my fault your stomach is the size of a lima bean."

"You're barely any bigger than I am!" Ida protests. "Forget health concerns, where are you physically keeping all that!?"

I open my mouth to answer, then close it. That's... actually a question I don't really want to think about. I'm probably using it to fuel my horrifying monster transformation, after all. I start shaking again, feeling pressure build up in my chest, but I take some deep breaths and try to calm back down. I feel my claws gouge deeper tracks into the inside of my shoes, which sort of helps me calm down but also really, *really* doesn't.

"...We should probably get back to school," I mutter quietly.

"Yeah," Ida agrees, giving me another concerned look. "Okay."

We make the drive back in silence, though Ida turns to me as soon as she parks.

"Hey, I get that you don't want to talk to me about stuff," she says. "I'll just want to scream and shake it all out of you, which you clearly don't vibe with. But talk to *somebody,* okay? Like your not-boyfriend or whoever. You're putting up more red flags than a first-act Marvel villain."

I glance at her with surprise.

"I didn't know you read comics," I say, slightly dumbfounded.

"I *don't!*" Ida groans."I watch movies! You absolute nerd!"

I wrinkle my nose. I guess the movies aren't bad, but the comics are better. Well, okay, the good comics are better. Which is definitely not all of them. But still.

"I appreciate the concern, I guess," I tell her. "But honestly, I don't even know where to start talking."

"Then start anywhere," she grunts, hopping out of the car. "Come on, Hannah. You used to be so clever and fun! That's why we became friends, you know? You were witty as shit and I *loved* it. But all semester you've been getting more and more closed off. You barely talk to anyone anymore. You're *obviously* depressed as fuck. What happened?"

"Nothing happened," I tell her.

"Bullshit."

"No it isn't!" I snap. "Nothing happened!"

Wait, no, something obvious and huge and awful and horrifying happened. It's just not what we're talking about.

"...Okay, something happened *today*," I correct. "I ended up spending gym class in the nurse's office. But like, nothing happened that ruined my semester, okay?"

"Then why are you so fucking miserable all the time?" Ida presses.

"I don't know!" I shout. "I have no earthly idea, Ida! My parents are annoying but not anything worse than that! My brother is the same as always, my dayjob is going well enough, I'm not struggling in any of my classes, and I'm making more and more money with my business! By all accounts, my life is *fine.* Great, even! I literally can't think of a single tangible complaint!"

Other than horrifying and possibly deadly monster problems, but those are all too recent to have contributed to the current trend. Because Ida is right, I'm kind of miserable. I've been miserable for a long time and I don't know what I'm supposed to do about it.

Ida looks me over one more time and sighs.

"Just talk to Brendan, okay?" she says. "Or preferably a therapist, but I know better than to push you on that. I know we're not besties or anything, but I still worry."

"Wow," I answer flatly. "Real human emotion coming from the evil goblin. I'm touched. ...In the head, probably."

Ida beams with glee.

"Yeah! See, that's more like it! Talk to you later, Hannah Banana!"

I wave goodbye, letting myself smile a little. She did it again, huh? I wanted to punch her in the face just a couple hours ago. Or maybe a day ago, depending on how you count horrifying dream world time.

I hate to admit she's right, since I don't want to talk to anybody about any of this. But she's totally right. I have enough self-awareness to know that things will get much, much worse if I try to handle everything all on my own. I just really, *really* don't want to freak Brendan out or accidentally put him in danger or anything like that. I'd never be able to forgive myself.

...But that would go against our Best Friend Code. If Brendan started growing talons and turning into a spider monster in his dreams, I would want him to tell me about it even if it would put me in danger somehow. Therefore, I should tell him. (The Code is also why he's the only person who knows I'm a lesbian. He was a bit disappointed at the revelation, but to be fair *I* actually took it way worse. I almost tried dating him anyway, but he said no.)

The rest of my classes pass me by as the stress of fleeing for my life fades into a much more familiar existential dread. I suppose if dying in the other world was going to kill me in real life, it would have happened by now. I just have to worry about the claws, and more importantly I have to worry about explaining to Brendan that I *have* claws. I successfully manage to avoid him for most of the day, but when we get on the bus together I know my time has run out.

"So..." he prompts. "Your feet?"

Ah yes, that classic Brendan subtlety is on display.

"Can I tell you tomorrow?" I ask desperately.

"Sure," he answers immediately.

Oh. Huh. I didn't expect that to work. Tomorrow is Saturday, so I'll have a lot more time to explain everything. I have my other job today, after all, and it's important I don't drop a huge bomb on Brendan like this without having enough time to actually let him process it. So this isn't really running away from the problem, when you think about it. I'm actually being responsible!

Satisfied with my obviously terrible self-justifications, I enter my home with my head held high and my guilt cutting deep. I successfully dodge my father on the way to the bathroom, ripping my shoes and socks off and noting with relief and a bit of surprise that the new bandages aren't bloody. I remove them as well, swallowing with horror as I give my new toes an experimental wiggle. They, uh, they look really sharp.

I want to claw something.

I shiver at the thought. It feels alien, but not really in the same way that the awful mind control monsters did. When they invaded my head and stuck their own thoughts in there, it felt... I don't know. Insidious? Like something was nudging my mind around to think in certain ways, and I could only tell it was wrong because those thoughts didn't make *sense.* I couldn't justify them to myself, and I am *really good* at justifying things. This, however, is the opposite. It feels like something someone else stuck in my head and forced me to think, but it's not. It's me. And I'm not sure if that's worse.

I put new bandages on even though the old ones were still clean, then sneak out of the bathroom to grab fresh, thick socks. My feet still look slightly weird, but with all the layers in the way they're not too bad. Then I hand wash my old socks in the sink, break a red highlighter pen all over them and my pants, then drench them all in Spray 'n Wash to disguise the stains as best I can.

I grin at my handiwork. I'd stick it in the washing machine as well, but I think it needs a bit more handwashing or else it'll ruin the other clothes, and if I wash it by itself my mom will definitely ask questions. By leaving it stained, properly soaking, and out in the open, my mom will come to a conclusion about what happened without needing to talk to me at all. It is truly the perfect crime.

Now, onto work. My earlier sobbing session didn't mess up my makeup as bad as I'd feared, but I still get some touch-ups on it after changing into a slightly lower-cut top. Something horrible is happening to me. When I go to sleep, I might wake up as a mind slave, or just straight-up dead. My body is mutating into something alien and I have no idea what the cause is. I am embroiled in insane fantasy nonsense which could very literally be the death of me, or worse.

But it's Friday night, dang it. I'm gonna play *Pokémon* and no one is going to stop me. Not even my constant need to feel like I'm being productive. Door: closed. Lights: on. Outfit: cute. Room: clean. Potential methods of doxxing me: removed. It's go time.

45

"Welcome to the stream, everybody!" I say into the camera with an exuberance I don't really feel, and my second job begins.

I am a professional streamer. Technically. Obviously, I still have another job because I'm not making enough money to support myself with just this, but it's a nice little supplement to my paychecks. And legally, I do this with the intention of making an income, and therefore it is a business! My mom really hated it when I said that. She thinks it's awful, dangerous nonsense because the internet is full of predators and video games rot my brain, but she hasn't explicitly forbidden it and that's good enough for me. No one bothers me when my door is closed and the recording sign is up, either, so it's one of the better ways to not be annoyed by family members as well.

So I start to play! I'm currently doing a basic runthrough of *Pokémon Legends: Arceus,* trying to complete the 'Dex and occasionally experimenting with interesting glitch opportunities in hopes of throwing the speedrunning community a bone. Unfortunately, *Legends* uses a strict flag system that makes finding time-saving bugs a major hassle, so I doubt I'll find anything good. Still, it passes the time, and I get to banter a bit with my modest chat as I play one of my favorite games. It's nice.

I don't have a ton of followers, but I'm steadily growing and that gives me some vain hope that someday I might. Streaming is a job, sure, but unlike my other job I don't hate it. Being able to do something I don't hate and make money off of it is supposed to be the dream, right? So here I am. I mostly do *Pokémon* stuff, which is a bit of a saturated market, but I'm good enough at the game to hold the attention of the type of person that obsessively browses Twitch for new *Pokémon* streamers, and also I have breasts, so that already puts me ahead of most of my competitors. But not all, obviously, and I'm really struggling to find something that sets me apart from the pack. I'm definitely not interested in playing up the sexy girl angle and catering to the horny crowd; I recognize that boobs selling products is a fact of life, but I have no desire to emphasize that. Power to all the ladies that get their money that way, but I'm just here for the silly little Nintendo games. The creeps I already get are way, way, *way* more than enough, thank you. I very much do not find that kind of attention flattering.

So that leaves... what? Challenge runs? It's a good idea, but the kind that's so good everyone already does it. Fangames? That makes it *harder* to get an audience before you're already established because no one knows what the heck *Pokemon Blaze Black 2 Redux* is. Having a winning personality? Ha. Funny joke. Maybe I should just rip something up with my claws on camera.

*Maybe I should just rip something up with my claws on camera.*

Agh, I mean, that would work. But also *heck no.* Geez, me, 'no showing feet' was an ironclad rule *before* I started mutating into something horrifying and inhuman and *dang it that's a thing that's happening to me, why why why?*

Ignore it. Play the game. Banter with the chat. *Relax.* Relax you moron! Relax before you have another panic attack like the weak little freak you are and your heart explodes! You're doing something you love, Hannah! You're making an income and securing your future, Hannah! You're doing everything you're supposed to be doing, Hannah, so *why aren't you relaxed!?*

I resist the urge to shudder, feeling my feet curl up, easily piercing my bandages and socks to rip gouges into the carpet. *Ignore that.* I'm on camera. I've been quiet for too long. I need a topic of conversation.

"Does it bother anyone else," I begin, "that none of the official *Pokémon* games ever really talk about what the Pokémon experiences when they evolve?"

I get a handful of answers from the chat, mostly agreement. The big paragraphs of counterpoints will no doubt be arriving in the next minute or so. I press on with my rambling anyway.

"I mean, it's sort of touched on here and there," I continue. "But think about it. Imagine being a Pokémon and suddenly getting wrapped up in golden light or whatever as your body rapidly shifts

47

into something completely different. You might grow new limbs, or maybe lose old limbs! And it all happens so fast! It must be terrifying for the poor things, don't you think? It's always portrayed as the newly-evolved Pokémon being awesome and kicking butt, like… woo, Charizard! Look at how cool Charizard is, he's flying around! How did he even learn to fly, though? Is it just all instinct? And if so… don't you guys think it would be terrifying to just suddenly have new instincts? To find yourself moving completely differently from how you've ever moved in your life, but still feeling natural? To be twice as tall as you used to be but never stumble? To just instantly be something completely new but being okay with that?"

I clench my toes again. I'll have to hide the carpet damage somehow. I don't care.

"I think that's terrifying," I say. "Do you think that's why they made evolution postgame-only in Pokémon Mystery Dungeon? To ignore how traumatizing it would be for everyone? They used amnesia to get around the trauma of the original change. Personally, I think more Pokémon games should have trauma in them. It'd be helpful! Teach kids early how to manage PTSD!"

It sure would be handy if I knew how to do that!

My mom has a strict time limit on how late I'm allowed to stream, but I willfully ignore it. The idea of going to sleep is impossible for me. It's too terrifying. If it was just a nightmare, maybe I could work up the courage to do it anyway. But the insanity of my life is real, as far as I can tell. It's real and the moment I pass out I will return to that horrible world of torture and fear. I can't bring myself to do it. I can't.

But I can't stay awake forever, either.

I wouldn't exactly describe myself as a morning person, but I'm definitely not a night person. Staying awake is very difficult for me. So as the early morning starts to pass and birds start singing in the pitch darkness of 4am, I feel myself fading. I can barely talk to the stream anymore. If I don't shut it off, I'm going to pass out on camera. So I sign off for the night, thanking everyone that stuck with me to the end.

It might possibly, actually be my end.

I'm tempted to go chug some energy drinks and try to stay awake forever. I'm tempted to text Brendan goodbye, to ramble into his phone while he's unconscious and cry about how I might be dying the moment I close my eyes. But instead of doing any of those things, I just fall onto my bed and pass out.

Then I wake up, and everything hurts.

There is only pain. My muscles burn. My breath is gone. I'm on fire from the inside. I'm sick. I'm delirious. *My death is right behind me.*

They've only progressed a little from what I remember. What... what happened? Did I only pass out for a moment? Did I experience over twelve hours on Earth while barely a few seconds occurred here?

No time to think about it. My body feels like it's about to explode but I still struggle to twist my legs, start standing again, start to move...! Slowly, agonizingly, I stand up, take a single step, then tumble to the ground. It hurts. It hurts it hurts it hurts. I can't go on. I can't. I should just give up and let my new friends help.

No! No, no, no! I have to move! I have to, except my body won't let me! If I keep trying, I might get irreparably damaged. My new friends wouldn't want me to be hurt. My friends are coming. It'll be okay. My friends are going to help. My friends. My friends...

I cough up a foul-tasting mix of bile and blood. I don't have any friends in this horrible, terrifying world. But fine. I'll wait. I expected to die anyway.

The monsters catch up to me. My friends are concerned. Fuck them. I want to scream at them, claw at them, hurt them, kill them! My legs twitch in desperation, but there's no way I'll be able to stand up. Instead, following some wrathful instinct, I rub the serrated edges of two legs together, and a furious hissing noise erupts from them like a demonic cricket's chirp. That seems to startle the monsters. Ha. One last lick before I die. I hate all of this so, so much.

The most human-looking of the new friends leans down at me, and I know he won't ever hurt me. Except I *saw* him hurt something this way, I know he did, *I am stronger than you, you monster!* You might take my life but you won't take my mind! He reaches out a hand and I hiss again. It hurts to even make that much movement, but it's worth it to make him stop. I don't want him to touch me. Just kill me, damn you! I'm already helpless, what more do you want!?

But no, he keeps reaching forwards. A horrid sense of foreboding washes over me, but there's nothing I can do to prevent this. His hand touches my carapace, and—

*It's okay because he doesn't want to hurt me. He is a friend. He is sorry. It is okay. He has water. He has food. It is okay.*

Ah. I'm safe, then. I start to relax immediately, but the feeling is so foreign to me that I jolt back to sanity.

*It's not okay!* I roar into the recesses of my own mind. *I just got chased all the way across who knows where by a bunch of horrifying monsters! I just got fucking persistance hunted ninety percent to death! I hate you!* I HATE YOU!

The monster touching me (who is *not* my friend) goes still. Not counting his hideous internal organs, of course, but I try my best not to pay attention to those. He doesn't remove his hand, though. Instead, my mind suddenly has a very different stray thought from every one prior.

*Wait,* I think to myself. *Did you just communicate with words?*

Huh? What? Oh my fucking god. No. *Fuck* no!

*Yes I can communicate with words!* I think as loudly as I can. *I'm a person you absolute fuck! What is wrong with you!?*

He seems distressed. Even more anger starts to bubble up inside me. I cannot believe this. This is so stupid.

*Leaves and branches, I am so sorry,* my mind thinks to itself.

*Go die in a horse's asshole!* I think back.

The freakish, twisting monsters glance at each other, then back to me.

*We would like to give you some food and water first, at least?*

He... he wants to... gah! I hate this! I hate everything! But I'm in so much pain I can't even move. I'm starving. I'm dehydrated. My tormenter is offering to help me, and ultimately I can't afford to say no, no matter how much I want to. If I just chase them off, I'll die. Plus, something in his backpack smells *really* good.

...Dang it. It's always the food that gets me.

*Yeah, okay.* I say, and the monsters break bread with me.

# 4

# PERSPECTIVE

*Are you* sure *you're human?* I grumble indignantly, swallowing some jerky the trio of terrors offered me. The bread didn't go so well. I'm apparently carnivorous.

*I certainly was the last time I checked,* the creepy psychic guy answers me, which I suppose is an answer I can vibe with. Me too, buddy. Me too.

I don't think he means it that way, though. Despite looking like a funhouse horror show, Mr. Mindfuck insists that he currently is and has always been a perfectly normal human being. He and his monster pals have set up a small impromptu camp next to me, mostly because I refused to be moved. I still don't quite trust them, because while they seem nice they also have creepy mind magic and that makes it rather difficult to trust anyone or anything.

The two monsters that *aren't* trying to claim to be human don't seem to be thralls, at least. The three of them work together to set up camp, acting as equals to gather materials, set up tents, start a fire, and so on. Or at least I assume they start a fire. My 'sight' still doesn't detect light at all, so while I can feel the heat, the fire looks nothing like fire to me. It looks more like... steam, kind of?

*You look... off.* I tell the 'human.' *Like you're human from some angles but not others. But most things look strange to me. I think I might not be seeing things as they actually are.*

*I'm not really sure how to interpret that,* the psychic admits.

Yeah, I'm not sure how to interpret it either. I spit out the jerky as well. It tastes delicious but I feel sick from my recent flight for my life. I have heat exhaustion, or possibly heat stroke since I literally passed out from overexertion, and I don't want to end up vomiting it back up.

*I'm overheating,* I say. *Can you take me to one of the barren zones to cool off?*

*What is that? I don't understand the concept you're sending.*

I would scowl if I was capable of it. The telepathy ability the 'human' is using to speak with me is interesting. Neither of us speak the same language, but the spell doesn't care; it interprets thoughts as raw concepts and associations, so that the intention of our words is conveyed rather than the words themselves. This is, apparently, why he can use the ability to control animals.

...And me. But I'm doing my best to ignore that, because these people seem inclined to feed me and nurse me back to health as an apology for nearly killing me, and no matter how much I don't trust them I still need them to do that. I can't even walk on my own, which is why I need help to get somewhere cool.

*Barren zones,* I repeat. *The places without plants that you couldn't follow me into.*

*Oh, is that how you see them?* The telepath asks me. *That must be your Space magic at work.*

*...My what?* I ask, startled.

*Space magic,* he repeats. *Is the concept sending correctly? For such a small creature, you have quite the powerful aura. That's, um... why we were after you, actually. Before we knew you were a person, of course! Again, I'm terribly sorry, we've never met an intelligent species that looks anything like you. Would it be alright if I ask what you are?*

*H-hold on,* I send back. *I need a moment to process all that.*

Space magic. He said Space magic, didn't he? I, Hannah the horrifying radial spider monster, have magic? Like obviously something that's basically magic is involved with whatever the heck is going on, but if I also have magic that I get to use on *purpose?* That's different. It's a siren call to my inner nerd, and I can't help but get a little bit excited.

All of a sudden, everything finally starts to sink in at that. I am a fantasy creature in a fantasy world. I'm basically a character in one of Brendan's favorite manga. Mangas? Whatever. The *point* is... okay, I don't actually know what the point is. 'What the friggin' heck,' I guess? This is insane!

But it doesn't have to be the *bad* kind of insane.

As much as I hate these three for the horrifying torture they put me through, as much as I don't trust their apparent generosity, as much as they are terrifying, horrible giants representative of how utterly insane my life has become... my nightmares finally caught me, and I'm okay. I might be in danger, sure, but it's not immediate. Instead I'm having a conversation about magic with a weird telepathic man who seems willing and eager to help me. The fact that I'm small, inhuman, and freaky looking doesn't matter to him, or to his companions for that matter. They seem to be really used to the idea of nonhuman sapients, and they seem to have like... a basic respect for that? Which already puts this place ahead of a lot of fantasy worlds I've read about.

Two of them clearly aren't human, after all. They have four long arms, thick fur, pointed ears, a prehensile-looking tail with what I think might be three fingers at the end of it, and a language that seems to involve a lot of growling. One of them is male and the other is female, which is obvious since their anatomy in that regard is quite similar to humans and my method of 'sight' doesn't care that they're wearing undergarments in the slightest. Not that they're really wearing a lot, which is almost as distracting as the fact that the woman has four breasts to go with her four arms. She has such thick fur on her torso that they aren't particularly noticeable even though she's not wearing a shirt... unless you have a weird, possibly magical spatial sense like a certain recently-arthropodic girl I know. I can see everything, but that comes at the cost of seeing *inside* her body as well, making the overall experience... less than enticing. I'm not sure if I'm thankful for that or annoyed by it.

...I really don't have time to think about this right now anyway. I'm a magical spider monster the size of a cat, this is no time to be ogling tits. Focus, Hannah! It's time to figure out your apparent magical powers!

*What does it look like to you when I step into one of the places you can't go?* I ask the human telepath.

*You disappear from... everything, really,* he answers simply. *You cease to be physically present at all. Then you reappear in a different location later. It seemed more like invisibility than teleportation, which is odd because most invisibility spells should be impossible for a Space mage. It's almost as strange as your legs.*

*My legs?* I prompt.

*Your magic is obvious in your aura, but it's even more obvious in your body,* he tells me. *We can't count how many legs you have. They seem to appear and disappear in impossible ways as you walk. It's like an illusion, though again you shouldn't be capable of that. It's more likely that you're not entirely in this realm.*

Well that's... concerning and strange, but also very appropriate. 'Not entirely in this realm' does seem to fit my situation to a tee, but I didn't expect it to manifest quite so physically.

*I have ten legs,* I tell him simply. *And they move normally from my perspective. You all, meanwhile, look like you stretch and shift around the barren zones, or have to take strange turns to avoid more straightforward paths. You zig-zag around a lot.*

*How interesting,* the telepath muses. *Well, I only know the basics of Space magic, but it sounds like you can go into places that don't exist for anyone else, hide in them, and use them as shortcuts. The ability to perceive these extradimensional locations must be warping your senses; we didn't zig-zag towards you like you describe.*

*Oh good, I'm eldritch,* I mentally mutter. *Wonderful.*

*I'm afraid I didn't understand that word,* the telepath answers.

Hmm! So the concept of 'relating to incomprehensible outer gods' doesn't translate? Is that concerning? I mean that's not the dictionary definition, but that's certainly how *I* use the word, so that's probably what the telepath is picking up. Agh, I have no idea. Let's just be safe here.

*If you don't know it I'm not explaining it,* I state firmly. *Just get me somewhere cool.*

He nods at me.

*Is it okay if I pick you up?*

I hesitate. He's been prodding me with a finger this whole time, since apparently it helps him with his magic. I don't like it, but it's better than not being able to communicate. Being picked up is a whole different thing, though. He's... huge. Huge and terrifying.

*Okay,* I allow anyway. It's not like I'll be walking anywhere on my own.

He delicately wraps his fingers around the core of my body, threading them between my legs. I squirm a little; I can't help it, getting touched freaks me out. In doing so, one of my legs actually passes into one of his fingers, causing it to twist and warp around the leg in the same way their bodies would warp around barren zones.

*...Did you feel that?* I ask, going still.

*Feel what?*

I guess he doesn't!? Gosh this is so weird. Some of my legs touch the human's hands normally, while others pass strangely through his fingers... and the strangest bit is that it doesn't stay consistent. A leg that used to pass through him will suddenly find itself perfectly solid while the leg next to it starts interacting strangely. What the

57

heck is going on? I guess I really am some kind of extra-dimensional creature. In more ways than one, I mean.

Then he actually lifts me into the air and I can no longer focus on anything else. Once again, I feel an urge to scream that I'm unable to fulfill. Holy crap holy crap holy crap! I squeeze his hands as tightly as I can with my legs as I'm rocketed into the sky like one of those amusement park drop towers in reverse. The human's motion is effortless, completely and utterly effortless. I probably weigh less than a gallon of milk, I *definitely* weigh less than the backpack I carry to school every day, and it's doubtlessly well within this human's power to crush my carapace with his bare hands.

Not to mention if I fall, I could very well die. A tiny, itty-bitty spider the size of your fingertip has a terminal velocity so low that it could jump off a skyscraper and be fine when it hits the ground, but I'm a lot bigger than that. Despite being so light, I might still be heavy enough to crack my body open if I'm dropped from high up. I'm currently closer to the ground than my own *head* normally is when I'm standing up as a human, but looking down still feels like I'm staring down a vast, impossibly high cliff with certain death sneering up at me from the bottom.

It's terrifying, but also weirdly exhilarating.

Though my screaming muscles still clench with terror and the warmth of the human's hands is highly unpleasant to my overheating body, as the giant carries me carefully to our destination I can't help but find comfort in the firmness of his grip. And as I let myself acknowledge that profoundly alien feeling of safety, more and more of the terror bleeds away into joy. It's... fun!

And then the terror hits again. I should not be this relaxed. That's *wrong.* And he's touching me, which means he could be doing anything!

*Get out of my head!* I think as loudly and angrily as I can.

*What?* the 'human' blinks with surprise. *I'm not doing anything.*

*Liar!*

*I swear on my honor I am not influencing you,* he insists, and I have no way to know if I believe him. Suppressing a shudder, I just focus on not falling and try to ignore the bubbling exhilaration in my gut. It's probably just more vomit.

Carefully cradling me in one arm, the human gets out a moderately-sized bowl and fills it with water before setting me down into it. It's cool, and a shudder through my body indicates it's exactly what I need. I don't care that I'm lounging in the pool, I still drink a bit, the glorious liquid soothing me on the inside and out. The others let me, busying themselves with duties around their camp as I rest there for what must be around half an hour, just sitting silently and feeling like garbage. I am exhausted, but still far too wired to be anything close to sleepy. Not to mention far too surrounded by people I don't trust. Though now that my body is no longer boiling itself to death, I'm starting to get very, *very* hungry.

I tap the edge of my bowl loudly to get attention. The human isn't casting on me, so I can't communicate with anyone. All three of them ignore me, though, so I rub two legs together to make another horrible eldritch hiss, which gets their attention much more promptly. They rush over to see what the matter is and I hold out one leg. The human touches it, and we speak again.

*Is something the matter?* he asks.

*No, I'm feeling better overall,* I tell him. *I just... can't talk? I didn't have another way to get your attention.*

*Oh,* he answers. *My apologies. We really do feel terrible about all this.*

*Well, how about you give me some more of that jerky and tell me what 'all this' even is,* I suggest. *Who are you people?*

*Ah, allow me to introduce everyone. I'll have to do this verbally, since the sounds don't transfer over the link. My name is—*

"Sindri," he says out loud.

*The [four-arm tree fur person war hunter agile tail] gentleman you see behind me is named* "Teboho."

*Hold up, I didn't quite catch one of those words,* I think at him. *The what gentleman?*

*Ah, sorry, the word is* "dentron," he clarifies, saying it verbally. *It is the name of the species my two companions are part of. The last of whom is the lovely lady* "Kagiso."

The dentron man named 'Teboho' is stoutly ignoring me, as he's busy pitching a tent. I watch with surprise as, after placing a tent stake, a hammer simply appears out of nowhere in his hand, which he then uses to pound the stake into the ground. The hammer then disappears, at least until he prepares the next stake, at which point it's back in his hand. Crazy! Maybe he's another Space mage? A hammerspace mage, to be precise! Hee hee, I'm hilarious.

Meanwhile, Kagiso (aka the woman whose chest I'm firmly refusing to think about) seems to be... whittling, I think? Oh, she has a bow. She's probably making arrows. Every so often she glances in my direction with a dour facial expression, assuming I'm interpreting her facial expressions correctly given the weird, twisty way I see everyone's faces. It helps to alter the angle I'm choosing to perceive her from, since some of them make people look more normal than others.

...Also, huh, I can choose to perceive things in my range at different angles? But only kind of, since I'm seeing all of it at once? Gah, thinking too much about how I work gives me a headache.

*Sindri, Teboho, and Kagiso,* I repeat instead. *The latter two of whom are 'dentron.' I see. My name is Hannah, but I guess you won't be able to interpret that.*

*Apologies, you are correct,* he says. *Sounds don't carry over the link, only meaning, which makes onomatopoeias and names particularly difficult to convey. When you think of your own name, I merely get an impression of a term you use to refer to yourself, not what the term is. Although now I find myself curious: why does your species have a phonetic language if you can't speak?*

Hmm. What's a true enough answer to not invite further questioning? I'm definitely not opening up about the whole 'from another world that I go back to when I sleep' thing until I have a better idea of what reaction that would cause.

*I've never actually met another member of my species,* I admit. *The language I know was invented by humans. I can't speak it, but I can understand and write it. I doubt you've seen it before, though.*

*Can't hurt to try!* he says.

Well, it totally *could* hurt to try, but... hmm. Let me think. I guess if they do recognize English that means I'm not the only isekai victim, and that would give away my situation immediately. Which could be totally fine or it could be really bad, but even if it's bad it means being able to communicate without someone touching me and worming their way into my head. That's a net win. I crawl out of my water bowl with no small amount of regret, staggering as I get back to my feet. With a claw I write out my name in the dirt, hoping that no weird dimensional shenanigans prevent me from being legible. Best I can tell, though, everything is stable.

*Hmm, you're right,* the human muses. I mean, Sindri muses. His name is Sindri. *I've never seen these runes before. Though if there was any doubt to your intelligence it's certainly been dispelled now.*

*Um, should I be offended?* I ask.

*Oh! Um, no, it's just that the other two can't hear you yet. They've had to take my word for everything so far, and they've been a bit frustrated about this entire hunt.*

I tamp the ground with my claws in irritation. Something about him saying that so casually pisses me off.

*You mean your hunt for me?* I grumble.

*Er. Well, yes, I suppose I do.*

*Yeah, thanks again for giving me the single most horrifying experience of my entire life,* I snap at him. *Can I send emotions through this link?*

61

*Um. Technically yes, if you... well, I mean, I generally pick up on that sort of thing.*

Ah, good. I do everything I can to focus on the absolute maddening horror my life has unexpectedly become, and *especially* this jerk's part in it. It hurts. I recall the pain of my body, the dangerously hot beating of my heart, the way every bit of me protested for mercy but I just had to keep *going* or face what I thought would be certain death. I shudder physically at the recollection, and do everything in my power to send it all over the link. It's a horrid self-torture to relive my recent memories like this. But for the sake of spite, I can do many, many things.

*I... you have made your point,* Sindri insists. *Please stop hurting yourself just to hurt me.*

*No.*

*What?*

*I said no!* I snap at him. *I'm mad, so that means I get to make stupid decisions!*

There's a pause as Sindri tries to figure out how to respond to that.

*Would you perhaps stop torturing yourself if I offered you more meat rations?* he asks helplessly. My stomach growls in response.

Dang it. Not again.

*...Okay,* I regretfully allow.

I am given my promised jerky by the jerk, which I nibble indignantly as Sindri starts to explain why my life was recently turned into a living hell.

*So... ah, where shall we begin? I suppose I'll start by saying my naturalborn element is Pneuma, and my innate magic focuses on coordination and cooperation. On a personal level, I am... less suited for combat than my two teammates. So I supplement this by convincing beasts of the wild to fight alongside me.*

My first thought here is, of course, 'what's with all these buzzwords?' I guess it's time to suss out the type of fantasy world

I'm stuck in. 'Naturalborn' and 'innate magic' obviously implies that some people get born with the ability to cast spells. Talking about elements means that we probably have an elemental-based magic system, or at least one where categories like that are relevant. Sindri has already mentioned that I use Space magic, and so my 'naturalborn element' is probably Space. That is very neat.

My second thought here is 'dang it, he's a friggin-fraggin Pokémon trainer, isn't he?' The fact that there are elements makes the comparison even more obvious. So that means there's only one reason he would try to chase me all over the damn place.

I'm a Legendary.

*You wanted to add me to your team,* I conclude. *Why?*

*We are on a hunt for a Chaos mage,* he explains, *and there could be nothing more useful than a creature with as powerful an Order aura as you.*

Gah! Order? What's this Order stuff? Is that in addition to Space being my magic, or does it mean something else?

*Back up for a second,* I say. *Do I have a Space aura, or an Order aura? And what does that mean?*

*Er... both?* Sindri explains. *Your aura reflects your naturalborn magic, and yours features a near-even mix of Order and Space. Which isn't terribly uncommon; I only have Pneuma, but a lot of people have more than one naturalborn element.*

*I assume 'naturalborn' is the name for people who are born with certain elemental spells just built in?* I ask. *I'm not sure I'm picking up on the meaning perfectly, whatever word you're using doesn't have a good equivalent in my language.*

*It doesn't?* he asks, seeming dumbfounded. *Well, ah, no, 'naturalborn' doesn't mean you're born with elemental alignments and spells, it's merely the term used to describe which elements you're aligned to. There's no need for a word denoting individuals that are born with magic, because* all *living things are naturalborn to at least one element, without exception. Even mindless creatures like plants, though their auras are generally so weak as to be unnoticable.*

Huh! So in *Dungeons and Dragons* terms, everyone in this world is a sorcerer. That's... wild. And extremely concerning!

*So like, does that mean any of the cute little chipmunk things around here might randomly be able to shoot fireballs?*

*Do you mean the small animals of the plateau?* Sindri asks, since 'chipmunk' naturally didn't translate. *Any of them could be Heat-aligned, yes, though they are weak creatures and it would be very rare for any of them to have an aura that could pose a threat to a person.*

Well hopefully we don't have bacteria with dangerous magic, in that case. That feels like it'd maybe be apocalyptic.

*Okay so circling back, then, you said you wanted me because I had Order in my aura,* I muse. *And that's useful because you intend to fight a Chaos mage. I take it that some elements naturally oppose each other, then?*

He nods slowly, and I get the impression that he's a bit weirded out by the fact that I don't know this stuff. Hey my guy, what do you want from me? You literally found me living under a rock. Cut me some slack.

*That's correct,* he says. *Order and Chaos are diametrically opposed, both magically speaking and in base concept. Chaos magic will be drastically less effective against you, which is important because Chaos is the most destructive and deadly form of magic there is. Where the rest of us might be obliterated into nothing, your powerful aura will protect you from the worst of it. Of course, this goes the other way as well; Order magic you cast on powerful Chaos-aligned targets will be relatively ineffective. Your aura will also protect you slightly from Chaos' complementary elements, but it won't help at all against most things.*

Gah! I'm filling up on new concepts faster than I can get him to explain them. So elements can oppose each other or compliment each other, and that alters their effectiveness. I know I'm at least a little bit obsessed with Pokémon but dang it I'm gonna keep comparing it to Pokémon until I have a reason not to.

*Are there any elements that are particularly effective against other elements?* I ask. *Super-effective, you might say?*

*No,* Sindri answers. *Not really.*

I drum my legs against the ground in a manner that definitely isn't a form of sulking.

*Your magic is at its most effective against auras that don't really interact with it at all,* Sindri explains. *Using an Order spell against, say, a Motion mage will be about as effective as using it on something without an aura at all. Or, for that matter, about as effective as using it on another Order mage. You don't resist your own elements.*

*What element does Space oppose?* I ask.

*Light,* Sindri answers.

Ah. That explains why he didn't think I could use invisibility or illusion magic. But also: what? Why light? Because Space is so big that not even the fastest possible thing can traverse it? Because black holes can eat light (along with everything else) and gravity is generally associated with space? Eh, I suppose I've internalized worse analogies for the sake of remembering type advantages. Like ground being weak to ice because of 'that thing where water gets into cracks in the ground and freezes which makes the ground crack, which is really actually more of a reason *rock* should be weak to ice, but rock isn't weak to ice so don't worry about it.' And bug resists fighting because it's really hard to punch a bee.

Dang it, now I just wanna go back to playing *Pokémon.* ...Although if the pattern continues, when I take a nap I'll likely wake up on Saturday morning and be able to do just that! Wild. On the other spider leg, I'm learning about real-ass actual magic right now. Why the heck do I want to go home and play video games instead? Maybe my mind is just starting to wander from exhaustion-induced delirium.

Besides, I won't get to play *Pokémon* when I wake up at home anyway. I'll probably end up spending an hour in the shower freaking out about my inhuman toes and then I'll have to go to Brendan's place and show him said inhuman toes, and I have *no idea* how that'll go.

Staying awake it is, then.

*Considering how your physiology seems to be related to your Space magic, I suspect it's an inherent part of your species,* Sindri continues. *Your 'sight' seems to use Space magic to function, since you don't have any obvious organs for such a purpose. I've never heard of an intelligent race reliant on an innate magic like that, but it's hardly outside the realm of possibility. I'd guess your entire species is Space-aligned for this reason, but many of you likely have a secondary element. Yours is Order.*

*Which is why you want me to fight a Chaos mage with you,* I reiterate. *Why are you after this Chaos mage, anyway?*

*Because those innately born to Chaos are destructive and dangerous by their very nature,* Sindri says firmly.

Ah! Now *there's* the fantasy racism I was expecting! Whew! I was worried for a moment, but now that I know he believes an entire category of person is 'destructive and dangerous by their very nature,' I can now confidently say that Sindri is, in fact, human.

Of course, this is a fantasy world, so it's not impossible that being born with Chaos magic *actually* makes you inherently destructive or dangerous in some way, but you're always going to see counterexamples. Part of what makes a person a *person* is the fact that they can make meaningfully informed decisions. They can comprehend right, wrong, happiness, and suffering, at least intellectually if not emotionally. It's certainly *possible* that being a Chaos mage strips you of that capacity and removes your ability to choose good entirely, but... well, color me skeptical.

*People are just born with random elemental affinities, right?* I ask. *Is that detectable as a baby?*

*It is,* Sindri confirms. *But the mother of this particular mage failed to slay her child as she was supposed to, so now we have to hunt them down.*

Ah, they practice baby-killing here. Skepticism rising.

*How did you find out about all this?* I ask.

*The mage turned Teboho and Kagiso's village into dust,* he hisses. *Dozens of innocent people died.*

Okay, skepticism... somewhat falling. I don't know if I'm on board with the 'all Chaos mages are evil' thing, but chasing down this *particular* mage for war crimes against innocents sounds reasonable, I suppose. I don't really know enough about the overall situation, or for that matter what Chaos magic even *is.* Chaos and Order are terms that get thrown all over the place in fantasy games and it seems like every universe has its own interpretation of what that actually means. Sometimes the forces of Order are the good guys and Chaos are the evil demons trying to destroy everything. Sometimes that's subverted and Order *acts* like the good guys but Chaos are actually the plucky rebels preventing the world from descending into a totalitarian dystopia. Though I use the word 'subverted' here pretty liberally because both tropes are so common it's really more of a tossup.

*So, Order is good and Chaos is bad,* I prompt.

*Pretty much, yes,* Sindri confirms. *Both are fairly rare elements, but it's always nice to see a strong Order mage, whereas most people ought to run the moment they see anyone naturalborn with Chaos.*

*Why's that?* I ask. *What do they do?*

*They do what they sound like they do,* Sindri answers, leaning down to sketch out a human shape in the dirt. *Order is... order. Structure. Codification. Complexity. All living things are naturally creatures of Order, because we are unimaginably intricate combinations of systems. As such, Order magic is most commonly associated with healing, as healing is fundamentally the art of taking something that is destroyed and making it orderly again. Order is the idea that there is a way things are 'supposed' to be in this vast and frightening world, and by imposing our will upon it we can control our fate. Chaos, meanwhile, is the opposite.*

He sketches out a little spider next to the human, then sweeps his hand across both, scattering the pictures into nothing.

*Chaos is randomness. Meaninglessness. The aggressive annihilation of simple probability. Where Order maintains a form, Chaos destroys it, reducing it to constitute parts... or perhaps turning it into something else altogether. But not in the way a Transmutation spell might change something; Chaos does not turn a man into a beast, or a monster into a... a swarm of insects or something. It's the kind of randomness that doesn't change meaning but destroys meaning completely. Most people, when targeted by the most basic of pure chaos spells, simply... disintegrate. Their bodies become something else, particle by particle, substance by substance, until no element of their physical form properly matches with any other. They simply become dust, or gas, or some terrible combination thereof, and they die.*

I pause for a while, chewing on more offered jerky as I soak that in. I'll admit, the way it's described is absolutely terrifying.

*I see,* I eventually say, not sure how else to continue the conversation. Thankfully, Sindri just barrels on without needing actual feedback.

*This is why we went to such lengths to capture you,* he explains. *I am a Chaos hunter. It is my job to deal with Chaos mages, and this one is a particularly major problem because they're human and killing people in dentron territory. The murders are bad enough in their own right, but this could also cause a diplomatic incident. Dentron-human relations are already... rather strained.*

*And you fight by sending mind-controlled beasts after your target rather than fighting them yourself,* I continue for him. *So when you saw a strong counter to your target you couldn't wait to get her to fight for you.*

*I... again, I apologize. I realize my strategy sounds cowardly, but—*

68

*It's fine,* I grunt. *I understand. From the way you describe Chaos mages, they seem prone to one-shot pretty much anything they can cast a spell at. Relying on meatshields is just good strategy, and if your meatshields are animals that's the best way to ensure no actual people get hurt. If your meatshields are Order-aligned animals, then hopefully not even the animals get hurt. It's a win-win.*

*Exactly!* Sindri agrees with relief. *You understand. Teboho and Kagiso are motivated by vengeance, but each of them also has innate spells that are well-suited to dealing with Chaos mages. If there is one weakness to the element of Chaos, it is that it tends to be fairly straightforward. There are only so many ways one can unconditionally destroy.*

*That sounds like the kind of assumption of weakness that will get you killed,* I idly note.

He laughs at that.

*I have been fighting for years against monsters and people with the ability to instantly disintegrate matter with but a thought,* he reminds me. *I assure you, I am only alive because my hubris has long since died.*

*Heh, okay,* I grant him. *Fair enough.*

*And after hubris, pride tends to be next to go,* Sindri continues. *So I am compelled to ask: will you consider putting aside your well-earned grudge against me and assist us in our task?*

I stiffen with surprise.

*What?* I ask. *Are you serious?*

*Of course I'm serious,* he confirms. *You are not a beast, so it would be monstrous of me to force you to come. But all the reasons I want you to come have not changed just because I mistakenly attempted something monstrous. You owe me nothing. Quite the opposite, in fact; I'm still clearly in your debt. But as shameful as it is, I must nonetheless ask for your help because I know it could save lives.*

I hesitate. The Call to Adventure, is it? Well sorry, fantasy world, I'm in no hurry to galavant off on a headhunting mission to murder a *disintegration mage*, of all friggin' things. My initial response is a firm 'no.' Why wouldn't it be? Even if I accept the idea of fantasy headhunters maybe not being bad guys if they headhunt mass murderers (which is *very* much not something I can just take at face value) I still don't want to *become* one! I don't wanna fight and kill things! Why would any sane person willingly choose to do that outside of extreme duress?

I quickly realize, however, that this train of thought might not apply perfectly to me, because *I am under extreme duress.* Not in the sense that I'm being forced to accept this decision, but in the sense that my current position is completely untenable. I know nothing about the world I'm in. I'm tiny and physically incapable of seeing more than a small distance around me. If I tell these people to screw off and they leave me here, *I'm* the one that gets screwed. I can't really search for civilization with how limited my senses are, and even if I find one I can't communicate with anybody so I might just immediately get mistaken for a dangerous animal and attacked! Again!

As spooky as Mr. Murderous Mind Mage is, he's still being nice and taking care of me when he doesn't have to, *and* he's my only method of communicating with people. While I hesitate to trust any of my feelings about him (because again, *mind mage*) he's affable and helpful and going out of his way to answer my questions, and I have *so many questions.* I need someone like him if I want to figure out anything about this crazy new world, and here he is, dropped into my lap just like that. It's frankly rather suspicious, but can I really afford to turn up my nose at it? Uh, so to speak.

*...Can I think about it and get back to you later?* I ask.

*I suppose so,* Sindri allows. *We'll be moving on in the morning, though.*

*Would it be okay... if I came with you?* I ask hesitantly. *This isn't me saying yes, I'm not sure if I want to join your crusade thingy. But you* said you're in my debt, right? Well, I need help. I don't know where I am or where I'm going. I don't know much about magic or... or really much of anything? I'm lost and you're the only person I can even talk to.

He smiles at that.

*Travel partners, then?* he asks. *I think that sounds quite reasonable to me. You won't be much of a burden on our supplies, considering your size. And I wouldn't want to leave you alone in the wilderness regardless.*

Okay! Okay, this works! I can travel around with these three weirdos, get my bearings, and learn about the world. And then once I understand what's going on a bit better, I can make an *informed* decision about the whole helping-Sindri-kill-a-guy thing. Which will probably still be 'no,' because like... murder.

*Travel partners sounds great,* I tell him.

*Well, it's the least I can do for you,* Sindri agrees affably. *I'll add you to the team's telepathic link tomorrow, and properly introduce you to the others. But for now I think we should both get some sleep, don't you?*

I hesitate. I don't really want to sleep, knowing what I'll wake up to. But I can't deny that my body is screaming for rest.

*I suppose so,* I admit. *Thank you, Sindri. For not killing me, and stuff.*

*Ah, you're welcome?* he says. *Sorry again for today, little one.*

*Do NOT call me little one,* I grumble. *I have a name!*

*Yes, but unfortunately until we trade languages I'm not sure what it is.*

*You're a telepath!* I grumble. *You don't need my name to get my attention.*

*True enough,* he admits, and then finally takes his hand off of me to wander off and return with a small blanket, motioning for me to get on top of it. I do, and once again I am rapidly lifted into the sky in an exhilarating fear-concoction of altitude and powerlessness.

Again I wish I had lungs, though this time I'm not sure if it's because I want to scream or because I want to giggle. Gah, why is this so *fun?*

I'm taken into Sindri's tent, which immediately freaks me out at first because like... being brought into a man's tent!? Except that's a stupid reaction, because I doubt Sindri intends to try and seduce an extradimensional spider monster. I'm not being treated like a woman, I'm being treated like a talking cat. Which... I guess I'm okay with, given the circumstances. The only other woman in the party is someone I don't even know and hasn't done much of anything other than glower at me, which I'm going to assume isn't really a great sign.

Sure enough, my blanket is placed on the ground next to Sindri's bedroll, which he promptly gets inside of and passes out. It looks like Teboho has first watch, leaving Sindri and... god, what's her name again? Kagiso? Leaving Sindri and Kagiso to sleep. I try to get comfortable in my little impromptu pet bed, but it just doesn't feel right. I keep trying to rip into the blanket with my sharp legs, aggressively kneading it in a manner that will definitely tear it if I'm left to my own devices. It's not right. I get up, quickly spin in a circle, and sit back down again. It's not right! On a whim, I step off of the blanket and, following the call of instinct, burrow underneath it instead. I carve a small indent into dry earth, squish my body into it, and wiggle around until the dirt caresses me comfortably. There we go. That's *much* better. Hooking the blanket with a bladed foot, I drag it overtop my body and quickly pass into slumber.

Then I wake up, and I wish I hadn't. My instinct-driven bliss immediately twists into terror as I realize my head is no longer covered by a protective layer of dirt, which is *bad* and *wrong!* I try to move my legs but they're all *gone* and my lungs burn because *I have lungs now* and my whole body spasms as I desperately trial-and-error my way through remembering *which muscle makes them inhale.* Ah, that's right. There we go. Slowly but surely, I remember how to move as a human. I'm human again, except for my feet of course. I'm back home. Wonderful. Well, at least I can use these lungs for what I've been wishing for since I passed out.

I bury my face in my pillow and scream.

# 5

# RIP AND TEAR

My pillow-muffled screams eventually die down as the anxiety of staying in bed for too long starts to catch up to me. My mom is going to pop her head into my room any minute now to make sure I'm not oversleeping, and I just *can't* deal with that so I guess it's time to get up.

I turn over and start dragging myself out of bed, causing my brand new claws to rip up the bedsheets with a loud, horrible tearing noise. I pull my pillow back over my face and start screaming again. If I'm going to be stuck in an isekai anyway, why couldn't I at least be spared from having to continue my original life too!? Or at least let this part of my life be tolerable! What kind of insane mess of a person do I have to be if turning into an extradimensional spider monster in another friggin' universe and getting persistence hunted half to death turned out to have a better conclusion than *just waking up in the goddamn morning!?*

I curl my toes with frustration and it just rips up even more of the bedsheets, but screw it. Screw it! I don't care! I'm a freak now and I don't know what's going on and I'm just going to have to put up with that! Carefully, I extract myself from my bed, the long claws protruding from my toes having had no issues poking through both my bandages and my socks that I'd futilely left on my feet. Ugh... what time is it? I reach over for my phone and scowl at it. 8:34am. I probably have another hour and a half before my mom actually walks in and starts badgering me, but all things considered I should still get up and get dressed.

I gather up an outfit in my arms and stagger into the bathroom, dropping the clean clothes by the door and quickly stripping out of my dirty ones to drop them by the shower. With every step, even before I remove my socks, my talons click horridly on the hard floor, sending vibrations up my toes that yearn to have commands to *tear* sent back down to them. I want to break it all, claw it up and feel the strength in my feet as I grip into the porcelain floor, into the wood beneath it, and feel the resistance of proper ding dang *traction.* The scrabbling is offensive to me; my claws aren't being *used* right and I know that somehow and it's this horrible, constant brainworm in the back of my head all throughout my shower.

I cut my shower short because of it. I can't even enjoy the most simple pleasures in my life right now. I'm far too busy becoming a monster. But it's fine. It's *fine!* Worst case scenario I go full cryptid and gallop off into the woods where maybe I can *actually relax from time to time* before getting shot by some wandering hunters. Or should I say best case scenario?

Gah. No. No entertaining thoughts of suicide. I fortunately don't have much trouble with that, despite my ever-mounting depression. I suppose my prodigious skill at distracting myself with constant work is to thank for that. Move on, one step at a time. It's the only way I can get through anything. It's a strategy that works really well until I encounter a problem that can't be solved in an afternoon of hard labor, and while I realize that's a lot of *really important problems* it is, by definition, none of my immediate, short-term ones. I kick butt at doing homework, at working my day job, at getting to my appointments on time, and at fleeing from my apparent impending death. These are all things inside my skill set. Long-term planning, though? Not so much. Talons growing out of my feet is not a problem I can just bash my head into until it's solved, and as a result I don't even know where to start with it. I have no idea how to deal with it beyond just ignoring it as best I can, and I *know* that won't work but I have nothing else. I just feel helpless.

Which is exactly why I need help.

**You awake?** I text Brendan, tossing my clean clothes over my body.

The response starts immediately, but it's nearly five minutes before Brendan hits send on a single word.

**Unfortunately,** is the ultimate response. I snort with amusement. Brendan is very much *not* a morning person.

**Everything okay?** I ask.

**There's this fucking bird**, he sends, his next two sentences each individual messages.

**Outside my window.**

**It is a bastard.**

Chuckling and shaking my head, I formulate a comforting response befitting my status as his best friend.

**Most birds are bastards, considering their lack of marital practice,** I send back.

**Okay but this one is a bastard and also a fuck. Because it will NOT SHUT UP. It has kept me awake since 4am. I hate it so much.**

**It's true, most birds also fuck,** I agree. **It's probably singing in an attempt to do so, actually.**

**No stop being witty it's too early in the morning for this.**

**I'm not really being witty so much as smarmy,** I argue. **Which is totally different.**

**What if, instead of witty or smarmy, you were murderous,** Brendan suggests. **Against, specifically, this fucking bird. Because I want it to die.**

**Killing a bird would be a fowl crime indeed,** I point out solemnly.

**Damn it you're with the bird aren't you,** Brendan realizes. **You have joined with it to torment me!**

Well obviously there's no better response to that than "**Muahahahaha!**" so that's what I send back. Brendan wallows in this cruel but inevitable betrayal for a while before I finally ask if I can head over to his place, which he agrees to on the condition that he also needs to shower first. I magnanimously release him from the iron grip of an entirely text-based conversation he can easily walk away from whenever he wants, and contemplate how I'm going to pass the time until I can get out of the house. I guess I should probably eat, but unfortunately that means going downstairs.

Actually... wait. I sniff a bit. Do I smell pancakes?

My anxiety forgotten, I make sure my shoes are on tight and curl my toes a bit to make sure they won't just get shredded. The soft padding gives way and once again fires waves of pleasure up my toes, but the shoes are tight enough and the soles thick enough that I'm in no danger of clawing my way out the bottom. That's all I really need. Rushing downstairs, I happily slide onto a seat at the dining room table and take in the delicious scent of my mom making pancakes.

"Hannah!" my mother greets me cheerfully. "Just in time. I've got a hot one coming up. You want any sausage with it?"

"Nice!" I cheer. "And yes please!"

A radiant pancake is swiftly deposited on my plate, which I coat with glistening butter (and then a lot more butter once my mom turns around) before topping it all with thick, amber syrup, mixing it with the buttery goodness and happily shoveling it all into my mouth. Pancake pancake, paaaancaaaake! It's impossible to predict when my mother will get the urge to make a big breakfast for everyone, but when she does it's always wonderful. The sausages are deposited on my plate before I'm even half done with the pancake, letting me enjoy devouring them together. An unexpected explosion of savory, salty goodness fills my mouth as I chow down, surprising me with how much I love it to death.

"Is this a new brand?" I ask, immersing myself in the joy of the mystery meat.

"Nope, same as always, honey," my mother informs me.

"Huh," I mutter. "Must be a new batch. It tastes way better than usual."

"Hmm. You think so?"

Well, I'm not going to look a gift sausage in the long-since-crushed-into-a-meat-tube mouth. I'm in heaven, and as I'm learning is probably going to be a trend, I'm very hungry. I devour twice as many pancakes as I usually do, though thankfully no one minds; my mom generally makes a lot of extra ones so we can reheat them throughout the week.

"So, you have any plans today?" my mom asks, and I immediately stiffen a bit, trying to focus on the delicious food.

"I'm, uh, going to Brendan's to hang out," I admit.

"Hmm. Are his parents home?"

"I dunno," I lie.

"Well, you know how I feel about that," my mother says. "Boys that age will take advantage of you if you're not careful."

I grit my teeth. I know she has my best interests at heart and I know she's just worried about me, but we've had this conversation a hundred times before and at some point I will not be able to listen to her baselessly imply my best friend is a rapist.

"I understand," I say. "Like I keep telling you, it isn't like that. He rejected me, remember? We're just friends."

"He's a teenager, honey. You need to be careful. A boy invites you over to his house alone and there's only going to be one thing on his mind."

Yeah, and it's probably *Pathfinder.* First edition, obviously. This is literally her entire argument: boys like to take advantage of girls, Brendan is a boy, quod erat demonstrandum. And like, yeah, I'm not some ignorant little church girl who doesn't understand that sexual assault happens. I *get it.* But it's pretty obvious that she keeps saying this because she just doesn't like Brendan, has absolutely no interest in trusting him as a person, and by extension doesn't trust my choice of friends. It doesn't matter that we've known each other since we were eight, it doesn't matter that Brendan has never done anything cruel to *anyone* because he's the best thing in my entire gosh dang *life,* she doesn't like him and she doesn't trust him. And she is *impossibly* stubborn about it, just like she is with everything.

There's no point in calling her out on it. If I get mad she'll play the victim. If I try to explain she'll never be convinced. If I try to vocalize my feelings she'll take offense to the fact that her attempts at protecting me make me feel bad. The worst part about all of it is that she loves me. She loves me a *lot.* She puts a lot of effort into doing what she thinks is right for me. She makes me food and helps me find good colleges, sure. She'll go full Karen for me if I let her, aggressively going after anything she perceives as a threat to my well-being with all her power as a lawyer. She dotes on me when I'm sick, she pushes me when I'm holding myself back, and she throws her all into planning family vacations that everyone will enjoy. She always has my back. She's not a selfish person at all, and I know if I give her a *task,* something she can work towards that I think will help me, she will pour her everything into it. It just has to be something concrete, something achievable, and something she can physically *do.* My mother will work hard at anything other than self-improvement.

She's just like me in that way, and I *despise* it.

I seethe silently through the rest of the captive conversation, and it's more than enough time for me to finally receive a text from Brendan that he's ready for me to come over. I take that as the perfect excuse to leave the table with the excuse of an obligation (my mom at least values punctuality, even if she doesn't value Brendan) and I start the familiar walk over to his house.

My mom does not, I notice, ever worry about me getting assaulted when I'm off walking alone, but I suppose to be fair to her we live in an *extremely* nice neighborhood. We're firmly at the tippy-top of upper middle class, what with both of my parents having doctorates and my father even having his own business. Unlike what my food service job's health insurance policy insists on, teeth are not exactly optional bones, and as long as humans keep existing they will keep having cavities and cleanings. And of course my mother makes good money at her law firm, as well... even if she almost certainly makes less than her male co-workers. Funny how even lawyers can't stop their employers from illegally applying a pay disparity. Still, as I wander past the fancy, two-story houses on this pleasant spring day, I can't help but notice again that I am lucky and my life is quite good. I wish my depression would just shut up and pay attention to that fact.

I walk up the beautiful garden path that leads to Brendan's house, noting with derision that no one in his family actually maintains it. Unlike what I told my mother, I'm supremely confident Brendan's parents aren't home, and it's for pretty much the same reason that I'd be willing to bet that Brendan sees the groundskeepers more than he sees his own mom and dad. Brendan's parents are landlords and stock traders, making their vast wealth through the unholy magic of late-stage capitalism. As such, a lot of their work involves leaving the state to check up on their many, *many* properties and investments. Even when they aren't working, though, their favorite pastime is taking long vacations to other countries, and resultantly they are basically *never* around.

Brendan's parents are another constant reminder of the fact that my parents really aren't that bad. My mother and father are present, helpful in their own ways, and consistently make an effort to do right by me. His mother and father tried raising a kid as a lark and then decided they didn't like it very much when he was barely ten years old, and he's more or less raised himself ever since. And frankly, he's turned out better for it! Brendan's mother actively claims his autism is caused by vaccines and the fact that she's so irrationally angry about that is pretty informative of how negatively she thinks of said autism (to which I'd like to emphatically say 'fuck her'). His father agrees with this general assessment, and is a generally belligerent and self-entitled man who I have nothing but horrible memories of during the many times I've unfortunately had to interact with him over the years.

So, in case I haven't made my opinion on Brendan's family crystal clear: I hope they all eat twelve cases of needle-shaped sticks of deodorant before vomiting it all, mixing it into a stew, and eating it again. My family is pretty much the one thing I never complain to Brendan about, because I *know* he's got it a thousand times worse.

Anyway, Brendan answers the door seconds after I ring it, the cute dork having probably been sitting on the stairs next to the front door waiting for me. He gives me a goofy grin and invites me inside, and I immediately stare with hesitation at the spot where I'm normally supposed to take off and leave my shoes.

"That bad, huh?" Brendan says, tilting his head to the side a little.

"At least I'm no longer limping, I suppose," I sigh. "Look, it's not really bad so much as… insane, I guess?"

"Huh. Well, you're probably just gonna dance around the issue unless we dive into whatever it is you wanna tell me, so… let's just do that now?"

Dang it, he's totally right.

"…Okay," I allow. "Let's head to the basement first, though."

He nods and leads me there, though of course I know the way. Brendan has basically claimed his house's entire basement for his purposes, and it contains nearly all of his gaming and computer stuff, as well as massive shelves of tabletop RPG books, figurines, and paraphernalia. His computer is open to a drawing program I can't identify, in which a half-finished picture of what I assume is one of his or his party member's TTRPG characters. She appears to be some kind of large-chested dragon woman, and perhaps fittingly for the occasion she does indeed have talons. That's an uncomfortable coincidence, but I suppose I'll give Brendan the benefit of the doubt and won't start to wonder if he's secretly the mastermind of my suffering until I start to grow scales, too.

"So," he prompts.

"So," I answer hesitantly.

"Come on, out with it," he says, putting his hands on his hips. "You're the one who called this meeting, after all."

I'm working up to it! Geez.

"Uh… you're not gonna believe me unless I show you, so… I guess I'll just do that," I say, plopping down on a nearby couch.

"This is gonna be some kind of wacky flesh-eating athlete's foot, isn't it?" he asks as I take my shoes off.

"If only," I grumble.

I peel off my rather useless sock and reveal my horrifying talons, stretching and wiggling my toes as they once again taste freedom. I could be wrong, but the bony area seems like it might have started growing up the toe knuckle, though it's a bit hard to tell. I haven't examined my feet super closely, if I'm being honest. It just makes me too anxious.

Dang it, I want to claw something.

"So, uh—" I start, but Brendan barrels through my words like a freight train.

"Did you get *way* better at makeup without telling me, or are those real?" he asks.

I blink, not expecting him to jump straight to the 'are they real' question without a bit more skepticism first. Does he know something about this? Or… no. It's *Brendan*. Best friend code. He would have told me.

"They are, in fact, real," I confirm. "They grew out of my feet in a bloody mess and I don't know what's happening, but it's freaking me out."

Don't make fun of me. Don't doubt me. Please, *please* don't tell me I'm crazy. I won't be able to take it. Not from you. But he doesn't, of course. Instead he kneels down on the ground, inspecting my freakish foot from a dozen different angles, getting so uncomfortably close to it that I can feel his breath.

"These just… grew," he clarifies.

"Yeah, in like a day," I confirm. "Maybe half a day? It was horrifying."

"It's like your bone structure is… hmm. Can I touch you?"

I stiffen up a bit, but I'm already mentally prepared for this particular question. Brendan doesn't touch people basically ever, which is a state of affairs I'm very happy with because I *hate* to be touched. But I figured he might want to investigate, so I swallow my anxiety and give my consent. He gently pokes around, squeezing the bone and the base of the toe where they meet, feeling out the reality that, yes, that *really is* part of my skeleton, and it *really is* protruding from ten different places on my body, and that is *not* how human skeletons are supposed to work!

"This is *incredible,*" Brendan breathes.

"I know, but I kind of don't *like* being incredible in this regard?" I whimper. "I'd really prefer someone else was the scientific marvel here."

"O-of course, sorry," Brendan apologizes immediately. "But still…"

He starts poking around near the tip and I go very, very still.

"C-careful," I caution him. "They're *really* sharp. I—"

"Ah!" Brendan yelps, pulling his finger back in pain despite my warning. "You weren't kidding! Geez, how are your bones that sharp without shattering? They should be too brittle for an edge like that. It's almost as if…"

I don't really hear the rest of it, because I'm too focused on the blood beading on the end of my best friend's fingertip and the horrible verve it seems to fill me with. My heart beats faster. Saliva pools in my mouth. Time seems to slow as the muscles in my legs bunch up, ready to kick out and rip more beautifully red gashes through the skin of the person I love more than anyone.

"Get out," I whisper.

Brendan shuts up and looks at me with surprise.

"What?" he asks.

"Out!" I shout at him. "Go upstairs! Bandage! *Now!*"

My sudden outburst gets through to him and he skedaddles, leaving me vibrating with murderous energy. I want to *chase him!* I want to tackle him to the ground and... and... agh! No, no, no! Bad horrible monster instincts! I'm *not* doing any of those things!

I'm not. It doesn't feel like I'm actively fighting against some terrifying inner beast that's going to rip itself free and commit murders on my behalf or anything. I'm not going to turn into a werewolf and wake up naked in the forest surrounded by corpses. ...Probably not, anyway. It feels more like I have an open bag of potato chips nearby, and I know I should probably close the bag and put them away, but I'd really, *really* like another chip. Like a mild addiction to performing actions I've never even done before. Except in this analogy eating the chip would involve injuring my best friend, and not even Chile Limón flavor is worth *that.*

...Though maybe if there's something nobody would miss, I suppose I could indulge myself and rip it to shreds. As a little present to myself. Just once, to see what it feels like.

I free my other foot while I wait and carefully flex my toes in an attempt to calm down. Brendan eventually staggers back downstairs holding a massive whiteboard, some dry erase markers clattering down the stairwell to herald his impending arrival. I want to go help him pick them up, but I end up not moving, rooted to the couch by vague anxieties and paranoid terrors that I can tell

85

are patently ridiculous even considering my current absurd circumstances. Oh well. He'll understand.

"Okay!" Brendan announces, setting up the oversized whiteboard on a stand in front of me and uncapping the black marker. "Let's write some stuff out and try to get a handle on the facts! Then we can figure out where to go from there. So... when did you notice something was wrong with your feet?"

"Um... yesterday morning, I guess?" I answer.

"Okay, yesterday..." he mutters to himself, moving to write on the board. The marker, unfortunately, passes across its surface without leaving a mark. Brendan scowls, tosses the black marker to the side, and fails to find any ink in the blue marker next. The red marker suffers the same fate. Only the green marker seems to function, so I guess we're doing this whole thing in green.

"Okay!" Brendan tries again. "Yesterday morning. What happened?"

"Well, my toes started bleeding in the shower when the bone first poked out of them." I say hesitantly. "Er... actually, no. We should probably back up and talk about my dreams."

"The digging ones?" Brendan asks.

"Uh, no," I say. "I mean yes, but not anymore. I... I got to the end of the tunnel, I guess. I finished digging. That's when this all started. Now my dreams are all super vivid and lucid, and I'm like this... spider monster thing? In a weird fantasy world? I guess!?"

Brendan blinks at me for a few long moments before turning back to the whiteboard.

"Well I'm not... I'm not really sure how to put all that into the timeline," he says. "How about you just... tell the whole story?"

So I do. I tell him what I remember about burrowing out of seemingly-infinite wood, catching a wild animal on a strange alien world, the fact that I'm apparently *fourth-dimensional,* at least in some limited capacity. I describe my horrific dash for my life, my new maybe-friend-maybe-mind-rapist associate Sindri, who gave me the most horrifying experience of my life on complete accident. I explain the limited things I know about the magic system, the whole Order vs. Chaos nonsense, and the offer I got to help three obviously-murderous strangers kill another, allegedly murderous stranger.

"And then I went to sleep in that world, so now I'm back in this one," I conclude. "Now I'm here."

"Damn," Brendan sighs. "Is it weird that I'm jealous?"

"Not at all, but you *definitely* shouldn't be," I insist. "All of this is horrific and terrible."

"But magic, though!" Brendan exclaims, throwing up his hands. "And super cool claws!"

I bristle a little at that.

"You think these freakish bone growths are *cool?*"

"Extremely, yes!"

I sigh, trying to ignore the slight flush on my cheeks. I should have expected that. Brendan is *such* a dork for fantasy stuff. I love him so dang much, I was completely serious when I tried to date him. Like... he's not attractive at all, not physically. But I don't click with anyone the way I click with him, and... gah! It sounds dumb to say but I don't know how to describe it other than 'he's not like other guys?' He doesn't creep me out the way most of them do, even when he sometimes not-so-subtly checks me out. What would be revolting from anyone else is flattering from him, and I don't really get *why*. I don't wanna have sex with him, but I want to do... I don't know. Everything else, I guess? Whatever that is? But he doesn't, because he knows I'm not really into him that way, and he's *fine* with that because he's wonderful but like... gah! I should not be thinking about this right now! Or at all! He's right, I'm way too gay for a relationship to work out, and I *know* that, it's just... ugh. Being a girl nerd is already a pain in the butt because all the *guy* nerds are constantly trying to get in my pants but I'm actually stuck with the

87

same problem they're stuck with! There just aren't enough girl nerds!

"Hannah?" Brendan asks. "Are you listening?"

"Huh?" I ask with a jolt. "Uh, sorry, nope. I missed all of that. What were you saying?"

"I was asking about the predatory urges you mentioned."

"Um... I'm not really sure what there is to say," I hedge.

"You said you wanted to claw things?"

Yes. Desperately. I need to rip something open with my feet and *I don't know why.*

"I mean, it's just a random intrusive thought," I say. "It's not really a big deal."

Brendan taps his chin.

"Let me get you one of the big dog toys Fartbuns doesn't use anymore."

"Where is stinky 'ol F-Buns anyway?" I ask.

"Asleep, probably. I'll be right back."

Fartbuns is, naturally, Brendan's dog. He's named as such because Brendan got said dog for his thirteenth birthday despite being *absolutely terrified of dogs.* He hated them as a kid. Being slobbered on and *especially* loud barking tends to set off his sensory overload, and to this day he hates the way they smell. Hence he bequeathed his 'thoughtful present' the scathing title of Fartbuns, although I'm sure there's something else his parents put on the collar as his 'real' name.

Thankfully for Fartbuns, Brendan has grown to love the perpetually happy little fuzzball over time. The huge Alaskan Malamute is pretty well-behaved as long as he gets his exercise, and thankfully our neighborhood has some great dog walking trails whenever the absolutely massive yard Brendan's home features isn't enough. Also thankfully for Fartbuns, he's unlikely to miss any given piece of his infinite mountain of dog toys, which is good because I am getting increasingly excited at the prospect of destroying one.

Brendan eventually returns with what is pretty much just a teddy bear, except for how it's styled to look ferocious instead of cuddly. Also, it squeaks.

"Here you are," Brendan says, tossing it at me underhand. "Go nuts."

I snatch it out of the air and stare at it. I suddenly realize I'm, uh, not actually sure what to do? I've never torn something open with claws before. Should I like... pin it between my feet while I'm sitting, or something? No, that's dumb, how would that even work? I'm not ripping it apart like plastic wrapper, I'm... I'm slaughtering prey.

I toss the bear to the ground, standing up slowly as I feel my breath get heavy. Instinct floods my motions in an intoxicating haze and I feel myself lifting up on the balls of my feet, my body coiling for violence. I carefully lift up a foot, balancing on my other leg as I line up my kill, and stomp down.

The floor protests and my body sings as my talons easily pierce into the fluffy stuffing of my hapless prey, causing it to let out a terrified squeak. My curved blades easily hook into its body, so when I lift my foot off the ground once again I bring the little bear with me, dragging it into the sky where I then stomp down on it again, and again and again until I finally smash the bladder making that defiant squeaking noise! Its struggles ceasing, I pin what remains of my catch to the ground and dig my free foot deep into its neck, ripping the skull from the body. I am victorious! Now I can... I can...

...I can clean up all the stuffing I got everywhere, I guess!? Um. Yeah, wow, let's not get ahead of ourselves, Hannah, that was a flippin' *teddy bear*. I blush furiously at the thought of how thoroughly I enjoyed that, sneaking an embarrassed glance at Brendan. He seems to be downright jubilant about the whole process of my budding monsterdom, and I'm not sure if that's less embarrassing or more.

"S-sorry," I mutter, kneeling down to start collecting my fuzzy victim's wool viscera.

"Are you kidding?" he grins. "That's the biggest smile I've seen out of you in ages! Something about that really... I dunno, nailed it home for me, I guess? That was just *not* a Hannah thing to do at all. You're really turning into a monster girl, huh? I gotta admit, I'm jealous."

"*Don't* be jealous," I hiss. "This is completely messed up!"

"Oh, definitely, but at least it's in a really cool way," Brendan says cheerfully. "Like... wow. *Wow!* I can't fucking believe this is happening, this is insane. Do you think you're going to keep mutating or evolving or whatever?"

"I don't exactly have any precedent to compare myself to," I grumble. "But I doubt I'm lucky enough for the changes to stop here."

"This is so fucking cool," he whispers.

"It's *not cool!*" I snap at him."Brendan, please! This is terrifying! I have *no idea* what's happening to my body, I have no idea what caused this, I have no idea what it's going to do to me, and I have no idea what anybody *else* is going to do to me because of it! And it's... it's infecting my mind! You just saw that, you *said* so! That... that wasn't a Hannah thing to do!"

I point a shaky finger at the eviscerated teddy bear, feeling my breathing start to accelerate dangerously.

"So stop being happy about this!" I demand desperately. "It's wrong and it's going to ruin *everything!* I don't need you to fanboy over me, I need a *solution!* A... a plan! Some way to hide all this before... before... before whatever the *fuck* is going to happen when this gets found out!"

Brendan frowns at that, seeming to contemplate for a moment.

"Oh," he finally says. "Okay. Sorry about that. Um… I mean, I guess I've thought about how I might handle something like this before, so I have a few ideas."

"…You've thought about this specific situation?" I ask incredulously. "Really?"

He shrugs.

"Not like, *exactly* this situation, but yes I've thought about what I'd do in a bodily transformation situation."

"Why…?"

"For the same reason I'm excited about it happening to my best friend: I think it's cool. Anyway, the first strategy is to become as open and public about it as possible, as quickly as possible."

"That sounds like the absolute worst strategy ever," I grumble.

"Hear me out," he insists. "It's 2022. It's the information age. And while there are certainly still crazy people and religious bumpkins out there in the world that will see you as a monster and nothing else, the vast majority of the world is going to see you as a human girl with a strange condition that categorically deserves the exact same fundamental human rights as everyone else. That means privacy and control over your medical records, that means protection from discrimination, that means continuing your life *mostly* as-is, and most importantly that means protection from being kidnapped or murdered. If we presuppose that there are other people like you and they're unknown due to some sort of dangerous masquerade enforcement system, be that the government or the magical society itself, then while going public draws their ire, going public *enough* means that they're only painting a bigger target on their backs if they make you disappear. As long as you don't go public too slowly, they won't have a window to get rid of you and will likely be better served by obfuscating your situation with pseudoscience and propaganda until people collectively lose interest in the fact that your body is strange."

"That… seems like a lot of assumptions," I point out.

"Of course it's a lot of assumptions," he counters. "Everything I have to offer is going to be like, eighty percent assumption. We know nothing, we can only extrapolate chains of logic based on whatever seems most reasonable to us. I'm not the one metamorphosing, you can't expect me to know any more than you do."

"Right, right," I sigh. "Yeah, that makes sense. What's your next idea, then?"

"My next idea is the opposite. Publish pictures of your talons online, with a link to like… a dummy account people can PM you on, but nothing identifying. Then hope someone who knows what's happening to you reaches out."

"Nope, I hate that idea," I shudder. "I'm just gonna get messaged by creepy fetishists and you know it. Plus, the hypothetical masquerade people would have to be able to dox the crap out of offenders in order to do their job, which means there's nothing stopping them from coming after me. What's your next idea?"

"Pretend to be a furry."

*"What!?"*

"As long as your transformations remain as things that could reasonably be a costume of some sort—and you could definitely manage that with your talons, as long as you don't let anyone get too close—you can just be kind of eccentric and people will happily assume that's all there is to it."

"Okay, but what if the changes get worse?" I ask. "Like, way worse."

"I mean, there's a lot you can probably hide behind a veneer of just being a little weird, but yeah at a certain point you're screwed, I suppose. Of course, we don't know how bad your changes are going to get, or if they'll even progress at all, and it's not like we can't change strategies if one of them becomes untenable."

"…I guess so," I grumble. "I'm not really a good actor, though."

"True, you're terrible at it."

Um? I know I said it first, but still. Ouch.

"Well if you don't like any of those, my last idea is to just try to hide all the changes," Brendan continues, shrugging. "Which is what you've been doing. The problem is that you're putting your reveal to chance; if you *do* end up getting revealed, it'll be in a situation you have zero control over. Furthermore, while you're most heavily denying the possibility of people coming to hurt you, you're *also* denying the possibility of people coming to help you. It's the low-risk, low-reward strategy that just kind of leaves the situation stagnant."

"Sounds perfect for me," I grunt.

"Uh… I mean, I know you meant that as a joke, Hannah, but—"

"I'll just keep hiding," I conclude firmly. "At least for now. Like you said, we can always switch the strategy later, and if we wait a little longer we'll be able to see if any other changes start to happen to my body or not."

"I… suppose waiting for a week or two to gather what information we can would be prudent," he agrees hesitantly. "I'm just worried you'll keep hiding a lot longer than you should because it's easy."

I pout mightily, but Brendan is too powerful for it.

"…Yeah, okay, that's fair," I admit. "If you don't push me I probably will. That's… why I'm here, I guess."

He smiles slightly, letting the conversation come to a natural close. As usual, I feel better about it now that I've talked with him, even though we didn't really come up with a plan. I knew that going in, though. There's no way to plan with no information available. There's no way to seek information without risk. And I'm far too terrified and too overwhelmed to try bringing strangers into it anyway. But talking to Brendan helps dull the panic of the situation, the feeling of isolation, and brings in one of the only people I truly, deeply care about into the mix.

I wish I could say anyone in my family falls into that category, but for whatever reason they never have. Which is another one of those things I haven't told anyone other than Brendan; the idea that I've never loved my own family makes me feel like a monstrous sociopath. *They* clearly love *me.* They're not abusive, they're not negligent, and while they have their problems they're not outright awful in any way. And yet I read so many stories about how family is important, about how people love their family no matter what, about how people that are put through horrible abuses far worse than my own *still* love their family despite all that, and I, meanwhile, just feel... nothing.

I suspect the only thing I'll feel at their funerals is a dull horror at the knowledge that I don't feel anything else. In many ways, I know that makes me even more of a freak than my feet do. Valuing your family is the right thing. The human thing. But... I don't. And I don't know why.

"Well... this is all pretty crazy, huh?" Brendan eloquently summarizes.

"Yep," I sigh. "I'm still not totally sure I'm not in a psychiatric ward somewhere."

"That's fair," Brendan grimaces. "That's definitely fair. Um... can I ask... what it felt like? To grow them, I mean."

I glance down at my feet, wriggling my toes as I idly note how quickly I seem to be getting used to them.

"...There's not much to say," I admit. "It just hurt. A sharp pain from them cutting open the skin, and a duller ache from the growing pains, I guess. That was about it."

"No flash of mana or whatever?" he asks with a grin.

"I don't even know if mana is a *thing,*" I admit. "I'll keep you apprised on the magical details as I work them out, I suppose."

"You'd better! I've got dibs on being the first person you teach spells to. Archmagi Hannah and Brendan shall drive this world into darkness!"

"Okay, I'll pencil in 'conquering the world with arcane might' immediately after 'actually learning the names of the other kinds of magic.'"

"Haha, okay, fair," Brendan admits, glancing at the whiteboard. "We've got, what, six kinds? Order, Chaos, Space, Light, Pneuma and you said he also briefly mentioned Motion. Unless Motion is the opposing element to Pneuma, which wouldn't make much sense, there's probably quite a bit more than that. And considering how vague the categories are, you've seemingly got either a really soft magic system or a poorly understood magic system, both of which are ripe for exploitation and abuse!"

"That's not reassuring," I grumble. "If the magic system can be abused, it's probably already *being* abused by people a lot more powerful and knowledgeable than I am."

"What, you don't think you can use basic logic to immediately become the best at a system that entire societies have already been using for thousands of years?"

"Well I didn't get any mental notifications about experience points or skill upgrades, so no, I doubt it's going to be that easy. I don't even *have* magic, I just sorta *am* magic in a weird fourth-dimensional way that mostly seems good for hiding. Which I will probably need to do a lot because I am tiny and weak."

"Yeah… you'll be okay, Hannah," Brendan assures me. "You'll figure things out and make it through this."

"Well, if I randomly die in my sleep you'll know I didn't," I answer sardonically.

We sit on the couch in silence for a little while longer, but Brendan stands up before I can wallow for too long.

"Let's go get Fartbuns up and take him to the backyard," he suggests.

I sigh and nod, grabbing my socks.

"Nah, leave your shoes and stuff off," Brendan suggests. "The only thing bigger than our yard is the fence surrounding it, nobody'll see."

I frown at that.

"I don't exactly like seeing my feet like this," I remind him. "I'd prefer the shoes."

"Humor me?" he suggests.

Gah. Fine. I follow him upstairs, carefully keeping my toes off the ground so I don't ruin the hardwood floors. Brendan easily wakes the family fuzzball with promises of "outside time!" and we head out the backdoor together, Fartbuns bounding happily ahead of us and quickly finding a nice spot to piss in the grass. The yard isn't very exciting; there's a decently-sized patio complete with a sizable gas grill, and pretty much everything else is a vast green field of wasted water. When we were little they had more things here; a miniature playground, a trampoline, and an inflatable pool in the summer. But that's all gone now, so everything is just grass, grass, and more grass.

Tennis ball in hand, Brendan plays a halfhearted game of fetch with Fartbuns as the two of us silently appreciate the beautiful weather. Once out in the grass I let myself relax a little, lowering my talons into the soft earth and relishing in the feeling of *grip* I get from it. I rock back and forth on the balls of my feet to my heels, trying to ignore my ever-growing instincts to chase the dog every time it runs off to grab the ball.

"You doing okay, Hannah?" Brendan asks.

"No," I tell him. "I feel weird. Really weird. I just..."

Brendan tosses that dang ball again and Fartbuns dashes off after it, causing me to instinctively crouch a little lower, preparing to run. Agh, I want to... I don't know! I want to move, to run, to feel the dirt in my toes and... and it's weird! It's weird and freaky and wrong, but like... it's just me and Brendan here. Is there any reason I *shouldn't?* As long as I don't claw Fartbuns, obviously.

"You just what?" Brendan asks, retrieving the ball from a returning Fartbuns.

"Just... just don't judge me," I beg, and when he throws the ball again I'm right behind the dog.

I don't generally like exercise. I'm *certainly* not a fan of running, and my recent experience of nearly running so hard that I die will forever get an honorary spot on my bulging shelf of traumatic memories. But nonetheless, as my feet grip into the ground and my legs explode my body forward at speeds I've never achieved before, I feel raw, unfettered elation.

Fartbuns quickly loses interest in the ball as I barrel after him, panting excitedly as he dodges around my charge and happily accepts this apparent upgrade to playtime. I pounce at him again and again until eventually, after a near-miss, the big happy doggo retaliates. He playfully nips my hand as I reach out to grab him, which is just the opportunity I need to double-down my assault and wrap my arms around my favorite fluffy boy. We roll in the dirt, eliciting another nip on my arm, to which I respond with the only thing a rational woman can do in this situation.

I bite him back. I don't even know why, I just get the sudden urge to chomp and I roll with it, winning a mouthful of dog fuzz and a light, toothy pinch on my new playmate. It's *fun!* Then Fartbuns quickly wriggles free of my grip and bounds happily around me, and the dance resets. I think at some point I start laughing, and I can't really bring myself to care.

I don't know how much time passes, but eventually Fartbuns and I are both left panting in the grass, my outfit ruined by countless green stains and my toes caked with three layers of dirt. Giggles still occasionally bubble up from my chest as I stare up at the blue sky, the back of my mind constantly jolting with terror at the question of 'what if someone sees me like this!?' But there's no one here but Brendan and I, and it's okay for him to know. It's okay.

I... had fun. I haven't had fun like that in a long time.

Brendan's towering figure eventually moves to loom over me, offering a hand to help me to my feet. I take it, still grinning like an idiot.

"Thanks," I tell him. "For... for all this. For being you, I guess."

"I'm glad I could help," he answers. "And Buns really appreciated it too, it seems."

"Yeah, I... I kind of hate how much I loved that?" I admit.

"Well don't," he says. "You're not allowed to hate any part of my best friend. She's too cool for that."

I smile wider.

"God. How are you not absolutely freaking the heck out, Brendan?" I ask. "I... how can you so blithely *accept* this?"

He shrugs.

"I guess I'm just better at freaking out on the inside."

I laugh. What else can I do? All of that was... I don't know. I don't know if this is a good thing or not. I'm happy now, sure, but... this changes nothing about the horror of the situation. I'm still afraid it's all going to keep getting worse.

"I need to feel normal for a while," I declare. "Let's go play *Super Smash Brothers.*"

"Sounds good to me," Brendan agrees as I try to wipe all the grass off my body. "You gonna stream today?"

"Yeah," I confirm. "But starting a little late won't kill anyone."

"You're not worried about suddenly mutating on camera?"

Oh, fuck. I mean, I am *now.*

"...My talons took a whole day to grow in and they hurt like hell," I hedge. "It's probably fine. I'm sure I'll notice before anything gets too wild."

"If you say so."

We head back inside and I put my shoes and socks back on, whiling away the next few hours playing video games. Eventually I can't justify staying any longer, though, so before long I'm heading home, feeling just the slightest bit better about my situation. I'll go home, I'll get my work done, and soon enough it'll be time for bed.

And then it'll be time to learn magic.

# 6

# MAGICAL MEETINGS

A comforting pressure surrounds me as I wake, though I'm immediately aware I am no longer in my bed. Yesterday went... pretty well. After getting home from Brendan's house I just streamed most of the day, which helped take my mind off of things. Brendan even found a set of foam blocks that I can stick on my claws to prevent me from ripping up my bedsheets any more when I sleep, and they *also* give that pleasantly tingly feeling of stabbing something, which helped a lot with my anxiety about getting in bed.

Now that I'm very, very far away from my bed, I nonetheless find myself comfortable and warm, my many-legged body nestled pleasantly in the earth. Ah, that's right. My weird burrower instincts took over last night so I dug *underneath* the blanket given to me and put it on top of me. Geez, I'm like a trapdoor spider. Trapdoor hyperspider? Whatever. I flex all my legs in sequence to make sure I know which ones are which, and start taking in my surroundings.

I assume it's morning, because Mr. Mindfucker and his pals are all up and about, cleaning up the campsite. I *guess* I should put more effort into mentally thinking of him by his name, 'Sindri,' because it would be kind of awkward to send over my nickname for him instead, no matter how fitting. The three of them seem to be quite experienced working together, effortlessly completing their individual jobs without a word and without getting in each other's way. That said, they also don't seem to be particularly *friendly* with one another, as while the two non-humans (who are called dentron, if I recall correctly) occasionally chatter a bit with each other, they barely acknowledge Sindri at all and seem to treat him with mild suspicion.

Which, y'know, fair. Mind magic is suspicious as fuck. On the other hand, it sounds like people don't get to choose the kind of spells they're born with, so it'd be unfair of me to judge the Pneuma mage while being hesitant to do the same to the Chaos mage.

Regretfully, I wriggle my way out of my comfy little dirt coffin, shaking off the detritus still sticking to my body for a moment before I get the urge to just step into a nearby barren zone instead. It just... feels more right. Hesitantly, I do so, and all the dirt caked on my body simply falls right off, unable to pass the barrier between dimensions. Huh! I check myself over with my spatial sense and can't find so much as a single speck of dust on my carapace. I've probably never been this clean in my life. In fact, I get the distinct impression that I couldn't choose to enter the barren zones with crap stuck to me even if I wanted to.

On the one leg, this is awesome. I'm so clean I probably don't even have microbes on me! Being this clean is so wonderful and good, it's like dopamine central for my various neuroses. On the other leg, this is creepy. I hate having all these new foreign instincts pushing me to do things, even if they're convenient in regards to figuring out how my body works. Something has fucked with my head, mind mage or no, and that's *violating.* And on a third leg... not being able to bring anything into the barren zones is going to be more of a hassle than it will be a benefit, I think. I won't be able to carry anything! For that matter, I won't be able to *wear clothing,* though I guess I don't really feel immodest. I suppose there's not much to be embarrassed about on my creepy ten-legged bug body. I haven't even had to go to the bathroom yet, which is good because I'm not at all excited to learn how the heck I actually do that. I, uh, try not to stare too hard at my own intestines. More importantly, though: I won't be able to carry equipment, materials, supplies, *food...* no spider-backpack full of meat rations for Hannah! It's a tragedy.

...Although presumably once I *eat* food, it doesn't leave my body when I enter a barren zone. So maybe I can carry stuff inside my mouth?

I step back out of the barren zone into the middle of camp, where all three other people there jolt with surprise as I seem to appear out of nowhere to their senses. I grab a small rock and close my mouth around it, walking into the barren zone and spitting it back out without trouble. Okay, neat! I take it back out to the normal realm, spit it out again, and pick it up between my teeth so that it's not fully enclosed by my body. This time, crossing over into the barren zone causes it to simply drop from my grip as if it stopped existing. It seems like I can carry things into my little pocket dimensions only if those things are completely enclosed by my body. That's a pain, but it's better than nothing.

I suppose while I'm in my little pocket dimension here, I should try to get a better handle on how it actually *works*. Now that I understand what I'm looking at a bit better, things are easier to wrap my head around. There are pockets of space I can enter which balloon within the physical area around them like bubbles in a bathtub. When someone else walks into a spot where I perceive one of these spaces, they simply flow around it, causing the strange twisting effect that kind of looks like gravitational lensing. I, meanwhile, step into the bubbles as if they're normal space and walk straight through them, giving me a 'shortcut' where other people have to 'go around' the bubble. The bubbles are all different sizes and shapes, scattered around the environment, and by changing the 'angle' I'm looking at things through my spatial sense, some bubbles will appear, disappear, grow, shrink, move, and so on. There are a set number and position of the space bubbles, but it's difficult for me to perceive them all at once. It might be *possible* for me to perceive them all at once, but that'd take a degree of familiarity with fourth-dimensional thinking that my pathetic human mind simply does not have.

...Meh. I can figure it out. I'm not going to give up on perfecting my cool new magic powers just because they require naturalizing myself to the w-axis.

I scuttle out of the barren zone again, startling my new companions for a second time. Teboho (the male non-human) babbles something at me in his weird language, which I don't really understand. I'm not sure how to convey that to him, though, so I just tap each of my legs on the ground once in sequence, lifting them in a little wave pattern around my body. Hopefully that's enough to acknowledge I'm paying attention, at least.

Sindri kneels down and holds out a hand, which I'm tempted to hop onto so I can be carried but I just touch it with a single leg instead. Let's not go crazy just yet.

*Good morning,* he greets me. *Did you sleep well?*

*I feel much better than I did yesterday,* I admit truthfully. *Thanks.*

*Of course! Now, would you like to speak with the others today?*

*That sounds like a good idea, if we're going to be traveling toge—ow!*

A sharp pain fires in my side as a pebble bounces off my carapace. What the fajita? Four-boobs threw a rock at me! I tense immediately, rubbing two legs together to produce that furious, warbling hiss to communicate my displeasure. Kagiso (which is *her name,* Hannah, get your mind out of the gutter) just scowls at me, the long ears on the side of her head twitching with displeasure.

*Well for my first question I'd like to ask her what the heck* that *was for!* I snap at Sindri.

*I'm so sorry!* he sends back. *I have no idea what has gotten into her!*

Both he and Teboho turn to chastise her, but she just tosses *another* pebble at me—this time with her three-fingered tail—which I dodge by scuttling to the side. This causes her to narrow her eyes at me further, but Teboho bodily steps between the two of us and starts pleading with her. She glances his way and starts

104

yammering an explanation, and the two of them exchange words for a while.

*A-ah, apologies again,* Sindri says, reaching out to poke me once more. *Kagiso can be... impulsive. It sounds like your body is interacting uncomfortably with her innate magic.*

*So she threw a rock at me!?* I protest. *That's not impulsive, that's just being a jerk.*

*Please don't think too poorly of her,* Sindri requests. *She's a bit... odd. I don't think she meant you any harm.*

*If you don't intend to harm someone you shouldn't throw any friggin' rocks at them!*

*I agree entirely, I assure you,* Sindri says calmingly. *How about we establish a method of communication so she can apologize to you directly?*

Ugh. This morning is off to a terrible start already.

*How does it work?* I ask.

*It's simple enough,* Sindri says. *I'll cast a spell on everyone that will join us together in a mental network. We'll all be able to send and receive information over the link. It's normally a faster and quieter method of coordinating in combat scenarios, but we can simply use it on a regular basis to maintain the ability to speak with you without needing me to be in physical contact all the time.*

Huh. Okay. I'll admit, that sounds like a handy use for mind magic. And it's not like it's any riskier than communicating only with Sindri.

*Let's do it,* I answer.

The four of us gather together, the three of them each grabbing another's wrist so they're all in contact with each other at the same time. They kneel down and I, with instruction, put a leg on each of their hands, Kagiso flinching a bit as I do. Teboho seems a bit more accepting of my presence, but both of the dentron are obviously uncomfortable with me. Hopefully, that will change soon.

A pulse of… something shivers up my body and settles into my mind, that tickling presence of Sindri's magic making itself known. It remains even as the others unlink hands and stand back up.

*Hello, everyone,* I send to them. *Can you all hear me?*

The dentron mutter a few words at Sindri, but then Teboho answers me.

*Yes, I hear you little one,* he confirms.

The mental voice he sends is startlingly different from the one I 'hear' when Sindri speaks to me. It's interesting. When Sindri speaks it almost feels like I'm just thinking to myself. The different cadence, word choice, and habits are the only things that make it obvious it's him. Teboho doesn't sound like that at all, though; he just *feels* like a different person, the voice deep, sturdy, and reassuring.

*Don't call me 'little one,'* I grumble.

*I will not,* he confirms apologetically. *Do you have a name?*

*It does, but it's unable to speak it,* Sindri confirms on my behalf.

*Uh, I'm also a 'she,' not an 'it,' thank you,* I correct.

*Is this not easily remedied?* Teboho asks. *She can write.*

*Not in any language I know,* Sindri shrugs.

*Then we will improvise,* Teboho insists. *We must know her name, Sindri. Give me a moment. Kagiso, apologize for throwing rocks.*

*Undamaged,* Kagiso sends in protest. Her voice is dramatically different from both Sindri and Teboho, stilted and somewhat fuzzy, as if it's being projected on a CRT television with a bad connection.

*Whether or not you hurt her is not important,* Teboho explains patiently. *Would you want someone to throw rocks at you unexpectedly? Would that not distress you?*

*…Oh,* Kagiso says, wrinkling her nose. *Apologies, creature.*

*Not as bad as 'little one,' but please don't call me 'creature' either,* I grumble. *Why were you throwing rocks at me, exactly?*

In response to my question, Kagiso grabs another pebble from the ground with her tail, which really is a fascinating little structure. A long, thin extension of her spine that reminds me most of a monkey in its flexibility and shape, the tail ends by splitting into three smaller tails, each about the size and length of a finger. Like her feet, which have longer, more flexible toes and small claws, her body seems more designed for grasping and climbing than a human's. Considering how much of her body is humanoid but *more*—tail, extra arms, bigger ears, fur, etcetera—her species probably has to eat a lot more food than humans do every day. I wonder why they evolved that way.

...Assuming this fantasy world functions via Darwinian evolution, anyway. I mean, I don't know how else it could work, but it's a fantasy world with magic, they could very possibly have been spat out by a divine entity as-is. What do I know? I should probably ignore that and focus on the fact that she just grabbed another rock, and the last two times she did that were not pleasant for me.

*Targets,* she says over the link, pointing at four different rock formations in sequence. Then her mouth moves, and a word is spoken. But not by her.

I understand the word. It makes perfect, clear sense in my mind, despite how I've never heard it before and will be hearing it for the first time no matter how often I listen to the sound. The word is something *other*, something beyond that touches me, peels me open, and holds the core of my being with the distant affection of a woman holding someone else's baby. It laughs at me, joyful and fond and utterly without obligation.

"**Ricochet**," something says with Kagiso's lips, and she throws the stone.

I'm so shaken by the word that I almost don't notice her flick her tail, launching at the first of her targets. The pebble bounces off the rock and, in gleeful defiance of all physical laws, *accelerates* as it bounces off into the next rock, then the next, dramatically increasing in speed every time until it finally smashes clear through a poor animal's skull and splatters its brains onto the ground behind it.

Literally none of that would be possible on Earth.

*I take it your naturalborn element is Motion, then?* I ask, trying to restrain my stunned terror. *Or was that something else?*

*Motion,* Kagiso confirms. *Know where shot will go. Always.*

She kneels down next to me, her eyes boring into my carapace.

*Unless. I bounce off you. You're… wrong.*

I shudder slightly, scuttling backwards.

*Well there's an obvious solution to that, don't you think?* I grumble.

Her eyes go wide.

*Tell,* she insists fervently, scooting towards me more.

*Just don't bounce things off of me!!!*

She blinks slowly.

*Not a solution,* she pouts. *What if need to throw you? Or use you for angle?*

*Wh—no!* I yelp, hissing at her and stepping back further. *Do NOT throw me!*

"Kagiso!" Teboho barks out loud, followed with a bunch of words I don't understand.

Kagiso's ears droop and she walks away from me as Teboho gives me an apologetic smile.

*Hey, come on over here,* he says. *I've got something I want to show you.*

*Is it that alphabet you've been writing?* I ask.

He seems surprised, but it's not like I can't tell what he's doing. Even though he's a good ways away, I get a bird's eye view of what he's writing in the dirt with that weird pole of his. I do not, of course, have any idea where he got the pole, but I assume it's more of his funky hammerspace magic.

*Yes. Do you recognize it?* he asks.

*No,* I admit. *I was just guessing, but it seems like the most logical thing you could be doing. It reminds me of an alphabet I've seen before.*

*Ah, yes, I see!* he nods happily. *Well, I was thinking that the easiest way for me to get your name would be to teach you which sounds are associated with which letters and let you write it out yourself.*

I drum the ground once with each of my legs in sequence.

*That's very thoughtful of you,* I tell him. *Thank you. Let's get started.*

And so we do, and I learn the basics of the dentron language. It is, as I feared from looking at how many damn letters it has, more comparable to Japanese than English. I don't know much Japanese, despite my heritage, but Dentronese (or whatever it's called) has the same basic structure to katakana: each letter is a *syllable* rather than a single phoneme, and accordingly there are well over twice as many of the stupid little squiggles than the English alphabet has. They use the odd guttural hiss as a consonant in a handful of letters, but the rest of the sounds are familiar. It's weird how they use mostly the same phonemes and syllable structure as my father's native language, but Dentronese still manages to sound way, *way* uglier. It grates on the ears even without adding in the occasional choking noise.

Still, it gets the job done. I point out the symbols for 'ha' and 'na,' quickly assembling a close approximation for my name.

"Ha... na," Teboho vocalizes. "Hana?" *Is that right?*

*Hannah, yeah,* I confirm. *That's close enough. Thank you.*

*Of course, Hannah,* he sends happily. *It's truly the least I can do for you. I'd like to apologize for the other day, as well as for my sister's conduct this morning. Please forgive her. She struggles to get along with others.*

I drum my legs again. I suppose it's as good a shrug equivalent as anything.

*It's fine,* I allow. *Strange doesn't mean bad, I'll figure her out. We won't have any problems as long as she stops assaulting me.*

*Ah, but what if she has to throw you?* he asks, shooting me an amused grin.

I hiss at him and he laughs, giving me a good look at his terrifying teeth. Hmm. Or perhaps not-so-terrifying teeth? They're a lot flatter than human teeth, his species probably eats a lot more plant matter than humans do. Certainly more than I do.

*I would like to give you this corpse as apology,* Kagiso says, having returned with the body of the small animal she recently exploded the skull of. She holds it out to me, its blood leaking between her fingers.

I stare at her. She stares silently back.

*Um, thank you,* I say. *That's... very thoughtful of you.*

Kagiso smiles very slightly.

*Yay,* is all she says, and then she wanders off to finish packing up the camp.

Hmm. I, uh, hope I haven't started a dangerous precedent. Should I even eat this? It's uh... got a lotta organs leaking out of it.

...Which actually makes it smell pretty good.

Okay, fine, waste not want not. I scuttle over to it and pull it into my mouth. Mmm, delicious raw meat. Let's not worry about how much I enjoy this and just let myself appreciate the flavor, okay? I have enough on my plate. And thankfully, my feeding practices don't seem to net me any strange looks from my companions. Well, not any that I think are because of the feeding practices, anyway. Before long the camp is collected into a set of packs which the group slings onto their backs, and very noticeably does *not* put into any kind of hammerspace. Hmm. Maybe the hammerspace mage doesn't have enough room for it all? ...Or maybe my guess was just totally off.

*So Hannah, just for clarity's sake, we're heading to the base of the branch and traveling further up the trunk,* Sindri explains. *You're comfortable heading that way, right?*

I mean, I don't know what that is, so... hmm. Wait. Branch? Trunk? And I dug my way up through wood, right? Holy bagels, am I on a *world tree!?*

*Um... is there a reason I shouldn't be comfortable heading that way?* I ask hesitantly.

Sindri laughs.

*Not unless you're wanted on the upper branches, I suppose. We shouldn't be going high enough to worry about the burning tunnels or anything like that. And with us around, you should be safe from any monsters along the way.*

Uh. Hmm. Yeah that more or less confirms the world tree theory, unless it's all metaphorical. It feels like the kind of thing that might be dangerous to ask about because they'll *definitely* ask why I don't already know the answer to that question, and I won't have any lies that don't sound dumb. There's another question I want to ask, though. One that I *do* have a good excuse for.

*I'm not sure I'm interpreting the word 'monster' correctly,* I hedge. *What's the difference between a monster and an animal?*

*Hmm. Nothing formal?* Sindri answers after a brief pause. *I suppose it's aesthetics, mostly.*

Alright, so there's not some entire category of crazy something-or-another that monsters have, they're just... dangerous creatures, I guess.

*Then let's get going, I suppose,* I say.

*Forgive me if this is an offensive question,* Teboho says, *but would you like a ride, Hannah? We are likely to keep a marching pace for quite some time.*

Translation: 'your legs are smaller than our flipping feet and we're not gonna slow down for you.' I admit, it's a tempting offer, but I'm a bit hesitant to be treated like luggage.

*I think I'll be okay for now,* I say. *I don't have to walk as far as you do.*

I punctuate my point by stepping into a barren zone, eliciting surprise and a slight chuckle from Teboho. Once everyone starts to set out, though, I soon find myself struggling. I don't have to be constantly sprinting for my life anymore, but my tiny body still has awful heat regulation and I don't have enough time to rest in the cooler barren zones before I get exhausted. I make it barely half an hour before throwing in the towel.

*Okay... remember your offer when we started, Teboho?*

He laughs and kneels down, both palms out to let me scuttle onto two of his hands. I do so, feeling that terrifying, elating rush of being lifted into the sky. He places me carefully on top of his backpack, and I hook a leg into a couple of the straps and over each of his fuzzy shoulders to secure myself. *Gosh* his fur is soft, I can even feel it through the muted sense of touch in my legs.

*You ready?* he asks.

*Yeah, sorry about this.*

*It's no trouble,* he assures me, and then the horrifying giant starts to walk and I try very, very hard to scream. Of course, I still can't, so I have to settle for screaming inside my own brain.

Holy gondola he's so flippin' fast! I clearly take being five-foot two for granted, if this is *walking speed* for someone at human height. Considering my little spider body might *maybe* reach one foot two if I stand on my tippy toes, I feel like I'm living through *Shadow of the Colossus* right now! Aaand now I have *Revived Power* stuck in my head. Ah, well.

Though I feel what I assume is the sun beating down from above us, our trip up the steep tundra just keeps getting colder. Motes of frost and occasional patches of snow get more and more common, which might make me wonder if we were just on a normal mountain climb if not for the fact that I can still 'see' that, under the layer of dirt at our feet, there's wood rather than stone.

*Ah, now that's a fantastic view of the trunk,* Teboho says to me. *It's majestic isn't it?*

*I'm blind,* I remind him. *I can only sense things close to me.*

*Oh, truly? My apologies. You're quite the strange little person, I must admit. I've never heard of anything like you. Does your kind hail from the Slaying Stone, like the humans?*

I hesitate. I have to admit I'm ignorant at some point, I suppose. I just need that to not be suspicious. There was a level of intense vitriol in the words 'Slaying Stone,' so I probably don't want to push at that too hard.

*I... don't think so?* I answer. *I'm sorry, I just... you literally found me living under a rock. I hardly know anything about the world. I've never met anything else like me either.*

*Ah, I see. I'm sorry to hear that. It must be difficult to be alone. If you're curious, I'm certainly happy to answer questions.*

*I appreciate that,* I say honestly. *I'm very curious about a lot of things, I've just never really had many people to talk to before. Is it okay if I ask stuff that might seem... I dunno, really stupid and basic?*

*Of course!* he assures me.

Well, now or never, Hannah. ...Well, okay, I mean it's actually more like 'now or any time after now, probably,' but let's pretend it's now or never to try and trick my procrastination instinct into shutting up.

*...Are we on a big tree?* I ask hesitantly.

113

There's a pause, and then Teboho bursts out laughing, jostling me unexpectedly enough to send a wave of terror through my body. Don't fall, don't fall…!

*Well! You could certainly say that,* Teboho confirms as his chuckles die down. *Merely calling The Mother Tree 'big' is rather underselling it, however. You have, ah, sensed a tree before? You are familiar with their structure?*

*Yes,* I say. *I'm able to sense details very well, I just can't see light or color or things that are far away.*

*I see, I see,* he nods. *A tree has roots, it has a trunk, it has branches, and it has a canopy. The Mother Tree has all of these things as well, though the difference in scale is so vast it is barely comprehensible. Entire countries may exist on a single one of Her leaves. We are at the base of one of the Mother Tree's branches, where we will soon meet with the trunk. You know how the trunk of a tree has grooves, yes? Jagged and wavy patches between the individual pieces of bark? We will walk into one, a vast canyon deeper than the eye can see, and from there we will enter the trunk itself.*

Yeah, okay. Standard world tree stuff.

*It sounds beautiful,* I say, trying to seem suitably awed. *I wish I could see it.*

*Perhaps you can,* Sindri chimes in. *I'll try to work out an upgrade to the coordination spell that can allow us to better share senses. I think it will be useful for a number of purposes.*

I shuffle irritably.

*Like letting people tell you their names? Well, either way, I agree. That would be useful. I'd like to be able to see.*

He nods and I return my focus to Teboho.

*My next question is about you, if that's okay,* I say.

*Go ahead!*

*How does your magic work? I thought you might be Space-aligned like I am after seeing you make a hammer appear out of nowhere, but now I'm starting to think I'm wrong.*

*A good guess!* he reassures me. *But no. I am dual-aligned to Matter and Barrier. I can create static objects at will, with a focus on sturdiness. I use this to form myself weapons and armor, create cover for my allies, and give my sister objects to use her spells on if needed. She and I have always fought together as family, and I believe it is a sign of our bond that our innate magic compliments each other so well. Though I have to admit, I'm pleasantly surprised at how well Sindri's skills enhance our own, despite his unfortunate humanness.*

*Why thank you,* Sindri sends dryly.

*Sorry, can we clarify all that a little?* I ask. *You say your innate spells create matter?*

*Nearly all Matter magic does,* Teboho confirms, not seeming to understand why I'm suddenly so exasperated. *It is the primary feature of that form of magic. I can also un-create the things I create, though that's only the things conjured by myself personally.*

Well crap in the peanut butter, that's... that's... what even *is* that!? The amount of energy required to make, like, a *single gram* of matter is in the terajoules! It's the kind of power scale where you start using gosh dang *atomic bombs* as a unit of measurement! Magic has to be absolutely cracked to the point of insanity unless mass-energy equivalence just isn't a thing in this universe... but if that's true then *that's* insanity. How would physics even work!? Aaaaaaaah!

*Is... is there any chance you could give me a quick rundown on all the types of magic?* I ask helplessly. If they're all as absolutely bonkers as Matter magic, I need to know sooner rather than later.

*Of course,* Teboho answers easily. *The pairs are Order-Chaos, Pneuma-Death, Art-Matter, Motion-Barrier, Light-Space, and Heat-Transmutation. With the exception of Chaos, which is quite rare for any being to possess, they are all fairly common.*

115

Huh. That's a decent variety, though there are some odd picks. Art? Barrier? I mean, Barrier is the opposite of Motion, so it's presumably about stopping stuff. Heat and Transmutation both seem like normal kinds of magic too, but why are they opposites?

*Are there any others that are considered evil or overly dangerous the way Chaos is?*

*Death and Heat are the two complements to Chaos, so they are rarely smiled upon. Your naturalborn element is a reflection of who you are, after all, and both types of magic are nearly always destructive in nature. Death in particular is magic that revolves around the creation and abuse of departed souls, so its users are generally depraved.*

And 'creation of departed souls' of course means 'killing people.' Cute.

*Unlike Chaos mages, however, the naturalborn of Death and Heat are rarely incapable of controlling themselves,* Teboho continues. *If they are destructive and murderous, it is due to their own decisions, and they are thus judged by their actions, not the circumstance of their birth. However, this is not so with those of Chaos. The lack of volition that Chaos imposes on its naturalborn is the reason they must be purged. I...*

He pauses, his breath catching a bit as I watch his tear ducts fill up ever so slightly from the inside. (Which is super gross, for the record.)

*...I should speak of something else, I am sorry,* he finally says.

*It's fine,* I assure him. *Don't worry about it, Teboho.*

*I am normally much more composed,* he insists. *I fear my sister is handling our situation far better than I am.*

*I'm sure she's hurting,* I tell him. *She probably just doesn't show it the way other people do.*

*Of course,* he sighs. *Of course, you're right. Thank you, Hannah. You are very kind. I appreciate your patience with her.*

116

I wriggle uncomfortably. I'd like to say it's just common decency, but I know better than to expect decency to be common.

*I'm just giving her the benefit of the doubt,* I insist. *Mistakes and misunderstandings are forgivable. But if she doesn't treat me well then I'll run out of reasons to do so for her.*

*That seems more than fair to me,* he agrees amiably. *Did you have any other questions?*

*I am an endless barrel of questions,* I answer frankly. *I am confused and overwhelmed basically all the time.*

He chuckles again, forcing me to squeeze his shoulders a bit tighter.

*Well, my offer to answer them remains open.*

Hmm. Well, now I have to choose one. I suppose I'll go with the greediest, most self-indulgent question.

*...How do I actually do magic?* I ask. *Like... I know you apparently chased me because I'm naturalborn to Order, but I don't actually know how to do any Order magic.*

*That's not uncommon,* Teboho assures me. *But ultimately, I can't answer that question. It's your magic. While you might be able to learn generalized Order magic, the Order magic unique to you will make itself known when you discover it.*

*Wait, so I can* learn *spells in addition to just being born with them?*

*Of course! Well, as long as you're compatible with them. You can learn any spell as long as it's an element you have or an element that compliments your naturalborn ones. You'll never be able to learn, say, Heat magic, but you have a solid variety of magic you could pick up.*

*Wait, why won't I be able to learn Heat?* I ask. No fireballs!? What sort of self-respecting wizard can't shoot fireballs? Worse, I won't be able to make magical air conditioning spells!

*Your two elements, Order and Space, each complement Transmutation. You might even be naturalborn to Transmutation as well, but that's unlikely. Your aura would look the same either way, so it's hard to tell.*

Hmm. I, uh, think I might be. No reason to tell him that, though.

*And Transmutation opposes Heat, for some reason,* I recall. *What's up with that, anyway?*

He thinks for a moment.

*If you think of Order as the element of maintaining a form,* he muses, *Transmutation is the element of altering, improving, and advancing one. And while you can think of Chaos as the absence of form, the element of Heat is the process of destroying one. Heat is not mere temperature, but also the inevitability of waste, the infantry in Chaos' war against Order. It is the idea that, with every change, some beauty is burnt away and never returned.*

*You're talking about entropy,* I realize. *Every reaction creates thermal energy that becomes unavailable for work in a system.*

*Pardon?* Teboho chuckles. *I'm not sure I understood even half of that.*

*I understood it,* Sindri comments. *How do you know about entropy but not basic magical theory, Hannah?*

Wait, how does Sindri know about entropy? Is the tech level here higher than I... no, wait, Kagiso uses a *bow,* and I don't see any post-industrial tech on Sindri. Why is science advanced enough to know about entropy but not make guns or clocks or whatever. Actually, now that I'm thinking about it, how the frizzle does entropy even *apply* to a world where people can *create arbitrary matter!?* Surely there must be some kind of hard limiting factor I don't understand there.

*I have had a very strange education,* is all I actually say in response. *So basically, Transmutation makes things more complex, while setting stuff on fire generally makes things less complex. That's such a strange and arbitrary dividing line.*

*I'm not sure where you got the impression that the nature of the world needs to conform to your idea of a proper dividing line,* Teboho chuckles. *We make the best explanations we can, but at the end of the day Transmutation opposes Heat regardless of whatever we think makes sense.*

*I guess so,* I grumble. *It's just that—*

*Destination,* Kagiso announces.

*Destination?* Sindri asks. *What do you see?*

*Village.*

*A village?* Sindri muses. *That's strange. There wasn't even an outpost the last time I was here. Though I suppose it has been a couple years since I was this high on the tree.*

*Ah, will we be getting proper beds to sleep in tonight?* Teboho asks. *That would be a welcome change of pace.*

*Hmm. I was hoping to make progress through the burrow before we rest. But a proper inn is tempting.*

*Ah, but if there's a settlement here, there's almost certainly a trader's burrow. You know where our quarry is headed, don't you Sindri? We can simply take a more efficient path. The Chaos mage wouldn't have been able to enter a village of this size.*

Sindri nods in contemplation.

*Yes... all right. Let's stop in the village. Lead the way, Kagiso.*

I grumble blindly as the conversation moves to discussion of a village that I won't be able to see until we're already inside it. I guess the rest of my magic lessons will have to wait. I've yet to even see a single structure in my range when a dentron man starts approaching us, wearing a heavy backpack and followed by a large sloth-like creature drawing a cart full of goods. I see textiles, mostly, with the occasional crate of fruit. The dentron man has a lot more clothing on than Kagiso and Teboho, presumably to show off his fancy wares. I wonder if they're dyed; I suppose they probably are, but I don't have any way to tell beyond asking. He's also

119

wearing an interesting pendant with what looks like a twisting centipede on it, though it's underneath his shirt.

He says something to us all as he approaches, probably buttering us up to try and sell something. Naturally, I can't understand any of it. Sindri politely declines whatever it is he's asking about three times before he finally lets us go. He glances towards me every so often throughout his yammering, though I suppose I can't blame him. I'm pretty weird.

*What a pushy guy,* I comment dryly. *He was wearing a weird pendant too. Some kind of bug?*

*Ah, he's probably a cultist,* Sindri comments as if that wasn't an utterly terrifying revelation.

*A cultist!?* I ask. *Like the human sacrifice kind?*

*What? No!* Sindri snaps. *They don't really do anything bad other than recruit rich merchants and exploit them for donations, preaching about the end of the world as if its coming wasn't obvious to everyone. The Tree of Souls has been dying for hundreds of years and it's taking the rest of the world with it. What would we need an apocalypse cult for?*

Oh boy. More plot hooks. I hope this world doesn't expect me to save the Tree of Souls from The Great Bark Beetle of Annihilation or something. Like, what am I supposed to do, exactly? Tremble, for I am the great hero Hannah! I'll nibble your kneecaps off, foul fiend! At least as long as I can reach them!

*Is the Tree of Souls the same thing as the Mother Tree?* I ask as we continue to approach the settlement. I can see a giant wall of wood off to my side now, which I assume means this place is built next to the trunk.

*Yes, that is what the humans call it,* Teboho confirms.

I drum my legs on his fuzzy shoulders. I don't want to save a dying world. I just want cool magic and somewhere I can relax. And frankly, today has been promising in regards to those things. As long as these cultists don't turn out to be a problem, I think I can chalk today up as a win.

As we continue to approach the wall of bark, I find something interesting inside it: a tunnel. A human-sized tunnel, in fact, resting just behind the natural wall of the tree with small slits that lead outside to where we are. Bolt holes, maybe? No one is manning them, though, and soon enough I find the entryway to a series of man-made tunnels that lead into the trunk, marked by a pair of banners flying on either side.

Oh, that's kind of cool. The village is *inside* the tree.

Sure enough, we wander in unaccosted and I quickly notice a small marketplace, most of the stalls and buildings crafted by excavating wood out of the tree rather than building anything inside it. It looks almost like everyone is living in a giant sculpture. The vast majority of people here are dentron, but there are some humans as well. I do my best not to look at their internal organs and compare them to the particularly tasty ones I ate this morning. That was an animal, so it's very different.

*I suppose we'll confirm the existence of a burrow that heads where we want to go, then find an inn,* Sindri says. *Our quarry already lost a lot of time heading to the upper branches, so we should gain on them even if we rest early today.*

Another one of the merchants suddenly approaches us, this one also with one of the centipede pendants. He babbles a bit at Teboho and points at *me,* producing a large sack of what I assume is probably money.

*Is he trying to buy me?* I ask.

*Yes... he is a beast trader.* Teboho confirms, seeming shocked. *I've told him you aren't for sale, though I suppose you should be flattered. You are apparently worth quite a lot.*

*I'm not a beast, though!*

*He insists you are.*

*Well he's rude! No selling me!*

*I would never dream of it, Hannah.*

I wriggle uncomfortably. I do *not* like the idea of a cultist trying to buy me. Cultists are always bad news. He's probably wanting to use me for ritual components.

*Maybe we shouldn't sleep here after all,* I hedge.

*You'll be fine,* Sindri insists. *I call them cultists but they're a recognized religion in most major nations. They're scammers, but not technically criminals. Besides, beast trading is a common and lucrative occupation for Pneuma naturalborn. He's not going to jeopardize his business or his life trying to steal from a Chaos hunter, not to mention two dentron warriors.*

*Okay but if something awful happens I reserve the right to say I told you so,* I insist.

*Seems fair to me,* Sindri smirks.

Sindri then wanders off to confirm that there's a 'quality burrow' heading to wherever it is we're going, and since that apparently turned out well we buy a pair of rooms at the inn.

*You said you were a woman, right Hannah?* Teboho asks. *Would you mind sharing a room with my sister?*

*I will not throw,* Kagiso insists, though after a pause she adds *...Unless emergency.*

*What kind of emergency would require you to throw me!?* I grumble.

*Will know when see it,* she insists.

I wish I could sigh right now.

*Just don't squish me or throw anything at me,* I request in exasperation. *If you can agree to that, I don't mind rooming with you.*

*I agree,* Kagiso nods immediately.

There's no way this could possibly go wrong.

# 7

# SLEEP

Kagiso carefully cradles me in two hands, idly brushing the top of my carapace with a third as she carries me up to what will be our shared room. I, of course, am holding onto her with a death grip, wary of being dropped—or worse, *thrown*. I admit, I don't actually know if I'll be hurt if I fall, but I've heard that tarantulas can get seriously injured from being dropped and that's about the closest equivalent I have to my current leggy body. I don't intend to test it.

I can 'see' the two rooms long before we reach them, and I have to admit they look nicer than I expected for a fantasy world. The way the whole building is carved out from the inside of the tree is incredibly cool, and I can't even imagine how most of it could have been done without magic. The walls are beautifully smooth, most of the furniture is artistically crafted out of the wood, and there are even small tunnels snaking between the rooms for what I assume are ventilation purposes. Not even I could fit inside those, so what sort of tool would they even use to carve something like that? I mean... I guess there probably *is* a tool of some sort that would work, but magic seems likely considering that it's largely ubiquitous. Not to mention... no way. Some of the little pipe-tunnels aren't ventilation, they're full of water! They lead to a *bath!* That's so awesome!

I do note with annoyance that Kasigo and I only have a single-bed room, while the boys get two beds. I get *why*. I am nowhere near large enough to justify giving me a bed to myself. But also, where am I supposed to sleep!? Do they expect me to just curl up on the foot of the bed like a cat? Or do I just slip under the covers with this four-breasted fuzzball and act like it would be physically possible for me to get any sleep that way? I just—ah, woah woah woah woah woah!

My thoughts are interrupted by a sudden increase in altitude, Kagiso lifting me up, placing me on her head, and then extracting her hands from my grasp, leaving me to cling in terror to her skull.

*You are a hat,* she declares.

*Wh-what?*

*Good hat. Pat pat.*

And then she just... pats me. I am absolutely stunned speechless. Her brother seems to be holding back a laugh, and even Sindri is smiling.

*What just happened?* I ask helplessly.

*I think she likes you,* Teboho says. *Are you getting along with Hannah, Kagiso?*

*Angles, bad. But! She is small.*

I get the feeling that this is somehow overall an assessment in my favor.

*I suppose that's good! I hope you're not too uncomfortable, Hannah?* Teboho asks.

I hesitate. Unprompted physical contact is not normally 'my thing,' and I don't really want to encourage it.

*It's fine,* I say anyway. I'd be blushing with embarrassment right now if I could, and I don't even know why. I just can't bring myself to call this a problem. Even if she's not all that much like him, Kagiso's weird charm reminds me of Brendan so I just can't be mad at her. ...Hmm. Now I'm thinking about getting picked up and carried around by Brendan and yep I think I know why I'm embarrassed now let's think about something else yep yep yep. God I need to get over the squish I have on my best friend.

*It's okay,* I say. *It's kind of a fun perch up here, to be honest. I get to feel like one of you big people.*

Teboho laughs at that, giving me a grateful nod before we part ways, he and Sindri entering their room while Kagiso brings us to ours. Kagiso carefully removes her bow and quiver, setting them by the bed before much more haphazardly peeling off and dropping her backpack on the floor. I watch Teboho and Sindri much more carefully unpack their things, since of course having a solid wall between us does nothing to prevent me from seeing them.

*I'm going to work on the sensory-sharing spell,* Sindri announces. *But while I do so, I'll have to deactivate our current communication spell. It takes too much focus.*

*Oh,* I respond. *So I'm not going to be able to talk to anyone?*

*Hats don't talk,* Kagiso points out.

*Well this hat does!* I counter.

*Hmm,* Kagiso considers. *Fancy hat. Hungry?*

*I suppose I could eat,* I admit.

*Okay. More food for Hannah. Goodbye.*

She reaches up with two hands and peels me off her head, putting me back down on the bed and giving my carapace another pat before slinging her weapons back over her shoulders.

*Wait, are you just leaving me here alone?* I ask hesitantly.

*There shouldn't be any problems with that,* Sindri notes. *But if there are, hiss as loudly as you can and we'll come help you.*

Kagiso, for her part, ignores our conversation and just leaves, wandering off alone to presumably murder some more unfortunate fantasy chipmunks.

125

*Can't I just hang out in your room until she comes back?* I whine. *There's no way I'm gonna be comfortable alone in a town full of cultists! One of which tried to buy me!*

*I assure you, they are annoying evangelists but otherwise harmless,* Sindri responds with a mental sigh. *Besides, Teboho and I are going to be bathing.*

Gah. If I were still human that'd be enough to drive me off. I'm *way* too gay for that crap. Unfortunately for spider-Hannah...

*Look, I appreciate you treating me as a woman instead of as a weird monster, but I can see through objects, guys. I've been looking at your gross dicks the entire journey, not to mention all your internal organs. Taking your clothes off—or for that matter, even having this wall between us—doesn't affect my perception in the slightest. But it does affect your ability to protect me from cultists, so I'd really feel a lot more comfortable in your room.*

I watch the two men glance awkwardly at each other before Teboho shrugs.

*It seems like a compelling argument to me,* he admits. *I say we let her in.*

*Fine,* Sindri sighs. *I'll come get you.*

*Thanks, I... hmm.* I stop. *Wait a moment.*

I wondered for a moment if I could just walk through a barren zone and ignore the wall between our rooms entirely, but now that I'm looking for one I'm seeing something strange. There aren't really barren zones here. Or... no. There are barren zones *everywhere*, but they're not empty. They're all full of wood. Whatever carved out these rooms only carved out the three dimensions normal people have access to, which... I mean, duh, of course they did that. But the wood extends *beyond* the third dimension. It's a completely solid wall in every direction that moves along the w-axis. Of course, a bunch of wood in my way is pretty much the opposite of an obstacle. Like... I could just burrow a hole in the wall, I've been burrowing through wood for years. Except that it *wouldn't* be a hole in the wall, not to anyone else. It'd be a... a fourth-dimensional hole. A little spider-burrow between locations.

I scuttle up to the wall, align my perceptions so I'm looking at the part of the wall that exists only for me, and then I rear up on my 'back' legs, readying myself to dig. Something... clicks, and warmth enters the legs I've lifted. When I pierce into the flesh of the world tree, they cut through it like butter.

I don't need to make a large hole. Just a hole that leads from one side of the wall to the other. I easily twist my legs into a simple circle, carving through the space I need, then push the fourth-dimensional chunk of wood out into the normal world, walking through the wall after it. From Sindri and Teboho's perspective, a one-foot diameter disc of wood just manifested out of their still-solid, fully intact wall... and then I did the same. They stare at me in shock.

*Hey guys,* I send as casually as I'm able, trying not to let my full-bodied excitement take over. I just walked through a wall! And I got to *claw shit* to do it! I'm magic and I'm awesome and I'm magic and I'm magiiiic! It's only when Teboho walks over and leans down to pick up the disc of world tree wood with a blank expression that I realize I might have just seriously messed up. His people revere the tree, don't they...? Aw poop aw beans aw lard.

*This is Deep Wood,* Teboho notes, twirling the disc between his fingers. Thankfully, he doesn't sound mad. *I suppose there's no doubt you hail from the Mother Tree now. That is reassuring.*

*Yeah, that's quite interesting,* Sindri agrees, rubbing his chin. *She's like a tunnel worm.*

*I don't know what that is but the comparison does not sound flattering!* I grumble in protest.

Sindri chuckles.

*Tunnel worms. They dig the tunnels we'll be using to head to a higher branch. Traveling to other branches would be absurdly impractical on foot otherwise. Even if you had an easy path to climb on the* outside of the tree, it would take months to get to the next highest branch. But the holes dug by tunnel worms somehow just... ignore that. They're Space-aligned, like you, and their tunnels are somehow far, far shorter than the distance between their entrance and exits.

Huh. That's neat. They're like wormh... oh gosh frigging darn it. They're *literally* wormholes. Uuuuugh, I hate that, why does this world have a pun monster.

*Unfortunately, I don't think I can bring anyone else into my space,* I say. *I'm kinda surprised I could push that out of it. I wasn't able to do so with a rock unless I put it in my mouth.*

*Is that what you were doing with that rock?* Sindri asks. *Hmm. Well, the Tree of Souls has long been documented to interact differently with spatial magic. The tunnel worms can't replicate their transport abilities back on Pillar. Although part of that could just be how they had to be modified to work with rock.*

*Can we not speak of your kind's perversions of nature?* Teboho grumbles. *You are a decent man, Sindri, but I cannot simply forget all that humans have done. The only creatures more destructive than you are the Steel Ones, which* you *created!*

*I most certainly did not,* Sindri grumbles. *Moronic humans from hundreds of years ago did that. Trust me, we're no more thrilled by those things than you are.*

*And yet you still dabble in that which is beyond you.*

*Woah, woah!* I say, mentally butting in. *Let's stow the casual racism, you two. We're all friends here, aren't we? Common purpose and stuff? There's no point in getting mad at people for something they haven't personally done.*

*Of course,* Teboho sighs. *I am tired, so I forgot myself. Please accept my apologies, Sindri. Would you mind if I bathe first?*

*Go ahead,* Sindri confirms. *I'm going to cut the connection now and work on the improved spell. Goodbye for now, Hannah.*

*Uh, bye?* I allow, and then that clawing feeling at the back of my mind vanishes, thrusting me into muteness once more. Oh well, I guess. I crawl up onto the empty bed and curl into what I have decided is morph ball form, tucking my legs up under my body so I can roll around a bit. Hmm. It's kind of fun to roll around, actually. And I don't get dizzy! Hehe. Rolly rolly rolly. I keep circling around the bed until I catch Sindri staring at me with amusement, at which point I quickly burrow under the covers in shame.

Dang it. Why is being a freaky hyperspider so fun? I should be having a panic attack but it mostly just feels neat. It's just... I don't know. Exciting? New, yet weirdly natural? Like sure, okay, the first day wasn't so hot, what with the fleeing for my life and nearly dying of exhaustion and all. But now I'm just hanging out with nice people, learning magic, and *not* transforming into a horrifying monster. I'm *already* a monster, sure, but everyone is super cool about it so it's not really a problem?

I guess I don't really care about *being* a monster so much as I care about being treated like one?

I contemplate this in silence as the boys get naked and clean themselves off, one after the other. As predicted, the process doesn't really bother me any more than my spatial sense already does. I'm just looking at an extra-detailed anatomy diagram of everybody all the time and slowly learning to ignore it. I stay under the covers in silent contemplation until Teboho sits down on the bed, prompting me to scuttle on out in case he wants to use it. He doesn't seem interested yet, but he does nod in thanks. I don't actually have any idea how close it is to nighttime, and I suppose I can no longer ask.

Teboho looks contemplative for a moment before motioning me over to where he's sitting. I crawl on over and curl up by his lap, where he proceeds to summon a *stone tablet* out of *thin air.* Holy geez. Etched on the stone talent is a familiar alphabet, the same one he drew out when learning my name. He clears his throat, points to the first letter, and starts to sing.

129

Oh my goodness. Teboho is a *terrible* singer. Like, I'm not sure a dying raccoon could sound worse than this. But that doesn't matter, because he's teaching me his culture's alphabet song! He's gonna teach me to read! I straighten up a bit to show that I'm interested, and we go through the song together a few times before he starts to quiz me. I wiggle with delight, drumming my legs in a circle around me whenever I get one of the letters right. By the time I see Kagiso return with a bag full of bloody animal corpses I'm getting about eight of the letters consistently (including 'ha' and 'na,' naturally) which I feel is pretty darn good for a first day.

I don't really have any way to tell him Kagiso is back with food, of course, so I carve another coaster-sized circle of what he called 'deep wood' out of the air, reaching into the w-axis with magically empowered legs to make the circle cut and then reaching in from a few other directions to chop it out of the solid mass of wood that exists in the barren zone realm. I carve a crude smiley face on it, sign my name with what I can only assume is absolutely atrocious handwriting, and gift it to him before jumping through the tunnel I made between the rooms right after Kagiso gets back with my dinner.

I'm starting to get a handle on how all this stuff works! It's just fourth-dimensional thinking; in the same way a two-dimensional image only exists in a single 'slice' of 3D space, 3D objects only exist in a single 'slice' of 4D space. Every single 3D object seems to exist in the same point on the w-axis (let's assume it's zero), so when I move across that axis, 3D objects can't interact with me anymore. Well I mean, they could interact with me if they *also* move along the w-axis, but they can't do that unless they take a ride inside my mouth.

The tree, however, is four-dimensional somehow. When I'm standing on top of a branch, I see 4D space as a series of barren areas with wood floors because the tree is beneath me and *only the tree* exists in that space. When I'm inside the trunk like I am now, every point on the 4D axis *except* the one dug out in 3D (i.e., w=0) is just solid wood. But I can still dig through that wood to make myself tunnels to hide in. It's... well, it's a lot! Complicated and somewhat brain-bursting. I don't seem to have perfect control over 4D movement, either, since if I did I could just waltz into w=1 space and then walk as far as I want before reemerging. But I can't do that when I'm out on the branches; the barren zones aren't infinite. I wonder why. Maybe it has something to do with how I can use them as shortcuts. Hopefully I'll get better at it the more I practice.

Kagiso doesn't seem the least bit surprised when I walk out of a solid wall and wave a leg to greet her. She just waves back and dumps a bunch of corpses on the floor, looking as proud as a cat. I have to admit, they *do* smell like delicious corpses, so I happily skitter over and start shoving them in my maw. I manage to swallow four magic chipmunks before I realize I shouldn't physically be able to hold this much food. My stomach looks pretty normal, though? Are my organs bigger on the inside?

Hmm. Well, more food for me I guess. I gleefully finish a fifth critter. Kagiso makes a weird noise that I think is a laugh and squats down to pat my carapace some more, which I stoically allow because she was kind enough to get me so much tasty animal flesh. I suppose I should probably be cooking it, but it's just so delicious like this! Surely that means my body is designed to handle it, right? It's not like I can cook it without hands anyway. Or, for that matter, a stove. This isn't exactly a hotel, there's no kitchen in the room. Just somewhere to clean up, somewhere to sleep, and somewhere to take a dump.

Kagiso herself apparently found some berries and leaves to munch on while she was out hunting. She eats them alongside one of the thick, dense-looking bread rations from her pack, which looks like enough food for two human-sized Hannahs. Either my guess about a higher metabolism was correct, or Kagiso just has the munchies tonight. Once she's done eating, she hops face-first onto the bed, spreading out over the whole thing without bothering to take off her clothes or get under the covers. She raises her lower right arm and pats the bed next to her, as if inviting me to join her.

I hesitate like the gay little mess that I am. It's obviously not any sort of proposition, since we're completely different species, but that *is* a shirtless woman that would probably be quite attractive (in a weird mutant fursona sort of way) were I not currently staring at her internal organs. I'm not sure how comfortable I am getting on a bed with her.

"Hana," Kagiso grumbles loudly into the pillow, slapping the bed again.

Ah. Hmm. Well I guess a little influx of social anxiety helps. Driven by her apparent insistence, I crawl over to the side of the bed and, on a whim, leap up like a cat. Ha! Oh gosh, I didn't expect that to work! I have *hops.* Wow, that was kind of fun. Anyway, I curl up on the spot Kagiso indicated. She places a hand on top of me and then shoves her face deep into the pillows.

Hmm. I wonder what her deal is. Does she just enjoy physical contact? Hesitantly, I scoot up next to her side, brushing my legs against her fuzzy ribcage. She makes a happy noise. It's kinda cute, but in more of a cuddly dog kind of way than an attractive girl sort of way. I give in and snuggle up, letting Kagiso hold me like some sort of arachnid teddy bear.

Despite my worries, sharing a bed with a shirtless woman is turning out to not be the least bit sexy. Now that I think about it, I haven't been even slightly horny at any point during my time as a spider-beast. I initially thought that's because of my weird perception, but now I'm starting to wonder if it's physiological. I haven't gone to the bathroom as a spider creature yet either, which I'm thankful for because I'm pretty sure I don't have any orifices other than my mouth. If my mouth actually functions as a cloaca and therefore does, shall we say, double duty? I'll be less than enthused. But I'm not an entirely comprehensible creature in terms of pure biology, am I? I'm a motherflippin' *magical beast,* maybe I take a dump via teleportation or something. How crazy would that be? Incomprehensible arcane might, all used to take fourth-dimensional poops. Regardless, the point I'm making is that I don't think I have genitals. Either that or this body is only sexually attracted to other hyperspiders, which... well! I don't want to think about that so I'm not going to. I'm just glad I don't have to be a creepy voyeur animal like Morgana from *Persona 5.*

...Though I guess it's possible I'll have a different interpretation of this particular memory back when I'm in a humanoid body. Gah! Just add that to the 'don't think about it' pile, Hannah.

Hmm.

Crap, I can't stop thinking about it. I'm probably not going to be able to sleep like this. I'm pretty sure Kagiso is zonked out, so I'm hesitant to extract myself from her grasp and wake her. Honestly, I'm hesitant to sleep at all. I... well, I don't really *want* to go back to Earth. I suppose it's Sunday tomorrow, so that won't be too bad as long as I can survive the agony of church service. Heh, I guess my weekends are twice as long now, kind of. ...Though I guess by that logic, my weekdays are too. Oof.

Mentally grimacing, I make an effort to busy my mind elsewhere. My impromptu fantasy adventure party is all sleeping peacefully, but the same can't be said for the entire inn. Many merchants are still awake in their rooms, and the inn proprietor still yawns behind the front desk. He has, I note, one of the centipede necklaces marking him as one of the supposedly harmless cultists, but naturally I don't trust that one bit. Sure enough, my suspicions start to rise when three other cultists, including the one that tried to buy me earlier today, all get together and start chatting with him, the conversation getting increasingly quick and secretive.

Obviously I can't hear a word they're saying and even if I could I wouldn't understand it (I'll put 'learn to lip read' on my to-do list) but I can't help but get more and more anxious as they seem to assemble and start to enact some sort of plan. I watch one of them break off from the others, heading upstairs to where our rooms are, and I start to panic, nudging Kagiso awake. She blinks blearily at me, seeming rather grumpy to be roused, but I just point at the door and let out a soft hiss.

Immediately, her exhaustion seems to vanish. She wordlessly grabs her bow, knocks an arrow, and draws it, pointing to the door. I stay still, waiting in terror... as the cultist passes us by and uses a key to enter the room next to ours. He begins to unload his stuff.

Gah! False alarm? No, wait! The other three are heading upstairs as well. I'm not really sure what they're doing. It looks like they're... stuffing their ears with something? Why? Wait, what's the guy next door doing? Is that an instrument? It must be! He pulls a small, harp-like object out of a fancy wooden case. A lyre, I guess? Or maybe some fantasy equivalent, I don't really know much about instruments.

He starts to play, and the world tilts.

Barely five notes have come out of the song and I feel my limbs getting heavy, my tense body slacking. Wh-what? Oh, crap! The music is carrying through the air vents, and the three other men put in *ear plugs!* Kagiso inhales deeply and starts to *scream,* her voice drowning out the sound for a moment and snapping some vitality back into my mind. Art! Art is a kind of magic! This is a sleep spell! I start hissing with five pairs of legs, rubbing them together to create an even more horrid cacophony. In response, the mage in the other room starts playing even louder. None of it seems to be noticed by any other patrons, our own friends included.

Out in the hallway, the three men are using the innkeeper's master key to unlock our door, presumably oblivious to the racket we're making. I spare a pair of legs to point at the door with more urgency, and Kagiso nods. She swings her aim to the side, pointing at a seemingly unrelated wall. Her scream starts to peter out, so I do everything I can to be as loud as I can, scraping and tearing at the bed during my hiss, and giving Kagiso the time she needs to take a breath. The next thing out of her mouth isn't a scream, though.

"**Ricochet**," something beyond either of us growls, and Kagiso's arrow flies. Bouncing off the floor, the ceiling, and three different

134

walls, her dinky arrow eventually punches straight through the solid wooden door, stabbing one of the men behind it through the arm. Blood splatters as the arrow passes *through* him and out the other end, and though the man grimaces he does not cry out. I, however, jump in surprise, which means for a brief and terrible moment, my stupid, moronic self let the room fall into silence. Except, of course, for the lullaby.

Kagiso's bow clatters to the ground. She's unconscious before she finishes collapsing onto the bed. Shit, shit, shit! I'm so exhausted I nearly do the same the moment I land from my terror-induced leap, but I start hissing again just in time to be awake when the door flies open. In a panic, I lift up a leg and *slash* Kagiso, drawing blood from her arm. She doesn't even twitch.

I do the only thing I can think to do. I run. Three grown men stomp into the room, each nearly six times my height and two of them lanky, four-armed dentron. They make a grab for me, but I barely manage to rush over to the wall, leaping through the extradimensional tunnel I dug for myself.

I suppose I shouldn't have bothered, because the music is playing here, too. I hiss and shriek as loud as I can, clawing away at the beds beside me. It's already too late, though. With all the running I had to do, I couldn't hiss at the same time. And without Kagiso's screaming to help drown out the music, I can't think straight anymore. I'm dimly aware of one of the men staying behind with Kagiso as two more rush over into the boys' room. That's... bad, I think. I left her. I left her to die. But... it doesn't really matter... anymore. All... I can do... is...

"**Sleep.**"

I wake up and scream.

# 8

# RELIGIOUS EXPERIENCE

No, no no no. Oh god. We're going to die. We're all going to die. The cultists had weapons, they knocked us out, we're *dead we're dead we're dead.* Or maybe I'll be the only survivor. They probably wanted to capture me alive, they wanted *me* because I'm some sort of valuable monster so they're going to steal me and lock me up and *kill my friends to remove the witnesses and—*

"Hannah!" someone shrieks. "Hannah, is everything alright!?"

My mother bursts into the room, ignoring the closed door because my room has no lock (I *hate* that my room has no lock!) and stomps her way to my side. No. Why. I don't want you here. I try to stop her, to shove her away, but my head is still scrambled and my instinct to move gets sent to a limb that doesn't exist. Get out get out get out *why are you here.*

"Hannah!" my mother shouts again, wrapping her hands around my cheeks. She looks so terrified, it's hard to stay mad at her. She says something else, but her voice is too hard to hear over the awful *noise* in the room. What's...

Oh, wait. That's me. I'm still screaming.

A few seconds later I figure out how to stop, taking gasping breaths as I force myself to focus on my body. My heart hammers at troubling speeds as I tug around at my own limbs, remembering which is which as I stare my worried, loving mother in the eyes and wish she would just *go away.* Curling my toes, I feel the foam blocks preventing my freakish talons from ripping apart my sheets. My whole body feels sore, a deep, bone-level ache permeating everything. For all I know, something a lot more horrible than toe-claws is growing on me underneath my blankets. It could be anything. *Anything.* I have no idea what sort of monster I'm turning into.

"Oh my baby, you're okay, it's okay," my mother coos. "It's alright. You're alright."

"Get out," I croak.

She seems taken aback. A bit offended, even. I suppose I was harsher than I needed to be, but I'm not in the best state of mind right now.

"...Are you sure?" my mother asks. Ugh. Do I look like I'm in the state of mind to want this kind of careful consideration!?

"I'm fine," I say, repeating the easiest of all lies. "I'm okay, I just... I'm gonna get dressed."

"The dreams again?" she asks.

I want to tell her to *get out* again, but I suspect I've already pushed my luck by being rude even a single time. And you know what, sure. 'The dreams again' may as well be a correct answer. It's certainly all I intend to explain.

"Yeah," I answer. "N-nothing special. I just need a moment to myself."

"Alright," she says, leaning over to kiss me on the forehead. "Church today, be sure to dress nice."

"I know," I tell her, and she finally *leaves,* closing the door behind her. I shudder and extract myself from bed, flexing my toes again before yanking them free of all the foam. Are they...? Shit. They are. The bone growth has started to crawl up the entirety of the toe, breaking into segments over the joints. It hardly even looks like bone anymore, it's more like... well, an exoskeleton. An ivory-white

138

carapace. Flexing my toes as much as I can, I try to peer into the crack between the joints, seeing what I think might be a hint of skin. Or... maybe not skin, but some other kind of flexible epidermis. It's dark. ...Actually, is my whole body getting darker? I look a bit more tanned than usual.

Gah, I can't tell. If it is, it's subtle. I quickly get my shoes on and rush for the bathroom, stripping down to give myself a more thorough examination with the help of a mirror. Ugh, my everything hurts. And I'm itchy! It's from an errant scratching on my leg where I find the next problem: a small section of bone growing from what I think must be my tibia, protruding ever so slightly from the skin. It's not bleeding or anything, it's just... there. In a tiny patch smaller than a fingernail, my skin just *stops* and there's bone instead. Creepy.

I'm on a time limit, aren't I? I'll have to figure this transformation thing out *fast* or it's gonna figure itself out all over my metaphorical front lawn. Of course, thinking about time limits is a bad plan, because now I'm back to panicking about *my impending death.* Or worse, the impending deaths of kind people which I may have just caused.

I jump into the shower out of a need to keep moving. I don't want to be here right now, existing as a human while a crisis is going down in another world. But what am I supposed to do, try to pass out again with my heart beating a mile a minute? I'm on the verge of another panic attack, there's no way I'm going to be able to nap. I'm pretty sure we don't have any melatonin pills or other sleeping aids in the house either. We *might* have Nyquil or something? I seriously doubt it'll do the job, though. It's nearly impossible for me to nap.

Guess I'll just be a twitchy neurotic mess all day! Last time I nearly flippin' *died* I passed out in the other world and woke up moments later, even after spending a full day awake on Earth. So it stands to reason that regardless of how short (or long) my nap is in the other world, when I sleep here I'll wake up over there whenever I would have woken up normally. Our timelines aren't in sync.

...Which, y'know, actually has terrifying implications. Is the relative time that passes between universes based entirely on when I zonk out in each one? If so, that would mean I have to be the only person on Earth who wakes up in that world when I sleep, or at the very least everyone else must be synched with me somehow. Or more likely, if there's anyone else like me, they could be going to a completely different world from the one I go to. Nothing else really makes sense.

...*Unless* time travel is happening. If causality has been ceremonially defenestrated then anything goes. But I hope it's not that. Nothing good ever happens because of time travel.

It's thanks to all these musings that I almost fail to notice a larger patch of skin falling off my leg in the shower, revealing more bone in the process. Unfortunately, I manage to *step* on the palm-sized mass of discarded epidermis, causing me to start screaming again. It sticks to the bottom of my foot and I flail around in the shower, scratching up the tub with my talons and nearly cracking my head open as I slip trying to shake it off. Aaagh it's too big to fit down the shower drain, oh gross oh no oh ew ew ew ew!

My body shaking, I carefully hold back my urge to vomit as I drop the patch of my own skin in the toilet and flush it down, immediately extracting myself from the shower and carefully drying myself off. The exposed bone of my leg is now large enough that it's clearly not *actually* my normal bones; there are muscles working underneath. I'm just... growing an exoskeleton, I guess. But it's not very chitinous, it's distinctly *bony.* I have extra bones. Bonus bones. More bone per bone. I'm going insane and my whole body is shaking and I just... I just can't.

Deep breath. In and out, Hannah. You can and you will, because you have to. That's life. Learn to deal with it. I mean, this isn't anything like *most* people's lives, presumably, but you have to learn to deal with it all the same. Look at the bright side! You're not bleeding this time! Clearly your aching flesh sack of a body is improving its technique. Which is an idea that I thought was going to be comforting but now very firmly is *not.*

140

Whatever. I'm dry. Clothes on. I'm wearing my modest little church-blouse-and-floor-skirt combo so I can cosplay as a straight person. I do not, unfortunately, go to a church with one of the cool denominations who have decided that being gay is a-okay, which is a big part of why I'm still in the closet. Those denominations are funny to me; the Bible is pretty explicit about 'gay is bad,' but it's also explicit about, say, 'divorce is bad,' yet multiple people in my church prove I wouldn't get shamed for *that.* We should get more people lobbying to make divorce illegal. Not because I think it should be, but because it would be funny to compare the utter lack of traction that gets just because 'people who have divorced' are not a minority. But hey, what do I know, I don't believe in any of it and every day I wake up as even more of an abomination that Yahweh would doubtlessly despise, so the narcissistic, abusive prick can go shove his divine knob into a carpentry saw for all I care. At least it wouldn't be another virgin.

Blasphemy aside, I still find myself shaking in terror as I sit in the backseat of my mom's car, my brother beside me and my dad riding shotgun. My claws are cramped horribly inside these awful church shoes, though after some quick tests they seem sturdy enough to keep my feet contained. The modest breakfast I wolfed down after getting dressed is nowhere near enough to calm my gnawing hunger pains, and I feel achy and sick all over. Maybe I'll burst forth from my flesh during the sermon today. That'd be a fun way to get outed as a demon. The gays were monsters all along! Muahaha! Then I'll eat them, and everyone will be happy.

I bite my lower lip, doing a double-take on that particular daydream. There was something weirdly euphoric about it, and that's... terrifying. Why did my head just go there? Most people in my church are *really nice* apart from the bigotry thing (and like yeah, that's bad, but we're hardly Westboro Baptists). They're just, y'know, a community of people whose existence makes it impossible for me to publicly pursue a relationship until I'm financially independent from my parents. So there might be some pent-up aggression at my congregation, I guess, but I don't want to *murder* them. I don't want to murder anybody! If someone stubbed

141

their toe because of me I'd do nothing but apologize for like, six hours. I really hope I'm not becoming a danger to society.

I flex my talons, and even as cramped as they are the movement sends joy up through my feet.

Church is boring. I avoid talking to anyone as much as I can, both because there's nothing I *want* to talk about with any of these people and because I'm still in the type of panicked state where I might start crying if I attempt to string more than two words together. Thankfully we didn't get here terribly early, and before long we're all in the pews, listening to an old white man ramble on about conscience and the Holy Spirit. I barely pay attention, since my mind is fully occupied with the infinitely-replaying thought of Kagiso getting stabbed through the heart while she sleeps. In my mind's eye I'm using my spatial sense to watch it all, seeing the moment the blade pierces that vital organ, watching it continue to beat over and over, pumping more and more blood out of the new holes now digging through its walls, until it rapidly falters, fades, and ultimately fails. She dies alone in her room, because I was too cowardly to stay and too pathetic to help. I tell myself there's nothing I could have done, but then I start thinking of a dozen things I could have done. If I hadn't messed up and stopped making noise to drown out the spell. Or better yet, if I had been fast enough, smart enough, *ruthless* enough, I could have dug right through the wall and silenced that Art mage myself. But I can't take a life like that. I don't *want* to. What other options are there, though? Give myself up? No, of course not, 'letting the murderous assholes win' is not how you deal with murderous assholes. But what else am I supposed to do!?

It's probably too late anyway. By the time my spider-body wakes up, it'll be long over. Automatically, I stand up with the rest of the congregation and mindlessly sing the hymns along with everyone else. I may not believe any of this stuff anymore—haven't for years—but I have to admit that *Benediction (May the Peace of God)* is actually an unironic bop, even if shortening 'heaven' to one syllable during the chorus kind of grates a little. How are we supposed to pronounce that, even? It's spelled "heav'n" in the hymnal, and like... what? What is that? The closest we tend to get is just saying 'hev.'

The one good hymn soon ends, though, and my musings end with it. It's back to panic mode. I politely excuse myself to the bathroom now that the service is over and spend a little while stretching out my poor, abused monster feet before I once again trap them inside my awful, awful church shoes. I don't take off my tights, but I do run my hand over the front of my leg, feeling out the patch of external bone and shuddering. At least I don't find any more skin falling off. Hmm, that reminds me.

**Help, my skin is falling off,** I text Brendan.

Almost immediately, those three little dots which indicate a person typing appear, and just that alone is enough to fill me with relief.

**Because you're in a holy building, or...?** he asks.

**Smartass,** I chide him. **No I mean like my skeleton is straight up hatching, Bren.**

**I'll get the trumpets and xylophones I guess?** he answers, and I snort out a laugh from inside the bathroom stall.

**I can't believe you're memeing me right now,** I grumble halfheartedly.

**Sure you can. Besides, I'm not sure what else to do? I mean, other than scream "holy shit go to a fucking doctor, Hannah!"**

**But I obviously won't listen to that,** I answer.

**Obviously,** he agrees. **You bleeding?**

**Nah,** I answer. **It's the benign kind of late-stage leprosy.**

**Small mercies, I guess?** he hedges.

**So they tell me.**

The next message takes quite some time to show up. No doubt Brendan tried to type something and then deleted it a few times before finally settling on a message.

143

**You streaming today?** is all he ends up asking.

**Yeah,** I confirm. **Gotta take my mind off of stuff. Are you finally going to tell me what your Twitch handle is?**

**Nope. But I'll be watching and commenting! >:D**

**Curse your shenanigans!** I whine. **I'll figure you out one of these days!**

**No you won't! Your chat is too popular due to how great you are!**

**Nooooooo! Liiiiiies!**

**Muahahahahahaha! Ok now you should probably put your phone away until you get home.**

**Yeah ok.**

Regretfully, I get off the toilet and return to society. No one thinks much of my extended stay, since normal humans can somehow engage in conversation with each other about topics other than Pokémon, Tabletop RPGs, or horrifying mutations of one's physical form, which is a technique I have yet to master. Still, it means they're all too distracted speaking with each other to try and speak with me, which is just the way I like it. I tolerate the wait in silent panic, but a short eternity later we're back in the car and heading to Taco Bell, which is *for some reason* our traditional after-church choice of dining. Nothing quite like praising God shortly before your intestines make you wish you were dead, I suppose.

"What do you want, Hannah?" my mom asks, which means it's time to *calculate.* I'm hungry as hell, but how much of her money can I get her to spend on just me without her questioning it? Probably no more than... fifteen dollars, max? She'll balk at that, but silently. I quickly order some of the larger things on the menu and, to my great relief, she just nods and asks my brother the same question. Mission accomplished, Hannah! Booya! You have successfully minimized social interaction with your own family at this juncture! Great job, very normal and well-adjusted of you!

...Well, whatever. I chow ravenously down on my collection of beefy potato burritos, their cheezy, oozing slosh helping quiet down the chaos in my mind. The increased food consumption is *obviously* fueling my transformation, but like... what am I gonna do? Starve? Then I would probably just transform into an underweight monster with hunger pains. Let's be honest with myself here: I'm absolutely doomed. I have no control over this situation and I'm too much of a mess to *get* control over this situation, no matter how much help Brendan tries to get me. I'm stuck on this ride until something catastrophic happens and then I will probably be shot to death by a local coven of rednecks.

But whatever. It doesn't matter. *None* of this matters, not when I might wake up in a cage with the blood of three good people on my legs the next time I pass out. Everything here is just so *pointless* in the face of that. What's the use of putting effort into caring about something horrible that will *probably* happen to me when something horrible is *already* happening to me *right now!?*

I'm helpless to do anything about any of it anyway, so why bother to try? Global warming is killing the world, half the country is trying to make sure COVID gets us first, wars are starting up all over the place and I'm slowly transforming into some kind of freakish pandimensional spider-girl. I even have a first and last name that start with the same letter! I'm a regular silver-age superhero! The point is, it's all garbage that's going to keep happening to me no matter what I do. That's just how things are. So my lot is even more insane than anyone else's. So what? Someone has to be the edge of the bell curve. Doesn't give me any more of a right to complain.

We all make it home without so much as a fart endangering us and I swiftly return to my room, closing the door and kicking off my awful, *awful* shoes. The rest of my outfit quickly follows, leaving me free to select an actually *good* outfit to stream in today. Hmm... something black, I think, to try to draw attention away from the fact that my skin might be subtly changing color. After a double check of the room and a triple check of my own face to make sure nothing monstrous is happening up there, I put on a bright grin and start the stream.

"Hello everyone!"

Sunday is one of the few times I semi-regularly stream, so chat is a bit more packed than usual. Still nothing huge or impressive, of course, but there were a good chunk of people *there* right when I started. Just... waiting for me. Something about that always feels good. I might protest and quibble with Brendan over it—I can't let myself get too big a head, after all—but my channel really is growing and I *love* watching it grow. It means nothing to my family, since I don't even make minimum wage yet, but to me this is beautiful. I get to do something I love, and other people love watching me do it so much that I make an income out of it! Like come on, I'm literally getting paid to play Pokémon. Sometimes it feels like, even if I only just make enough money to survive, that'd be worth it, you know? But that path leads to ruin, unfortunately. Bills will pile up somewhere, most likely from the fucking protection racket that is the American healthcare system. I've got to make a lot more money than the average food service worker or Twitch streamer if I expect to survive with any degree of comfort.

...Unless I mutate into a monster and rampage through downtown instead. One more point in that category, I suppose.

YaktaurCaptain u ok, DD?

AllTricks she'sTHIMKING

LavAbsol Pokémon is a game that requires INTENSE FOCUS

NougatKin DD has achieved zen

PentUp is she even breathing lol

Lucarivor29 DD please notice us ;-;

SwalotRancher RIP DD

Oh, crap! A quick glance at my chat reminds me that I've been silent for far too long, which is a quick way to lose my audience. "DD" is me, obviously. I go by DistractedDreamer online.

"Ah! Sorry, chat," I tell them, shaking my head as clear of thoughts as I'm able. "It's been a pretty rough few days, my head's caught up in all sorts of things."

I immediately get a chorus of 'what's wrong' and 'oh no!' and realize my mistake. They're curious. Now I'm expected to *explain,* and I really, really don't want to do that.

Obviously, I could decline to do so. Nothing stops me except my own obsession with channel growth. Managing relationships, or at least the appearance of relationships, is an extremely important part of my job. I *am* my brand, and brand loyalty is a big part of how a business grows. I don't want to encourage parasocial relationships, of course—they're as creepy for me as they are unhealthy for everyone else—but it's sort of unavoidable since personal interaction is essential to my job. People caring about me personally, about *my life,* is what will keep them on my channel rather than migrating to one of the more popular and more skilled streamers. I'll never physically meet any of these people, but I want to try to remember them, recognize them, and form that vague sort of internet familiarity with them because that's going to be the foundation on which more people get attracted to my content.

Streaming is fun, sure, but it's also a job. So... how do I explain? How do I discuss my problems when they all sound like insane fantasies? ...Hmm. Well, I suppose there's a pretty easy way to talk about insane fantasy stuff as if it was happening to me.

"Does anyone here play GURPS?" I ask. "The tabletop game? Generic Universal Role Play System?"

I get a few 'yes' answers but mostly 'no.' That's okay. It gives me more story to tell.

"GURPS is wild," I continue. "It's pretty much exactly what it says on the tin: an attempt at a *universal* role play system, one that can be used to simulate any fantasy or sci-fi world you can imagine. Even the real world, if you're into that for some reason. You can make absurd things with the GURPS ruleset, from eldritch gods to swarm-minds to hyper-advanced robots to ancient magi. It's a phenomenally powerful system, mainly held back by the fact that it goes *really* hard into physics simulation and realism. If you're not very, *very* familiar with the rules, you're going to spend literal hours in every single combat encounter, looking up all sorts of wacky edge cases and *still* ignoring half the game's rules just to make *that* bearable. I'm not personally a fan of the system much because of that, but I can't deny that it does an absolutely incredible job of accomplishing what it sets out to do."

Time for the small lie, I suppose.

"Anyway, I'm currently in a GURPS game. And it's fun, but it's kind of messing with my head."

I hesitate a bit, trying to think of the best way to frame my life as a fantasy.

"...So, the premise of the game is that... our characters have amnesia. To the point that we don't even know what we are or what we can do. The GM has our character sheets and was the one to make our character. We have to figure ourselves out as we go, and we've got all kinds of weirdos. A human mind mage, a pair of four-armed siblings, and I'm a friggin *spider* with some sort of space magic. It's pretty wild. Anyway, uh... the last session ended with like, our whole party getting hit by a sleep spell from some cultists. I think they wanted to capture me, but they have no reason to keep the rest of the team alive. And I feel *awful.* I did what I could to stop it, but it wasn't anywhere near enough. Now I've gotten everyone into a situation where they all might die. The session *stopped* there, too, right when everyone passed out. We don't know what might happen."

LavAbsol The GM isn't gonna randomly kill you all like that lol

"Yeah, you don't know my GM, Lav," I sigh. "Trust me, it's a real risk."

AllTricks u got space magic right? Teleports?

"Pseudo-teleports, yeah. More like I can step into another dimension for a while. I have to sorta... dig through the other

148

world, I guess? At least in the place I'm in now. But I can make my legs sharp for that."

PentUp OK it sounds like you're spec'd for an ambush character. GURPS is high lethality, so that's good for stealth play. Step into another dimension, wait for a good sneak attack, kill cultist. Step back. Repeat.

"Uh… I don't think my combat stats are very high. Also, I *definitely* have the Reluctant Killer disadvantage."

AllTricks atk from behind so u don't take the -4 from seeing ur victims face

"I, uh, have some kind of unique omnidirectional sense which makes that impossible."

PentUp Then your build is trash and you're fucked lol

AllTricks ya lol

Lucarivor29 big oof

"Wow," I sigh. "Thanks, chat."

I suppose I probably should have known better on that one. Panic starts filling me once again so I drown it out in video games, chatting as much as I can. I'm not doing well tonight. This is a bad stream. This will hurt my metrics. But I keep going, because the alternative is being alone with my thoughts.

Unfortunately, no amount of distraction seems to be enough. What's going to happen to me? Will I wake up in a cage? Perhaps I could escape that easily enough, but then what? I can't even communicate with anyone unless I have Sindri's help. In the best-case scenario, my friends are free and alive, but I'm still probably kidnapped. Will they be able to find me? Will they try? It's more likely that my friends are *dead.* No loose ends and all that. It would be child's play to kill them all while they're unconscious. Hours pass and the despair just keeps creeping in on me. Maybe they captured my team alongside me? I don't know why they *would* but they certainly *could* have. They're cultists, perhaps they want to sacrifice us! But by that same token, maybe they don't want to capture me at all. Maybe they want to kill me and the sleep spell was just their best way of accomplishing that. Over and over, each imagined scenario worse than the last, I torture myself until well after the sun sets and my body starts becoming too exhausted to continue. It's almost a relief when the stream ends, the foam goes back over my toes, and I snuggle into bed, quickly passing out despite my raging heart rate.

I wake to a furious roar shaking me to my core, and blood splattering over my body.

My spider-self has no eyelids to blearily blink open, only a perpetual sense of everything surrounding me, so the chaos hits all at once. A fuzzy arm, cradling me. Pulped and peeled organs, smashed and cut. Blood pooling inside bodies, but outside veins. Death. Pain. Danger. Movement.

Teboho is holding me in the crook of his left lower arm. Another arm holds a large shield. The last two hold a spear, which currently has its point impaled through the neck of the lullaby-spell user. One of the other three cultists has a sword impaled through his belly; he's alive, but likely won't be for long. The other two are busy smashing through walls of stone that have somehow grown out of the wood of the tree. And speaking of the tree, two brand new holes have been smashed in it, presumably by the sledgehammer at Teboho's feet.

Holy crap. Teboho somehow woke up *during* the sleep spell, blocked the two cultists entering his room with a stone wall, smashed *through* the wall separating our rooms to stab the cultist going after Kagiso, and then smashed through the *next* wall in our room to stab the Art mage. Once again, I can't have been asleep for more than a few seconds.

Is this... a best-case scenario!?

A crashing sound rings out as the two upright cultists break through the stone barrier two rooms over. Agh, let's not be hasty here! The scenario is *still going!* Teboho rips his spear out of the Art mage's throat, quickly stabbing him two more times for good measure before turning back into my room. Kagiso and Sindri blearily blink awake for only a split second before jumping into combat mode, which fortunately saves Sindri's life as he barely leaps out of bed in time to avoid a super-speed stab from one of the cultists. Motion magic, probably? With another furious roar, Teboho hurls his spear into the room, forcing the Motion mage to dodge and giving Sindri time to scramble over to the weapon and pull it out of the far wall. A crack like thunder rings out as the other cultist points his hands at Sindri, though, something striking him in the chest and causing him to let out a hoarse scream. I watch some of the blood vessels in Sindri's arm *explode,* his whole body seizing painfully for a moment. What was that!? It sounded like lightning! Shoot, it might *be* lightning, what with how it traveled down his arm and boiled his blood. I have no way to know, I can't see light! Kagiso scrambles for her bow, grabbing arrows to nock, and the chaos escalates from there.

I feel paralyzed by terror, the nature of my strange senses contributing to a feeling that I'm not really here, just watching this horrifying scene in third person. Yet I know that's not true. Each pump of rapidly-leaking blood spilling from the bodies of the cultists near us is a reminder that these deaths are *real,* and it is only by some miracle that Teboho is the one dealing them rather than the one bleeding out on the floor. Dimly, I realize that I'm restricting his ability to fight by clutching onto his hand like this, so with shaky limbs I dig through the air and hop into an extradimensional cubby, hoping against hope that somehow, everyone will be okay.

It's all I can do.

Teboho seems to notice me scurry off, quickly forming himself another hammer out of thin air and rushing to Sindri's side with the weapon swinging. In the arm that used to hold me, he now has a dagger. Kagiso has finished nocking her first arrow, but she fires it point-blank into the head of the dying cultist at her feet before joining the fight proper, a chilling execution that I'd probably have nightmares about if I was capable of them.

Though I suppose, arguably, this world *is* my nightmares.

The speedster-cultist jumps into the room with Kagiso and his ally unleashes another crash of thunder, this time hitting Sindri *and* Teboho. Suddenly, our archer is stuck fighting in close-range while our two melee combatants are held back by a mage. Everything's going worst-case again, and I'm just sitting here, hiding!

Trembling.

I don't want to be a killer.

*Step into another dimension. Wait for a good sneak attack. Kill cultist.* The recent murderhobo advice rings in the back of my mind, and I feel myself start digging. Kagiso and her enemy are both Motion mages, and though she's struggling she's still defending herself. She probably has some degree of magical speed as well. There's no way I could ambush them. Sindri and Teboho, meanwhile, are getting fried. ...And their enemy is standing still.

Can I stop him? How would I even do that? Attack his legs? His arms? He's a mage and the magic of this world doesn't require limbs to use. I'd have to knock him unconscious, but I don't know how to do that safely. I don't even know what to *try,* and even if I did it'd risk either death or failure depending on how I mess it up. My friends scream as their bodies burn, wracked with deadly magic that I can't even see.

I can save them, though. I just... I just have to kill.

Teboho tries to throw up another stone wall, but the zap-mage focuses him down, leaving him a writhing mess on the floor. My tiny valve of a heart beats as fast as it can, my legs throbbing with power as I dig to my target. My tunnel is more or less suspended in midair, starting from the spot I crawled out of Teboho's grasp at waist height. It doesn't take terribly long to find myself huddled in terror behind the cultist's neck, my claws ready to strike.

"Hana!" Sindri shouts my name in desperation, leaping behind a bed for cover. "Hana!"

I barely hear him, what passes for my ears consumed by the pounding sound of my own blood and Teboho's screams. I don't want to kill. I don't want to kill him. This man in front of me attacked us, unprovoked. He's going to kill us all. He's evil. He's scum. He's more of a monster than I ever could be.

I don't want to kill him.

But I have to. I have to. I'm shaking. I have to kill him. I can't but I have to. The speedster nicks Kagiso in the arm. She's going to die at this rate, but the boys can't help her. No. No, no no. Have to. I have to. I create my tunnel exit, shredding the wood inside my mouth so it doesn't fall out into 3D space and alert my prey. The back of his neck is right in front of me. Exposed. My legs tense, magic filling them and begging for release. I feel the pull, the *need* to sink them deep into flesh, remembering the ecstasy of cutting things open with my talons back on Earth.

I don't want to kill him. Two of my legs flash forwards, one aiming for the spine and the other for the jugular. I don't want to kill him. My bladed body swims through bone even easier than it does wood. I don't want to kill him. My instincts know what to do, leaping onto his severed neck and sinking my teeth into the wound. I don't want to kill him. He tastes like iron and victory.

I clatter to the floor atop a corpse, tearing into it voraciously as Sindri rushes into the adjacent room to flank the last cultist. The speedster isn't so easily cornered, but he quickly catches onto the fact that he's outmatched, disengaging immediately and rushing out the door. Sindri swears, or at least it sounds like he does, before staggering back into this room—the room where I am currently eating a man that I just killed—to try and drag Teboho to his feet. The dentron is in terrible shape, which I suppose is the natural consequence of being struck by lightning multiple times in repeated succession.

"Hana!" Sindri barks at me, but I ignore him because I'm still very busy eating. Because I killed a man, and now I'm eating him. I killed a man and I'm eating him I killed a man and I'm eating him *I killed a man and I'm eating him what am I doing what am I doing stop stop stop stop stop—*

Two strong hands reach down and pull me out of the bloody mess of viscera I've ravenously dug myself inside of, and I immediately freak out. Flailing as hard as I can, I hiss with multiple pairs of legs, trying to squirm out of the tight grip. Despite all the blood making my carapace slippery, however, I am lifted up, up, *way* up until I find my shrieking body placed carefully on top of Kagiso's head.

"Fala hana, nata nata," she coos, tapping the top of my body once for each 'nata.'

*Good hat,* I intuit. *Pat pat.*

I stop struggling, swallowing the last bits of flesh caught in my mouth. I'm just shaking now, my body unable to scream or cry. I'm a murderer. I saved my friends, but... god. Oh god. *Fuck!* I just... I just...!

*We need to go,* Sindri's mental voice suddenly blares in my head. *Now!*

Ah. Yeah. The speedster might be getting backup. I don't answer, but I don't need to. I just keep a firm grip on Kagiso's skull, careful not to cut her as she and Sindri each support one side of Teboho and the three of them all flee together, taking whatever they can carry before legging it out of the inn. Outside of the confined spaces, my limited sensory range now *feels* confining. I see Kagiso grab a stone from a pouch on her side, speak her spell, and throw it... but I don't know what her target was until we run past the corpse of a human woman, face-first on the ground with a hole in the back of her skull. Another cultist, judging by the necklace, but not the speedster that was fighting us. I have no idea what she might have done to earn Kagiso's ire.

The little rest stop village we're in isn't very large, and we're soon at what is obviously the end of it. Multiple human-sized tunnels are dug into the wood at the town's edge, each quickly twisting into an impossible direction. Sindri looks them all over briefly before decisively picking one, and we rush into what I can only assume is one of the wormholes. Once inside, it quickly twists into w=1 space, but somehow enables the human and dentron to follow the path anyway. I can somehow *feel* the magic here, but I have no capacity to focus on anything right now. I feel as dead as the man I just killed.

Sindri and the others have a brief conversation, and a barely-conscious Teboho makes another wall, sealing off the tunnel behind us. Sindri and Kagiso set him down as carefully as they can, then collapse from exhaustion. Sindri makes everyone clasp hands the way we did when establishing the last communication spell, and I numbly step off of Kagiso's head and add a leg to the mix.

*Well,* Sindri heaves. *I suppose I owe Hannah an apology. The cult... was definitely a problem.*

I don't answer.

*Brother save us,* Kagiso comments. *Hat save brother. Good hat.*

*How did he save us?* I manage to ask numbly. *Why wasn't he...*

I don't manage to finish communicating the thought, but Teboho figures out my question anyway.

*I'm a Matter mage,* he says. *Matter and Barrier. Matter opposes Art. You screeching underneath my bed was enough to wake me up.*

Oh. *Oh,* I'm so dumb! He resisted the spell because of his element. Gah, I'd *just* learned that, how did I forget?

*Thank you,* I mentally mutter.

*No, thank* you, *Hannah. If you hadn't woken me up, a blade through the chest probably would have. You saved my life twice just now!*

And I ended a life. I ended a life for the first time. I'm still covered in sticky, wet blood. I drank it from him. I *liked* it.

*I'm the only reason they attacked,* I answer numbly. *I put you in danger in the first place. They wanted me because I'm valuable, right?*

*Most likely,* Sindri confirms bluntly.

*That hardly makes it Hannah's fault!* Teboho protests. *They wanted to steal her like an animal, and kill us to get her! What occurred was nothing but justice against foul men so cruel and corrupt that they doubtlessly would have found a reason to attack us regardless.*

*Perhaps,* Sindri answers noncommittally. *But whether they wanted Hannah or not, the important thing is that we stopped them and made it out alive. We should be largely safe here in the worm tunnels, at least for a while. And if they DO come after us here, Teboho and Kagiso can set up an absolutely brutal killzone. So for now, let's lick our wounds and rest.*

*Lick, lick,* Kagiso purrs, having taken Sindri's advice literally and decided to slurp at the gash on her arm. Then she glances at me, takes her arm out of her mouth, and offers it to me.

*Hannah want?* She asks, motioning to the blood leaking out of her.

*N-no!* I yelp back at her. She shrugs and goes back to licking herself.

*Yes, about that,* Sindri sighs. *Please don't eat anyone else, Hannah. It's not acceptable in civilized cultures.*

I jump a little at that, my legs nervously drumming through 4D space.

*I didn't mean—I mean, I won't! I don't want to, I just... I won't. Sorry. I'm sorry!*

*She saved your life, Sindri!* Teboho protests. *Leave her be. You aren't hurt anywhere, are you Hannah?*

*N-no, I'm fine,* I insist. *I'm fine.*

I'd ask the same to him, but I can't bring myself to do so. I can see *exactly* how bad Teboho is torn up on the inside, and it's horrifying. Less than an hour later, though, I'm back on Kagiso's head and everyone else is back on their feet, staggering up the wormhole to our next destination. I spend the whole trip replaying my kill over and over in my mind. Remembering my panic, my horror, my regret, and my reluctance.

And how it all washed away at the bite.

# 9

# TASTE FOR BLOOD

We don't talk much for the rest of the day. Or... is it nighttime? I guess it probably is, considering our rude awakening, but it's impossible for anyone to tell inside this spatial tunnel up through the trunk of the Mother Tree, or Tree of Souls, or whatever a given culture wants to call this thing. My vote is 'Absolutely Massive Woody.' God, that's so bad. What the heck, brain?

Regardless of the time, we're all exhausted, frayed past our breaking points. My thoughts are a constant anxious loop, replaying the moment I murdered a man over and over in my mind. The way my legs slid through him with only the slightest resistance, the way the smell of his viscera erupting from the wound drove me into a frenzy, the way his sticky blood still covers my body, gunking up my joints and providing a constant reminder of what I just did. It's sickening. It's horrifying. It's revolting.

It was probably the right thing to do.

I mean, by any halfway decent legal system that wasn't murder, that was justified self-defense. They escalated to lethal force, we responded reasonably in order to protect ourselves. I guess you could argue Teboho was the first to kill someone, but if I woke up in the middle of being magically disabled to see two shady men with weapons drawn looming over my bed... yeah, I think anyone would be justified in assuming they were trying to kill us. And by the time *I* got involved, my victim was already frying my friends with goddamn lighting bolts. If I got tried in court, I'd probably get off scot-free if I had a reasonably competent lawyer.

Literally none of that justification makes me feel better, of course. The law does not decide what's moral or what's right, and it certainly doesn't decide how traumatized I'm going to be after an event like this. If someone else had done what I did, I would tell them that they did the right thing. They saved people that were in danger via the best method they had available. I know that. It just... doesn't matter. Because I did that, *I* had to live through it, and *I just killed someone.* I will never, ever be able to take that back.

At least I'm not alone in my trauma. The only one of us who seems unaffected by the experience is Kagiso, who just seems sleepy more than anything else. Though all three big people trudge up the tunnel with obvious fatigue, Teboho and Sindri are both noticeably subdued in ways that feel like they go beyond mere exhaustion. I want to ask them about it and see if there's anything I can do to help, and I've almost worked up the courage to speak up when everyone suddenly halts.

*Kagiso, hide Hannah,* Sindri orders.

*Wait, what?* I ask, but I'm immediately peeled off of Kagiso's head and stuffed into her backpack, which is sealed overtop of me. *Oi! What's going on?*

*People ahead,* Sindri explains. *They're heading down, we'll meet them. They're probably merchants, which means there's at least a half-decent chance that they're cultists. I seriously doubt every member of their group is going to try and kidnap you, but... well, better safe than sorry.*

I stop struggling and curl up into a little ball, doing my best to act like luggage.

*That makes sense,* I allow. *Why do you think they were after me in the first place?*

*Same reason I was, I suppose,* Sindri answers. *If you were just a monster, you'd be ridiculously valuable.*

*Did you not explain to the merchant who wanted to buy me that I'm a person!?*

*I did,* Sindri insists. *I suppose he just didn't care.*

*What makes me so valuable, anyway? It seems like you have tons of Space-aligned monsters, and I'm sure there are plenty of Order-aligned ones as well.*

*Hannah, I just saw you decapitate a Light mage with a Space spell. Those are opposing elements. Remember how magic resistance works? You completely ignored being electrocuted—which is normal enough, if admittedly impressive—but you* also *ignored your target's resistance to* your *magic. That speaks of a massive difference in relative power.*

Wait, I was being *electrocuted* that whole time!? I didn't even feel it! I guess it was loud in there, but I assumed he was still zapping Teboho! Gah, I really wish I could see! Still though, I suppose it sounds like I have the standard bullshit isekai power level. That's... something, except I'm fairly certain it doesn't translate to anything like hit points. I can still quite literally be squashed like a bug.

*I... I had no idea,* I admit. *So they just wanted me because I'm powerful?*

*Yes,* Sindri confirms. *That's my suspicion. It probably had more to do with the fact that one of them was a beast trader than the fact that they were cultists. The Disciples of Unification are a borderline pyramid scheme, sure, but they're not a bunch of bandits. They'd strongly disapprove of anyone wearing their emblem engaging in that sort of behavior.*

*What do you mean by a 'borderline pyramid scheme?'* I ask.

*Becoming a high-ranking Disciple of Unification requires sizable donations to ensure your dedication,* Sindri explains. *The more you pay, the more the 'truth of reality is revealed to you,' or some such nonsense. Anyone with basic sense knows to stay away from them, but they still manage to subsist off of aggressive evangelism among the merchant class.*

Oh my god they're scientologists. That's... I hate that so much. I get sent to a fantasy world, but instead of deep and interesting cultures of tree-dwelling peoples who worship provably real deities that enact miracles directly on the world, I'm stuck still mucking around with the lowest common denominator of religion.

*I... I see,* I manage to answer, and then the incoming merchants come into my sensory range.

It's three dentron: a man, a woman, and a small male that I assume is a young boy. They have a strange wagon-like... thing, but rather than being pulled by an animal it rests on top of a large, flat lizard-like creature, which has no apparent trouble with the rough, steep tunnel even with an entire caravan and three people on its back. The creature is wide and low to the ground, both of its eyes resting on top of its head. Oversized feet grip so solidly into the wood that I suspect it could travel via the ceiling of the tunnel if it were so inclined, though its cargo might not appreciate that. Its body is longer than a pickup truck, not counting the tail, and on its back is what I suspect might be the life's wealth of the family driving it. Securely covered and attached, the storage area has crates upon crates of glass bottles filled with unidentifiable substances, from powders to liquids to animal organs to dried plants. There's enough empty space back there for the group to huddle up and sleep together, as well, so there are beds laid out and plenty of crates that just have travel food. It's all very interesting, but I'm more concerned with the risk they pose than the goods they sell. I search through their outfits, and to my dismay I find that both of the adults have the same centipede-engraved pendants that the other cultists have.

*They're Disciples of Unification,* I confirm to my team.

*How can you tell?* Teboho asks.

*Pendants under their clothes,* I answer. *Centipede symbol, right? Long twisty bug, lots of legs?*

*That would be them,* Teboho confirms.

*There's no reason to assume they're involved with the group that attacked us,* Sindri assures everyone, but it doesn't stop him and the rest of the team from tensing up for combat, muscles coiled and ready to fight in an instant. Kagiso doesn't draw her bow, but she subtly palms a stone in each hand while Sindri rests one of his own on the short sword at his hip. Teboho, of course, is neither armed nor armored, but the entire premise of his magic is the ability to change that in an instant.

Our tension must make the cultists nervous, as it spreads to them the closer they get to us. They don't make any aggressive moves, however, simply ordering their son to hide in the covered parts of the cargo before politely (or what I assume is politely) hailing us. They keep their huge (and kind of adorable) flounder-skink as respectful a distance away from us as they can, but we'll have to pass very close by in order to get around them.

*Hannah, can you see what goods they sell?* Sindri asks.

*A bunch of weird stuff,* I answer. *Glass bottles full of crap. Maybe they're apothecaries? Magic potions or something?*

*There's no such thing as magic potions,* Sindri chides. *They could certainly be selling medicine, though.*

*Need medicine,* Kagiso points out. *Hurt. Stabbed.*

*You want to buy stuff from the people that tried to kill us?* I ask incredulously.

*It's better than going untreated, I suppose,* Sindri grumbles. *We need a doctor to look at Teboho's injuries, and we need to make sure Kagiso's wounds don't get infected, and I could probably use someone to look at my arm as well. Just... keep Hannah in the bag. Don't let them see her. Alright?*

*Hide the hat, no pat pat,* Kagiso confirms seriously.

*I can just hide in one of my dimensional pockets,* I point out.

*Your what?* Teboho asks. *I don't think Kagiso's pockets will be big enough.*

163

*Did that not translate?* I ask.

*I understood you,* Sindri sighs. *Do what you think is best, just don't be seen.*

*Okay, I'm hiding in higher dimensional space then,* I say. *Just don't leave without me. I'll sneak back into the backpack when you guys are ready to go.*

I reach through the direction that shouldn't exist, carve out the wood in my way, and pass into the cool, familiar space of tunneled world tree, the blood caked to my body all dropping into Kagiso's backpack as it's unable to follow. It's second-nature for me to dig through the trunk like this, probably because that's what I was *doing* every night of my life until I finally emerged less than a week ago. ...Geez, was it really less than a week ago? That's insane, it feels like so much longer.

Anyway. The team is going to go talk to cultists on purpose, even though we *just* got nearly killed by a group of them. That seems incredibly stupid to me, but I guess it's not my call. I need to stay out of sight. And if something happens, then I'll be in the perfect position to... to...

Oh god, please don't make me have to kill anyone else.

Ignoring an urge to vomit, I shakingly dig a tunnel towards where the cultist merchants have stopped, shoving the carved-out wood down my seemingly-endless gullet. Sindri speaks with them for a while, giving me the time I need to move behind their necks. Just... just in case. The merchants wear armor underneath their clothes, but have no weapons. That means nothing, of course. Weapons are somewhat less important when anyone can randomly be born with a deadly spell. Everyone is *always* armed, though most people have no idea what anyone else is armed *with*, making everything even more terrifying. Pneuma mages have it lucky, what with being able to see whatever 'auras' are.

I skitter in a circle, chasing the unfocused thoughts from my mind. This is dangerous. This could be another catastrophe and I have to be *ready* because if I'm not ready people could die! ...And if I am ready then people will die *and* it will be my fault, but at least it won't be people I like. That's... fuck. Fuck! I hate this! I hate having to think like this! Why is every part of my life collapsing all at once!?

I wait, claws at the ready as Sindri negotiates with the cultists. I'm ready when he approaches them, showing proof that he can and will pay. I'm ready when a deal is agreed on, I'm ready when Sindri reports it's a *good* deal and these kind people aren't taking advantage of our desperation. I'm ready when clothing starts to come off so wounds can be treated. I'm ready. I'm ready through it all. If they attack, I'll make their kid an orphan. I'll do it. That's the reality of this world, so I'll do it.

An eternity later, my friends are thanking the traveling merchant-doctors, the two groups parting ways. I slip back into Kagiso's backpack, trying to ignore the small bed of dried blood shavings that I inadvertently created inside. Nothing happened. Everything was fine.

*See, that's how things usually go with the Disciples of Unification,* Sindri grunts. *Those four we fought were just rotten, greedy bastards.*

*You speak as though you have a history with this group,* Teboho comments.

*I wouldn't say a history,* Sindri hedges. *I just travel a lot, and they're one of the few organizations prominent on both the Tree of Souls and Pillar. They accept basically every sapient species to their ranks and mainly recruit other travelers, like merchants. They're usually quite fair merchants, too, they just have a horrible tendency to constantly prod at me and try to get me to join their organization. They're annoying, is all.*

*Talk too much,* Kagiso groans. *Sleep soon?*

*It'd be bad form to set up camp inside a tunnel,* Sindri insists. *Not enough room in here. Just a little further, everyone.*

*But sleepy,* Kagiso whines.

*Your brother nearly got fried to death and he's not complaining,* Sindri sighs. *I mean it. It's just a little further.*

I think it's a little weird that we're avoiding rest when we nearly all just died, but I guess I'm the only member of the group that didn't get injured and I'm *also* the only member of the group that doesn't have to walk, so I figure I don't deserve a say in the matter. Sindri isn't lying, at least. Less than half an hour later, we make it out of the tunnel onto another branch, the cool wind indicating we once again stand under open sky.

I'm sure it looks beautiful to everyone that can see it. To my senses, it's just a few structures and a bit more dirt.

There's no village here, just a small outpost. We avoid it, Sindri navigating us away from anyone else and setting up camp somewhere secluded. We agree on a watch rotation, and since it's apparently dark enough right now that my senses see *further* than everyone else's, I'm included in the shifts. Sindri takes first watch, followed by me, and ending with Kagiso. Teboho is excluded, since he's the most heavily injured.

*Hannah want?* Kagiso asks, patting the dirt next to her sleeping bag.

*I think I'll sleep somewhere no one can get to me,* I tell her. *Thanks for the offer, though.*

She pouts a little, but nods. I start trying to burrow into the tree… and realize that we're out on a branch again rather than inside the trunk, so I'm not able to burrow in whatever direction I want. I have to find a nearby barren zone and step into it. I'm not sure why it works that way, but that's the way it works. There's a small barren zone nearby, though, so into it I go.

I curl up, dig a bit to get myself comfortable, and then wake up on Earth. My alarm is going off. It's Monday morning. I guess it's time for this traumatized little murderer to go to school. Once I remember how to walk, anyway.

The morning routine isn't so bad today, at least. It doesn't take long for me to figure my limbs out, and I head to the shower without any trouble. My horrifying mutant bits are still horrifying and mutant, but other than my skin getting a little bit darker and the exoskeleton slowly growing up my toes I don't see anything notable. I don't even lose another patch of skin from my leg, although *that* patch of bony exoskeleton sure is a thing still.

Nope, it would seem I've hit a new normal. The only odd part about today is how I start shaking like an insane person every time I stop moving for more than five seconds, having to think about the taste of glorious, horrible blood in my mouth as I burrowed into a man's chest cavity. It makes my toes curl and my leg itch and my stomach growl for bloody meat. Will I kill someone here on Earth, too? Will it be in self-defense again, or will the changes to my body just drive me mad?

No. Don't think about it. Press forward. I get long, thick socks on to hide my mutating leg and claws, with a basic T-shirt and jeans covering... hmm. No. I put a jacket on, one with a hood. Then I find some gloves and stuff them into my pockets, just in case. *Now* I'm ready. Or at least as ready as I can expect my useless preparation skills to be capable of. I walk to the bus stop and immediately realize my mistake.

I have to wait. There's nothing to do here. I pull out my phone in a desperate attempt to acquire distractions but it's too late, I'm already thinking about human flesh sliding down my throat. God, why did the one cultist I ended up killing have to be the human one!? I mean, would it have been better if he was a dentron? Is it racist to say yes? Oh good, now I'm a murderer *and* a bigot. Great work, Hannah, you're really striking off the unforgivable monster bingo card! Keep this up and you'll be going for a blackout before the end of the month! I'm sure you can find someone to torture if you put your mind to—

"Hey, Han—"

I *leap* away from the sound, twisting in the air and trying to get a half dozen limbs that don't exist up and ready to protect my face from the predator that somehow just snuck up on me. How did it do that!? I can see... I can... wait.

I land in a slight crouch, my heart throbbing a mile a minute and my breathing heavy. It's just... it's just Brendan. It's Brendan, it's fine, it's okay, it's Brendan. It's okay. I'm fine. There's no attack.

"Hannah...?" he asks slowly, opening and showing both his palms.

I open my mouth to tell him I'm okay, and a hiss leaks out. Brendan takes a step back, which immediately makes me want to *chase him claw him predator danger kill eat* I'm going crazy oh god I'm going crazy help me *help me!* I feel my breathing get faster, my eyes grow wider, but I'm *not* going to hurt Brendan, I refuse, I refuse, I categorically *refuse.* Not the best thing in my life. He's fine. He's safe. I'm safe.

...Except I'm clearly not safe. Not safe to be around, not safe to *exist.* I'm still stanced like an animal, still completely certain that something is trying to kill me and I'll have to kill it first if I want to live. Just like last night. He had to die. He had to. I had no choice.

"Hannah," Brendan repeats, kneeling down slowly. Smaller. Less aggressive. Good. "You in there, Hannah?"

Yes, I'm in here. I'm in here and I need help. I know how to say the words but they won't come out. I feel tears start to form in my eyes. I'm completely, mortally terrified, and I don't even know what of. I want to run, I want to fight, I want to scream until the sun dies, but as usual the action that comes easiest to me is doing nothing at all. Stay the course. Maintain status quo. I stay stock still, not trusting myself to attempt anything else.

Brendan takes a slow step forwards. I let him. He takes another, and another. Cautiously, treating me like the wild animal that I am, he extends a hand forwards. I track it carefully with my eyes—I don't think I could choose to *not* track it—but I continue to otherwise stay still until it inevitably reaches its target.

Brendan pats me on the head, the motion rough and uncomfortable.

"There... there?" he says awkwardly.

Something about that—maybe the odd humor to it, maybe the sheer absurdity, maybe the contact itself—breaks the dam of tension and I break, my body dropping out of fight-or-flight mode like a stone. I gulp for air and then have to *stop* gulping for air, worried about hyperventilation. Brendan catches me as I stagger, then quickly releases me once I get my balance back. I look up into his worried expression, embarrassment sparking inside me but lacking the energy to flare.

"...Bad night?" Brendan asks.

"Y-yeah," I confirm. "Yeah. Pretty bad night."

"Maybe you shouldn't go to school today," he ventures.

"I'm fine," I insist. "I'll be fine."

"Hannah..."

"I'm *fine!*" I snap."I just... let me pretend."

He stares at me, not knowing what to say for a while.

"Tell me about it?" he eventually asks.

I take an involuntary step back, my body starting to shake with stress again.

"I..."

I killed someone. The words are on the tip of my tongue but they don't come out. I killed someone and I ate them. I was almost kidnapped and my friends almost died.

"I-I..."

Hannah you pathetic imbecile, just say the words! The Best Friend Code demands it! Yet the bus arrives before I can choke out the truth, and before I know it we're at school, getting off the bus and neither of us have said a single word. We're going to have to split up to get to classes. Now or never.

Come on, Hannah. You're not *this* weak.

"I killed someone," I manage to choke out.

Brendan stops and stares at me for a while, taking in the severity of my words.

"You should definitely see a therapist," he says simply.

I'm taken aback by the comment for a moment, feeling offended and betrayed.

"I-I'm not going to see a therapist!" I snap.

"Okay, but like, intellectually you understand that you *need* a therapist, right?" he presses.

I hiss at him. Again. Because apparently I have a hissing response now. I'm still too exhausted and angry to be embarrassed about it.

"I know you hate therapists, Hannah," Brendan says, putting his hands up placatingly. "But bad experiences with them doesn't mean you don't still need one. No, actually, it means you need one *more.*"

"So I can do what?" I challenge. "What am I gonna say, Brendan? That I wake up in an alternate universe every night and I ate a man because he was shooting lightning? I'd get thrown in a looney bin!"

"I think you're more than lucid enough to avoid being forced into a psychiatric hospital," Brendan answers calmly. "You're not... okay, I mean, you *are* a danger to yourself, but not because you're insane."

"Oh, har-dee-har!"

"Hannah, that was *emphatically* not a joke."

I hesitate at that. He's really serious. Even worse, he's not wrong. I'm obviously traumatized, I'd have to be a thousand times more dense than I already am to not see that. Therapy is how you deal with trauma. The problem, of course, is that I'm traumatized by therapy.

"You can go to a completely different treatment center, Hannah," Brendan points out. "Hell, there's no way your parents would *let* you go back to that place. That's not how things normally go and you know that. You had a good therapist for *years.*"

"I had a useless therapist for years," I counter. "It never *helped,* it was just... not that."

The bell rings, announcing our impending tardiness. I turn to head to class, hesitantly looking back at Brendan one more time.

"We'll talk more about this after school," he insists.

I nod glumly, hurrying off to my first class of the day. It's just English, so nothing particularly interesting or difficult, which is good because I have biology next and there's a big test today. Ignoring whatever nonsense about *The Scarlet Letter* the teacher is droning on about, I pull out my science textbooks and start to get some last-minute review in. The teacher calls on me with a question part way through class to try and gotcha me into paying attention, but that only works if I can't answer the question correctly. Obviously, I can. No complaining, teach, I have straight A's and you know it. Leave me the heck alone.

Studying biology isn't exactly productive, but it's engaging enough to work as a proper distraction and that's what I need to get through the day. I expect the test itself to be similar. Not difficult, but definitely taking my full attention to accomplish. I sit down, manage to distract myself with my phone until the bell rings, and then it's testing time. Multiple choice, too, just the way I like it. I look forward to forgetting all of this crap in a few months. Who needs life skills if you can just regurgitate information without context? It's not like our society has created a searchable database of nearly all human knowledge or anything. Memorization is definitely the most important thing to focus on. ...Although what I should *really* be focusing on is this test.

As time passes, that quickly starts to get more and more difficult. There are a few questions about blood, and just thinking about them brings up horrid memories, horrid *tastes* that creep into my mouth and refuse to let go. Warm, wet iron sliding down my throat like syrup. Pooling in my mouth. I've heard that human meat tastes like pork, but I can't say I agree with that. Maybe that's true when you cook it, but when you devour it raw from a still-spurting neck? It just tastes like blood.

My mouth tastes like blood. So much blood. More and more, I try to lock my focus on the test in front of me, but I just keep tasting that awful, revolting, *glorious* blood. I fill out an answer as it fills up my mouth. I can't get the taste out of my mind. It's so real, almost like I—

A drop of liquid leaks out of my cloth facemask and stains the test paper red.

Oh. *Oh.* My mouth tastes like blood because it's *actually bleeding.* I don't even know if that's better or worse. I move my tongue around, and *wow*, okay, there's actually a lot of blood collecting in here. Where's the cut? What's happening to me *now?* I prod at one of my teeth on a whim and... it moves.

It comes loose.

I'm so startled I open my mouth, just a little, an audible *splat* of blood hitting my desk as a result. Now that I'm scared of it, I can't help but apply pressure to other teeth—poking them, sucking on them, just a *little*—and one by one they all start to collapse out of my gums, filling my mouth with enamel and blood. Oh god. Oh god! In a panic I jump to my feet, hand over my mouth as my chair clatters behind me. Everyone looks my way. Everyone sees the blood oozing through my mask, over my fingers, and dripping onto the desk. The teacher shouts my name as I run out of the classroom, but I don't listen. I rush for the bathroom, no nurse, not again. I rush to a sink, block the drain, pull up my mask and *spit.*

Every single tooth in my mouth clatters into the porcelain, all of them drenched red. I... I don't have any teeth anymore. I don't have *teeth.* And that is a lot of blood. My blood. All that blood is coming out of my face. It's still bleeding. Oh no. Oh no oh no. Stop. Please stop.

My chest starts to ache. I guess we're doing the panic attack thing again. I hardly even feel like I'm in my body this time, like I'm some casual observer feeling this pain, seeing this bloody-faced girl in the mirror start to hyperventilate and nearly choke on her own blood. C-calm. I have to calm down. Face down, let the blood drain out. Don't swallow it. It'll stop. It'll definitely stop. You're lightheaded because of the panic attack, not because you're dying. I don't know if that's true but I'll keep telling myself that. Oh, fuck, what's happening to me? *What's happening to me!?*

I mean... I suppose there's only one thing it could be, when you think about it. I've already lost all my baby teeth, of course, and my father is a dentist for crying out loud. My teeth were *impeccably* healthy. The only thing that could have pushed them out is new teeth coming *in.* I prod my gums with my tongue, quickly finding telltale points starting to emerge. Because of course they're so damn pointy I nearly cut my tongue on them before they're even poking out of my gums.

I suppose I'm a maneater now, so it only makes sense I grow the teeth to match.

# 10

# URGES

I do not have the supplies and tools I'd *like* to have for cleaning up this much blood, but I suppose I'll just have to make do.

I should probably try to stop producing more blood first, though. Or... well, I mean, I'm going to need to produce blood to make up for all the blood that's falling out of my face, but I need that blood to *not* fall out of my face, so... god, what am I even thinking about? Am I still having a panic attack?

Hmm.

Yep, chest still hurts, body still feels like it's screaming, breathing is only stable due to effort. Definitely a panic attack. Is this what dissociation feels like? Huh. I don't like it. What was I thinking about? Oh *right,* the blood. Thankfully I still have a bunch of crap in my backpack all about dealing with blood, so I quickly close my mouth, rinse my hands, and stick a bunch of gauze in my mouth. Awesome. Now what should I do with the thirty-two teeth that I just dropped into a sink?

Something about that thought hits me like a brick to the face, and I'm slammed back into the full terror of my situation all at once. *All of my teeth just fell out of my face.* I am bleeding from the entirety of my gums at the same time. I am losing a *lot* of blood and I might need to go to the emergency room, at which point it will be discovered that I am a horrifying freak of nature whose existence probably defies everything we know about how biology works and

*I don't know,* maybe that'll go just fine, but maybe I'll be kidnapped and tested on or outright killed and I have no idea what will happen, I have no way to know *what* will happen, so I just have to keep it all a secret even though there's no way that's going to last I just... I can't! I can't handle anything else!

So, again: teeth. Do I just flush them down the toilet or something? I mean, that might work if there was just one of them, but I have an entire *mouth* full of teeth and I'm worried they might get stuck in the pipes. Imagine an irritated old plumber trudging out to the school to fix a clog just to open up a pipe and have thirty-two teeth just tumble onto the floor. He'd think someone was killed and murdered to death! They'd call the police, the police would check the dental records, they'd *find* my dental records and find out I'm alive and well but they'd *definitely* want to talk and figure out what all that was about and just... *aaaaaaaaah!*

So none of that plan is happening! Instead, I reach my hand into the horrible little soup of blood I've collected in the sink and retrieve all my teeth, depositing them on top of five layers of paper towel. I rinse them off, transfer them over to a new set of dry paper towel, then stick them all in a ziplock bag and drop it in my backpack. Good. Now if anyone finds my teeth, they won't think I'm a murder victim. They'll just think I'm a murderer instead.

Which is true.

And speaking of, this entire process has gotten a *lot* of blood everywhere, so I quickly change out the red-soaked gauze in my mouth, put on a fresh N95, and start compartmentalizing the crap out of all my various forms of panic so I can move my body in automatic mode. I'm not sure why, but I've always liked cleaning. I'm certainly *good* at cleaning, and it's something that I can do with my hands that's just engaging enough to fully occupy my brain. It's distracting in exactly the way I need right now, or at least in exactly the way I've traditionally used to handle stress which probably isn't *actually* what I need but is the only thing I know that helps, even temporarily.

I've always considered myself weirdly self-aware for someone who repeatedly runs face-first into the same problems over and over. They say the first step is admitting you have a problem, and *dang* am I really good at that, but all the other steps sure do tend to give me trouble. ...Wait, did I just hear the bathroom door open? Oh, crap-and-mustard sandwich someone's coming in! No no no no no!

"O-occupied!?" I squeak desperately, even though that's not how this bathroom works because it has four different stalls in it.

"Uh, Hannah, right?" an oddly familiar voice calls out to me. "Mr. Frank said to check if..."

A freckled girl's face peeks around the corner into the bathroom proper and immediately goes white as a sheet, presumably because of all the blood all over everything, myself included. It's Autumn, of all people, the girl who *also* saw my bloody-as-a-horror-movie toes back in gym class. She has brown hair, green eyes, and a somewhat thin face with high cheekbones that would probably look sharp and intimidating on someone who didn't look like she was about to scream and/or throw up. Outside of that she looks incredibly plain, wearing the kind of nondescript, almost uniform-like outfit that's so boring I can almost forget what it looks like while staring right at her. Which I am, in fact, doing, because someone just walked in on me cleaning up pools of my own blood with nothing but hand soap and a panic attack. We deer-in-the-headlights each other for an awkward fifteen seconds or so as Autumn's face gets increasingly more panicked, her breathing accelerating and body shaking until she suddenly squeezes her eyes shut, takes a deep breath, and twists her expression into something more like confused, mildly irritated bewilderment with what seems to be sheer force of will.

"Okay," she manages to say, sighing deeply. "What?"

"What?" I parrot back like an utter fool and complete moron.

"What," she grumbles, fishing into her back pocket for a small notepad and pulling it out, "is going on, exactly?"

"I, uh. Bloody nose," I lie poorly. My voice is a horrid muffled mess because of all the gauze in it, and *also* because of the lack of teeth in it, but maybe I can just talk quietly and pretend it's the mask getting in the way.

"Do you have a fucking artery in your nose, or something?" Autumn asks incredulously, glancing at her notebook rather than me. Her eyebrows scrunch together as she reads it, but she just puts it back in her pocket afterwards.

"The sphenopalatine artery, yeah," I answer numbly.

She blinks at me. I blink back.

"...Would you like help cleaning that up?" she asks with a sigh.

I mean. I suppose this is a lot of blood for one person.

"Thank you," I mumble. "I have some latex gloves in my backpack, if you want them."

"Of *course* you do," Autumn sighs. "That's not creepy at all. Is your mask stuffed with gauze or something? You sound like you're talking through a wall."

"Not the whole mask," I assure her. "But I mean, there was a lot of blood, so..."

"A lot of gauze," Autumn agrees as if that's perfectly reasonable and I'm not a crazy person covered in liquid human, which I have to say is rather nice of her. "Get me those gloves, I definitely don't want to catch whatever explosive blood problem you seem to have. Are your feet okay?"

"Uh... well, they're not bleeding anymore," I answer awkwardly, pulling a whole box of latex gloves out of my backpack that I guess I must have stuffed in there during my morning fugue. What else is in here? Bandages, Band-Aids, some other useful stuff I guess I stole from my house's medical supplies. Well hey, good job, me. I'll have to pack some cleaning equipment tomorrow, too. I toss Autumn the box.

"Y'know, once is unfortunate, but twice is suspicious," she points out, catching the box and pulling out a pair of gloves to wear. "You gonna explain any of this?"

178

I stare at her, trying to figure out the best way to answer.

"No," I ultimately decide. "No I am not."

Autumn gives me a rather nonplussed look, but to her immense credit she grabs some paper towels, squirts some soap on them, and starts cleaning up regardless. Which is *exactly* the response I needed. Honestly, kind of a girlboss move to see someone who was literally drowning in blood moments ago and be all like 'hey, you need help wiping up all your gross human juice?' Something about that—probably the fact that it's horribly timed and doomed to failure, given my track record—makes my heart flutter in what I've come to recognize as the beginning of a crush. Which, y'know, is the last possible thing I need right now, but my body being a piece of shit and doing whatever it wants with no regard to how it affects me has become somewhat of a theme lately. Ugh. I was just thinking about how Autumn looks plain, but the moment she does something nice for me I'm staring at those adorable freckles and long brown curls in a completely different light, trying to avoid letting my gaze fall below her neckline, and generally just activating all of my gayest neurons. This happens *way* too often for my liking, I really wish it would stop. But also, I really wish she'd take off that offensively plain shirt and—*hmm* nope stopping that thought. You know what? I've got blood to clean up. Let's clean up the blood. I peel my eyes away from my uncomfortably attractive classmate and get back to work.

"Thank you," I manage to gurgle out, doing my best to ignore how catastrophically stupid I must sound with my gums stuffed with gauze. "I really appreciate the help."

"It's whatever," Autumn grunts. "At this point I'm just trying to get a good excuse to take the science test some other day. I feel like helping you with all this is probably enough of one."

"Well, you said Mr. Frank told you to come check on me, right?" I ask. "He can't get mad at you for doing what he said to do."

Autumn is silent for a moment, her eyes squinting almost imperceptibly, but she nods slowly.

179

"Right, yeah," she answers blandly. "Good point."

If there's one advantage to a sudden, intrusive, and entirely unwanted budding crush on a girl I have talked to a grand total of two times, it's that it somehow manages to distract me from the horrid feelings in my frighteningly-empty mouth, the throbbing ache of slowly-closing blood vessels, the painful pang of new teeth growing in, and the general lightheadedness of having lost all of the blood that I'm currently wiping up. The bleeding does, at least, seem to be rapidly slowing down, as my fresh gauze still tastes more like spit than iron. Together, Autumn and I quickly contain and sanitize the mess as best we can, making it look less like a slasher flick. I only need to remind myself that she's probably straight about fourteen times throughout the process. My brain is just annoying like that. I'm *very* much not able to handle a relationship right now, with everything going on. I mean heck, at this rate I'd probably try to eat her or something! Plus, she's not wearing a mask, and I *refuse* to date anybody not wearing a mask. I don't care that it's not required indoors anymore! Every little bit helps! My stupid hormones ignore all of this perfectly reasonable logic, of course, but it's no big deal. I get these sorts of crushes all the time, and they are yet another thing I've gotten very good at repressing. Nobody else is gay in this stupid southern-state Christian town, so sixty percent of my crushes end up making cartoon awooga eyes at the beefiest football players, thirty-five percent loudly agree with my pastor when he decries homosexuality as sinful (which I guess doesn't mean they *aren't* gay, but it certainly means I don't want to deal with their baggage) and of course the last five percent is Brendan, who I assume is there just because the part of my brain who crushes on people that are nice to me went so far into overdrive that it temporarily tossed my gayness out the window, or something. I dunno. I'm probably just *unspeakably desperate.*

"I guess I owe you double for this," I tell Autumn, my mouth still a muffled mess. "If you need anything, just let me know."

I'm not sure if I'll be of much help with my life rapidly shattering to pieces like this, but I'm certainly going to *try.*

"I'll be sure to write your favor down," Autumn answers dryly, peeling her soapy gloves off and tossing them in the trash before pulling out her notepad and, apparently, actually doing just that. Unfortunately, she has the notepad angled so that I can't see it. Probably on purpose. Still though, I want to ask.

"Do you collect all your debts into that ledger, or just the particularly bloody ones?" I joke.

"What can I say," she drawls. "It pays to know who'll be willing to spot you some cash. Literally."

I chuckle even though it isn't funny, half because of the budding crush and half because I'm experiencing a major adrenaline crash and my brain is completely shutting off. Though in her defense, Autumn generally seems very... flat. Uh, like in the amazing, dry, witty sort of way, not the chest way, which actually looks rather... y'know, not, um. Flat. *Anyway,* point is, even if that particular joke didn't particularly land, I liked the *delivery* of it. For some reason the deadpan really hits me. Also, as previously mentioned, I'm unspeakably desperate.

"Let's see if we can get that test rescheduled for tomorrow," I offer. "And maybe if we can get some janitors in here to properly sanitize the place. I'm not sure I trust the bulk-bought hand soap."

"That's probably wise on all fronts," Autumn agrees. "Hell, if we play our cards right, maybe we can get out of gym tomorrow."

"Hah! I doubt it, but we can dream. Really, thanks again, Autumn. I appreciate the help."

And more than that, I appreciate the fact that she seemed utterly unfazed outside of her initial shock on entry. She didn't press any questions I gave obviously evasive answers to, and she was content to work in silence once we really got going on things. And I *definitely* liked... no, wait, stop. Bad brain. *Stop crushing.* You

181

basically just met this girl, you awful collection of hormonal garbage.

"No problem, gauze-face," Autumn answers. "Which is what I'm going to call you until you tell me your name."

Oh! Gosh, did I forget to tell her my name!? Rude, rude, rude, Hannah! How could you be so rude?

"Agh, I'm sorry! It's Hannah. My name is Hannah!"

"Hannah, right. I'll remember it this time."

I nod, and the two of us head back to the science room. We politely ask the teacher to reschedule the test for tomorrow—I could probably finish in the time we have left since I'm a blisteringly fast test taker, but I don't want to make it awkward for Autumn to ask—and he agrees, probably in part because I took the opportunity to strategically change out some of my bloody gauze. With the N95 still on, of course. I gotta say, my favorite thing about facemasks is that they hide your face. Helping prevent the spread of a deadly disease is a close second, though. The bell rings shortly afterwards, Autumn and I parting ways without a word as we head to our next class. Gah, I still can't believe I forgot to give her my name!

Except... wait a second. Didn't Autumn say my name when she walked into the bathroom? *That's* why I didn't tell her! She already knew it! I guess she was just messing with me? Or something!? Ah, whatever. It doesn't make much difference. I guess I can just ask her next time I see her.

Welp. Only one thing left to do then. I pull out my phone and send off a succinct text to Brendan.

**Hey so literally all of my teeth just fell out.**

The three dots that mean 'this person is typing' appear, disappear, appear, disappear, and appear again for the entire short break between classes before Brendan finally hits send.

**Smoothies for lunch then?** he asks. I snort with amusement. Cheeky dork. But also… yeah that's a good idea actually.

**I guess I don't have any other options!?** I admit. **I wasn't really thinking about that.**

**Is there a more pressing train of thought for losing all your teeth than "how am I supposed to eat now?"**

I mean, there apparently is when cute girls are around. But as tempted as I am to simply respond with the word 'titty' (which I'm sure Brendan would understand, considering all the curvy monster girls he draws in his free time) I do actually have a more coherent excuse and I'm going to use it.

**The worryingly large amount of blood leaving my face was actually my primary concern,** I tell him. **That and the fact that someone else saw it. Not the teeth, but the blood.**

**Who?**

**Mr. Frank sent a girl named Autumn after me. Same one that saw my bloody feet. She was nonplussed, but she helped me clean it all up so she's cool in my book. You know her?**

**I know who you're talking about, but no, we've never really talked.** Brendan informs me. I kind of expected that answer; Brendan has a couple other friends but otherwise doesn't talk to much of anyone.

**Hmm. I'll ask Ida about her at lunch, I guess,** I respond, entering my third period classroom and sitting down.

**Oh, yeah, we'll need her car if we want smoothies,** Brendan agrees.

**You okay with that?** I ask. **I know you two aren't really friends.**

**I can't say I'm thrilled but I'm not going to leave you at Ida's mercy.**

**She's not that bad,** I protest.

**She is and you know it.**

I sigh. This particular line of conversation won't go well, so I change it.

**I'm surprised you're not bugging me to get more extreme help than a smoothie, considering my situation.**

Five minutes later, when class has started and Brendan is *still* typing his response, I realize that particular diversion may have been a tactical error. A big block of text enters my phone all at once, and I read it with the fear that it will explode inside my heart.

**I care about you, and your health, significantly more than I care about anyone else. Myself included. If I could get you the medical attention you need, I would. If I could fix all these problems for you, I would. What's happening to you is interesting and neat in the abstract, but I know that, to live it, it's horrific. And you're handling it the same way you handle all the problems in your life, which is to just pretend it's not there and try to keep everything the same until it gets worse and worse and worse and ultimately blows up in your face. You shut down, close yourself off, put on a big smile and act like you aren't going insane because the worst, most awful, most unthinkable shit in the world is happening to you. Stuff you should NOT put up with, stuff that you NEED to act on, but you refuse. You always do this, and if anyone tries to push you out of your cycle you just push them away, dig your heels in, and make it a contest of stubbornness that I don't have a chance of winning. So yeah. I'll be happy if I can just make sure you eat enough fucking food, Hannah.**

I feel my toes curl, my gums masticating a bit on the gauze, the itchy spot on my leg where skin gives way to something terrifyingly firm. I was right. That hurt to read. In the awful, stressful way of something I want to deny, I want to get *mad* about, but I know that he's right. Brendan is right, but as usual I already knew that. I just can't fix it.

**I don't know what else to do,** I answer lamely.

**I gave you three other things you could do,** Brendan reminds me. **You're just refusing to try them.**

A flash of irritation passes over me and I fail to push it away. I know he gave me other options. I *know* that. He doesn't have to tell me.

**I can't,** I insist. **There's too many unknowns. None of my options are good, but hiding gives me more time to figure stuff out!**

**Hannah, you know that's not why you're hiding.**

I grit my gums instinctively, which is painful so I immediately have to stop.

**I just can't, okay?**

**Yeah, I know,** he answers. **I'm used to you by now.**

What the strudel does *that* mean? I scowl, which turns out to also be a terrible idea. Ow, ow, ow. Stupid budding monster teeth. ...Wait. Am I getting to the point where I've successfully compartmentalized enough trauma that my response is just 'stupid monster teeth?' Gosh, I mean, that's probably really bad, but it's also incredibly refreshing! Like, *finally*, geez. Panic attacks are exhausting.

I look up and notice the teacher glaring at me, which I correctly interpret as an order to put away my phone and at least pretend to pay attention. I wonder what my next horrifying mutation will be? I hope nothing happens to my eyes or the upper half of my face, since that'd be a pain to cover up. What *wouldn't* I mind is another good question. If I'm going to end up being the villain in a horror B-movie I should at least get to be a cool one. Hmm... extra limbs is an obvious answer. It'd be nice to fill the slots I always wake up missing. Ooh, and magic is cool. I like magic, I like having magic, and if I had magic on Earth it might make my life here a little more manageable. ...Actually, wait, *do* I have magic here on Earth? I, uh... haven't tried yet.

It would make sense though, wouldn't it? Going by the theory that my current transformations are due to the aptly-named *Transmutation* category of magic, because why wouldn't they be, magic exists on Earth and I'm doing it, albeit unwillingly. If I figure out more about magic, maybe I could even control the changes! It's gotta be worth a shot, right? The problem is that I don't actually have any idea how to *do* magic, since all my powers are passive. The spatial sense is always on, the barren zones are just *there,* and the ability to move in 4D space likewise just feels normal when I'm in hyperspider mode. I don't *have* any active... er, no, wait. I do have one. I used a spell to cut that delicious cultist's spine in half, didn't I?

...I mean evil cultist. Not... not the other thing. I shudder. Fuck, okay, not totally compartmentalized there.

A-anyway. Magic. Magic cutting spell. I have one, and I guess it *might* be a bit of a trauma trigger but it's still *magic,* it's the only active spell I know I have, and... I just want to see if it works? I guess being in public and surrounded by people is a terrible time to practice supernatural mojo I barely understand, though. I should definitely wait.

I successfully wait five minutes. I'm honestly inclined to consider that pretty good. It's *magic,* for fritter's sake. My toes have been curling with excitement just thinking about it. How am I going to test a cutting spell, though? I guess I should get like, a piece of paper or something else that has no real consequences for destroying. Easy enough, I have lots of paper. I position a sheet on my lap, drag a fingernail along it, and try to get it to cut. Which, uh, doesn't work. I suppose I should have seen that coming.

I don't exactly like thinking about... the killing I did. I guess I also use the spell to dig but I still associate it with murder, and it hurts to think about. I should just... forget about it. At least for now. It's probably smarter to figure it out over in world tree land anyway. Distractedly, I let class pass me by, doing my best to ignore the increasingly uncomfortable gauze, the urges to drum my claws on something, and all the other constant reminders that after a few weeks of this I probably won't look even remotely human anymore. I'm getting resigned to it, at least. Being human isn't all that great anyway.

When lunch begins, I quickly find Brendan (he is very tall, which makes it very easy) and the two of us approach Ida, who's chattering away with some girl I don't know. I wave her down and she quickly wraps up whatever conversation that was, all but skipping over to us.

"Hannah! Hey!" she greets me cheerfully. "I heard your face exploded!"

"I... I mean, that's not *inaccurate,*" I hedge.

"What?" Ida asks, blinking with confusion. "I can't understand you."

Bah. Stupid gauze mouth. Stupid lack of teeth!

"I'm calling in the second lunch you owe me," I say, enunciating as carefully as I can. "I need a smoothie or a milkshake or a soup or something."

"Ah. Something with your mouth then? I would have guessed your nose."

"If anyone asks, I'd prefer you tell them it was a bloody nose," I grumble at her. "But yeah, it's my mouth."

"Well sure, I'll ferry you out to get something edible for you, I guess. Is tall, dark, and nerdy coming with us?"

"If that's not a problem," Brendan mumbles quietly, not looking Ida in the eyes.

"Sure, no skin off my back," Ida shrugs. "You're paying for your own lunch, though, I only owe Hannah."

Brendan nods, and the three of us exit the school and head for Ida's car.

"Speaking of debts," I mention idly, "I now owe a girl named Autumn, she helped me out today. You know her, Ida?"

"Uhh, vaguely," she hedges, to my immediate surprise. I thought Ida knew everyone, and I tell her as much.

"Hey, I certainly make the social rounds, but Autumn's a bit of a weird one," Ida says defensively. "Girl with the notebook, right? Curly brown hair, freckles, that Autumn? Yeah, she doesn't really talk to anybody. I don't know anyone who hates her or whatever, I don't think she's being bullied. She's just kind of... skittish, I guess?"

Huh. 'Skittish' is not how I would have described Autumn, but the rest of that description seems spot-on.

"Uh... let's see," Ida continues, starting to count things off on her fingers. "I think she's on the swim team, and I think she does martial arts? So she's athletic. I've spotted her hiding in the library with her nose in a book during lunch, too. I dunno, she's nice enough, she could probably fit in with basically any clique, she just... doesn't? So, y'know, fifty-fifty on being an nth-level introvert versus being horribly traumatized. Either way I think you'd probably get along well with her!"

"...Hey," I protest lamely.

"Dunno if she's gay, though, so I can't help you there."

"Hey!" I protest even harder, thanking my mask for hopefully hiding the blush creeping up my cheeks. Ida's snickering makes me less than confident about that, though.

She starts up the car and I cede shotgun to Brendan, who immediately sets the seat back as far as it will go since his absolutely massive legs need all the extra space he can squeeze out. Ida's back seat has all sorts of knick-knacks and items of various usefulness, from the obviously important blankets to the questionably tasteful collection of antennae toppers that I'm just now realizing she probably swaps out every few days. She has a bunch of them, from Mickey Mouse to Rick and Morty to Jason Voorhees, not to mention a collection of various non-copyrighted cute animals. It's all rather adorable, actually.

I want to rip one apart with my claws.

188

I peel my eyes away from the floppy, cartoony, *shreddable* things, but it's too late. The need to cut and tear has wormed its way into my brain, my feet tapping with pent-up energy. Gah, why am I like this now!? I cross my legs to try and get them under control, but it doesn't help in the slightest, my eyes constantly flicking back to the pile of novelty antenna toppers. Oh come on, what a stupid friggin' problem to have!

Come on, Hannah, think about something else. Resisting the urge to cut things is a skill you are *absolutely* going to need to develop, so you'd better start now! Gah, but the only topic that comes to mind as sufficiently distracting is magic, which is *also* a bad idea! Not the least because it's basically the *same idea,* since my magic is also just cutting stuff! In a lot of ways, the way I feel about these stupid little rubber figures is comparable to how I felt shortly before opening a man's throat, just... y'know, without the terror, the revulsion, the life-threatening situation, the horrid crashing thunder rumbling through my exoskeleton, and so on. More like... in the sense that my instincts are calling for something. Some part of me, the part that has lived every night of my life digging up through the wood of a world tree, knows this feeling, and how to summon it. Magic is part of me. It has *always* been part of me, for as long as I can remember. I just never knew it until I finally dug myself free.

I clench and unclench my toes, digging my claws deeper into the grooves they've already carved in my shoes. I know this feeling. All I need to do is reach out a little, and it's mine. Just like in the other world. It's the same, after all. The magic is waiting for me, off in that direction my human self can't quite reach towards yet. But it's still *there,* if I call for it.

So I do. I can't help myself. I want to feel it, *need* to feel it, to pull something cool and good out of this nightmare. To my irritation, though, my prior confidence seems to be for naught. The magic is there, itching to fill my toes and imbue them with cutting energy, but the path is... clogged, for lack of a better term. Misdirected? Blocked by something that shouldn't be there? I peel away at the problem in silence, ignoring Ida's singing, Brendan's uncomfortable stares out the window, even the antenna toppers that were, until this moment, the subject of my need to destroy. I *need* to figure this out. It shouldn't *be* here, whatever it is. It's my fault and I have to fix it.

When I asked Teboho how magic is cast, he said he couldn't tell me because the process was too personal. He said that my magic will "make itself known to me when I discover it." No one else can teach me my spells, because they're *mine,* and to cast them proficiently I have to understand what *makes* them mine. Is my own lack of understanding causing the problem?

Yes. Of course it is. I've been thinking about it wrong. I've considered it a claw augmentation, a cutting spell, but my magic is Space magic, and Space does not *cut.* To cut something is to apply force to it. Pressure is force over area, and thin, slicing edges work by maximizing the amount of pressure applied with the same quantity of force. That is what allows them to *cut,* and my spell is not some paltry application of basic physics. I'm a Space mage. I don't cut, I *separate.* It's not force that gouges holes in my foes, it is simply the creation of space where before, there was none, and the world recognizes the newly-formed break by simple tautology. The two halves are separated, therefore they are separate. *That's* my magic. It is power. It is pure. It is so batshit broken it may as well be *divine.*

Again, I call upon it, but I realize now that it needs a name. *Deserves* a name. Given my proclivities, there's only one name that comes to mind. A pearl of wisdom, you could say. I open my mouth to speak it and my breath is stolen away, inhaled by an amused goddess, invisible and perhaps imagined. For a stolen moment, the world stops, myself included, and I'm left choking motionlessly as some infinite creature decides whether to use my air to speak or simply laugh at me. She caresses my face, tousles my hair, and pinches my cheeks, all without ever being here. How small she must think I am. How cute and helpless. She makes her decision, and when time moves again, so too does my mouth. But I no longer have my breath, so she speaks in my place.

190

"**Spacial Rend**," my mouth says on its own, the sound impossibly perfect despite the mask, gauze, and current plane of existence. The world shrieks as I tear deep gouges in the bottom of Ida's car, opening the interior to the roar of the road.

Ida, of course, starts shrieking immediately afterwards.

# 11

# SECRETS SPREADING

"What the fuck!" Ida screams, slamming the emergency lights button in her car and pulling over to the side of the road. "What the fuck what the fuck what the *fuck!*"

I can't respond, of course, since I'm too busy pressing both hands against my mouth and trying to pull my claws back up through the gouges I just dug into my shoes. I'm such an idiot! What the heck was I thinking, trying to cast magic in a moving car? With my friends around? *With the verbal incantation I can apparently now do!?*

The car jerks to a stop once Ida gets out of the way of traffic, twisting around to send a look of utter panic in my direction.

"Did you just summon *fucking Cthulhu* into my car!?" she shrieks.

Holy crap what does she know.

"Cthulhu!?" I blurt. "Is Cthulhu real? Is that who that was!?"

"Wh—no! God no! I mean, I hope not!? I was fucking kidding, Hannah, I do *not* like that your reaction is apparently 'that sounds concerningly plausible!'"

She says the last bit in an exaggerated, mocking tone that just *gets* to me in a way I feel normally wouldn't. I'm raw right now, lightheaded and dizzy and just coming down from a panic attack followed by a self-induced horror show. My body starts to shake. I feel my toes curl, immediately undoing my progress of pulling them out of the soles of my shoes and causing them to grind up against the tears in the metal I just dug into the floor of Ida's car. I remember it all happening, the way the goddess—I don't know *what* that was, really, but it can't be anything other than divine—just... had her attention here. Her judgment, her *presence.* I got to name my own spell, but she got to judge the name, decide its worthiness. She spoke the words, after all, and she's no mere tool I can use at my whim. I get the impression she was faintly amused by my naming scheme, but had she *not* been amused? Had 'Spacial Rend' not been a name she approved of? I've no doubt that I wouldn't like what she'd choose to use my breath for, in that case.

I got the impression the goddess *liked* me, but not in a way that feels remotely comforting. It was an appreciation akin to one I'd give a photo of someone else's cat. Cute, certainly. Something I enjoy seeing. But the moment that picture goes away, I'll never think about it again, because there are a billion cat photos in the world and most simply aren't all that special. It is the sort of imperceptible, instinctive fondness that only lasts as long as we choose to indulge it. How many cute pictures have I seen of animals that are no longer alive? Of animals that have suffered abuse, neglect, pain, and torment? I'll never know, because I never even think about those pictures outside of a passing entertainment. Of course, unlike the goddess, if I *did* know an animal was being hurt, I would actually care. But to her I'm just... an abstract amusement.

But I was at least amusing enough to get her to speak two words, and what an experience that was. I mean, the loss of bodily autonomy was *horrifying,* the way something else reached out and seized my muscles with as much effort as a blink and spoke words that needed no voicebox, no lungs, and no mouth to emerge from my body fully-formed and brimming with power. Which, in retrospect, makes the entire experience *more* terrifying, because like... why bother forcing me through that at all, in that case?

...Though before I start trying to justify anything to myself, I should probably establish that while *activating* the spell involved my body

194

being briefly taken over to speak the wacky universal magic language or whatever, the stupidity that followed was 100% home-grown Hannah. I'd felt the spell coalesce around my claws, wreathing the exoskeletal weapons with spatial energy which extended maybe a couple inches past the tip of the curved blades. The moment they came into being, the moment I felt them pulsing in my feet, I *had* to cut something. The overwhelming need of it boiled over, and I proceeded to choose the stupidest possible target: the bottom of Ida's car.

It turns out car frames aren't particularly thick; only a few inches of it separates the riders from the road. That means the ten thin gouges I dug through the backseat floor are all exposed to the air outside, resulting in a terrible roaring noise when the car moves at high speeds. So yeah, I just dealt expensive damage to an expensive vehicle, loudly broadcasted that something supernatural is going on to Ida, and generally fucked up in the biggest way possible.

And it felt *so good.* The way the metal just peeled open like tissue paper... god, it gives me chills just thinking about it. I can *feel* through the spell, kind of, as if it's an extension of my own body. The easy glide through solid material was far from the sort of vibrational, visceral feedback I usually get from digging my claws into things, but differently pleasurable is certainly still *pleasurable.* I want to do it again. I can cut metal. I can cut *anything!* Can we just go to a scrapyard and... agh, no! No no no no!

"What happened to my car!?" Ida yelps. "Those look like goddamn claw marks! Oh my fucking god Hannah, if you don't explain what's going on *right now—*"

"I don't know!" I snap at her, trying not to choke on all the gauze still in my mouth. "I don't know, just... just give me a minute!"

"Are we in any danger, Hannah?" Brendan asks evenly, though I know his calm expression and demeanor mean he's anything but. When things get intense, he gets... flat. It's how he handles stress. Were he happy or comfortable he'd be a lot more expressive, if not in voice then at least in body: tapping his feet, rubbing his hands together, possibly even wiggling his whole body if he was in a particularly good mood. He gets self-conscious about it all when he's stressed, though, causing him to focus on shutting all of that down and being as emotionless as possible.

"I... I don't think so," I manage to choke out, trying to take deep breaths. "I'm sorry. I'm sorry, I just... this was my fault. There's nothing else going on."

"Was... was there someone else here?" he presses.

Was there...? Oh, he means the goddess. They heard that. They *felt* that. Maybe not exactly the same way I did, but there's no way they believe that's natural. I mean... I'm sure a lot of people could convince themselves it was just a hallucination, but I doubt Brendan and Ida are the type.

"I... kind of, I think," I tell him. "But I don't know. I don't know if that was a person or... or something else. Look, please, I just... I need a minute."

Brendan nods, while Ida just gives me a look mixed with stress, fury, and general 'are you fucking serious' energy... but she shuts her mouth and lets me take a while to compose myself. I take a few shaky breaths, curling myself into a ball by perching my heels on the edge of my seat, letting my toes dangle in open air where they *can't fucking cut anything.* My shoes are still on, of course, even if the soles are mostly shredded, but that's enough to prevent Ida from seeing the freakish changes. Once I feel capable of it, I say the first thing on my mind.

"I don't want to talk about this."

It's not fair, but... it's too much. It's too much to face head-on. I can't handle it, and I *definitely* don't want Ida to know about it. I know it's not fair, but maybe if I just request it politely I can pretend this never happened.

"Too goddamn bad," Ida grunts. "You don't get to speak in tongues and make my car look like I just ran over a velociraptor and then *not explain.* Fuck that."

I wince, but I guess I should have expected that. Words won't come, though, so with shaky hands I just start removing my shoes instead of saying anything. It feels *so good* to not have my feet pinched into a shoe that's now two sizes too small for the extra length on my toes, so I allow myself a small shudder of pleasure as I go ahead and take my knee socks off as well, stretching out my claws. They look the same as they did this morning, the bone growing up past the knuckles of my toes and forming sharp, exoskeletal joints. They're not entirely even, with something craggly and primordial about them that gives off an air of danger that both terrifies and enraptures me. I'm so busy admiring my own feet that I almost miss Ida's gaping expression, though I do look up and catch it when she starts making an 'uhhhh' noise.

"...You're shitting me," she whispers. "Hannah, are you turning into a goddamn *werewolf* or something?"

"I... I mean I think it's more of a were-spider?" I squeak.

"Hannah isn't any kind of therianthrope," Brendan says, almost automatically. "She's turning into *something,* but it seems to be mono-directional, not a kind of shapeshifting. Though I guess she might qualify for more spiritual kinds of therianthropy, considering she's apparently a spider in her dreams, but that's not really how the word is used much anymore."

Ida turns and blinks at him once.

"What?" she manages.

"Werewolves turn into wolves or wolf-hybrids under certain conditions, then turn back into humans when the conditions are no longer met. Same with other were-creatures. Hannah does not seem to be changing back."

"Yes, thank you for the reminder," I grumble.

"I'm just clarifying," he answers flatly.

"So... so back up," Ida insists, rubbing her face with exasperation. "Basically, magic is real and those claws are real and Hannah is

197

turning into a monster somehow? That's what you're saying? This has gotta be some kind of insane, stupid prank, right?"

Well, nothing for it. The spider's out of the dimensional pocket now. I reach up under my mask, pulling the bloody gauze out of my mouth as I reach into my backpack and retrieve my ziplock bag full of human teeth. Ida stares at it in horror as I plop the gauze in there (I don't want to get her car messy, after all) before putting it all back in my backpack. I stretch my jaw a bit, moving it around with satisfaction. I'm not bleeding anymore. That's nice. Ida just gapes at the whole scene, and since that's apparently still not enough for her I pull up my pant leg and show her the exoskeletal growth starting there, as well. Brendan raises his eyebrows at that, a flicker of interest passing over his features, but he's too overwhelmed to ask to touch it like I expect he wants to.

"Feel free to independently verify," I offer, feeling the comfortable yet horrible numbness of disassociation start to set in. It immediately starts warring with a fresh spike of adrenaline, though, and who knows which one is going to end up winning this particular faceoff.

Ida looks down at my leg, which I extend out to allow her ease of access. Then she looks up at my face, then back down to the leg, then up at my face again before finally reaching over to touch the exposed bit of exoskeletal bone. She pokes it, sending a strange and somewhat uncomfortable sensation through my leg. The touch isn't anywhere as dulled as I would have expected from not having skin there anymore; in fact, it still feels almost exactly the same as it would have normally... if not for the fact that there is no feeling of *give*, no depression to make from the force. My exoskeleton is utterly unmoving where skin would bend or squish, and that is, somehow, the biggest difference in sensation I get from the experience.

"Is this... is this actually bone?" Ida hisses, poking around at the edges where the skin thins out and reveals my mutation. "You're fucking with me, right?"

I try to answer that, but Ida presses on a particularly itchy part of skin around the area and I end up involuntarily letting out a small, happy noise. Sensing blood in the water, Ida seems to immediately forget that I'm turning into a monster and grins mischievously, rubbing a bit more around the area in an attempt to elicit more noises from me. It *does* feel nice—as getting someone to massage an itch generally does—so even though I put my hands up over my mouth I end up making another happy grunt or two.

"This is weird," Ida says, though she's grinning like a demon. "This is so fucking weird. Seriously, what the fuck is—"

With much the same sort of satisfaction that I felt when I took my restricting shoes off, a rush of relief suddenly fills me as I watch Ida's idle scratches suddenly peel off a palm-sized chunk of skin, which catches underneath her nails and sticks to them. She screams, flailing her arm and ripping the chunk of dead epidermis off my leg, eliciting a hiss of pain and relief from my lips. The patch of skin soon flies free of Ida's wild movements, landing on Brendan, who is visibly disturbed... though he at least reacts to that by freezing stiff rather than screaming painfully. I, for one, just stretch my ankle a bit, watching the now-revealed joint slide around plate-over-plate like a robot from a sci-fi movie. The revealed exoskeleton now reaches from my ankle up my shin to nearly my knee, like it's trying to move down to meet up with the bones crawling up my toes. Between them, my skin feels normal, but pressing around the revealed areas indicates that more fresh exoskeleton is growing underneath the skin that's still attached. Little by little, it's all going to fall off, and at this point I'm so resigned to it that it barely even registers as something I should be panicking about. Ida knows and my life is ruined. She'll tell everyone. I'll be outed as a freak and this is the end.

Oh, well. Honestly, I couldn't have expected this to last much longer. I feel an urge to giggle bubble up and I just let it happen. Why not? I'm turning into some kind of bone monster, I just invoked *divine magic* in the middle of town—so y'know, any secret organizations looking for that kind of shit absolutely just found me—and my ankle has some kind of freaky interlocking ball joint that I can't stop staring at and moving around because I'm *pretty sure* it's a scaled-up iteration of some of my hip joints when I'm a hyperspider, albeit minus one dim... well. It *might* be minus one dimension. I can't actually see into the w-axis right now, so who knows?

"Hannah?" Brendan asks quietly. He sounds pretty concerned, presumably because I've been staring at part of my body that just had the skin ripped off and giggling to myself.

"Hi Brendan," I answer, grinning under my mask. This doesn't seem to make him feel any better for some reason.

"...Can you take some deep breaths for me?" he asks. Which, okay, that seems reasonable, but it's pretty hard to control my breathing right now between my laughter and gasps for air. I do my best, though, trying to slow down my overtaxed lungs and get some air. I meet with moderate success.

"So this is real, then," Ida gulps. "Really real."

"Yes," Brendan confirms for her. "We're not sure what's happening, but it's definitely real."

"Holy fucking shit," Ida breathes. "Well. That's absolutely fucking terrifying, but alright. I guess I live in a movie now."

"How are you feeling?" Brendan asks me, turning away from Ida without answering her.

"Very lightheaded," I answer, since it's true. "I'm dizzy. And hungry. And thirsty, I think? I have a bit of a headache, at least."

"Right. You... said you lost a lot of blood alongside your teeth, right?"

I feel my hands shaking. So much blood. I'd wished it was someone else's.

"Yeah," I confirm. "I *really* need more blood."

"Oh my god don't say it like that," Ida insists. "Look, just... Brendan, there should be a roll of duct tape in the door next to you. We're

200

gonna patch the floor with that and... put a mat over it or something, okay? For the noise. You didn't hit the drive shaft or anything, did you Hannah? Brake line, maybe? You must have missed the exhaust or we'd smell it."

I blink, looking down into the gashes I made in the floor.

"I don't see any car bits other than the frame," I tell her. "But you probably want to check for yourself."

She groans and sticks her torso back between the front seats, getting a closer look at the damage.

"...Nope, I don't see anything, we should be good," she sighs, holding the palm of her hand out towards Brendan. "Duct tape, tallboy."

He dutifully hands her the roll, and she quickly patches the floor while I very carefully twist my body to keep my claws the heck away from her. She quickly patches up the hole and swaps the foot mats on the left and right sides in order to cover it further.

"That should help with the noise," Ida grumbles, sounding resigned. "I'm not looking forward to explaining this shit to a mechanic, but whatever. Liquid meal time. A smoothie isn't gonna cut it, we're gonna get you tomato soup or something. Maybe a bread bowl? ...No, wait, our Panera doesn't have a drive through."

"Huh?" I manage to vocalize.

"Hannah, your shoes are shredded, we can't take you inside a restaurant," Ida dismisses. "That'd be against health code."

"...Huh?" I repeat.

"You're being awfully calm about this," Brendan comments.

"Look, I had my freakout," Ida snaps, looking into the rear-view mirror and fixing her hair before starting the car again. "We did that, it's done. Now it's time for me to make sure the woman growing goddamn monster teeth in my car doesn't get hungry. There's no fucking way I'm gonna die because I didn't get Hannah enough chicken wings. What's your shoe size, by the way?"

201

"Um. Six?" I supply.

"Great, we'll get you some size seven and eights on the way back, too," Ida grunts.

"...Please don't buy me anything expensive," I squeak, since *that's* somehow the most uncomfortable part of this situation.

"Fuck you, I do what I want," Ida answers, and slams the car into drive.

The rest of the car ride is somewhat of a daze to me, partly because it's full of awkward silence but mostly because I have, for like the third or fourth time today, burned out on adrenaline. I feel like that's too many times in a day, y'know? Though I mean, the day's barely halfway done, so I probably shouldn't be tallying up the record yet. *Wow* my life is bad. Just. Golly!

At some point I'm broken out of my daze by the tantalizing smell of soup, which I quickly devour. Or I guess chug, depending on your perspective. Doing so, of course, necessitates taking off my mask, allowing Ida and Brendan an eyeful of my raw gums and the tiny, *tiny* tips of sharp white starting to poke out from within them. I make the mistake of poking them with my tongue and end up cutting myself, trickling the taste of blood into my mouth once again, pushing that flashback into the forefront of my mind. Thankfully, I have a second bowl of soup to wash it away with.

"Hannah, wait, that's ho—"

Too late. I gulp it down like an alcoholic during happy hour. I used to love tomato soup, but now I find it kind of... bland. Whatever. It was the only soup that didn't have a bunch of noodles or vegetables or delicious meats in it, and I unfortunately need that since I can't currently chew.

"What the fuck, Hannah, are you okay!?" Ida gapes at me. "Just holding the container for that nearly burned my hand!"

I blink at her with surprise.

"It... felt normal to me?" I hedge. "Like, warm enough to be good, but not so hot that it hurts."

"Is fire a kind of magic?" Brendan asks, staring at me. "And if so, what does it oppose?"

Ah, I see where he's going with this.

"Heat opposes Transmutation," I inform him. "So I guess I'm probably heat-resistant. But at the same time, that'd be really weird, because when I first popped over to the other world I was having *serious* problems regulating my body temperature."

"Maybe that's why?" Brendan hedges. "You oppose Light, and you're blind. You oppose Heat, and it's difficult for heat to enter your body *or* leave it. You oppose Chaos, and nothing seems to be more toxic to you than deviating from your schedule."

"...I don't think that last one is magic-related."

"You can't oppose chaos!" Ida protests. "I *embody* chaos!"

"I oppose it metaphysically, not ideologically," I say defensively. "It's not exactly something I have a choice in."

"And if you could not interject when you don't even know what we're talking about, that would be great," Brendan grumbles.

"Woah, shit, tallboy's spine just straightened itself," Ida quips. "Never thought I'd see him actually man up."

"Stop," I snap at them. "Please, just... don't prod each other. Please?"

"Sorry," Ida says, waving it off. "Habit. I'm gonna go buy you some of those really thick-soled shoes that lesser short people wear to hide their true power. I figure you'll need the extra sole so you don't just delete the damn things. You two stay in the car and *don't break anything*."

Oh, huh. We're parked in front of a shoe store now. When did that happen?

"Bye," I tell Ida, but she's already out of the car and slamming the door.

Brendan and I are now alone, and immediately I see some of his tension fall away. He starts bouncing a leg, watching her walk away with one of his many varieties of unreadable expressions.

"I don't like her," he announces.

"I know," I sigh. "If it makes you feel any better, it's not personal. I don't think she has anything against you, she's just... like that."

And Brendan is pretty sensitive, so the kind of thing that just rolls off my back really, really gets to him. But I don't say that out loud, since that would sound like I'm blaming him for her being rude, and that's not appropriate or helpful. Ida is abrasive. That's her flaw, not his.

"That doesn't make me feel better at all," he says. "Being rude to everyone is *worse* than only being rude to me. Besides, I thought you didn't want to tell her any of this stuff."

"I don't," I mumble. "I just did something moronic, is all."

"I guess that sounds like you, yeah," he admits.

"...Hey," I say. "You, uh, seem a lot more rude than usual yourself."

"I guess so," he agrees. "I'm stressed. About you, about all of this. But you and I are friends. Ida and I are not friends. It's different."

I shrug.

"I guess you're right," I agree. "It's probably good we went with her to get food, though. As out of it as I was, if I didn't do the big stupid magic thing in her car, I probably would have done it in a classroom."

"What *was* that, anyway?" he asks after a short pause. "What said those words?"

"I don't know," I answer, "and I get the feeling I'm probably safer that way."

Another awkward pause stretches between us, the silence only broken by the tap of Brendan's leg.

"...Spatial Rend is a Pokémon attack, isn't it?" he asks slowly.

I feel a blush creep up my neck onto my face.

"It, uh, yeah," I admit. "Signature move of the legendary Pokémon Palkia. 'Spacial Rend,' spelled s-p-a-c-i-a-l instead of s-p-a-t-i-a-l, because spatial is spelled with a c in the UK and I guess they just decided to translate it that way for all English versions of the game?"

"Is it any good?" he asks.

"I-in Pokémon?" I ask.

"Yeah," he confirms.

"I mean, it's pretty good, yeah," I mumble. "Sometimes Draco Meteor is better for specific needs, but Spacial Rend is still a one hundred power high crit STAB move on a Pokémon with base one-fifty special attack. Though they kinda did it dirty in Legends by making the base power actually go *down* when Origin Forme Palkia uses it? Like yeah, the crit rate goes up and becomes the highest crit rate move in the game, and that's neat, but I like the consistency, you know?"

"I've always found it funny how much you like competitive Pokémon, an *incredibly* luck-based game, but you hate luck."

"It's not... it's still a skill-based game! Luck swings things, but not enough to prevent top players from consistently winning! Like, yeah, Scald is bullpoop and Focus Miss is just the *absolute worst,* but like..."

I'm babbling. I know I'm babbling, and I hate that, but it's okay because it's just me and Brendan and I'm pretty sure he just baited me into babbling in the first place. Both of us start to relax as the words flow out of me, a conversation (more of a rant, really) that I'm sure I've had a dozen times but it's okay because it's just me and him and my freaky monster toes wiggling around in my

205

mostly-shredded socks. Things probably aren't going to be okay, but they're okay *right now,* and frankly that's more than I've had in what feels like way, way too long.

So naturally, my brain has to go and ruin it by blurting a question I don't want to think about the answer to.

"What if I hurt you?" I ask.

The question is full of meaning and fear that I can't fully articulate, the horror of urges I don't understand creeping into more and more of my brain and body. The *physicality* of it all terrifies me, the violence pulsing underneath my rapidly-degrading skin which makes me feel aberrant and dangerous because of *course* it does, normal, healthy people *do not get urges to do these things.* And now I do, and I feel like I'm always teetering a step away from giving in at the worst possible moment.

Brendan regards me in silence, perhaps picking up on the fear I'm leaving unsaid but perhaps not. To some extent, it doesn't matter. He'll know someday, and he'll understand. He *always* understands, in the end, even if it takes hours or days of late-night texting sessions and impossible heart-to-hearts that I could never even *think* of breaching with my parents, or anyone else for that matter. And I know that, to him, I'm the same. Brendan doesn't have many friends. He's more or less had to raise himself, stuck with parents that don't understand or even particularly care about him. He does not trust easily, because his childhood was nothing but beratement and apathy. I didn't know it back when I first latched onto him in elementary school, but I was all he had for a long, long time.

"Then I'll forgive you," he answers, and it's not what I wanted to hear. "Just don't do that stupid thing everyone does in the movies where you try to leave for my sake, okay? That's just going to make everything worse, and you know it."

"Okay," I promise him, because what else can I say? "I won't."

Ida returns shortly afterwards, tossing two shoeboxes at me before pulling the car door shut behind her with a grunt.

"These are yours now," she huffs. "Figure out which one fits better."

I'm too stunned to respond, instead simply gaping at the fact that Ida just threw well over a hundred dollars of gifts into my lap. These aren't *expensive* shoes, but they sure as sugar aren't cheap shoes either! My mind is absolutely *shredded* by this insanity. I am a *very* frugal person and this kind of casual waste of money is just... aaagh!

"Ida, you can't—" I start, but the little imp is having none of it.

"I. Do. What. I. Want," she snaps at me. "So take the damn shoes. You *need* them. I'm a spoiled rich girl, Hannah, I didn't have to earn a cent of what I just spent. So chill out and cover up your monster claws already!"

I shut my mouth and nod numbly, slipping a foot into the first pair of shoes. Immediately, I know these are a million times better than my old shoes, and that thought magnifies a hundredfold when I end up curling my toes and sinking my claws into the inch-thick soles without piercing through the other side. The warm buzz from penetrating the leathery, fleshy texture feels like the relief of getting in a hot tub on a cold day, and I'm far too exhausted and frazzled to resist the pleasure of it. I barely have enough energy to put the other shoe on before I collapse into the backseat, closing my eyes and just... letting myself stop for a little while.

But not sleep. It's much too early to sleep.

"...So, how many other people know about this?" I hear Ida ask, the car starting to pick up speed down the road.

"Nobody," Brendan answers. "It's just us. We'd like you to keep it that way."

"I know I'm a blabbermouth, but I'd just seem like a crazy person if I gossiped about this," Ida grumbles.

"Glad to know you can keep secrets if it's your reputation on the line rather than someone else's," Brendan says.

"I've never claimed to be anything but a hedonist," Ida answers. "So frankly? I don't want to be involved with this shit. Don't come crying to me if you need help hiding a body."

"Please don't joke about that," I groan. "I already killed someone last night."

There's a painfully stressful pause.

"...*Fuck*," Ida hisses vitrolically. "Fuck, fuck, fuck. I can't *believe* you told me that. Are you stupid? I'm going to have to testify that you said that or else I could be tried as an accomplice!"

"I don't think she can be tried under an American court, considering that it happened in another universe," Brendan supplies.

"What!? No, wait, actually, fuck that. Don't answer. I'm not getting wrapped up into your crazy movie bullshit, you two can just save the world without me. You understand? I want no part of this. We're going to go back to school, get chewed out for missing fourth period, and then when the day is finally over I'm getting so fucking blown out of my mind on LSD that I will not even know who you two are tomorrow."

"You know," Brendan supplies, "now we'll have to testify that you said that or else—"

"Oh, *fuck you!*"

"I, for one, approve of this plan," I mumble. "Just pretending it didn't happen works well for me."

"Don't you dare say that, Hannah, or else I'll have to be self-aware about how stupid this plan is," Ida grumbles.

"...I said I *liked* the idea, though?"

"I know!"

Another awkward silence fills the air. This time, I'm the one to breach it.

"Thank you for the shoes, Ida," I tell her. "I like them."

"...You're welcome," she mutters. "I made sure to get you black ones to hide any bloodstains."

"That's thoughtful of you," I admit. "Thanks again. You've always been really nice to me. I don't know why you're so nice to me. You're not usually nice to people."

She flinches a bit at that, drumming her fingers on the steering wheel as she keeps her eyes planted firmly on the road. The car speeds up a little more, even though she's already well over the legal limit.

"It's because I want to fuck you," she says. "Obviously."

I blink, slowly and numbly. I blink again. My mouth opens, then closes, then opens again.

"Oh," I manage to say.

"I do not know how to articulate to you how much of a dumb fucking lesbian you are, Hannah," Ida continues. "Even Brendan figured it out, and he has a special education action plan longer than the damn English final."

"Maybe I'm just more observant than you think," Brendan supplies, "and you're just worse at flirting."

So much blood is going to my face right now that I'm afraid my gums are going to start bleeding again just from the pressure. I try to formulate a response and only manage to let out a confused squeaking noise.

"Fuck you, you don't know shit!" Ida snaps at Brendan. "You've never seen a vagina without tabbing into 4chan first."

"Ida!" I say, finally finding the power to step in. "Uncalled for!"

She shrinks down a bit from her bristled posture, Brendan turning away from her to look out the window and quietly fume.

"...Sorry," Ida manages. "I speak before I think."

"Something like that shouldn't even be used as an insult," I continue. "No one should ever be *expected* to—"

209

"I know, I know! Jesus, Hannah, I get it. I'm glad you seem to be feeling better."

"Huh?" I ask, dumbfounded.

"Your fucking... preachy moralizing. I haven't heard that from you in a long time. It's annoying, but it's better than the silence we've been getting instead."

We pull into school, Ida having to find a parking spot at the back of the lot since we're so late. We'll be in trouble, but we probably won't be in *much* trouble, since we're pretty much never late. Or at least Brendan and I don't. Ida might ditch all the time, for all I know. She doesn't ever ditch the classes *I'm* in, but... well. That might be for a different reason, I guess?

"I definitely think you're attractive," I admit to Ida.

"Oh yeah?" she drawls. "Damn, and here I was thinking that you constantly stare at my tits for heterosexual reasons."

I blush again but press on, because Ida is a good friend and she deserves a clear answer.

"Wh... I, uh. Anyway, I don't think a relationship would be a, uh, good idea. For a few reasons, but the current situation is... a big one."

"Yeah," Ida says. "I figured. It's pretty fucking wild. I don't even know what to say, other than like... I hope it works out for you? Like, what else is there? This is so far beyond my ability to help with, so far beyond what makes sense in reality, that it's just... I can't. I wasn't telling you I think you're hot in order to ask you out, I'm telling you to remind you that I'm a shallow cunt and giving you a reason to cut ties. I just wanted in your pants, Hannah, but I don't fuck with crazy. I'll keep your secret, just... keep away from me. I don't want your eldritch goddess doing something to my head again, understand?"

"I really, really do," I assure her. "Trust me, if I had the option to just walk away from this, I would take it in an instant."

I clench my toes at that, delighting in the feel of digging deeper into my shoes. Something about my words just now felt a little hollow, but... whatever. I could definitely live without freaky monster instincts. It'd be greatly preferable, in fact.

"You are nice and great and I hope everything works out for you," Ida says. "Now get the fuck out of my car."

We oblige, trudging back to school in awkward silence. I'm late enough to be considered absent to class already, so I just head for my next class of the day to wait. It's the only class I share with Brendan, actually, so he follows me and waits outside the door alongside me.

"So," I manage, "that could have gone much worse."

"Well we're no longer friends with Ida, so all things considered I think it went quite optimally," Brendan answers.

"Hey!" I protest, elbowing him in the hip. "I know you don't like her, but *I* like her. At least be supportive of that."

"She reminds me of my mom," Brendan says bluntly. "Except with more swear words."

Oh. Shoot. I don't... have a good answer to that. There probably isn't one.

"I'm sorry," I say.

He doesn't answer, but I didn't expect him to. We wait outside class together, and just the proximity is enough. Today has been... quite the roller coaster, I have to say. Way too much panic, way too much terror. I'm rubbed raw from having to kill for the first time and spitting all my teeth out of my mouth and just... everything going on. But as terrifying and alien as it was, I *did* love getting to access my magic. It's a spell that destroys, which I'm not thrilled about, but it's just the beginning, right? I'm also an Order mage, so maybe I can get a spell that heals, too. A spell that fixes things. Pretty much by definition, magic opens up countless possibilities that weren't there before. Maybe if I get good at it, I can take control of what's happening to me. Now that I'm fed and not in pain and coming off the high of getting shoes that actually feel good on my feet, I can start to feel a spark of hope that everything will be okay.

"So what do you think Ida meant," Brendan says suddenly, "when she said 'I don't want your eldritch goddess doing something to my head *again?*'"

...Ah, never mind. The terror's back. At least I'm starting to get used to it.

# 12

# NEW NORMAL

The rest of my day is startlingly normal. No secret organizations kidnap me for using magic in the middle of a street, no body parts form or fall off of me, and no one else learns of my freakish mutations. Ida, unfortunately, seems to have blocked Brendan and I's phone numbers, or at the very least she's *pretending* she has, so my inquiries into her experience with me accidentally drawing a divine entity's attention go unanswered. I hope she's okay, but as Brendan pointed out we can't help somebody that refuses to communicate with us. If she's in trouble, we just have to hope that she'll reach out.

"Good work today, Hannah," my boss says just as I finish cleaning the floor. Yeah, I went to work today. Yeah, that was probably stupid. But frankly, the idea of going to work was a lot less stressful than the idea of trying to explain to my parents why I don't want to go to work.

"Of course," I answer. "Thanks for letting me stick to back-of-house stuff tonight."

"No problem," my boss nods. "You sound a little funny today. Something up with your mouth?"

I have, for all the obvious reasons, kept my mask on all shift. I'd be doing that even if I didn't have monster teeth growing in, what with the global pandemic and all.

"Yeah, talking all night wouldn't be pleasant," I confirm.

More importantly, I'm still feeling a bit too raw to deal with customers all day. Making food, though? I can get into kind of a zen mode for that, completing whatever orders pop up on screen and cleaning the rest of the time. My boss was happy to have me in back-of-house, which is how we refer to kitchen work. We have one of those kitchens that's open to the main room so everyone who orders can watch us make stuff, so it's really all one room. The 'positions' are front-of-house—which handles customer orders, cleaning the dining room, and so on—and back-of-house, which does all the food prep and dishwashing (even though everyone is *supposed* to handle dishwashing). There are technically a bunch of sub-positions for back-of-house that focus on the different foods we offer, but I can do it all and when we're understaffed like we were tonight, I tend to need to do exactly that. It's stressful, certainly, but it's a very *human* stress, something that takes a lot of effort and attention but is very much my element. There's a list of things I have to do, and I need to get them all done as quickly as possible, and I'm never lost for the next step. It's very... well, I guess I'd describe it as orderly, but considering that I'm Order-aligned in terms of magic I'm a little leery about that. I'd like to assume your personality just determines what magic you get somehow, but unfortunately I know that, due to how Chaos mages are apparently killed at birth, your type of magic is *assigned* at birth. So while my preference for structure could be a coincidence, I very much don't like the possibility that it *isn't*.

"Is it ever?" my boss asks, smirking at me as he cleans out the inside of one of our grease traps. My boss is a decent enough guy, though I don't really have strong feelings about him either way. He's thirty-something, with short brown hair, brown eyes, light stubble all over his face and a generally pretty positive disposition. Our store is low on employees right now, so he's almost always in the thick of things alongside us, making food and taking customer orders like a common grunt. I think I lucked out a bit with this job, since I've heard all kinds of horror stories about food service bosses and he doesn't really match up to any of them. That said, I

214

still just mentally think of him as 'my boss' and not by his name, since I can't even remember it, which I think kind of communicates my general opinion on the man better than anything else.

"It kind of depends on my mood," I admit. "Sometimes I prefer front-of-house to back. Managing customers and cleaning the dining room is *easier* than making all the food, it's just a matter of how thick my skin is feeling that day. If I can't handle getting screamed at, it's better for me to stay in the back."

Which is exactly how I felt today, hence asking for kitchen duty. It's past 10pm now, so we're closed and putting the finishing touches on all the cleaning we have to do before going home for the night.

"Eh, you know that if anyone starts giving you shit you can just come get me, right?" my boss insists. "I will absolutely kick out a customer that starts yelling at my employees, and if somebody's that mad you should be grabbing me anyway."

See? He's a good boss. I wiggle my toes a little, feeling my claws slide into and out of the gouges I've dug into my new shoes.

"It's not fun to be yelled at even if I have an immediate way to leave the situation," I point out. "But thank you."

"No problem," he confirms. "You need a ride home tonight, by the way?"

I hesitate. That's... a perfectly innocuous question. I *do* usually carpool home, and the girl I usually carpool with is one of the two people that called in sick tonight (and wasn't *that* fun). I can and often do call my dad to have him pick me up, but I prefer *not* to do that since he tends to be really late and also, y'know, car ride with my dad. So honestly I have every reason to accept that offer, except for the obvious and glaring fact that I do not at all want to get into a man's car alone with him.

I don't think my boss is at all inclined to sexually harass me, let alone do anything worse than that. He doesn't give off that kind of... creepy vibe, you know? And the creepy vibe metric is a pretty darn good metric, frankly, and I will not allow anyone to tell me otherwise. Sure, it's technically profiling, but like… I'm not a cop determining who needs to be arrested, I'm a young underage woman trying not to get raped. I really, really wish that didn't have to be the sort of thing I need to worry about, but it absolutely *is.* If anyone tries to convince you otherwise you should punch them in the dick.

So! High-speed personal safety mental calculation time. I've already been hesitating for too long, which means *he* probably suspects I'm trying to determine the odds that he's going to try to rape me, which, y'know, most people kind of take offense to, even if just silently. So I make a show of saying 'uhhhh' and pulling out my phone to look at the calendar app as if it has my carpool information in it, which it does not. Does my boss pass the creepy check? Yes, no real bad vibes from him. Does he pass the leering check? Mmmmostly, yes. Better than most guys, which is unfortunately a technical pass because my standards have been lowered enough to grade on a curve. Does he pass the accountability check? Yes, there's one other employee here tonight who could confirm we left in the same vehicle. Does the situation pass the personal safety check? I think… yes. I can have my phone out for the whole drive to quickly call the police if needed, and if things get *really* bad I can pretty easily kill him with one foot.

I blink at that thought, reeling it back a little and letting it play again. I, uh… huh. I can kill him with one foot. I can trivially overpower an adult man. That's… *incredibly* comforting, in a way I never expected it to be. Like, obviously I don't want to kill him, but… well, I'm a five foot two teenage girl who doesn't work out, any incel off the street could easily force me to the ground because testosterone just cheats like that. I've got *less than half* the upper body strength of the average man, because I am a below-average strength woman. That's just *life.* But now I have a literally magical equalizer, and that's a weight off my shoulders that's been pressing down hard for a long, long time. A horrible fear that I always have to keep in the back of mind is now just… quieter.

"I think a ride would be helpful, thank you," I tell him, and get back to cleaning.

"No problem," he agrees, and returns to scrubbing as well.

We're done with the closing routine just under an hour later, which is *way* longer than it's supposed to take but that's the reality of only having three people on a five-man shift. I buckle up in the passenger seat of my boss' truck and direct him back to my house, all of which occurs without incident. Which is what I expected, but... y'know. Still a relief.

The rest of my family is asleep at this hour, so I quietly enter the house and creep up to my room before peeling off my clothes, dutifully sticking foam cubes over my claws, and squirming into bed. As usual, I start to feel the exhaustion take me almost immediately.

*Hannah! Are you asleep?*

I try to open my eyes, but I don't have them anymore. I roll around a little instead, getting my legs underneath me before uncurling myself into a stretch. Sensory information floods me all at once, the entire material composition of everything within fifty feet of me rushing into my mind before I mentally blink it back into submission, focusing my attention enough to comprehend what I'm looking at. We're... in our camp. Teboho and Kagiso are asleep. There doesn't seem to be anyone else around.

*Sindri?* I think groggily. *What's up?*

*It's your turn to keep watch,* Sindri answers. *I can feel your presence, but I can't see you. Where are you?*

*Ah, right, sorry. I slept in a barren zone. Or I guess a dimensional pocket? Same thing I guess.*

I crawl out of my little extradimensional sleeping cubby next to where Sindri is standing, startling him enough to make him jump a bit. Hee hee. It's a shame I can't laugh in this body, because I totally would if I could.

*Woah! Hey there,* he greets me. *I'm glad I managed to wake you up, I suppose, because otherwise I wouldn't be able to find you. It's your turn to keep watch.*

Oh right, I did agree to do that.

*Sure thing,* I confirm. *Quick question, though. How will I know when my shift is over? I don't know how to tell time.*

Sindri nods and pulls out a small lantern, though rather than oil or something to fuel it, the inside only has a single, tiny candle that can't possibly emit much light. Not that light helps me in the first place, so why... oh! I see. There are notches built into the lantern next to where the candle rests.

*Is that a candle clock?* I ask.

*Yes, exactly. The candle will burn down and you can see how much time has passed by how much wax is left. Each small notch is a [time increment, medium-short length, fraction of fraction of day], while each longer notch is [time increment, medium-long length, fraction of day].*

*Your units didn't convert for me,* I inform him. *How many notches am I waiting?*

*Two of the long ones, Hannah.*

*Okay, thank you!*

Sindri nods and yawns mightily, rolling a stiff shoulder.

*By the way, forgive me if this is a rude question, but is something growing on your carapace? Your coloration looks a bit different.*

*Huh?* I ask.

*Between each of your legs there. At least, if I'm not mistaken?*

Huh. I suppose I haven't really checked myself over since waking up. I focus on my own body, glancing at the area between each leg, and sure enough there's... something happening. The exoskeleton seems to be thinning out, a membrane developing under it alongside a nerve cluster to match. What the heck? Does my spider-body mutate too? That's... kind of really annoying, actually. I'm not sure *why*, but it is.

*You're right, something is different,* I agree. *Not sure what, though. Hyperspider puberty, maybe?*

He chuckles a bit at that.

*It must have been very difficult growing up as the only member of your species that you know,* he sympathizes, and I'm not really sure how I feel about that. It's somehow completely inaccurate yet extremely relatable. *Your species name didn't quite translate there, by the way.*

*It's not the real name for the species anyway, since I don't know what that is,* I admit. *It's just what I call my species. Mix of the words 'hyper' and 'spider,' because that's how my native language refers to fourth-dimensional objects. The 4D equivalent of a cube is a 'hypercube,' etcetera.*

*Ah, interesting. Thank you for explaining.*

*No problem.*

He smiles down at me before heading into his tent to get comfortable for bed. I don't follow, because there's no real need—I can still 'see' him and 'hear' him exactly as well as I could when we were right next to each other.

*I must say, you seem to be doing a lot better than you were before,* Sindri says. *It's good to see.*

I stiffen a bit at that.

*...I mean, don't get me wrong, I'm extremely traumatized,* I tell him frankly. *I've... never killed anyone before. But sleep helped, I guess.*

Mainly because a bunch of other crazy stuff happened, from my teeth to using magic on Earth to Ida finding everything out, and while all of that was terrible in the moment, things... kinda turned out decent? Other than Ida not speaking to me anymore, I guess, but I'm not super worried about that. It's... a very Ida thing to do, and I'm kind of expecting it to not last very long.

...I'm not sure how I feel about her having a crush on me, though. That's... odd. Because I *used* to have a big crush on her, for sure. I spent like a year and a half smooshing it to nothing because I was sure she was straight, though, so now I *don't* have that crush, which makes things... a bit odd, emotionally speaking. Hannah from a year ago would be ecstatic. I'm just... confused. That's not even bringing in the whole terrifying monster transformation thing, which probably means she's not interested in me anymore regardless.

*Honestly, it's heartening that you haven't had to see much death before,* Sindri sighs. *But I'm afraid you'll probably have to get used to it. The Tree of Souls is a fairly lawless place with relatively few central governments. It's mostly villages and city-states, and only the biggest ones bother to patrol the areas outside their walls for bandits and monsters. Travel is dangerous, and we are travelers.*

*Huh. That really sucks. Can we even get the guy who ran away arrested?*

*In the strictest sense of the word, the people who attacked us weren't even doing anything illegal, so no. Though practically speaking, if we could prove the merchants responsible performed such banditry, they'd likely be expelled from from their guild if they're in one, or possibly even barred from entering some of the nearby towns, but... well, I don't really have the time to go around trying to convince local ruling councils to do things like that. Likewise, I don't have the spare funds to devote to putting up a bounty, which is the most common form of retribution for richer folk to employ.*

Sheesh, it's pretty wild-west out here, isn't it?

*That really sucks,* I say, because what else is there to say? *Society seems like a mess.*

*It's the natural consequence of having large numbers of small, disparate communities of people who seem disinclined to engage much with each other. Things are much better organized back on Pillar.*

*Okay, so question about that,* I say. *The word 'Pillar' mostly translates, but I don't know much about it. Is it the same thing as what Teboho called 'The Slaying Stone?'*

*It is,* Sindri confirms. *It's where my people come from. Humans. The ground there is rock, rather than wood.*

*Where is it?* I ask.

*A very long way below us,* Sindri shrugs. *I'll be returning there after killing the Chaos mage we're hunting, and if you have nothing better to do you're welcome to join me.*

*I might take you up on that,* I admit. It's not like I have anywhere else to go, and Sindri is a pretty cool friend.

*We'll talk more about that all later, then,* Sindri says. *For now, I need to rest. If you feel yourself falling asleep, please wake Kagiso early. It's better than having no one awake, and she's mostly unharmed from our recent fight.*

*Will do, Sindri.*

*Thanks again, Hannah. I know that what you did weighs on you, but never forget that you saved our lives in doing it. To protect innocents by killing aggressors is not evil, it is brave.*

*I guess so,* I admit. *I just wish nobody had to die at all.*

*Were only the world so kind,* Sindri sighs. *Good night, Hannah.*

*Good night, Sindri.*

Well. I guess I'm keeping watch now. The general idea of it seems pretty straightforward—if anything dangerous-looking comes within fifty feet of us, or if I hear anything suspicious enough from outside my range, I wake everybody up. Easy enough. The hard part, I suspect, is staying focused and awake.

Or, well... at least awake. I don't think I can really *fail* to notice something big enough to be threatening entering my range, not unless I was particularly groggy. And since I *am* kind of groggy, priority one right now is waking myself up. I scuttle in a circle, spinning my body and getting my blood pumping. For some odd reason, this feels a lot weirder than normal. Uh, insofar as spinning around as a little radially symmetrical spider creature can feel normal, anyway. Still, something feels odd, almost like something is pressing on me in a particular direction. But it's not... touch, really? I'm not sure how to describe it, it's just... new. Is there anything in that direction that's noteworthy? Let's see... there's Sindri's tent, I guess. A small colony of ant-like creatures is over that way as well, kind of. And the candle clock is next to me, I guess.

...Oh, wait a minute! The candle clock! I stop spinning myself silly and walk around it, feeling the... *whatever* I'm feeling match whatever side of my body the candle is on. I walk away from the lit candle, noticing the feeling get dimmer. Then I walk behind a tent and immediately notice the feeling disappear.

...I think I'm sensing light!

It's the new organs between each of my legs, it has to be. They're rudimentary light sensors, the evolutionary precursor to eyes. I mean, probably, anyway. It matches my observations and would make sense, and like... *dang* I really hope it's eyes. I don't like being blind one bit. My spatial sense is really nice, don't get me wrong, but it's sort of... claustrophobic. Fifty feet seems like a long distance up until it really, *really* isn't.

One way or another, my body is definitely changing. The thick nerve clusters underneath each part of my weakening exoskeleton just kinda weren't there before, so it's pretty obvious. Assuming this is the same sort of Transmutation effect as the one affecting me on Earth, this might be a good time to try and figure that magic out, maybe even learn to control it!

...Though on the subject of control, I should probably start with the spell I already know. I focus on the feeling of my Spacial Rend, at least as best I can. Spacial Rend, Spacial Rend... I know it's called that, I know it's *named* that, but it also isn't. That's a representation of the name, but the *real* name is **Sp—**

I shudder, feeling the goddess' attention on me for a fractional yet infinite second. I... I recall Kagiso demonstrating her spell by

222

incanting its true name to me, so I doubt the goddess minds all that much about being summoned frivolously, but... I don't know. It still seems rude to do it without a reason. Like calling someone on the phone, or sending them a Discord ping. Some people can just *do* that, but I sure can't. It's intrusive! I'm curious if I can use the verbal incantation without being able to talk, but not curious enough to... y'know, bother somebody. What if I accidentally wake my friends if I succeed? They'd assume we're under attack!

Anyway, inviting the goddess to speak the true name of my magic is an entirely optional part of casting the spell. It *empowers* things, from what I'm told, and it probably does so considerably. This just comes at the cost of all the many downsides of, y'know, *saying the name of your spell out loud,* a trope that has been criticized to death. This world doesn't run on anime time, for starters, so enemies won't stop trying to kill you while you talk. Plus, the name of the spell describes the spell, and that gives information about your spell that people otherwise might not have. It *certainly* isn't stealthy, and screaming "I'M CASTING A SPELL!" is pretty bad on its own, but... I feel like the name has to actually, legitimately describe the spell, as well. Your target *will* get information regarding what you're about to do when you say the name. No trying to game the system and trick people with the name. I don't know why I feel that's true, but I do. The goddess just... wouldn't like it, probably. Maybe. Blah, I genuinely don't have a logical reason to believe this is true, which means I *should* submit the belief to scientific rigor, but... maybe not personally. I'm sure someone else has tried. I'll ask the others about it when they wake up.

So. Magic. Let's try to focus here, Hannah. My goal is to figure out my shapeshifting magic in order to try and control it a bit better. I feel like shapeshifting is somewhat of a potentially catastrophic kind of magic to fuck up, and considering that I don't want to *Akira* myself I'm gonna try to take this slow. I'll start with the one spell I *can* cast, and see if figuring out the details of actually casting it can help me extrapolate from there. Spacial Rend, my cutting-that-isn't-cutting magic. I will never be able to cast it without remembering my first kill, I think, so that's the memory I turn to, the feeling I force myself to relive. I hope it is always as haunting and disturbing as it was then.

I am, as I so *often* am, immediately disappointed in myself. The bloom of power comes easily and it feels comfortable, like putting on a snug sock. The memory of blood and terror and evil performed by my own claws doesn't torment me like I feel it should. I just... activate the magic, casually dig a small hole with it, then let it fade away. It's *easy,* as easy as breathing. It's my magic, after all, and it's as much a part of me now as any muscle or limb. And I'm actually pretty good at trying to flex muscles that don't exist.

Though... surely that's not all there is to it, right? There's no way I can learn to control my transformation spell by just feeling around for other threads of power to pull on, can I? That doesn't seem quite right, but it doesn't seem quite *wrong* either. Agh! I hate that! I hate how... *instinctive* everything is. I hate *feeling* my way through this rather than understanding and knowing! I like hard magic systems, ones where the magic is basically science in the sense that it's consistent, predictable, and an inherent part of the world. This wacky personalized stuff is... uncomfortable to me, yet at the same time it got me my first spell, so... here we go? Feeling around for threads of power. This will work, kind of, I think... because I know what I'm looking for. I know the spell I'm seeking. It's the spell that *changes me.*

That feels fundamentally incorrect, but also sort of close enough. There's some basic resonance from that: yes, the spell does change me, at least in the sort of 'no duh' way which is basically meaningless. I'm missing important elements here. I roll the idea around in my mind a while, accompanied by me curling myself into a ball and rolling around the campsite a little bit. Hmm... hmm hmm hmm. Rolling does weird things to my budding light-sensor organs. I'm radially symmetrical but not spherically symmetrical, so the light sensors are rolling along with me, spinning in ways that would make my human body quite dizzy. Or, well. My human*oid* body. I'm not really human anymore, what with the exoskeleton I'm growing.

An exoskeleton. *Hmm.* My spider body... also has an exoskeleton. And it has claws, though they're not shaped quite the same way as my toe claws. The teeth, though. My spider body has *very* sharp teeth. My human body might be growing parts that are more like my spider-self. And the budding eyes, well... my human body has eyes. Not ten eyes, though. It doesn't quite match up perfectly, but I think I'm onto something, and while I'm tempted to go pulling on what my instincts say is *kind of* the right magic muscle, I'm not currently anemic enough to think that's a good idea a second time. Instead, I idle away the hours until the candle finally burns down and then skuttle into Kagiso's tent to wake her up.

She's curled up in her bedroll on the ground, so I just head up to her face and bump into her a few times to wake her up. She tenses, her eyes shooting open... but then she glances at me and relaxes, making a tired groaning noise and trying to curl up deeper into her bed. Which... hey! She can't do that! It's my turn to sleep!

I bump her a few more times, to increasingly annoyed groans, before she finally starts wriggling out of bed.

"Fala hana, nata nata," she mumbles, patting me on top of my body. I drum my feet indignantly, because I am *not* a hat, no matter how often I end up on top of her head. She ignores my silent denial, however, stretching like a cat and yawning before grabbing her weapons and standing up.

For some reason, I follow Kagiso out of the tent rather than just curl up into the nearby barren zone and pass out. She sits down on a rock, nods at me, and pats a small space beside her, so I jump up and curl into a ball next to her thigh. Kagiso pulls out a set of whittling tools as well as the chunk of the deep wood I left in her backpack after tunneling into it, and starts turning it into arrows. Neat. The two of us sit in silence, partly because we can't actually talk to each other while Sindri is unconscious but partly because that's just who we are: a pair of introverts in the mood to enjoy each other's company in utter silence.

It doesn't take long after I get comfortable there to find myself waking up in bed. Once I spend the requisite few seconds figuring out how to breathe again, I let out a sigh. Nothing actually bad happened. No one tried to come after us in our sleep. That's quite a relief.

For the first time this week I crawl out of bed without being on the verge of a panic attack. Alien feelings in my jaw and careful movements of my tongue indicate I should probably keep my lips firmly shut until I lock myself in the bathroom, but I expected this. It'll... it'll be okay, I think. As long as there's nothing extra tagging along with my new teeth. I enter the bathroom, strip down, and do a quick check over my body. Everything looks the same. My toes are now entirely exoskeletal, and they're starting to infect my feet. My slowly-changing leg has more growing under the skin than it did yesterday, but I don't have that itch I tend to have when the skin is ready to fall off. Satisfied with my checkup, I bite the bullet, stare into the mirror, and finally open my mouth.

Uh. Wow. Holy steamed casserole, okay, that's... that's some teeth. I stare into the mirror and huge, glistening-white triangles shine back at me like an upscaled shark mouth. A full set of horrifying saw-like edges, not a single one built for chewing. I am made to tear chunks off flesh and swallow them whole. I open and close my mouth a few times, focusing on the strangely disturbing feeling of my upper teeth and lower teeth slotting in next to each other, passing into the gaps side-by-side rather than settling on top or in front. It's almost mechanical, in a way. They slot into each other *too* well, to the point that any slight warping would leave me stabbing my own gums or unable to close my jaw. A naturally-evolving creature couldn't rely on having perfectly ordered teeth all the time, that's just genetic variance, but I suppose my magically-induced changes have no such limitation.

I open my mouth as wide as it will go—and holy moly that's a *lot* wider than it used to be—then snap my jaws shut with a satisfying *clack.* Woah, that's... loud. I used a lot more force than I intended. My teeth are extremely sharp, extremely dangerous, but whatever part of my brain that instinctively wants to be careful with my own teeth and not stress them too hard has apparently been shut off. I'll have to be sure not to bite my own fingers off when I'm eating! Hell, I could probably bite my own hand off if I tried. Or, y'know, someone else's. Heh.

...I should get in the shower so I can go eat breakfast. I step in and let the hot water run, rinsing myself down and looking over the skin on my legs for hair to shave. I've thankfully never been all that hairy—it's annoying shaving what little body hair I *do* get, I can't imagine having to do both legs every day—but I don't spot anything. Hmm. Not too strange, I suppose, but I feel like I should have regrown some body hair by now. I guess my skin knows it's eventually going to die and fall off, so it has stopped bothering with frivolities. I do still have to shave my armpits, but I suppose the exoskeletal advance army has yet to reach such heightened shores. I giggle a little, and now that my mouth is open I just *have* to snap my teeth together again. Then again. *Clack clack.* Man, that is worryingly satisfying. I need to find someone to chew. I mean something to chew.

Ha ha, I'm definitely going insane. I should probably be panicking about this. I *could* be panicking about this, if I really started focusing on how fucked up it all is. But... I'm extremely tired, *especially* of panic. I've been doing that so often lately that I just feel numb to it. It's probably healthy to take a rest day or two to refill my panic reserves for later, right?

I luxuriate in the shower for a good while longer before finally getting out, wiping the steam off the mirror and watching myself clack my teeth together one last time for good measure before drying off and getting clothes on. Including, of course, my mask. There's almost a hint of resignation in me as I put it on, for whatever reason. It's human Hannah time. My routine is calling, and it's school, work, sleep, repeat. Just get through things, taking one step at a time and hoping my problems just go away, even though I know they won't. That's my life. It sucks, and it's terrible, but it's mine and the idea of letting it go just terrifies me too much to consider.

I spare one last longing glance at the mirror, then exit the bathroom to face the day.

# 13

# FUEL FOR THE FIRE

The simple act of trying to eat breakfast is enough to alert me that something a bit more fundamental has changed than just my teeth. I eat cereal for breakfast every day, unless my mom decides to cook something on the weekend. I mean that. Every single day, I wake up, I shower, and I chow down on a bowl or two of sugary, oaty, wheaty goodness drenched in milk. I like cereal; it's simple and easy and tasty and quick. It's a great meal all around, yet the mere thought of eating it now makes my stomach churn. After a hesitant, confused back-and-forth of trying to complete my usual routine but being deeply repulsed by it, a cycle of opening the cupboard, shaking in place, closing the cupboard, then opening it again, I head to the fridge instead. This feels more natural, somehow. An urge takes me and before I know it I've swallowed four eggs whole.

...Huh.

I... really hope I don't get salmonella. What the heck, monster brain? At least let me cook them. I didn't even chew the darn things, just... gulp. Like a friggin' snake. I mean, I doubt raw egg would taste good anyway, but... uh, hmm. I glance at the egg carton. Hesitantly, I put another egg in my mouth. I'm not really able to chew things anymore, since I have no molar structures and my teeth just do cutting now. Eggs don't really need more than that, though, so I burst it open in my mouth and jolt at the explosion of flavor that rushes out of it. This is *weird*. Really weird. Eggs used to taste so bland to me, but now it's just like... mmm. Tasty unborn children juice. I swallow it all, the broken eggshell scratching uncomfortably but not painfully as it slides down my throat. I'll need to eat a few dozen more eggs each day to catch up with Gaston, but I'm starting to see the appeal of his routine all of a sudden.

Whatever. I'd better get out of the house before my brother comes downstairs. It's raining outside, which in some nebulously narcissistic way makes me feel somewhat cheated. Days upon days of constant panic and horror have finally left me somewhat numb to the idea that my humanity is slowly dripping away. Not... not *totally* numb, not by a longshot. The thought is horrifying. It's just that I'm so incredibly *exhausted* from being horrified all the time that the feeling is sort of sliding off of my brain a little. I feel like there's a subtle difference between coming to terms with something and just... lacking the mental bandwidth for additional panic attacks. But maybe not. Maybe this is what acceptance feels like. I guess I'll take it, either way.

I grab an umbrella from the stand by the door—it rains a lot here, so my family is prepared for it—and start my walk to the bus stop. Brendan arrives not long after, giving me a wide berth as he circles into my line of sight in an attempt to not surprise me. I smile at him, not that he can see it behind my mask.

"Hey," I greet him.

"Hey," he answers, relaxing noticeably. "Uh, how's things?"

"Not terrible," I admit.

"That's... good news, I suppose," he nods. "How was last night?"

"Pleasantly uneventful," I admit. "I was only awake for about two hour-ish fantasy time units. We were keeping a watch rotation."

"Ah. Yeah. Classic adventuring stuff."

"Exactly."

"Good that nothing happened," he comments awkwardly.

"Agreed," I say. "I think spider-Hannah is starting to grow eyes though, maybe?"

"Oh! Is that good?"

"Well if they let me see it will be, yeah."

He nods, and the silence that follows makes me restless instead of comfortable like it usually does. Absentmindedly, I open my mouth just a little bit and let my jaw snap shut. *Clack.* Brendan gives me a startled look.

"Teeth came in," I explain, pointing at my own mouth. "They're, uh, really big and sharp. Also I had a weird urge to eat like five raw eggs this morning, so if I start vomiting later that's probably why."

"You seem, uh, calmer about that than I would have expected," Brendan admits.

"I noticed that too, yeah," I agree. "I think I'm just too tired to panic, but it might be mental corruption, so... I'm trying not to think about it too much, honestly."

He relaxes a little.

"Well the corruption can't be too bad, you're still you enough to purposefully ignore it," he jokes, and I glare at him. This only seems to amuse him further, so I really don't know why I bothered. I clack my teeth at him again, and *that* seems to do a better job of getting my point across.

"...I *really* wanna see what you have going on under that mask," Brendan admits.

I glance around. We're the only two people at the bus stop and the bus is nowhere to be seen, so I shrug and lift the mask, opening my jaw up as wide as it'll go. I feel it drop down, down further, and nearly unhinge all the way down to touch my neck to my chin, even as I stare up at Brendan. His expression is... complicated, to say the least. I watch his eyes flicker around to various parts of my face, a mix of interest and mild horror and something I can't really identify all warring together in a messy mush of emotion.

"Close your mouth and smile," Brendan says.

Seeing no reason not to, I snap my teeth shut again *(clack!)* and give him a tight-lipped grin.

"Woah, that's creepy," Brendan mutters. "Your cheeks stretch *just* enough to put you in uncanny valley there, Hannah. Be careful with that if you're ever caught without your mask."

"Oh, good to know," I nod, putting said mask back on. "I guess that makes sense, considering how wide I can open my jaw now. Think of how big of a burger I could eat!"

Although, frankly, I'd prefer to just remove the patties and bacon from the burger and just eat that. Maybe the cheese, too.

"It's always food with you," Brendan snorts.

"Hey, mutating into a horror beyond human comprehension takes a lot of calories, okay?"

"I dunno, you seem pretty comprehensible right now."

"Just wait until I start phasing out of reality! I'll reach halfway through the fourth dimension and you'll get to see all my internal organs and stuff."

"Lucky me."

Unfortunately, our banter is cut short by the arrival of the bus. Once surrounded by humanity, the talk of my budding *in*humanity has to end, so I prod Brendan for more information about the misadventures of his tabletop characters. The mermaid who summons battle mounts to get around on land hasn't even gotten another game since I first started mutating, so instead I'm learning about a clawed psychic woman who flies around everywhere *completely naked* because GURPS gives you a discount on defensive force fields if they prevent you from wearing anything while they're up for some reason. Consequently, she functionally has more hit points than the rest of the party put together, because hardened ablative psychic barriers are better than hit points anyway. I choose not to judge the fact that Brendan clearly decided not to convince his GM that the 'no wearing equipment under the force field' shouldn't apply to clothing that provides no mechanical advantage, even though he absolutely could have done that. I am in no position to complain about someone who fantasizes about flying naked ladies.

We soon get off the bus and the school day begins. Vaguely wondering what sort of horrible mutation will ruin my life today, I'm surprised to find lunchtime rolling around entirely without incident. Unfortunately, (or perhaps fortunately, given my teeth situation) I don't really get to eat today. I have a science test to make up.

I find Autumn already waiting outside the science classroom when I show up, scribbling something into her notebook. She quickly puts it away when she spots me, nodding a somewhat nervous greeting. She seems kind of uncomfortable in general, hunched over slightly with her arms tight against her body.

"Hello, um... Hannah?" she says. What, did she forget my name again?

"That's me, I'm Hannah," I confirm, stepping beside her to wait for the teacher to arrive. "Worried about the test?"

She shrugs awkwardly and declines to answer.

"What about you?" she says instead. "Are you doing okay?"

"The bleeding stopped, if that's what you mean," I respond carefully. It's simultaneously a more reassuring and more correct answer than just saying 'yes,' even if it's misleading because of that.

Autumn just gives me a funny look for a while before turning away.

"That's good," she says.

"Thanks again for all your help back then," I tell her before I can chicken out. "Really, it means a lot to me."

"Don't thank me for that," she answers firmly, which surprises me. That didn't sound like modesty, that sounded like a legitimate request. Self-esteem issue, maybe?

"Uh, I'm not sure I can stop myself from *being thankful*. Like, that was a *lot* of blood you helped out with, but... I'll go ahead and be thankful silently, I suppose," I manage.

She just nods, not even looking at me. Shoot, I handled that badly and I don't understand how. She seems *really* uncomfortable all of a sudden, so I take a subtle half-step away to give her some space and shut up. If she appreciates that, I can't tell, but it's still probably my smartest move so far. The science teacher arrives not long after, letting us into the classroom and giving us our tests back. He didn't bother to give us new tests, apparently not caring about the possibility that we looked up all the answers overnight. Which is fortunate for Autumn, because she blitzes through the test with a speed that implies she did exactly that.

I finish my test (even though it still has bloodstains on it, which I feel like should probably be a biohazard) and turn it in at around the same time, leaving Autumn and I free to go actually eat something before our next class. I glance into the cafeteria to see what they're serving and see some vegetarian pasta thing that smells absolutely revolting, so lacking any real way to get food I just end up turning to Autumn.

"You wouldn't happen to be going out to eat, would you?"

She shakes her head, causing her brown curls to bounce adorably.

"I have a car, but I don't normally go out. I packed lunch."

"Well darn," I sigh. Then, on a whim: "Mind if I come sit with you anyway?"

She gives me an odd (and cute) look before turning away.

"...I'm just going to the library to read," she mutters.

"I'm okay with that," I tell her. "I have some homework to do."

That's only half true; I would normally do the homework next period, but... y'know. Crush brain says proximity to girl is good. Follow. Befriend. Bask in presence. Other perfectly normal and not-creepy behavior. Like yeah, everything I thought yesterday about

234

relationships being a bad idea when I'm mutating into a monster is *true*, and also it'd probably suck for Ida if I start pursuing someone else right after she admitted she wants to get in my pants (which is still kind of weird and confusing, what the heck), but I'm not really in a position where my logic brain is in charge here. But hey, if I want a logical reason to do this, here's one: Autumn is the kind of friend that's willing to help me clean up giant bloodstains, and I'll probably need more of that in the near future.

Though I guess she might change her tune if it ends up not being my blood. Hopefully we won't have to find out.

Thanks to the joy of rich-person taxes, my school library is actually pretty well stocked. I don't have time to read anymore, but I used to enjoy it quite a bit and I consumed a lot of the books on offer here during my freshman year. Autumn awkwardly plops down at a table, pulling a book and a lunch bag out of her backpack before lifting said backpack up on the table, as if to use it as a shield to prevent her from having to look at my face. Which, y'know, probably not the best sign. I have *no idea* what this girl thinks of me, but... I guess that's what I'm here to find out?

I hear a pencil scribbling as I get out my textbooks—probably Autumn taking notes again—and settle in to study. I don't want to come off as too weird (or too desperate) so I resign myself to stay quiet until lunch ends unless Autumn starts a conversation. She doesn't, but that's okay. Silence is pretty comfortable for me, a lot of the time. When the bell finally rings and we start getting up, I finally manage to catch a glimpse at the cover of her book, which just has a single, large word on it: *Thud!*

Oh nice, she has good taste!

"Are you reading Terry Pratchett?" I ask. "I love Terry Pratchett!"

Slowly, she peels her eyes away from the book, blinking owlishly for a moment as she slings her backpack over her shoulder.

"...What's your favorite thing he's written?" she asks, testingly.

Uh. Hmm. That's a good question. Pratchett has a *lot* of great books, but...

*"Monstrous Regiment,"* I say, since I'm trying to hint at the fact that I am a lesbian. "But I also really love *Going Postal*. Only Terry Pratchett would have the gall to name the main character of a story 'Moist.' Like dang, that is an *impossible* amount of confidence on display. The dude really made me read the word 'moist' thousands of times in a row *and like it,* and I think that is all the evidence you need to prove he is the most powerful author to have ever lived."

She giggles a bit at that and my heart flutters, my face flushes and a feeling of unparalleled success washes over me, utterly unearned. All I did was speak a few sentences about how Terry Pratchett—whose books have sold over *one hundred million copies* worldwide, who is technically, in fact, *Sir* Terry Pratchett because he was *knighted* for being *so good at words*—is a pretty good author, actually. An utterly worthless, smooth-brain thing to point out.

And yet, it made a nerdy girl laugh. *Aaaaaaaaaaaaaaaaaaah!*

"My favorite is *Carpe Jugulum*," Autumn supplies. "The whole witches series was what hooked me. I'm rather disappointed the witches don't show up much in the other books. Most of the Ankh-Morpork characters do to some extent."

"Well, that's what happens when most of the books take place in Ankh-Morpork," I agree. "You're right though, it is a shame. With a series as huge as Discworld, though, it'd be impossible to have everyone showing up all the time. I always wished for more Susan, myself."

"Susan is neat," Autumn agrees. She agreed with me about a book! I can't help but grin, which probably makes it extra fortunate that I have a mask on. Look at me interact socially! Aww yeah! Unfortunately, it looks like we now have to part ways, because Autumn doesn't seem to be heading in the direction of my next class.

"So, uh, do you usually eat in the library like that?" I ask.

Autumn immediately tenses, her expression immediately becoming twenty times more anxious.

"...Um, yeah?" she answers after a long and conspicuous pause.

Woah. What was up with *that?* Ida said she was pretty sure Autumn wasn't getting bullied, but that was... not the face of someone expecting something good to happen as a result of asking where she eats. This is so weird, she's acting really funky compared to yesterday. I should make sure to give her an out.

"Well, um, I was wondering if you would be okay with me dropping by and eating with you sometimes, or if you'd prefer to eat alone," I say carefully.

She stares at me briefly, not seeming to know what to say.

"I'm not gonna stop you from going to the library," is all she settles on, and I decide it's best not to press. She turns and hurries off, the unexpected quickness of her movements making my muscles tense with an instinct to pounce. Thankfully, I ignore that instinct and do not chase down, tackle, and bite my crush. That's like, third or fourth date stuff.

...Uh, wait. Back up on that one. Really, brain? I shake my head and wander off to my next class. It's boring, uninteresting, and uneventful, as is the class after *that.* Things are going suspiciously well, and since I don't know how to feel about that I do my usual strategy of ignoring it. I have work today, too, which means I'm not expected to eat dinner with my family, which means I don't have to spend a whole meal trying not to show my teeth when I eat, and that's pretty nice too. Even work goes off without a hitch. It feels like my old routine is back, despite all the changes. It feels... weird. I'd expected it to be more comfortable after all the panic and insanity and madness. I suppose none of that is disappearing, though, it's just... delayed. I'm probably just stressed in anticipation.

Whatever. I head home after work, trudge up to my room, and quickly pass out. Then I immediately start flailing and hissing because it feels like somebody just *peeled my eyelids back and forced me to look at the sun.* I try to shriek in agony but nothing happens because I can't *breathe.* I flail around instead, screaming silently as I flail to get the agony out instead. I roll in pain, other parts of my mind dimly starting to wake and take stock of the situation. I'm in fantasyland, I'm a hyperspider, Kagiso is standing over me looking horrified and repeatedly calling my name. But none of that matters because pain, pain, pain, *pain!* It feels like something is boring itself into my skull from a dozen different directions, ripping me open and setting the holes on fire. I'm in pain. I'm under attack! I need *safety!* I jump into the closest barren zone, entirely on instinct.

Darkness descends instantly. The pain vanishes like a popped bubble. I still wish I could scream, but the need is less instinctive and more... me.

"Makana!" Kagiso cries out, looking around desperately. "Hana makana! Makana! Makana makana!"

I don't know what that means, and I'm worried for her, but we don't seem to be under attack by anything so I don't have the mental bandwidth to focus on it. The pain is... kind of coming back. It's not *really* there, almost like the memory of pain rather than pain itself, but sometimes it throbs in a way that makes me immediately fear it's about to return. Teboho and Sindri wake up as a result of Kagiso's shouts, rushing out to speak with her in hushed tones. I get the expected mental contact shortly afterwards.

*Hannah?* Sindri asks, causing another spike of agony to ram into my brain.

*Ow!* I hiss back at him. *I'm here. I'm alive. I'm in pain.*

*Kagiso is apologizing over and over,* Sindri says, which hurts more so I hiss at him mentally. *What happened?*

*I have no idea,* I answer. *I literally just woke up.*

*She says she hurt you.*

Huh. That seems odd. I don't feel wounded or anything, I feel more... a stabbing ache. Like a migraine. I check my body over

238

anyway, and... wait. There's some chitin missing between two of my legs. Oh. *Oh!* The light-sensing organs! The thinning chitin that had been covering them is falling off! A quick check next to where I was sleeping on the rock next to Kagiso does indeed show a chunk of chitin that fell off.

*Not her fault,* I tell him. *I'm partially molting. It hurts. I think I'm growing eyes.*

*You're what?*

*Growing eyes,* I repeat, looking deeper into my own body. Yeah, those nerve clusters are really bunching up and meshing with my brain. Kinda creepy. *I think I just overloaded an undeveloped organ system. My nervous system is still adjusting to stuff. I should probably stay here for a while.*

*May I ask why?*

*Well, it's dark in the fourth dimension, and I don't have eyelids.*

There's a pause.

*Fair enough,* Sindri eventually allows. *I'll let the others know the situation while we get camp cleaned up, and then we'll figure out the best way to handle things.*

I send back an affirmation and stretch my legs a bit, scuttling around the inside of the barren zone as I try to think. It does seem like I'm getting my wish, as least as long as I'm interpreting my new senses correctly. My guess for how things went down is as follows: I fall asleep next to Kagiso, my body still changing. Kagiso gives me pats and scratches as she is wont to do, but accidentally ends up removing part of my body covering up my still-developing eyes. It probably came off really easily since they're just... dead chitin at this point, entirely intended for being harmlessly removed. They were just removed too early, before the changes to my nervous system were ready for the sudden influx of light and information. So under this assumption, all I can really do is rest and wait for my body to finish changing. The main problem with that being that I am very, very hungry.

*Sindri,* I think as 'loudly' as I can, for lack of a better term. *Sindri, can you hear me?*

*Of course,* Sindri answers. *How can I help, Hannah?*

*I think I need food,* I admit. *Meat. A lot of it.*

*Transmutation pangs?* He asks.

*Huh?*

*You need mass and fuel for your changes,* Sindri explains. *The speed of the change and the symptoms you're experiencing point to Transmutation magic, so I think this is pretty obvious evidence that you're triple-naturalborn. Which, again, is* extremely *uncommon, but certainly not unheard of. Most Transmutation magic focuses on the self, with shapeshifting spells and whatnot, and it's one of the more energy-intensive forms of magic. It tends to make the caster hungry. We call that hunger Transmutation pangs.*

*Oh, that... makes sense, I guess,* I admit. *Honestly, this is all really weird and strange to me, so it's really reassuring when you treat it like it's normal? If, um, that makes sense.*

*Of course that makes sense. And it* is *normal, Hannah. I would not consider your situation in general to be normal, I suppose, but the individual pieces? Of course. Humans categorize and record everything we can on magic, and it's part of my job to be up-to-date on our general well of knowledge. Mostly so I don't get killed by my own ignorance. You're fascinating and unique in many ways, but many people have magic that allows them to step through space, or that changes their body over time. I'm happy to help share what we've learned from their experiences.*

In that moment, I am very, *very* tempted to tell him about Earth. Maybe he won't think that's crazy either. Maybe he can help me find people like me. Sindri is nice, Sindri is a *friend,* and he's proven that he's willing to put real effort into helping me when he doesn't have to. I don't, though. It's a conversation I don't want to have.

For some reason, I kind of like not having to talk about being human.

Curling up into a ball, I roll around a bit to get comfortable since I know I'm just going to be waiting around for a while. I am currently watching *my own eyeballs grow*, which is a bit of a surreal experience. They aren't growing or changing very fast, not by a longshot, but they *are* shifting at a visible rate, the ends of new nerves slowly snaking to their destinations, the membranes of the eyes themselves thickening and adjusting little by little. It's kind of fascinating.

*Kagiso caught you some food, Hannah,* Sindri reports. *Where should she leave it?*

Ah, right, actually getting the food into the barren zone will be a problem. I scuttle over to the edge of the area and stick one limb out, wiggling it around for Kagiso to notice. She drops the animal corpses nearby, deliciously raw and bloody. Resigning myself to a moment of pain, I scuttle out of my barren zone, keeping the budding eye she accidentally revealed at the back of my body as I quickly grab a bite and return to the dimensional pocket to swallow it. Repeating this a few more times, I actually start to feel full by the time I finish off her pile of unneeded apology presents. I tell Sindri to tell her thank-you.

Getting food in my system seems to speed the growth process for my eyes significantly, though I mean that as a very scientific kind of significance, not to in any way imply that things are now moving fast. There might be a way to speed it up, though. Let's try to tackle that problem in the least stupid way I have available, though.

*Hey Sindri,* I ask. *I was thinking of trying to purposefully use my Transmutation magic. Right now it just kind of does its own thing, and I was hoping to get a bit more control over it. Any advice?*

*Not the first time you've woken up with new body parts, then?* Sindri muses. *Hmm. Your own magic generally isn't at risk of harming you, unless you go out of your way to be reckless and stupid with it. Even then, reckless and stupid people generally get magic they can't irreversibly injure themselves with, so generally speaking I'd say you're likely to be fine. The same can't be said for the rest of us,*

241

*though, so make sure to direct whatever magical energies you conjure up away from Kagiso, Teboho, and I, okay?*

Huh. That's weirdly nonchalant. "You'll probably be fine" is not an answer I expected from Sindri, he seems like an extremely cautious man.

*Of course, I won't expose you guys to anything if I can help it,* I confirm. *But I have to admit, I was hoping for more concrete advice. I barely have any idea how magic even works, I've just kind of been flailing around and trying to do what feels right, and that's* annoying. *I like to know how something works, why something works, and only act once I have some solid idea of the expected outcome. But I'm just kind of doing everything blind! Er, no pun intended.*

Sindri laughs.

*Well,* he muses, *I must say, it's easy to believe that you were raised by humans.*

*What, just from that?* I ask. *I know lots of reckless humans.*

*Of course, of course, we can be just as thoughtless as anyone. But a dentron wouldn't have that philosophy towards magic at all. It's sacred to them. A deeply personal thing. Dentron are like that in general, very uninterested in looking towards the 'how' and 'why.' I have to admit, it's very refreshing to be traveling with someone who bothers to ask those kinds of questions. Unfortunately, much to the endless frustration of our scientists, magic continues to defy our understanding. The most common theory is that it's managed by some sort of greater intelligence, but I personally have my doubts.*

*You do?* I ask, personally quite surprised. *I felt... I mean,* someone *says the true names of spells, don't you think? When they're cast that way, I mean. The voice sounds like it's coming from a person.*

An unfathomably alien person, but still a *person,* in the broad sense of the definition. Sindri just shrugs, though.

*I am a Pneuma mage,* he says simply. *I am somewhat naturally suspicious of the veracity of unexplained, magically-induced certainty, even if it's a phenomenon shared by nearly all sapients to*

242

*some extent. I do not claim there is no guiding intelligence, I only claim what I said: I have my doubts. Wrapping back to your initial concern, however, my point is that magic is frustratingly personalized. Attempts to standardize magical teaching ultimately amount to mindfulness exercises like meditation and personal therapy.*

Oh no, they have therapists here. I shudder.

*So I just kind of have to figure it out,* I conclude.

*You just kind of have to figure it out,* Sindri confirms. *But the flipside of that is this: you* can *'just figure it out,' on your own, without help. Go ahead and let your instincts guide you. I merely ask, again, that you direct your tests away from our general direction.*

*I suppose if I must,* I answer jokingly, and try to figure out some magic. Fortunately, I already did most of the groundwork for that last night. I know what lever of power I have to pull. I don't know its name, I don't really know what it does, but I know it's *there.* If I want to know more, I'll have to see what it does with my own ten eyes. So with a twist of a muscle that isn't real, I cast some magic, and I'm in two places at once.

Power flows into me, and power flows into me. I'm here, waiting in the darkness for my eyes to function, and I'm there, four-limbed, motionless, and dreaming, deep in REM yet somehow aware. My magic takes hold, thrumming in the space between universes. An impossibly long line of power connects each half of me, my magic reaching out to grasp it, full-fisted. Grip firmly established, my magic activates, and all it does is *pull.*

My changes accelerate in both bodies at once, and my familiar friend panic makes her triumphant return. Immediately, I clamp down on the spell *hard,* ending it before it can change too much. My awareness of my mostly-human self ends, but the damage is done. *Something* will be wrong when I wake up, that's for sure. At least here and now, in my small little spherical spider body, things have more or less gone to plan. Nerve clusters finish filling themselves out and attaching to my brain. Membranes protect the light-sensitive organs, while the rest of the dead chitin covering them falls off. I still can't see a darn thing, but I suspect that's just because light doesn't seem to enter the fourth dimension at all. Even once the changes stop, though, I'm a bit hesitant to go outside because *I don't have any friggin' eyelids.*

I get that spiders don't have eyelids, but... really, body? You're going with the spider theme rather than basic sense? I'm going to have to be looking in every direction simultaneously, all the time, because I have *ten eyes* and *none of them can close.* That's, uh, a little overkill, don't you think, goddess?

If she's listening she doesn't make herself known, which in retrospect I suppose I'm thankful for.

Hesitantly, I crawl partially out of my dimensional pocket and fail to squint at the bright, painful light I'm greeted with. I'm gonna have a constant headache, aren't I? It takes way too long for my eyes to adjust, stepping uncomfortably out into the open where my three friends have recently finished packing up camp. This *hurts* and I can't see crap but slowly, very slowly, my vision starts to clear and my new eyes start to be comprehensible. The worst part is how *overwhelming* it all is. I don't even know why it's overwhelming, I'm currently seeing everything in every direction including stuff that's inside other stuff, so why is three hundred and sixty degree vision a problem? I suspect that I'm just too used to monodirectional vision; I know what vision is *supposed* to be like, but this is around four times more than that. I take a few hesitant steps, slowly rotating my body and trying to keep my focus towards the ground, watching my own little spider feet tap around. My chitin, I notice, is bone-white. Funny, that.

*Hannah?* Sindri asks. *Are you okay?*

*This is indescribably weird,* I answer.

*I suppose I can only imagine. Here, can I at least borrow a leg so I can get us all in the communication network?*

I drum my feet in agreement and lift a leg in his general direction, which he, Teboho, and Kagiso all touch at once so Sindri can allow everyone to talk. The first voice is, of course, Kagiso.

*Hannah!* she chirps immediately. *Sorry!*

*It's fine, Kagiso! Really, you didn't do anything. My body is just a bit cruel to me sometimes.*

Y'know. Just a bit. Kagiso just responds by projecting a general feeling of anxiety in my direction, which like, mood.

*Uncountable legs, and now uncountable eyes,* Teboho comments. *You are truly a uniquely beautiful creature, Hannah.*

*Thanks, I think?* I manage. *But it's ten legs, ten eyes. Neither is uncountable.*

My legs *do* seem a bit hard to keep track of with my eyes, I suppose, but they look perfectly normal to my spatial sense.

*I'll take your word for it,* Teboho chuckles. *But the fact that I have to do so is rather the point, isn't it?*

*I guess,* I admit, trying to focus on the legs and feet of my comrades. Teboho's fuzzy legs are a somewhat woody reddish brown, matching what I can only assume is the giant, upscaled bark of the world tree in the distance. It looks like a giant wall that replaces the sky in a certain direction, but I can't really see much of it thanks to my low-to-the-ground position. Kagiso's fur, meanwhile, is stark white. I'm not sure if that's albinism or just a normal variation in her species, but I decide not to ask.

Tilting my tiny body, I start moving my gaze upwards (and also downwards, as the other half of me starts pointing towards dirt). The more of my friends I get to see with my eyes, the more I start to realize how insufficient my spatial sense is in terms of experiencing the world. Like sure, I already knew Teboho was smiling at me, but I knew that because I knew the muscles of his lips were tensed into an upturned position, not because I was *looking at the guy and seeing him smile.* There's a world of difference between knowing an expression and *seeing* it, letting every social instinct in my brain chug into reciprocation mode, feeling my mood noticeably improve due to the proof that another person is happy with me. I can *see* again. Holy crap, I missed this. Also, while I'm still seeing the inside of them all the time, which is kind of super gross, I now get to actually *look* at all four of Kagiso's fuzzy boobs which, uh, is certainly a very different experience now than it was before, and... that's really all I have to say about that! *Also* also: Sindri is black. I did not expect that at all and as a result I now feel vaguely racist. So. That's a thing.

*Hello, everyone,* I manage to think at them. *It's really nice seeing you for the first time.*

*Not too ugly a view, I hope,* Teboho jokes.

Not at all. I mean like, Sindri's a human man so he's not really all that interesting to look at, but the dentron are actually really neat! Their four long orangutan-esque arms seem kind of creepy to a human aesthetic sense at first, but now that I've been on the receiving end of many fuzzy pats I'm really growing to like them.

*Kagiso is the cutest,* I announce. *But I suppose you two aren't terrible looking.*

Kagiso grins smugly, grabbing me with her tail. Her tail then transfers me up to a hand, which ultimately transfers me up to her head. The whole process is *dizzying,* but I do my best to keep my bearings and ignore the overwhelming sensory data flooding into my head as my view gets moved around.

*Good hat,* she says happily.

*I'm not a hat,* I protest.

*Then why on head?* Kagiso counters, a foolproof response that no one could ever possibly argue against. I rub two legs together to make a hissing noise in lieu of an answer.

That earns a few chuckles from everyone, which I stoically ignore. I'm still busy looking at new things, after all. The problem with my spatial sense is seeing distance, after all, so I'm trying to get my brain to actually focus on and comprehend the absolutely *vast* amount of visual information I'm now getting thanks to my high vantage point. Around us, the ground just looks like pretty normal ground: dirt, shrubs, etcetera. It seems like it's pretty dry here, but other than that things seem normal. The further I look, however, the crazier things become. Out in the distance, it becomes clear that we're on a raised plateau of land, one that extends far, far out into the horizon, thinning and splitting off into branches of branches of branches until they finally end in what are undoubtedly leaves, even if they, too, are covered in dirt and foliage—a *lot* more foliage than where we are by the trunk. The closest leaf I see is at least a few miles away, but on it is an entire *forest,* countless normal-sized trees all growing on the leaf of the giant tree we're already standing on. A waterfall plummets from one of the leaf's edges, painting a rainbow in the air as the impossibly long drop separates the column of water into mist. Beyond it all, puffy white clouds intersperse with the edges of longer branches, the sky a mix of white and green without a hint of the clear blue I'm used to from home. I'm not sure if that's because the sky here is just white or if there's just too many clouds to see it. I look forward to discovering the answer.

That's just looking outwards, though. I'm on a world tree, so the real view is looking *up.* My family often goes to Dollywood for celebrations and the like, which is a theme park based on Dolly Parton which somehow exists and is actually real. This is relevant because Dollywood offers log cabins in the Smoky Mountains, and we'd rent them because my mom finds that kind of thing incredibly romantic. And really, it's a pretty cool vacation. The Great Smoky Mountains are absolutely gorgeous, and like most mountains they are also very, very tall. My experiences in hiking around the smokies defined a lot of what I find gorgeous in nature, even today. Majestic, powerful, and *huge.* I thought there was nothing else that could come close.

And then I went to the *Rocky* Mountains, and my mind was absolutely blown out of my ears. The topographic prominence of Mount Elbert is *double* that of the highest prominence in the smokies, and in terms of elevation it hits an absolutely ridiculous *fourteen thousand feet.* Sure, there are more impressive mountains in the world, but for little twelve-year-old Hannah? I thought I was climbing the gosh dang Tower of Babel and sneaking my way into heaven. There is nothing quite like the awe of yet-unforeseen scale, of having the idea of what you thought was big suddenly and impossibly dwarfed into nothingness by comparison. And *that* is what it's like to look up the trunk of the world tree.

The wall of wood has no apparent beginning or end. Simply looking *forward* gives me vertigo, because what I'm looking at is so vast, so all-encompassingly solid, that my brain insists *it must be the ground.* I shift my weight on Kagiso's head, however, and start looking up, up, *up,* further and further, higher and higher until finally I'm looking straight vertically and there's nothing but canopy, leaf, wood, and fire.

...Wait, fire? Oh shoot, that's definitely fire! There are countless branches and leaves between us and it, it has to be like, a hundred miles above us or something. It's hard to judge distance at this scale, but peeking between the gaps in the leaves is undoubtedly a roaring inferno on an impossible scale.

*Uh, Sindri?* I ask. *Is the Tree of Souls* supposed *to be on fire?*

*No, absolutely not,* he answers. *But there's nothing* we *can do about that, so let's get moving, shall we? We have a Chaos mage to catch, after all.*

*Um. Okay?* I manage, nervously clinging a little tighter to Kagiso's head, which prompts her to give me a pat. The four of us head out together, following whatever it is Sindri uses to determine where we're supposed to be going.

*If you think that's bad,* Teboho comments glumly, *wait until we get a chance to look down.*

I don't like the sound of that at all.

# 14

# WHEEL OF FORTUNE

Since everyone has apparently agreed to collectively ignore the fact that the world is ending, our journey resumes with only moderate urgency. We are, on one hand, chasing a dangerous, murderous criminal who needs to be stopped as soon as possible. On the other hand, Sindri is already confident that we have them cornered. They're here on this branch, which means we're between them and the trunk. It's only a matter of time before we either catch up or drive them to the edge of the branch where they can't run anymore anyway.

*How do you know where they are, by the way?* I ask.

*I'm an animal tamer, remember?* Sindri reminds me. *I have a pair of birds tracking our target. I can send and receive very basic information from them over a very long distance. They're my only two assistants right now, but since we've made it to the branch we'll be facing our foe on it's time for me to collect allies in earnest.*

*I hope that doesn't mean I'm going to have to fight a bunch of monsters.*

*Fighting shouldn't be required with me around,* Sindri says, a little smugly. *Though there's always the possibility of bandits, I suppose.*

Kagiso bobs her head back and forth slightly, making a humming noise and causing me to swing precariously around. I endure it. I'm starting to get used to being six times my body height up in the sky all the time. I do get revenge, however, by pinching Kagiso's long ears between two legs each and tugging each of them back and forth. She squeaks in protest.

*There's no need for glum talk of battle!* Teboho laughs. *We will be ready if it comes. Hannah, why don't you cease torturing my poor sister and work on your letters with me? Or I could teach you more about magic!*

*Magic,* I answer immediately. Literacy is awesome but magic is awesomer. This is simply an undisputed fact of the universe. *I've gotten the name of every kind of magic, but not the description, and some of the magic types seem a bit esoteric. Also, I think you mentioned something about complementary forms of magic? What's up with that?*

*Ah, yes!* Teboho nods happily, summoning a stone tablet with what looks like a carving of a spoked wheel on it. At the end of each spoke is a word and a symbol, though of course I can't read any of it. *So! Think of it as though every kind of magic rests on the edge of this wheel here. Order, Pneuma, Art, Motion, Light, Heat, Chaos, Death, Matter, Barrier, Space, Transmutation, and finally looping back around to Order again. The two forms of magic on either side of any given type are its complements. So Order is complemented by Pneuma and Transmutation, Light is complemented by Motion and Heat, and Matter is complemented by Barrier and Death. With me so far?*

*I think so,* I admit. *What do complements do?*

*A few things. You'll slightly resist the elements which complement any elements you oppose, but the effect is minor. More importantly is the fact that you can learn other people's spells if they complement your elements, as long as you know the true name of the spell. Spells copied from other people in this manner are substantially weaker than the original, but there are a lot of helpful spells that don't rely very much on power.*

*Ah, yes, that's right,* Sindri chimes in. *I was going to teach you Aura Sight, Hannah. My magic, Pneuma, complements Order, and Aura*

*Sight is one of the best Pneuma spells to know. Very useful for determining how dangerous an opponent is and what their likely capabilities are, not to mention some hints on their personality.*

*Do people's personalities show up in their aura somehow?* I ask hesitantly.

*No, people's personalities are reflected by the magic they have,* Teboho explains. *The Mother gifts us magic that fits who we are. You are an orderly person that often needs space to herself, are you not?*

I wriggle uncomfortably.

*I mean, yeah, I guess.*

*Don't be ashamed!* Teboho reassures me, laughing. *My Matter magic opposes Art, and guess what I don't have a lick of talent at?*

*Teboho singing against law back in village,* Kagiso comments blandly.

*Ha! Yes, the chief did ban me from doing so, didn't she?* Teboho agrees with a bittersweet smile. *The point is, it's useful information to know.*

*Well, give me the rundown then, I guess,* I sigh. I'm not so sure about this magical profiling stuff, it feels kind of... horoscope-y. It's too vague to be useful. Who *doesn't* need space to themselves from time to time? You could apply that to anybody!

*Right then, where to start... I suppose Order is the standard place. It's at the top of the circle here, with Chaos all the way at the bottom. As we've mentioned before, Order is the magic of complexity, meaning, and systems. Most notably it encompasses healing magic, as all living things are impossibly complex constructions of the Mother. That's far from its only use, of course: some Order mages are born with impossibly keen minds, capable of putting together disparate facts or complicated equations in moments. Others get magic revolving around directing a community or building complex structures. Order magic is fundamentally helpful, however, and almost always shines best in conjunction with other people. Conversely, Chaos magic is entirely about destruction. It is volatile, difficult to control, and harmful to all life. Chaos magic is about scrambling, randomizing, and mashing something until it is utterly unrecognizable, reduced to uselessness. For obvious reasons, it is reviled.*

I send a few mental confirmations that I'm listening, but don't speak. I feel like Teboho is getting into lecture mode, so I let him continue talking without interrupting. I wish I had something to take notes on.

*Pneuma is the magic of the soul,* he continues. *Specifically, the magic of the* living *soul, encompassing mind, thought, personality, breath, self-image, will, and to some extent, our connection to magic itself. The soul is where our magic arises from, so the rare Pneuma mage can manipulate that connection, strengthening or weakening it. Most, however, dwell within the realm of the mind, be that reading minds or influencing them. Pneuma mages tend to be somewhat controlling, no offense intended, of course.*

*None taken,* Sindri answers easily.

*Pneuma opposes Death, the magic of corruption, subsumption, and unlife. Like Pneuma, Death mages influence the soul directly, but rather than manipulate its connection to the living body, their spells pervert the soul, ripping it from where it belongs and using it for foul and selfish intentions. They can create unliving servants, weaken the body and mind, or just outright kill. Death complements Chaos, which is another mark against it to be sure, but it is also a perfectly natural part of life, and an... acceptable form of magic. I would not go so far to say it is well-liked, of course, and the tendency of Death mages to be incredibly selfish does little to assist with that.*

*Next we have Art, complement to Pneuma and Motion. It is the magic of emotion, sound, and beauty. Art magic is as esoteric and varied as art itself, though it often requires the active presence and practice of art to be used: singing, painting, sculpting, dancing... these things accompany the use of Art magic and its effects on the world. To be affected by Art magic, you must be affected by art itself, and upon being moved by beauty you are moved in a magical sense as well. Art mages can incite certain emotional states, empower or weaken those who behold their work, or just shatter your eardrums with a blast of sound. Art mages tend to be self-conscious and somewhat flighty.*

*The opposition to Art is Matter, and while I may be somewhat biased I daresay Matter is the most straightforward form of magic there is. There are no complexities like there are in Art, it creates matter and very little else. Some people can only create certain kinds of matter, some people can only create certain amounts, some people make matter that disappears on its own, and some people—like myself— have only a certain amount of matter that can form at any given time, and can remove anything we create at will. Matter complements Death and Barrier, and as their centerground its creations are lifeless and inert. Like the magic itself, we Matter mages tend to be rather uncomplicated individuals, focused and blunt.*

Huh. That's interesting. So Teboho has a limit to the amount of matter he can produce at once. Is that how his magic avoids conservation of energy problems? It's still an absurd amount of energy, though. Plus he just said not all Matter mages have that restriction. Gah, magic is so crazy! I can't decide if that's frustrating or cool!

*Next, we have Motion, which rests between Art and Light. It is also relatively self-describing: it is the magic of momentum, velocity, acceleration... it moves things! Motion mages tend to be impatient and easily distracted.*

Kagiso blinks slowly, radiating disapproval.

*...But they're also quick and decisive thinkers, good at accomplishing things efficiently!* Teboho quickly adds. *Motion opposes Barrier, the magic of halting, limiting, preventing, weakening, and warding. Barrier magic focuses not on enacting one's own will on the world, but denying others and protecting the caster. It is steady, sturdy, and fundamentally defensive. The types of effects they can produce are varied and powerful, but also stationary. Barrier mages tend to be resolute and determined.*

*...Obstinate and stubborn,* Kagiso corrects, causing Teboho to laugh awkwardly.

*Anyway, next we have Light,* Teboho continues. *It focuses on the manipulation of light itself, of course, and also lightning as I'm sure you're aware. More esoterically, however, some Light mages can manipulate magnetic objects as well.*

*Well they can do lightning so that makes sense,* I agree. *It's all electromagnetism. Which is probably what the category of magic should be called, by the sound of it.*

*Pardon?* Teboho asks.

*Don't bother trying to explain electromagnetism to the dentron,* Sindri says wryly. *Believe me, we've tried. Though I am* very *curious to learn where you hail from, to know about that but not write in any language I've seen before.*

*...A story for another time, I think,* I deflect. *Please continue, Teboho.*

*Yes, of course,* Teboho agrees. *Anyway, Light mages can damage and destroy things with burning sun rays and lightning, of course, but they can also create fantastic illusions, render themselves invisible, and countless other tricky effects. Light mages tend to be optimistic and upbeat, yet struggle to form deeper connections. Light opposes Space—the vast and infinite gulf through which not even light is fast enough to travel. I'm sure you're quite familiar with Space magic, but for completeness' sake: Space covers dimensional movement, teleportation, and occasionally gravity. Unlike Motion which allows people and objects to get from place to place very quickly, Space magic moves the concept of 'place to place' itself, having no effect on those actually doing the moving. Space mages tend to frequently swap between needing close interpersonal contact and strict alone time.*

...Hey. What? Okay, that hits pretty hard, actually. I'll die without being able to hang out with my friends, but I'll *also* die if I have to hang out with people too often. I don't like being called out there.

254

*Next up is Heat magic, which is the second complement to Chaos and therefore not well-liked. It is destructive, as while heating and cooling things is certainly capable of being used for mundane purposes, with enough power any change in temperature is a deadly one. Heat mages manipulate fire and ice, certainly, but also the more invisible aspects of their craft. They tend to be impatient and impulsive.*

*Finally, we have the last form of magic: Transmutation, your third naturalborn element. It is a complement to Order, but where Order focuses on making things how they* should *be, to whatever degree that is perceived, Transmutation is about how things* could *be. Where Order is structure, Transmutation is improvement. It is the magic of evolution, alteration, and actualization. Shapeshifting is the most common form of the magic, though more permanent changes like yours aren't unheard of. It's possible your species hasn't been seen before because you're one-of-a-kind: some other creature, animal, or person that was changed by your magic into who you are today. Or by someone else's, I suppose. Transmutation mages are creative and brilliant, but tend to struggle to fit in with society.*

Ah, see, there's the weak link. None of that sounds like me. I have been working my ass off to fit in with society and I feel like I was doing a pretty darn good job until Transmutation magic itself strolled in and started making problems. That's a self-fulfilling prophecy, not any part of *my* personality. I'm getting straight A's, I'm working a job and a half, I'm making a little nest egg so I can go through university without indebting myself for life, I'm going to graduate with a good degree and find a nice girl to marry and adopt a kid with or whatever. I don't smoke or drink or do drugs or really break any laws at all. Other than the homosexuality I am a prim and proper American woman, and even the gay stuff is rapidly (and correctly) being accepted as okay in... well, parts of the country that aren't mine. But I can just move to a better place and it'll be fine! That was my plan, to fit in and work hard and get rich and hopefully find some way to be happy with the money I make ten years from now. And sure, I'm miserable now and I'll be miserable until then, but you don't get good things without putting in the work for them. The magic messed everything up, and then the *magic* says I don't fit into society well? Nuh-uh. Now all my plans are screwed because nobody's gonna hire a fourth-dimensional bug lady to be a department manager and basically everything I've done in preparation for that future is now worthless. I'm just glad I'm too busy worrying about the fourth-dimensional bug lady bits to panic all that much about the plans-are-ruined bits. Honestly, I haven't really had time to care about any of that.

...Hmm. Well, uh, let's not start now, shall we? I have plenty of more important things to worry about. Like that magic!

*So every kind of spell is one of those elements, right?* I prompt.

*One or more!* Teboho corrects. *People like you and me that have more than one element often have spells which use multiple elements simultaneously. The spell I use to conjure protective walls, for example, is both Matter and Barrier, the Barrier element of the spell making the walls significantly more durable than mundane material would be otherwise. Though my spells are relatively boring in that manner. You will no doubt see more unique and exciting magic when we reach [location, destination, proper noun].*

*Sorry, what was the name for that?* I ask.

"Grawlaka," he rumbles out loud, the first syllable animalistic and guttural.

*That sounds like what you'd name a tiger king, not a city,* I comment. *But alright.*

*Grawlaka is one of the largest city-states on this branch,* Sindri explains. *They're a couple leaves ahead of here, and while our quarry is almost certainly going to avoid the area, it's still an ideal place for us to rest and obtain supplies. It's a beautiful city, I'm sure you'll like it.*

*What if our quarry doesn't avoid the area?* I ask hesitantly. A chaos mage entering a major city sounds bad.

*Then our job becomes significantly easier, as they will be slaughtered by the city's defenders without us having to lift a finger,* Sindri answers easily. *Cities of that size keep a careful eye on those trying to enter, and while Chaos mages are undoubtedly dangerous, they aren't dangerous enough to survive the combined efforts of a major militia.*

*Well, I guess that's reassuring,* I admit. *Why don't the militias handle it, then?*

*Partly because any Chaos mage that lives past a few years old needs to be very, very good at hiding from them, and partly because local militias don't tend to be any more inclined to get killed by a Chaos mage than the Chaos mage is inclined to get killed by them. There are an abundance of smaller villages that Chaos mages can prey on instead.*

Teboho scowls, since the implication is obvious. Everyone he used to know other than his sister is dead. That's... insane to think about. It's a miracle he and Kagiso can still function. Maybe the thought of revenge is all that's keeping them going. ...Though maybe not, since Kagiso doesn't seem to react at all. Perhaps she's just not listening to the conversation.

*So how do I go about learning that aura sight spell, then?* I ask. Magic magic magic! More magic!!!

*I think it might be wise if you start by learning the local language,* Sindri answers. *Just for the sake of convenience. Teboho, if we could switch the lesson plan up a bit?*

*Oh, certainly,* he agrees to my immense disappointment. His magical wheel diagram disappears and is soon replaced with an alphabet tablet. *Shall we review, Hannah?*

I groan internally, but agree. Knowing how to understand what everyone is saying *does* seem important. So the lesson begins. And continues. And continues. ...And continues.

This world, I note, does appear to have a sun. This is pretty obvious, since as the hours pass the glowing, flaming pain-ball very clearly moves across the sky above our heads. It's often hard to see it between the branches and the leaves, but it's there. For obvious reasons I'm avoiding looking at it too much, yet my gaze still wanders up to it every so often. There's something weird about it that I can't quite seem to put my claw on, but I suppose this *is* a fantasy world. I shouldn't expect the light source for a magical world tree to be anything like the one I have back home on Earth. Whatever's bugging me, I don't figure it out before the glowing ball descends below the branch, cutting it off from view. But not, apparently, cutting off most of the light.

Instead, a muted, sunset-like glow washes over everything, the world colored vaguely green as the majority of light reflecting down on us first bounces off of the leaves above. It quickly gets cooler out, which I personally find quite welcome, but despite the sun setting below what counts for our horizon it does not appear to be getting any darker from here.

*This is kind of pretty,* I comment. *What's nighttime like? Does it ever get darker than this?*

*Yes,* Teboho confirms. *The sky will darken again when the great flame dips underneath the Slaying Stone, then once again when it moves to the opposite side of the Mother Tree. The fire up above will provide some light through the night, but we're too low for it to do much.*

*We'll have to make camp soon,* Sindri comments. *We probably won't make it to Grawlaka for another couple days.*

A pit of dread settles inside me at the thought of having to wake up as a 'human' again, not knowing what horrifying changes I've managed to force onto my body. Will tonight be the day that I'm finally discovered? Did I screw myself already? I feel myself start to knead Kagiso's hair, running my legs through the long strands of white for a while before a given leg moves out of synch with her slice of space, letting the hair fall right 'through' me. I immediately get embarrassed when I catch myself doing it, but then Kagiso makes a quiet but happy trill. Permission to keep going, if not an outright request. Hesitantly, I continue, taking care not to accidentally cut her. My legs aren't *that* sharp without magic enhancing them, but they're still clawed.

*You really get along well with her,* Teboho says after a while. I realize he's been staring at us and embarrassment immediately returns.

*Is there a reason we wouldn't get along?* I counter defensively.

*Don't like smelly people,* Kagiso murmurs. *Loud people. Nosy people. Tall people. Blue people.*

*Wait, do you know anybody that's blue?* I ask.

She thinks for a moment.

*No,* she admits. *But wouldn't like them if I did. Blue is not an accurate color.*

*And green is not a creative color?* I supply, knowing that probably zero other people in this entire universe get the reference.

*Hmm. That is good to know,* Kagiso nods, taking me seriously.

*See, this is what I mean.* Teboho chuckles. *What are you two on about?*

*We are vibing about colors, obviously,* I tell him. *Colors are neat. I'm feeling kind of yellow right now, personally.*

*Mmm! Yellow is good,* Kagiso says, nodding profusely and nearly flinging me off her head. *Red is favorite though. Red is good. I like red.*

*Like blood, or...?*

*Yes,* Kagiso confirms. *I like blood.*

I pause for a moment, trying to decide how I feel about that.

*...Blood can be pretty, yeah,* I conclude. *It's not red when I'm looking at it my usual way, but I can 'see' the blood moving through your bodies. It's kind of hypnotizing the way it pumps around to the beat of your hearts.*

*Oh. Yes. I like that,* Kagiso agrees, her four hands slowly clenching into fists, then unclenching, then clenching again. *Helps you aim? Sindri. Make sensory share spell. You promised.*

*It's nowhere near the priority it used to be, since Hannah went and grew her own damn eyes without me,* Sindri points out.

*Make. The spell. I would like to see the blood, Sindri.*

*Well, when you put it like that,* he chuckles.

*Sindri. I want to watch your heart beat.*

*I think he's going to make it, Kagiso,* I assure her. *My heart is pretty interesting as well! It's much smaller than yours and less complex, lacking a lot of the chambers yours has.*

*Oooh,* Kagiso trills happily. Well, I guess I found her hyperfocus. No wonder she likes hunting things for me so much.

*How does 'making' a spell even work, anyway?* I ask. *I thought you had to discover your own spells.*

*You do,* Sindri confirms. *But this is the sort of spell I believe is part of my gifts. In the same way you're not born with knowledge of everything you can do, I'm not either. But I feel as though this is possible for me, so I'm trying to figure it out. My magic shares thoughts. Why shouldn't it share more complex thoughts, like sensory data?*

*I guess that makes sense,* I agree.

*We should get back to teaching you the language,* Teboho chimes in, and I sigh. I suppose he's right.

Time passes until it finally starts getting dark. I feel like I just spent an entire school day in a single class. It's boring, but I'm good at handling boring things so I make decent progress. A simple set of mnemonics makes memorizing the alphabet easy enough, but the hard part is putting them together and learning words. It's not something I expect to get a handle on for weeks, but I'm pleasantly surprised by my progress. Learning the language is a lot easier than I thought it would be. Maybe Sindri's mind magic is helping somehow? I *am* in constant telepathic contact with three people who think in this language. I ask him, but he says he doesn't know. He's busy setting up camp so he doesn't really think about it too hard.

I cannot, unfortunately, delay the coming of night and the need for sleep. I try to, though, by volunteering for first watch. I don't want to go to sleep, don't want to face how badly I messed up back on Earth. But no amount of time being alone with my thoughts in the night has any hope of helping with my anxiety. When the candle clock melts down, I wake Sindri and wander into Kagiso's tent to sleep. I want to rest beside her, but I *also* want to dig a hole and hide in that to rest. It's so frustrating that, on a whim, I decide to scuttle into the bedroll with her, snuggling onto her fuzzy back with the blankets pressing down on top of me. I end up waking her up, but she seems happy with the arrangement and promptly passes out again. Ah, this is what I need. Cozy, warm, safe, and soft. The advantages of being the party's mascot, I suppose.

I fall asleep not long after her, and then I wake up. It's a relatively easy transition, unlike how gaining consciousness in my human body tends to go. Usually I find the whole experience quite jarring, but I went to sleep with so much dread that waking up with it just feels kind of natural. It's just me and my sleep paralysis demon now, no fuzzy maybe-albino alien girls to keep me company. Unfortunate, but that's life, I guess. Let's get this show on the road.

Limb one... nothing. Limb two is therefore probably also nothing, and... yep, I don't feel anything move. Limb three... ooh, that's my left arm. Which probably means limb four is my left leg, so I move that next, and... uh. Um. That doesn't feel right.

Oh geez, did I grow another *limb?* I quickly cycle through muscle groups and figure out where my actual arms and legs are, and *yes,* there's something extra. Crap, crap, crap, crap! I manage to sit up, twisting my body around to look at myself, but I don't see anything. What's going on? I feel *something* moving around my lower back, but I don't see it!

I scramble to my feet, hissing with displeasure as I put weight on my mutating leg. My blinds are closed so I go ahead and rip off all my clothes in my room, checking myself over. Agh, my leg is... wrong. The whole thing feels itchy, the skin from my knee to my foot sagging and clearly dead. That stuff is gonna fall off today, and I am *not* looking forward to ripping it into pieces to flush down the toilet. I feel around my other leg, looking for the signs of exoskeletal growth, but when I press too hard on my fingers pain shoots up them and they start to bleed. No, no, no! This is too much at once!

...And this isn't even the worst of it, is it? Advancements of prior changes in my legs. Expected matching changes in my hands. I quickly grab a handful of tissues to catch the blood from my now-leaking fingers. This is fine. All this, I was prepared for. What I was *not* prepared for are limbs five and six coming to life. I can *move* them. Now that I'm naked, I can watch them bend underneath my skin, pulling and deforming the sides of my abdominals like a fat, bony leech swimming through my body. I *feel* them, anchored to my spine a short way above my pelvis. I can move them, pushing on my intestines as they stretch for the first time. They're useless things, at least for now. Still trapped inside my soft epidermis, still small and ungrown. But they're *there.* My limbs. My fifth and sixth limbs that I'd always known I was missing. *They're finally here.*

*Clack.* I snap my teeth together, letting my lips twist into a grin. Anxiety and euphoria go to war inside my head and for the first time in a fucking *year* I feel euphoria win out. I should not be excited for this. I'm a freak, I'm going to get kidnapped or killed, this is going to ruin *everything in my life.* I should not be excited for this. But as I flex my budding limbs, I can't bring myself to feel anything else.

I am tempted, *very* tempted, to call on the magic again and accelerate this further, but then there's a knock on my door.

"Hannah!" my mother calls, and immediately I'm back in panic mode. Oh no oh geez what if she comes in!? No no no no no! I leap back onto my bed and throw the covers over my body.

"What's up, mom?" I say in as normal a way as I can. My voice only cracks a little.

"I'm running a little late, so could I shower first?" she asks.

Oh. Right. That makes sense. She doesn't use the same shower that my brother and I do, her bedroom has an attached bath. But she doesn't like showering at the same time as anyone else for water pressure and temperature reasons, and frankly I agree with her on that.

"...Sure!" I answer. "I'll grab breakfast first?"

"Thank you dear!" my mother calls, and leaves me a panicked, disorganized mess. What was I *thinking?* Accelerating the changes further would just... agh, shoot, I'm bleeding on my sheets! Nooo! I forgot about my stupid bloody fingers! I peel myself out of bed again and get bandages on my newly-budding claws, putting gloves on overtop them. And now that I'm entirely naked *except* for those gloves I fish out my dirty clothes from yesterday and quickly put them on. I'll get clean clothes on *after* I shower, thank you very much.

Underneath my shirt, I flex limbs five and six, and my body shudders. No time for that, though. I head downstairs so I can grab more eggs without anyone around to look at me.

I've gotta keep pretending to be human, after all.

# 15

# ONCE-MEAT

I'm so friggin' hungry that even when I finish off the last of the egg carton I still need to microwave up some frozen sausages and eat those as well. *Geez,* they taste good now, all savory, salty, umami heaven. They're not even like, high-quality sausages, they're the kind you're *supposed* to cook in the microwave, nothing but fat and sodium and once-meat. But once-meat is, apparently, good enough for my newly carnivorous taste buds. My teeth slice through the tubes of industrially-compressed flesh like they're cotton candy. I swallow the chunks without chewing and wash it down with milk.

I quickly write in eggs on the grocery list and head back upstairs just in time to slip into the bathroom before my brother. I strip down again, being careful with my bleeding fingers, and hop into the shower the moment I hear my mom finish hers. I feel like I'm in a fugue state, but unlike my usual post-panic disassociation it's not really a *negative* one. It's more of a zen-like flow, where I keep encountering problems with my routine—my mom messed up the order of operations, I can't eat cereal anymore, touching anything with my fingertips yields blood and pain—but it's not really bothersome in the way it normally is, it just adds a new task to the list to be solved with the same efficiency as any other. It's *nice,* at least up until the moment I automatically sit down to shave my legs and remember that all the skin is falling off one of them. Literally all the skin, at least from the knee down. It's *very* itchy and I am going to have to *dispose of it somehow,* which just... eyugh!

It feels *so gross,* partly because it no longer has feeling at all. The skin is dead, so touching it feels like someone is touching a particularly slimy, squishy pair of pants that I'm wearing. It's even more disgusting than it sounds, and that's without even factoring in how gross it *looks.* Graying from a lack of blood, it sags and shifts slightly whenever I move it, just a simple tug away from falling off. The idea of just pulling on it and letting it tear is horrifying, though, like trying to pull at a hangnail rather than clip it off. If only I had something sharp to… cut it… with.

I lick my lips, my stomach bubbling at the thought. No. Absolutely not. I'm not going to *eat* my own dead skin! That's *completely revolting.* Like, sure, on the small scale I do stuff like that, like when there's dead skin on my lips. I normally just peel that off with my teeth and swallow it, which um… might be normal? I have no idea if that's normal, but either way a tiny little fleck of skin is nothing like eating the entire epidermis off my gosh dang leg! Plenty of animals do it, I guess, but *I* sure don't want to. Though, uh, I guess my alternative is tearing it off by hand, ripping it into small pieces, and flushing them down the toilet. That or ignoring it until it falls out of my pant leg in public, and while that *does* sound like the kind of thing I'd do normally this is just way too itchy for me to be able to reasonably leave it alone. Turkey dumplings and piss, is this really what I'm going with? Am I even flexible enough to reach my calf up to my mouth in the first place?

Hesitantly, I grab my leg and pull it up to my face, genuinely surprised that I *am,* in fact, that flexible. Unfortunately, now that my leg is *right here,* I find myself biting into it before I know what I'm doing. I suppress an instinct to shudder as I feel my teeth sinking painlessly into the dead flesh, tearing through skin and peeling it off my body with ease. I cut carefully, my teeth scraping safely against the outside of my yet-to-be-freed exoskeleton without penetrating any part of me that would actually hurt. One mouthful of horribly clammy former Hannah parts later, I swallow. It's… unpleasant, but not disgusting like I thought it would be. I feel like I'm eating plain, unseasoned and unsauced lasagna noodles. Mostly tasteless, but still technically food. That realization is all the push I need to finish the job, cutting and slurping and swallowing the remaining humanity still futilely clinging to my right leg. My exoskeleton is free now, and it gleams in the clear water of the shower.

As before, my organic armor is bone-white, though streaks of red wash down it as I poke it with my bleeding fingers. The joints aren't perfectly covered, though, so when I bend my knee or my toes it's possible to spot softer, pitch-black flesh underneath, providing an impressive contrast. I flex and move my leg as I swallow the last of my dead skin, enraptured by the alien movements that are somehow *mine.* My body, my leg. It's terrifying, certainly, but nowhere near as much as I expected. Honestly, the fear comes from thinking about the *implications:* the problems this will cause, the what-ifs and oh-noes. I am scared of the consequences of my leg. I'm scared of what other people will do to me if they find out. But… I'm not really scared of the leg itself, am I? This feels like it should be inherently disturbing, but somehow it's *exciting* instead. I feel stronger, I feel more *right.* There's a euphoria bubbling under the fear, and I'm hesitant to find out what happens if I embrace it.

Shivering with… *some* sort of emotion, though I'm not sure what, I stand back up and finish washing myself off. It's mildly worrying that my fingers are still bleeding, but they aren't bleeding *much* and I've recently dealt with far, far worse. I dry my hands off with toilet paper since I don't want to get blood all over my towel, then bandage up my hands before drying the rest of myself off. As before, I have multiple layers of clothing over my legs: thigh socks *and* pants, just in case. Some fashionable gloves are added to my outfit for the day, and I guess also to every outfit from now on, forever. There's no way I'm going to be lucky enough to grow retractable claws. …I should go shopping soon. I'd *like* to go shopping with Ida. She's always fun to shop with because she has the energy to keep me going, the intuition to make sure I don't dress myself like an idiot, and most importantly she doesn't waste time. Unfortunately, she still hasn't responded to my texts. Brendan hates shopping with a passion so he's out, but I really don't want to go alone. Maybe Autumn will go shopping with me?

...Aaaaand I'm already blushing just thinking about that. Dang it, Hannah! Why do you have to be so gay!? I mean, I could do it, though. I normally would stream today but I think that's potentially on hold with the whole mutation situation, so I'm *pretty much* free, and there's no reason not to at least ask if she's *also* free, so... hmm. We'll see how socially useless I am when I meet her face-to-face, I guess. It's all a moot point if I'm too busy being distracted by GIRL PRETTY to actually ask.

Well, let's go over my mental checklist one last time. I'm dressed, I have medical supplies and extra gloves in my backpack, and I can't find any more dead skin. Because checking for parts of my body that are about to fall off is part of my morning routine now. Isn't life grand? Everything seems to be in order, though, so I hoist my backpack on, luxuriate in the alien feeling of moving my budding limbs underneath my skin, and march out to the bus stop.

God, I'm such a freak. I should be a *lot* more weirded out by this, shouldn't I? I guess there's a level of validation to it all. I've seen doctors and therapists (ugh) about my dreams, and the general consensus was always that I just experience a weird form of sleep paralysis, not that I was ever actually missing limbs. And I mean, sure, I believed that too, because why wouldn't I? I still love the fact that they're all wrong, though. They're wrong! My insane fucking therapist was *wrong!*

"Hannah?"

I whip my body towards the noise and *hiss,* my hands up and my budding claws throbbing. Then I spot Brendan, who has introduced himself from a *very* respectful distance away this time. I blink twice, take a deep breath, and feel blood flushing my cheeks as I relax my body. Dang it, this is twice, now! Being snuck up on freaks me out, but at this point it's just my fault for getting so distracted. I clear my throat awkwardly and look away.

"Oh, uh, hi Brendan," I greet him casually. Nothing happened, nothing happened, don't worry about it.

268

"Hey, Hannah," Brendan answers slowly, eyeing my gloves. "Hand claws growing in?"

"Oh, ah, yep. A lot of things are growing in, actually. I, uh, tried to figure out how to control whatever spell is transforming me and I just kind of ended up… accelerating things."

"Oh yeah?" he asks, raising an eyebrow and walking up next to me. "Like what?"

"Here, here!" I grin, making grabby hands at him. Obligingly, Brendan offers his arms and I grab his wrists, putting his hands on my waist so I can wiggle my new limbs around. His eyes bulge and his cheeks flush and I immediately wish I'd had the presence of mind to take a photo of it, it's *hilarious.*

"Wiggle wiggle," I giggle to myself, poking at him from inside my own body. His face gets *even redder* and he pulls away, prompting me to laugh even harder. He's such a dork!

"What… what are those?" Brendan asks quietly.

"I don't know!" I answer excitedly. "They're limbs, I can tell that much, but they're sort of low to be arms and high to be legs, so I think they're going to be something a bit funkier than either. I guess I'll find out!"

"Uh… yeah," Brendan nods, scratching his cheek. "You seem super stoked about it, actually? Which is… surprising, but really nice to see."

"Don't get me wrong, this is freaky," I assure him. "I had to eat half the skin off my leg this morning, it's like… all exoskeleton below my right knee. I am utterly *horrified* of people finding out, but like… I dunno. You already know and you're cool with it so it's cool I get to talk to you about it, I guess? I think I'm more scared of what people are going to do to me because of the changes than I'm scared of the changes themselves. Cuz like… I don't really *mind* being a spider monster when I sleep, you know? It doesn't feel weird in a world where everyone is okay with it."

Brendan nods slowly.

"That's… honestly really good to hear," he admits. "I know this is freaky for you, but since you're changing *anyway* it's nice to know you're changing into something you like? It would really suck if you had dysphoria on top of everything else. It's kind of weird that you don't, I guess, but it's a good weird."

"It's your kind of weird, right?" I joke, elbowing him in the hip. "You sold any commissions for your art, yet?"

"Oh, um… yeah, a few, actually," he confirms awkwardly.

"Are you finally going to tell me what your account is so I can *buy* one?"

"Nnnnnope."

"I'll let you play with my leeeeeg," I tempt him.

"You'll do that anyway," he counters immediately. "Speaking of, you wanna hang out today? Or are you going to go public on your Twitch?"

"Uh… actually, I was thinking about going shopping for new clothes. Y'know, since I need some more stuff to help cover up. But if that doesn't take long I could come over afterwards?"

"That's fine," Brendan shrugs. "Who are you going with? You and Ida make up?"

"…No," I grumble. "What makes you think I'm going with anyone?"

Brendan just gives me a flat look.

"Ugh, fine. I want to ask Autumn to go with me, because she seems cool and I want to thank her for cleaning up a bunch of my blood."

"If someone tried to thank *me* by taking me shopping, I don't think I'd like them very much," Brendan says matter-of-factly.

"I know that!" I protest. "But… y'know! She's a girl, and… well, I guess it's sexist to assume that means she likes shopping—"

"It is," Brendan helpfully assures me.

"*—But* I'm hoping it's one of those situations where she'll at least enjoy it a little with company? And then like, y'know, we'll be at the mall so if it's going well maybe I could see if she wants to see a movie or something."

"What?" Brendan asks. "Sorry, you started mumbling *really* quietly there."

"Nothing! It's nothing."

"It certainly didn't *sound* like nothing," he prods, amusement tingeing his voice.

"I'll bite you, Brendan," I threaten. "Don't think I won't."

That shuts him up, at least. He even glances away like he's embarrassed. Well! Good! He should be embarrassed about trying to make fun of me like that! This is just unexpectedly effective revenge. The bus arrives shortly afterwards, and since I don't really want to talk about my mutating monster bits in a crowded public transit vehicle Brendan instead regales me with the adventures of Scrixel the tabaxi fist warlock, a catgirl who summons knuckle dusters as her pact weapon, empowers them with demonic energy, and then beats the snot out of people in the name of her blood-obsessed patron. Apparently, 5e doesn't officially have stats for fist weapons, but that sort of thing is trivially easy to homebrew and the DM let it slide. She is, obviously, evil... and she's the only evil member of the party, so Brendan gets to have a lot of fun letting Scrixel be an unhinged little gremlin held back from slaughter only by having been de facto adopted by the party's Paladin of Redemption. Brendan doesn't really like 5th edition all that much compared to 3.5, but D&D is still D&D and the real fun comes from roleplaying the characters rather than the mechanics anyway.

"Besides, tabaxi are cool," Brendan insists. "They pretty much have the best racial abilities available, barring the obligatory hashtag-variant-human. Climb speed *and* an activatable double-speed that's super easy to refresh? They're crazy good. Their stat bonuses are perfect for melee warlocks as well."

"Are you self-conscious?" I tease. "You don't have to justify being the cat species, Brendan. I, of all people, am not going to judge you for being a monster girl."

He snorts at that.

"...Thanks, I guess."

"I've always got your back, dude," I assure him. "Anybody messes with you, I'll bite 'em."

"What is with you and biting people all of a sudden?" Brendan grumbles.

Well. It's because I kinda want to bite somebody.

"I have to be careful every time I open my mouth, so I've got teeth on the brain," I say instead. "I'm sure it's not at all indicative of anything concerning."

"Well, I would have agreed with you up until the point where you said that," Brendan sighs.

I hiss at him, which only makes him chuckle instead of be afraid for some reason. I guess it's not really a proper hiss, only a rush of air out of my freakish and mostly-muffled mouth. There's no eldritch screech component to it like when I rub my legs together over on the world tree. Oh, well. We arrive at school soon enough, Brendan and I parting ways. Let's see... today's Wednesday on a B-week, so... no gym today. Awesome! I have no idea what I'm going to do about my new leg in a class where shorts are required, but I can figure that out tomorrow. Sucks to be future Hannah!

I *do* have Biology, though, which means I get to see Autumn before lunch. I guess I get to do that every day, since Autumn is also in my gym class. Huh. That'll make coordinating lunches easier. English class is boring, so I spend the whole time reading ahead in our assignment. Biology is *also* pretty boring, though I spend half the time glancing towards Autumn rather than doing homework like I should be doing. Stupid, stupid, stupid. This is why I only have two friends. Guys get creepy around me but I get creepy around girls!

...Though I guess I'm a monster now. Maybe monsters are *allowed* to be a little creepy. You know, as a treat.

I chuckle to myself and focus on homework as best I can. Monster creepy and stalker creepy are different things, so I'll have to nip that idea in the bud, I think. When class finally ends, though, I do actually work up the courage to approach Autumn. I honestly wasn't expecting that.

"Hey," I greet her eloquently.

She freezes halfway through getting out of her seat, turning to look at me.

"Hello, Hannah," Autumn answers hesitantly, her head bobbing in acknowledgement.

"Sorry, I didn't mean to startle you," I assure her, scratching my cheek awkwardly. "I just, um... wanna eat lunch together again?"

Slowly, she finishes extracting herself from her desk and gets her backpack on.

"...I'm not going to be any better of a conversationalist than I was last time," she warns me.

"And I'm not going to be any less swamped with homework," I assure her.

She stares at me for a moment, gives me a nearly imperceptible nod, and then starts walking away. I follow her, budding limbs wiggling with delight underneath my skin, but then I realize I forgot to pack a lunch again. I peek into the cafeteria as we pass it. Meatloaf, huh? Kinda gross, but maybe it'll actually taste good to my weird new senses. It already smells better than usual in there.

"Let me go grab food and then I'll join you, okay?" I say.

"Sure," Autumn shrugs.

The meatloaf, it turns out, does actually taste a lot better now... but I still wouldn't call it *great*. Soggy, mushy, and not at all satisfying. Especially annoying is how I have to scuttle off to a bathroom stall to eat it, since I don't want anyone to see my teeth. The presence of

Bathroom Smell doesn't do anything to enhance its flavor, that's for sure.

Once I finish, I return to the library and find Autumn at the same table as before, reading the same book. She hasn't put her backpack up on the table like a shield, though. I plop down across from her, pull out the work I need to do, and get working. It's quiet for a good while, but to my surprise it's Autumn that breaks the silence first.

"Why are you wearing gloves?"

I look up, blinking with surprise. Well, shoot, how do I answer that? Honestly, just giving her a chunk of the truth is probably best here, she's already witnessed things getting pretty weird for me.

"Blood," I admit. "My fingers were bleeding."

"Were?" she prompts.

I shrug.

"They might have stopped by now? I haven't checked. But they're all bandaged up and I didn't really want people bugging me about that, so... gloves."

"You, uh, bleed a lot, then?" she asks.

"I have a very weird medical condition that likes to intrude on my life at the worst possible times," I tell her flatly.

She smiles a little and it makes my toes curl, my claws digging into my soles.

"I get that," she sympathizes. "That sucks."

Huh. Was that general empathy, or is she implying that she *also* has an intrusive medical condition? She certainly seems to have experience dealing with the aftermath of blood geysers. I'm not really sure if it's appropriate to ask, but I guess she brought it up.

"Is that coming from personal experience?" I prod.

She bristles slightly.

"I don't randomly start bleeding all the time, if that's what you're asking," she deflects.

"Fair enough," I allow. I don't want to get too nosy, especially when it might prompt her to do the same.

We return to silence, books once again being at the center of our focus. Before long, the lunch bell rings and we start heading to our next classes. It's now or never, Hannah. Ask her. Just ask! She might say no, she might think you're weird, but you should still *ask!* Ask ask ask ask ask, dang it!

"Would you like to go shopping with me after school?" I blurt.

...Holy cannoli I actually did it. What!?

"What?" Autumn asks, parroting my thoughts.

"U-uh, I, um..." Dang it, Hannah, don't mess this up now! "I need new clothes. I... y'know. More gloves. New pants. Maybe another pair of shoes. Stuff I can wear to cover up. A-and the friend I usually shop with isn't talking to me, and... you seem nice?"

God. Just. *Great* job with that, Hannah, real eloquent. You look like a loon. Autumn's eyes widen imperceptibly, her lips quietly mouthing 'oh.'

"I, uh... I can't," she answers simply.

Agh! Stupid, stupid, stupid, I'm so stupid!

"Right!" I say as cheerfully as I can. "Of course, that makes sense, we don't really know each other all that well! Um... bye, then!"

"Hold on," she protests. "I... I can't today, but... maybe? I'll get back to you, alright?"

"Oh! Cool. Cool cool cool." I am a clown of unparalleled proportions, but not by profession. "I'll... talk to you later, then?"

"Yeah," Autumn agrees. "Um, talk to you later."

I turn and swiftly walk away, blush so deep it's making my cheeks feel heavy. She said 'talk to you later!' She's thinking about it! She doesn't want to ghost me! Aaaaaah! ...Geez, why am I even doing this, though? I *do* actually need more clothes, but inviting my probably-straight crush who I only met a few days ago is... stupid? I'm mutating into a horrifying monster, I should be *minimizing* contact with people. Yet I'm going to the dang mall. Uugh, what part of me thought this would be a good idea!? Thankfully my phone buzzes, knocking me out of my self-depreciating spiral.

**How'd it go?** Brendan asks.

**She can't today, but she said she'd think about it,** I text back.

**So you're free. Wanna hang out?**

**I dunno,** I hedge. **I should probably stream.**

**With a mask on, or...?**

**Yeah,** I confirm. **People will think it's weird but it should work.**

**I wanna see your leg though :(**

I chuckle.

**Can you imagine what my mom would say to you inviting me over so I can take my clothes off?**

**Well she lectures you without bothering to figure out if I'm actually going to do that or not, so... exactly the same thing she says normally?** he answers, which makes me wince. He's got me there.

**I'd like to hang out, but I think I need to take a slow day,** I admit. **I promise my leg isn't going anywhere.**

**Okay,** he allows. **I still question your strategy of 'turn your favorite form of relaxation into a job,' but whatever works for you, I guess.**

**Thanks, Brendan.**

The rest of the school day passes without anything notable happening. I feel a bit twitchier than normal, I get a few comments on my gloves, and whenever I get a moment to myself I take a while to luxuriate in feeling of my new limbs, both budding and recently transformed. My exoskeletal leg still functions basically the same as my old leg, just… sturdier. Stronger. It's the same size as my left leg but the difference in power sometimes makes me feel like I'm limping, unexpected bursts of energy adversely affecting my gait in subtle ways. It's a bit unpleasant, but also empowering. I *know* I'm stronger now. Much stronger than I used to be. I don't know why, but I really, really like that.

Once I get home I grab some food so I don't have to head downstairs for dinner later and turn on my stream, spending the rest of the day on that. People ask about my mask so I give vague non-answers and act all mysterious, since maybe that'll increase viewership or something, I dunno. I'm just here to play Pokémon until it's time to pass out, and eventually that time does indeed arrive. I actually got through a full day without a major incident. Go me.

I pass out on my bed and wake up in Kagiso's, though she's not in here with me. She must have gotten up without waking me. I feel groggy and vaguely embarrassed. Did I really get into *bed* with Kagiso last night? It doesn't really get any more suggestive than that, but… well, at the same time, it doesn't really feel like anything? Kagiso is warm and fuzzy and comfortable, but my status as a tiny, ten-legged arthropod of indeterminate sex and dimension has somewhat understandably killed my libido. And besides, Kagiso invites me to cuddle with her almost every night, so it's not like it's unprecedented. Just… weird. I *like* it, I guess I can admit that, but it's definitely weird. I grumble internally and scurry deeper into her bedroll, which feels *very* strange, like my own skin is fighting against me. Except that… I don't have skin. Huh?

I focus my spatial sense on myself and figure out the issue immediately: I'm molting. How lovely, I guess I get to eat more of my own discarded flesh today. I step into an intersecting barren zone, leaving my molt behind inside the bedroll before stepping back into normal space and scurrying back inside, dragging it out by my teeth and making sure the inside of Kagiso's sleeping space is devoid of dead Hannah. Once I'm satisfied that everything is clean, I start chowing down on my molt and *that's* the moment

Teboho decides to open up the tent flap, naturally. The light hurts my eyes and I spend a while adjusting to that as he stares at me, looking vaguely queasy. I stare back for a bit, then resume my meal. It's not like I can talk to the guy until Sindri sets up our network. Teboho silently departs, leaving me to my meal.

*Hey Hannah,* Sindri reaches out. *Teboho says you've found breakfast?*

*I have found my own discarded epidermis, yes,* I confirm. *Though I could definitely eat more, this is pretty bland.*

*Ah, so your species molts, then? I guess you're still growing.*

*I guess so!* I agree.

*I'm sure Kagiso would be happy to catch some breakfast for you. Unless you'd like to hunt your own food?*

I stop eating and think about that for a moment. Immediately, my reaction is that I *do* kind of want to do that, partly because I think I might enjoy it but largely because I think I should get *practice.* I want to be self-sufficient, for one, and for two I'm kind of worried I need more practice fighting. Killing people is horrifying and I never want to do it again, but killing animals for food? That's fine. There's nothing wrong with that. I *am* a carnivore.

*Sure,* I agree. *I guess I'll hunt something.*

*Great!* Sindri agrees. *If you can, try to catch something big enough for me, too.*

Wait. That wasn't the deal. Oh shoot, did I just get set up?

*It'll help you learn to fight, won't it?* Sindri presses.

Gah! Yes, I suppose so.

*Fine,* I grumble in response. *But I'm not carrying something big back to camp!*

*Hah! Fair. I was thinking you and Teboho could go? He can keep you safe while Kagiso and I handle camp. As long as you stay within a [distance, long] or so, the two of you should still be able to talk.*

278

*I guess I'll trust him to know how far that is?* I hedge.

*Oh, right. Yes, that's another good reason to bring him. Good luck!*

*Thanks,* I say, sending him a mental sigh. What am I getting myself into? Oh, well. I did nothing but sit on Kagiso's head all day yesterday. It'll be good to finally stretch my legs and kill something. ...Wait. Hmm. Okay, I mean, that's actually what I'm setting out to do this time, so I suppose I'll let the frighteningly murderous Freudian slip pass just this once. I'm hungry and I don't really need to make excuses about that.

Let's go hunting.

# 16

# CLEAN KILL

*So Hannah,* Teboho asks me as we trudge away from camp, *exactly how much experience do you have, in terms of hunting and fighting?*

I squirm slightly, firmly attached to his fuzzy shoulder as he walks. When we get closer to our destination I'll get off and walk by myself, but until then it's more efficient to hitch a ride.

*Uh... well, remember those cultists we fought?* I ask.

*I'll never forget it,* he assures me solemnly.

*That's it,* I say. *That's the first time I've fought anyone or anything.*

*Have you never even hunted?* he asks. *How were you feeding yourself when we first found you?*

*Well I ate tiny burrowing animals,* I tell him, since I guess I did do that once. *Nothing like what we're supposed to get today. They couldn't hurt me at all. Other than that...*

I... I'm not actually sure what I ate before that. Because my spider body has been *alive,* right? It's been alive just as long as my human body, or at least as far as I can remember. Was I eating the wood of the tree? I've swallowed that stuff before, but it never really felt all that filling. I guess my two bodies are connected somehow, though. Maybe I was sustaining both of them with the food from Earth, or maybe I *can* eat wood even though it tastes all bland and... I dunno, woody.

*I have mostly been fed by kind humans,* I decide to admit, since it's true.

There's a pause, and I feel a confused mix of worry and amusement coming from Teboho.

*...Ones that got too close, or...?* he prods.

What's he... *AGH OH I GET IT, FRICK.* I sputter with indignance and terror, my flailing wild enough that I end up falling off Teboho's shoulder.. He quickly twists around and catches me, chuckling lightly.

*I don't eat people!!!* I insist. *Other than that one time! That... I don't know what that was! It was a stressful situation!*

*So you only eat people when stressed,* he muses. *Good to know, good to know.*

I hiss at him and scuttle down his torso and leg, unwilling to dignify his japes with my proximity.

*Why is this so funny to you?* I grumble. *I ate someone! Isn't that super messed up?*

He calms down his laughter and gives me a more sympathetic look.

*Ah, that's right, you were raised by humans,* he muses. *Killing a person for the purpose of eating them would be a grave crime indeed, but to simply eat the corpse of a man who was slain in self-defense? Most people of the Mother Tree would find no fault in that. We dentron do not eat much meat at all, but many of our neighbors do and this sometimes includes the bodies of intelligent people. The nychtava in particular are known to devour their enemies en masse when they are moved to war. To consume the flesh of the fallen is a natural thing, Hannah! It is not shameful for the predator and it is not shameful for the prey.*

I hesitate, very unsure of how I feel about all that. It *feels* wrong, but it makes sense. Murder is bad, maiming someone is bad, that's all bad. But if someone is going to be dead anyway, well... a corpse is just a thing. People might get really upset about corpse desecration, but that's just part of human culture, it doesn't hurt anyone outside of sorta rubbing in the trauma of someone being dead on those still living. Most of the really bad things eating bodies *can* do are things that just happen to whoever does the eating: diseases, mainly, but also stuff like mercury buildup I think? I dunno, I'm not really an expert, I just know it isn't healthy to eat your own species.

*Isn't it likely to make you sick, though?* I ask.

*For dentron? Yes, certainly,* Teboho agrees amicably. *We can't handle much meat in our diet in the first place, however. I don't think it's healthy for humans, either, but I'm not sure.*

*It's a pretty bad idea,* Sindri confirms, startling me slightly. I... I mean, I guess we're using his spell to talk, so it makes sense that he's hearing our conversation, even though he's nowhere near us anymore. *It's disgusting in general, but it's very much unhealthy as well. Do 'prions' mean anything to you, Hannah?*

*Those are like, the weird things that kill you by making your brain proteins fold wrong or something, right?* I ask.

*Hmm, that's very close to correct,* Sindri confirms. *Interesting. Regardless, while I certainly wouldn't recommend you eat people, it might not be a problem for you depending on your personal biology. Plenty of living things, particularly predators from the Tree of Souls, have a robust set of resistances towards the types of diseases and issues one would normally associate with the dangers of cannibalism. I'm not sure if you're among their number, but if your instincts are telling you that corpses are food I'd say it's at least somewhat likely. Perhaps your Order magic assists you in that manner as well. Still, maybe just don't.*

*Or do!* Teboho encourages. *You're not human, you don't have to think like them.*

I scuttle through the grass, not really having any way to respond to that. He's right. I'm not human. If I ever was, I'm obviously not now. In the stories, this is usually a pretty big plot point. The plucky protagonist wakes up as a monster and their goal is to fight their way through trials and tribulations to be reborn as a human once more, to reclaim the humanity they've lost over the course of their journey. That's what I'm *supposed* to want, but... I don't, really. My body is weird and annoyingly tiny, sure, but... it's fine? I don't hate it and I don't understand why I should. At least this way I have all the limbs I'm supposed to.

Teboho, thankfully, picks up on my silence as the desire to end the discussion that it is. We're descending pretty far down the branch now, and I'm noticing a lot of consequences of that which remind me of descending in altitude, even though we're still way higher up on the tree than the branch we were on before. Regardless of why, the air seems to be getting thicker and more humid, and the temperature is rising a bit as well. Consequently, the foliage is growing thicker and thicker, until eventually I'm walking through grass that's even taller than I am.

...Oh my god I'm a random encounter. Some ten-year-old-jerk is going to stumble into me and throw an animal at my head any second now! ...Except not actually because being stuck in overgrown foliage doesn't stop me from having perfect knowledge of everything within fifty feet of me. I'm still less blind than I was before my eyes grew in, so it's not really a huge deal.

No, the truly weird part about this experience is the fact that I can't blink. When I lift a leg off a blade of long grass and it comes shooting back up towards my eyes, my instincts get *confused.* I want to scrunch my eyelids together and pull away, yet I also want to step forward and lash out. So I end up doing a lot of both: sometimes I jump and twitch away, bringing up a leg to protect my eye. Other times one of my legs lashes out on its own, cutting a blade of grass that moves too quickly past my vision. All of it, I soon learn, is unnecessary: whenever the moving grass gets past my defenses and pokes me in an eye anyway, it doesn't even hurt. Whatever my eyes are made out of, they're not squishy or vulnerable like my human eyes are. They don't rotate, they don't move. They're just solid orbs, and I'm fully capable of poking or pressing on them directly without discomfort. It's very strange.

About fifteen minutes later or so, the first trees pop into my spatial sensory radius. They're gnarled, twisted things, with jagged, uninviting branches and needles instead of leaves. Conifers, I suppose, though they don't look anything like the straight-trunked pine trees of home. There's something odd about them, about the way their branches split and seek outward, like the stepped leader of an incoming lightning bolt.

*Ah, a forest of devourer trees,* Teboho muses. *That's a good sign. Let's go in there.*

Uh. Devourer trees?

*That doesn't sound like a good sign at all!* I protest. *That is, in fact, the least reassuring name for a tree I've ever heard!*

Teboho chuckles.

*Ah, worry not, Hannah. They are harmless to us, only devouring other trees, you see. Look at where their branches meet.*

I do that, following the tangles of wood wherever they grow towards other trees, and sure enough I see it. When a branch tip encounters another tree's branch, or even the trunk itself, it doesn't stop growing. Instead, it *burrows,* lodging itself into the bark like a parasite. Each one of the trees is stabbing all of its neighbors, drinking their sap and creating an incestuous network of consumption and counter-consumption. Even their roots, now that I'm tracking how low they go, seem to jut straight down, digging as deep as they can go and searching not for fertile soil, but the flesh of the world tree itself.

*Devourer forests are fairly common,* Teboho explains, *and they are prime hunting grounds. Devourer tree branches are sturdy, rigid, and often anchored at both ends, allowing much larger creatures to live high in the treetops without risking the collapse of their handholds and footholds from their own weight. Many of my own people prefer to live in devourer trees as well, though these look a bit too small and young to support a dentron population.*

I send a mental acknowledgement of the information, scuttling closer to the forest and keeping a careful eye out for any animals around. I'm a bit anxious, what with us being here to try and kill likely-dangerous creatures and all, but I'm also weirdly energetic. Like, in a *good* way, that way which happens in the month before a new Pokémon game comes out and my brain wanders over to thinking about the days until release and everything I'm looking forward to and just *overloads* with joyful energy that makes my body wiggle and kick in happy ways. I guess this isn't anywhere near that exciting for me, but... yeah. 'Exciting' is the right word, isn't it? I'm excited to go hunting. What a weird thought.

I start moving forward a little faster, enjoying the rhythmic tapping of my legs against the lush dirt. It doesn't take long to reach the trees, and on a whim I decide to see if I can climb one. The movement comes naturally to me, my claws digging ever so lightly into the bark and easily giving me the grip needed to ascend the trunk just as quickly as I would run across the ground. I want to laugh, to giggle, but my body can't so I just send the feeling over the mental link, the need to share this utterly unexpected joy strong enough to overcome my usual preference for keeping things like that to myself. Teboho grins below me, and with an impressive leap he reaches the lower set of branches, grabbing onto them and pulling himself upwards with ease, following me up into the tree with natural, monkey-like movements. He called this forest 'small and young,' but all the conifers around us are still probably seventy feet tall, at least. I guess it makes sense that the people of the world tree have high standards for forests.

I find a branch that connects to another tree's trunk and start skittering along it, my legs not having any problem traversing a walkway thinner than my body for what I'm fairly sure are just naturally good coordination reasons, not fourth-dimensional reasons. Teboho seems to be enjoying himself as well, swinging around from branch to branch with acrobatic leaps and catches that alternate between all four of his arms. I reach the next trunk and scuttle straight down without any sort of vertigo, making it to the next branch and rushing across that to try and keep pace with my fuzzy, four-armed friend.

*Enjoying the forest, Hannah?* Teboho prompts, grinning nearly from ear to ear.

*Yes!* I confirm. *I can see why you like these trees, they're fun!*

*Indeed!* Teboho laughs. *You take to it like a natural! Perhaps you're not from the Slaying Stone after all!*

*Thanks, I think?* I answer him. *I'm not sure how to take that!*

*Neither am I,* Sindri grumbles.

*Haha! I mean nothing by it, friend!* Teboho assures him. *Those from your rock aren't often very good at climbing, is all. Now be sure to stay vigilant, Hannah! We're getting deep enough in to start seeing some good prey.*

I don't need him to tell me that. There are weird fantasy animals all over the place, and I've been eyeing them with interest. I've already seen a dozen different types of birds, uncountable amounts of bugs, a weird-smelling sack-plant that I'm fairly sure is eating those bugs, and a collection of fuzzy snakes that remind me of those adorable little worm toys, which I have decided to name 'friend noodles.' Mmm. Yummy. I wanna eat a friend noodle. Chomp and slurp!

While appreciating the many noodles of the forest, however, my focus falls on a creature that just entered the edge of my range, lounging lazily on some lower branches. It looks like a giant starfish the size of a human being, with five radial limbs the color and texture of bark. Wrapped sinuously around the trunk of the tree, it appears more like the kind of weird growth common to randomly occur in tree trunks than any kind of animal, at least to my eyes. My spatial sense knows better: judging by the many sharp teeth I can see inside of its closed mouths, this thing is almost certainly an ambush predator.

And yes, I really do mean 'mouths.' Plural. Rather than a singular mouth in the center of its body like I have—or for that matter, like starfish have—this creature has *five*, a massive, gaping maw on the end of each limb. This isn't a giant starfish, not really. This is a star*hydra.*

*I think I see something I'd like to hunt,* I tell Teboho.

*Oh?* he answers, immediately stopping at the next branch. *What is it?*

I stop as well, pointing at the creature... and then realize there's currently a tree between me and it so I scuttle a little closer and then point again.

*That thing,* I tell him. *With the five heads.*

*Five... hmm. I don't... oh! I think I see it! A [dangerous, monster, magical, threat], probably!*

*Yeah, I didn't understand that, so I'm going to call it a starhydra.*

*A what?*

I feel the need to sigh, but since I can't, the energy ends up being used to quickly rotate my body in a circle. Sindri's mental communication spell can be a bit silly sometimes.

*The name isn't important,* I tell him. *Is hunting it a good idea? I picked up the fact that you thought it was dangerous.*

*They're dangerous because of their potential for magical potency,* Teboho explains. *It might have a particularly powerful spell or two, and without Sindri here there's no way for us to get a hint as to what kind.*

*Teach me that Aura Sight spell already, Sindri!* I whine at him.

*Okay, okay, we can work on that today,* he answers. *After you get us breakfast, of course.*

Bah! Why's he so insistent on getting me to kill some food for him, anyway? ...Well, I guess now that I think about it, I should do this regardless of his reasons. I've more or less been freeloading off of these people, eating their food and riding their heads and getting them nearly killed and not really doing anything for them in return. Like sure, they owed me to some extent for the horror of how we first met, but that was definitely paid back and then some after the whole cultist problem. Plus, they're my *friends!* I should be helping them out, and this is something I can do to help. It wouldn't be fair for me to *not* do this. And since I'm certainly no vegetarian, I don't have any moral problems with killing animals to eat them.

I'm just slightly worried about how excited I am about it. Killing to eat is fine. Killing for fun is... a bit worrisome. But I guess it makes sense for a predator to get excited about the thing it has to do in order to eat? Like, biologically speaking. Though I guess cats seem pretty excited to hunt things and so they end up killing a lot of stuff they don't eat, like the cute little jerks they are. I don't know. I suppose I could say that I just won't do that, but I'm not exactly confident in my capacity for self-control. Still! Sindri wants food, I should get him some food. If there are problems, I'll likely understand them better after I've given this a shot.

I drum my legs on the branch I'm perching on, anticipatory energy coursing through my body. I need a plan of action. The starhydra and I are both ambush predators, and while it's a much *bigger* ambush predator, I'm (hopefully) smarter, and most importantly I'm the one actually doing the ambush in this situation. My Spacial Rend spell is crazy powerful, and while the starhydra is very big it's also pretty flat. I think I can stick my claws deep enough into its body to hit something vital. Assuming, of course, I can figure out where its vital areas *are.*

The inside of the starhydra's body is *weird.* It doesn't really have five heads so much as it has five mouths and *zero* heads. It certainly doesn't have five brains; my best guess as to its nervous system is decentralized throughout its entire body, with a relatively small node in the center but a pretty substantial chunk of neural matter winding down each neck-arm. In essence, I'm not confident that stabbing the central bit of brain matter will be lethal to this weird little goober. Like, it's certainly not going to *enjoy* the experience, but I've heard that an octopus tentacle has a similar sort of brain structure and those things can keep trying to grab stuff after they've been cut off. This guy has octopus tentacles if tentacles had mouths as big as my entire body, so... let's just not take that risk.

Unlike octopi (which I know is technically less correct than 'octopuses,' but I've always liked it more), the starhydra only seems to have one heart, so that's probably my best bet at killing it in one shot. I'll have to sneak up on it from above, pop out of the fourth dimension, stab it through the center of its body and retreat until it bleeds out. Easy!

*I think I can take it,* I tell Teboho. *Or at the very least, I want to try. If things go badly, can we get away? It doesn't look very fast.*

*It's faster than you might think,* Teboho muses. *But it's still slower than I am. We're also close to the edge of the forest and I doubt it will follow us past the treeline.*

*Hunt safe, little Hannah,* Kagiso sends, feelings of worry spilling over the mental link.

*I'll do my best,* I promise her.

*Go for your killing stroke, Hannah, then retreat towards me,* Teboho instructs. *Don't wait to see if it dies first, just immediately start running. If it is dead, great. If it isn't, you'll be glad you didn't hesitate.*

*I understand,* I tell him, and start scuttling along the branch network to the space above my target. The slow rise and fall of its body suggests that it's napping, but it's hard to say for sure. I search for barren zones when I get close, and... wait, what? There aren't *any?* There are normally a ton! Why aren't there... hmm. No, I'm probably looking at things wrong.

I pause, focusing my perception on fourth-dimensional space. It's a difficult thing to consciously wrap my head around, even if I have quite a bit of intuition guiding me. It's not like adding an axis merely increases the volume of stuff; adding an axis makes the *concept* of volume insufficient for completely describing space. 4D space *has* volume, sure, in the same way that 3D space has area. But it also has *hypervolume*, and it's just... gah. I'm glad there's no light in the barren zones, because I'm an actual fourth-dimensional being and even I have no clue what the heck that would look like. Projections only go so far.

My point is, it takes more than a metaphorical flick of focus to properly survey the nearby fourth-dimensional space. There's a *lot* of it, because adding one dimension makes every choice of movement many times more complicated. I wait, perfectly still, as I figure out what's going on with my perception. Why could I move into 4D space whenever I wanted while I was inside the trunk, but I can only move into barren zones now? That doesn't feel right. I *am* 4D. I should be able to move along the w-axis any time I like. I should just be a small step in... *woah!*

I stumble slightly, nearly falling out of the tree as I make an experimental movement outside of normal space. I was right! I *can* do it whenever I want! So why they heck can't I see anything in that direction!? It's like there's nothing there, which... uh. Which... makes perfect sense, actually. Gosh, I'm an idiot.

The wood of the world tree is fourth-dimensional, like I am. I can go into w=1 space in the trunk any time I want because there's *wood* in every direction, there's something to sink my claws into. But out here on a branch, the wood of the world tree is a good forty-plus feet below me most of the time! In normal space, there's a huge layer of dirt and rocks on top of the branch itself, on which all the plants grow and all the structures are built and whatnot.

I *can* enter w=1 space outside the barren zones... but only if I want to fall four stories and splat painfully on the ground below. When I see 'barren zones,' that's just my brain filtering areas where the wood in 4D space has bulged upwards and actually given me something to stand on. And now that I'm up in the branch of a tree *on* the branch of *the* tree, I'm so far above my higher-dimensional footholds that no knurls or branchlets of wood reach me. I'm surrounded by a sheer drop on all sides.

This makes my ambush significantly riskier.

*Hannah?* Teboho asks. *Everything okay?*

*Yes,* I tell him. *Sorry. Planning my approach. My spatial movement is very limited up here.*

*Oh? How so?*

*Basically, my movement is better the closer I am to the Mother Tree,* I summarize. *Out on a branch there's a lot of dirt between us and it, and up on a tree we're even further away. So I'm much more restricted in the places where I can step out of view.*

*Hmm,* Teboho rumbles, seeming vaguely pleased about my magic's limitation. I guess when his religion reveres the world tree as a creator goddess, that makes a lot of sense. *You still think you can do it?*

*I'm certainly still willing to try,* I confirm.

*Then I'm ready when you are.*

I send my affirmation and slowly creep across the branch, my spatial sense guiding my claws to soft bark that won't crack or make a sound. I can *see,* in that ephemeral way that isn't sight at all, how the internal structure of the bark is laid out, where it's dry and thin, where it's wet and flush with life. Carefully, ever so carefully, I make my way over to the same tree as the starhydra, crawling silently onto the trunk. I barely feel the slightest hint of vertigo as I creep down the sheer vertical surface, stepping around a slowly-breathing mouth and right next to the creature's core. The heart is in pretty deep, but I'm sure I can reach it with magic. I lift a leg and channel my energy into it, the essence of *extra space* pushing aside the air around my claw. Hmm. It's hugging my leg a bit too closely, I need it to be a bit longer. More powerful, but not so much that I accidentally get the goddess to say Spa—

The world seems to stop. A personified pressure crushes me with the weight of its attention, her casual giggle like drumbeats hammering into my mind. The air is pulled from the vents on my side that I have instead of lungs, thin pages of gill-like filters which whisk oxygen passively from the air. She steals it from me, inhaling it with a horrible, razor-sharp smirk on her invisible face.

"**Spacial Rend**," the goddess commands the world, and the world obeys. Power blooms from my claw, adding an extra six inches to the length of its blade—just about doubling it. But also, of course, waking up basically everything in the forest.

Crap in a sack of beets. I stab as quickly as I can, my extra range cutting a deep, bloody gouge into my victim... who is unfortunately already awake and moving.

"Hana!" Teboho cries out fearfully, but I hardly need the warning to know I need to jump. Two gaping, drooling mouths of razor-sharp teeth converge on my location from mere moments ago, and though I swipe my bloody claw at them as I retreat, I already know I've messed it all up. I missed the heart, and while it certainly has a chance of bleeding out from the deep gash I gave it, it isn't going to be quick.

I let myself drop, gravity accelerating me downwards just a few feet before my legs latch onto a branch and I start to skitter away as fast as my tiny little claws can carry me. I've gotta get to Teboho so he can protect us! Yet behind me, the massive monster *also* drops from the tree, reaching up with one of its limbs to *bite* the branch above us and start swinging mouth-over-mouth like a horrifically toothy monkey. It is angry and it is coming for me and I *so* wish I could scream right now.

*Hannah!* Teboho mentally cries out. *Why did you incant? You were doing so well!*

*It was an accident!* I snap back. *I wasn't trying to speak the spell, I don't even have a voicebox!*

*Wait, did you say Hannah spoke an incantation?* Sindri asks. *How? Isn't she still learning the basics of her magic?*

The branch I'm scuttling across jerks violently, nearly flinging me out of the tree as the starhydra chomps down on the wood just behind me, yanking it downwards. It *roars* at me from three different mouths, furious and aggressive beyond what I expected from an injured animal. Spittle flies, teeth dig deep into wood I'd been running across moments before, and my death rushes ever closer all the while.

*Can everybody just shut up and focus on the monster that's trying to kill me!?* I shriek over the mental link.

*Help?* Kagiso asks.

*Backup would be good just in case,* Teboho confirms, *but I think I've got it. You're almost to me, Hannah, just a little more!*

Just a little more. He's right. He's right in front of me on the branch, one arm grabbing the trunk, one arm reaching out to me, and the other two gripping a long stone spear. He stabs it right at me, and I'm immediately thankful because I can *also* see the starhydra chomping upwards at me from below. The spear barely passes by my back legs, and Teboho manages to lodge it into the roof of one of the starhydra's mouths, saving me from an untimely demise. I reach his legs and scamper up the side of one, and Teboho quickly drops his spear, takes a deep breath, and—

"**Stone Shield**!" the goddess says with Teboho's voice.

Darkness flares around us as light is cut off, the wood cracking dangerously beneath us as it's suddenly an anchor to a hollow orb of rock, encasing us safely inside. A horrible slamming sound rings out as the starhydra bashes against the exterior, but the rock easily holds. Teboho has encased us in a cocoon that the beast can't penetrate.

*There. See? I got it,* Teboho sighs. *Now we just wait here for it to bleed out or leave. It's just an angry animal, it'll rush off to lick its wounds when it figures out it can't reach us.*

*Thanks,* I shiver, crawling up to his shoulder. *Sorry for screwing up like that.*

*Ah, well, we all learn to speak to the goddess in our own ways,* Teboho reassures me. *You didn't do badly for a first hunt.*

*That's kind of you to say,* I send back, not really believing him.

*It's the honest truth!* Teboho insists. *Why, on my first hunt, I—*

He stops sending words, wincing as a horrible sizzling sound rings out from above us. I focus on the area, and to my horror I see the stone start to melt away, something invisible to my spatial sense devouring the rock at terrifying speeds. A gas, maybe? The starhydra starts wrapping its body around the stone shell like we're a clam that needs prying open, its five maws all leaking the horrid *something* that's eating away at the rock.

*Teboho!* I yelp. *Why didn't you tell me these things have acid breath!?*

*They normally don't!* he protests. *That must be its magic! Death, maybe? Or Matter? It could be Chaos for all we know!*

*Both of you calm down,* Sindri says firmly. *Kagiso is en route.*

*We're out of time!* I insist. *It's about to break into the shield!*

I scamper down Teboho's back as at that very moment, a hole is burned through our protections. Light streams into our once-protective ball, and with my eyes I can see my guess is correct: a faint green vapor pours from the starhydra's maws, eating through stone and gradually sinking down towards us. Teboho drops his protection and leaps away, but ends up jumping right through a cloud of the stuff on our way out. I wish I could scream again, but Teboho manages one that's agonizing enough for both of us.

In barely a second, Teboho's upper body is scoured of fur, and the skin starts to bubble away immediately afterwards. I don't fare well either, my exoskeleton no more resistant to the acid than Teboho's rock was. I instinctively stick all but three of my legs out of normal space, but the three I need to hang onto Teboho with feel like they're being boiled into nothing. The moment passes and we make it into open air, Teboho out-swinging the starhydra even with his badly damaged and bleeding arms, but despite no longer being in the cloud of death his wounds—and mine—keep getting worse. It's not a gas anymore, not after making contact with our bodies. It *clings* to us, eats at us, and just keeps digging deeper into our flesh. Teboho tries to grab a branch and his arm just *gives out,* nearly causing us to plummet to the forest floor before he thankfully catches himself with one of his three other hands. But we won't last

295

at this rate. We're dying. If we can't get this stuff off of us, we might already be dead.

An arrow whisks past us, clattering into the trunk of a tree behind us, yet somehow *bouncing off* instead of imbedding itself. It hits a branch, then another branch, picking up speed with each sudden change in direction. The entire length of the arrow somehow rotates instantly whenever it hits something, flying straight and true even though there's no way physics could have given it its new vector. In the blink of an eye, it finds its ultimate target, stabbing deep into the starhydra's flank. It's then followed by a second, a third, a fourth, a fifth, and a sixth all in frighteningly rapid succession, pincushioning the poor creature from every direction and finally forcing it to plummet to the forest floor, not quite dead but definitely dying. The chase is over.

...But the burning remains. The acid isn't *going anywhere.* Teboho quickly drops in altitude, using a few branches to safely land us on the ground where he promptly collapses in agony. I'm in much better shape, as while I can see and feel the acid eating away at my flesh, I'm now on the ground. I leap into a nearby barren zone, leaving the acid behind to plop on the ground and start dissolving the grass. Then I emerge on the other side of Teboho, injured but safe. Teboho himself, however, has no such cheat. He groans in agony as I try to figure out what the heck I can do. Water, probably? Water can wash off most things, there's even an emergency shower in our chemistry classroom that I've never seen anyone use. Kagiso rushes towards us, firing another few arrows into the unmoving body of the starhydra for good measure, but nearly makes a grave mistake as she skids to a stop next to us.

*Don't touch him!* I warn. *It'll stick to you, too!*

*Dying,* Kagiso sends, her mental voice as flat as ever. *Needs help.*

*Do you have water? We might be able to wash this off.*

She nods, pulling out a waterskin and starting to pour it over the worst of the burns. ...It doesn't seem to help. Why isn't it helping!? Gosh dang magic! I start to panic as more and more of Teboho's blood starts leaking up from his rapidly-dissolving skin, mixing with the acid and being no more effective at removing it than the water was. What can I do? What can I *do?*

Kagiso reaches over, a firm hand gripping the top of my carapace and squeezing hard enough to hurt. I freeze, confused and terrified by the gesture.

*Save him,* she commands me. *Order magic. Heal.*

Oh. Oh, she's right. I *am* an Order mage. But... I don't know any Order spells!

*Hannah has never healed anyone before!* Sindri reminds us. *Do not use unknown magic on an injured person! I'm on my way, just keep trying to dilute the acid!*

*Hannah strong,* Kagiso grunts back. *Hannah heal.*

*She might not be able to, Kagiso!* Sindri insists.

Her grip just grows tighter.

*Hannah heal.*

Is... is that a threat? No. It's stress. She's terrified of losing her brother. I force my terrified brain to *think,* to focus on magic. To try and get back into that calm realm of self-reflection that I used to accidentally accelerate my transformation. But rather than look for my Transmutation magic, I need to look for my Order magic. I have to heal him. I have to heal him. I have to *heal!*

...Nothing. I feel nothing. No resonance, no instinct, just... nothing. If I wasn't panicking before, I certainly am now. I can't have *nothing.* I'm supposed to be a super-powerful Order mage! That's the whole reason I'm hanging out with everyone here in the first place! Why can't I do this? I *should* be able to do this! Order magic heals!

No. No, no, no. Wait. Order magic *is order.* It is the application of systems. Order is not the bringer of life, life is merely one of its many facets. But... but what if that means I can't heal him? No, stop, *focus.* Life is one of its many facets. I have to find *my* facet. What makes me Order-aligned? Where is *my* place in its domain? I think

297

back to how it felt to use my Transmutation spell, how I saw the ephemeral thread between my sleeping, partially-human body back on Earth and my hyperspider body here on the world tree. I remember how I took that connection and *tugged*, drawing the two closer. That's not what I want. I focus on that thread, focus on the incredible *power* flowing through it, the impossible magical might connecting two completely different universes together, and I draw it into myself. I feel it flow into me. I'm ready. I'm ready to... uh. Hmm.

*I need a bucket,* I realize, sending the message to my team. *No, wait. I need like... a beaker. A glass cup, basically. Teboho, can you make glass?*

*I'm currently dying,* he reminds me with startling calm.

*Yes, and before you do that I* really *need you to make glass.*

*Is this truly important right now!?* Sindri demands.

*I don't know!* I answer honestly, the magic roaring inside me, *demanding* an outlet. I can't hold it for much longer. *Teboho, can you do it or not!?*

He groans in agony, but manifests a crude glass container on the ground next to him. Perfect, now... agh, something's still not right!

*Dump out the rest of your waterskin!* I tell Kagiso, and she does it without hesitation. *Now* I'm ready! I let the magic flow, the power rushing out of me... and nearly all of it flowing right back into that thread between my bodies. Hey, what the heck!? But the rest of it *does* enter this world, it does what I command, washing over Teboho, passing over his body, *into* his body, and... not healing him in the slightest.

But the acid is gone. The *blood* is gone. My heart soars for a moment, but Teboho quickly continues bleeding a moment later. No, no no no! What did I do wrong? I followed my instincts! Hmm, wait. He's not covered in acid anymore! That's good, that's *really* good! In fact, for a brief period of time, Teboho's body was completely, perfectly clean.

Oh my gosh it's a cleaning spell. My mighty magical aura has finally shown the full extent of the potential I was nearly mind controlled into slavery for, and it's a gosh dang *cleaning spell.*

I... have no idea how to feel about this.

"Fala Hana!" Kagiso shrieks happily, releasing my body and quickly retrieving bandages from her pack to start binding up Teboho's wounds. I glance over at the crude beaker that Teboho made, and sure enough it's full of horrible, murky green acid. I cleaned it up. That's what my magic does. To my surprise, though, the acid bubbles furiously against the glass, and somehow it actually starts burning *that too.* What the heck? It's *supposed* to go there and stay there, because glass is the proper receptacle for acid. It needs to be in its proper place! That's very annoying in the nagging OCD way I usually just ignore, so I do my best to ignore it now. I guess the acid isn't going to get the ground *dirty*, really. ...Oh, and what matters is that Teboho is safe. Obviously.

*First it's electrocution, now it's a magical dissolving spell,* Teboho groans, letting Kagiso poke and prod at his wounds with only the occasional whining noise. *You're saving me from a lot lately, Hannah.*

*Not before you end up saving me from something that's my fault in the first place,* I answer back. *You only keep getting hurt because you keep helping me! Please, please don't die.*

*Will be dizzy,* Kagiso grunts. *Not bleed out, but maybe bad infection. Need healer.*

I notice Sindri running towards us, the man finally entering my sensory radius.

*We'll march as fast as we can for the nearest town,* he promises. *Is the [animal, dangerous] dead?*

Another jolt of panic re-fires the parts of my brain that had recently stopped producing adrenaline, and I quickly focus on the last place I remember the starhydra lying. ...And it's still there, dead as a doornail. No heartbeat, no breathing. Kagiso got it good.

*It is, it's over there,* I tell him, pointing briefly before realizing there are way too many things between the two of us for him to be able to see me. Agh, I'm so dumb. I drum my legs to try to let off some stress, but *that* just reminds me of all the pain in my body which happens to be rapidly getting worse as the stress hormones die down. Yeah, okay. That hurts. That hurts a lot. Frickadoodle fries, that hurts *so* much wow wow wow wow. I lie down in the grass and mostly give in to my body's sudden urge to completely shut down, but annoyingly the pain prevents me from passing out. No going to another universe to escape the consequences of my actions, unfortunately.

Sindri finally reaches us, rushing past us a bit to go check on the starhydra corpse that he apparently didn't need my help to find anyway. He balks the moment he sees it, returning to us with a furious look on his face.

*Teboho!* he demands. *Did you seriously let her fight that!? It's fully grown, what did you* think *was going to happen?*

*She wanted to hunt it,* Teboho says, chuckling lightly for a breath before wincing in pain. *Who was I to tell her no?*

*Have you absolutely no sense of self-preservation?* Sindri demands.

His smile drops at that, and his lack of answer is an answer in and of itself. Oh, gosh. I wish I could comfort him somehow. He's so positive most of the time, it's easy to forget how much he's lost recently. He and Kagiso both grieve... strangely.

*Well,* Sindri sighs, his anger quickly deflating at Teboho's response, *I'm very glad that everyone is safe. We're not far from our destination, so even if Teboho falls ill we should be able to get him treatment before it's too late. Hannah, I certainly hope you've learned your lesson about aggravating monsters outside your weight class.*

*Yeah,* I agree. *Sorry. That was stupid of me.*

*It's okay,* he sighs. *Learning is what matters. Kagiso, can you carry your brother once his wounds are tended to?*

300

She nods, and that seems to be the end of the conversation. Sindri returns to camp to finish packing it up, carrying his, Teboho's, *and* Kagiso's gear as Kagiso carries her brother in a piggyback... and once again insists I rest on her head. I snuggle up onto her scalp, clinging to her body with four of my uninjured limbs and resting the three heavily burned ones in the cool darkness of higher-dimensional space. The trudging walk begins, my body alternating between intense pain and intense *itchiness.* Gah, I just molted, but I'm going to have to molt again to heal all of this, aren't I? Maybe even more than once. That's certainly one advantage of having skin.

*I suppose I promised to teach you Aura Sight, didn't I, Hannah?* Sindri muses.

*Uh, yeah, I guess you did,* I confirm. *I'm guessing there's more to it than just saying the incantation?*

*Always,* Sindri confirms. *Be careful when you say the names of spells, Hannah. You must be certain you fully understand the spell you're trying to cast, or at least fully enough to satisfy whatever arbitrary system judges that understanding. I highly, highly recommend never speaking the true name of a spell—or trying to name one of your own spells—until after you've cast it normally at least a hundred times. If your name isn't approved, there are painful consequences.*

*What happens, exactly?* I ask.

*It depends on what you were trying to cast,* Sindri answers. *Generally, it spawns a magical effect of the same category of what you were trying to cast, except it's always highly dangerous and directed exclusively at you.*

*The Mother Tree's displeasure is fickle and fearsome,* Teboho agrees. *But I would not worry so much. When I heard her speak your words, Hannah, I got the impression that she liked you quite a bit. She will be lenient with you where others might suffer.*

*Regardless of whether the essence of magic truly has opinions,* Sindri grumbles, *prudence is always wise. So I'm going to start by explaining the nature of the soul as we understand it, so that you can understand the nature of aura.*

He pulls a waterskin from his belt, idly uncorking it and bringing it to his mouth.

*So far as we can tell,* he continues, since drinking something doesn't prevent telepathic communication, *the soul doesn't actually con—*

He sputters, coughing, hacking and looking down in horror as he chokes up a hideous mix of blood, viscera, and dirt, all of it dripping from his mouth *and* the waterskin in his hand as he spits furiously, desperately trying to clean out his mouth. Ah. Uh. I guess when I cleaned up the acid and put it in the beaker, I put *everything else* in the waterskin.

*S-sorry,* I whimper over the link. *That's my bad.*

*Wh... is this blood?* Sindri yelps back. *Is this* Teboho's *blood?*

*Don't worry, Sindri!* Teboho grins. *We've already discussed my views on cannibalism! Go ahead and take another swig!*

The *look* we get from Sindri makes me suspect I won't be getting a Pneuma lesson today after all. Fooey. Though on the bright side, I guess I *do* have a new opportunity to test my cleaning spell.

# 17

# GOOD MOOD

I wake up, and it hardly feels like I've slept at all. Because, y'know, I sort of haven't.

A quick limb check gets me out of bed sooner than usual. I know to expect six in my Earth body now, though I'm hoping to get up to ten. And isn't *that* a weird thing to think? 'I sure hope I grow more horrific bug limbs!' In my defense, I've been waking up feeling like I don't have enough for my entire life, so the prospect of finally fixing that is undeniably exciting. Not exciting enough to make me not feel exhausted, though.

Sleep is important, and it serves multiple functions. Physical upkeep is an important one: the brain needs to reformat, clear out junk data, form more permanent connections, and do general maintenance tasks on itself and the body. Without sleep we eventually lose the physical ability to function. And luckily for me, I'm pretty sure my bodies are still doing all those things. When one brain is awake, the other rests. Easy enough.

My *mind*, however, is always awake. My continuity of consciousness gets a bit disoriented when I flip-flop between universes, but it never gets a *break*. I really, really hope that's not going to start driving me crazy. I could definitely use a bit more rest in my life.

No time for that now, though. I sit up in bed, stretching my arms above my head and my budding extra limbs underneath my skin before finally flipping the covers back to examine my sheets. Sure enough, a lot of bloodstains are visible among the tears and claw marks. Old stains by the foot of the bed contrast much newer stains around hand-level, which I confirm as probably from the claws on my fingers once I unwrap their bloody bandages. They're fully grown now, the bony, half-inch long protrusions sharp and deadly. Unlike the curved talons of my feet, my hand-claws are relatively straight, the ends of my fingers naturally tapering down into an exoskeletal point after the bone emerges from the last knuckle. I hope I'm running out of transformations that involve me losing so much gosh dang blood all the time. It's a wonder I'm not critically anemic after this past week. Plus, it always makes a mess.

...Though perhaps I don't have to care about that anymore. I pick up the small waste bin just inside my door, put it next to my bed, and then *focus*. The magic I'd been practicing all day as a hyperspider comes to me easily, and the dried blood all over my bed and hands swiftly removes itself, gathering as a fine dust on top of the other bits of trash where it belongs.

*Gosh* that feels so satisfying to do, I can't help but grin a little. It's official: cleaning spell is best spell. I can do the same with the dried sweat in the sheets, with the lint, with every impurity and improperly present substance. I can't repair the many tears in the fabric, though I suspect there are probably Order spells which could. I don't seem to be able to use them, though. My magic is exclusively about cleaning, or more accurately it's about *sorting.* I spent pretty much all day after the fight with the starhydra getting a handle on it, and I think I have a pretty good idea how it works.

On paper, it seems like it's a really weak spell. It does nothing other than grab stuff and move it somewhere else, but its weight limit is super low and even if it *does* grab something it won't work unless that something is *misplaced.* It's not telekinesis: I can't grab and move anything manually, I can't choose the path the substance takes when it's being moved, I can't do any of that. I just target a substance, and then I target a place for that substance to go and that place has to result in... a superior state of organization, basically?

It's a little wibbly, and it's unclear how the 'superior state of organization' is determined. My best guesses are either that I'm subconsciously determining that through some method I haven't figured out how to trick, or the goddess just judges it for me. I hope it's the former for many, many reasons, though Teboho insists it's the latter. Either way, I can't do crazy stuff like 'cleaning' the entire mucus lining out of someone's eyeballs (though I *can* remove any excess discharge), and though I intend to check I'm probably not able to 'sort' the engine of a vehicle into its component parts. Mucus belongs in the eye, a car engine belongs in a car, and I can't convince myself (or the goddess) that there is a superior location or configuration for either. So really, the spell just seems best for cleaning.

I am completely, one hundred percent okay with this.

I *like* cleaning. One of my favorite things to do at work is to clean. I don't have the time or energy to clean much around the house anymore, but that used to be something I would do to relax. I'm way more comfortable in clean places than dirty ones, and now I can finally just *turn any place into a clean place.* With my gosh dang mind! It's the *best!*

I grin wider, and on a whim I open my mouth and shut my jaws with a resounding *clack.* It feels almost as satisfying as wiggling my new limbs, even as trapped under my skin as they still are. I guess I should check up on the rest of myself, now that I think about it. My claws finished growing in, so I'm probably due for some new horrific transformation that I'll need to scramble to conceal with increasingly-improbable excuses. See? I have pattern recognition. I know how this goes.

I strip down and start investigating myself, prodding my body in various places to look for any new changes. Surprisingly, there aren't really any. A bit more skin comes off of my right leg, so I pop that into my mouth and slurp it down, but other than that I seem more or less the same. Maybe I've hit a temporary equilibrium where my body is busy trying to finish growing its many changes-in-progress that I won't have anything new added today? That'd be a nice change of pace. Maybe I'll actually get some relaxation in.

Someone knocks on the door to my bedroom and it takes everything I have not to scream.

"Hannah?" my mother calls.

"Don't come in!" I shriek hurriedly, quickly jumping under the covers in case my words aren't heeded. I'm sure they will be, my mother doesn't ignore closed doors for no reason, but that doesn't stop me from immediately thinking of a dozen terrifying scenarios in which she walks in on me anyway. My heart is pounding out of my chest so hard I probably have more adrenaline in my body than I did after almost getting eaten by a monster.

"Calm down, honey," she sighs. "I'm just letting you know that your father tested positive for COVID."

Well *that* certainly doesn't help my anxiety at all.

"Is he okay?" I ask hurriedly.

"Oh, yes, he'll be fine," my mother dismisses. "His lungs are strong, I doubt it'll affect him worse than a cold. It's what he gets for sticking his nose so close to other people's open mouths all day."

That's... true. I can't help but be worried about him, of course. COVID is scary, but my dad's not that old and overall he's very healthy. I want to worry about him more, but in the back of my brain all I can really think about is how this gives me a *great* excuse to wear a mask around the house to hide my teeth.

"...Well, he *is* a dentist," I point out. "He doesn't have much choice in the matter."

"Details. Anyway, I'm just letting you know he's going to be home for the next couple weeks, and that I'm going in late today as well to cook everyone breakfast. Join us, would you? We've barely seen your face lately."

Aw, crapbaskets. There goes the only upside to the situation. Hiding my teeth is going to be a chore and a half when I'm *eating.* I don't want to eat with them. I don't want to be around them at all. What are they going to think of me when they find out? My thoughts on the manner feel pretty much identical to how I feel about coming out as gay, I suppose. Dad won't understand. I don't think he'll do anything bad but he'll still think I'm a freak in his mind. And mom will try to *control* it all, somehow. She's like me in that way, always needing things to be going according to plan, according to schedule. But only *her* schedule. Never anyone else's. She has to be in charge of everything she's involved in.

"Sorry mom, I've just been really busy lately," I mutter loudly enough to be heard through the door.

"I know," she answers fondly. "You've always been my busy little worker bee. But you're not too busy to eat a good breakfast before school, and you're going to make sure of that. Understand?"

"Yes ma'am," I answer, feeling a metaphorical coffin close around me. I can't get out of this now.

"Good," she confirms, and then heads down the hall to give my brother the same ultimatum.

I peel myself out of bed for the second time, dread pooling in my belly. How am I going to get out of this? I mean, I guess I'm *not* going to get out of this. Skipping will put me in more trouble and make mom more likely to pay more attention to me, which will of course lead to more problems. Instead, my best bet is to try to learn how to eat with a mask on, and... honestly, that's a skill I'll probably need to cultivate anyway. The trial run is just going to be a little more high-stakes than I'd like, I guess.

I wait for my mom to head back downstairs and start cooking before getting out of my room and slipping into the shower. I'm tempted—very tempted—to just shower through the entire meal, but I know that won't work. It'll just result in my brother pounding on the door until I let him in. So I speed through my shower instead, not really having time to savor it as I think about my strategy for not letting my family see my teeth. Honestly, I'm lucky I haven't cut my own tongue off with these things, they're crazy sharp and way bigger than my old teeth. I wonder what my dad would think of them. He'd probably have a ninth-level freakout, honestly. He was always pretty invested in the quality of my old teeth. ...Which I still have in a baggie in my backpack. I, uh, am not sure what to do with them. This whole teeth situation is so freaky.

At least they're fun. *Clack.*

There's no time to enjoy myself, though. I take a deep breath, drum my claws on the floor, then stick my little foam packing cubes on them to prevent them from cutting anything. I squeeze my transformed calf, still impressed with how *solid* it is without any apparent loss of touch, but then I get my thigh socks on and the mutations are covered up. Then I get my pants on, my bra on, my long-sleeved shirt on (just in case) and my gloves. Hopefully, my natural heat resistance will allow me to survive being overdressed for the humid spring day, but I'll be inside an air conditioned building the whole time so it shouldn't be unbearable either way.

I can do this. I get my mask on and head downstairs.

Our kitchen, dining room, and main living area are all more or less the same huge room, the difference between kitchen and dining room indicated only by a counter and the border between dining room and living room just being the swap from tile floor to carpet. Skillets crackle as my mother works to prepare a big breakfast, my father sprawled out on the living room couch, watching the news.

"There she is!" he announces, turning to grin at me as I walk into view. "How's my Hannahgator?"

"Doing good, dad," I lie. "How are you?"

"Oh, I'm fine," he grins, waving me off. "It'll take more than a deadly plague to put your old man down. I've just gotta stay cooped up inside so I don't spread it to anyone else, is all."

"Stay inside *and rest*," my mother insists. "And don't get any of the rest of us sick! That couch is the quarantine zone now, Hannah, stay away from it."

"Can do," I confirm.

"Now come on, sit down!" my mom presses, motioning to the chairs at the counter. "Tell me how your week has been!"

"Uh..." I mumble, not quite sure what sort of lie to tell. "It hasn't really been all that eventful. Just work and more work."

"Has your stream thing been going well?" she asks. "With your games?"

*With my games.* What does that even mean? I swear, she's aggressively ignorant about everything I actually care about. She can't even say 'stream' without putting 'thing' after it, or something similar.

"It's been going fairly okay," I admit. "The numbers are slowly crawling up, so I guess I'm doing something right."

"I still can't believe people sit around and watch you play those things," my mother comments idly, seeming genuinely dumbfounded. Not... offensive or anything. Not accusing me of something. And yet I still feel an immediate need to defend myself as if I'm being verbally attacked.

"Is it really that strange?" I ask. "You and dad sit around and watch people play football and stuff."

"Yes, but those people *move*," my mother counters.

I don't really have anything to say to that. Not because I can't keep trying to explain, but because I should have known better than to start. We've done this sort of back-and-forth before, and I'll just get accused of being argumentative if I don't let her have the last word. I guess I can't really say *nothing* either, or that becomes a problem, but my mom pretty exclusively wants to talk about things that I very much don't want to talk about. I should change tactics.

"How has your work been?" I ask.

That gets her complaining about the corporation she's currently contracted for and all the legal work she has to do for them, though heavily edited for confidentiality. ...Most of the time. Sometimes she lets some things slip that she's legally not allowed to, but I kind of like it when she does. It helps to be reminded that she's a person that needs to vent sometimes. She gets overwhelmed, she makes mistakes. She needs a human connection from time to time, too. That's why she's so insistent on forcing my brother and I to spend time with her. She doesn't actually have any friends outside of work, and she spends so much time complaining about her co-workers that I'm not sure she has any *at* work either. I think her legal firm has in-house parties every so often, and sometimes she goes to those, but honestly I think she likes big social gatherings even less than I do. And that's *saying* something.

Neither of us have been diagnosed with anything, but no one in my family is exactly neurotypical.

"Ask me about *my* work!" my father says once my mom is finally done with... whatever she was saying. I just kind of made noises at her and pretended to listen.

"Honey, we're about to start eating," my mother protests, dropping some pancakes on my plate. Mmm. At least I get pancakes.

"Aw, this one's not that gross," he insists. "A man came in the other day, he must have been late twenties, early thirties? And he still had a bunch of baby teeth because of an impacted canine that grew in *sideways* and blocked off an incisor as well. A real big one! His other canine came in fine and it was like a damn vampire fang on the left side of his mouth, but the right was just a worn-away baby! Barely longer than its neighbors. It struck quite the amusing contrast."

Huh. I wonder if vampires are real. My guess would be no; magic is real, sure, but the one magical creature I know of (me) is nothing like any urban fantasy novels I've read. Whatever magic secret society that probably exists keeps a tight lid on stuff, I'll bet.

"He's probably the one that gave you COVID," mom grunts.

I let the two of them carry the conversation, taking advantage of their distraction to quickly lift up my mask and sneak a bite of delicious, syrupy pancake into... my... mouth. Huh. This batch doesn't seem as good today, for some reason.

...No. No! *Do I not like pancakes anymore!?* I take it all back! Curse you, horrible monster transformation! Curse you a thousand times! You have given me my limbs, but you have taken away my love!? How could you ever—ooh, wait, mom's also making sausage. She plops some on my plate and I gobble it down, the savory flavor—or 'umami,' as dad would call it—multiplied a hundredfold and firing off every endorphin generator in my brain. Okay monster transformation, I forgive you. Feel free to return to your regularly-scheduled ruining of my life.

My brother wanders downstairs shortly afterwards, yawning and plopping himself into the chair next to me without so much as a hello. Which I'm perfectly okay with. My little brother and I are about as opposite as they come: he's tall, I'm short, he's athletic, I'm nerdy, he's tan, I'm pale, he's talkative, I'm quiet. He doesn't even have any interest in video games, which I think is a big ripoff. A sibling that I could play *Super Smash Bros.* with would be awesome, but nope. Somehow, the *girl* of the family is the gamer, and the boy of the family is the gossipy asshole.

It's fine, though. Now that he's here, he can take all the attention off of me. Mom grills him for information harder than she grills the sausages, but at least she still cooks enough for me to get extras. A *lot* of extras. I wish there were eggs, too, but... well, I ate them all yesterday. I have no idea what I'm going to eat tomorrow, but I'll figure that out when it happens. I hate how thankful I am that dad catching a potentially deadly disease means I can get away with wearing a mask at the breakfast table. Before this transformation started I'd probably be freaking out at the idea of someone in my family being sick. I *really* don't want to catch the plague, and I have no idea why everyone else seems so laissez-faire about the whole thing.

"I'll be getting us some of the saliva tests from work to make sure none of us are infected," my mother comments. "But for now just stay out of the same room as your father."

"A whole forced vacation and no one to spend it with!" my dad laments. "Nobody make any judgy comments about our Netflix history this week, I'm going to be desperate."

I was already going to be desperately avoiding my whole family, but now I just have an additional reason to. I feel like my mom and brother aren't going to be quite so diligent about not spreading things around. They're certainly not wearing masks indoors. ...Though I guess they're not dealing with their teeth mutating either. Still, though!

I glance at my phone to check the time, and decide it's close enough to when the bus arrives at the stop for me to be able to politely excuse myself. I wait for my family to be distracted and shove the rest of my food into my mouth at once, pancakes and sausages together, but when I try to close my jaw I realize two things: I just unhinged my jaw, and my teeth aren't designed for chewing anymore. I'm forced to swallow the entire mass of cake and flesh whole, causing me to make a weird involuntary grunting noise in the process. My brother turns my way so I quickly turn my back to him and grab some water to wash it all down with before getting my disguise back in place. I continue to pretend not to see him as I grab my backpack and make for the door, my face burning red.

"You heading out, Hannahgator?" my dad asks. "You can use my car if you want."

I blink. Huh. I guess he's not going to be driving to work, is he? But... agh, I don't wanna leave Brendan alone on the bus.

"I think I'll take the bus to school, but I'll drive myself to work tonight if that's okay?" I hedge.

"Of course that's okay," he agrees. "You're not going to be able to get to work otherwise."

"Right. Yeah, that makes sense."

"Love you, Hannah!" my dad calls out.

"Love you too," I call back, guilt clawing at my heart since I know that's a lie. I desperately wish it wasn't, but it is.

I exit the house and immediately realize I'm an idiot for denying the car. I could just *drive to the bus stop and pick Brendan up myself.* And then we'd have a car to go out to eat with! Stupid, stupid, stupid. I didn't think about that, I just kind of instinctively didn't like the idea of driving to school for some reason.

I guess it's just not my usual routine.

I meet up with Brendan at the bus stop, give him the bad news about my dad, and let him know my finger-claws finished growing in. More importantly than that, though, I tell him about my super awesome amazing cleaning spell.

"Of course you'd be more excited about getting one-sixth of prestidigitation than everything else that's been happening to you," Brendan comments dryly.

Wh... the nerve of him!

"Hey!" I protest. "My magic is way more awesome than a fractional cantrip! Get me a bag of Skittles and I'll instantly sort them all by flavor into separate little baggies."

He opens his mouth to respond, then closes it, then opens it again.

"...Shit, okay, that *is* pretty good," Brendan admits.

"Right!?"

"Now I'm just imagining a goddess showing up and being told to sort candy for you," he muses. "Imagine how that would feel."

"Oh, I mean, I can't actually summon her for this spell yet. I haven't named it, and she only shows up if you speak a spell's name."

"...So the whole car incident is even more unnecessary than it already was?"

"Shut up! It was an accident!"

313

We depart the bus still engaged in friendly bickering, parting ways soon afterwards. I really need to get around to showing off my recent monster parts to him, but unfortunately I'm working today. I guess I could probably get today off if I call in saying my dad has COVID, but I don't have any symptoms so that feels like it's just me being lazy. Arguably, I should stay home just because of the risk that I might transfer COVID to a customer, but I haven't even *looked* at my dad without an N95 on for over a week. I seriously doubt I've gotten anywhere close to catching it, but I'm still really, really scared that I will.

...Actually, wait. *Can* I catch COVID? I'm like, half bug person, and I'm slowly becoming more and more of a bug person every day. COVID barely affects other mammals and it conclusively can't infect invertebrates, birds, reptiles, or amphibians. I guess I'm technically still more mammal than anything else, since I still have hair and breasts and stuff. ...Aw, geez, I didn't think about that. I'm becoming less and less of a mammal! I hope my bazoingas don't fall off, I really like them.

My day is pretty boring until gym class happens, because gym class means I have to change into gym clothes, and changing into gym clothes means I have to *take clothing off.* Fortunately, I am super smart, and I prepared for this. Gym clothing has to be a t-shirt and shorts, plus a sports bra if I don't want my aforementioned badonkadonks to get sore. Normally I'd change into all of that at school because I don't like wearing sports bras all day, but to minimize the risk I'll be changing that habit on gym days. At some point I'm gonna have extra limbs poking out of my body, and I'll definitely not be wanting to take my shirt off anymore. So my sports bra and t-shirt are already underneath my long-sleeved shirt, so I just have to take the latter off. Swapping from pants to shorts is a little risky, but it's fine for now: my thigh socks go well above the spot where my leg is mutating, so as long as they don't fall down too much I should be golden!

Confident in the iron-clad guarantee of normalcy my exceptional planning skills have granted me, I step into the girl's locker room without worry and almost immediately get all thoughts yeeted clean out of my skull when I spot Autumn changing her shirt. She… she has abs. Oh my *god* she has girl abs, oh geez oh frick oh no I want to put my face on them aaaaaaa!

My plan forgot to account for how gay I am. Rookie mistake. Autumn's normal outfits are always so bland, I never really got the impression that she was *buff* underneath them. It's not the gross kind of buff that ignores the fact that humans *need* body fat in order to be healthy, and women need more body fat to be healthy than men do. Autumn doesn't have abs that look like tank treads, you couldn't grate cheese on them or whatever. But she's very obviously *toned.* Easily on par with someone from a varsity sports team. She's not on any teams, though. She's not in any clubs, as far as I know. But who cares, the *important* thing is that I did not expect her to be this hot! She tricked me!

Her shirt drops over her tummy, cutting off my view and shocking my brain back into functionality. Shoot, agh! I can't get caught ogling, that'd be so embarrassing!

"Oh, hey Hannah," Autumn greets me. "Need something?"

"Buh?" I ask.

"Hmm? Oh, sorry, I thought you were staring at me," she says.

I can *feel* my face about to turn red, so I quickly turn away and shake my head rapidly.

"N-no! Nope! No, I just… got really distracted there, sorry!" I lie terribly. "Haven't been getting enough sleep lately, I guess. Haha."

"Right," Autumn answers flatly. "Well if you're not about to start getting blood all over the place again, I'm gonna go line up."

"Nope! No blood today so far!" I squeak.

"How reassuring," she grunts, then steps past me and out of the locker room. I quickly get changed according to plan and follow her. Class starts soon after, and we do our stretches before starting a warm-up jog. Both feel very, very strange to me. For reasons that

I suppose should be obvious, my exoskeletal leg is noticeably less flexible than my purely-skin-covered leg, and by the same token I can't really strain the exoskeletal leg all that much. When it reaches the edge of its ability to rotate, it's because two chunks of bone-chitin have clonked up against each other and are no longer able to budge, no matter how hard I try. The act of stretching it at all feels somewhat pointless, since I'm just kind of... *not* stretching it. But of course, I go through the motions anyway. The worst part is when I get a piece of lint stuck *inside my joint,* which itches like crazy and feels really, *really* uncomfortable. I immediately cheat a bit and clean it out with magic, shuddering at the alien feeling of it sliding around inside me.

The jog gets to me because I just feel lopsided. My mutated leg is *much* stronger than my normal leg, and while it's not too difficult to tone it down to normal human levels to match, I don't *want* to tone it down at all. My body wants to leap with every other step, pushing me harder so I can feel the wind rush past me. I do my best to ignore the urge, sticking to what I feel like is a normal pace for me as I watch Autumn run. I never really paid much attention to her before, but she's pretty solidly near the front of the pack, huh? The track team outruns her but that's pretty much it. That's really cool. She starts getting close to lapping me, and I'm not really feeling all that tired so I do my best to speed up, letting her get close to passing me and then matching her so I can chat for a bit.

"Don't take this the wrong way," I huff, "But I never expected a fellow book nerd to also be super active!"

Autumn glances at me and opts to slow down slightly to help me keep pace. Which is nice of her, even if I don't really feel like I need to.

"Uh, yeah," she agrees, giving me an oddly searching look. "What can I say, I'm multifaceted. Did you need something?"

"I, uh, was just wondering if you'd given any more thought to the thing I asked you about at lunch," I say sheepishly. "No rush! I know you said you wanted time to think about it, but... uh, y'know."

She grimaces.

"I... had forgotten, actually," Autumn admits. "Sorry. Ask me again at lunch?"

"Oh, no problem," I assure her. "Um... do you wanna partner up for all the partner stuff today? We're playing volleyball, right?"

"We are," Autumn confirms. "Hmm. No offense, but... are you *also* a book nerd that's super active? I don't want to do everything at a reduced pace."

Hmm. I'm *still* not feeling tired, and we've run nearly a half mile.

"Go ahead and speed up," I challenge her. "I may not be as buff as you, but I'm faster than I look."

"Hmm," she mutters doubtfully. "Okay."

We start to speed up, and I do my best to keep pace without my form getting too weird. It's a lot easier than I expected. Did I not get any external changes today because I'm getting internal changes instead? I guess I don't really have any way to know. I just have to be careful about overheating and/or accidentally letting my socks slip. They're doing a good job of staying up so far, at least.

"So," I comment idly, my breath finally starting to huff a bit. "You work out, huh?"

"You *were* looking at me," Autumn accuses, though she at least seems amused rather than grossed out. That does nothing to prevent my face from getting red, of course.

"I... I'm just curious!" I protest. "You're nice and I want to get to know you! You don't really seem to have any other friends, which makes you all mysterious and junk."

"Maybe I just don't want any friends," Autumn grunts.

"Pfft, okay Sasuke Uchiha," I snort.

She just gives me a weird look.

"Wh... what?" I protest. "Have you not seen *Naruto?* I don't even like anime and I've seen *Naruto.*"

317

"Mm-hmm," she mutters. "Well if you're really dying to know, I do martial arts. Self-defense stuff."

"Oh!" I grin. "That's super cool! Is that why you were busy after school yesterday?"

She gives me *another* weird look, distinctly different from the first and completely incomprehensible to me. Gah, am I doing something wrong? Is my disguise slipping!? No, no, everything seems to be in place. It's just me, normal human Hannah, doing normal human things with my fellow normal humans.

"Yeah," Autumn eventually confirms. "That's what I was doing after school yesterday."

"Nnnneat," I say, snapping the T a little as my mind screams a mile a minute. Autumn's always a little weird, but I feel like I'm missing something big that I just absolutely do not see at all.

Autumn is... not very talkative for the rest of gym class, which my anxiety interprets as an abject failure on my part. I don't even know why I'm doing this. Trying to be friends with someone *because I have a crush and want to date them* is a little bit... ugh. Like, I'm just setting myself up for heartbreak, aren't I? There's like a ninety percent chance she's straight, and even if she's gay she's not going to want to date a gosh dang bug monster! I should really just leave her alone.

...Or so I tell myself, but after Autumn and I part ways and I get through my third class of the day, lunch rolls around and I find my feet taking me to the library. I ended up eating in a bathroom stall again, so Autumn is already there when I arrive, her nose buried in the little notebook she's always looking at and scribbling stuff in.

"Um... hey, Autumn," I greet her awkwardly.

She jolts, briefly giving me a wide-eyed look before she seems to figure out words again.

"Hannah. Hi."

Well, she figured out a couple words, anyway.

"Hi," I say. "Um... is it okay if I sit?"

"Oh, uh, yeah," she confirms, motioning to the seat across from her. "Feel free."

"Sure, thanks," I agree, sliding stiffly into the chair. We stare at each other for a bit, and I can't help but ask. "Did I make things awkward in gym class?"

"What?" she asks. "No? I mean, I don't think so?"

"Oh. That's good."

Another awkward pause descends. I'm tempted to pull out some homework and start it, but I feel like the conversation isn't really finished. It's just delayed.

"...Does Saturday work for you?" Autumn suddenly asks.

"Huh?" I blink.

"Saturday," she repeats. "I thought about it, like you asked me to. Do you want to go to the mall Saturday?"

Do I have work Saturday? Oh shoot I don't. I'm free that day. We can go and get new outfits. Me and Autumn. Er, Autumn and I? Cute girl with abs and idiot bug. I bet she could pick me up really easily.

"Um... sure," I manage to force my mouth to say. "That sounds awesome. Thanks."

"Cool," she says quietly. "I'm, uh, really bad at shopping though. Just a fair warning."

"I bet I'm worse," I admit. "Don't worry about it."

She chuckles a little, and it's so cute it almost hurts. I don't really see her smile much, but she definitely looks better that way. I hope I can make her smile more and more. Although... maybe I should be more careful about that, thinking back on our conversation in gym.

"Hey, uh, I kind of made fun of it at the time, but... were you serious when you said you didn't want any friends?" I ask.

She stiffens up immediately, and I almost regret asking, but... well. Communication is important, and friends don't let friends say vaguely cryptic red flags about depression without offering a bit of support.

"I, um... I suppose that sounds like something I might say," she mutters bitterly.

"Yeah, I made a joke out of it at the time, but that was probably rude of me, thinking back," I admit.

She shrugs.

"It's fine," she says. "Please don't worry about it."

Shoot. That was definitely the kind of 'it's fine' that means 'it's not fine,' wasn't it? Do I know her well enough to press on this? ...Ugh, no, I don't think so. I want to be her friend, but we've only met a handful of times now. Maybe if the d—*the friendly outing* goes well, I'll feel comfortable pushing. For now, I feel like it's best to back off and just be there if she wants to open up. Maybe continue the conversation in a different direction.

"I have... one and a half friends, I think," I admit. "The half-friend is Ida. I don't know if you know her, but we got in an argument and we're not really talking right now, but I think she'll come around. My best friend is Brendan, we've been pals since elementary school. But that's pretty much it. I don't really reach out to other people at all."

A pang of guilt stabs at me as I realize I do, in fact, have three other friends: Teboho, Kagiso, and Sindri. I haven't known them long, but they're undoubtedly my friends. Still, I can't really talk about them here.

"You're reaching out to me," Autumn points out. "I'm honestly surprised you haven't already decided I'm a weirdo and stopped trying."

"Uh... well, I like that you're a weirdo, I guess?" I admit. "I'm also a huge weirdo. Like, probably way weirder than you think. I think weird is good. And like, sure, you don't talk much, but that just

320

means you're not flapping your mouth when you don't have anything to say."

"That's hardly the strangest thing about me," Autumn protests.

"Well, I look forward to learning what else there is!" I insist. "My eyes just glaze over when normal people bond over normal things, it doesn't mesh with me at all. I don't know why, I just... can't focus on anything outside my own little zones of interest, I guess. Like... Pokémon, or tabletop games, or fantasy novels, or... you, I guess!"

She blushes a little. Actually blushes. What? Oh *god* did I just flirt? I didn't mean to flirt! Aaah!

"I'm one of your zones of interest?" she presses.

*Code red! Code red! Abort, abort!*

"Uhh, that... kind of came out wrong," I stumble over my words, my mouth feeling dry. I can't believe I said that, aaagh! "I just... I mean you've been really nice to me. Helping me clean up blood and stuff. You do martial arts. You're *cool*. So... I wanna hang out with you more."

Another unreadable expression flashes over her face, but she quickly buries it in a book, no longer looking at me. Did I make it too weird? Or... is she also...?

"So... Saturday is good?" she mumbles.

"Um... yeah," I agree. "Saturday is good."

The rest of my day is just a blur of me trying not to let out a squeal of lesbian triumph. I know my gaydar is made out of two broken toothpicks and a slice of cheese, but if she's maybe, possibly *also* in the same boat I am, that would just... aaaah! No. No, calm down, Hannah. You're reading too much into things. The only interpersonal thing you're insightful about is noticing when someone is trying to deflect away from a serious problem, and the only reason you're good at *that* is because you've used all those techniques first.

I'm just... projecting, probably. I can figure things out once I get more data from the shopping mall trip. It's *way* too early to be fantasizing about touching our foreheads together, or getting to feel her biceps, or biting into the meat of her thighs and letting her blood run down my throat. I want to hold her close and dig my claws into her back, I... I'm going to take a cold shower when I get home. Holy carp on a hook, those are *not* good fantasies to have! That would *kill her,* you stupid brain! What the heck!

...I'm never going to be able to have a relationship, am I?

Maybe I can cancel the shower. That thought is plenty chilling on its own. None of this matters, does it? The friendship doesn't matter, the maybe-date doesn't matter, Autumn's sexuality doesn't matter. I'm not going to be human long enough to enjoy it. I do my best to hide it, to forget about it, but what's happening to me isn't going to go away. The threat of being outed won't vanish. I am a monster and I'm becoming more monstrous all the time. It doesn't matter if I hate it or enjoy it, it's going to *happen* and I might not even be the same person when I come out the other side. Autumn isn't a potential date, not really. She's just another distraction, and before long that won't be enough.

I hug myself tight, clutching my triceps so hard I almost puncture my gloves with my claws. What's going to happen to me, when the world finds out? Just thinking the question is enough to make my good mood die on the vine. For a while there, I was really starting to believe I didn't mind the idea of being a monster. It's scary, but also exciting. It feels like *me,* in some way that being human somehow doesn't. It's right and I like it, so why... why am I afraid again?

I guess no matter how much I'm okay with being a monster, I'm still mortally terrified of being a freak.

# 18

# GUILT

A freak. An outcast. A pariah. That's the core of my fear, isn't it? Sure, there are people who will accept me for what I am. There are people that already do. But society as a whole? No. Definitely not.

It's similar to being gay, really. I do not live in what I would describe as a queer-friendly community, so I keep my mouth shut about it. Does that mean that the average person on the street would attack me if they saw me kissing a girl? Probably not. A good chunk of people won't care in the slightest. A good chunk would be happy to see it, even. But a good chunk of people, my family included, would glower judgmentally at me, complain about the sin of the youth, and be just a little bit angrier the next time they go chat with their friends... or go to the polls.

And in the wrong parts of the wrong towns, yes, I absolutely might get attacked for it.

For obvious reasons, I don't want to deal with that. Even before this whole mutation problem, I was very purposefully trying to get through life without adding to my list of issues. It's easier to just not think about it, to bury the thing people will hate me for deep down inside, to avoid the disdain and the ostracization by pretending I'm just like everyone else. I know not everyone does that. We had pride parades in town last June, even. Ida invited me to come with her to one and *wow* I thought she was making fun of me at the time, I could not have been more wrong. But the point is that I know I'm not trapped. There are people braver than me who created ways for me to safely come out. I just... can't. I don't want to. I'm *scared* of stepping out of line, of the disapproval of my family, of being dragged to church every Sunday with that much more vitriol behind the expectant glare of my parents. I can't... no. That's a lie. I *could* handle it. I know that. I just don't want to. I wish I didn't have to make this decision at all.

Honestly, I hate being a lesbian.

If I could just be straight and date my best friend and live a normal life, that would be *awesome.* I mean, for a certain kind of normal life. I get that I'm weird even without the gay stuff and the turning-into-a-monster stuff, but it's it's not the same. Nerdy girls that barely talk to anybody unless it's about video games or fantasy novels, who don't like going out and don't fit in with any cliques and don't bother remembering the names of most of their classmates are *weird,* sure, but it's a different kind of weird. A socially acceptable kind of weird. 'Eccentric,' I think the word is. Sure, I'd probably have more friends if I wasn't introverted, or geeky, or fashion-ignorant, but all of those things are still okay to be in society. All of those are things my family and community can forgive. Being gay isn't, so that's what I end up crying about in my room.

I feel like a traitor to the queer community for thinking this way. These kinds of feelings are exactly *why* 'pride' is emphasized, because we're raised in a culture that has been trained for generations to *shame.* I know, intellectually, that there's nothing wrong with me. That my family's bigotry doesn't make me a lesser person. That the things I've been taught by a religion I don't believe in do not dictate my reality, and that it is okay to be who I am. But my emotions don't care. I still feel the shame of being other. I still feel the *fear* of being a sheep in wolf's clothing, surrounded by the pack. I hate it. It's not fair. I should have never had to deal with any of this. And now it's worse, because my body is giving society even more of a reason to think I'm a monster.

If I start walking around as openly homosexual in this town, I'll be hated. If I start walking around as openly inhuman, I'm pretty sure I'll be *shot*. Not by anyone I know, and not right away, but there's no doubt in my mind that *somebody* in this town is a crazy, neo-confederate bastard with no doubts as to my lack of personhood and ready access to plenty of methods to relieve me of it anyway. I'm sure I can convince my family that I'm still Hannah, and I'm sure they'd be on my side, but only in that very particular way that they're always 'on my side.' Which is to say they'd try to bring me to *their* side, dictating everything I do because they know better, insisting on having control of the situation and—most frighteningly—doing their best to remove me from the situation entirely.

They would view what's happening to me as a problem, and they'd only be right because they'd *make* it one.

My grip tightens on the broom in my hands as my claws dig deep into the thick soles of my shoes. Without really thinking about it, I let out a low hiss, as if trying to intimidate the crumbs on the floor. I'm at work now, the rest of the school day having not been all that exciting. Somewhat predictably, though, thinking about all this garbage has put me in a bad mood. It isn't helped by the fact that my boss gave me a bunch of crap for wearing gloves.

I can't really blame him though, since he's just doing his job. Gloves and food service have a tricky relationship, to say the least. Food safety protocols are *complicated,* and in many cases purposefully excessive. Which is a reasonable policy, if I'm being honest. Lazy teenagers comprise a pretty large percentage of food service workers, and the amount of times I've seen my coworkers casually disregard the health code is frankly rather terrifying. By holding everyone to a ridiculously high standard, they prevent the vast majority of inevitable slip-ups from actually hurting anybody.

So! Gloves. Common wisdom would suggest that you *want* food service workers to wear gloves. And oftentimes, you do! Hands are gross. But while the gloves I wear to hide the fact that my fingers are powerful, deadly weapons are pretty stylish (if I do say so myself), from a health perspective they are significantly more gross than my bare hands because they aren't designed to be washed in a sink.

Gloves in food service are only sanitary if they are *disposable* gloves, and only if they are actually disposed of and replaced often. Wearing gloves prevents dirty hands from touching food, but it does not prevent dirty *gloves* from touching food, and it's often more difficult to notice when gloves are dirty than when hands are dirty. My workplace actually doesn't want us to wear gloves at *all* most of the time, preferring that we use tongs and ladles and what-have-you to keep our hands away from the food completely. As such, it's against company policy to wear the kind of gloves I'm currently wearing at all, even if I'm not working in the kitchen. It's a uniform violation, one I had to get around by insisting to my boss that I have some really gross crap growing on my hands that I thought customers would be concerned about seeing, which is technically true. The compromise is that, when I step foot in the kitchen, I have to wear disposable gloves over my normal gloves and change them out often.

Honestly, it's not that big of a deal, really. My boss wasn't happy about it, but I've earned enough brownie points by being a good worker that he's willing to let it slide. I'm technically violating company policy, but as long as I use disposable gloves properly I'm not violating the *health code,* and that's a compromise he is begrudgingly willing to make for me. I still hated needing to have the conversation at all. Needing to draw attention to myself, needing to be an exception to the rules that all my coworkers will at some point ask about or find out about. And the worst part is that it's all unnecessary, it's all performative. My gloves will never be dirty again, not unless I choose to let them be.

Though that thought is a bit annoying, it makes me smile a little, too. I love my cleaning spell. I could start using it right now and make this restaurant cleaner than the day it opened. I won't, but I *could,* and something about that makes me very happy. I sweep efficiently away at the floor, tidying up the dining room just in time for another customer to come in and return my focus to the register. I may not have been thinking about very pleasant things today, but I'm glad I've been thinking about them. The customer is a regular, an annoying and belligerent one, but I patiently help them anyway, recording their ridiculous order and all the off-menu peculiarities that we never complain about to their face. We have a lot of strange regulars that order difficult-to-make things, but no one ever grumbles about the ones that are actually nice to us. Funny how that works.

I wish that people would accept the weird parts about me as long as I'm nice enough. Maybe I could find some pride for who I am, if that were true.

A lump starts to form in my throat and I swallow it down, trying to will away the uncontrolled burst of depression I feel coming. As usual, my emotions brazenly defy me. No, no, no! Don't start crying now! I'm busy, I'm working, I'm in a professional environment! My shift just started, we're not even at the dinner rush yet, I can't fall apart *already!*

The tears start to drop. Silently, without looking at any of my co-workers, I quickly turn a hundred and eighty degrees and walk into the back room, where my manager is sitting at the store's computer and looking at his phone.

"Hannah?" he asks, looking up and noticing my tears the moment my name leaves his lips. His eyes go wide. I pretend not to see his facial expression.

"Could you man the front for a little bit?" I ask quietly, forcing my voice not to waver.

"Yeah," he says, nodding once and getting up to do just that. I collapse into the chair and start to sob. My coworkers will probably all think I was driven to tears by that jerk of a customer, even though I've dealt with him a hundred times and I deal with him well. They're going to think I'm emotional and weak. They're going to be right, even if for the wrong reasons.

327

I banish those thoughts from my mind. I barely know them and shouldn't care what they think. I care anyway, but I *shouldn't.* My focus right now needs to be pulling myself together. I take deep, slow breaths, each of them shaky and accompanied by the wetness of my cheeks. I try not to think about how my life is going to fall apart, how I'll have to live as a sideshow freak if I even get to keep living at all, and focus on those breaths. Keep them even. Calm myself down. Through sheer force of will, I start getting the tears to halt. I brought my backpack to work today, and I'll keep bringing my backpack to work in case I need any of the supplies I've been stuffing it with. I pull out a small hand mirror once I have a bit more control of myself, and to my dismay I find my makeup smeared and messy. It's not too bad, not enough for most people to notice, but any other women that get a good look at my face will be able to tell I've been crying. I don't have a makeup kit in my backpack, though. I'll need to buy a portable one for when I inevitably need it to cover up my skin falling off, but I guess for now I'll have to head to the bathroom and wash it all off. Better no makeup than smeared makeup, no matter how light it happens to be. It *annoys* me. The placement of makeup is important, that's a big part of why it works. It's subtle, that's the *point.* Even people who can't tell *why* it's wrong will get the feeling that something is wrong. It can't function if it's... disorderly.

Huh. I wonder if...

A twist of will and a pleasant thrum of power later, I watch the smeared cosmetics return themselves to how they were before, the extra salt and water from my tears separating from the compounds and evaporating back into the air. The makeup looks better than when I put it on this morning. I smile.

I seriously have the best spell ever.

I take in a deep breath and let it out in a refreshing huff, putting my hand mirror away and returning to the front to get back to work. I assure my boss I'm okay when he asks, and the rest of my shift proceeds fairly normally. No more outbursts, no more tears. I only fantasize about killing three different customers, but that probably isn't even the monster thing. I asked the girl running the other register and she admitted to wanting to strangle five.

Fantasizing about *eating* them though, that's probably the monster thing. I get over the urge by stealing some raw chicken from the walk-in fridge and slurping it down. It's all slimy from the marinade but I pretend it's blood and that makes things more fun. I don't even have to worry about getting messy anymore! It's kind of weird how standing in the fridge doesn't really feel cold anymore, though.

...I really, *really* hope my immune system is up for dealing with raw foods, because I've had weird teeth for like, a few days, and I'm already addicted to ripping apart uncooked meat with them. It's just not the same when the meat is cooked, there's no... *pop,* if that makes sense. There's no moment between not enough pressure to penetrate and then *enough,* where you suddenly break through all at once, like biting into an apple but more... soft? Even? It doesn't resist being pierced because of skin, but because it's bending to absorb the force, I guess. It's hard to describe, but there's nothing else quite like it. The feeling of cutting it apart, of letting my teeth slide through the flesh, is completely different when the food is cooked. Tender meat is easier to chew for pathetic omnivore teeth, but I like mine tough and dripping. It's satisfying on a much more primal level than simple flavor.

Also nice is that it means I can eat the restaurant's chicken without paying for it and without anyone suspecting that I'm the reason for the shortage, since no one will ever see me cook the stuff. Woo for stealing from soulless corporations! ...Exclusively in ways that can't be traced back to me, of course. I'm a hungry, hungry lesbian, not a revolutionary.

With that as the highlight of my night, I eventually drive myself home and scoot into bed. I'm still not feeling great, all things considered, and while I'd normally be happy to get to sleep for that reason—one of the absolute best cures for bad days is a good night's sleep, after all—I don't get that sort of luxury anymore. My bad night will carry over as a bad morning in the other world, because my day never really ends anymore. Still, though, a change of scenery might help, not to mention getting to wake up surrounded by friends.

Or more accurately, wake up with a friend surrounding me. When my eyes close on Earth, my eyes are already open on the Mother Tree thanks to my complete lack of eyelids. Of course, I still can't see anything, because I'm snuggled up deep inside Kagiso's bedroll, with three of her arms wrapped around me and hugging me tight against her chest. I adjust my legs slightly, all too aware of how the minute movements press up against her fuzzy boobs. Damn. I'm finally getting to touch another woman's breasts, and I don't even have the libido to appreciate it.

Thankfully, I can still appreciate every other part of this situation. The way the bedroll ecompasses me is delightful to my burrowing instincts, and the joy of cuddling a friend I care for and trust with my life is possibly all the more vibrant now that I'm not distracted with thoughts of sex. The warmth of Kagiso's fluffy arms around me is one of the most profoundly comfortable things I've had the pleasure of experiencing, so I'm more than content to just stay still and enjoy letting her sleep.

The sheer comfort of the moment makes me happy to not have hormones making things weird, but unfortunately the moment I have that thought I'm brought back to thinking about how I resent my sexuality. I've always struggled to make friends, but being attracted to or the object of unwanted attraction from any potential candidates made that struggle all the more difficult. It's a big part of what trained my brain to avoid physical contact with people: it makes me feel like a total creep. Just brushing shoulders with another girl would set my heart fluttering, and that always started up a chain of self-loathing which contributed to my distance from everyone else. It's certainly not *all* of it, I'm sure I'd still be an incorrigible introvert if I was straight or asexual or whatever, but it's still another thing to add to the pile. I hate how just having an upcoming maybe-date is forcing all these thoughts back into my head. I shouldn't have bothered with—urk!

I twitch with surprise as Kagiso suddenly gives me a firm squeeze, prompting me to phase a few legs into 4D space to avoid them getting crushed. She starts mumbling something in her sleep in a language I can't understand, and I stay still for a moment before hesitantly bringing my legs back to wrap them around her arms and torso. I squeeze her back, and she quiets down, returning to restful sleep.

A warm feeling bubbles through my body and, on a whim, I start stroking a claw through her hair. It's so weird how quickly I've warmed up to Kagiso, considering all my hangups. Sindri and Teboho, too, though neither of them are insisting on cuddling me to sleep so it's a much less extreme example. Maybe it's because they keep saving my life? As reasons to trust people go, that's a pretty damn good one. Whatever it is, though, I'm glad for it. I'm glad that my friend group has basically doubled thanks to this other world. I'm glad there are more people in my life that I can touch and talk to and joke with and enjoy being around. This world is crazy and terrifying, but I'm really starting to love it thanks to my friends. If only Brendan could be here. He'd love it, too.

...Gosh dang it, I'm introspective lately. I don't like it. Let's think about something else. Uhh... according to the one-half rule, the fact that dentron have four breasts means that their average litter size is two, but having up to four children at once wouldn't be uncommon. So it's pretty likely that Kagiso and Teboho are twins. It's also fairly likely they're triplets or quadruplets, and their other siblings are just dead. Oh geez. I... don't know if I should ask them about that. Probably not? Wait, was Kagiso having nightmares earlier? Is *that* why she keeps wanting to cuddle with me at night? *Oh no poor baby.*

I squeeze her a little tighter, eliciting a small, happy noise from the sleeping fuzzball. She gets to cuddle me as much as she needs to, ding dang it. In the meantime, I distract myself by keeping tabs on the camp with my spatial sense rather than trying to think about more things. Thinking has been somewhat of a loser's game today.

It's easy enough to find Teboho, snoring away in his bedroll as he is. At least he doesn't seem to be dreaming. Sindri, meanwhile, seems to be... talking to a bird? Hmm. That's probably a normal thing for a person to do if they're an animal tamer. The owl-like creature looks large enough to pick me up and fly away with me, though it's hard to be afraid of it with how happily it's gobbling down chunks of shredded starhydra meat pinched between Sindri's fingers. I wonder if this is one of the birds Sindri is using to track the chaos mage or if it's a... 'new hire,' so to speak. Hopefully it didn't have to get run down like I was, but Sindri mentioned that his power is intended for animals rather than people anyway, so it's probably a lot more effective on them. It's kind of strange that it worked on me at all, but I suppose I'm a bit... animalistic. It sucks that people keep assuming I'm not a person, but I guess I can't really blame them for that. I definitely have 'weird critter' vibes.

Since I'm awake anyway and Sindri seems a bit distracted, I turn my focus to keeping watch on the camp perimeter, settling into a familiar watch routine. I only realize it's morning when Sindri puts out the last embers of the campfire and heads into Teboho's tent to wake him up. The bird is long gone. I hope for a moment that he lets Kagiso rest, but unfortunately he's tapping on the outside of our tent flap right afterwards and Kagiso's long ears perk up instantly, rousing her from slumber. She pats my carapace good morning and extracts herself from the bedroll, leaving me to begrudgingly follow. I scuttle up her leg and onto her head as she exits the tent.

Teboho waves and says something that I can actually parse as 'good morning, you two!' thanks to all the lessons I've been getting on the dentron language. I wave a leg back at him and he grins, the four of us coming together so Sindri can cast the mental communication spell on us. It's a nice morning ritual, one that's particularly welcome in this crazy world where my normal routine means absolutely nothing. It's nice to start the day by joining hands with all of my trusted friends.

*...And there we go,* Sindri announces. *Good morning, Hannah.*

332

*Warm hat,* Kagiso agrees happily.

"Good morning, Hana!" Teboho says aloud. "You [gibberish] me, right?"

*All but one word,* I answer. *I'm far from fluent, but I'm starting to pick things up.*

"[Glibblegorble] fast!"

I do my best to commit the sounds I don't understand to memory so I can try to remember them from context before I answer.

*Yeah, I didn't think I'd learn this quickly,* I admit. *Either my magic is helping me somehow, or more likely I think Sindri's magic is.*

*I couldn't say for sure,* Sindri admits. *It's definitely plausible, though. Sharing information between minds is well within the realm of Pneuma magic, and this communication spell is relatively new and unnamed. We tend to think our thoughts in our native languages, so whenever Kagiso and Teboho send you their thoughts you're getting that information along with the meaning of the words. I can see that being a very effective teaching aid, but considering that you're the first person who has attempted to learn a new language under the influence of this spell, I can't say for sure.*

*Yeah, we need more data points,* I agree. *It's pretty darn useful if it does help, though. Learning a new language in a week and change is crazy.*

"You negative [glurpleburple] yet, Hana!" Teboho reminds me.

*...But I haven't finished learning yet, yeah,* I agree. *I'll get it, though. I appreciate you all helping me out so much.*

"Think small of it!" Teboho assures me with a laugh. "You are being very pleasurable!"

Um. Oh! He means I'm enjoyable to be around. Gah, I'll have to mentally translate things less literally, as well.

*Well, we have a long day of walking ahead of us,* Sindri reminds the team. *So let's get camp packed up and get to moving.*

333

We do—or rather everyone else does, since I continue to be pretty useless at basic object manipulation—and then we get walking. ...Which I guess is also just something that everyone else does. I need to find more ways to help out. I kind of wonder why they put up with me, now that I think about it. Are they just going to leave me in the city when we finally make it there? ...Well, I guess I'm not an entire human's worth of logistics either. I don't help very much, but I don't really make their journey that much harder either, barring that time we were almost murdered. Still, they're all going on a really dangerous journey. It's weird that I'm tagging along when I barely even know how to fight.

Oh. Wait. *That's* why Sindri wanted me to go hunting. He wants me to practice killing. He wants me to fight the chaos mage for him. He wants me to murder another person. Am... am I willing to do that? Even to the monster that slaughtered Kagiso and Teboho's village, I'm not sure I can.

I... I guess that's why I need practice? If I'm not going to bring anything but trouble to my friends, the least I can do is help them safely deal with a threat to their lives, not to mention countless other lives. I don't realize how hard I'm gripping Kagiso's head until she reaches up and scratches the base of one of my legs, letting out a quiet trill. I relax, resettling my weight. It's okay. I'll be okay. I'll figure something out.

Shortly into the walk we encounter a forest, and with Sindri having to trudge through the thick undergrowth on foot, I finally get a chance to walk under my own power rather than just ride. Kagiso, Teboho and I take to the trees while Sindri struggles below us, which gives me time to hunt. Kagiso purrs with approval as I successfully sneak up on and assassinate a fuzzy little friend noodle, gobbling it down and savoring the bloody meat. The furry snakes are surprisingly delicious! I expected all the hair to be a bit unappetizing, but nope, it's still yummy. I gleefully hunt two more and eat them before Sindri eventually gets fed up with his slow progress and mind controls what looks like a giant tardigrade-sloth combo to clear the way for him. It also looks tasty, but since it's currently an ally I guess I shouldn't stab it through the skull and suck its brain out through the hole before tearing the rest of its flesh from its bones and oh my *gosh* I'm really hungry, why am I still this hungry after eating so many friend noodles? I've probably close to doubled my weight in food intake, not that I'm actually any heavier. ...Hmm. I'm gonna go eat more cute fuzzy snakes.

Hours later, I decide to reinstate my usual position on Kagiso's head after being electrocuted, immolated, splashed with acid, driven into a mindless terror by a cute little noodle song, and utterly flummoxed by a little fuzzy worm that just grew wings and flew away when I got close. Only the latter two actually stopped me from eating them, since the lightning and fire didn't really hurt and the acid was easily cleaned off my body with my spell. Still, it served as an important reminder that potentially everything in this world is dangerous, no matter how cute or delicious.

*Which is why I could really use that aura sight spell,* I remind Sindri. *You're not still mad at me for the blood in the waterskin, are you? I promise I'm really sorry.*

*It wasn't just blood in there, but alright,* he acquiesces. *I'll quit being a grump and teach you. To use aura sight, it's important that you first understand what aura is. Therein lies our first and largest obstacle: we don't know.*

*We don't know?* I repeat dumbly.

*Nope,* Sindri confirms. *We don't know what aura is, beyond the fact that it only appears on creatures with souls. And we don't have a great idea what souls are either, but they're a lot easier to interact with so we can start there.*

*Okay, I wanna stop you right there,* I say. *When you say the word 'soul,' that's being translated as a word in my language that has a lot of cultural baggage. Like, we're talking 'the part of you that goes to the afterlife and lives forever when your body dies' kind of cultural baggage. 'The part of you that is most truly and essentially you,' cultural baggage. 'The ephemeral essence of a person that separates thinking beings from mindless apes,' cultural baggage. Can I get some clarification here on how accurate that is?*

*Hmm. A good chunk of it is,* Sindri confirms. *Souls are hardly exclusive to people, though, nearly every living thing has a soul.*

*Souls are granted by the goddess the moment a living being takes their first breath, and they are returned to the goddess the moment a being takes their last,* Teboho chimes in. *That's not merely a poetic turn of phrase, either. The first breath of a child summons her as surely as a spoken spell, wherein she takes that breath and fashions a spirit from it. It is thus via the soul that we interact with the divine, as the soul is inherently divine in nature.*

*Uh, what about creatures that don't breathe?* I ask. Y'know, since I'm currently one of them.

*You still respirate,* Sindri shrugs. *The common wisdom for the trigger is an organism respirating under its own power rather than being supplied by its mother or an egg, though this is largely disproven by the existence of ensouled synthetic life forms.*

*Woah, woah, what!?* I ask. *You guys have robots?*

*Unfortunately, yes,* Sindri grumbles. *That's not important right now. What* is *important is that—divine or not—the force responsible for magic is responsible for souls, and souls are extremely influential. Pneuma mages can manipulate them to affect your personality, and Death mages can communicate with the recently deceased, so the idea that your soul contains your personality and continues to retain it after death is a fairly compelling one. Best we can tell, the aura is just... some sort of energy that a soul passively gives off. The stronger the mage, the larger their aura. The aura sight spell magically attunes your mind to detect the energy of whatever you're currently focusing on. Calling it 'sight,' however, is a bit of a misnomer. It's a unique sense that most people equate to sight, but it's... odd. Difficult to describe. Foreknowledge of the experience thankfully isn't required to learn the spell, but the odd sensory inputs do make things difficult to parse at first.*

*I'm getting used to having weird new forms of observing the world that don't seem to make any sense,* I answer casually. *I'm not too worried about it.*

*Hmm, yes, I suppose using sight as a comparison would be a somewhat different metaphor for you,* Sindri agrees, giving me an odd look while I pretend that I *definitely* was referring to sight when I said that, yep.

...Though I guess being able to see in three hundred and sixty degrees is pretty darn weird. On one hand it kind of feels like I just have way more peripheral vision than normal, but that's not quite right. It's more like I know I *can* focus on additional directions at once, but I'm so used to only focusing on one that I never do that without putting in the effort to. The rest of the time it feels more like I just have one eye that can rotate in whatever direction I want and kind of detect movement in whatever direction it isn't looking. I guess my brain isn't powerful enough to unconsciously handle all the sensory input yet.

*In any case,* Sindri continues, *Aura Sight is a powerful spell in its initial state. Because Aura reflects the soul, experienced and skilled users can discern a lot of information with this spell alone, watching fluctuations in the natural emissions of the soul to determine thoughts, moods, opinions, strengths, and weaknesses. You need to know this because it's important you understand the nature of the spell itself, even if you'll never be able to accomplish that sort of refined ability with it.*

*Wait, I won't?* I ask. *How come?*

*Because your learning is third-hand and you aren't even a Pneuma mage,* Sindri answers. *Spells are substantially weaker when taught rather than innate, and weaker still when taught by someone other than their originator, and the fact that you only have an adjacent affinity compounds both of those problems immensely. Your aura is so powerful you'll be able to push raw strength through those maluses, but you'll still only get the bare basics. My guess is you'll only be able to manage viewing a single person at a time, and you'll only get their affinities and* maybe *their relative strength.*

*Geez,* I sigh. *That's some stiff penalties. Learning a bunch of spells doesn't sound like a great strategy when you put it like that.*

*Mmm. It depends. Even a massively neutered version of Aura Sight grants you essential information: your target's affinities. Thus, as long as you can cast it at all, there's little reason not to find someone to teach it to you. A lot of spells are useful even without significant power behind them, so those are the ones that get passed around. Most people will charge exorbitant prices when teaching spells, of course. It's a valuable resource, and time-consuming for the student and the teacher if you don't want things to end in disaster.*

*Uh... disaster?* I hedge.

*I doubt that's a concern in this instance,* Teboho protests.

*Teboho, do you have any idea what a Pneuma miscast can* do *to a person?* Sindri snaps.

*Woah, woah, don't fight!* I yelp. *We'll do this the safe way, there's no reason not to do this the safe way.*

*Exactly,* Sindri agrees. *Thank you, Hannah.*

*So, uh, what* does *a Pneuma miscast do?* I ask hesitantly.

*I assure you that you don't want to know,* Sindri answers firmly.

Yeah, okay, he's right, I don't want to know.

*Anyway,* Sindri continues, *you know the basics now, so most of the rest is getting a feel for the spell in action.*

*Which means what?* I ask.

*Paying attention while I cast the spell,* Sindri answers simply. *Exposure to the spell being used is statistically proven to increase your chances of success. So if you'll come over here...*

He holds out his arm and I hop on, scuttling up to his shoulder.

*Just wait and get a feel for it,* Sindri instructs. *You won't see anything. The spell won't do anything to you. But the feeling of the invocation itself is something you should try to commit to memory. Cultivate an affinity for it over the course of a few weeks. Ready?*

*Yep,* I confirm.

He takes a breath, and then the goddess takes it back, tasting the air from his lips with the same amusement as always. She acknowledges him for only a moment before switching to me, her attention stroking my carapace with equal parts affection and schadenfreude. She licks her nonexistent lips with a tongue of horrors and speaks the words Sindri meant to say.

"**Aura Sight**."

From my perspective, nothing else happens. Sindri presumably feels the effects of the spell. The goddess, however, does not leave. Her gaze remains on me, crushing me from without and within, playful and expecting. Inviting me. Daring me, almost. It's tacit permission, and while I'm curious why she's extending it I'm far more terrified of what might happen if I deny her.

I let the intent flood through me, and she rips the air from my body, laughing with delight. Knowing me a fool. She says the words anyway, because what would a goddess gain from a lie?

"**Aura Sight**."

And *then* she's gone, leaving only one last cackle that I'm not sure anyone else hears. Not that 'hear' is the right word to describe how one experiences the sounds she makes. I don't have much time to be horrified by the interaction, because Sindri grabs me and yanks me off his arm, throwing me away from the others as hard as he can. My heart nearly bursts with terror as I fly like a football, instinctively curling my legs up underneath me and holding myself in a tight ball. I hit the ground, bounce, and roll quite a good distance before I re-extend my legs and skid to a stop, my body shaking with adrenaline and sore with damage.

*What the FUCK were you thinking!?* Sindri roars furiously into my head, and Teboho starts to laugh. Sindri ignores him. *I JUST told you that kind of shit is dangerous, Hannah! You could have killed yourself! Or WORSE!*

*I told you!* Teboho laughs. *The goddess favors her! It's obvious!*

*She might have become a mindless beast!* Sindri snaps back. *She might have gone insane! She could have turned into a completely different person! She could have done that to* all *of us!*

*But she did not!* Teboho continues to chuckle as I get back to my feet and start to painfully limp back to the team.

*Only because of dumb luck!* Sindri counters. *Dumb fucking luck!*

I want to be angry, but I *know* that was stupid. Sindri only threw me because he was afraid that I was about to hurt everyone. It hurts, but it's my own dang fault.

*It wasn't luck,* Teboho insists. *The Mother Tree speaks to you, doesn't she Hannah?*

*...I don't know if 'speak' is the right word,* I answer noncommittally. *But I do feel a sapient intent behind magic, yeah. I know it's not exactly scientific, but... I don't know. I was urged to try it. I was scared of not trying it. I'm sorry.*

The apology comes out easily, years of experience guiding me to downplay what happened and immediately admit fault. I can tell in an instant from the look on Sindri's face that he's still angry, though. It takes all of my willpower to avoid hiding in another dimension.

*That sort of recklessness isn't something you can just say sorry to,* Sindri hisses. *You will not be learning any more spells.*

Any 'more' spells? I don't exactly see any... oh, wait. I tilt my gaze up and look at Sindri with my eyes rather than my spatial sense, and I focus. Sure enough, the magic I activated shows me... something. It's like a halo of light, but it glows *Pneuma* rather than white or green or blue. Its color is a meaning, not a sight. It makes my head hurt. I look at Kagiso next, who sure enough glows with Motion. My glance at Teboho has a bit of extra strangeness: he glows with Matter and Barrier, but the two are similar and blend together in odd ways. It's sort of hypnotic, like a lava lamp or something.

Kagiso runs up to meet me halfway, lifting me onto her head and giving Sindri an angry glower.

*Only I throw Hannah,* she growls at him.

*Wait, what?* I protest. *How about nobody throw Hannah!*

*No. Only me!*

*Why is the person doing the throwing the thing you're worried about!?*

*Enough!* Sindri shouts, saying the word out loud as well. *This is not a joking matter! Hannah, you need to understand the severity of the risk you just took. Learning spells is not that easy. You had well over a ninety percent chance of ruining your life forever by speaking those words. Promise me you won't invoke a spell's name like that again without my approval.*

I let my legs droop, hanging limp on Kagiso's scalp.

*I promise,* I tell him.

*Good,* Sindri says firmly. *Good. Okay. Let's get moving again. Teboho, keep teaching her the local language.*

*Fine, fine,* Teboho agrees. *Though I do think you don't understand as well as you think you do, Sindri.*

*The feeling is mutual,* Sindri grunts.

*Some people are born with a deeper connection to the Mother Tree than others,* Teboho insists. *She has favored children, I think. I may not know as much about numbers as you do, but aren't outliers exempted from averages?*

They start bickering a bit more about that, though I mostly tune them out, a lump of dread settling into my body. Teboho is right, isn't he? I'm pretty obviously different. Favored. My situation is exactly the kind of weird that evokes a chosen hero with a grand destiny. I've been living my life in this world day to day without thinking about *why* I'm here, about what could have caused my situation in the first place. I've read stories where people get reincarnated in another world to fight demon lords, corrupt kings, or... or apocalypses. Such as, perhaps, the one the *crazy apocalypse cult that almost killed us* might be worshiping. Oh, god. Is that why? What do they know about me? Am I going to have to keep fighting them? What are they trying to accomplish? What sort of horrible fate am I supposed to prevent? No, no no no. This is crazy, right? I'm not arrogant enough to think that this world revolves around me like that. I'm not a hero. I'm *nothing* like a hero.

I can't even get through a week without crying. How the heck am I supposed to save the world?

# 19

# TASTE FOR FLESH

"It's about time you finally came over again," Brendan grumbles, glowering half-heartedly down at me as I walk through his front door, Fartbuns happily bouncing behind him.

It's Friday afternoon already. Time seems to have flown by. After learning the soul sight spell and royally infuriating Sindri, the rest of the day was thankfully not all that eventful. I pretty much just spent it sitting on Kagiso's head and learning the dentron language some more, stopping occasionally to hunt friend noodles for food. Boring, yes, but a good sort of boring. By the end of the day, I'd settled into somewhat of a comfortable routine. We should reach the city we've been heading towards either the next day (tonight's sleep) or the day after (Saturday's sleep). My day here on Earth has been equally uneventful, with Autumn and I being awkwardly quiet around one another as our mall maybe-date looms on the immediate horizon. I'm excited and I'm stressed and I'm especially glad I finally have time to hang out with Brendan. The two of us don't usually have lunch together for various reasons, so I've been missing the guy.

"Can't say I disagree," I tell him, slipping my shoes off as he closes the door. "It's good to be here. Really good, actually. Can I hug you?"

He seems briefly taken aback, but nods and holds open his arms. I flop my face into his belly and squeeze his waist, since he is too gosh dang tall for me to hold anything else. He stiffens up and makes an uncomfortable gurgling noise when I squeeze him, causing me to let go in a panic.

"Ah! Are you okay?" I yelp.

"Yeah, yeah, I'm fine," he assures me, rubbing his back. "Pretty sure you're getting stronger, though."

"Oh no, I'm sorry!"

"Seriously, I'm okay," he waves me off. "You're not Supergirl yet. Come on, let's go."

I don't need to be told that he means for me to go to the basement, so we head down there promptly. Fartbuns bounces down the stairs after us, the huge fluffy dog full of energy as usual.

"So," Brendan says conversationally, "you seem to be doing a lot better."

"Do I?" I ask. "I guess that's good. Better than doing worse!"

Brendan gives me a knowing stare. Oh no. He's about to go on the offensive.

"...Looking forward to your date tomorrow, huh?" he asks.

"It's probably not a date!" I yelp immediately.

"Sounds like you definitely believe that," he answers dryly.

Agh no he's going to bug me until I explain. Curse my conditionally hyper-observant friend.

"Look, I just... she was blushing at me a lot today," I admit. "Just, really awkward. And considering that she caught me staring at her abs yesterday, I think she figured me out."

"Autumn has abs?" Brendan asks, seeming surprised.

"Oh my goodness she has *really nice* abs," I confirm, nodding excitedly. "Just like, toned enough to be noticeable, to be *strong*, but still all... I dunno. Girl soft?"

"Girl soft," Brendan repeats flatly.

"Girl soft!" I insist, flopping onto the couch. "Like, y'know, girls. We're soft. Men have less body fat and gross rough skin, all rough and tough and... bleh. Um, no offense."

"None taken," he answers in a tone that implies there was at least some amount of offense taken. "So. You think Autumn knows you're gay, but that just makes her blush a lot and she hasn't called off your date, so you're thinking she's also gay. And neither of you have bothered to just *ask* if the other is interested in that sort of thing."

"It's arguably a good sign that she isn't asking," I nod sagely. "Being a complete mess is the lesbian love language."

"Hannah, you've literally never dated another lesbian, you're just saying that because *you're* a mess. You don't get to pretend it's not a problem by projecting it onto other people."

I fishmouth at my friend a little, my jaw opening and closing wordlessly as I put a hand over the heart he just so brutally wounded. Fartbuns makes a happy 'boof' noise and puts his face on my lap.

"I can't believe my dearest friend would so mercilessly wound me," I intone as dramatically as possible, the hand not clutching the gaping hole he just dug into my heart moving automatically to scritch behind the dog's ear.

"I'm just trying to get through to you about the fact that your life would be so much easier if you'd just *talk* to people about this stuff," Brendan says, exasperated.

"I'm just not ready to come out, okay?" I fire back at him.

"Then why are you trying to date a woman!?"

I open my mouth, lips peeling back to reveal deadly fangs as I *hiss* at him, a sound that carries only a hint of the eldritch vibrations that I can make in my hyperspider form, but it's still enough to quiet the room into silence. It surprises what little part of me is still looking out for that sort of thing during the instinctive impulse, making me wonder what part of my throat now dips ever so slightly into angles impossible to represent in a mere three dimensions. The dog's muscles freeze with tension underneath my fingers, the prospect of having claws so close to his neck suddenly not as appealing as it was seconds before. Brendan goes silent, averting his eyes from my glare as I wait for my brain to catch up with what I just did. The hiss just *slipped out,* it wasn't a conscious decision on my part. I take a deep breath, removing my hand from Fartbuns and consciously relaxing myself.

"Sorry," I manage to get out. "I didn't mean to... do that. Anyway, there's honestly a good chance it won't be a date, and I actually *do* need the clothes we'll be buying, so there's that. But also, I just... I'm afraid I won't have the chance to do this kind of thing again pretty soon. You know?"

Brendan's face falls.

"Hannah..." he starts, but I cut him off as Fartbuns retreats behind his legs.

"The transformations have slowed down a bit," I tell him. "I haven't gotten anything new these past few days. But the old changes are growing and I probably don't have all that much time before everything comes to a head. I just... I wanna feel normal while I have the chance."

"Being normal is overrated," Brendan says quietly, his expression inscrutable.

"You're probably right," I admit. "But still, this is my last chance at it."

"...Can I still see all your cool monster bits, though?" he asks.

I chuckle.

"Brendan! Imagine what Autumn would think if she knew I took my clothing off for a man!"

"Imagine what your *mom* would think," he counters, and I shudder.

"Yeah, okay, let's not go there. I'll show you."

346

I start rolling up the right leg of my pants, though the thigh sock underneath it still covers up everything important. I *could* take off my gloves first, but honestly I've gotten so used to having my claws covered up that I'm a little worried I'll cut myself. I mean, I guess I probably can't cut my own exoskeleton, but... whatever. This order of operations works. Plus I get to torment Brendan a little by doing things the slow way. ...No, wait, bad brain. Don't think of this as a strip tease. This is just normal teasing which merely happens to involve stripping, *entirely by coincidence.*

After the pant leg is rolled up, the shoes and socks come off, as well as the little foam blocks, revealing the brilliant bone-white chitin of my leg. The sight of it steals my breath a little, even though I know what to expect. It's so hard to believe that this is my body, yet I feel the sensation when I run a finger across it, I watch it move when I flex the joints. I am, somehow, becoming a creature beyond the understanding of modern science. A fantastical beast, a monster of legend, a dream from a storybook. The white armor of my leg, pristine to the point of gleaming thanks to my magic, perfectly frames the contours of my body, deviating only to protrude the occasional spine or ridge reminiscent of my other body's limbs. I curl my toes, revealing the deep contrast of black in the flexible material underneath the armor, visible only within bent joints. Brendan kneels down to investigate and only then do I remember he's even *here,* self-consciousness blooming inside me as he grabs my calf and starts prodding away at my body. He pokes at the inside of my knee, between my chitin plates, and I almost take his finger off with a twitch.

"Th-that feels weird," I protest. "Don't poke there."

"Weird how?" he asks.

"Uh... I dunno. Like you just stuck a finger up my nose? It's sensitive in that 'this part of the body isn't supposed to be touched' kind of way."

"Mmm. Okay, sorry," he says, removing his hand from the soft part of my joint. "It's an interesting structure. Kind of... wiry, and it

347

tenses up when you move. It's either closely attached to the muscle or it *is* the muscle."

"All the more reason not to poke it," I grumble.

I take off my gloves next, though Brendan is still pretty engrossed in investigating my leg. The chitin tips emerging from each of my fingers are delightfully sharp-looking, giving me the immediate and concerningly familiar urge to cut something. Though honestly, without Spacial Rend active I doubt I could do all that much damage. *Can* I cut things with these claws? Yeah, definitely. It's not going to pierce skin if I don't put a lot of force into it, though.

I still wanna.

"Hey Brendan, do you have anything I can tear to shreds?" I ask.

"There's a raw steak in the fridge," he grunts.

Oh fudge truffle *yes*. That's the most yes thing I've ever heard. I practically leap to my feet and dash up the stairs, claws digging delightfully into the carpet before I bound into the kitchen and do a sort of clatter-slide once that traction suddenly vanishes on the hardwood floor. Fartbuns does the exact same thing, smacking into me right after I skid to a stop and nearly knocking me to the ground. I can't help myself; I start laughing.

"Fartbuns! Hey, boy, you be careful, alright?" I giggle, kneeling down to give him some careful scratches. He seems to like the feel of my claws, thankfully, so I indulge him a bit more before returning my attention to the fridge and throwing it open in delight. Sure enough, in front of me is a huge slab of glorious dead cow meat, still on the bone. I extract it lovingly, resisting the dangerous urge to try and lick my lips, since that's unlikely to go well with my teeth as huge and sharp as they are.

"Hannah, please don't make a mess," Brendan sighs, having finally caught up with me. I turn and give him the biggest grin I can fit on my face.

"You fool," I tell him. "You utter imbecile."

Then I rip the packaging in half with my claws, splattering bloody marinade all over the kitchen. I take a moment to savor Brendan's bug-eyed expression before locking my vision firmly on the meat, ripping a chunk off of it with my bare hands and swallowing it whole. I bite and tear and rend it to shreds, relishing in the delightful feeling of meat sliding down my throat. I'm laughing whenever I'm not swallowing, knowing full well that it makes me look completely unhinged, but what do I care? It's just me and Brendan here, the one and only place where I can be truly and completely me. I don't feel out of control, I feel *in my element.*

Even the T-bone is no impediment to my greedy fangs, letting me bring the meal to my mouth and crunch down to finish off the rest of it. There's a very different appeal to gnawing on bone than devouring meat, a more methodical yet no less visceral process. While I can bite large chunks of bone off at once, it wouldn't be comfortable to swallow them. Therefore, while I can't chew in the same way I did with a human mouth, I still have to perform my best equivalent in order to get at the tasty marrow I crave, slurping up the bits of meat still stuck to the lumbar vertebra that I'm happily crunching down on.

"Nom nom nom nom," I coo happily once I've calmed down a little, delighting in the contrast between the bloody mess and my dumb little noises.

"Holy *shit,* Hannah," Brendan breathes.

I chuckle, swallowing my current mouthful and licking the tasty blood off my claws. We lock eyes, a nervous swallow descending slowly down his throat, betraying a delicious fear that makes me want to pounce on him, sink my teeth into him, and shake him around like a toy until he goes limp. But that would be insane, and also probably murder, so I do not do those things. The urge isn't a strong one, just a passing thought that makes me warm and happy to consider. Maybe I can just tackle him without the biting? No, wait, he doesn't like to be touched. What am I even thinking, *I* don't like to be touched! At least, normally I don't, but I've been kind of...

weirdly touchy recently. Maybe I just get touchy when I'm feeling relaxed.

...Oh, woah. That's what this is. I'm feeling *relaxed.*

"Thank you," I tell Brendan emphatically. "I really needed this."

"You really needed to make a bloody mess of my kitchen," he grumbles, glancing away from me.

"Oh, pishhh, come on Brendan!" I say, blowing a raspberry at him. "Did you forget that I'm a super cool magical mage with the best spell of all time!? Behold! Spell-I-Haven't-Na... actually no I'm not going to name it even as a joke, she might take it seriously."

"Um. Maybe you shouldn't—"

I ignore him and snap my bloody fingers (entirely for dramatic effect) and activate the cleaning spell at the same time. If there's anything dangerous about this spell, it's too late to warn me now; I've been subtly using it all over the dang place. Here, though, I have no need to be subtle. The blood flies off my body and dances into the sink in beautiful red streams. The remains of the packaging pick up off the floor and plunk themselves into the trash. I stand up and take a quick sweep around the rest of the kitchen while I'm at it, collecting dirt and hair and food and other detritus, leaving the entire place looking squeaky clean. While there's absolutely a visceral satisfaction involved in ripping stuff apart, putting it all back together like this might be even more intoxicating. It's clean! It's all clean! Hehehehehehe!

"...Woah," Brendan breathes, finally getting to see the full power of my spell in action. It doesn't have very much range or power, but I can cast it repeatedly so as long as I get close enough to my target I can get it clean pretty trivially.

"Ha! Pretty awesome, right?" I preen, putting my hands on my hips and puffing out my chest triumphantly. "Who's only one-sixth of prestidigitation now?"

"I concede, you're clearly making me eat my words," Brendan rightfully reneges. "That spell is a lot more impressive than I thought it would be. It seems... ripe for exploitation, actually."

"I *know*, but I still can't find anything broken with it!" I whine. "The target limits are pretty strict and the weight limit is super low. I can't figure out anything more useful than cleaning. Still, though! I'm in love with this spell."

"I can only imagine," Brendan nods, letting out a big huff of air. "That.... was *magic*. The way everything just moved on its own, it just... I don't know. Somehow, that seems more real than the changes to your body. The world has magic. Fiction is fact. And I'm a *part* of it, even adjacently."

I drum my toes on the floor, happily soaking in the goofy smile that's barely touching the corners of Brendan's lips. This is what he's always dreamed about, right in front of him. It's exciting, but I bet on some level it's tearing him up a little that he's not the one with the powers. ...Although, maybe that's not quite the case. Magic is real, after all, and at least in the other world *everyone* has it. Maybe Brendan does too.

"Hey Brendan," I say conversationally. "You know that spell I was telling you I learned last night?"

"The Aura Sight spell, the one your friend justifiably got super mad at you for ignoring all safety protocols before using," Brendan summarizes.

"Yeah, that one," I say. "I haven't used it on Earth yet because I can't activate it without invoking the goddess to speak the words for me, and that's somewhat conspicuous."

"Yeah, reasonable," Brendan nods.

"But it's just you, me, and Fartbuns here," I say, motioning at the dog who is disappointedly trying to find more delicious floor flavor after I made all of it magically disappear. "Less risk of exposure than the whole car incident, and... well, I could maybe figure out your magical aptitude."

I can tell he was about to firmly insist on the stupidity of my idea until that last sentence there, but I know magic is his weakness. He hesitates.

"Do I even *have* a magical aptitude?" he asks.

"I have no idea!" I answer cheerfully. "That's what we'd be figuring out, I guess."

"Is it *safe?*" he presses.

"Um, I mean, we'd be figuring that out too," I admit. "But as long as I do things the same way as before and don't try to shove too much power into the spell, I don't think there's any chance of miscasting. We already know I can cast spells here, and there's no reason Aura Sight would be an exception."

"There are *lots* of reasons it could be an exception," Brendan groans. "It's learned rather than innate. It's in a different world. It's being cast without the goddess' attention and permission already on you. We have no idea how many of these things could be significant variables, Hannah. Not to mention that summoning a goddess from another universe here could *itself* have dangerous consequences we don't know about."

"So what do we do, then?" I ask. "Just sit on the spell and never use it?"

"You could always come clean to the people that *you yourself* claim to be friends, explain to them about the alternate world stuff, and get their significantly more educated opinions," Brendan grumbles.

I hesitate.

"They're my friends," I say, just to have said it out loud.

"Yeah," Brendan nods.

"They are. I like them. I just... I'm not sure I trust them with that. I'm not friends with them the same way I'm friends with *you,* Brendan. I've only known them for a couple weeks. And I kind of want to tell Kagiso, but... I can't tell her *anything* without Sindri hearing it. Which is... I dunno. It's never really all that much of a problem in the moment, I don't really *need* privacy from him, but it's still creepy when you think about it in the abstract."

"Waiting to learn the language so you can communicate privately is, I'll admit, a decent reason to wait," Brendan sighs.

"Ha!" I cheer triumphantly.

"...But isn't Sindri the person most likely to have the knowledge you need to answer these questions in the first place?" Brendan continues. "Based on what you've told me, his culture seems to be pretty advanced for a fantasy world, scientifically speaking. Magitech was implied, he knows about stuff like entropy and enthalpy. Multiverse theory probably isn't much of a stretch for his knowledge base."

I hesitate, thinking on that.

"I prefer to be seen as a denizen of that world, for now," I tell him. "I don't know what will happen if I tell him, and it's not something I can undo. I want to learn a bit more about the culture and mythology of the world before I do anything that might be stupid. Maybe after we get to the city? Or I can ask them about those things and prepare, I guess."

"Alright, that's a sensible enough plan," Brendan nods. "And speaking of plans, now that you're done going feral we should head back down to the basement. I have some stuff to show you."

"What if I'm not done going feral?" I ask, moving to follow him anyway. "It seems to be an ongoing process, really."

He gives me a sideways glance before heading down the stairs.

"Please don't joke about my friend losing her sense of self," he grumbles.

"...Okay, sorry," I tell him. "If it makes you feel any better, I don't feel like I am. Things are a bit weird and different, but I still feel like *me,* even when I'm... I dunno. Doing things I wouldn't otherwise do?"

"Yeah," Brendan nods. "It does make me feel better. You seem happy, actually. I'm jealous."

"Having positive emotions is a strange and novel experience, but I do recommend it," I agree, plopping back down onto the basement couch. Fartbuns, having long since got over the prior spook with my hissing, joins me immediately, flopping onto my lap and crushing me under his massive floof. I give him a hug, which he seems to appreciate. Brendan, meanwhile, goes to get his whiteboard. And a corkboard. And a bunch of books. And a laptop.

"Um, what is all this stuff?" I ask hesitantly.

"Research," Brendan grunts. "On world trees, mostly."

"World trees?" I ask, reaching forward and barely managing to grab one of the books before the weight of a giant goofy puppy forces me back to the couch. Sure enough, it seems to be a collection of norse myths. A post-it note marks pages with references to Yggdrasil.

"The Norse world tree is the most well-known," Brendan says, returning with his last stack of books. "But the thing about mythologies is that there are a lot of them, and there's no reason to assume the most popular interpretation of a myth is the most accurate one. So I've pretty much collected every resource I can find to try and compare it with your current situation. I have to admit, though, the Norse interpretation is looking like one of the more solid ones."

"Oh? Why's that?" I ask. "I don't actually know much about other world tree myths. Heck, I don't know much about real Norse mythology, only the modern interpretations."

"Well, that's partially because there's less of it than you might think. Norse mythology was mainly an oral tradition, and the resources we use today were composed by like, Icelandic scholars or something. There's more to it than that, but the point is, in terms of actual text I could get a hold of, there isn't actually much said about Yggdrasil. But that's okay, because again, there's no reason to think that the original text is more likely to be accurate than the modern interpretations."

"Wait, there isn't?" I ask. "Why not?"

"Why would it?" Brendan asks. "Why would any of these stories be more likely to be divinely inspired or written by actual witnesses just because they're *old?* Statistically speaking, since there are so many more people now, the odds of someone having a legitimate source rather than making up stories out of their ass is higher now."

I blink at him, reach out to a paperback with a big number on the spine, and read the title. It says '*High School DxD.*'

"This is a harem manga," I point out simply.

"It's… it's explicitly referenced on the wikipedia page for Níðhöggr," Brendan answers defensively.

"Pony poop," I challenge, whipping out my phone to call his bluff. One quick google search later, I scroll down and… well dang, okay, there it is. Huh.

"Was Wikipedia a mistake?" I ask idly.

"No, Wikipedia is one of the single greatest achievements of mankind, period," Brendan answers immediately. "But I admit that, upon actually reading it, I seriously doubt that *High School DxD* holds the answers to any burning questions we could possibly come up with. But the possibility existed, so I *looked for it.* What exactly do you think I've been doing with all my free time lately?"

"Right, okay," I say, giving my friend a soft smile. "Thank you, Brendan. It means a lot to me. What stuff in this pile of possibility *has* stood out to you, then?"

"Most world trees, or at least the *classic* world trees, are more like trees *of* worlds than trees that *are* worlds," Brendan explains. "They're often symbolic, with the whole underworld-Earth-heaven thing being represented or outright connected via the roots, trunk, and branches. We're looking for non-symbolic trees, literal actual megaflora which aren't just important for being magic, they're important because they *connect multiple realities,* and Yiggdrasil

355

fits the bill. It's far from the only one, but there are *really* limited resources on, say, Samoyed mythology."

"I don't even know what that is," I admit.

"Exactly. I'm going to keep looking for stuff, because there's a *lot* of it, but we're starting with Yggdrasil. The whole thing with how it connects multiple worlds together is an obvious reason we care about it, but also notable is the fact that things *live* on Yggdrasil. Not a lot of things are mentioned, of course; hell, one of the most notable parts of the myth is just called 'the unnamed eagle,' but there are some points of importance. Notably, the reason I subjected myself to trashy self-insert wish-fulfillment junk fiction: Níðhǫggr, the serpent that eats the tree."

"...I don't see how that's relevant," I grumble.

"Hannah, by your own reckoning, you spent *seventeen years* eating a world tree."

...Oh.

"Th-that doesn't make me Nidhogg!" I protest. "Lots of things eat the world tree! There are literally creatures bred for the purpose!"

"I know, I know, the hole-worms," Brendan placates. "I don't actually think you're the herald of Ragnarök, Hannah, there are too many inconsistencies. You not being a serpent is sort of a notable one, as is the fact that you don't hang out in the underworld or get nasty rumors spread about you via a lying squirrel. Níðhǫggr is also supposed to eat the roots, while you appeared on some random branch. It's flimsy at best. Though, again, accuracy to the original text doesn't necessarily mean actual accuracy. Maybe Norse mythology *was* describing you, but it was filtered through an unreliable narrator and the original myths are what's wrong. All things considered, though, I believe the most likely situation is that the world you go to when you sleep isn't any of the world trees discussed in mythology. Or at the very least, if there are kernels of truth in the mythologies we know about, they're mixed too deeply with falsehoods that it's impossible to tell."

"...Which puts more evidence in the pile for 'someone out there is suppressing magical knowledge,'" I conclude.

"Either that or you're the only person on the entire planet with access to this alternate universe that you never even intentionally sought out, yeah," Brendan confirms. "I love you, Hannah, but I don't think you're *that* special."

That gets a chuckle out of me.

"So. Your main conclusion so far is that we still know nothing?"

"Yep," Brendan nods. "The most boring and most likely conclusion of all research."

"I guess we'd better get cracking at the rest of these books, then?" I suggest, since I know he didn't stack these all up just to show off. Even if he did, Brendan has been working so hard for me and I need to help. Taking care of myself is, technically, more my job than his. Even if he's obviously way better at it than I am.

As the hours pass, we do get some research done. We also ramble about games, talk about what dead skin tastes like, play with Fartbuns, order pizza and chicken wings, and generally just *hang out* until well after the sun goes down and it's time for me to get home or risk a scolding from my parents. Regretfully, we eventually part ways and I head home, my nascent limbs wiggling with joy underneath my skin. Today was a good day. A *great* day, even. I'd forgotten what those feel like. When I get in bed and pass out, there's finally some real optimism behind it.

Immediately, of course, I wake up. Kagiso is shaking me conscious for last watch, which unfortunately means I'm not waking up cuddling next to her. Gosh, that's still such a weird thought. More evidence that I'm getting over my touch aversion with startling speed. I wonder why that is.

I stretch my groggy body and regretfully crawl out from deep within the bedroll. I'm not really comfortable sleeping as a hyperspider unless I'm fully encompassed, though being in a human-sized sleeping bag is of course more than enough to accomplish that requirement. Being one foot tall has its perks, and comfiness is a big one. Being constantly surrounded by terrifying giants tends to put a damper on the comfort, I'll admit, but I've mostly gotten over it.

"Fire burn?" Kagiso asks, her raspy voice quiet in the dead of night. She's asking if I want her to refresh the campfire that's been burning all night. It's one of the many tasks I can't do on my own, but it also doesn't much matter to me if the fire burns or not. I don't need it to stay warm thanks to my body's resistance to external heat sources, and I don't need it to keep watch thanks to my spatial sense. Still though, I like being able to see things with my normal eyes, and I can trust my friends with fire pits enough to let the thing burn all night without too much worry.

I scratch the dentron words for 'yes' and 'please' in the dirt, and Kagiso makes a happy rumbling noise before exiting the tent to put more wood on the fire. Sindri, Kagiso, and I are still handling all of the watches ourselves, letting Teboho sleep through the night undisturbed. The poor guy is still severely injured after getting half his skin burned off by acid, because why wouldn't he be. Though with how consistently upbeat he seems to be in spite of that, it's sometimes hard to tell.

"Done," Kagiso rumbles as I scuttle over next to her. "Night be peaceful, Hana."

I hug her fuzzy leg with two of my own and she makes a happy noise, reaching down to pat me before exhaustedly staggering into her tent and getting in bed. The night passes slowly after that, my eyes hypnotized by the waves of smoke drifting up from the damp logs. Our choice of firewood was less than ideal tonight, but I'm at least happy that I can help everyone by being the one to cut it all into the right sizes. Whenever I find a chore I can take care of for people, I try to put my all into it. I don't like being such a dead weight.

Night watches are another good way to help out my friends. Now that I have eyes, I don't even need the candle clock to do the last shift of the day; my watch ends when the sun comes up, or I guess whenever it gets into a position in which things won't be dark. I'm still not entirely clear on how the sun actually works. If it's just moving in a circular orbit, wouldn't most of the branches never actually get blocked off from seeing it? You'd only get true night if the sun was completely blocked by the trunk, right? Because when the sun is merely below our branch we get the pretty green-sky evenings. I guess if there are enough other branches in the way, they could block stuff. Maybe that's it; just sheer mass of branches between us and the sun causes nighttime. ...But no, wait, that still wouldn't work for every branch, unless the sun had a really irregular orbit. Which I guess it might? Gah, this is so confusing! I should just ask for more—

A snapping sound breaks me from my thoughts. That's very much the sound of something alive, stepping on something as it moves through the forest. I'm already looking in the direction it comes from, but I can't see anything, neither with my eyes nor my spatial sense. Just to be safe, I slip into a barren zone, the light from the fire completely winking out of my perception. With or without the fire, my eyes can't see any farther than my other senses in the dark of night anyway.

Though now that I'm on edge, I'm quickly coming to realize how incredibly short those senses travel. Fifty feet is like, the length of a semi trailer, give or take. Not even the trailer and the truck, just the trailer. That distance, in every direction, is my entire world. It's enough to encompass the camp, but not much beyond it.

Which means I won't know if anything is coming our way until it's right on top of us.

I guess that's not much better than anyone else being on watch, but that thought makes my situation no less nerve-wracking. Still within the barren zone, I wander closer to the direction I heard the noise, hoping to pick something up on the edge of my senses. If an animal wanders into the camp proper, I'm not actually sure what to do about it. The fire does a decent job at keeping things away, but it might *attract* certain animals with Heat affinities, depending on how their magic manifests. I can kill most things in the forest, I suppose, but I'd rather not have to. I continue approaching until eventually I sense some moving creatures in my range. They're... wait. They're not creatures at all. They're dentron.

They're *people*, and they're armed.

Terror flooding me, I reverse direction and scuttle quickly into Sindri's tent, reappearing in normal space once inside it and poking him awake. More and more people start entering the edges of my sensory radius, coming from multiple different directions. At least six of them, all men, all armed, surrounding us from all sides. What do they want!? They don't have cultist necklaces or anything, so why are they here!?

Sindri wakes up the moment I place a clawed leg on his face, his hand twitching towards the knife under his pillow for a second before he registers it's me. Using the contact, he opens our mental connection in silence.

*Trouble?* he asks. I have never been more thankful about his to-the-point attitude than at this moment.

*Six dentron, armed,* I report. *We're surrounded.*

*Fuck. Bandits, probably,* Sindri grumbles. *They saw the campfire smoke. Odd to have dentron bandits, though.*

I want to ask why that's odd, but the smarter part of my brain reminds me that now really isn't the time. Bandits, though? Really? I take a closer look at the people slowly and stealthily approaching us, dressed in dirty clothes and armed with axes, bows, and other cheap equipment designed more for hunting and forestry than combat. The hard determination in their expressions shows only a hint of the stress they must be feeling, approaching a camp of people they don't know with intent to kill. That, more than anything, makes me believe they've killed people before.

*What do we do?* I ask.

*I'll wake everyone and attempt diplomacy,* Sindri grunts. *When it inevitably doesn't work, I want you already in position to kill as many as you think you can.*

Some part of me expected an answer like that. These people wouldn't be sneaking towards our camp in the middle of the night with weapons out if they were intending charity. Intellectually, I know that. This world is harsh. It's mostly lawless. People fight each other and die. I know that. I've *experienced* that. But I still don't want to kill people. The thought mortifies me, and unfortunately Sindri seems to pick up on it, or at least anticipate it.

*Hannah, I'm sorry,* he says. *But there's six of them and Teboho is injured. I need you to do this. We all need you.*

*I... okay,* I answer numbly, trying to decide which of the bandits seems most likely to be in charge, or at least particularly dangerous. The one with the newest-looking axe is grouped a bit closer with a comrade than the others, who are now getting close to the last few trees between them and our camp. That'll be my target then. My kill. My little act of greater-good.

Ice flooding my veins, I step silently into the nearby barren zone, approaching my target as closely as I can without stepping out. I do, unfortunately, have to step out; I'm not lucky enough to have a straight shot to my target and even if I did he's moving around. Instead, I exit at the base of a tree and scuttle quietly up the trunk, my tiny body quiet even in the hush of night. Sindri is awake and quickly gathering weapons and what armor he can put on, mental jabs to Kagiso and Teboho waking both of them up. When he exits his tent and calls out to the people approaching us, they freeze in place, letting me more easily find a branch directly above their heads. Sindri and the bandits exchange a few words, but I'm too terrified to try and translate either side of it. I'm too busy staring at the bandit's heart. Watching it beat. Tracing the veins and arteries that snake out from it in every direction, noting which ones seem most likely to be a quick kill if severed. The blood pulses, streaming quicker and quicker throughout the body. It annoys me how his heartbeat doesn't sync up with mine, like when I'm watching the blinker of a car at the stoplight in front of me flash just the *slightest bit* out of time. Both heartbeats are starting to go faster, though.

I imagine the kill, over and over, in this endless, torturous minute before I take a person's life. What will the fall be like, where will I aim, what are my backup plans if he moves? Over and over, the same few answers pop into my head, and yet I just turn around and ask myself the same questions again. Will he even feel it, when my tear in space splits his body apart? Will I? I can't just kill one man and be done with it, either. I'll have other targets to go for as well. It's a good thing that I can't breathe manually, or else I'd certainly be hyperventilating right now. I feel like that'd probably be loud enough to give away my position.

I will probably die if that man ever looks up.

The thought flits by, and selfishly it fills me with even more terror than the prospect of murder. I feel disgusted by that, but it's hardly a surprise, is it? That's why I'm here, plotting a man's death. Because I'd rather kill him than die. I wonder why this man would rather kill us than whatever happens if he doesn't. Is he starving? He doesn't need us to die for us to give him food, I'd bet. Is this just the sort of man he is? A lover of violence and death? A raider? A villain? Or is he more complex than that? Could I understand him if we could speak to each other? Could we someday be friends?

He moves. I watch muscles start to pull all around his body. I see him inhale deeper than ever before in his conversation with Sindri, preparing to shout. His heartbeat goes faster, faster, faster. Maybe now it will match my own.

*Do it, Hannah!* Sindri orders me, and I immediately drop, power flowing through my legs. With a flick of a half-dozen different legs, I sheer into flesh and puncture through veins, pools of blood blooming all over the bandit's body. I miss most of my strikes, but I doubt it matters: the most damage of all was dealt by the one leg that didn't move, that I simply held straight as I fell, digging a deep gash through the back of the man's skull, down his neck, back, pelvis and tail. It's by no means a clean cut, weaving in and out of the spine in multiple places, but in the second it takes me to hit the ground, it's more than enough to cripple him, assuming he isn't already dead. I don't wait to find out before slashing his calves and leaping to his head when he falls. I plunge a foot through his skull like a boot through fresh snow. He might have been dead before. He's definitely dead now.

With my omnidirectional senses, I can see the whole fight play out, watching myself take part in the combat as if I'm not even the one doing it. It's like a third-person action game, one where I can see the whole battle at once and make snap tactical judgements. Not that I do, I'm just vaguely aware that I *could* if I wasn't a terrified mess, scrambling in horror for the nearest barren zone to escape into before the bandit nearest my victim notices me. I can only assume I fail, since the ground beneath me twists into a terrifying claw of dirt and stone, trying to clamp around me and smash me like the bug I am. I barely manage to step away before it closes around me, breaking line of sight by retreating into a higher dimension. The bandit starts looking for me, so I just make distance between the two of us, instead targeting one of the ones that hasn't even seen me yet. Unfortunately for them, they're close enough to the exit of a barren zone that I can pop out right behind them, removing their ability to stand with a quick swipe and their ability to live with another before retreating back to safety.

The battle continues. An arrow takes a bandit in the throat. The battle continues. Sindri duels the one with earth-hands, eventually managing to bury his short sword in the mage's belly despite the aggressive terrain. I don't know if I end up killing a third bandit or not. I stop paying much attention at some point.

But when the battle is over, I know that dentron meat is sweet.

# 20

# CLICHÉ

Bone marrow is one of the most delicious things I've ever tasted.

The smooth, buttery texture, creamy and savory and sweet, will live in my memories forever. Not because I've never had it before; I've crunched on quite a few bones since being human became a past-tense situation, but these are special. These are a lot sweeter than any other bones I've tasted. They're honestly the best I've ever had the pleasure to eat.

They come from a person.

I bite down again anyway. Sweet. They're so *sweet!* Though they're technically omnivores, dentron mainly seem to eat fruit and sap more than anything else, only having occasional, small portions of the meat that Sindri and I subsist almost exclusively off of. I guess all that concentrated sugar leaks its way into the muscle and fat somehow, marinating the meat while it's still alive. Or something like that, anyway. I don't know why different animals taste differently. Different meats. Different people. I'm eating a person. I'm eating a person and I *don't want to stop.*

Part of me is desperately trying to hyperventilate, but of course I can't do that because I don't have lungs. Instead, the only movements of my body are the greedy dips into torn and bleeding flesh, my knees bending so I can smash the underside of my circular form into skin or wound or protruding limb and close my teeth around a chunk, ripping it off and swallowing with a precise speed that doesn't slow, doesn't have any desire to savor even in the face of such a heavenly meal. If anything, thinking about the flavor only makes me want to eat faster. To get this over with. To finish this corpse and finally have nothing left that was once a person to engorge myself on.

I'm very small, though, and dentron are very large. The drying blood on my body is quickly replaced with fresh, oozing globules of red. I'm only vaguely aware of a desire to clean myself. My actions and my thoughts are... disconnected. They have been since the fight started. With my spatial sense, I'm watching myself devour these bodies—bodies that I killed, *people* that I killed—from a somewhat detached perspective. Sure, I'm still moving my legs, biting with my teeth, feeling the meat of my kills slide up my esophagus, watching it shrink as it travels up into my body before eventually disappearing... but there's a distance to it that there normally isn't. I guess I'm disassociating. That's a stress response. A pretty major one, I think. Like panic attacks. I also have panic attacks. I might currently be having a panic attack. Why am I still eating? Can't someone stop me? Shouldn't they?

Another bone breaks in my jaws, and I suck out more of the creamy nectar within. I wonder where it all goes. I don't seem to have a stomach, and I don't defecate. Just another thing that makes me a freak, I guess. Adrenaline, or whatever my alien equivalent of it is, thrums through each and every muscle in my body, urging my fight-or-flight instinct to continue fighting, continue *feeding*, as if my life depends on it. Kagiso and Sindri both approach me, and I hiss furiously at them, overcome with anger and possessiveness and a burning need for them to leave me alone and let me eat. I don't want them to leave me alone. Please, don't go. Help me.

They don't hear my silent pleas, and they leave me be. My new eyes, unfortunately, cannot cry. Perhaps they would have stayed if I was capable of showing any expression, any sort of hint that my conscious and subconscious minds are at war and I can't do this alone, I *can't* let myself keep digging into the blood and death and delicious, delicious taste of my mistakes. Yet they have no way to know, so here I remain. I am full of horror, full of joy, and full of a person's flesh.

Except I'm not really full at all.

No matter how much I eat, I'm not satisfied. I do not feel *hungry* anymore, far from it. I have been eating plenty and I know that, to sustain myself, I do not need to eat any more. But I *can,* so I do, because I love it as much as I hate it. *God,* I love it as much as I hate it. Why? Why is it so *good?* What about this situation makes this meal so special? Do I just like eating people? Do I just like *killing* people? Or do I want to eat it all because it's something that I, personally, killed?

...I mean some*one.* But still, there might be something to that thought. This man—oh god, he was a living, breathing person with hopes and dreams and a life and I took it all away—is the biggest thing I've killed on my own, barring of course the *other* people I killed all on my own. All three of them. I killed three people this fight, plus the one cultist. I've killed four people. Four kills, incidentally, is just enough to count as mass murder. Anyway, I like to eat the things I kill. I swallow the smaller things whole, but when I hunt bigger things I act in a similar way to how I'm acting now, just... without the guilt. Because hunting animals for food is okay, but killing people for food is *absolutely not, why am I still doing this, stop please stop!*

I manage, for a moment, to pause. To take a bit more stock of my situation. I'm safe, the enemies are dead. My kill, and my right to it, are being respected. There's plenty more food, and plenty more need for it. My hunger goes beyond just self-sustenance, it is a burning desire for fuel, materials, and strength. These people before me are already dead. They attacked us, we didn't attack them. Arguably, their deaths are justified, but even if they aren't... does it do them any good for me to leave their bodies alone? To ignore my needs for the sake of a morality that, logically speaking, is not something that should apply to me? The culture of this world, of the *very people I just killed,* believes getting eaten to be an acceptable equivalent to burial. The only thing to fear beyond that is my personal health, and my biology is so vastly different from that of my prey the idea of getting diseases from them seems rather silly. I know, in my chitin, that I am built for this. For the consumption of flesh. I want it. I need it. I take another bite, not feeling the slightest bit better about the act but no longer having the will to deny it.

I really like maraschino cherries. Or... at least I did, back when I was human. I probably don't anymore. But my *point* is, whenever we'd go out and get milkshakes or mocktails or what-have-you, I'd always beg the rest of my family for their cherries because those things are *delicious.* One time, my mother did an at-home mocktail party as one of our little 'family events' that we're required to go to since my brother and I wouldn't otherwise, and she bought a jar of maraschino cherries for it. Of course, a jar of maraschino cherries has vastly more of the little red jewels of sugar than one can reasonably consume in a single four-person party with one's mom, so the jar just kind of sat there in the fridge after that particular event. One day, I decided to eat one. This was, in my young mind, a dastardly act of theft. The consumption of unauthorized sweets was highly illegal in my household, at least back when I was little. I swore I'd only eat one, though, and no one would ever know.

Minutes later, I'd eaten a second. A day later, the jar was empty. And now, years later, I drench my throat in red syrup once again, savory and sharp. My self-control, it seems, has not improved one whit since then. Each bite, I find myself demanding 'this must be the last one,' and knowing in my heart that it won't be. The dread just keeps stacking as the mouthfuls keep coming, with no end in sight. Do I have weird monster instincts urging me to eat this man? Yes. I obviously do. But is it still me, taking each and every bite? Absolutely.

They say the first step is admitting you have a problem. As always, I am *incredible* at the first step, and absolutely nothing else. So I keep devouring this trauma, knowing that it will sit inside me forever and never digest.

When the last of this man's body finally gets pushed up my throat (except the area around his bum, since not even weird monster instincts can convince me to eat poop) I immediately start looking for one of the other two people I killed today (other two people I killed today *other two people I killed today)* which of course is an easy thing to do with my spatial sense. I take a shortcut through a nearby barren zone, which also has the unexpectedly delightful effect of removing the many sticky layers of blood all over my body. The sudden *cleanness* smacks into my conscious mind like a shovel, the joy of getting into a shower after being covered in sweat shaking me just enough to give me something to hold onto, something to focus on beyond the horrid addiction to blood and muscle and marrow. Stop. Wait. I really, honestly, don't have to do this. I want to, I really, *really* want to, but... but I...

I'm a seventeen year old high school student that has killed *four people.* Fuck! I just... I did that. I did all of that. Worse, I'm apparently *good* at it. Six people attacked us. Sindri killed one, Kagiso killed two, and *I killed three, I killed them, they're dead and it's my fault.* I dug my claws into their bodies, I made their hearts stop beating, I cut them open and let their life pour onto the forest floor. It was horrible. It was easy. A quick slash to the legs hamstrung them, allowing access to their vital organs at ground level. With enough barren zones around I can strike silently from virtually anywhere, and I took advantage of that, cutting from behind the moment my target tried to focus on anyone else. My *target.* That's all they were. I collapse to the cool ground, darkness all around me as my body tries and fails to figure out how to heave out stomach acid that does not exist. I can't cry, I can't vomit, I can't even scream. My whole body shakes, horrified and alone, invisible in the dimension only I can access. I can't do anything *more* than shake. I'm so fucking inhuman I can't even emote my despair.

...No. There's one thing. It's not something a human would do, but I'm a monster and it's all I've ever been. Just a wretched fucking monster. I bring my legs together, all ten of them touching a partner, and rub a mournful, wailing hiss out into the infinite darkness of the higher dimensions. A cry and a scream all in one.

Why? Why did I have to do this? Why am I like this? Why, goddess? If you made me, why did you make me so horrible and wrong?

From the way I see my friends stiffen with my spatial sense, the sound I'm making apparently reaches them, on some level. I take some satisfaction in that, in knowing that my eldritch equivalent of sobbing can reach through the barrier between my realm and theirs. But it's a tiny and meaningless satisfaction, utterly incomparable to the weight of the lives I've just taken. So I screech my horrid sounds well into the morning, when the sun finally rises and the time my watch *should* have ended finally comes to pass. I'm exhausted, I realize, and it doesn't take much time after that for me to finally stop screaming and fall asleep.

Immediately, I wake up. My eyes and cheeks are wet, my nose runs with a fountain snot. The knowledge that I have apparently been crying in my sleep is vaguely comforting, in a horrible, weighty sort of way that replaces pain with dread rather than actually making me feel *better.* I can cry now, I can vomit, I can scream, but I absolutely shouldn't do any of those things because unlike my friends in the other world, my family will not understand and the absolute last thing I want is to be comforted by them. Not when it will just lead to more questions, more things I have to deal with that I absolutely, positively cannot deal with right now. So I have to hold it in. I have to pretend everything is fine. I have to minimize the amount of questions and attention I get because I can't *afford* that sort of thing right now, I don't have the mental bandwidth for it.

Small mercies, at least: it's strangely easy to get out of bed today, my limbs feeling more normal and natural than usual. I inhale a shaky breath, trying to force myself calmer and halfway succeeding. I need to clean my face. I almost cast the spell for it, but magic doesn't feel very fun all of a sudden. I use a tissue instead. It doesn't do a very good job, but whatever. I'm about to shower anyway.

Inhale, exhale. Steady breaths. Barely feeling functional, I stagger into the bathroom and strip, using the mirror to help me check my body for new changes. The claws on my hands are starting to creep up my fingers, gaining territory over my first set of knuckles. The wiry black flesh within is now visible in the joint, and my hands consequently feel a lot stronger than they used to. My right leg has a bit more dead skin (skin, I ate so much skin. It tastes far better when it's still juicy with blood.) and my left foot does as well, signaling that it's starting to change beyond the claws. Wiggling my extra growing limbs, I find them still firmly trapped inside my torso but noticeably larger, long enough to reach up from where they anchor above my hips and touch the bottom rung of my ribcage. Doing so isn't particularly comfortable, but it sure is a thing I can do now.

None of these changes are big, and none of these changes are new, but I can't help but note that there are a lot more changes than I had when I woke up yesterday, or the day before. Is this what excess food does? Or is it just a coincidence? Thinking about it nearly makes me vomit, so I ignore the thought and get into the shower, cutting off the hanging flaps of dead skin so they don't fall off on their own at inopportune times. Despite the revulsion churning throughout my entire body, I still eat them, because I am a messed-up, horrific *thing* with absolutely no self-control. Would it be stupid for me to go to school today? Will I lose control? Wait. No. There is no school today. It's Saturday. I have my maybe-date today.

Holy gonzoli, I have my *maybe-date* today. For some reason, that's impossibly funny to me. A laugh bubbles up in my chest and I lean into it, letting it out full-force. I double over with mirth, hot water running down my naked body as the horrible, horrible irony washes over me. The date I've been convincing myself is okay to go on because I might be too monstrous to have one later is *today.*

Literally one day too late.

Oh, sure, I can probably still *pass* as human as long as I doll myself up how I usually do. If I'm doing really, really well at suppressing my emotions I can probably even pass as a human who isn't having a complete mental breakdown. Pretending everything is fine has always been one of my best and most practiced skills! But I am still mid-panic about the fight to the death I just had and the people I just killed during it and *boy howdy that does not seem like it'll be conducive to romance!* I should not be going to the mall, I should be going to a therapist.

...Except there's absolutely no way I'm ever going to a therapist again, so screw it. I guess I'll go to the mall, if for no other reason than to not have to suffer the utter mortal terror of texting Autumn to cancel. And *yes,* I am saying that as someone *literally currently getting over a bout of immediate mortal terror.* And yes, I know that's stupid.

Whatever. What's the worst that could happen, she thought to herself with the most agonizingly massive girth of irony conceivable to exist within this pathetic fragment of the presumably infinite multiverse. I will go to the mall, not because it is a good idea, but because it's on my schedule for the day, and it's a good enough reason as any to maybe, hopefully, think about something other than the actual people with rich inner worlds as complex as my own which I just snuffed out of existence and then devoured like cattle. I guess.

Shower, over. Clothes, on. Makeup, perfect. Outfit, cute. Other than the fact that my current heart rate is more comprehensibly measurable in bps than bpm, everything seems to be going swimmingly. I head downstairs and exit the front door without talking to anyone or eating any breakfast, because *for some reason* I do not feel like doing either of those things.

Autumn and I traded addresses, figured out that we're both in walking distance of the mall, and decided to walk there, presumably because we're stupid and forgot that we would be buying things. Her house is closer than mine, so I'll be walking there to meet her. Consequently, I'll get to see what her house looks like, which is something that has always felt a bit weird to me. I wonder if other people feel weird when they see someone's house for the first time. It's not really the kind of thing I've ever thought to ask someone else, but *dang* does it always make me feel weird. As I walk towards where my phone says the address is, however, I start feeling significantly weirder.

It starts with the lawns. I mean, it probably *doesn't* start with the lawns, but they're what I notice first. Overgrown gardens, patches of brown, walkways blocked by untrimmed foliage. Cars are a bit older, a bit rustier, a bit more often parked on the street. The houses have flaking paint, the windows are dirty, and the fences damaged. Disrepair escalates. Poverty becomes obvious. I am now in what my parents refer to as 'the bad part of town,' and my coddled, privileged white girl brain immediately starts to worry about that.

This begins the familiar thought process I've lovingly dubbed the "Am-I-Racist Train." I am uncomfortable in this part of town. I live in Tennessee, and therefore 'this part of town' has a lot of people that are not white. While this is a true demographic fact regardless of whether or not any given person on Earth is racist, acknowledging it certainly *feels* racist, because it's making the claim that I'm uncomfortable in an area that is, to a significant degree, not full of people of European descent. But *I'm* not even fully European in descent (though I do kind of look like I am) so does that count? I certainly don't feel like I'd be *more* comfortable if this neighborhood was all extra-pale neo-confederates, but... no, that doesn't work, I can't equate the people here with the lowest common denominator, that's obviously racist. ...And actually, while it's true that we have these 'demographic facts' as my brain just somewhat concerningly put it, I don't actually know what the demographics of this specific neighborhood is, I just made an assumption, and *aw dang it* that is *definitely* racist. Agh, no, I didn't mean to! I'm just scared because the crime rate is higher in places like this! Isn't that a good reason? *No wait crap how do I stop!?* Look Hannah, maybe this place *looks* scary, but it could just as easily be full of neo-nazis instead of gangs or whatever.

...Which I am assuming as the logical alternative because it looks poor. Why is 'this neighborhood has bad people' my assumption at all? Great, now I'm racist *and* classist. Why would I even think about neo-nazis in this situation, all *sorts* of rich and powerful people are neo-nazis! *Oh great, now I'm worried about that instead!!!* And the best part of all is that absolutely none of these thoughts are making me more comfortable to be walking around alone in this WONDERFUL NEIGHBORHOOD THAT I'M SURE IS FULL OF GREAT PEOPLE DOING THEIR BEST. Oh good, there are cop cars in front of that house over there! I am sure that the cops are being bastards, as cops are purported to be, even though I've never had a cop do anything other than be very nice to me and help me out because I am a petite white woman that does not break laws! Other than homicide! But that's pretty recent and no cops have talked to me about that, I only talk to cops when, say, a man flashes me when I'm in the middle of taking his order at work (which is a real thing that happened that I'm honestly more confused about than traumatized over) and the police were very nice to me when I called them about that! So basically all the bad stuff feels wrong, even though lots of extremely reputable sources insist it is right, which *should* be more than enough to override my stupid personal biases from my stupid Karen-mom upbringing but it *isn't* and I *hate it* and I'm a *bad person* and aaaaaaaaaaagh!

I've almost managed to work myself into another panic attack when my phone's GPS loudly informs me I've arrived at Autumn's place, but at least this panic attack is about a different thing than the one I was having this morning. I like how there are so many interesting and unique ways for me to be a bad person.

I walk up to the front door (cracked walkway, weeds in the garden, porch looks unstable) and ring the doorbell (doesn't work, have to knock). I manage to get the attention of someone inside, hear the requisite shuffling, and do my best not to think about the ridiculous and purely paranoid possibility of the person on the other side of the door pointing a gun at me when they open it. I don't even know why my brain is considering that possibility, I'm just so outside my element and flushed with stress hormones that everything seems possible as long as it would be really bad for me personally, and ideally everyone around me as well. Thankfully, an armed stranger does not open the door. Autumn does, and the gay part of my brain immediately joins the anxious part of my brain in bullying the logical part.

Girl pretty.

Autumn's school clothes are always plain, but it's a very particular *kind* of plain. The sort of plain designed to be generic, uninteresting, default. Her outfits are generally practical but somewhat baggy, hiding her figure and bouncing attention off of a shield of meh. Her Saturday clothes are a very different sort of plain: the adorable kind. She doesn't look boring, she looks like a librarian. And reading is hot.

She's got the ankle-length skirt. The long-sleeved cardigan. The homey color scheme of woody browns and dull maroons. Really, the only things she's missing are glasses and books in the crook of her arm, and I bet we can fix that second part at the mall today. I, conversely, look exactly the same as I usually do. Sure, I picked out my fanciest outfit that involves long pants, thigh socks, and gloves, but the whole reason we're going to the mall is that I do not have many outfits which satisfy that criteria. It's hot and muggy out at this time of year, and gloves are not exactly a common fashion accessory in weather that makes every confined body part leak sweat like spring rain. Out of the entire town, Autumn is probably the only person other than me wearing something that covers up so much skin.

...Which, uh, actually brings up the question of why she's doing that. But before I can think too much on the matter I realize that I've been staring without saying anything, and that she's blushing slightly, and holy cannoli she is *so cute* when she's blushing and now I'm blushing and oh my god Hannah *say something, you dumb bug.*

"I like your shkirt," I say, almost successfully completing a single sentence.

"My... 'shkirt?'" she asks, because of course it would be obvious that I am stupid.

"I like your skirt," I clarify. "And also your shirt."

"Thanks, um, you too," she answers. "Your shirt I mean. Since... you're not wearing a skirt."

There's a pause.

"...But I also like your pants," she manages to finish.

Well. At least we seem to be equally bad at this. I smile at her, and then remember I'm wearing a mask so she can't actually see me do that.

"To the mall, then?" I ask.

"Um, yep!" she confirms. "To the mall!"

And so, we start walking to the mall, at first in more awkward silence but eventually in significantly less awkward conversation. All of said conversations pretty much involve us trading book titles until we find one that we've both read, at which point we babble about it in each other's general direction. I get the distinct impression that she's probably not all that good at talking about anything that isn't fiction, but that's okay because that's honestly a pretty big mood. I don't have anywhere *near* her number of consumed books, but getting her to open up and talk about something I haven't read is weirdly difficult. I know she *could,* she can really get talkative about books sometimes, but for whatever reason she doesn't seem to want to.

Should I open up about a thing I like to talk about but she doesn't know much of to indicate that it's okay? Or would that just be seen as me being selfish in response to her consideration? What would I even talk about? The main thing that comes to mind is Pokémon, but that's a terrible idea, I'll ramble for hours and ruin the whole date if I start talking about Pokémon.

"So, um, what's your favorite fictional universe?" Autumn asks as we finally make it to the mall.

"Pokémon," I answer.

Aw, cracker barrel.

"Pokémon? Like the kid's show?"

Hannah, I swear to Arceus, do *not* rant angrily about the massive adult following of Pokémon.

"That's the one," I manage to say. "Though it's *way* more than a show, there are a bunch of different canons across the franchise."

"Oh. Really?"

"Yeah, really!" I confirm. "I mean, none of them are really high-effort on the writing front except Adventures-slash-Special, the canon is always full of contradictions and vagaries and really just... not a whole lot in the way of story at all, really? But something about the world and setting have always captured me anyway. There's both a gorgeous utopic bent and a horrifying underbelly of fridge logic in the world of Pokémon, and I love talking about it."

"But you said the writing wasn't any good," Autumn points out.

"Yeah, the official material is kind of terrible. But like, the potential is there, which makes it really, really fun to think about."

"Have you tried reading any fanfiction?" she asks.

Agh oh no I love her.

"There's some *really good* Pokémon fanfiction, yeah," I agree happily. "I can recommend some if you've never tried any."

"Um, sure!"

Fanfiction is awesome, with its only glaring weakness being the incomprehensible fact that most people do not think it's awesome. You can't talk to the average person about fanfiction at all without it being really awkward because there's this weird cultural stigma surrounding it that assumes all of it is embarrassing garbage written by tweens. And sure, there's a *lot* of embarrassing garbage fanfiction written by tweens, but first of all how is anyone supposed to become a good writer without starting with embarrassing garbage? And second of all, *so much of it is so fudge-in-a-cupcake good.* There are some genuinely, unironically *brilliant* works of fiction that the average person will never even hear the title of for no reason other than it being fanfiction, and that's a horrible state of affairs. Taking stories other people make and using them to inspire your own is one of the most fundamentally natural methods of human storytelling, and it has been going on since the dawn of history. Just think about it for like two seconds, and it becomes pretty obvious: every single vampire novel ever is *Dracula* fanfiction. The entire extended Cthulhu mythos is Lovecraft fanfiction. The wikipedia page for *Divine Comedy* claims "it is widely considered the pre-eminent work in Italian literature and one of the greatest works of world literature," and it's literally, unambiguously, inarguably a self-insert fanfiction of the gosh dang Bible. It's not even *accurate* to the Bible!

Then capitalism walked in and was like 'yeah, but what if we prevent humanity from doing this anymore so we can make a bit more money' and suddenly fanfiction is in a really weird spot of intellectual property law that nobody wants to touch. Only the copyright holder can make derivative works, but is fanfiction a derivative work or is it fair use? There's arguments for both and there *isn't* a lot of legal precedent on the matter, and frankly it's probably better that way because nobody wants to risk a corporation actually trying to *get* the legal precedent that they'd no doubt be gunning for. As a result, fanfiction survives and thrives by simply being made by people who do not monetize their labor, creating beautiful stories (or terrible ones) purely for the enjoyment of doing so without receiving compensation for it, which, while bullshit, is at least something that most companies don't care too much about. But that's dumb, and fanfiction writers should be able to monetize their fanfiction. If you've ever actually tried to write one, you'd know it's a ton of work, creatively and otherwise. It's nothing like rote plagiarism.

"So what about you?" I ask. "Favorite fictional universe?"

"Real life," she answers.

"Huh?"

She shrugs, her lips twitching in an almost-laugh.

378

"I, um, really love urban fantasy," she explains. "Stories that have magic but take place in a modern-day world which could believably be our own."

I am briefly overcome with a temptation to just peel back the edge of my mask, grin a little too wide and say 'oh?' It'd be so *wild*, so… exhilarating. Magic *is* real, Autumn! Just look at what it's done to me. You live in that world, and here's just a hint of it.

"U-uh, yeah," I stutter out instead. I'm not daring enough for anything more, and frankly Autumn doesn't deserve to be caught up in my crap. "I used to like that a lot. I don't know if it'd be to my tastes anymore. I don't have a lot of time to read, but lately I want my fantasy worlds to not remind me of real life at all."

Which, among other things, means no world trees. *I've killed four people on a world tree. I'm a monster.* All of a sudden, the enjoyable conversation melts away and I become hyper-aware of my freakish body, the chitin of my leg, the way my claws dig into my shoes, the constant thrum of magic within myself that's waiting to be unleashed into the world. I don't belong in this normal place, not when I can't stop thinking about what the people around me would taste like. I'm a freak and a fraud, playing at a guise of humanity that's paper-thin, one bad day away from a disaster.

"Hannah?" Autumn asks, sounding a bit worried.

"Wha?" I gulp, blinking my attention back to the now. "Sorry, did you say something?"

"I said that makes sense," she answers nervously. "The world is pretty bad right now, what with the wars and the plague and stuff."

Ah. Yep. That's definitely what I was referring to.

"Uh-huh," I manage to choke out. "By the by, I think we walked past like three clothing stores already, but I don't actually know how to go shopping so I've just continued walking straight."

"Oh!" she answers. "Um, haha, I thought you had a plan so I've just been following you."

379

"Yeah, nope, I never have a plan," I admit a bit too honestly. "I'm just a total loser whose mom buys her clothes."

"That sounds kind of nice, actually," Autumn answers. "Well, I can take the lead then. I'm sure you've noticed I'm not super fashionable, but I know how to find things, at least. You need, um, gloves you said? And stuff to go with gloves?"

"Yeah, this is my only pair," I confirm.

"Why the sudden need for them, anyway?" Autumn asks curiously.

"Um… it's better than walking around with my hands visibly covered in bandages," I answer honestly. Well, as honest as a sentence I've specifically constructed to mislead can be, I guess.

"Oh, right. Gosh, I'm sorry. Are you okay?"

No. Not at all. I'm so far from okay that I'm pretty sure my only chance of feeling okay again is to literally go insane.

"Yeah, I'm fine," I say out loud. "You of all people don't have to apologize, Autumn. You were a big help."

She doesn't respond, awkwardly turning away and walking into the nearest clothing store instead. From that point on, conversation is mostly about outfits and bargains and checking between stores for options before deciding on a purchase. Hours pass before I even buy one thing, which probably isn't conducive to a proper date. Though I guess Autumn doesn't really seem to mind. She checks the time a fair bit, but when I ask her if she has anywhere to be she insists that she doesn't.

"Although, um, are you not hungry?" Autumn squeaks. "It's nearly three-thirty."

Oh gosh, really? I mean, I'm not hungry, but only because I've been doing everything in my power to disassociate my mind with the very concept of food. No longer able to hide, the hunger and the trauma both crash into me at once and I almost physically stagger.

"…Food would probably be a smart idea," I admit, horrible and delicious flavors singing through my memories.

"Cool," she nods. "Food court?"

That sounds like a good place for food. There are plenty of people in the food court.

"Sure," I answer quietly.

Are my hands shaking? Oh geez I probably look completely insane. Change the subject, Hannah, change the subject!

"Is it really three-thirty?" I ask.

"Yep, just about," Autumn answers. "Sorry, I should have asked to eat sooner, but we were finally getting some progress..."

"Ugh. Yeah. Maybe the only reason I hate shopping is just because my methodology is unbearable. I feel so pushy and annoying dragging you around all over the mall."

"It's fine," Autumn insists. "It's nice to pass the time with someone else."

"It's nice seeing you be kind of talkative for once, too," I joke. "I'm glad I haven't frightened you off, yet. Sometimes you seem so tough, but usually you're like a nervous little mouse."

Her brown curls spring adorably as she nervously tugs on a lock of hair.

"...Do you like me better tough?" she asks.

Oh gosh is that... is she...? Aaaaah, abort, abort! Except... wait. You know what? I don't have the mental bandwidth to be embarrassed about this. So belay that, full speed ahead.

"Um... I, uh, wouldn't say that," I admit. "I just... like you. I've been having a lot of fun talking to you. And you've been really helpful today, I don't think I could have bought any of this stuff without your help. You're cool when you're tough, but... you're cute when you're nervous."

Holy beans on toast I actually said that. I blush. She blushes.

"I see," is all she says, though I manage to catch her doing the smallest little wiggle. My heart. Oh gosh.

I ride the high of this interpersonal victory all the way to the food court, where I promptly realize that even if I *did* have the emotional wherewithal to eat right now, I can't actually take my mask off in public and am therefore screwed. At school I just eat somewhere private, but I can't exactly buy food and rush off into the bathroom to scarf it down here, now can I? That'd be disgusting and *super* weird. Oh, I don't necessarily have to, though! I could get something food-adjacent that I can slurp down with a straw. That should do the trick. A milkshake isn't exactly a meal, but it's better than nothing and my rapidly-carnivorizing digestive system can hopefully-probably still handle milk without much issue. I'll have to check how tasty it smells.

I will say that, on a whole, the food court is absolutely full of tasty smells, and it's really reassuring to know that those tasty smells are not people.

"Well, um, what were you thinking?" Autumn asks. "Looks like there's a Chinese place, a Mexican place, an 'Italian' place that's really just a pizza place, and something called 'Nathan's World-Famous Hot Dogs,' even though I've never actually heard of them."

"Well, I feel like the advantage of a food court is that we don't necessarily have to agree on a place," I point out.

"Yeah, but then we have to wait in two different lines," she counters expertly.

"Oh, right. True. Um... I'm fine with anywhere that has a milkshake, that's probably all I'm going to be getting."

"Oh, gosh. Not hungry?" Autumn asks. "You must have had a big breakfast."

I mean, does an entire human-sized person count? I flex my claws and talons, extra limbs in my torso shifting uncomfortably.

"Something like that," I answer.

Autumn frowns.

"Are you okay?" she asks. "You've seemed pretty distracted all day."

"I'm... well, okay, no. I'm not fine," I admit. "But I will be fine. Hopefully. I just... some stuff happened yesterday."

"More medical stuff?" Autumn asks.

I glance over to her. That *is* the logical assumption, isn't it? Based on what she knows, she probably thinks I'm dying. She might be right. Considering how violent the other world is, I'll be lucky to survive a month. Forget the whole turning-into-a-monster problem, will my body over here even still be *alive* if my body over there gets chopped up in its sleep? No wonder I'm so desperate to go on a date, I'm basically trying to fill out my bucket list. And Autumn doesn't even know. If she thinks this is a serious date that might actually end up as a relationship, I'm just leading her on.

"I'm not doing so hot in a lot of areas," I tell her. "I'm sorry. I just... I'm kind of using you, aren't I?"

"H-huh?" she stutters, looking startled. "I'm not... I don't feel used? We're just shopping."

"And if I asked if you wanted to see a movie with me once we're done eating, what would you say?"

She gives me a deer-in-the-headlights stare for a moment, but manages to answer.

"I'd... like that a lot," she squeaks.

I stare at her. We're both pretty short people, so it's easy to meet her eyes. Anxious and surrounded by loud, rude humans in line for crappy mall food, I realize that I have become so overwhelmed with horror that my brain has stack overflowed all the way into fearless. I take the plunge.

"Autumn, are you aware that I'm gay?" I ask her.

Her blush deepens.

"I, um, did manage to pick up that impression from somewhere," she admits.

"So is this a date?" I ask.

"...Historians in the future may or may not refer to today as a date," she hedges. "It depends on if it goes well or not. Though we can't let any information about any hypothetical dates get back to my dad."

"Same goes for my family," I sigh. "But that's really not the only problem. I don't know how long I'll be *capable* of dating, Autumn. It's not fair to you if we start something when I know I'm just going to have to call it off. I'm being selfish."

She doesn't get the chance to answer immediately, since it's our turn to order food. We fumble a bit at doing so considering the mental gear-shift required, but I get myself a plain vanilla milkshake (I figure chocolate might be risky) and settle back into waiting for the inevitable rejection.

"Maybe it's okay if we're selfish, for once," Autumn says instead.

I give her a surprised blink.

"...What do you mean?" I ask.

"Exactly what I said," she answers. "I'm here because I want to be, Hannah. I'm having fun. Can we continue?"

"Oh, um... sure."

I awkwardly collect my milkshake and stick the straw behind my mask, earning an odd look from Autumn that I only shrug to in response.

"We should normalize kinds of food that can be eaten with masks on," I mutter. "There's a dang pandemic going on."

"I guess it makes sense that you have to be pretty health-conscious, huh?" Autumn chuckles. "At least you seem hale."

"Except for when my blood all decides to fall out, yeah," I confirm. "Although speaking of stuff in my body that needs to fall out, I'm gonna head to the bathroom. Watch my shake?"

"I'll protect it with my life," Autumn promises.

"Cool," I nod. "Uh, don't actually do that though, please run if there are any threats to your life. Be right back!"

I jog to the nearest bathroom, my need to use it a lot more urgent than I expected. What did Autumn mean by that? 'Maybe it's okay if we're selfish?' If nothing else, I guess it sounds like she's okay with it if this turns out to be a pretty short-term thing. Which is... nice. Definitely reassuring. Holy crap though, did I really just *admit that I'm gay* in a public setting!? I mean, it's a public setting with a zero percent chance that anyone was bothering to listen in on me, and even if they were I didn't recognize anyone nearby, but *still*. What the heck, me? I'm going to give myself a heart attack with something like that.

I sit down on the toilet, moving my right sock down to expose my knee so I can pick the lint out of the joint. Having things inside my joints, it turns out, is *extremely* uncomfortable, and lint really likes to get stuck between the plates. I could just magic it out, but... I dunno. I guess I have to wait here for my large intestine to cooperate anyway. It's a big one, which is odd since I haven't eaten anything, but I didn't poop this morning so I guess this sort of thing happens. Unless... no. Nope, nuh-uh, I'm not going to think about that. I do my business as quickly as I can, wipe up, and resolve *not* to look into the toilet itself when I stand. I immediately fail.

I feel like it's weird to look back and check your own turds after pooping, but like... surely everybody does that at least sometimes, right? Gosh I'm on my first date ever and I'm lamenting about my own feces. It's not like there's any way that it... that... um.

Are those shards of bone?

They are. Oh god, they are. Packed in with the brown rot of my own excretions are chunks of hard white, proof positive of what I've done. How is it here? How did it chase me across *dimensions?* Why would... how did... *fuck!*

Vomit joins shit in the toilet bowl, a powerful heave upending a waterfall of horrible orange acids from my throat. No. No! Everything was going so well! Why did this have to happen now? Why can't I even have one good day? I'm going to ruin everything, not just for me but for Autumn too! I just... no. No! I can fix this!

385

No more feeling weird about my spells, I need them. Magic cleans me up well enough, and a flush of the toilet removes the rest of the evidence. Making sure my clothes are all on right, I walk out of the toilet stall and use the mirror to double-check myself, taking deep breaths and forcing my body to at least *appear* calm. I can do this. It'll be fine. Maybe I can't have a good day, but she can. Poor, cute Autumn. I'm not sure she *has* any other friends, so I'll be the best friend she's ever had. And if she wants things to go further than that... well, hopefully I'll still be around.

I return to the food court with a spring in my step that I don't really feel. I give Autumn a smile she can't actually see.

"So!" I say. "Movie?"

She agrees, and we head to the theater. I let her pick something without even really registering what it is. Something live-action fantasy. I've never heard of it before, but glancing at the ticket I'm startled by the nearly three hour run time. Sure, though. Whatever. It's not like I have anything better to do. Multiple hours of loud, in-my-face distraction sounds like exactly what I need right now.

I'm so out of it I don't even cringe when Autumn buys some of the overpriced theater snacks, I just offer to carry all of the bags so that she can hold her sugary spoils. I might be able to get away with a few bites of food when everyone is distracted by the movie, but I don't know if I can even digest popcorn and candy. I don't want to think about digesting things anyway.

Time slides by. I don't remember the movie, but Autumn seems to be pretty into it. That's good. She's good. I think. I guess I barely know anything about her. But she seems like a good person to me, and that's enough for now. When the credits start to roll, Autumn insists we wait and see if there's an after-credits scene. There isn't one. We leave. The sun is starting to set when we make it outside.

"Everything okay?" Autumn asks quietly.

I blink, turning to look at her.

"Yeah," I lie. "Sorry. Just... a bit out of it."

"Was the movie too long...?"

"No," I assure her. "No, it was fine."

"Sorry," she mutters. "I picked a really long one."

"I don't mind," I tell her.

"I was just being selfish."

I know, in my gut, that I should probably challenge that statement. I don't think I have the energy to, though, so we walk together in silence. Since we're walking, it's probably another forty-five minutes to an hour before we finally get home. Autumn seems more and more nervous the closer we get, and I can hardly blame her. I'm not looking forward to going home either.

It's a good thing my phone is giving me directions, because I wouldn't recognize where anything is in the dark like this. Sure, this is my hometown, but I don't actually know it all that well. Outside of a few specific places, I never really go anywhere. It's not all that late at night, but wherever we are is still pretty dead in terms of activity. Besides Autumn and I, there's only one other person on the street. He's approaching us from behind, which is a little concerning on general principles. I don't really want to turn around and actually see what he looks like, though. ...Wait, if I haven't seen him, how do I know he's there?

I glance backwards, and sure enough, there's someone approaching us from behind. They've got a hood up and they're staring at the ground, so I can't see their face. Both hands are in their pockets. Their pockets are bulging rather suspiciously.

No way, right? Not... not like this. Not *now.* Not even the movie we just watched was cliché enough for this.

I put a hand on Autumn's shoulder and subtly nudge her to start walking faster. Unfortunately, we're both short, and the person behind us keeps gaining ground anyway. What should we do? Scream? I don't think there's... no. I *know* there isn't anyone else around. But how...? I don't seem to have access to my actual spatial sense. I try to look at things that way, but it just isn't there. Still, something more instinctive seems to insist on knowledge that I don't know how I could be aware of in any other manner. My heartbeat thumps faster as I feel out the nearby streets and alleyways, trying to find one out of sight we can duck into. Best-case scenario, he's just some dude in a hurry and he walks right past us. Worst-case scenario... well. I'll want witnesses even less than he will.

What's a fifth, in the grand scheme of things? The thought makes tears start to form in my eyes, but I ignore them. He's just gonna walk right past us anyway, right? I'm just being paranoid.

"Be quiet and stay behind me," I whisper to Autumn, and nudge her into an alleyway between two run-down businesses. The man behind us picks up speed. He'll be in view soon. Walk past us, walk past us, please walk past us.

He turns into our alleyway. He draws a knife. Tears start to fall down my cheeks in earnest.

"Y-your money," he demands. He's wearing a COVID facemask. The one damn guy I see actually wearing a mask during the pandemic, and he's using it to commit a crime.

It's funny. I've read a lot of superhero comics. Oftentimes, some of the best parts of superhero stories are the origins, the moment the hero first gets their powers and embraces them as tools of justice. Now obviously, we know that in the real world you can't actually make the world a noticeably better place by beating people up, and the vast majority of superheroes can do more good by using their powers for volunteer work than by using them to punch criminals in the schnoz, but the opening moments of a superhero's career are very, very often exactly like what I'm seeing right now. Bad guy, wearing a mask so the audience can't empathize with him, accosts a woman in an alleyway. Superhero punches him in the schnoz. Superhero is praised by woman, superhero realizes the joy and responsibility of heroism, superhero career begins. It's so stupidly common, so incredibly cliché that even the subversions of the trope are cliché. Even the times you know for a fact that, at the end of the scene, there isn't going to be a hero walking out of the alleyway.

I take a shaky breath, standing up straighter. I don't really know how to fight, certainly not in a straight one-on-one battle like this. I'll probably get stabbed when I attack, but if I kick him with my right leg then my chitin should be plenty tough to shrug such a tiny blade off. In return, my magically-enhanced claws will rend deep into him. He'll probably die. I'm hungry enough to dispose of the evidence, at least.

"I said give me your money!" the boy snaps. God, he sounds so young.

"Please just go," I beg him. "Don't become my cliché."

He seems a bit taken aback by my words, but he doesn't leave. I figured as much. This is just my life now, isn't it?

I take a deep breath, and the goddess reaches out towards my lungs.

# 21

# FACE-OFF

The goddess smiles a faceless grin as she takes my breath. It is a joyful smile, though not at all a kind one.

I recognize the goddess' presence as a simple fact of reality, the same as I know my heart beats in my chest even when I'm not feeling for a pulse. She's here, right in front of my face, drawing in the air from my lungs and leaving me breathless. Yet she's barely a consideration as my eyes focus on the knife in front of me, the threat, the *danger* that I only have one way to remove. Speaking a spell takes time, time that I'm not sure I have. The weapon is close, plenty close enough to stab me in the time it takes to say two words. I need to already be moving, already be striking. With the incantation spoken, my claws reach nearly a foot in length. More than enough to take his wrist... or his head. I open my mouth, twisting my body to strike as I and the goddess say—

"Hannah, *stop!*"

A hand grabs my shoulder from behind, and for an instant I'm certain I'm about to die. Someone is behind me and I'm not *ready* and *I can't stop their attack.* Then I remember there is no one behind me but Autumn, and there is no attack at all. Not even the mugger is moving, his eyes wide and hands shaky. Is he afraid? I know I am. The incantation catches in my throat. The goddess twitches in annoyance, my words left unsaid on the tip of her tongue.

"Are you fucking insane?" Autumn hisses at me, pulling me back and glaring at me face-to-face. "Don't *attack* an armed mugger, you moron, just give him your money!"

Stunned, I do nothing but stare at her for a moment. I open my mouth to respond, but no words can come out because my lungs are still empty. The goddess holds my breath.

Autumn sends a nervous glance towards the kid with the knife.

"...You're not gonna like, rape us or anything, right?" she asks him bluntly.

The mugger jolts a bit, rapidly shaking his head. Autumn turns her attention back to me.

"Yeah, see? He just wants our money. We just give it to him, nice and easy, and we go on our way. Let's not get ourselves stabbed over whatever's in your wallet."

I blink at her, still unable to respond. Unable to *breathe.* Though she has no limbs, I feel the goddess tap her foot impatiently.

"Your *wallet,* Hannah," Autumn snaps authoritatively, and I fumble for it, pulling it out of my pocket and handing it to her. She opens it up and pulls out the bills. I probably have eighty to a hundred dollars of bills in there, collected from various twenties I would get in birthday cards and then never use because credit is more convenient.

"Y-your phones, too," the boy says.

"You don't want our phones," Autumn firmly insists. "Tracer apps."

...Is that a thing? I feel like even if it is a thing, it's a thing that can be negated by just removing the battery. The mugger hesitates anyway, and by then Autumn is already collecting the drastically smaller number of bills from her own wallet and handing them over to him, staying towards his left side. The unarmed side. She's watching the knife very, very carefully, but the mugger doesn't attack her. He just snatches the bills and stuffs them in his pocket, jabbing towards the shopping bags I dropped on the ground with his knife.

"A-anything valuable in there, too," the mugger insists.

"It's women's clothing," Autumn says, stepping away from it. "Do you even know what's valuable?"

Her question isn't a mocking one. It's genuine. He's staring at her now, confusion obvious on his face.

"You want purses. You want shoes. You want jewelry. We didn't buy any of that. You can rummage through there anyway if you want, or you can make me do it, but the more time you drag this out, the more likely someone is to walk by."

And the more time we drag this out, the more my lungs *burn.* Pain crawls through my chest as my body screams for air, the goddess still waiting on me. But I don't want to cast anything! I made a mistake!

A smothering pressure closes in on all sides, a thousand misty limbs wrapping me, crushing me, *demanding* to know of me: a mistake? *Really?* I called a goddess, I *summoned the divine,* for a mistake? For a waste of time? Exactly whose time do I think I'm wasting? Did I forget my place? She strokes my face, slowly and sensually, and the brush of unwanted intimacy almost makes me scream. It would have, were she not still holding my breath. I am still favored, she promises. I am still loved. But love only forgives so much.

The goddess opens her mouth, her face so close to mine that I feel her breath on my cheek. *I feel my own soul on my cheek,* the tiniest puff of air nearly crushing me to death. Her wispy fingers crawl into me, peeling open my lips and winding down my throat, wrapping around my voicebox, pulling and twisting and forcing words that I cannot refuse. The mugger glances between Autumn and the shopping bags one last time before scampering off, leaving Autumn alone with me in the alley.

"Poor kid," she mutters. "You okay, Hannah? We should be safe n—"

"**Spacial Rend**," the Goddess says with my body, and my world becomes blood and pain.

No familiar pulse of magic engulfs my claws, because though I spoke the words it is the Goddess' magic and the Goddess decides what is done with it. This is the lesson She teaches me as a hundred claws tear open holes in my body, separating skin from skin and muscle from muscle with the effortless grace of the omnipotent. My own spell turns against me, and I feel the agony of it. No blade slides between my ribs, no sword cuts into my flesh, yet the wounds form all the same, obeying the natural laws of the world even while those laws are taken out back and shot in the head. There is space between two parts of me. Therefore, I was cut.

I collapse to the ground immediately, streams of red erupting from countless wounds. The Goddess glares down at me, watching and waiting, as I finally manage to take half a breath before choking on my own blood. Coughing makes everything hurt even more. I'm already lightheaded.

"Hannah? Holy shit, *Hannah!*"

My whole body is in agony. I feel my clothes getting soaked, wet ooze blossoming all over. It's impossible for me to know how many times I've been cut, there's simply too much pain. But I'm choking, aren't I? My throat was slit by my own miscasted spell. I'm going to bleed out in seconds. I'm going to die.

The Goddess watches, and She waits. I'm not going to disappoint Her twice in a row, am I?

I'm vaguely aware that Autumn is squatting next to me, putting pressure on me, doing something with her phone. But my vision is blurry and I don't have time to consider her, not in the seconds I have left. The prospect of trying to cast magic right now is utterly horrifying, but what choice do I have? If I don't figure out a healing spell, a *powerful* healing spell, I will die. But healing is Order, and the last time I tried for a healing spell I got something completely different. Which makes sense, if magic reflects who we are. I'm nowhere near a good enough person to be a healer. I was about to kill someone in order to... what? Save myself a hundred dollars?

So that's it, right? I'm dead? The Goddess sneers at me, turning away in disgust and irritation. Why? How can She expect better from me? She's the one that gives spells, so She should know if I have a solution. Which... which means I do. Right? So how can I heal my wounds? ...No, wait. That's the wrong question, isn't it? The real question is 'how do I prevent myself from dying?'

An idea starts to form. A stupid idea. I don't have enough power for it. I need... I need a named spell. That's why She's still here. She knows I have to say it out loud. But... She cut my throat. I can't speak! ...No, wait, I'm a fool. My body in the other world can't speak, but that's no obstacle to a Goddess.

I have, of course, been thinking about what to name my magic. My first spell was somewhat of a whim, but I think it worked not just because it was perfectly descriptive, but because it was perfect *for me.* Spacial Rend, the name of an attack from a game that is near and dear to my heart, that I have invested myself into and obsessed over more than any other thing in the world. In some stupid, nerdy way, Pokémon is part of me in a true sense, and with one spell already inspired by it, I like the idea of naming all of my spells with the same theme.

The Goddess' gaze turns back to me, her ethereal lips quirking upwards. She likes the idea, too. Good. Without her favor, I'm dead. She smiles more broadly.

My favorite spell is a cleaning spell, but it's more than *just* a cleaning spell. It is a spell of Order, a spell that presupposes the idea that there is a way that *things should be,* and makes it so. What makes it more than a cleaning spell is that it's really more about 'putting things in their proper place.' To cast it, I need something to be in the wrong place, and I need somewhere that *is* the right place to relocate it to.

My blood is in the wrong place. The right place is my veins. The Goddess beams with delight.

"**Refresh**," She intones, my coughing ceasing long enough for my mouth to mime the words.

To restore. To stimulate. To wash. The word 'refresh' has many relevant meanings. In Pokémon, it's a move that cures the negative status of the user, removing conditions and restoring to the default. On a computer, refreshing a page is often the first and most useful troubleshooting tip online, clearing up errors by starting things anew, returning them to their initial state. It is a word that fits me well, leaden with the implications of cleanliness and Order, and the Goddess approves.

My blood runs backwards. The stains in my clothes unsoak themselves, sucking backwards out of the fabric and into the wounds. Blood slithers out of my lungs, out of my perforated organs, and I'm allowed a real, complete breath for the first time in a long time.

Then my heart beats, and it all pours back out my wounds anew.

"**Refresh**," I hiss, the Goddess delighting in copying my intended intonation. Each blood vessel, each artery, each vein... it all has a direction it is supposed to be traveling in. The proper state of blood is not a singular place but *in motion,* and whenever it incorrectly falls out of a severed tube it needs to be relocated to the other side of the cut, stuffed back into the far end of its broken road, to continue properly on its way. Raw power bridges the many gaps in my flesh, each cut now perfectly dry but for the tiny, lightning-shaped patterns of dancing red indicating where an unsevered vessel is supposed to be.

But the cuts are still there. I don't have a healing spell. I can't mend them.

"What the fuck," Autumn breathes. "What the fuck what the fuck what the fuck."

"Ma'am?" her phone chirps. "What was that? Are you still there?"

Magic churns through my entire body, guiding the flow of my life where my heart alone is no longer capable of doing the task. The Goddess gives me a condescending pat on the head before Her presence vanishes, leaving only the power of the spell literally thrumming in my veins.

"Ma'am, just stay where you are," the voice on the phone commands calmly. "We have an ambulance and police en route."

Oh, fudge sunday. She was on the phone. *They have a recording of my spell!*

"Off," I order Autumn, gesturing shakily at her phone. "Turn it off."

"What... what just...?"

"Turn it *off!*" I snap, and she fumbles for the device, quickly complying as I unsteadily get to my feet. A certain amount of oxygen belongs in my brain, and it's there now. The lightheadedness is gone.

"We have to go," I insist, leaning against a wall as I feel the *holes in my body* twist and move alongside me, each side of the many cuts scraping against their matching face. "Grab the b-bags."

"Wh... the bags!? Really? Hannah, I just saw you—"

*"The receipts have my name on them!"* I bark at her, holding back an adrenaline-fueled hiss. "I can't go to the hospital, I can't talk to the police, we have to *go.* Now!"

She stares at me for a moment, a shell-shocked expression on her face. I have no idea what she sees when she looks at me. There are cuts on my face, my clothes are shredded, my mask is in pieces. She sees what I really am, at least in part, and as her eyes twitch to take in details I can't help but be terrified of whatever it is she's thinking. What if she runs? What if she leaves me here? Can I escape on my own? Can I even *walk?*

"Okay," Autumn says simply, none of the stress she's under audible in her voice. She stands up, and rather than leaving she collects all the shopping bags on one arm before offering me her other one. Her face has locked down completely, showing no expression.

...Which is for some reason *extremely* hot, but I can't exactly afford to focus on that right now so I just take her hand, struggling to walk on my deeply lacerated legs. My mutated limb doesn't need anywhere near as much magical maintenance in terms of keeping the blood going where it should, thanks to how rigid it is, but a lot of the cuts are still deep enough to damage muscle. Autumn takes my arm around her shoulder and I let her guide my body as we flee the scene together, most of my focus occupied with maintaining the magical 'cleaning' spell that's somehow barely keeping me alive.

"...Where are we going?" Autumn asks.

"I don't know," I snap without really meaning to. The pain seems to be making what parts of my lips that still actually work curl up into a sneer, and I'm certain that I'm only conscious thanks to adrenaline. By all rights, I shouldn't even be able to think with my body in this much agony.

"You don't know?" Autumn repeats. "Well I sure as hell can't take you back to my place."

"Understandable," I grunt, trying to keep the edge out of my voice. She's helping me. She's staying with me. Holy crap she's *staying with me.* "I can't really go home looking like this either."

Autumn just nods, like that's the most natural thing in the world.

"I know of some places we can hide out," she admits. "Are you gonna be okay without medical attention, though?"

"Autumn, I'm a freak," I growl. "Will I be okay *with* medical attention? What would a hospital even do with me?"

She glances down to where my shredded pants and shoes are slowly revealing more and more of my mutant leg as we walk.

"...That's a good question," she acknowledges. "I almost want to ask if this is all real, but..."

"It is," I confirm. "Unfortunately."

"Yeah," she nods. "I heard... I don't know what I heard. You spoke and then someone *touched* me. I didn't like it one bit."

"Yeah, that was the Goddess," I groan. "By the way, religion is solved and magic is real."

She chews on her lower lip a bit, biting off some dead skin and glancing down at my leg again.

"...That is not going to be fun to process later," she decides, her voice flat.

"I am surprised and very, *very* appreciative that you're not freaking out about it right now," I tell her. "Thank you."

Autumn shrugs very slightly, which is very painful.

"Crisis management is what I do," she dismisses, taking a sudden turn and crossing the street with me. Off in the distance, I hear sirens, but I can't see where they're coming from. Turning my head hurts like a habanero anyway.

"...Like the robber?" I say, trying to keep talking because it's *something* other than agony and the jittery heat of blood-sorting magic.

"Well technically that was a mugger, but yeah," Autumn grunts. "What the hell were you thinking? Were you about to cut up that poor kid the way you cut up yourself?"

"'Poor kid?' He drew a knife on us! I freaked out and thought we were about to die!"

"Well, we weren't," Autumn grunts. "He was even more terrified than you were. Total amateur, that was probably his first mugging. Fell for some obvious lies. People like him don't commit crimes unless they're really, *really* desperate."

I look her way, peeling my eyes up from my own feet and enduring the pain required to actually *see* her rather than just soak in information from my budding spatial sense—which is a thing I've been doing, apparently—and really *look* at her blank expression, the way the hardness of her face and the experience evident in her words paint a clear picture that even I'm not too dense to understand.

Autumn has some significant criminal experience. That is not going to be fun to process later. As of right now, though, I can hardly fault her. She's being far more awesome than I have any right to.

"...Thank you," I manage to choke out. "For stopping me, and for stepping in. I... I'm pretty sure I would have killed him if you hadn't done that."

Autumn doesn't respond at first, leading me off the road down into a ditch, and into one of those big concrete tubes with roads built on top of them that are probably used for drainage or something. She sits me down on the damp ground, then extracts herself from me to sit on the far side, facing me.

"You ever kill anyone?" she asks.

I swallow, looking away. I guess at this point she deserves to know.

"Yes," I admit. "I have."

Her emotionless demeanor cracks a little bit at that, her eyebrows raising.

"Huh. Okay. Well, at least you seem pretty torn up about it." She wrinkles her nose. "...Uh, poor choice of words on my part, sorry."

I wince, which hurts and causes me to wince harder.

"It's, um, fine."

"You doing okay?" she asks.

I could try to blow this off, I guess. Deflect, try to salvage like I always do. But that's too much work. Too much of my head is dedicated to the image of my blood flowing correctly and Orderly through my body, maintaining the link to an outpouring of magic that suffuses me. I'm in too much pain to add a lie to the anguish.

"...I'm using magic to circulate my blood," I explain. "Everything hurts. The only thing currently stopping me from having a panic attack is the knowledge that if I stop focusing on keeping this spell active I'll die."

"That sounds bad," she hedges.

"It's pretty bad," I confirm. "On the other hand, I'm kind of freaking out about the fact that I can apparently do this at all. Like… look at this crazy gumbo."

I peel off a ruined glove, then peel *back* a deep cut on my hand, opening the lesion wider so that internals are visible, pale skin on fat on muscle on bone. All throughout it, thin spiderweb lines of red snake through the air that's now between them and the other end of the cut. Blood and guts and internal organs look very, very different to my spatial sense than they do to my eyes, but even so I don't feel much disgust in the action. I'm simply too inured to the insides of bodies on a daily basis to care much about seeing my own fat and bone exposed to the air.

"I'm doing this," I marvel, ignoring the sharp increase of pain that comes with the demonstration. "I'm holding myself together, my own life clenched in two fists. With a *cleaning spell.* I'm just… I'm really not human anymore, huh? Shame I don't know how to actually heal the wounds, so I'm kind of stuck in a holding pattern here."

I glance over at Autumn, who is very stoically trying to avoid letting her queasiness show on her face. I let the cut on my hand go, hiding the insides from view. The way she looks at my face makes me suspect there's something similarly gross there, though.

"…But hopefully I can start working to fix myself," I assure her, continuing to babble as is my wont. "No healing spell is a problem, but… maybe I can spoof one with a Transmutation spell? Like, I have a spell which accelerates my mutation into a horrifying inhuman monster, and maybe accelerating my changes will also accelerate my healing?"

"Um, so about that…" Autumn starts, motioning vaguely in my direction.

"About what?" I ask, since it really could be anything I've said in the past five minutes.

"...The, um. The monster thing."

I don't know why, but her sudden hesitance makes me grin with the half of my mouth still capable of it. Heh, I forgot my lips can stretch this far.

"Y'know, I'd really like to know the answer to that myself!" I say with false cheerfulness. "This just sort of *started happening* one day, and like, I could give a lot more context and details behind that but frankly I'm pretty sure all of it would just make things more confusing. All I really know is that one day while I was showering my bones started growing out of my toes, and now... well."

I wiggle my toes, my monstrous limb having long since been freed from my torn-up shoes.

"...That's why your feet were bleeding in gym," Autumn realizes. "Not because you cut yourself open like this, but because you were changing."

"Yes! Exactly. I don't usually rip myself to shreds and have to barely hold on for life, I promise. Having magic at all is actually more recent than the monster thing."

"So you started mutating, and then you got magic," Autumn clarifies. "You didn't use magic to start mutating."

"Correct," I nod. "Well, I mean, magic is probably *responsible* for me turning into a monster, but I certainly didn't cast that spell on purpose."

She nods slowly, grabbing her chin between her thumb and forefinger as her eyes go distant. She's back to not looking stressed, just... calculating.

"...You're taking this *really* well," I note. "Like, suspiciously well. Are you okay?"

She frowns slightly.

"I'm not really sure that it's sunk in yet," she admits. "This is a lot, even for me. A big part of me keeps trying to explain this, to rationalize it. But even if your limbs and teeth are just strange prostheses, your wounds and blood... there's no way. I can't figure it out. And I don't think you're lying about being in danger of dying, so either way it's kind of not the top priority right now."

"Oh, right, I guess I should probably try to stop myself from dying, huh?"

"Preferably yes?"

There are two problems with that, though: one, I'm not sure I can focus on Refresh and unnamed-Transmutation-spell at the same time. Accidentally halting the only spell that's keeping me alive is probably A Bad Plan™. At the same time, though, the current situation isn't at all sustainable so I'm not sure I can afford to *not* take the risk. This leads to the second problem: I don't want to. Accelerating my changes means I come out of this even more of a monstrous freak than before, and I'm already a maniac that's jumping to murder as my first option in dangerous scenarios. I don't want to cast a spell that basically just uses magic to make all of that worse. Obviously though, just like with problem one, I don't have a choice. I'm forced into this horrid situation by my own mistakes, and it's time to pay the piper. I'll become a freak and my chance at anything normal or good in this world will be over.

"Is there anything more I can do to help?" Autumn asks.

...Unless she stays with me. And she *is* staying with me. Why? No, no, stop, now is not the time for my self-esteem issues, *I am dying.* Anything she can do. Hmm. Well, I've been ignoring it all day for trauma reasons, but I haven't eaten anything but a milkshake and I'm very, *very* hungry. If I'm going to repair myself and grow new body parts, I'll need fuel.

"...I need meat," I tell her, trying not to think about the fact that she's made of it.

"Alright," Autumn nods, pulling out her phone. "Chick-fil-a is closeby."

"I'd prefer meat from a company that isn't owned by a bigot that keeps donating to anti-LGBT organizations."

"Well it's the closest place and you just fucking filleted yourself, so you're just going to have to deal with it?"

She's got me there.

"...I guess I've given in to worse excuses to pay a bigot."

"That's the spirit," Autumn sighs. "Be back in like... ten minutes. Please don't die, my fingerprints are all over you."

And with that, she turns and sprints away. Woah, she's fast. Now I'm alone. At night. Torn to shreds and visibly inhuman. ...Nope can't think about that, have magic to do. I close my eyes, doubling down on the feeling of power moving my blood through my body. I can't lose my focus on this, even when I'm casting another spell. I mean, now that I'm thinking about it, I'm not sure if it's *possible* to cast two spells at the same time. Maybe there's an arbitrary limit. ...Still don't have a choice, though.

Okay. Don't panic. Just... work through this. My blood is where it belongs. My *body* is not, but I can't heal it just by moving things around. My body has to heal itself, and that means it has to *change.* I need to focus on the Transmutation magic in my soul and channel that alongside my Order spell. So... focus. Transmutation. Change. Order is complexity, and Transmutation is the pathway to increasing complexity, the ever-advancing nature of life. Order says *there is a way things should be.* Transmutation says *but what if we make it even better?*

...For a certain definition of better, of course. As much as I might be stronger, faster, more dangerous, more *powerful...* it's not all upsides. Although those things *are* pretty cool. I mean, I don't wanna murder people, and those attributes mostly just make me better at murdering people, but... I dunno. Not important! Focus on transforming!

I find the energy that's somehow Transmutation-flavored, drawing it out slowly like I did before. Last time, I tugged at a link between

404

my two bodies, but this time I want to try to avoid messing with that if possible. It seems... I dunno. Ominous. It's like, part of my soul probably? I don't exactly like the idea of yanking on my own soul.

...Ugh, I used to be an atheist. I guess I'd be a pretty crummy skeptic if I ignored *literally having divine magic,* though. So sure! Souls exist! Why not! It's as good an explanation as any in regards to sharing a consciousness between *entire universes.*

Oh, right, I need to focus so that I don't literally die. As terrible and terrifying as my life is, as dangerous as I'm afraid I'm becoming, I absolutely, positively do not want to die. The idea of death is terrifying, even more so now that I've met god. Er, I mean the Goddess. She's... kind of scary. Incredible, sure, but definitely scary. So that means I need to make this *work.*

I find the feeling of Transmutation inside me easily enough. I carefully fill myself with it, making sure not to drop Refresh while pulling more and more of the energy into my body. I breathe in, and I breathe out, ignoring how alone I am, how I can feel the damp ground soaking into what's left of my underwear, how easy it would be for Autumn to abandon me, how every single insect and night-creature nearby is marked in my mind as a potential threat every time they move. There's just me and the magic. Nothing else.

Time drags by, and I don't start feeling any better. I pull on more and more Transmutation magic, trying to use it to fix my body, but it spills out between my metaphorical fingers, refusing to touch me. I mentally grab for it, chasing it like a cat would a laser, but it's as ephemeral as smoke. What am I doing wrong? Am I going to have to pull on my soul after all?

"I'm back," Autumn announces. "Please say something."

"Hey," I answer quietly, my eyes still closed.

"Um, hey. I have chicken for you. Are you doing something? The air feels kind of... tingly."

My eyes shoot open at that, panic making me drop focus on the Transmutation magic and nearly doing the same with Refresh.

"You could feel that?" I ask.

"Um, yeah? I could feel *something*, anyway. Is that bad?"

She hands me a box of chicken tenders, which I hesitantly take and start shoving into my mouth.

"It might be?" I admit between bites. "I was experimenting with Transmutation magic, so…"

"Transmutation magic? Like, the stuff that's probably… urk. Gah!"

She suddenly doubles over, breath going fast as she starts clutching her stomach, groaning in agony as she staggers towards me.

"What… what's…"

"Oh god, Autumn, I'm so sorry!" I shriek, dropping my foods I gape at the absolute, unparalleled fuckup I just caused. Is she changing!? Did I ruin her life in the same way I ruined mine? Oh no oh no oh no oh no I—

"Just kidding," Autumn smirks, standing up straight.

I stare at her, open-mouthed. She stares back.

"Don't *do* that!" I yelp, throwing a waffle fry at her. She laughs, plopping down to start eating her own share of food.

"Eat and get back to trying to fix yourself," she orders. "Don't worry about me."

"…Alright," I allow, and close my eyes again.

If it's really been enough time for Autumn to get food since I started trying to use raw Transmutation magic to fix myself, though, I bet it's the wrong track. Why, though? The spell that transmutates me is probably a Transmutation spell, I figure? Hmm, wait. Of *course* it's a Transmutation spell. It's just not *only* a Transmutation spell. I don't control what I turn into. I don't get the option to stop it, either. The spell keeps going, keeps applying itself, because my transformed state is a predetermined goal. It is, at least in the spell's eyes, *the way I should be.* And that way is clearly inspired by my second body, in color and design and even number of limbs. There's a body I'm *supposed* to have, and this spell is slowly but surely shifting me into that. It's shifting *both* of me into that. That's why it felt like I was tugging the line: I'm figuratively pulling my two bodies closer together.

Somehow that... that feels right.

I've never been fully human, have I? Some part of me has always been that fourth-dimensional spider from another world, scuttling along barely a foot off the ground. And I *like* that. It feels right to me. But so does being human. As a spider, I'm too small, too restricted. I'm slow and I don't have hands and in many ways I'm more of an accessory than a person. I love some parts of that, but I want more than that. Growth. Change. Merger. *The way I'm supposed to be.*

I take a deep breath, feel the power in my soul, and tug the line.

This time, the feedback is immediate, the familiar thrum of a successfully activated spell filling my body. No... filling *both* my bodies, at least to the limited extent that I can feel the sleeping form of my hyperspider self. But my desperate hunch is right: 'full of cuts and holes' does not match the form my spell is shaping me into, and so they will be transfigured. The pain of my many lesions multiplies and pairs with a horrid itching sensation, my magic sealing up the broken flesh and undoing the damage dealt. It's such a terrible feeling that it finally breaks my wavering concentration on Refresh.

Panic flows down my throat along with the contents of my jugular, my mouth opening to re-speak the spell. The Goddess arrives between slivers of moments, pouring into our world and happily wrapping Herself around me, giggling joyfully as my life's blood leaks onto the ground.

"**Refresh**," I silently croak, and She sings the words real, seeming to luxuriate in the moment like a cat stretching in a sunbeam. Autumn shudders, her stoic mask cracking and nearly shattering before the

Goddess finally has mercy on the mortals in Her midst and the weight of Her attention leaves.

"...Do you get used to that?" Autumn asks quietly.

"I certainly haven't yet," I answer, and return to focusing on my body.

I can see why Sindri was so afraid of miscasts, now. I take a deep, shuddering breath and pull on the line between bodies again, letting the fiery itch of healing pass through my flesh, the horrible feeling knitting my wounds slowly, *oh* so horribly slowly back together. And I know that this isn't *just* healing, not really. As my chitin repairs itself, bubbling and growing and hardening anew, I also feel it reinforcing itself, growing further up my leg. Each flap of skin seals itself shut with the promise that one day, something that isn't skin at all will take its place. Worst of all and best of all are the parts that don't seal up at all. On each side of my abdomen, just above my waist, a cut doesn't close. It's waiting for something to grow first. My dear limbs number five and six.

I usually don't move the parts of me that are trapped inside my body, since why would I? I wiggle them when I'm happy from time to time, but overall they just feel weird to move. Still, I find it as natural as breathing to maneuver them, feeling them grow larger and stronger, questing for the exit to the prison of my skin. I let out an involuntary grunt of pain, pushing one through the inside of an open wound, stretching it white and gleaming out into the open air of night. There's no blood on it, of course, since that's not where my blood is supposed to be.

"Ohhhh holy fucking shit Hannah, I swear to god if you're chestbursting right now—"

"Nope! Nope, it's fine, this is fine!" I hiss, crying out in pain as I navigate my other extra limb into the world as well. It's... nothing special at all, really. Just a leg. Almost exactly like one of my other body's legs, even down to the barely foot-long length. One joint at the base, two more joints along the length of the limb, ending in a sharp tip that can be used as a weapon. It's beautiful. I love it. It's completely and utterly useless.

"I'm okay," I continue, speaking the words out loud and being surprised to mean them. "I'm fine. I'm healing, I'm getting better, I'm going to be fine."

Autumn spares a worried glance at both of my new limbs as I wriggle them freely in the air, the holes they emerged from slowly but surely starting to close up after them. It feels so, so good to have them. I don't care how terrible this is for me in terms of my daily life right now, I'm just excited to be alive and to be just a little more free from the agony of the morning. Six limbs down, four to go. Autumn lets out a huff of air, visibly centering herself before reaching into her back pocket and pulling out the little notebook she always carries, flipping through it quickly. A scowl grows on her face as she does so, getting deeper and deeper until she finally growls in frustration and puts the notebook away.

"What is that, anyway?" I ask. "Your little book. Why are you looking at it all the time? What do you write in there?"

Normally I wouldn't pry, but I'm somewhat curious and this seems like a good environment as any to be spilling secrets, considering Autumn just learned pretty much all of mine. Not that I'm going to try to press her into answering because of that, it's just... y'know. A good opportunity. I guess that's manipulative, but it doesn't seem like it's manipulative enough to actually work. My question only serves to make Autumn seem more irritated.

"...So you haven't figured it out yet?" she grunts. "And of *course* you haven't been told."

"Um, I mean, who would tell me if not you?" I ask. "It's okay, though. You don't have to say anything if you don't want to, I really don't mind."

"It's not really a decision for me to make alone," she answers, shrugging. "Though I guess it's starting to seem like she doesn't really care about that sort of thing anymore."

409

I nod, my curiosity increasing drastically but my restraint actually functioning for once in my life regardless.

"I understand if it's not really the sort of thing you talk about on a first date," I assure her. "All this magic stuff certainly wasn't planned on my part."

Autumn jolts in surprise, her head suddenly whipping up to stare at me like a rabbit stares at a fox.

"Wait, back that one the fuck up," she demands. "You and Alma went on a *date!?*"

# 22

# FRIENDS

"What?" I yelp, startled. "I thought you and I... who's Alma!?"

Autumn lets out a frustrated growl, clutching her face with both hands.

"Oh, of course!" she snaps. "Of course! That's why she's not fucking writing anything about you! She's going behind my back and getting us into commitments like I don't even exist! Fuck, fuck, *fuck!"*

"A-autumn?" I stutter. "Are you okay? Did I do something wrong?"

She inhales through grit teeth, then lets the breath out slowly, looking up at me.

"No," she answers firmly. "If you don't know what's going on, then none of this is your fault. Probably. You kind of just completely destroyed my concept of reality so I'm second-guessing most things, but I'm *pretty sure* this isn't your fault. It would be stupid if it was."

"Okay?" I hedge, not sure if it's appropriate to ask what the heck she's talking about. She doesn't seem to be paying me much mind, though.

"Fuck it!" she laughs, a worryingly maddened cackle given the circumstances. "Fuck this, fuck all of it! I've tried so *goddamn hard* to do right by her and she goes and tries to start a *relationship* behind my back? Without even talking to me? Something this big? Fuck it! I don't care anymore!"

"A-autumn, you're scaring me a little," I admit quietly.

She laughs even louder at that.

"Of course I am," she chuckles. "God, that's fucking rich considering that you're a *literal magic monster.* But hey, it's funny, right? Scaring you is what she's scared of!"

"What *who* is scared of?" I ask, flinching away a little.

"Right, right, sorry, sorry," Autumn laughs some more, waving me off. "I shouldn't take this shit out on you, if anything you're a victim in all this. You deserve to know. Basically, uh, do you know what plurality is? I assume you don't because you're still looking *really* confused."

"Um… plurality as in like… grammar?" I hedge.

"Okay, that's a no. I have Dissociative Identity Disorder, Hannah. There's two of me, and we don't share memories. We're *supposed* to communicate, yet I was certainly never told that we'd be going on a goddamn date with anybody."

"Oh," I say, blinking slowly as I think back at the thousand little weird things I didn't really understand about Autumn. The notebook, the forgetfulness, *everything.* "Oh gosh. I'm sorry, I feel really dumb. I think I sort of get what's happening, but also not really."

"It's fine. Most people have never even heard of it being a thing outside of *Sybil,* so I don't really expect you to be educated about it."

"…What's *Sybil?"* I ask.

"It's this book-slash-movie that… actually, you know what? Keep being ignorant about *Sybil,* that's totally fine. My situation isn't really like that anyway. Most people's aren't. There is *so* much controversial media bullshit about DID and I don't really wanna get into it!"

"Okay?" I gulp, swapping my focus over from magical recovery to devouring chicken fingers, since I don't have the energy or attention span to do the former right now. "So, um, if I was at the mall with 'Alma,' does that make you 'Autumn,' or…?"

"We're both Autumn," Autumn (?) explains. "Autumn is our legal name and our 'system name,' so it refers to both of us collectively and is the name we use for people that don't know we're a plural system. My personal name is Jet."

"Okay," I nod slowly, doing everything I can to absorb and categorize all the new terminology flying at me at the speed of light. I can only guess as to what the schnitzer any of that means, so I fall back on standard politeness tactics. She gave me a name for the first time, there's an easy response here. "It's nice to officially meet you, Jet."

She flashes me a lopsided grin at that, so I guess I said something right.

"Hey, nice to officially meet you too, ya weird bug girl. You're taking this awfully well."

I flinch and quickly stuff my face with more chicken. Not having anything to chew makes it a rather short distraction, though.

"…Recent events have made me pretty receptive to stuff I don't understand," I mumble, wiggling my new limbs for emphasis. "You having a split personality is hardly outside the realm of believability."

"Okay," Jet nods, her smile fading. "For the record, though, we don't like being called 'personalities.' *Everyone* has multiple personalities, that's part and parcel to how people present themselves. Alma and I are individuals. Two whole, entire people."

"Alright," I nod, a blush rising to my face because apparently I'm being *really rude,* but how was I supposed to ever know that, but it makes *sense* when she explains it so maybe I should have figured it out? I'm so stupid! "I'm sorry, I don't really know anything about this. Just correct me when I say something dumb?"

413

"Yeah, alright," she agrees, and the smile returns. It makes my tummy twist into knots. Curses, I am no longer in too much pain to be gay.

...I *am* still in a lot of pain, though. My transformation-induced regeneration has progressed enough that I'm no longer in danger of dying the moment I stop focusing on magic, which is *extremely* relieving. I feel like I woke up the day after having twelve different surgeries, though, where it's just healed enough that the morphine wore off and just fresh enough to be agonizing. I'm in bad, bad shape and don't trust myself to walk, but in terms of immediate threats to my life I am hopefully more or less in the clear. So I finish devouring my first box of chicken and move onto the second, because Autumn is wonderful and amazing and didn't need to be told that the mutating monster needs lots and lots and *lots* of meat. I mean... Jet is wonderful and amazing. For doing that. Alma is also wonderful and amazing but I guess she has no idea that this is going on. Er, I think?

"...Um, is it okay if I ask some questions?"

"Of course, yeah," Jet agrees, taking a big bite out of her sandwich. "You're already knee deep in it."

"You said that you and Alma don't share memories," I start. "So... how much is she going to be aware of... all this, I guess?"

"None of it, and even if I try to tell her by writing it down I doubt she'll believe me. Because like, why would she?" Jet shrugs. "She already thinks I'm more of an embarrassing psychosis than a person, despite our current therapist's insistence to the contrary."

"Right, okay," I nod meekly. "Um... how does that work, exactly?"

She chews for a moment, taking an extra bite and swallowing it before answering.

"...Weirdly," she decides on. "It's not exactly cut-and-dry. She doesn't remember the things that I do, and I can't talk to her when I'm fronting or vice-versa. But we can still sort of... feel each other out, if that makes sense? Like if Alma had a shit day I'll sorta get the impression that we're having a shit day when I start fronting. And there are some moments when we're kind of... I dunno. I describe it as 'Autumn soup.' We're sort of both there and both not there, if that makes any sense. We can both remember those moments, but we still can't really communicate during them, the state kind of falls apart if we focus on it. I'm *pretty sure* it's brought on by both of us 'being in our element,' so to speak. Like, I tend to come out when Alma gets overwhelmed or shit otherwise needs to get done in an immediate manner. Most of the time, though? I just feel like me, and then there's a weird period when I stop feeling entirely like me, and then things kind of... fade away, until suddenly I'm somewhere else and there's something I need to take care of. Like being mugged, or gym class."

"Oh!" I grin. "So that *was* you in gym class!"

"Uh, yeah," Jet confirms, pointedly glancing away when she spots my teeth. "Yeah, Alma's really scared of the gym teacher. Plus I like exercise more than she does."

"The gym teacher *is* super scary, to be fair."

"He's not scary," Jet grunts. "He's just an asshole. *You're* scary."

I flinch a little, which hurts a lot.

"...I-I'm sorry," I stutter. "I'm not trying to be scary. Thank you so much for helping me."

"Mmm," Jet grunts noncommittally. "Well, I can sort of tell that Alma has grown attached to you, so I couldn't just leave you there to die. And now that I know you're a terrifying magical monster, I very much want to stay on your good side, because I literally have no good options for dealing with the possibility of you being a threat."

"Oh," I say lamely. "Well, um, the degree of pragmatism that went into your decision-making doesn't affect how thankful I am. So... thanks, Jet."

She gives me an odd look, but breaks it off with a shrug.

"You're welcome, I guess. What else do you need from me? I feel like sitting under a bridge all night isn't exactly your idea of a good time."

"I, um... I guess I need to finish healing once I'm done eating," I ponder. "And then... I guess I need to change into the new clothes I just bought for... basically this exact reason?"

I motion at my current torn-to-shreds outfit that's currently revealing all my monster bits. I am *incredibly* lucky that the goddess was kind enough to spare my undies.

"And then... I dunno," I shrug. "We go home?"

"Just like that, huh?" Au—I mean, Jet smirks. "No reporting me to your magical secret society about a containment breach?"

"I am not a part of a magical secret society," I tell her. "I'm the only person I know of in the world that has magic. Which is not to say that there isn't anybody else, I just don't know them. So like, maybe there will be scary magical government spooks coming after us for this? But it hasn't happened to me yet."

"Hmm. So either government incompetence or something *really* scary is going on. Fun."

"My bet is on something really scary," I nod sagely. "That's been a moneymaker so far."

"Normally I'd bet on government incompetence, but that only happens when the government is supposed to help people, so yeah. Something scary. Fantastic. Alma just *had* to pick you of all people to get a crush on, didn't she?"

I wince. Gosh, that brings up a lot of worrying things to ask and I don't really have any good way to ask them, so... bad way it is, I guess.

"Sorry. Um. I have another potentially insensitive question: does this mean you *don't* have a crush on me? Or, I mean, that you never did, even before the freaky monster stuff."

"...Of course not," Jet grumbles. "Why would I? All I know about you is that you're the freaky blood girl who runs *way* too fast for someone with a limp. Don't get me wrong, you're nice and I can see why you'd be Alma's type, but outside of a bit of feedback I get from her? Fuck no. I don't want you to touch me. She likes you, but *I'm not her.*"

"I... okay, I'm sorry, that's super fair. And I can see why you'd be very angry at, um, Alma? For not telling you? Like, I mean, I don't know what you're going through, but that sounds like a really awful thing to keep someone in the dark about if you share a body with them."

She stares at me for a moment, then nods.

"I appreciate that," she admits. "I wish there was a simple answer to the situation, but unfortunately there isn't. I don't want to date— or otherwise be involved with—your weird buggy ass. You scream danger to me, and I don't like it one bit. But I can't just write this all down and expect Alma to believe me, and I don't particularly want you to come clean to her considering the unknown risks. So here's what's going to happen: I'm going to tell Alma that I told you about us. She's going to be furious because we agreed not to do that, but she started it so fuck her. As a result, she'll probably avoid you. If she doesn't, please leave us alone anyway because you are a walking time bomb. Seriously Hannah, why the fuck are you still going to public school?"

"How exactly am I going to get *out* of going to public school?" I grumble back. "Hey mom, hey dad, could you call me in sick? I'm growing chitin!"

"I don't know! Like, maybe yeah, maybe you just say that. Just don't drag us into your mess, okay Hannah?" Jet sighs. "It's nothing personal, honestly. You seem like a great person. But I don't want any part of this."

I scrunch down, swallowing the last of the Chick-fil-A in despair. Dang it. I should have known I can't have nice things. I just... can I not even have *friends* anymore? First Ida, now this! Everyone who finds out about me leaves and they *should* leave because I'm a dangerous freak and I nearly killed a kid today because I'm *also* a man-eating monster! And just when I thought that maybe, *maybe* I could have something fun and happy and normal, whoops! Autumn is two people, actually, and one of them is breaking off the relationship for both of them! I don't get to have *anything!*

Oh, no. My breath is starting to get shaky. I'm going to start crying, aren't I? On top of everything, I'm about to have a complete breakdown in front of the hot girl-or-maybe-girls that just half-dumped me out of what might have been a half-relationship. Oh, fudge biscuits, here come the tears. Why? Why does my life have to be this bad?

"Oh, shit," Jet says quietly as I start to sob. "Uh…"

I hug myself with my extra legs, despite the pain from my wounds, as I clutch my face in my hands. This is too much. It's just too much! How am I supposed to function like this? I'm just some girl, some seventeen-year-old loser, and I have to handle mutations and alternate universes and a scary Goddess and bandits and cultists and nearly bleeding to death under a bridge! Then I finally get one good thing, one *person* I think might be a sign that things can get better, and now I'm not even allowed to see her anymore!

"Um, fuck, uh… Hannah, if you cry like that, someone might come looking for us…?" Jet says hesitantly, her cool attitude breaking entirely under the force of my tears.

"Can't we at least be *friends!?*" I whine, choking for air as the forceful sobs aggravate my wounds and cause pain to blast through my entire body."You don't wanna date me, I get that. I'm a weird freak and I don't even know if you're gay and you're *right* I could be a huge danger to everyone without even knowing how but… but I *like* you! Yeah, it's in the dumb crush way, but it's also just… you're so nice! Both of you are! You're the one that helped me when I was bleeding in the bathroom, right? And you're super cool and you do martial arts and you stopped me from fucking *killing a child* which I just, oh Goddess thank you. Thank you so much. A-and I like Alma too! She's cute and she has great taste in books and she lets me sit with her at lunch when Brendan's busy with his gaming group. You guys are the first new friends I've made in *years!*"

"Um... well, I—"

"A-and do you even get to decide what Alma does?" I ask, the waterworks still flowing. "Like, like I get that for some things it'd be super unhealthy for both of you not to agree on something, but you *just* got mad at her for going behind your back, right? Shouldn't she get to choose if she gets to be my friend? And—"

"Okay!" Jet snaps. "Okay, okay, okay, Jesus! You can talk to her if you wanna talk to her, fuck! Just be quiet!"

"Sorry," I hiccup, doing my best to calm my tears. "Sorry, sorry."

"It's okay, it's fine," Jet hisses. "You're right, okay? You caught my bullshit. I just... I'm trying to keep us safe. It's what I *do.*"

"Sorry," I say again.

"I said it's fine! God, you are the lamest, most blubbery movie monster ever, you know that? I can see why Alma likes you."

I have nothing to say to that, so I just keep quietly sobbing, slowly getting myself under control. I don't know how to feel about that breakdown, honestly. On one hand, I got permission to be friends, and that is *really* important to me. I don't want to lose Autumn after all the wonderful things she's done for me. I need to make it up to her. On the other hand, I feel... dirty. Like I just manipulated her into agreeing by bursting into tears. And like, that's probably stupid, because I certainly am *not* crying on purpose, it's just... I don't know. Everything I do has to be bad somehow. That's what it feels like. I can't have a clean win.

"...You really don't care about the whole 'two of us' thing, huh?" Jet asks.

"Wha?" I sniff. "Should I? You both seem really nice."

She scoffs, standing up and starting to pace around.

"Well first of all, I'm really not that nice," she insists. "But... I don't know. You're weirdly cool with it? Like, I've gotten *so* much shit for this when I've had to explain it to people. We both have, that's why we agreed to stop telling people and try to live normally. Our first therapist was all gung-ho about it, he was fucking writing a paper about DID and kept making us try a bunch of stuff for that cuz he knew we couldn't leave. Then our *second* therapist insisted that our condition was actually just caused *by the first therapist,* which I personally think is bullshit, and he mainly focused on trying to get me to stop existing, which I didn't really appreciate."

"Therapists are the worst," I growl.

"Fucking tell me about it. I mean, things have gotten better since, we found a pretty okay one finally. But there's still all the normal people that think I'm just delusional or lying and don't put any effort into interacting with us like we're separate people, which is just... really awful, not to mention disorienting. Like bitch, stop trying to have a discussion with me about something I was never a part of! Not to mention just general assholishness and... fuck. Why am I even ranting about this? I need to shut up."

"N-no! No, it's okay!" I assure her. "You can unload on me, I get it. I mean, I don't get it *exactly,* but I get people being jerks that refuse to listen. My best friend has days where he can't talk to people or touch anyone, and he's *really* bad with meeting new people, and he gets overwhelmed easily, and all those things can negatively impact how I might want to engage with him on a given day, you know? But it's not *about* me. I learned how to react to those situations, how to help with those situations, when I *shouldn't* be helping with those situations, and it takes a lot of work! But it's worth it, because I'm also pretty weird, and... well, I need help sometimes too, now more than ever, and he's there for me. Not like, in a transactional way, just... we both want to help each other as much as possible, so we do. And the best way to learn how to help someone is to just *listen* to what they ask from you. I can't say I'm not a little *surprised* that you're two people sharing one body, but if that's what you say you are... okay! I believe you. I'll figure things out as best I can."

Jet stares at me for a while, her expression blank. W-was that too cheesy? Did I sound like an idiot? Agh, I said too much about Brendan, too, that's not really my place to say. What's Jet thinking? What's she going to say!?

"...This is the weirdest fucking day of my entire life," she decides.

Oh.

"Well yeah, I mean, that's fair," I agree.

"If we're doing this—and this is still an *if*—we're doing this my way," she insists. "We are going to keep this under wraps, between us and Alma. We are going to learn everything we can about this fucking 'magic' bullshit, and how to defend against it. You're going to come clean to Alma about whatever the fuck you are, assuming she even wants to talk to you after learning you know about me. And then you are going to use that magic bullshit to help me with some things, no questions asked. Alright, 'friend?'"

This is gonna be illegal stuff, isn't it? On one hand, that's terrifying. I barely even jaywalk. On the other hand... be gay do crime? And I'm *definitely* gay for Autumn.

"I'm gonna be really bad at the 'no questions' part," I say. "I reserve final veto rights, but... okay. I'm all for helping a friend."

Those were some of the most terrifying words I've ever said in my life. I just *agreed to do crime things.* I mean, maybe. It'd be great if Jet just wants help with her laundry, but I'm not exactly getting those vibes here. I'm intellectually aware that not all crime is 'evil,' per se, it's just... well. I'm an upper-middle-class young woman in the rich part of town, why would I fight the system when I'm the person the system benefits? Not that I *like* the capitalist hellscape I live in, I just... y'know. Do not have a lot of solid motivations to put myself at risk within it. But if it's for Autumn? I can... try. I suppose. And if it turns out to be really nasty stuff, maybe I can help her claw her way out of whatever pit she's fallen into. Metaphorically. ...Hopefully metaphorically. Oh Goddess we're so boned.

"This is a terrible plan and I'm going to hate myself later," Jet grunts.

"Heh, that's pretty funny," I grin. "I was just thinking the same thing!"

That seems to surprise her for a moment, but then she grins, barking out a laugh as she stands up.

"Alright you fucking psycho," Jet chuckles, "let's get you dressed, healed, and home."

Oh yeah. Self-care. I forgot about that. Nodding, I close my eyes and pull at my link again, shuddering as the itch of healing races across my body. As my scabbed-over wounds repair themselves, so too does the chitin crawl up my hands and legs, growing and solidifying under skin that I know I'll have to cut loose soon. My right leg has chitin all the way to my upper thigh now, and soon it'll start encroaching on my pelvis. Hrm.

I, uh, am just gonna come out and say it: I'm pretty concerned as to what's going to happen to my vagina. Like... I don't know anything about bug sex and I don't *want* to know anything about bug sex, I am perfectly happy with my genitals as-is. So. Y'know. If you're taking requests, body, maybe kindly leave my gonads alone? Thanks.

Thankfully, I don't have to figure out the fate of my loins today. With my wounds mostly healed over, Jet keeps watch while I change into less-shredded clothing and stuff the ruined outfit underneath some other clothes in our shopping bags. My new limbs are a bit more difficult to hide than my other changes, unfortunately, because they pop out of my body right around waist height, where my pants meet my shirt. Twisting them up so they rest against my body and hug my ribcage hides them well enough as long as my shirt isn't too small, and while that's not the least bit comfortable and something I'll have to worry about people bumping into, it's the best we can do for now. I'll probably end up having to bind the new legs up in cloth to hold them in place, although that idea is *really* depressing for some reason. I mean... I

422

guess I know the reason, I like my new legs, but I can't exactly show them off to people. With one last mournful wiggle, I hide them in my shirt.

Now armed with a slightly newer version of what is basically my old outfit, we start heading home. Walking is terrible and it hurts. Jet also wasn't lying to the mugger when she said we didn't buy new shoes, which was kind of a stupid oversight on my part, so my thickest socks and the tattered remains of my actively-disintegrating current pair have to do for now. Every movement of my battered body screams in agony, a constant reminder not to fuck around with the Goddess lest I find out again. And *boy* did I find out.

"...Wait, is this the right way to your house?" I mumble.

"No, we're going to your house first," Jet grunts. "I can get home safe on my own. If you go alone you'll somehow manage to get mugged twice in one night."

"I hate that you're right."

There isn't much conversation from there on, which I guess is pretty fair. Jet has plenty to process, and I do too. I'm not sure how I feel about kinda-sorta-unfairly pressuring her into staying-slash-becoming my friend. She kind of has a point. I'm dangerous. It's probably best for everyone if I run off and become a hermit in the woods or something. It's all just too much for me, though. I'm too selfish to push her away like I should.

"Alright, this is my house," I announce once we arrive. "I'd invite you in or something but I don't want you to have to deal with my mom. She'll interrogate you about what we did today, and... yeah."

"Mmm. Nice neighborhood," Jet comments, glancing around with a critical eye.

"Oh, um... yep. My parents are, uh, pretty loaded. Anyway though, thanks again for all your help. It really means more to me than I can express."

"Mmm-hmm. It's what I do. Take care of yourself, Hannah, and try not to get in any more messes."

"I will," I promise. "But I'm probably going to fail miserably."

"Yeah, that checks out. G'night, bug girl."

I wince when she calls me that, glancing around for witnesses even though there's no way anyone else could get the context or find it suspicious without that context. She smirks at me, shakes her head, and walks off before I awkwardly remember to wave goodbye.

"See you, Jet!"

She gives me a singular wave without turning to face me, which is kind of unnecessarily cool of her and it makes me smile. Untrigintuple-checking myself for any out-of-place clothing, I take a deep breath and walk up to the front door of my own house, something that probably shouldn't be as terrifying as it actually is. Sure enough, when I open the door I'm swiftly greeted by the happy voice of my father.

"Hannahgator! Hey, you! Where have you been all day?"

And thus, I am trapped against my will. I hesitantly clutch all my shopping bags close, trying to decide whether or not to leave them here, run to my room to drop them off, or bring them with me as I face the conversation in front of me. I ultimately bring them with; it's not likely that anyone would rummage through the bags while I'm not around, but I'm certainly paranoid that they would. I *do* quickly slip off my ruined shoes and hide them underneath some clothes before walking down the main hallway and into our huge living room/dining room/kitchen, though. The moment I peek my head in I find my father and mother sitting on the couch together, watching one of the ten quintillion different television shows with Gordon Ramsay in it.

"Um, hey mom, hey dad," I say, waving. "I went to the mall with a friend."

"Did they drive you?" my mom asks. "I didn't hear a car."

"Oh, um, no. We walked."

"Mmm. You shouldn't walk around that area late at night, Hannah. Call me next time, your father or I can pick you up."

If not for the fact that I was literally just mugged, I wouldn't even consider ever doing that. Now that I've nearly died, I give it serious consideration and then decide to reject it.

"I'll do that," I lie anyway, because that is the only way to escape this conversation.

"Who did you go with?" my dad asks.

"A new friend, you don't know her. Her name is—" oh god she has three names which name do I give my parents "—Altum."

"All-tum?" my dad clarifies.

I mean hoo boy she has a *great* tum, but holy *geez* I cannot say that out loud ever.

"U-um, Autumn. Her name is Autumn. Sorry."

"Did you have fun?" my mom asks. "It's good to see you spending time with some other friends. That Ida girl is always so polite."

Ida just knows how to turn the charm on when she needs to, and also you'd hate her if you knew that she wants to bone me. But sure.

"I hope Ida and I can hang out together again soon," I say honestly. "I haven't seen her for a while, though."

"Oh, you young people are always so busy. You'll see her again," my mom promises, despite knowing absolutely nothing about the situation. "So, what did you buy?"

"Oh, um, just clothes," I say. "A lot of my old clothes are getting kind of worn-out."

"Mmm. I hope you didn't spend too much?"

"I never do," I answer honestly.

My mom nods approvingly, and I'm kind of annoyed how happy and proud I am to see that. If there's one virtue my mother likes to espouse that I'm genuinely good at, it's saving money. The secret is to have a mom that's really insistent on money management and therefore be pathologically terrified of spending anything in the first place. I've been reliable enough with my good spending habits that my mom even believes me when I claim to have them, which is an extremely rare smidgen of respect and always a nice feeling.

"Alright, well, let us know where you're going next time, okay?" she asks. "Us parents get worried, you know."

"Of course, yeah," I lie. "I'm gonna, um, put this stuff away, if that's okay?"

"Alright. We'll be going to bed soon, so try to keep it down."

"Okay," I nod, and then finally get to retreat to my room, shutting the door behind me. I hide my destroyed clothing and put my new outfits away before exiting my room and locking myself in the bathroom instead, stripping down to check my recent wounds. There's scarring all over my body now, even on my face, though thankfully the face scars are so light that they weren't noticeable from where my parents were sitting. Other places on my body have it much worse, places where cuts went deep and my bootlegged healing couldn't quite get the job done. Goddess, gym on Monday is going to be absolute hell. Just walking home was bad enough.

As for my actual mutation, I manage to make myself giggle by waving at my reflection in the mirror with my new limbs. As I feel around my body, I start to suspect that limbs seven and eight might be coming in soon as well; there's some severe tension under my shoulderblades that feels like more than just bad posture cramps. I hope it's more arms. Seems like it'd be a weird spot for dinky little spider legs. I mean, I guess any spot on my mostly-humanoid body is a weird spot for dinky little spider legs, but whatever. A girl can dream. Unless that girl is me because I guess I don't dream anymore and I arguably never have.

426

It is what it is, I guess. I successfully hide from my parents for the rest of the night, doing my best to calm myself down before the inevitable breakdown that will be waking up back on the world tree. I'm absolutely exhausted, though, which I suppose nearly dying probably tends to do to a person. I crawl into bed, pass out, and wake up. I am a lot smaller, and the world is a lot bigger. The barren zone I went to sleep in is still cold and dark and lifeless, but what little of the world outside that I can perceive with my spatial sense is at least somewhat different. Notably, camp is almost entirely packed up and someone had the good sense to move the bodies outside my line of sight. I'll have to thank them. Though I don't really get the ability to rest thanks to the odd way sleeping works for me, and my day hasn't exactly been a pleasant one back on Earth, I'm still doing better than I was when I first passed out here. I take a deep breath and stand up on ten shaky legs, as ready to face the day as can be expected.

...Wait. I take a deep breath?

Holy cannoli I'm breathing. I have lungs! What!? The moment I move to stand, I get that horrid, itchy feeling of my outer chitin layer molting off, so I have to cut myself free of that while I peek at my own internal organs, marveling at how my collection of book lungs have twisted and evolved to support diaphragm muscles, letting me inhale and exhale manually. Wow! Will I be able to talk now?

I try to say a word and it comes out of my body as a horrible eldritch hiss, because of course it does. Well darn, I'm still stuck writing and going through Sindri to communicate. But hopefully things will be better soon!

My horrible noises seem to have caught the attention of my friends while I munch idly on my discarded skin, causing them all to look not-quite-correctly in my direction. It's kind of funny how wrong they are, but I guess it's not their fault that their necks can't rotate along the w-axis.

*Hannah?* I think to myself. No, wait, that's obviously Sindri.

427

*Sindri, hi!* I greet him. *Sorry for, um... sorry. I'm okay now.*

*I'm pretty sure at least one of us would be dead if not for you,* Sindri answers. *You have absolutely nothing to apologize for. Thank you, Hannah. Truly.*

I'm not sure how I feel about that. Both disgusted and proud, I suppose? I step out of the barren zone back into normal space, flinching at the light. The sun's almost straight overhead already? Did I sleep through the whole morning?

*Oh gosh, did I make you guys wait?* I yelp. *Sorry, everyone! Sorry!*

*Don't worry about it, Hannah,* Sindri reassures me. *We all needed rest after that. I took the time to collect some animal companions as well, to help take the load off of any future fights. It tends to be difficult to convince most creatures to leave their natural habitats or enter settlements, but, ah... well, with the right incentives they can be convinced to protect us for a time.*

*Oh, that's neat,* I say, trying not to think about how the right incentives might be the reason the corpses are missing. The thought of those animals eating the bodies I killed makes me kind of jealous, and that's... well, it's not a good start to the day to realize how messed up my head has become.

*Yes, our new [large, four legs, hunter, dangerous] will be joining us soon, though I have him out scouting ahead for now. I'd like to ensure today's travels are as uneventful as possible.*

*Oh, alright! Sounds neat! I hope he's friendly!*

*Don't worry, Hannah, I'm very good at making friends,* Sindri assures me. *And I'm very lucky that my friends are so good at protecting me.*


I make a few embarrassed burbling noises and spin around in a circle a little, which makes Sindri chuckle.

*I'm not... I don't... I really, really don't like killing people, Sindri,* I whine. *How often does this kind of thing happen?*

428

*Unfortunately, 'this kind of thing' is frighteningly common,* Sindri explains as Kagiso notices my distress and walks over to pick me up. I flail my legs a bit when she grabs me by the top of the carapace, but she'd never drop me so I eventually just let her lift me up without resistance. Rather than put me on her head, she cuddles me in two arms and then sits down to sand down some arrow shafts with her other arms.

*So people just attack each other randomly?* I grumble.

*Well, it's hardly random,* Sindri explains. *Those men were from a dead branch. Normally, dentron communities tap the veins of the world tree and subsist mainly off of the plentiful rivers of sap. But sap is somewhat rapidly becoming less plentiful. It's flowing more slowly, and many leaves or entire branches are starting to die. Consequently, the normally-peaceful dentron are experiencing resource shortages that they've historically never had to deal with. When people from destroyed communities can't find a home because their neighbors don't want to feed them, they often turn to banditry.*

Oh. Huh. That's a problem, yeah. I suppose impending apocalypses are rather dangerous. It's funny, really; normally when you think of an apocalypse, you think of some huge, cataclysmic event that ruins everything immediately. What's happening to the tree seems like more of a long, drawn-out death, though. The highest branches burn, and the tree dies, but it sounds like this has been happening for hundreds of years. Everyone is so used to the idea that no one is panicking about it, it's just *how things are.* Yep, the world sure is on fire. Whatcha gonna do?

Honestly, it sounds concerningly similar to Earth.

*Is the dentron city we're visiting going to be okay?* I ask.

*Should be,* Sindri confirms. *This branch seems fine for now. Speaking of the city, are you prepared to start traveling again, Hannah? We'll still be able to reach the city tomorrow if we get marching.*

*Yeah, I'm ready I think,* I confirm. *What about you, Kagiso?*

Silence answers me. Kagiso doesn't seem to hear my question at all.

*Oh, haha. Sorry, Hannah, it's just you and me that are connected right now,* Sindri explains. *I haven't had the time to set up the team link this morning.*

*You haven't… oh, right! You do need to do that every morning, huh?* I remember. *Sorry, I'm still a bit out of it. But… wait, hold on. Don't you normally need to touch me to start this link as well?*

*You poked me when you woke me up, Hannah,* Sindri reminds me. *I haven't gone back to sleep since the fight.*

*Right, yeah, I remember,* I nod. *So… huh. Have you been maintaining the mental link while I sleep?*

*Just for your little after-battle nap there,* he says. *Don't worry, I don't pick up anything you're not purposefully attempting to send me.*

Oh. Okay, that's good. It would have been really freaky for him to have mentally gleaned information about Earth from my 'dreams.' I don't know how I'd ever explain something like that. Still, now I'm kind of freaking out about it.

*…Um, sorry, I don't mean to be rude,* I say, *but now that I'm thinking about it, how do I know that's true? I don't really have any idea what you can do with your magic.*

*Sure, but why would I lie to you?* Sindri asks. *We've been traveling together for a good while now, and we've gotten each other out of some really tight situations. I should hope you know me at least fairly well by now, and I certainly feel like I know you. In fact, I respect you, Hannah. I can't prove my own inability to do something—that's a logical impossibility—but surely I've done enough to earn your trust?*

Ah, of course. He's right, I'm being stupid, getting paranoid and thinking about terrible situations for no good reason.

*Of course I trust him,* I think to myself. *He's my friend.*

# 23

# AND I FEEL FINE

The day's travels are actually pretty fun, all things considered. Sindri's new tamed animal is a tiger-lizard-weasel thing that Kagiso decided to name Bulupunu, which I'm pretty sure means something like 'bald moron.' She named him this after I declared I wanted to try riding him, and in her defense Bulupunu did kind of turn out to be pretty uncomfortable to sit on. His huge, sinuous body is covered in small, rough scales that would probably tear up my skin if I had any. It feels fine on my carapace, but the way the wiggly boy bounces and twists and jumps like an extra-long cat kind of rattles my brain around and forces me to cling desperately to his back lest I be tossed off like an old rag. I quickly return to my usual perch on top of Kagiso's head, much to her smug satisfaction.

I have to admit, though, Bulupunu makes our journey a lot easier. He's naturalborn to Light, and much like the human being I killed and ate that one time *in self-defense,* that manifests as the ability to create and control lightning. Bulupunu uses this both to hunt—by latching onto something with his huge jaws and pumping them full of volts until they pass out—and to scare away potential hunters by making his body flash bright light and crackle like thunder, which does wonders for deterring beasts that might actually be dangerous to a lizard-tiger that shoots lightning. Scaly longcat is a good boy and a good friend.

Overall, though, the day isn't very eventful. Teboho and I practice the dentron language some more while Sindri and Kagiso mostly stay quiet, as usual. It's only a half-day of travel instead of the usual full day, and I rest for most of it, avoiding hunting for the time being. I'm hungry, and I twitch to go after the various friend noodles and other small animals in the area, but I'm just not up for it right now. My friends seem to understand, and they just let me munch on meat rations without comment. I'm given last watch again when we make camp and Sindri takes first, letting Kagiso and I snuggle up in her bedroll for the night. I'm a bit bigger than I was yesterday, but not by a lot. Molting is not a speedy method of growth, I guess. Wrapped up in the fuzzy arms of a friend, I drift to sleep.

I wake up and inhale deeply. I no longer need to worry about forgetting to breathe in the morning, since my hyperspider form finally has lungs. The reflexes match. Everything feels just a little bit more right. A relaxing day over on the world tree is exactly what I needed to get a bit of a mental reset after the chaos of the day before, and I spend a few moments basking in it before my alarm goes off and my phone reminds me that it's Sunday. I need to go to church with my family. Joy of joys.

Groaning, I quickly do my mental limb check and get myself in order before slithering out from under the covers, dropping on the floor in a crouch. Goddess, my entire right leg is chitin now and it honestly looks kind of sweet. Gleaming, pristine porcelain-white, hard and angled with the occasional protruding spike, all with just a hint of pitch black hiding inside the joints. Just looking at it makes me feel *powerful*, like I could kick through a wall. Hell, maybe I can! My left leg is starting to grow similarly, with my entire foot and some of my shin feeling like it's ready to be freed from the skin. Even more notably, *I'm not in pain.* Looking around my body, I still see the occasional light scar from what the Goddess did to me, but the agony I went to sleep with is gone completely. I guess my Transmutation magic works a lot better when I'm asleep?

432

I grab my phone to shut the alarm off, swipe the screen, and then... nothing happens. Blinking with surprise, I poke a finger and realize that they're *also* covered in dead skin. Ripping it off with my teeth, I quickly learn that all ten of my fingers are fully chitinous now, all the way to the palm. Creepy-looking.

...But the thing is, this shouldn't actually be preventing me from using the touch screen. I've been using my claws to operate my phone for days now, so why is that changing now? Capacitive touchscreens just function using electrical currents; living things are generally great conductors, which is why it works, but anything that can carry even a bit of electrical charge can do the trick. It doesn't even need to have an electrical charge running through it, or at least not an appreciable one. Like, you can use a capacitive touch screen with a soda can if you want to. So how come... wait. Oh gosh.

I don't have any more fingers with living skin, but I still have plenty of skin and that *should* use a touch screen just fine. But the palm of my hand doesn't work, my elbow doesn't work, my nose doesn't work... the capacitive touch screen can't pick up my body *at all*, it doesn't seem to matter whether or not I'm touching it with skin. The problem isn't that I'm chitinous, it's that I'm *Space-aligned,* and Space opposes Light. I've apparently become *too electrically resistant* to interact with this quintessential piece of modern technology, which is kind of a big stinky pile of cow poo.

Fortunately, I have a workaround. Thin gloves don't prevent you from using a touch screen, but thick gloves do and I need thick gloves for creepy monster finger reasons. So the gloves I bought yesterday are capacitive; there's some copper mesh in the fingertips that lets me use my phone. Of course, I'll have the problem of looking like a complete weirdo for wearing winter gloves in late spring, but it's better than the problem of being trapped at church without even a phone to run away and use in the bathroom to replenish myself from the sanity-draining field that is my congregation.

Well, it is what it is. I shrug to myself with my little spider limbs and bundle up in clothing just so I can walk to the bathroom and strip everything off again. It's the same routine as always, just how I like it: shower, eat my dead skin, try not to carve new holes in the bathtub, get the shampoo out and lather, rinse, repeat. An hour later and I'm stepping out to dry myself off around the same time my brother is waking up. Clothes, makeup, triple-check everything... yeah, we're good to go.

I'm in a weirdly good mood today for how terrible yesterday was, but I'm not going to complain. My brain doesn't seem to particularly enjoy dispensing the good chemicals, but maybe this monster transformation will wipe away a bit of the depression while it's up there giving me creepy urges to claw people apart. Honestly, wouldn't that be nice? This is probably just a temporary thing, though, so I resolve to enjoy it while it lasts.

My mom is already making breakfast when I head downstairs, and I ask for a bunch of eggs and sausage instead of pancakes, which she seems surprised by but accepts without comment. My father is nowhere to be seen, though, which is odd for a Sunday.

"Where's dad?" I ask.

"He has COVID, remember?" my mother chides. "He'll be staying home."

Oh. Oh *right*. I totally forgot about that, now I feel terrible. But... wait, wasn't she sharing a couch with him last night? Gah, she's going to infect my whole church, isn't she? I really, really hope she doesn't kill any of the old people that attend with us. Though honestly, most of the elderly at my church do wear masks, so maybe they'll be okay? My church was actually super cool about encouraging people to get vaccines, so props to them for that. It's a shame they're bigots!

I manage to get through breakfast without outing my freaky teeth or even having a conversation with my mother, which is more evidence that today is going to be an uncharacteristically good day. Eventually, my brother graces us with his presence, shoves some food down his throat, and all three of us waddle into the car and rush off to the stupid building that worships a fake deity like complete idiots. Guess what, losers? Religion is real, *but yours isn't!*

Heh. I wonder what would happen if I spoke a spell at church and got the actual Goddess to show up? She'd probably think it would be funny, which actually maybe isn't a good thing now that I'm considering it. Hmm. So, Teboho is totally right, I'm apparently favored by the Goddess. She even told me as much. Does that make me some kind of prophet? Gosh, I hope not. The Goddess is scary.

I'm still considering this when we pull into church and file into the main room, waiting for the old white guy behind the pulpit to teach us more nonsense. Today's sermon is apparently about Moses on Mt. Sinai, specifically the part where Moses asks to see Yahweh face-to-face. And Yahweh pretty much goes 'gosh, I mean, I really like you my guy, but if you actually *do* see my face you'll literally die. But tell you what: I'll head down there and turn around, and you can look at my butt if you wanna. Unlike my face, my posterior is not too powerful for mortals.'

Which, first of all: weak! If you were really as powerful as you say I bet that your divine bumcrack would smite people just as hard as your stupid gay-hating face. Second of all, this brings up so many questions about my personal divine experiences. I've never actually seen *any* part of the Goddess, despite how I tend to get impressions from Her that are best described with visual comparisons. As far as I know she doesn't even have a physical form. But what if she *does?* What if there is some physical representation of the Goddess? Would seeing it kill me? Would it drive me mad? Is there a way to miscast so hard that the Goddess appears personally to blast your brain out through your nostrils? I really, *really* don't want to find out. Honestly, it's kind of terrifying thinking about the fact that entire societies of people use spell incantations regularly. There's no way they all experience the Goddess in the same way I do, right? Sindri doesn't seem to notice Her at all.

...Hmm. When did I start mentally capitalizing the Goddess' pronouns? It just started to feel right after she nearly murdered me. That's... probably not healthy. Oh snickerdoodle this is so utterly terrifying, let's think about something else!

The hymns provide a welcome distraction as I finish quietly surviving through church because quietly surviving through church is one of my primary skills. I send Brendan a text or two from the safety of the bathroom but he unfortunately doesn't answer, likely due to being unconscious. Church service tends to end just after noon, which is not usually weekend Brendan hours.

That's okay. I lurk on Reddit for a bit, search for any crackpot sightings of weird monster girls staggering around last night on a whim, and relax a bit when I don't find anything. Eventually my bathroom safety time comes to a close and I have to pretend to care about all the people that would immediately try to "fix" me if they knew who I was for a while before the hell that is Church finally ends and our family Taco Bell run finally begins. Burritos are an interesting experience for me, because the cheese and meat tastes way better than it used to but the tortilla is no longer a flavorless filling dispensary service, it's actively kind of gross. I eat it all anyway, since the experience is still pretty decent overall. Hopefully it won't upset my stomach.

Other than the bit where I'm secretly hiding the fact that I have claws and chitin and a concerningly above-average number of limbs for a human (as opposed to a normally above-average number of limbs for a human), the day so far remains comfortably routine. I don't even really think about the fact that Sundays are usually streaming days; when we get home, I immediately go upstairs and start changing into a better outfit for streaming, fixing my makeup and triple-checking my setup for everything I need to do my second job. Hmm... what to play today? I finished *Legends: Arceus* last time so it's probably good to start something new. I'm tempted to start *Pokémon: Uranium,* I hear that fangame is super good, but I don't want to anger the Nintendo gods, or worse, the Nintendo legal team. You know what? Screw it. I've been saving a SoulSilver Nuzlocke for a rainy day and 'mutating into a horror monster and completely losing control over my life' sounds like primo rainy day material to me. I grin as I start the stream in the 'starting soon!' screen, watching my piddly little viewer count slowly tick upwards and happily absorbing the dopamine that my brain produces as a result. It's super nice to be liked, even in a weird parasocial way.

Alright. Check my cover-ups, verify my camera, start my emulator, set up my display. Everything's in working order. It's go time.

"Welcome, everybody! We're in for a treat today, I think. I'm going to be Nuzlocking my favorite Pokémon game: SoulSilver version. You know the rules: one 'mon per route, if it faints it's dead, and we nickname them all so the death actually hurts. Let's go!"

There's not much to do in the early parts of a Pokémon game, so I mostly spend the time gushing about why SoulSilver is the best. As I name my character "DD," I bring up the obvious points like how it's the first game to implement universal follow Pokémon and, thanks to the fact that it's a sprite game, it's the first one to work without being ugly as sin. I'm *not* a fan of 3D Pokémon models and never have been, I feel like the game's developers just don't put enough work into them to make them anything other than awkward-looking. With sprites, you don't need to worry about that problem as much. Beautiful sprite animations are great, but simplistic sprite animations don't *bother* me the same way simplistic 3D animations do. The nature of a handheld game with a zoomed-out top-down camera like the old Pokémon titles means that the world design, map layout, and character sprites on the overworld are all very representative and simple. They're sixteen-by-sixteen or thirty-two-by-thirty-two pixel sprites, for crying out loud. They leave a lot to the imagination by necessity, and that works really well for Pokémon since the sheer number of the little buggers really is a workload issue. That strategy doesn't translate to 3D at *all*, though, and Game Freak didn't adapt. So yeah. I guess I have Opinions™. What's the point of being a professional streamer if I can't subject my audience to them?

AllTricks hey DD what's with the mask

SwalotRancher ya is this a bit

...I guess they care more about what I'm wearing today. Thankfully, I have a good answer.

"My dad caught COVID the other day," I explain. "I'm just trying to stay safe."

Xenoversal oh shit I hope he's okay?

Lucarivor29 wait for real

LavAbsol Stay safe, DD!

"Thanks guys," I smile under the mask. "He should be okay, he's not stuck in the hospital or anything."

Lucarivor29 alright well what's with the gloves tho

...Aw crap I don't have a good excuse for that one. I hesitate, pretending to be focused on the game to give myself time to think. I'm going to get outed someday, right? It's inevitable, and Brendan's plan for that eventuality is to out myself to as many people as possible in order to reduce the ability of magical spooks to disappear me. I'm definitely not prepared for that right now, especially not with my barely twenty-one subscribers, but this *is* my chance for that. I swallow and gather my courage.

"The gloves are very much a bit," I answer, doing everything in my power to keep my voice steady. "If I hit fifty subs I'll show you what's going on."

PentUp oh shit hand pics!?!?

SwalotRancher oh no DD is becoming an egirl

"It's not...! Oh my Goddess, it's not like that," I protest. "It's not gonna be *creepy*, it's gonna be *cool.* At least so long as you guys don't make it creepy!"

ZirconCommando goti t. Operation: make it creepy is go.

LavAbsol Don't break the rules. She'll ban you.

Lucarivor29 "Oh my goddess?"

438

SwalotRancher more of the bit I guess?

"Uh, yeah," I confirm halfheartedly. "More of the bit."

Xenoversal sus

Shut up, Xenoversal. You know nothing. Unless you're secretly Brendan, I still have no idea what his Twitch name is. Hoping my mask hides at least most of my blush, I return my attention to the game, where I'm using game clock and repel manipulation strategies to guarantee myself a Gastly from Sprout Tower. There's really no reason not to, since the alternative is Rattata. Though Rattata is surprisingly dangerous from levels sixteen to twenty or so just because it learns Hyper Fang, which is a base 80 power STAB move that hurts like a truck at low levels when everyone else's moves are barely half as good. Gastly, meanwhile, is comparatively kind of garbage at this stage of the game, but the ghost type is *way* better long-term. I successfully catch one by just tossing normal pokeballs without even attacking (Gastly's catch rate is 90 so it's better odds than risking a crit) and name her My Future. Get it? Because she's dead!

With the help of my Geodude (who I named Fratricide because I'm going to teach him Rock Smash to deal with Whitney) I easily destroy Falkner and clear the first gym without trouble. The waves of nostalgia radiating through my body as I play this game are soothing enough to get me into a pleasant zen state, not even the inherent danger to a challenge run that lets Pokémon die enough to break me out of it. Pokémon SoulSilver is one of those games I know basically everything there is to know about, and I very much enjoy describing my strategies and showing off as we make our way through the game. The chat seems to like it too! I even get two new subscribers! ...Which is a lot for me, thank you very much. I hear if you average twenty viewers per stream you're in the top 1% of Twitch, so I guess I'm a prime roller (haha, Twitch joke). Fear me and the fifty-seven dollars and twenty-seven cents I'm due to make this month! ...Gosh this train of thought is embarrassingly stupid, I'm going to change it now.

Unfortunately, all good things must come to a close, especially when they are my good things. Day passes to night and I start getting sleepy, which means I'll ruin my good stream if I keep going. It's important that the stream *ends* as well as it starts; that's what keeps people coming back. So I keep going until right before the next major fight and then announce the end of the stream, much to everyone's dismay. Sorry, chat! Cliffhangers improve retention, engagement, and overall enjoyment. I have no mercy for you.

With the stream off, I head to the bathroom to wash the makeup off my face, take a dump, and finally get in bed. No bones in my poop today! That's nice. That's just great. Always good to see. It doesn't take long after that for me to close my eyes and fall asleep.

My eyes are already open when I wake up, though it's somewhat disorienting to feel Kagiso poking and prodding them for the purpose of doing so. Having solid rather than squishy eyes is weird. I'm not quite sure how it works, but I suspect my depth perception and ability to focus on things would be absolutely awful if not for the fact that I can use my spatial sense to supplement that information on most things.

Kagiso is out of the bedroll and about to get in, since she had to slink out for middle watch. I regretfully exit, wiggling my body and stifling a yawn. Gosh, I can *yawn* now. How funky is that? It feels like I'm going to molt soon too, but my carapace hasn't quite fallen off yet so I successfully manage to scuttle out of the bedroll without leaving any body parts behind.

"Watch good," Kagiso says, and it's neat that I can mostly understand her now. I bob my body in confirmation and she gives me a pat before curling up and getting comfortable for sleep.

Welp. Time for a hopefully-boring watch of me trying not to have a panic attack every time I hear a noise. Though honestly, most of the noises nearby are made by Bulupunu. Tiny blasts of lightning sometimes spark out of his nose as he snores, the buzzing crackle punctuating through the quiet of night and scaring away nearly

440

anything that gets close. It's a shame that Sindri never found a strong animal companion like this earlier. I'm sure he has his reasons, though.

Despite my brain's loud insistence that things are about to go very, very badly, they somehow don't and the sun eventually rises without incident. I scuttle into tents and start poking people awake, to a chorus of exhausted 'good mornings' and 'thank-yous.' Soon enough, camp is packed up, I'm back on Kagiso's head, and our journey resumes.

"Say speak opinion me vocal Hana," Teboho says, and it takes my brain a moment to rearrange all the grammar in my head and figure out that he's suggesting that the team speak out loud today rather than use the mental link to help me practice my language skills.

"That's a good idea," Sindri agrees (and it takes an equally long brain-twister for me to parse that one), "but Hana still needs the link so she can talk."

"Oh, true," Teboho concedes, and we quickly link up.

*Also noteworthy is that you all pronounce my name weird when you say it out loud and I don't really like it,* I comment, though it's mostly playful.

"Apologies!" Teboho answers immediately. "Though I'm not sure what to do about that... is it true you're growing—" ...and then he says some gibberish word that I assume means 'lungs.'

*Yeah, I have lungs now!* I confirm. *But no voicebox. Maybe later. Transmutation magic is super weird. I don't have much control over it.*

"That's odd," Teboho muses. "It's rare for non-Chaos mages to have magic they can't consciously control."

*Actually, I'm pretty sure it's because the spell that's changing me is Transmutation and Order. Spells can be more than one type at the same time, right?*

441

"They can indeed," Teboho agrees. "And I think I see what you mean. The Order component makes the spell only go one way, rather than shifting back and forth between possible forms as Transmutation is naturally wont to do."

*Sure, I guess?* I hedge. *You'd know more about that than I do. I just think it's both because it feels like both.*

Sindri clears his throat and speaks next.

"Were you familiar with magic category—" he says a word I don't know "—before learning the Aura Sight spell?"

*Sorry, am I familiar with what?*

*Qualia,* Sindri says over the mental link. *Were you familiar with magical qualia? As in, the unique feeling they each give off which makes them so easily recognizable and namable.*

*Oh, yeah,* I confirm. *Yeah, I kind of get the feeling of which kind of magic I'm using when I use it.*

"Hmm. That doesn't happen to me," Sindri muses. "But I'm only naturalborn to one element."

"I get the same impressions as Hana," Teboho nods. "My different elements are different."

"Only have one, but Motion feels like Motion," Kagiso grunts. "Sindri just stupid."

He twitches a bit at that, and I can't help but do a little hissy giggle. Teboho, Sindri, and Bulupunu all flinch at the sound, though Kagiso just pats me on the head like I deserve a reward.

"Good Hana. Taunt fools. Kill enemies."

*U-um. Thank you?*

"Ahem. Well. Be that as it may," Sindri deflects, "we should make it to the city of Grawlaka just after noon. If you've never seen a dentron city before, Hana, I think it'll be quite the sight."

*I look forward to it!* I agree happily.

442

And I really do! Fantasy civilizations sound neat, and hopefully there won't be quite as much horrible murder going on there. Or well, at least not as much horrible murder that I have to personally participate in. The excitement is a bit intoxicating, so I spend a lot more time today scuttling around through forest branches and catching small critters for my seemingly-bottomless stomach to consume. There are some neat little flying-squirrel-like creatures, some pretty supersized butterflies, and even some freaky, many-tentacled tree octopuses, camouflage and all. They're all quite tasty, but the wormy, fuzzy little friend noodles remain my favorite snack.

With the delicious distractions of hunting occupying my morning, it doesn't take long until I notice the ground we're traveling on start to slowly slant steeper and steeper downwards, until eventually the ground is no longer at a safe angle to walk on. While Teboho, Kagiso and I can ignore this by sticking to the trees, Sindri has no such luck and so we need to backtrack a bit uphill—which is doable, because the slope is mostly parallel to our traveling direction. With the way the trees thin out, though, I bet it would be possible to reach the edge of the forest fairly easily, just by heading down the slope far enough that there's no longer any soil stuck to the mighty branch of the Tree of Souls. I resist the urge, though, and soon enough we find an entirely different edge to the forest, one that I didn't expect to witness: an absolutely massive set of stairs.

"We're here," Sindri announces. "Grawlaka Bridge is right ahead of us."

The stone stairs are carved and installed into the side of the branch, a huge sloped road that's gotta be at least a hundred feet across. A smattering of dentron travel up and down, and while we get a few weird looks when we step out of the forest looking like vagabonds, people seem to lose interest after a few seconds. We're just some weirdos, and weirdos are a dime a dozen. Ah, it's good to be back in civilization.

Up the stairs, there isn't much to see. At some point they stop needing to *be* stairs and presumably even out into a much more normal road, but there isn't really much to see in that direction. It's *down* the stairs that has the really gorgeous view.

I have been told that I live on a world tree. I have *seen* that I live on a world tree: whenever I go to the tops of the branches in the forest, I can spot the massive trunk rising up into the sky, vanishing into the foliage it supports. I can see the mighty branches twist out from the trunk, beautiful and enormous beyond comprehension. And that's the problem; it's *beyond comprehension.* It's similar to the awe of staring up at the night sky: gorgeous, humbling, and yet completely beyond my ability to truly fathom the scale of. The human (and hyperspider) mind can't deal with orders of magnitude all that well, and some of the scale is lost in translation just because I can't really contextualize it. There's no sense of scale.

As I watch people walk the staircase, walk down to the *bottom* of the staircase, and start crossing the massive stone road *built atop the stem of a leaf,* a leaf which grows out from the middle of our current branch, longer and thicker than the golden gate bridge, ultimately terminating in a massive, island-sized flat green platform on which a redwood-scale forest grows, *I have the context for the scale.* It's as breathtaking as the Goddess Herself.

*Holy cannoli burrito and fries,* I say, awe overtaking me.

"What?" Sindri and Teboho both ask.

*I... it's just... woah! This is so huge and cool and crazy! There's a city over there!?*

"There certainly is," Sindri confirms. "Most of the leaf is the city, in fact. It's the largest dentron state on the branch."

*That's so cool!*

Teboho chuckles.

"Just wait until we get there! The city has some wonderful sights once you're in it, as well!"

*Yeah! Okay! Let's go let's go let's go!*

Now this is the cool part of being in a fantasy world! Wow! I bound happily down onto the stairwell, skittering down the little wall between the forest and the start of the steps proper. Almost immediately, my chitinous bladed legs scrabble tractionlessly on the stone and I stumble, causing me to fall down the steps. I instinctively curl up into a ball, which only seems to make the problem worse as I start rolling, rolling, rolling down the staircase, clonking my noggin with each fall.

*Ow! Ow! Ow! Somebody help!*

Unfortunately, rather than run after me and pick me up like kind people would and should, my friends all immediately burst into laughter. Even Kagiso! Sweet, lovable Kagiso! How could you!?

*Taunt fools!* she mentally reminds me as she doubles over and snorts with glee.

*Curse youuuu!* I call after her as my spherical body continues to roll and bounce and smack into stairs for nearly twenty flights before I finally stop. Shakily extracting my legs from my core, I carefully, *carefully* stand up on the slippery stone, waiting for my friends to come pick me up while my body pulses with adrenaline. But for once, it's not *bad* adrenaline. I'm not really hurt, just... a bit sore and disoriented.

*I'd like to be a hat again please,* I whine, causing Kagiso to grin and bound over to pick me back up.

"Hat is friend," Kagiso declares happily, since 'hana' and 'hat' are the same dang word. She places me on her head where I hug her skull nice and tight. It's gonna be sad when I grow to be too big for this.

My friends catch up with us and we make our way down the stairs together, the giant green stem getting closer and closer until eventually we're on top of it, walking down startlingly even and well-maintained cobblestone streets. I wonder how they make these? Where do they get all the stone? Is it possible they just use Matter magic to conjure it up!? Oh gosh, that'd be so cool!

"Someone's excited," Teboho comments as I bounce around on top of Kagiso's head, angling my body in different ways so I can see all the sights.

*I said it before and I'll say it again!* I answer. *You literally found me living under a rock! I've never seen anything this awesome before in my life!*

At the far edge of the stem bridge are what looks like defensive emplacements: large stone walls that would box any invading force in from three different directions, forming a nearly impenetrable kill zone. The stone seems to crawl down the sides of the stem and somehow hug onto the nearly-vertical edges of the cylindrical ground, making it impossible to approach from any direction other than the front. Of course, there doesn't seem to be any sign of conflict, and the gates are wide open, with only a handful of guards manning the three-story walls and waiting in front of the city. The stone itself is pristine and beautiful granite, or at least something that looks like granite, with only the occasional patch of what looks like green moss. Though when we walk by a patch of green moss, Sindri scowls at it, points, and then Bulupunu blasts it with lightning, frying the stuff to a charred heap.

*Woah! What the heck, Sindri?* I ask. *Was there something bad about that moss?*

*It's not moss,* he answers. *It's Stonerot. Terrible stuff.*

*Stonerot?* I inquire.

"Stonerot," he repeats out loud, giving me the word for it in the dentron language. "It's more or less what it sounds like. Invasive, corrosive, dangerous. I assure you, no one will complain about me killing some."

Hmm. So it's like evil magical kudzu or something? Sounds terrible. We approach the gates and get stopped by the guards, but it looks like everyone gets stopped by the guards so I'm not super worried.

446

Sure enough they're just looking for taxes, and since we aren't merchants and are obviously not here to sell goods they don't care a whole lot about us beyond recording our reason for entry, which is mostly just 'to sleep in a real bed for once.' We step past the gates and finally get to witness the city proper, the road shrinking down into a main thoroughfare lined on either side with countless merchants advertising their wares. Past them, the stem finally opens up into the leaf proper, and the stone road gives way to a massive forest of devourer trees that dwarfs the one we've been traveling through up until now. Some of the trunks have to be nearly a hundred feet in diameter, maybe more, and within them are carved-out homes and businesses, not just on the ground floor but all the way up the trunk. Dentron scamper easily up and down the natural multi-tiered structures, rushing straight up and down the bark without need for stairs or elevators. Huge bridges and large pulley structures do span the vast distances, but they seem to be exclusively used for freight and supplies, designed for workers moving heavy objects with carts and draft animals. The vast majority of individuals just *climb,* and there are certainly a lot of them. The city is incredibly busy, incredibly loud, incredibly *chaotic,* with people arguing, children playing, musicians performing, merchants haggling, and food sizzling as far as the eye can see. It's incredible.

"Say Hana, have you had your fill for impressive sights today, or do you have enough for one more?" Sindri asks.

*There's more!?* I ask. *What else could there be?*

"Well, we're away from the branch now, so we can see off the edge in the opposite direction. If we look down from here, I can show you my home. The Pillar should be easily visible."

*Oooh! Yes yes yes!* I bounce happily.

"Just be warned, Hana," Teboho says. "The Slaying Stone is not quite as beautiful a sight."

"Be glad I'm not patriotic enough to argue that," Sindri chuckles. "Come on, let's see if we can find a good view. Just be careful not to fall. You would, for obvious reasons, not survive."

We break off from the road and travel along the outside of the leaf, and it doesn't take long to find a lookout point. The dirt doesn't seem to stick well this close to the edge, so as we make our way off the beaten path, away from the trees and the city, we slide down a slope and end up on the actual skin of the leaf, all vibrant and waxy and green.

*Hey, if there's forest growing on top of the leaf, how does the leaf itself get any sunlight?* I ask.

"The leaves get sunlight mostly from below," Teboho explains. "When the sun dips underneath the branch."

...Oh holy crap that's right, I forgot about that. World trees are so cool, what the heck!

"Here, this looks like a good spot," Sindri announces, sidling very carefully to the bright green cliff face. "Come here, Hana."

I do so, although my method of doing so involves staying completely still as Kagiso does so instead. Sindri points down and I follow his finger past the branches below us, taking a moment to calm the pounding, horrifying vertigo of planetary-scale heights. Once I can focus, though, I see it. It's hard *not* to see it. The Pillar, or as the dentron call it, the Slaying Stone.

I think I know why it's called that, considering it's impaled straight through the trunk of the Mother Tree.

An *impossibly* giant cylinder of stone stretches out below us, far larger than any branch. Just over three-quarters the diameter of the trunk of the Tree of Souls, it's punched straight through the bark and wood like rebar tossed by a hurricane. Great waterfalls of sap gush out from the wound, coating the intersection point in an ocean of glistening, sticky syrup that reminds me altogether too much of blood. It seems the world tree hasn't taken this mortal wound lying down, however, as the Pillar is in fairly bad shape itself. Deep

448

canyons of green run along the outside of the stone in fractal patterns, like an alien artifact pulsing with unnatural energy. The color is clearly out of place on the hard, inorganic exterior, and I can't help but notice it's the same color as what Sindri called "Stonerot."

*...I... oh Goddess,* I whisper over the link. *This is horrible. When you said the World Tree is dying, I assumed it was because of the fire in the branches, not this!*

"Oh, it's not even just this," Sindri sighs, his tone resigned. "Keep looking. Follow the trunk lower."

So I do. Beyond the Slaying Stone, below the great wound of dripping sap, the trunk continues lower. Down and down and down, where branches get less and less common as the tree is closer and closer to the ground. Though before I can *see* the ground, the tree seems to spread out into a strange set of wide, gnarled wooden roots, twisting and drooping like tired tentacles. From thick, snaking vines to thin, almost web-like lines of lateral roots, they can't possibly be anything else. But they aren't planted in anything, they're just... floating in midair. The whole tree is suspended in a cloud-filled void, but it doesn't look like it's *supposed* to be. Clumps of brown dirt cling to the roots or float suspended around them, caught within the web of wood. The implication is both obvious and terrifying: the tree clearly used to be planted in something, but not anymore.

Something uprooted *the entire world tree.*

# 24

# FRIENDS (REDUX)

I think the worst part is that it would all be so beautiful if not for the horrifying implications. The roots floating in midair, reaching out in every direction like the Goddess' fingers, clumps of dirt levitating around them like islands in the sky... it's breathtaking. So too is the Slaying Stone, its pulsating green chasms a beautiful mix of color along the backdrop of dark gray. But then I remember people presumably live there, and that the Stonerot is poisonous. It's as sure a sign of death as the glistening sap that flows out of the world tree's wound. Everything about this world is broken and wrong, and it's impossible not to wonder how things ever got this bad.

*Three different apocalypses,* I send over our mental link. *Any one of these would have been enough, but you have three. The upper branches are on fire, the middle of the tree is impaled, and the roots are starving. Is Stonerot a fourth?*

"Functionally yes," Sindri nods. "We're doing what we can to slow it down, to reclaim what it has taken, but it carves through civilizations like acid through paper, devouring stone and metal to multiply itself. Our pre-cataclysm cities have been abandoned, and the stores of knowledge there are largely lost. We had to rebuild everything we know from the memories of surviving scholars, and now everyone that lived through that era is long dead."

*How are you so calm about all this?* I breathe. *This is completely insane.*

"I don't disagree, but what are we supposed to do about it?" SIndri shrugs. "Do you think I know how to put out a fire the size of an entire world? How to plant a tree into soil that does not seem to *exist?* I do what I can to make the world a better place with the skills I have, Hana, because maintaining what we have is all we can do."

"He's right," Teboho sighs. "These problems are beyond the scope of mortals, I fear. They are the domain of the Goddess, or perhaps Her chosen."

I'm glad I don't have a face to grimace with. The domain of Her chosen, huh? What the hell am I supposed to do about it, though? All I can do is cut things and be a stylish fashion accessory. Do you really expect me to fix this, Goddess? And if not, why *am* I here?

I'm here for some reason, aren't I? The magic that links me between two worlds belongs to the Goddess, granted by Her with purpose. I have Her attention, I have Her favor, and as best I can tell I feel Her more intimately than anyone else. But unlike the shows, games, and stories where the hero is whisked away from Earth by a divine being, I was never given a task or a purpose. The Goddess brought me here, that much I know. But I still haven't really *met* Her, per se. She's just... been around, watching with expectation and quiet amusement. I suppose I could just ask Her, at least so long as I'm willing to risk wasting Her time again. I can't say I find myself terribly keen on that idea, but it's certainly an option.

Maybe She just knows that She doesn't need to say anything. I don't need Her to give me a divine quest to search for answers and solutions. I guess that's my plan, then. To try and help. To look for ways to slow or reverse the apocalypse. Once I finish getting my bearings *and helping my friends stop a dangerous murderer* then that'll be my next step. I'll tour all of this world's various ongoing ragnaroks and see what I can do to help. I certainly can't think of a better use of my time than that.

"Well then, I suppose it's time to get back to business," Sindri announces. "Kagiso, Teboho, could you get us somewhere to stay while you're out finding a healer? I'm going to search around and see if this city has any Chaos hunters that would be willing to join us. My birds report that our target is holed up in a cave barely a day from here, so our fight will be tomorrow night. Best to be as prepared as possible."

Oh gosh. So soon?

"Don't worry, Hana," Sindri smiles at me. "You'll be ready."

I shudder, remembering the near-complete lack of feeling as my claws slid effortlessly through those bandits.

*If you're wrong, then I have good reason to be worried,* I tell him. *If you're right, I have even more of a reason to be worried.*

"You are so kind, Hana," Teboho smiles at me. "But you are also strong. I am grateful that you are willing to help us seek justice for this."

"No worry, Hana," Kagiso says, patting me. "You are hunter. Will be easy."

I sigh. *Kagiso* is a hunter. I'm not sure she really understands that I'm uncomfortable with the act of killing. Teboho shrugs apologetically at me, seeming to be of the same opinion. The two of them are so very different, aren't they? I'd never know they were siblings. ...Though I guess my brother and I are even further apart than they are. Even before it became concerningly literal, I would have described the two of us as completely different species.

Sindri motions us away from the edge and we head back into the city, the vibrant noise of it all tearing my thoughts away from my family. I didn't notice before, what with being so overwhelmed, but while the vast majority of people here are dentron there's an occasional smattering of non-dentron people. Humans are the first and most obvious. I can't help but note that every human I've seen so far has been dark-skinned, which is interesting. Much more interesting are the small, two-and-a-half-foot tall bat people that I

453

initially thought were some kind of animal until I noticed a pair of them chatting with a dentron while clinging to the trunk of a tree thirty feet above me.

I'm embarrassed to have assumed they were anything but people from that point on; they even have human-like faces, barring rodent-like incisors and long, fuzzy ears jutting up from the tops of their itty-bitty heads. The tiny little guys are actually really cute, with fuzzy bodies and large wings for forelimbs, tipped on the ends and joints with clawed, finger-like appendages that they use to latch onto the sides of trees, hanging and crawling at whatever angle they choose. Like humans, they only have four limbs counting the wings, but their stubby little feet don't seem like they'd be much use for walking; flat and thin, their legs barely even seem useful for crawling around. While all four limbs have hooked claws for clinging to trees, none of them seem to be even remotely useful for manipulating objects. Thankfully, they also have a dentron-like tail, thin like a monkey but tipped with three fingers that seem fully capable of holding onto anything they might need. And of course, while they're incredibly slow at crawling and climbing, that's because it isn't intended to be their forte at all. Whenever they please, they can leap off a tree and take to the air.

The bat-people immediately stop seeming clumsy once freely in the sky. Their funky little back legs become dexterous ailerons, their oversized forelimbs become powerful wings, and they zip through the air with the speed and grace of swallows. Interestingly, wherever they go a second one always follows them, never far behind or far apart.

*What are the cute little flying people called?* I ask.

Teboho chokes out a laugh as Sindri grins and says "Sciptera."

*Sciptera?* I ask. *Kind of a mouthful.*

"Sciptera are delightful people," Teboho says, a wisp of nostalgia in his voice. "A good many pairs of them would fly down to visit our village from time to time."

454

"Pala and Lula were there," Kagiso comments, her words emptier than usual.

"...Ah," Teboho says quietly, his fists clenching. "I was afraid of as much."

"Well. Let's make sure that tragedy never strikes again, hmm?" Sindri sighs, earning determined nods from both dentron. "Get a healer that can bring you back to your best, Teboho, and then get us somewhere to sleep. It'll be a long day tomorrow."

Gosh, it's so easy to forget that Teboho is severely injured. He hides it well. Despite those injuries, though, Sindri apparently still considers him the most reliable member of the group. Sindri hands Teboho some money and splits off from us, leaving him and Kagiso as my guides.

*Wait, hold on!* I call out. *Shouldn't I go with you, Sindri? I can't talk to people without you.*

"Isn't that what you've been practicing writing for?" Sindri calls back. "Get Teboho to make you a tablet."

"I can't make chalk," Teboho protests. "It's too soft of a material."

"She doesn't need chalk with her spells," Sindri dismisses. "Try to get a place on the ground floor for me, okay? I'd rather not suffer the indignity of being carried in and out of our room."

"Alright, alright," Teboho agrees, waving goodbye before summoning a thin stone slab in his hand and giving it to Kagiso. "Can you write on this, Hana?"

I skitter off Kagiso's head and down her shoulder, latching onto the forearm of the hand holding the tablet. Activating a weak Spacial Rend on one claw, I crudely carve my answer into the rock.

**This works.**

My handwriting certainly isn't going to be winning any awards, nor is my loquaciousness. It's slow going trying to carve out letters that I have to wrack my brain to even remember, but it gets the job done. Something about that feels really good, too. It's a level of independence I haven't felt in this world since first becoming fully lucid.

"Excellent!" Teboho grins. "I suppose I'll just unsummon it and summon you a new one whenever you run out of space?"

**Yes.**

I guess needing Teboho to give me writing material is a bit of an issue, but I suppose I'm not *unable* to communicate without that. Just unable to communicate without destroying stuff. It lacks the convenience of instant mind-to-mind communication, though.

"Now then," Teboho announces jovially, "I should probably admit I have no idea what we're doing."

"City big," Kagiso agrees, staring up at the treetops.

Oh gosh they're country bumpkins, that's right. But I'm super sheltered and from another universe, so am I any better off?

**Ask for directions?** I suggest.

"Oh! Good idea, Hana!" Teboho agrees.

We approach one of the merchants hocking wares, who glances at us for a moment before doing a sudden double-take when he spots me hanging on Kagiso's arm. Immediately, I panic, remembering the merchants from the trade stop that ended up trying to kill us. I direct my senses out and around us, searching for necklaces. I almost relax when I see the person we're approaching lacks one, but panic quickly seizes control again when I find five different cultists all in various parts of the crowd. One of them stares at me, though the others are minding their own business, either ignorant or uncaring of my presence. I poke Kagiso purposefully with my leg, pointing surreptitiously towards the man looking a bit too purposefully in our direction. She glances that way and spots him immediately, and I feel her muscles tense up under my legs.

"Mmm. Teboho," she growls quietly.

"Hmm?" he asks, looking up from his conversation with the merchant and taking only a moment to notice the hunter's posture

456

in his sister. "...Ah. Well. Thank you for the directions, my good man. It seems we'll be taking our leave now."

As we expected and feared, the cultist follows us from a distance as we head deeper into the city, moving towards the Order healer Teboho was recommended by the local merchant. Together we creep through the crowds, staying on the ground to try and put as many people between us and them as possible, but they manage to keep pace with us. It's a dentron man, and he looks nervous.

**What should we do?** I write.

"Secluded location," Kagiso suggests. "Hana dispose body."

Woah, woah, what!? No, no no no! Thankfully, Teboho comes to my rescue before I have to write out an objection to the murder-and-cannibalism plan.

"We're not killing anyone as a first response, Kagiso," he chides. "Let's just get me healed, no one is going to attack in broad daylight in the middle of a busy commerce sector."

"Can't decide place for sleep if being stalked," Kagiso hisses.

"True. We have a while to figure something out, though. Here we are."

We walk into the clinic, a ground-floor alcove carved out of the trunk of a massive tree. The 'door' is just a simple cloth hung over the opening, but it's still enough to block line of sight from the outside. Kagiso nudges me and I understand what she's worried about immediately.

**He's staking out the building,** I report, since needing line of sight is for losers.

She gives me a pat and we sit down in the waiting room, Teboho behind a decent chunk of other people also in line for non-critical healing. We're going to be here a while, and I get to spend the entire time watching a cultist stalk us. He's not even all that good at it; the dude is looking increasingly nervous as time goes on, not seeming to be sure whether or not to keep his stakeout going, walk in after us, or go do something else. Eventually, he makes his decision, though, and I'm not sure whether it's a good thing or a bad thing.

**He's leaving,** I scribble hastily.

"Hrm. Follow?"

**Me?**

"I no leave Teboho. But you are sneaky. Better stalker than the fool."

I'm not sure I like the idea of going alone, but Kagiso has a point. I *am* very good at hiding from things, even without the ability to pop into another dimension. I'll probably *have* to go without that, since there don't seem to be any barren zones on the leaf. It's just as flat in the fourth dimension as it is in 3D space, meaning that anywhere I want to step out of w=0 space will have me falling through where all the dirt should be and splattering on the leaf below it. I'm starting to think of a few tricks to make that less of a problem, but now isn't a good time to test them. I'm a bit too stressed.

**Okay,** I write. **Stay here so I can find you.**

As crazy as it is to follow this man, I feel like we *do* need to know where this stalker is going and if he's going to be a problem. The prospect of him returning with friends to murder us is a horrifyingly real one considering that it has already happened once, so I wait for him to be looking away and scuttle out of the room after him, rushing up the side of a tree so I don't get stepped on.

Tailing him is trivial, because as long as I stay within fifty feet of the man I never have to give him an opportunity to see me in the first place. I may not be able to pop into a barren zone here, but I can just keep a branch or trunk between the two of us and let perfectly normal physics do the work. I get some odd looks from other climbers as I scuttle by, even scaring the crap out of a few people, but people seem largely content to ignore me as soon as they figure out that I'm ignoring them. Weird little creatures crawling through the trees is one of those things that just kind of happens in forests.

The feeling of my heavy breaths as I rush after my quarry is strangely alien to me. My book lungs were garbage in terms of oxygen efficiency and temperature regulation, making my stamina with them absolutely terrible. They were, however, extremely quiet, and they didn't constantly inflate and deflate inside my body like creepy balloons. In all honestly, I'll probably miss them, as strange and inconvenient as they were. I'm no longer even radially symmetrical, at least on the inside. My lungs are growing larger and more human-shaped, it seems. Still, they help a lot with letting me keep pace with a fully grown dentron man despite him being nearly six times taller than me. I mean, he's just walking and I have to sprint, but at least I'm not dying trying to keep pace for so long.

I must be skittering after this stupid cultist for a solid twenty minutes before I finally find something that looks like it might be a destination: a building adorned with the same centipede symbol as the cultist necklaces that let me so easily identify them all. ...I guess if I'd known this was here it'd be pretty obvious. *Gosh* it's counterintuitive to think that the cultists would just have a big public building in the middle of the city, but I guess it's like Sindri said: they're recognized as a legitimate religion. Calling them 'cultists' is probably really insulting, but they tried to kill me so I don't really care.

The man I'm following rushes inside, and I sneak across a branch to grab onto the outside of the tree that forms the cultist headquarters. Peeking inside is easy enough when I get close, so I take the opportunity to spy on the enemy. It all seems pretty normal, honestly: a couple bedrooms, a couple studies, a big chapel-esque room that takes up a whole floor, and a series of offices on the ground floor, in one of which Sindri is chatting with a dude that looks like he might be a cultist leader.

Wait. What?

459

Instantly, my heart rate spikes a hundredfold. Why the habanero is Sindri here!? The cultist I'm following almost completely forgotten, I scurry along the outside of the trunk until I'm right on the outside wall to the room he's in. Sindri is talking to a large dentron man sitting behind a fancy desk. The dentron is wearing bulky, heavy-looking metal armor, which I find strange considering how difficult that must be to climb in; I'll admit to not knowing a ton of them, but I've literally never seen a dentron wearing that much, not even the city guards. Behind him, snugly sitting in a weapon stand is a large spear. His upper pair of arms have their fingers threaded together, elbows resting on the desk as he listens to Sindri speak. A lower hand drums its fingers on his thigh, as his tail lashes back and forth with apparent concern. Scuttling close to a nearby window, I do my best to listen in.

"—your cooperation," Sindri finishes. "Are you interested?"

"Very much so," the dentron cultist agrees. "I am a Chaos hunter, same as you. The thought of *not* working alongside you with such a mage hiding out this close to my home city is absurd."

Oh. Oh! Huh. I mean, this *is* exactly what Sindri said he was going to do, so I guess this isn't all that suspicious. I don't like that he's doing it with a cultist, but—

"And information about the white-carapaced creature?" Sindri presses, and my blood runs cold.

"Well, I can certainly tell you that they're important to the Disciples of Unification," the dentron warrior answers. "But you must understand, that sort of knowledge is generally restricted to the upper echelons of our organization. You would need to show some degree of dedication to our cause before we can discuss it."

"Your racketeering gig, of course," Sindri sighs. "I don't work for people that insist on keeping secrets."

"I don't necessarily mean donations when I speak of dedication," the dentron dismisses smoothly. "I don't keep secrets to extort you, I keep secrets *because they are secrets.* We don't share information with people that aren't dedicated to our cause. But I can tell you

460

this: if the familiarity you speak of this 'creature' with is any indication, you are in far more danger from it than you realize."

The two men stare at each other, sizing each other up for a moment before the guy I was *actually* supposed to be watching suddenly bursts into the room.

"Paladin!" the stalker yelps. "I saw a... oh."

The apparent paladin raises an eyebrow at the stalker as he realizes that Sindri is in the room and hesitates.

"Uh, should I...? I believe this is important, but..."

"By all means, continue," the paladin says. "I suspect it may actually be relevant to the current conversation."

"I... I saw it, Hagoro," the stalker stammers. "The Founder's kin. Young. It looked like a headless spider."

The paladin, Hagoro, nods.

"We'll speak of the details later," he orders. "You may go."

The stalker leaves, and Hagoro turns to Sindri.

"Sound familiar?" he asks.

"...That man sounded rather frightened," Sindri comments dryly.

"Because you are dealing with something frightening," Hagoro shrugs. "And I think you know that. I think that's why you're here. So how about this: you tell me why you came to me, why you decided to seek out a paladin from a religion that you yourself claim attacked you, and I will do what I can to explain."

I wait with bated breath, conscious thought stalling in my head as I try to put together all the pieces here. Sindri is *scared* of me? He went to our enemies because of that? What did I miss?

"I... am a Pneuma mage," Sindri explains slowly. "My specialty is in communication. I can link together thoughts in a large group and use it to direct battles more effectively."

"A useful magic," Hagoro answers amicably.

"To a limited extent, it... also can be used to read minds," Sindri admits. "I'll often pick up on things people don't consciously mean to send over the link. The... what did you call it, a 'founder's kin?' Her name is Hana. She's been traveling with us for many days now, and she's a kind person, not used to fighting. I didn't know what she was when we met, but I wanted her help with handling the Chaos mage since she has such an impressive Order aura. The more I spent time with her, however, the more I knew something was... off. She knew things she shouldn't have any way to know, and was ignorant about things she shouldn't have any way to miss. Through our link, I learned that she dreams of living in an entirely different world, full of technology advanced enough to be found in an ancestral ruin. It feels too real to just be a fantasy."

"I see. That is... more than I expected you to know," Hagoro admits. "And you're right. This 'Hana' is an invader from another world. And she is here to seek our ruin."

*What!?* No I'm not!

"I was afraid you'd say that," Sindri hisses. "Even the way she moves reminds me of those monsters from twenty years ago. But I've spoken with her soul to soul. She can get a bit... violent at times, I'll grant you, but she doesn't have a speck of malice on her. I'm confident in that. Honestly, training her to fight has been a pain and a half."

Yeah! You tell him, Sindri! ...Wait, no, actually maybe stop telling him about me at all, what the heck are you doing. And when have you ever trained me to fight!? You've just kinda gone 'hey Hannah, go kill that guy for me!'

"Hmm," Hagoro muses, rubbing his chin in contemplation. "Truly? If that's the case, I'd quite like to meet her."

"Well, if you hunt with us you'll get the chance," Sindri points out.

Woah, woah, woah! Don't I get a say in this? This paladin guy is part of the organization that has been stalking and occasionally attacking me for no good reason! This is a terrible idea, isn't it? And how come Sindri went to this random jerk instead of just talking to me about it!? If he'd confronted me about it I probably would have come clean, if for no other reason than the fact that I'm a huge pushover.

"I think I'll do that," Hagoro agrees. "Come find me when you leave?"

"Mmm. The bridge to the city, at first light," Sindri grunts. "And then we'll see about this 'dedication to your cause.'"

"Of course," Hagoro agrees, and Sindri gets up to leave. I scuttle up the tree and find a branch to follow him as he leaves, silently fuming. I can't believe he went behind my back to set up all this crap! We're friends, aren't we? This is distinctly unfriendly of him! I haven't been this angry at him since he nearly persistence hunted me to death. Which... sure is a thing he did. He's kind of done a lot of mean things to me that I've just kind of forgiven, huh? Like throwing me when I successfully casted the Aura Sight spell. I understand why he did it, but he never even apologized! I'm getting really mad now, scuttling after Sindri from above as he weaves along the ground floor of the city, walking further and further away from where I know Kagiso and Teboho are waiting at the healing clinic. Where is he even going?

Sindri pushes through some brush, walking farther and farther from the city proper and into the quiet, residential parts of Grawlaka. I almost think he must know someone here when he suddenly stops in the middle of nowhere, without anyone else around.

"Alright, Hana," he says. "Come on out."

I jolt with surprise. He knew I was following him? Well, you know what, fine! I need to give him a piece of my mind anyway. Sindri chuckles for some reason, *and I don't think about why.* Descending to the ground in front of him, I start furiously scratching in the dirt.

**Why were you talking to cultists about me!?**

"Why were you eavesdropping?" he counters.

463

**Because the others and I were getting stalked by cultists, and when I followed one I found you talking to his boss! These people attacked us, Sindri!**

"That's part of why I was talking with them," Sindri explains, reaching down to touch me and activate our mental link. "To learn their motivations."

*Then you should have told us you were doing that!* I protest. *You could have asked me about half the stuff you discussed in there! You didn't have to go to the creepy zealots that nearly killed us!*

"It was a calculated move, and I think it paid off," Sindri shrugs. "Can I ask you to just trust me?"

*No!* I fire back. *You can't! You're not allowed to tell people about stuff you found in my head without ever telling me you were in my head looking at those things in the first place! That's a pretty enormous breach of trust, Sindri!*

Sindri frowns, sucking on the inside of his cheek like he's distracted by thought. Then he sighs, seeming resigned.

"Are you sure I can't convince you?" Sindri asks. "We've been through a lot together. We're **Friends**, aren't we?"

She's here in an instant. Chuckling as She speaks the word lovingly into my ear. **Friends**. Of course, I've been so stupid. Why wouldn't I trust Sindri? He's my friend! Thank you for reminding me, Goddess. She just howls with laughter, gone without a trace.

I feel... disoriented. My anger from before is gone, and I just feel kind of embarrassed and foolish for having it in the first place. I've been the one being nosy and mean without any real reason. Ugh. I can't believe I've been such a bad friend.

*Sorry,* I send him.

"It's fine," Sindri smiles. "I understand. Now, you want to lead me back to the others?"

*Yeah,* I agree, crawling up his leg and perching on his shoulder. I point in the direction we came from, and we're off.

Feeling vaguely miserable, I stay quiet for the rest of the trip back, only speaking up to guide Sindri where we need to go. By stroke of luck, we make it to the clinic only shortly after Teboho's treatment is complete. He grins at us, jumping up and down a few times to show off how well he's doing. We find ourselves a room at an inn that night, opting for one large one instead of two smaller ones so we'll be together in the event of an attack. We spend the remainder of the day resting in our room, preparing ourselves for the fight that we'll be seeking tomorrow.

"Zarebo was a skilled tanner," Teboho says without prompting.

"Huh?" Sindri asks, looking up. Kagiso's long ears perk up, and she stares at Teboho intently.

"Apogo made delicious, delicious foods. We had no need to cook, our sap was plentiful, but Apogo went out of his way to make things for us anyway. His daughter Putoniba was nearly as good."

"Yazo," Kagiso grunts. "Bulana. Doragi. Abegraw. Strong warriors, all."

Oh. Are these people from their village?

"Fori was a wise old man," Teboho continues. "Talked me out of many stupid things. Helen, a skilled artist. At both paintings and sculptures, she was a master. I wish we'd known her longer. Tagrawko was beautiful beyond words. I kept trying to work up the courage to ask her to lay with me."

"She'd say no," Kagiso grunts.

Teboho laughs at that.

"Yes, I suppose you're right," he agrees. "She probably would have."

More and more names pass through the siblings' lips, over and over, a private eulogy between the only two people left to remember them. Time seems to stretch between each one, at first in solemnity but later in memory, the pair seeming to scour their brains to remember each and every name so as to not speak the ones that were so obviously missing. But eventually, the time comes. A long period of silence stretches out, until Kagiso finally breaks it.

"Borupu. A good brother. Grawna. A good mother. Mago. A good father."

"Yes," Teboho agrees. "The best."

"Tomorrow, we hunt," Kagiso promises. "For them."

"For them," Teboho agrees.

Nobody else speaks for the rest of the night. Eventually, with the sun down and our bodies weary, we drift off to sleep together. I wake up with tears in my eyes, full of secondhand grief for people I can never meet. Poor Kagiso. Poor Teboho. They are all they have left.

My breath shaky, I go through my usual morning routine. I figure out my limbs, I get out of bed, I crawl my way into the shower, glorious hot water soothing my body as I groggily recall the events of the day. Today is Monday, right? So I'm going to school today? I'm going to go help my friends assassinate someone tomorrow and I'm going to *school* today. This is totally insane. Honestly, we're in a city now, I could just stay there while the others go enact justice or whatever. Skip out on the whole 'cultist paladin joins the party' bullcarp. How the heck did Sindri even convince me to go along with that, anyway?

I blink, water rushing down my face. Huh. Wait. Wait a gosh dang second! I stand up straight, the exhaustion in my body vanishing as I yell furiously at the shower wall.

*"That motherfucker mind controlled me!"*

# 25

# EROSION

It takes a minute for me to register that the smashing noise and clatter of ceramic is because I just punched a hole in the bathroom wall.

I barely even felt it. My chitinous knuckles and feet can *feel* things, certainly, but the sharp shards of hard-fired clay would hurt a human hand, and the lack of pain—even the dull kind of pain I'd expect from punching a wall *without* breaking it—causes a few seconds of confused disconnect as my rage-fueled brain catches up with reality. I broke a *wall.* I didn't even cast any magic! Which I suppose is fortunate, because a pipe ultimately stopped my fist and I do *not* want to bust a water main before school. The metal pipe seems... fine, I think? I gave it a pretty solid hit, but I'm either not strong enough to mess up metal or the wall itself took enough impact to save it.

Still, though. This is, uh, pretty bad. I hear footsteps approaching from down the hall before someone knocks on the bathroom door.

"Hannah!" my mother calls out. "Are you okay? What was that noise?"

"I-I'm fine!" I answer, jolting a little at the sound. I direct the water away from the hole in the wall, do a quick rinse and shut the shower off. "I, uh, tripped? And accidentally broke the wall?"

"You *what!?*"

"I'm sorry! I fell!" I lie, the fear of *having* to lie hopefully making it sound more real.

"Let me see."

"Let me get dressed first!"

I quickly extract myself, drying off and bundling up in my clothes before unlocking the door and letting my increasingly-impatient mother in.

"Oh, God," my mother swears, pulling back the shower curtain to survey the damage. "You sure you're not cut anywhere?"

"Yeah, I'm fine, I got lucky," I lie. "I'm sorry."

"Take your gloves off, let me see," she orders. "Why are you wearing gloves indoors anyway?"

I swallow, instinctively taking a step back.

"I... I just want to," I answer, my heart beating like crazy.

She frowns at that.

"Let me see," she insists.

"No mom, don't be weird," I press. "I'm fine."

"Hannah..."

"I said I'm *fine!*" I snap, regretting the shout the moment it leaves my mouth. My mother's eyes narrow.

"Do not raise your voice with me, young lady," she intones. "That's not going to get you out of this. Do you think I'm stupid? Do you think I can't see that something is going on?"

She steps towards me and I take another step back, my body reflexively scrunching down, my hands grabbing onto my sleeves to hold them in place. Just in case. She's not going to touch me, right? She knows better than to touch me. I just... I can't take this. Not now. Not with everything going on. I glance away, unable to meet my mother's blistering gaze.

"Hannah," she says, a little calmer this time. "Look at me."

I hesitantly glance back up again. My mother doesn't look mad anymore. She looks... worried.

"Hannah, have you been hurting yourself?"

I blink, caught off guard by the unexpected question.

"I... what?"

"How did you get these scars on your face?" my mother asks. Oh, shoot. I forgot. They're light enough to be hard to see, but there are definitely still scars from my wounds all over my body, even the parts without skin. Chitin heals weirdly.

"I... I don't know," I lie lamely.

"Hannah," my mother frowns, clearly not buying it. "If... if you're not going to talk to your father and I, you should at least talk to a therapist."

I go stiff. She... what!? This is her way to get me to open up, isn't it? Because she knows, she *knows* I'm not going to... how dare she. How *dare* she!? What kind of bullshit false dichotomy is she supplying here!? I just found out my f—my *travel companion* is a Goddess-damn mind rapist, I am *not* dealing with my mom pressuring me on this bullshit by threatening to make me go back to therapy.

"No," I hiss.

"Hannah, please, your father and I have been talking. You've been avoiding us more and more, and now you won't even show us your face! I—"

"I'm going to school," I growl, stepping away from her.

"Oh, no you don't," my mother fires back. "Stop *right* there, young lady."

I pause, a decade and a half of well-trained fear of her tone ringing through what's left of my bones. I don't turn around to face her, but I stop.

469

"I don't know why you're getting angry at me but I'm not having it," my mother snaps. "You do not get to raise your voice. You do not get to be *rude.* Do you understand me?"

"Yes, mother," I seethe.

"All I want, all I am *asking,* is to see if my daughter is okay. Is that unreasonable? Is that something that warrants me being yelled at?"

"No, mother."

"Then show me."

I take a deep breath, forcing myself with every ounce of my strength to stay calm, to not hiss or bite or brandish my extra bladed limbs at her. The claws on my toes puncture clean through the foam protecting my socks, digging gouges into the carpet below me. Hopefully they won't be large enough to notice.

"...I'd rather go to therapy," I say, barely getting the words out.

I'm not looking at her but I can *feel* my mother's surprise, the shape of her shocked expression, alongside the positions of the rest of my family. The way my brother waits behind the door to his room for this awkward conversation to end. The way my father pretends to be asleep on the couch downstairs. My house is quiet. Honestly, it feels like a silly, stupid thing to shock people with. I'm mutating into a monster, I have real actual magic, I've killed four different people and eaten their corpses, I got mugged yesterday and nearly killed *myself,* and yet out of all the absurdities in my life, *this* manages to shake my family. This is still the baseline for 'surprising' that they live on. I probably wouldn't have had the courage to say those words if my life hadn't tossed me around so hard that my standards for stress shot through the roof and out of the atmosphere, but I did. Just to buy myself another week, maybe another couple days, before I actually have to face the real problems. If this gets my mom off my back *right now*, then I'll do it. And it will get her off my back, I know that. I can talk to her and dad, or I can talk to a therapist. That's what she offered. She just can't believe I chose a therapist, and I can hardly blame her.

She made sure to put my last one in prison, after all.

"I... okay," my mother nods. "If you're sure you can't talk to us, we'll respect that. And we will make *sure* you get the best, most trusted therapist we can possibly find, Hannah. There will be no chance of any problems. I promise. We'll help, okay? We love you."

I nod, and respond with the most commonly-spoken lie in my life.

"Love you too."

I don't hate my family. At worst I mildly dislike them, and even that feels ungrateful considering how much they've done for me. My biggest problem with them is just that they feel entitled to my time and attention, and arguably they are. It's certainly the argument they would make, anyway, and from a utilitarian standpoint I have to admit that the amount of suffering I go through by being around them is usually nil, and the amount of suffering my mom seems to go through when she doesn't get time with my brother and I is pretty substantial. She cares, she loves us, she goes out of our way to help us, and I should honestly be putting up with her more.

But I don't like her. I don't like my brother, either. My father can be okay just because he doesn't usually push me on things, but I still don't love him. I don't know why, but I've never had the sort of instinctive care that people are supposed to have for their family. If not for the fact that I live with them all, they are all the sort of people that I wouldn't even bother to remember the names of. None of them are interested in any of the things I am interested in, none of them even *understand* any of the things I like or want or feel, and my mother in particular has spent a large amount of her life subtly insisting that the things I like and want and feel are maybe not the best for me. Have I ever thought about going outside and engaging more in real life, she asks. It's not healthy to look at a screen all day, she insists. Take up a sport, make new friends, go camping with us, go to the beach, go and do all these normal things that normal people like, you'll surely like them too if you just give them a chance. It will make you so much happier and healthier to pretend to be someone you're not. Mother knows best.

471

So I fake it. I'm good at faking it. But that's all I am around my family: a fake. If not for Brendan I'm not even sure if I'd know what the real me is like. I sometimes wonder if I'm somewhere on the autistic spectrum like he is. Maybe that's why we get along so well, understand each other when no one else seems to. Thing is, I'm way better at faking it than he is. Am I neurodivergent enough to claim the title if I'm spending all day very successfully acting normal? If I have that capability, isn't that what being normal *is?*

I don't know. I feel like I'm a pretty empathetic person, but if other people aren't faking the way they seem to like the world as-is, I certainly don't have any intellectual or emotional understanding why. I'm not sure I *want* to have any.

"...Get me some plastic wrap and tape so your brother can shower?" my mother asks.

"Okay," I nod, and head downstairs to do exactly that. Wordlessly, I return with the materials she needs to patch things up, then head back downstairs and storm out of the house. With my dad resting in the living room, I don't want to go through the stress of hiding the fact that I've been eating raw eggs every morning. Better to go hungry. I trudge out to the bus stop with fury and resentment bubbling in my veins. I have real problems to worry about. Namely, 'how do I stop somebody with mind magic from continuing to mess with my head?'

I suppose the first option would be to kill him.

I shudder, my extra limbs flexing inside my shirt and scraping up against my skin. No. I won't do that. I know I won't do that, not just for moral reasons but because I don't think I have it in me. When the chips aren't down, when lives aren't in danger, when raw mortal terror isn't fueling my every movement, could I kill a person? I know that I'm the kind of coward to kill when my life is in danger, but I'm also the kind of coward to hesitate in every situation outside of that. Sindri probably knew that. That's why he was training me, encouraging me to hunt and to fight. He needs me to be a killer if he wants me to kill the Chaos mage for him.

472

I wonder: how much was planned? How much was staged? How much of my adrenaline-fueled murders was me firing the gun, and how much was him curling my fingers around the trigger? Was that cast of Friends the first time he directly controlled my mind? Or has every interaction with him been tainted, been him digging his claws deeper into my brain? Goddess, when You spoke that word with his lips I fell apart like a flower in a storm, trusting beyond trust that he'd never do wrong by me. I felt so weak and stupid and foolish for even thinking a bad thought about him that I threw all those thoughts away. In that moment, with that magic, he was more important to me than Brendan.

I flex my claws, terror and fury swirling together in a dangerous torrent. Maybe I'm wrong. Maybe I can kill him after all.

"Hannah," someone says, and I turn on them, hissing in warning. I can feel the air pass up my throat, warping and twisting into impossible noises before passing between my teeth. My extra limbs twitch, my talons gouge. But of course, it's just Brendan. He holds up his hands in surrender, keeping a respectful distance, and I calm down as best I can.

"Brendan," I sag slightly. "Hey. Sorry."

"Maybe you should just like... face this direction while you wait?" he suggests. "I promise I'm not trying to sneak up on you."

"Honestly, I'm not sure why you startled me," I admit. "My spatial sense is starting to kick in over on this side of things. I guess I'm just really distracted."

"Oh yeah?" Brendan asks. "Whatcha been up to?"

"Contemplating murder," I growl.

His face goes blank, defaulting to his usual unreadable expression. From anyone else, I'd be worried about being judged.

"Are you okay?" Brendan asks before anything else.

"Physically? Yes. By basically any other metric? No."

"But in a different way from usual," Brendan clarifies.

"Yes, in a different way from usual," I confirm, rolling my eyes. "Remember the Pneuma mage I travel with on the other side? Sindri?"

"Please tell me it's not mind control," Brendan sighs.

"It's definitely mind control."

"Fuck."

"Yeah," I confirm. "That's about where I'm at. He seemed all nice and normal for most of the trip, but then he goes and does something sus and the moment I call him out on it, he hits me with a spell called 'Friends.'"

"What, like the D&D spell?" Brendan asks.

"Uh... I don't know," I admit. "Maybe? When he invoked the Goddess to cast it, I just... stopped thinking he was capable of doing wrong, basically. And it lasted the rest of the day! I only figured things out when I woke up this morning. It either wore off or it doesn't affect both of my bodies."

"So you're worried you'll be mind controlled again when you go to sleep tonight. Okay. Yeah, that's pretty scary."

"I genuinely, actually thought he was my friend," I seethe. "Like, I thought he was my friend before the mind r... mind control. Or at least before the *obvious* mind control, who knows what sort of messed-up stuff he was doing to my head without me ever noticing. And I just... I don't know what to do about it! He just has to say one word, Brendan. One word and I'm a f-freaking slave!"

The bus arrives then, and it's only at that point that I realize I'm shaking. I'm not sure if it's anger or terror. Both, I guess. I'd been betrayed, I'd been *violated,* free will and independent thought stripped out of my brain like wrapping paper from a shiny new present. Everything I thought I knew about someone I thought I trusted has been thrown into doubt. As Brendan and I get onto the bus, a thousand paranoid fears flit through my mind. Are Teboho and Kagiso okay? Have they been slaves this whole time? Is their village even destroyed? What if those 'bandits' weren't bandits?

474

"Shadowruns, huh?" Brendan mutters.

"Huh?" I blink.

"Oh, uh. There's a tabletop game called Shadowrun, and the setting is pretty dystopian. The party is generally supposed to be a group of mercenaries who usually do jobs for like... evil megacorporations? And about ninety percent of the time whatever job you're on is a trick, a setup, something designed to cover up a far worse situation than you could have ever anticipated. And once that happens enough times, the players start to get paranoid. They see problems and threats everywhere. But it doesn't actually get any easier to figure out the truth just because you're freaking out about knowing that you've been lied to."

I blink, taking a moment to parse the analogy.

"...What are you saying I should do, exactly?" I ask.

"Focus on taking care of yourself. You can't stop the bad guy if you're not safe. So let's make a plan around that, and figure everything else out later."

"There's not much to plan," I grumble. "I figure the moment I wake up I'm either already caught or I have a few moments to act before Sindri notices I'm not under his control. I am *very* tempted to just slit his throat, but I'll probably try to run."

"Can you cast his spell first?"

"What? No."

"Why not?" Brendan presses. "It's Pneuma-aligned, you can learn Pneuma spells, and you heard the incantation."

"It's *not* that easy, Brendan," I insist. "Like, firstly, even if I *could* do that it'd be astronomically weaker than Sindri's version and might not even do much. But secondly and most importantly, I am not at *all* confident I understand the spell well enough to mess with it, and I am *not* risking a miscast. Miscasts are horrifying."

"Uh. Hmm. Last time we talked you seemed kind of laissez-faire about them? But you also said *Sindri* was scared of miscasts, so uh.

475

This entirely reasonable caution you have strikes me as a red flag. You sure I don't need to enact master-stranger protocols?"

"Enact what? Wait, you think I'm compromised? No, I just... oh. Oh, beans. I forgot to tell you about Saturday."

"I'm not going to like this, am I?" he sighs.

"Well I almost killed someone, then I almost died, and also Autumn knows about me. Kind of."

He rests his face in his hands as I spend the rest of the bus ride explaining the mugging and subsequent aftermath, though I leave out the bits about Autumn having DID since I think she wants that private. I'm up to the part where she's kind and thoughtful enough to come back with a bunch of extra chicken when we arrive at school and have to part ways for first period. Gosh, what the heck even *is* my first period? It feels like it's been forever since I last went to school. Uhh... it's an A-week, I think? And Monday? So I guess I'm going to... English? Sure, that sounds right. I head for my first class of the day, my mood rapidly dropping as my proximity to Brendan decreases.

For once, I not only fail to pay attention in class but I fail to do anything productive in it either. English comes and goes with my brain doing nothing but being a jittery, paranoid wreck. What do I do when I close my eyes tonight? Fight or run? Fucking Sindri's been putting so much effort into teaching me that it's okay to kill, so maybe I should take him up on that lesson! ...No. No, the fact that he's trying to turn me into a killer is just all the more reason to spite him. I don't want to give him a victory like that, no matter how pyrrhic. I should just run away. But... wait. If I run, what happens to Kagiso and Teboho? Crap, crap, crap!

I'm panicking so hard that I barely even register Autumn's presence when I sit down next to her in biology class. I'm vaguely aware that she jumps a little at my arrival, tensing up, but I only really consciously acknowledge these facts when she clears her throat and I *jolt*, my chair making a sharp screeching noise across

476

the floor as I nearly fall out of my seat. She returns the wide-eyed look I give her with one of her own.

"A-autumn!" I stutter. "Oh, gosh, I'm sorry, you nearly gave me a heart attack. I'm just... jumpy, sorry. Um, are you...?"

She fishmouths a little, opening and closing her jaw without saying anything. Class will start in a minute or two, so now is a pretty bad time to have an in-depth discussion about anything, but if this is Alma (and it kind of seems like she's Alma) then she probably has *no idea* what happened Saturday other than the fact that I know about Jet. She just continues staring at me, though, so I guess I have to start the conversation on my own.

"Um... sorry," I chuckle awkwardly, scratching my cheek. "It's... Alma, right?"

Her breath catches. Her expression quickly shifts from confusion and surprise to utter dread. She turns away from me, and I know I somehow fucked up really, *really* hard.

"Don't call me that," she mutters. "Not here."

"Oh," I answer softly. "Okay, I won't. I'm sorry."

She doesn't respond. Class begins, and the number of things to distract me and freak me out have doubled so I'm not exactly any better at paying attention. My time is split between freaking out about maybe losing Autumn as a friend (or friends) forever, and freaking out about upping my murder status from 'under duress' to 'first degree.' Suffice to say I am not having a great day. Once my second class ends, it takes everything I have to work up the courage for a single question.

"Um... wanna talk at lunch?" I ask Autumn.

"No," she answers, and my heart breaks in two.

"O-okay," I manage to stutter. "I'm not... I mean, I'd still like to be friends. Is that okay?"

She doesn't answer, just scrunching in on herself like it's raining on her and swiftly walking away, leaving me in a mire of self-hate.

Good job, Hannah. You made more of a mess than a milk truck hitting a sewage line. Not only are you rapidly running out of friends, but you don't get to be *Autumn's* friend, and she really looks like the kind of person that needs one. But again, not you, because you're an idiot.

I struggle through my third class and actually head to the lunchroom for lunch, against my better judgment. I just kind of don't have anywhere else to go. I didn't eat breakfast and I didn't pack a lunch, and while school naturally means I'm constantly surrounded by meat the fact that I am legitimately tempted to take a bite out of someone means that I definitely should be putting something in my stomach right now. I'm too wired up on adrenaline to compound the problem with hunger. Let's just ignore the fact that it's entirely my fault that I'm this hungry in the first place and get some grub.

The lunchroom is crowded, noisy, and full of bad food, but at least they have Salisbury steak today. Which is, uh, a sentence I never thought I'd say in my life, because Salisbury steak is usually quite disgusting *before* it's put through whatever degenerative process seems to be required of all school food. It's not even actually steak, it's just a wad of vaguely steak-shaped mystery meat in half-assed mushroom gravy. But it means I'm lucky enough to get a school lunch that I can actually *digest,* and that's a rather important attribute to food in my personal experience.

Brendan is sitting in the lunchroom with his school RPG group, as usual. I don't usually join him here because his friends are all boys and all really awkward around me in ways that I find kind of uncomfortable. They're not rude or misogynistic or anything, they're just... I dunno. They certainly don't pass the leering test, I'll say that much. It's the sort of mild background discomfort that I deal with pretty constantly as a person with boobs (and pretty nice ones, not to honk my own horns) but I'm the type of person that tries to avoid those sorts of situations rather than confront or just put up with them.

It's whatever, though. I'll deal. I wander up to Brendan's table and sit down next to him, wordlessly cutting into the deeply cursed lunchmeat and slipping a bite of it underneath my mask. Hrm. Definitely better than I remember, but not even my recent taste bud transfiguration can make it taste actually *good*. Why do they bother drizzling it in gravy if the gravy literally has no flavor whatsoever? It's just uncomfortably thick water.

"Oh, hey Hannah!" one of Brendan's friends greets me. I don't remember his name and don't really care to. He is staring at my chest.

I hiss at him. Loudly.

I don't think about it at all. I haven't even been caught off guard, I'm just *annoyed* and I need to make it known. The whole table, as well as most of the people sitting at nearby tables, goes quiet. I'd be lying to myself if I said that didn't feel strangely satisfying, and not just in the sense that not a lot can get a high schooler to actually shut up. It was accidental. Literally effortless, yet it got me what I wanted. I got to see him flinch. I like that he's afraid of me. It makes me feel a little less powerless.

"Uh, sorry," Brendan apologizes awkwardly. "She's had a bad weekend."

...Aaaand there's the embarrassment. Holy guacamole I just hissed at a ton of people I barely know I must look like a gosh dang crazy person! Aaaaagh, what am I doing!?

"That sounded kinda awesome, actually?" one of the other guys at the table chuckles nervously. "Like damn, I felt that in my bones. I kinda wish I could hiss like that."

What. He's... jealous? Of my weird eldritch hiss? Goddess darn it why am I feeling flattered about that?

"Brendan, is your whole friend group as obsessed with monsters as you are?" I grumble, sneaking in another bite of chaos loaf.

"Nah, Brendan and Jacob are the only furries in the group," a guy behind a Dungeon Master screen pipes up. "Speaking of, Brendan, it's your turn. What's your tabaxi doing?"

"I'm gonna punch him," Brendan answers, already rolling a handful of dice. "Twenty-three hit?"

"Yep."

"Fourteen damage."

"Oh, nice. He is bloodied!"

"Can I taunt him, too?" Brendan asks.

"What, like, goading him to focus on you?" the DM asks. "That'd be another action."

"...Can I taunt him *ineffectually?*"

"Ha. Sure."

Once the Dungeons and Dragons gets going in earnest I stop having to worry about awkward boys leering at me, since they're all way too invested in the grid on the table. I finish my lunch in silence, listening in on the game just to have something to occupy my attention other than dread and shame. At least I get to walk part of the way to class with Brendan. It helps calm my nerves a little bit, but a little bit goes a long way when I'm this much of a mess. On a whim, I tilt my body slightly to bump my shoulder into his arm. I should have asked before touching, but he doesn't react poorly to it. He just looks down at me with a concerned expression. We part ways soon afterwards and I head to my fourth class of the day. I sit down and pull my books out of my backpack in a futile attempt to convince myself I have the slightest chance of being able to focus when one of the so-called 'popular girls' walks up to me with a rather unfriendly look on her face.

"What's with those gloves?" she sneers.

I sigh. Why is it shit on Hannah day?

"My hands are injured," I respond lamely.

480

"And you thought *those* would look better?"

Wow. Wow wow wow. I'm actually getting fashion bullied. This honestly doesn't happen to me all that often. Who is this loser, anyway? I take the effort to actually look at her face and vaguely recognize her as one of the girls that hangs out with Ida sometimes. Doesn't Ida take this class with us? Yeah, there she is at the far end of the room, pretending she doesn't see me. I've been trying to respect the fact that she told me to leave her alone, but I don't really have the patience for this today. I lean past whoever-this-is and call out to my (former?) friend.

"Hey, Ida!" I bark. "Can you get your remora off of me?"

She flinches the slightest bit, probably not enough for anyone else to notice. Then she stands up with an affected sigh, pretending to fix her hair with one hand as she walks over.

"Are you saying I'm a shark?" she drawls.

"You're certainly as smooth as one," I say automatically. Goddess, what does that even mean? Ida laughs anyway, probably at least getting the reference but definitely playing up her reaction.

"What's even going on over here?" she asks. "I've never seen you two speak more than a sentence to each other."

"Not surprising, since Hannah never talks to anyone," girl-I-don't-care-about mutters. "I thought you'd given up on her too, Ida."

"And so you also thought to yourself 'oh hey, I should insult her gloves for *no reason*,'" I say, rolling my eyes.

"The reason is that they're ugly fucking gloves and it's the middle of April."

"Is your, uh, 'condition' getting that bad?" Ida asks me, ignoring the other girl. Which is a good tactic, honestly. It's one of the better snubs we can give her in this situation. I play along, keeping my attention entirely on Ida.

"Yeah, it's on my fingers and all the way up one leg now," I tell her. "The gloves are a bit heavy but I needed something capacitive."

481

One of the weird things about Ida that I've never understood is the fact that she spends a lot of time hanging out with people that she doesn't actually seem to like. When we first met in middle school she was already firmly integrated in the popular crowd, which by the natural law of middle school was also the bullies. And don't get me wrong, Ida *was* a bully, probably sometimes still is. She likes proving she's more clever than other people, and ultimately I think that's why we first started hitting off so well. I'm not as mean as she is, but I like that too.

When bullies came after me, I always tried to outmaneuver them. The plan was to make them feel stupid for talking to me enough times that they eventually decide I'm not worth the effort. Of course, being a middle schooler, I didn't really anticipate the fact that I'd be awkward and genuinely hurt at least as often as I was eloquent, and even if that wasn't the case the bullies would be too dumb to stop badgering the quiet kid anyway. At least that would have been the case, if not for Ida.

Ida likes hanging out with bullies. Heck, the little chaos gremlin is nominally *friends* with those bullies. But half the time I started biting back against their abuse, Ida would immediately turn on those very same friends and help me make fun of them. We'd banter back and forth, deny them what they want, and make them feel left out all while Ida remained firmly within their group and I remained firmly within mine. She was my little traitor on the inside, and I don't think it was because she wanted to be nice to me. I think she just wanted some intelligent conversation for once. She stifles herself, hanging out with them and obsessing over fashion and boys and gossip and whatever other inane things normal girls do. I've never gotten a straight answer when I've asked her why.

"What condition?" glove-insult-girl asks.

"Oh my god Gloria, you can't just *ask* her about a serious condition like that," Ida wheels on her immediately. "Do you not know how rude that is?"

"If you're scared of having to wear gloves, don't be," I chime in. "It's not contagious. Probably."

"Uh, probably?" Ida emphasizes.

"Probably!" I confirm innocently.

The bully whose name I swear I just heard looks a little uncomfortable at that, though *Ida* looks especially worried. Whoops, I forgot she was actually scared of my monster bits.

"Okay, whatever," G-something dismisses turning to walk off. "Have fun being diseased."

"Catch up with you in a sec, Gloria!" Ida calls after her happily, as if the two of us didn't spend the last thirty seconds explicitly trying to make her feel bad. She turns back to me, lowering her voice to a whisper. "You never mentioned it was fucking contagious!"

"That was just a bit!" I insist. "I mean, I guess I don't really know if it's contagious or not because I don't know what causes it, but no one else has started mutating yet."

She gives me a level stare.

"Um, that I know of?"

"Do you have a way to *check?*" she groans.

"I don't think s... hmm," I pause, remembering that I haven't tried the Soul Sight spell on Earth yet. "Uh, I guess maybe, actually? I don't know if it's a good idea, though. I am really flying by the seat of my pants on this stuff, Ida."

"Don't care," she grunts. "Do it."

"It's... not something I should do in public. It's, um, obvious. Like last time."

She shudders.

"...Okay," Ida nods. "How private do we need to be? Bathroom after class?"

"Back of the building, after school?" I hedge. "Just to be safe. But you'll have to be my ride home."

"Okay," Ida agrees, tapping her foot nervously. "...That really was all real, right?"

"Yeah," I confirm.

"Fuck," she swears emphatically, turning around and heading back to her seat. I can't say I disagree with her, though I'm a bit concerned about what's got her so worked up.

The teacher starts class soon after, though, and my mind is pulled back through spiraling about all my problems. Sindri most of all. The more I think about it, the more I need to not just decide how to try and prevent being hit with his magic again, but contingencies for if I *am* hit with his magic again. Ways to try and prod at the edges of his spell and look for weak points. Things to try that I won't *stop* having the incentive to try if I start unconditionally trusting Sindri with my life again. As Brendan would put it, I need to seek out excuses to give myself more will saves. The problem is that the dungeon master I'm trying to convince is my own future self, and that dumb jerk will have already thought of all this!

Stop, back up, don't panic about the shadowruns. All I need to worry about is giving myself the highest possible number of opportunities to stay alive. I pull out my notebook and start scribbling out ideas on the page after the actual class notes I'm *supposed* to be taking. I'm going to have an excessive amount of homework with all the in-school time I'm missing, but school is pretty rapidly plummeting down my priority list. I honestly don't care all that much anymore.

My fourth class ends, my fifth and final class begins, and I spend it doing much the same sort of planning. Can I use Refresh to 'clean' my mind of foreign influence? Probably not, since the spell works by physically moving things. Maybe investigate and/or try to manifest a more conceptual version? One of the big problems with being adjacent to Pneuma on the element wheel is that it means I don't have the slightest bit of resistance to Pneuma. I can't really

484

leverage my supposedly-huge aura to do much about it, so I'm stuck with more mundane methods. Mental tricks, promises to myself that I'm not sure if I'll keep, bargains and strategies and all sorts of little things that probably would never have a chance of working on their own... and if I'm being honest, probably don't have a chance of working in tandem. Because ultimately, the problem with fighting off mental influence is that it takes self-control. And I do not have that. Like, at all. So... that's a problem.

The school day ends and I barely remember to send Brendan a text to not expect me on the bus, as engrossed as I am in my plans. I wander to the back of the school, wishing I could chew on something or claw something to shreds to get rid of this ever-growing stress. I've already snapped two pencils today, though it's not a huge deal since I carry around about twenty. They just kind of seem to collect themselves in my backpack somehow. I spot the little chaos gremlin known as Ida and do my best to blink away my thoughts of tonight, but unfortunately she seems to catch on.

"Y'know, I uh... should have asked, before," Ida says awkwardly. "Are you doing okay?"

I shrug.

"No," I admit. "Not at all."

"Fuck," Ida swears. "I'm sorry, Hannah. I just... I've been freaking out about this, okay? Ever since you summoned that invisible scary lady into my car and used fucking actual magic I just... the world just feels fake. Does that make any sense?"

"Um, yeah, I guess," I nod. "It's a bit of an Earth-shattering revelation to have fantasy and reality swapping places like that."

"N-no," Ida shakes her head. "I mean yes, but also like... literally. If I stop focusing on it, then things literally, physically start to feel like they're fake. Like I'm just dreaming and if things were a little more lucid I could reach out and... I don't even know. Do something real? I'm sort of rapidly and very unwillingly turning into a solipsist."

Oh. Oh gosh. Okay.

"...Reach out how?" I ask hesitantly.

"I don't know," she admits, sounding uncharacteristically small.

"Okay," I nod. "There's... a way I can check to see if you have magic. I'm not sure what happens if I use it in this world, though. It'll probably be fine, but it might be *really* bad?"

"Did you say another world?" she asks.

"Yeah, I uh, I live in another universe when I sleep."

She opens her mouth to comment on that, but then she just shakes her head.

"You know what? Sure. Fine. I just... I accept whatever risk this is, Hannah. I feel like I'm going crazy. Just... do your thing."

"I'll have to summon the, uh, invisible scary lady again. The Goddess."

I add the last two words without even thinking much about it. It feels wrong not to clarify that I mean *Her.*

"Which is why you wanted us alone," Ida sighs. "Sure. Go for it."

I nod, inhale, and make my intent known.

"**Aura Sight**," the Goddess says, blooming into glorious existence around Ida and I, swirling and caressing us. She pats me on the head, pinches Ida's cheeks, and then disappears like she was never here. Ida and I both shudder, terror passing through us both in equal measure.

"So what did that do?" Ida asks nervously, looking distinctly like Order.

I blink. I look again. Yep, Order. Ida the chaos gremlin... is aligned to Order. And *only* Order.

"Well, congrats I guess," I tell her. "You have magic. I'm pretty sure if you pull on that feeling hard enough, you won't just be a lucid dreamer. You will metaphorically wake up."

"What, just like that!?" she asks, halfway between incredulous and hysterical. "Would... will she come back?"

"Uh, hopefully not," I say. "She only shows up if you speak the name of a spell out loud, and you should *not* be trying to speak any spell names out loud. It could seriously mess you up, maybe even kill you."

"Then why do *you* say spells out loud?" she snaps.

"Because I'm stupid," I tell her frankly. "And also a funky multidimensional monster. Don't do what I do. We should probably go to a better place than behind the school if you wanna test out your magic."

"What if I *don't* wanna test out my magic?" Ida hisses. "What if I just want things to make sense again?"

"Then maybe your magic does that! I don't have any clue, Ida. You're an Order mage like me, you could have all kinds of bullpoop. I have a cleaning spell."

"Wait, seriously?" she asks.

In response I just lick my wrist, bring it up to my face to smear my makeup, then snap my fingers for show, which makes a surprisingly satisfying popping sound even through my gloves. With a quick pulse of Refresh, my face is looking better than before the smudge.

"Okay, shit, I want magic now," Ida gapes. "That's *way* cooler than freaky toe claws."

"Uh, thanks, I think?" I smirk. "Come on, drive me home and I'll teach you what little I know about not causing yourself to explode."

"Is that a thing that can happen?"

"Yeah, I nearly bled out on Saturday," I nod.

"...Can I change my mind again?"

I chuckle humorlessly, heading out towards the school parking lot and motioning Ida to follow. Whether she chooses to cast or not, I still need to tell her as much as I can about what I know. It's only fair, not to mention much safer for her, to be informed. After some brief hesitation, she follows me and the two of us walk to her car, dozens of other students doing the same around us. Out of curiosity, I glance at one at random to try and see what magical alignment they have... and I don't feel anything.

Glancing back at Ida, I focus and confirm that yes, she still feels like Order, and yes the Aura Sight spell is still active. I glance at a different student. Nothing. Another new student. Nothing. A bird, a bug, a teacher, a tree... nothing. No auras on any of them. The bus passes by, and through the window I manage to catch Brendan's eye as he waves at me. I wave back, and of course give him a magical vibe check. Art. His aura very clearly tastes like Art. But that's it. Out of everyone I can see, the spell only reacts to Ida, Brendan, and of course me.

My friends and I are the only people in school that have souls.

# 26

# ARROGANCE

"Hannah? Hey, Hannah? Earth to Hannah Banana!"

"Huh? Eh? What?" I sputter, blinking rapidly as I peel my eyes away from trying and failing to find anything else of interest with my Aura Sight.

"You spaced out for a second there," Ida says. "What's up?"

"Oh, uh, nothing, I'm just sort of coming to a terrifying existential realization maybe?"

"Well in that case don't tell me, I'm way too sober," Ida grunts. "Come on, let's drive."

Aura sight sees auras, and auras come from souls. Right? Right. Now logically speaking, there could be plenty of explanations for why most people don't have auras. Their souls could just be too weak for me to see, or too magically inert to have an aura. But at the same time, something in the back of my head keeps bugging me, insisting that that's *wrong.* Souls are inherently divine in nature. So without the grace of the Goddess, how could there possibly be souls?

I had an edgy atheist phase for a bit after I accepted that I was gay and couldn't mesh that reality with what my pastor kept spouting about sin. I got really mad at the concept of religions and gods and decided that there isn't an afterlife and no inherent meaning exists in the universe. I mellowed out a bit after that and went from firm atheist to wibbly skeptic. My new position was that there probably isn't an afterlife because everything is statistically improbable until evidence for its existence can be observed by humanity, no religion possesses evidence about the immaterial, and therefore all religions are equally unlikely. They could technically exist, but with it being literally impossible to determine that existence, spending brainspace on it is a waste of my time.

I still consider myself a skeptic, I suppose, but part of being a skeptic is that when you *do* find evidence of something, you don't go "hmm, this seems fake because I'm skeptical," you say "oh dang, that's evidence" and adjust your worldview accordingly. And the Goddess observably exists.

Do I know what the Goddess is? No, not really. Do I know what souls are? Nope, not that either. But Death magic exists, and I've been told it proves that souls persist after death, containing the identity of the person who once held them. Therefore, consciousness exists after death... as long as you have a soul. So the idea that most people on my entire planet might *not* have a soul is honestly kind of terrifying.

I don't want to stop existing. I honestly can't think of anything that frightens me more. I'm tempted to thank the Goddess for confirmation that I won't, but I think I'll wait until I actually know what the afterlife is like. Oblivion seems bad, but Hell seems worse... and my Goddess can certainly be a wrathful one when the mood strikes Her.

I sit down in the passenger's seat of Ida's car, trying to banish the stress of this new revelation, or at least properly slot it in line behind my plethora of more immediate stressors. Ida has magic, so I should teach her about magic. She starts driving, keeping the radio off for once as I figure out where to start. I guess if I don't know where to start I may as well start anywhere. The element wheel is as good as any.

Ida is *not* happy to learn that she opposes Chaos, but honestly it makes a certain kind of sense. The sort of chaotic fae energy she has still possesses a sort of logic, which falls under the realm of Order. Chaos in the magical sense is true randomness, the absence of methodology, and it's fundamentally incompatible with life. Ida very much has a method to her madness, even if it's only understood by her.

Unfortunately, teaching Ida what she needs to know mostly just emphasizes how much *I* still need to know. I tell her about learning spells vs. having spells, I tell her about aura strength, I talk about how the Goddess seems to favor some people more than others and how she gives everyone their magic personally. I also, of course, tell her about the dangers of miscasting, but also how it's supposedly pretty safe to cast magic as long as you're not speaking the incantation.

"That's kind of a weird contradiction," Ida frowns. "Magic is super safe until it's super deadly?"

"I don't know what to tell you," I shrug. "When I'm casting a spell without speaking its name, I just... cast it. Once you figure it out it's pretty much automatic. But the incantation is a whole *thing.* You have to understand the spell you're trying to cast at a pretty deep level, and then you have to pick a name for it that the Goddess approves of. It has to be descriptive and... I think she also likes it if it's clever? Or at least interesting? It's not really needed, I suppose, because some spells have lame names like Aura Sight, but I think she was distinctly happy with me when I chose a theme."

"Huh," Ida frowns. "What's your theme?"

"Um," I say, a blush starting to form on my cheeks.

"Oh my god it's really geeky, isn't it?" Ida sighs. "It's a theme for absolute fucking dorks."

"It's Pokémon attacks," I confirm quietly.

"Of course it is. Fuck, that gives me *so many* questions. Does this goddess from another dimension know about goddamn *Pokémon,* of all things? How?"

"Um. I mean, She's a Goddess. It could literally be any number of ways. At minimum I'm pretty sure She knows everything I know. She responds to thoughts pretty directly."

"This is so fucking insane," Ida grumbles. "So I just... have magic now, huh? I just have to focus on it and then boom! It'll happen?"

"Yeah. Maybe don't try it while driving though."

Ida rolls her eyes.

"Hannah, I know you're a mere mortal restricted to seeing the world from her own viewpoint but *most* people are not the sort of fucking disaster to test something unknown and dangerous in a moving vehicle."

Well. That's just rude. But probably accurate. Ida doesn't react to my indignant scowls, though, and soon enough we're parked right outside my house.

"Well, you can test your magic while I get ready for work, then," I grumble, moving to open the door. "It's probably better if I'm not around, in case it turns out to be dangerous."

"Wait," Ida says, staring blankly forward and not shutting off the car. "I think you should stay."

I frown a bit.

"Your magic almost certainly won't hurt you," I tell her. "But that doesn't mean it can't hurt *me*. It's safer for you to test it alone."

"I don't... I think you should be here," Ida says slowly. "I don't know why, I just... is that weird?"

Huh. *Is* that weird? I mean, this is Ida, she's probably not saying this because she's clingy. Honestly, it's super plausible that her magic is giving her hints about stuff it needs in order to activate. Mine did that.

"Uh, no, that's not weird," I assure her. "Having feelings about that kind of stuff is how I learned to cast, so my vote is to trust it. I'd prefer you not cast anything you don't understand on me, though. Can you try it on like... a bug or something?"

"You are a bug," Ida snorts, shutting off the car. "But no, I don't think so. I... can you just stay here? Please?"

Hesitantly, I nod.

"...Okay," I allow. "I hope we don't regret this, though."

"Yeah," Ida confirms. "God, I can't fucking believe I'm taking this fantasy bullshit seriously. If I didn't know how hilariously useless at manipulation you are I'd think you were gaslighting me into this somehow."

"Is that... a compliment?" I hedge. I feel like having gaslighting skills isn't a good thing.

"No," she grunts. "Okay. Fuck it. Here goes."

She closes her eyes and takes a deep breath.

"Okay, nope this won't work," Ida says.

"What's wrong?" I ask.

"This isn't enough. It wants something else. I need to... no, we should... fuck, I dunno. Play me in rock-paper-scissors. First to ten."

I blink in surprise as she raises her fist to the starting position, but nod, raising my fist in kind. Why not? What could go wrong in a nice, friendly game of rock-paper-scissors? ...Haha don't actually answer that, me.

"On scissors. Ready?" she prompts.

"Ready," I confirm. "Rock, paper, scissors!"

I play scissors. She plays rock. I lose. Seems reasonable. We play again, and that time I win, which prompts Ida to scowl, scrunching her face together in a determined expression. We play nine more hands after that, and I lose every single one of them.

"Holy garbanzo beans," I gape after the ninth consecutive loss. "Luck manipulation?"

"What? No, fuck you," Ida snaps. "It's not luck, bitch. Rock-paper-scissors has a lot of skill to it if you actually know what you're

493

goddamn doing. There's a bunch of psychology to it, not to mention ways to cheat."

"Wait, have you been cheating?" I ask.

"Not if you can't prove I am," she smirks. "Otherwise I'm just the best!"

"Alright, but was that your magic at play or can you always kick this much ass at rock-paper-scissors?" I ask, rolling my eyes.

"I... I mean, it was definitely the magic," Ida says. "But it was *also* me, I think? It's fucking freaky. Like, I was still doing everything, I somehow just *knew* how to do everything. I had all these predictive and muscle reading skills that I never had before and can barely even remember now. ...Fuck, how *did* I do that? Shit, this is so fucking messed up. I guess my magic makes me better at stuff?"

"What does that mean, exactly?"

She opens her mouth to respond, then shuts it with a scowl, taking a moment to think.

"...I don't know," she ultimately concludes. "No, I'm just wrong, I'm not better *at stuff*. I think? I feel manic as all hell, like I do when I get fucked up and try to do dumb shit like fight MMA professionals just to show I'm hard enough. I think I can win at anything, but then I get my ass kicked."

She looks down at her hands, seeming to barely even be paying attention to me anymore. A grin slowly works its way up her face, starting cute but morphing towards worrying at high speed.

"...But I didn't lose just now," she chuckles. "Holy shit. Holy *shit.*"

"Um, you okay, Ida?"

"I'm better than okay!" she laughs. "I'm the best that's ever been! Go get changed for work, I'm gonna keep messing around with this."

"Uh, okay," I nod. "Just be careful, and don't let anyone see you."

"Sure, sure," Ida dismisses, waving me off.

That's not very reassuring, but I guess I didn't notice her using magic, and I *am* magic. I sneak into the house as best I can, thanking the blaring television that currently distracts my father. I quickly head upstairs, change into my work clothes and take most of my school stuff out of my backpack. I bring the rest of my backpack to work, because I don't really want to be caught without medical supplies and extra clothing again. I take the time to individually bind up my mutant fingers in bandages as well, since I suspect whoever's managing today might challenge me on my gloves. Showing that I literally can't use the cash register touch screens without them should get me some leniency, but I'll have to take my gloves off to actually do that.

Slinking back downstairs and returning to Ida, I find her scowling as she picks a bunch of playing cards up off the floor of her car.

"What's up?" I ask, plopping into the passenger's seat. "Figure anything out?"

"Well I figured out that I can't even win a game of solitaire, and I'm not totally sure why," she grumbles. "Spell wouldn't even activate. ...God, that's so fucking weird to say. Anyway, it sucks, because I *feel* like I should be able to be the best at everything."

I raise an eyebrow at that.

"You think your magic is supposed to make you 'the best at everything?'" I ask. "I mean, magic's crazy, but that's a bit arrogant, don't you think?"

"Huh!" she exclaims, thinking for a moment before twisting around and looking towards the back of the car. "Yeah, it... it kinda is, isn't it? But maybe that's it. Like, you said Order magic is about thinking there's a way the world should be, right?"

"Uh, kinda, yeah," I nod. "Like, the concept of 'clean' or 'sorted' isn't objectively defined, it's totally subjective. But my subjective definition of those things seems to drive the objective functions of my magic. There's a more orderly way I want the world to be, and my order magic makes the world that way."

"Well, subjectively speaking, the world is objectively better when I am the best at everything," Ida insists, crawling halfway into the backseat to pull the foot mat off the duct-taped holes I dug into the floor of her car back when my mutations were just starting. "If that's arrogance, then I think I have arrogance magic."

I blink, not really having any words for that. Arrogance magic!? Oh beans on toast, I can't even claim that doesn't make sense. Of *course* Ida would develop arrogance magic.

"The world would also be better if my shit wasn't broken," Ida continues. "My stuff should always be the best stuff. So let's see if I can do anything about *that.*"

She rips a strip of duct tape off and focuses for a moment. I stay quiet, letting her work. Then, I start to see it. The metal twists, shifting and even *growing* when necessary to get back into place, and when it's done there's not a shred of evidence that the damage ever occurred. Ida takes a deep breath, admiring her work with an ever-growing grin.

"Oh my fucking god," she chuckles. "I take it all back. Magic is the coolest thing ever."

"Goddess," I correct automatically.

"Huh?"

"You have a Goddess now," I remind her. "Not a god."

Ida glances back, giving me a concerned look.

"Oh," she answers. "Uh, right. Yeah."

"I just... y'know, if you have arrogance magic I think you should be careful about that, is all," I stutter, my brain doing its best to catch up with my words and figure out why I'm so insistent on this. "Arrogance is probably fine, I'm sure the Goddess thinks it's great if she gave you that. Just be careful it doesn't evolve into *hubris,* okay? She's dangerous, Ida. She can and will smite you if you make Her mad."

"Duly noted, I guess," Ida shrugs, ripping off the next piece of tape to expose the second of ten holes in the floor. "Can't say I wouldn't do the same if I were a goddess."

Uh. Huh. Gosh, the idea of Ida and the Goddess having similar personalities is simultaneously terrifying and enlightening in a bunch of different ways I really don't want to think about. I stay quiet as she struggles through repairing the rest of the damage I did to her car, not wanting to disturb her and not sure what to say. She actually starts sweating a bit when she gets halfway through repairing the damage I've done, leaning down in the space between the front seats and bumping up against me as she works, her butt sticking right up in my face.

It's a pretty nice butt, honestly, even as skinny as Ida is. While she can look pretty young from a distance, being very short and skinny, Ida makes an effort to accentuate her assets with tasteful makeup, expert accessorizing, and very, *very* tight clothing. Though they aren't as pronounced as most girls our age, Ida doesn't let anyone forget that *she has curves,* and when her shirt starts riding up to reveal her back and belly I have no choice but to muster all my willpower and redirect a deeply blushing face to look out the window until she sits back up.

"Fucking... finally," Ida huffs, her face shining with sweat. "That is *awesome*, but it is exhausting. I need a rest, you drive."

She tosses me the keys, which I fumble to catch, and then she shoos me out of the passenger seat. I get out of the car and head around to the driver's seat, experiencing the surprise of having to adjust the seat *back* for once. It's so strange not being the shortest person driving a car.

"You sure?" I ask. "You never let other people drive your car."

"Well don't fucking crash and I won't have reason to regret it," she mumbles. "I'm fucking tired and I agreed to give you a ride to work, so you can do it yourself."

"Alright," I nod, and start the car. It's very weird driving a car other than my dad's, but I take it slow and we get to my work safely. Ida spends the entire trip insulting my driving skills, but we still make it there. I park and move to get out, but Ida grabs my wrist before I can open the door.

"Hey," she says. I wait for her to continue, but she doesn't seem forthcoming.

"Hey?" I prompt.

She squirms a bit, slouching down in her seat with one leg bouncing nervously. She spends nearly half a minute looking like she's on the verge of saying something before she finally comes out and actually says anything at all.

"You're in some deep shit, right?" she manages.

Instinctively, I want to brush her off. To not say anything, to keep all my problems to myself, but that's not fair to her. Not when she already knows this much. So I wiggle my extra limbs, pulling them free of the bindings around my stomach that hold them in place and letting them peek out from underneath my shirt, the clawed spider legs revealing themselves with my best take at a shrug. Ida's eyes widen, though she carefully doesn't react.

"I'm not really human anymore," I say quietly. "And that's far from the worst of it. When I go to sleep tonight, my free will has a good chance of being stolen away by a mind rapist who plans to use me as a living weapon. I've been panicking about it all day because I don't know if there's anything I can do about it."

"Is that something I'm gonna end up getting stuck in?" Ida asks. "This other world?"

I shrug.

"Not to my knowledge," I tell her. "But my knowledge is next to nothing so it's a possibility. Nothing all that bad has happened on Earth yet, though I feel like that's just a ticking time bomb waiting to happen."

"Okay," Ida nods. She's still holding my wrist. "Hey, Hannah?"

"Yeah?"

"I'm a hedonist," she says. "I think there's no fucking point to life if I don't spend it living my best one."

"I *did* always get that impression from you, yeah," I agree, smiling softly. "It's fine. I'll keep leaving you alone, keep you out of the drama. If you're not overt with your magic I doubt anybody will bother you."

"No," Ida growls, giving me a frighteningly intense glare. "Fuck that. Fuck that until it tears in half. Hannah, I... this is insane, but I'm with you, okay? One hundred percent, one thousand fucking percent, I'm with you. I was a complete piece of shit for ditching you before when it first got weird."

"I... it's fine, Ida," I insist, pulling my hand away. "Really. It's probably better if you just avoid me and lie l—"

"No! Shut the *fuck* up, Hannah!" Ida shouts, pointing a furious finger at me. "Look at me! *I do what I goddamn want!* And I'm all-in on this. You don't get a say, because you do stupid shit with your say like forgive me and pretend you don't have any problems when on the inside you're fucking dying. And I saw you doing it! All last fucking week, whenever you weren't making goochie-goo eyes at that Autumn bitch, you were miserable. And I just... that hurt to see, okay? I can't stand that shit. I'll kill anybody that makes you feel that way."

She turns away from me, sinking a little lower into the passenger's seat and crossing her arms over her chest. I gape at her, feeling more than a little bowled over by that furious tirade. It's not fun being yelled at, even if that was ostensibly a pretty intense emotional declaration of... friendship? Maybe *more* than friendship? Gosh I don't want to read too much into that and don't know what I would want the answer to be if I did. She may have already admitted to wanting to have sex with me, but knowing Ida that definitely isn't something that requires love on her end.

You know what? Right now, it doesn't matter. I have Ida back, one way or another. Realizing that shoves everything else out of my mind, a soothing waterfall of relief filling me. *I have Ida back.* I didn't mess up our friendship after all. She has my back, and I literally have no choice but to embrace that. Which is perfect, because she's right that I probably wouldn't have accepted it otherwise.

"Thank you, Ida," I tell her, holding back a sudden urge for tears. "You're the best."

"I fucking know," she grunts. "Now get out of my goddamn car."

I smile, taking a brief moment to wrap up my extra limbs again before exiting, leaving her keys in the ignition. I head into work and get my day started, occasionally glancing out the window to see Ida's car sitting motionlessly for nearly fifteen minutes before she finally gets into the driver's seat and leaves.

Work is terrible, which is arguably a good thing because I'm so busy I don't have time to freak out about what's going to happen tonight. Three people call out sick, leaving my boss and I alone with one other employee to handle the entire dinner rush. I'm stuck up front because the extra employee was hired barely a week ago and only knows how to work one station in the kitchen, leaving my boss to do basically everything else in the back while I handle every single customer getting increasingly irate about our long wait times. At one point I turn away from the register and see four different full trays of orders ready to be bagged, and I am very, *very* tempted to just speak Refresh out loud and forcibly move them all where they're supposed to go at once. I don't, but it's a pretty close shave with my limited self-control. I wonder if I can be fired for using magic on shift. I guess *legally* I probably can, it's not like 'mage' is protected under equal opportunity laws, but would I be? ...Nah, probably not. My boss would think cleaning magic is pretty sick.

I *do* use some silent cleaning magic when I'm out in the dining room making sure everything looks nice. Subtle stuff where I give a table a cursory wipe-down with a towel and secretly make the whole thing ultra-clean, or force all the crumbs on the floor to obey my broom in a single sweep. Not that I have a whole lot of time to clean in the first place between taking, bagging, and tabling orders. Once the shift finally ends though I pretty much use as much magic as I can get away with to speed through the closing routine and make sure everything is clean for tomorrow, because I am exhausted and I have no desire to stay here any longer than... huh. I forgot that I really, really don't want to go to sleep tonight. Steak on toast, I'm really stupid. If anything I should be slowing down.

I mean, I *shouldn't* slow down, because that would be really unfair to the people I'm working with who very much want to go home, but oh Goddess I do not want to go home, I do not want to be faced with the combination of my own exhaustion and easy access to a bed. After all, I still haven't decided if I'm going to run away and leave my friends with a mind-controlling bastard, or if I'm going to... to kill him. I... no, no, no, I hate this. I hate this so much. I don't want to kill him, but I don't know what else I can *do.* Murder is bad, it's wrong, but Sindri can steal and twist *free will.*

I've called him a mind rapist before, and to some degree it feels wrong. It feels like rape—one of the and arguably *the* most terrible thing you can do to another person—can't possibly be used as a point of comparison without hyperbole. In reality, though, I think I've been generally avoiding the term in order to avoid thinking about how horribly, disgustingly, terrifyingly *accurate* it is. Sindri's violations aren't sexual in nature, no, but having someone worm their way into my mind and rip away the parts of me that want to scream 'no?' What... what other analogy can I use for that!?

I find myself kneeling on the floor, vaguely aware that I'm starting to hyperventilate, tears forming in my eyes. When I go home I am consigning myself to waking up in the same room as a man who intends to discard my personhood like a worn-out toy. I might escape, I might even end up killing him, but nothing will change the fact that I have to take that dive, I have to know that he has already twisted me and he very possibly will do so again. Maybe he'll find a way to retain his mind control when I'm here on Earth. Maybe I'll stop being anything but his puppet, his little fake 'friend' who sticks with him because she's physically lost the capability to identify

501

abuse. I could wither away to nothing, become no one, end up being his little monster pet in truth, just like one of the animals he thought I was. And the worst part is, I can't stop it. I'm doomed to have to face this possibility, to face *him,* and none of my plans give me a surefire way out. I'm going to go home, I'm going to get in bed, and I'm going to risk being raped. Those are the stakes. That's what I'm consigning myself to. The one fucking thing that's basically guaranteed to get me even more traumatized than I already am, and I just... I just... fuck! Fuck, fuck, fuck, fuck, fuck, fuck!

"Hannah? Hey, Hannah!"

My boss is kneeling on the ground next to me. The cleaning supplies are scattered on the floor around me. I'm sobbing in earnest, at least when I can manage to successfully take a full breath. My chest hurts. Oh good. A panic attack. Again.

"Fine," I somehow manage to choke out. "I'm fine."

"Do you need—"

I don't pay attention to the rest of my boss' sentence because he reaches out to put a reassuring hand on my shoulder and it takes all of my willpower to not claw his fucking throat out. I freeze, utterly motionless, not trusting myself to so much as breathe. He's touching me he's touching me he's *touching me like that bastard did* but it's not the same, he's trying to help, it's fine it's fine it's fine *it's fine it's fine it's fine!*

"...Off," I hiss, and thank the Goddess that's enough for him to get the message and remove his hand. My panic attack has fully evolved into predator fight-or-flight response and I'm seconds away from biting anything in range. I have to leave. To separate myself from people. The... the walk-in fridge has a lock on the inside. A thick door. I can hide there. I stand up and start to move, tears still falling down my face as I wordlessly step past my boss, step into the fridge, and collapse into a sobbing mess. I'm not human enough to feel cold anymore, so the temperature doesn't even bother me.

The smell does, though. I don't have even the slightest bit of willpower left to resist the urge to take off a glove, rip open a bag of raw chicken with my claws, and just devour the entire thing. One bag of chicken, incidentally, is ten pounds. Twenty cuts of meat, each slippery with marinade, torn into chunks by my teeth and swallowed by the mouthful. Ferociously gluttonous, I devour bite after bite of stolen meat and silently imagine each and every one as a person: Sindri, my boss, my old therapist, my own mother, my friends, the dumb preppy girl who made fun of my gloves earlier today, the various customers that yelled at me. Dead, dead, dead, dead, all by my tooth and claw, my dominance made manifest. Only when I reach into the bag and swipe at nothing but the remains of uncooked chicken juices does my fugue end, my stomach painfully bloated but somehow not burst. I waste a bit of time shuddering in revulsion, but then I realize I have to hide the evidence and get back to my job. Having a panic attack like that is really going to hurt my chance for a promotion.

A few quick casts of Refresh set the walk-in looking pristine, and with my budding spatial sense it's easy to find an opportunity to exit the fridge and throw away the empty chicken bag without anyone seeing me. I head back out to the dining room, where to my eternal embarrassment I find my boss finishing the last of my closing duties. I let out a shaky breath, feeling my cheeks turn a bit pinker. It's fine. I just let everyone down, but they're not going to be *that* mad. Probably.

"Sorry," I say automatically, reaching out to take the mop from my boss.

"It's fine," he says, probably lying. "It's been a rough day for everyone. I was really impressed with how clean you got everything else, actually."

"Um, thank you," I shrug awkwardly. "I'm good at cleaning. I like it."

"I guess you've found a good job then," he chuckles. "Just finish this up and we'll finally get out of here, okay?"

Oh. Goodie.

I get through the rest of the closing routine on autopilot. It's all I have left. I catch a ride home with my boss, successfully do not murder him, and with terror suffusing every bone and exoskeletal feature in my body, I trudge up to my room. A normal person, I think, would get in bed and be kept wide awake by this sort of panic and fear. But I know that when I lie down on that mattress, I'll be out like a light. And then I'll have to face it all. I can't do that. I collapse to the floor of my room, and shakily send off a text.

**Help.**

The response is almost immediate.

**What do you need?**

Thank you, Brendan. Thank you.

**I have to go back,** I text him. **I have to go back and he'll be waiting and I'll have to kill him.**

**You could run.**

**No. He's a rapist. A monster. I have to kill him.**

The typing symbol starts and stops, over and over. He's taking too long. I need to hear his response now.

**Just say something,** I send him.

**I believe in you,** he answers back.

**I don't.**

**I know,** he says. **But I do. And I think I'm right to. You'll make it through, Hannah. No matter what. I'd bet the whole world on you.**

**Okay,** I say. Then I follow it up with something I don't normally say, and maybe should more often. **I love you, Brendan.**

**I love you too, Hannah,** he answers immediately. **I'll talk to you tomorrow.**

He's implying a lot in that statement. He's saying I'll still be alive tomorrow, and I'll still be me.

**Okay,** I agree. **I'll talk to you tomorrow. I'm going to bed.**

**Good night, Hannah.**

**It won't be. But good night to you, Brendan.**

My body shaking, I strip my clothes off and get into bed. Soon I wake up, surrounded by wood and beds and full-bodied terror. Sindri! I have to kill Sindri, or else he'll—

"Good morning, Hana," my nightmare says.

He's standing by the window. I rush towards him immediately, magic collecting in my legs, but... wait. Am I really prepared to murder someone? No, agh, I have to commit!

*Aren't I overreacting?* my own mind wonders. *Sindri and I have have been through a lot together, and he's been on my side through all of it. What if I'm imagining this? Can I really kill him over something like that?*

Oh, this motherfucker! I'm not letting him gaslight me like this! I rush closer, preparing a strike on his leg to force him to the ground, but the thoughts he put in my head—*did he put them in my head?*—keep squirming, twisting, making me doubt. I don't... I don't want to kill him. I don't think I can do it! We saved each other from bandits, cultists, acid-spewing forest monsters, and all sorts of things! He's taught me so much, he's *helped* me so much, can I really doubt our friendship like—agh, no, not that word! He's not my friend!!! If I can't kill him, I have to run!

"**Friends** should hear each other out first," Sindri disagrees, and I stop in my tracks. He's... he's right, of course. I mean, well, the fact that he can remove free will makes hearing him out suspect, but he wouldn't do that to me. I'm... I'm not thinking straight. I have to go. Or... no. That's stupid. I'm not thinking straight, so that's all the more reason to get help from a friend.

*Sorry,* I apologize instinctively.

"It's fine, Hana," Sindri reassures me, a slight smile on his face. "I have to admit, I was surprised—and a little worried—to see you acting so aggressive all of a sudden."

*Yeah, that's... well, y'know. I thought you were mind controlling me, which... well. Um. No, wait, I heard you speak that incantation. I guess you are mind controlling me. But... that's... fine?*

*That's a very rude accusation, Hannah,* Sindri says, immediately making me feel ashamed. *My spell doesn't control anyone.*

*Oh? Gosh, sorry then. You're right, I feel so...! Wait. No, your magic definitely controls things, that's how you fight. It's not at all unreasonable to assume you can control me. You're controlling Bulupunu, after all. And those birds that you follow the Chaos mage with!*

*Hannah, I promise that I'm doing no such thing.*

Oh. Well. Hmm. That doesn't make a lot of sense, but I trust him. He's doing no such thing. But... well, just in case, I guess I should mention something.

*Okay, I believe you,* I tell him. *But we should look into this mind control thing anyway.*

*Oh?* Sindri asks.

*Well, because I was really, really convinced that you were mind controlling me when I was awake on Earth,* I tell him. I'm not sure why I'm mentioning Earth, but it's whatever. I trust Sindri. *I guess all my reasoning about you being an evil rapist seems kind of silly now, but there was definitely something affecting my state of mind. If you're a soul mage, you should help me get rid of it.*

*And why's that?* he asks.

*Well, because if you don't, I'll kill you,* I explain.

He blinks with shock, which is really embarrassing so I barrel onwards.

*Sorry, I mean, I don't want to kill you,* I assure him. *But I'm worried that I will when I go to sleep. The mind control stuff is a big deal to*

506

*me, you know? I thought of all these tricks I can try to break free of it, things I can attempt or try to force or whatever. I don't really want to do any of those, but I do want to warn you that I'll keep trying. I will find whatever's messing with my head. I will rip it to shreds. I will eat its corpse.*

My body is shaking as I say these things, and I'm not really sure why. I must be worried about Sindri. I used to be *really* convinced it was his fault, for some reason. That's why I have to tell him these things. So he doesn't get hurt.

*I'm very dangerous,* I tell him. *You've seen me fight. It would just take a few seconds. If there is anyone messing with my head, and they can understand me now, I suggest that they run. I know that you know I don't like killing, Sindri, but for this I will kill. Sleep far away from me. Get up early. Exclude me from night watches. You have to stay awake every hour I'm conscious, Sindri. Please.*

"I'm sure it will be okay," Sindri says hesitantly.

*Please, Sindri,* I beg him. *I don't want to kill my friend.*

He swallows, seeming nervous for whatever reason.

"For now, let's just wake the others," he says. "We have an important day ahead of us."

*Okay,* I agree happily, and jump up on Kagiso's bed to poke her awake. We have a Chaos mage to fight, after all. I should focus on that and put this entire conversation behind us.

That must be why I feel like I'm on the verge of a breakdown. Can't think of anything else it would be.

# 27

# CHAOS

It doesn't take us long to be ready to depart. As Sindri promised, the four of us are out of our room and waiting by the bridge at dawn. Kagiso yawns, stretching like a cat as morning's first rays of light wash over the multi-layered city. We're far from the only people up and about this early, the main road already full of noisy merchants and rowdy customers. Together we're waiting for that paladin cultist, Hagoro. I'm *really* worried about meeting him, but I know my friends will have my back if something bad happens.

Clinging to the top of Kagiso's head like usual, it's easy enough for me to spot the man when he approaches: he's the only dentron wearing full-plate armor, after all. His big spear—or I guess maybe it's a glaive or something, I'm not a weapon nerd—is just over six feet long from butt to tip, and pretty fancy-looking, with countless engravings down the entire length of the shaft that probably give him no tactical advantage whatsoever. It's a nice stick though, I'll give him that.

His armor is much cooler, even having a cute little chainmail sock for his tail. His chest piece also has a big fancy artisanal representation of the centipede symbol that the cultists normally wear on necklaces, which I guess is probably good publicity on a guy as huge as Hagoro. Although... hmm. Big fancy art on objects, huh?

509

"**Aura Sight**," I say on a whim, startling Sindri. He gives me a concerned look.

*Just checking the paladin guy,* I reassure him. I wonder what he's worried about.

Order and Barrier. That's what Hagoro tastes like. Interesting combination, but it feels like a good one for a paladin. To heal and protect, and all that. Also, I'm wrong as hell, those engravings feel like Art magic and absolutely provide some kind of tactical advantage, as does the design on the armor. Dang. Although that all said, it's *really* weird that those inanimate objects feel like anything, isn't it? Aura sight doesn't normally pick up on the presence of magical energy; it didn't show me anything when Ida was casting spells, for example. It picks up on energy given off by *souls*. So does that mean the armor and glaive have souls? How? Why?

*...It's Death magic, most likely,* Sindri explains. *The soul of an animal—or maybe a person—has been placed in those objects. They'll eventually degrade away, but until then they can use whatever Art magic is radiating off of them.*

Huh. I didn't think I was trying to send that thought, but whatever. That's interesting! Death mages are the ones that make magic items in this world, huh?

*Magic items aren't common, nor is the magic needed to make them, and the effects of any magically imbued item tend to either be restricted in some major way or temporary. But yes, for this particular kind of self-sustaining aura? Death magic.*

"Hello, everyone!" Paladin Hagoro hails us. "You must be Sindri's companions. I am Hagoro, Paladin of Unification. I'd like to extend both my sincere apologies about the mess my nominal allies have put you through, as well as my services on your quest."

Huh. I wonder what kind of cool subclass a Paladin of Unification is.

*I didn't catch one of those words, but the cultists are called the Disciples of Unification, Hannah. He's just referencing that.*

Oh. That makes sense.

"Silly Hana," Kagiso says, patting me in a very patronizing way that I definitely don't find at all endearing.

"As appreciated as your apologies are," Teboho says, crossing one pair of arms, "we *were* almost killed by members of your cult. I have to say, I'm less than thrilled at the idea of you accompanying us, even with Sindri's recommendation."

"Understandably so," Hagoro nods, though he winces a little when we call his religion a 'cult.' "But I assure you, it is my every intention to make up for that grave crime against you all. It *certainly* isn't the will of the Disciples of Unification for innocent travelers to be attacked in their beds. Unfortunately, I can only speculate as to the reason such action was taken against you."

*Uh, didn't you basically confirm the other day that your cult is after me?* I ask.

*He can't hear you, Hannah, he's not part of the mental link,* Sindri reminds me, though he does immediately translate on my behalf. "Weren't they after Hana? You mentioned yesterday that the Disciples have an interest in creatures like her."

"Well, that's certainly true," Hagoro confirms. "I admit to no small amount of interest in speaking with Hana here, but I want to emphasize that killing her is very much not on my itinerary. There *does* exist a heretical sect which would want to see her dead—and it's very possible that's what you encountered—but they are my enemy as much as they are yours. It's also entirely possible that they were too low-rankling in our order to even know what makes Hana important, and the situation was what you first assumed: they were greedy beast merchants looking to steal a powerful creature from a better man."

I flinch a little. Hmm. Why did... oh, I mean, I guess he dehumanized me there. Er... depersonized me?

*I'm not a 'creature,'* I grumble.

"True," Kagiso agrees. "Friend is Hana."

511

*Yes, I'm... wait, you're saying I'm a hat, aren't you?*

"Best hat!"

*Okay, well be that as it may—*

"Hana?" Hagoro interrupts, though I suppose he can't hear me so it's not really his fault. "I'm sorry to ask, but you *can* understand me, yes?"

I turn 'towards' him (which is mostly just reorienting to give the appearance that I'm doing so) and wiggle my body up and down to mimic a nod.

"Do you have a way to communicate on your own?" he asks.

I wiggle a few legs at Teboho and he obligingly summons a small tablet and hands it to Kagiso, who holds it up for me. I put a minor Spacial Rend on one claw and carve out a simple response.

**I can write.**

"Ah, good," Hagoro nods. "That's quite reassuring. Did your friends here teach you?"

**Yes,** I confirm.

"I can just add you to our communication spell, Paladin," Sindri offers. "If you're going to be joining us in the coming fight, it would be best to do so."

"Ah, I'm afraid I can't," Hagoro says, smiling apologetically. "Policy forbids me from allowing an unauthorized Pneuma mage from casting on me. It's nothing personal, I assure you."

Sindri frowns, but nods.

"A reasonable precaution, especially for a man with secrets to keep," he allows.

"I'm so glad you understand," Hagoro agrees. "Though in the interest of team communication, I believe it would be best to share our elements and general specialties, so that our strategy against the Chaos mage can be planned. I understand that this is sensitive information, so I have no issues going first."

512

He starts to walk out of town as he says that, heading across the bridge and away from the busy city full of prying ears that might be interested in 'sensitive information.' The rest of us follow, and Sindri nods at him.

"I agree that's worth doing. Team, I know we've had a nasty run-in with the Disciples of Unification before, but I believe Hagoro when he denounces them. He's a skilled Chaos hunter in his own right, and has every reason to work alongside us today."

"Is fine," Kagiso shrugs.

"If you're certain of this, Sindri, then I have no objections," Teboho nods. "I just want justice for my family and friends."

*I'm more than a little worried about the things Hagoro said about me yesterday,* I tell Sindri. *Specifically the part where he said I was 'here to seek your ruin.' That sounds like a pretty solid motivation for betraying us to me. I'm against it.*

*Those are, frankly, very valid concerns,* Sindri agrees. *But the journey over gives us an opportunity to speak with him and hear his explanation for that claim. And if your fears come to pass, Hannah... well, it'll be four on one. We're with you, no questions asked. Friendship inherently goes both ways.*

I wiggle nervously.

*Okay,* I ultimately answer.

"We're all in agreement, then," Sindri confirms, nodding to Hagoro.

"Excellent!" Hagoro smiles, clapping his hands once in a surprisingly endearing way. He just seems genuinely excited to be hanging out with us. "Well, I'm an Order and Barrier mage. My primary spell manifestation is Zone of Law. I can create areas in which certain things are banned. It's flexible and powerful, but it affects myself and my allies just as much as it does our enemies, so I don't tend to use it in mixed company. I am quite skilled in martial combat, however, and my weapons and armor will resist disintegration and ward against Chaos to a limited extent."

"I suppose I should go next, then," Teboho nods. "I'm a Matter and Barrier mage, and my magic focuses on rigid material creation. As long as it's not flexible and doesn't have moving parts, I can summon it with a thought. I use it mainly to create weapons, armor, and tools."

"You make armor that has no moving parts?" Hagoro asks.

"It's not very comfortable armor," Teboho chuckles. "There's a reason I don't wear it all the time. It's very restricting, but I can un-summon it and re-summon it to cover or reveal parts of me as needed."

"Hmm. Interesting."

"As you already know, I'm a Pneuma mage, with a focus on coordination and communication," Sindri says, apparently interested in moving things along. "I use the ability to make pacts with animals."

"Like Bulupunu!" Kagiso clarifies, pointing to our lightning lizard tiger.

"Like... Bulupunu," Sindri sighs.

"You named him bald idiot?" Hagoro asks, a smile twitching onto his face.

"Yes? Has no hair and is also stupid," Kagiso confirms matter-of-factly.

Bulupunu sneezes, a crackle of lightning ejecting itself out of his nose.

"No brain in head. Dumb." Kagiso nods happily, as if Bulupunu had just agreed with her.

"I... I see," Hagoro chuckles. "And your magic, Miss Kagiso?"

"Motion," she says. "Precision. Chain reactions."

*Chain reactions?* I ask. *Not just ricochets?*

"Have more than one spell," Kagiso says, wrinkling her nose in offense. "Ricochet just most useful."

514

"She means it's the least likely to kill us all," Teboho smirks.

Kagiso crosses her arms and pouts.

"Praise me for restraint," she orders, and her brother laughs.

"Well, that just leaves you, then," Hagoro says, turning to me. Fortunately, I've been spending the whole time writing, so I've had the opportunity to actually explain.

**I don't think my spells have a theme,** I say. **I have a bunch of weird ones. A Space spell that lets me cut anything, an Order spell that lets me sort and clean, and a Transmutation spell that's constantly changing my body.**

"You've also got the magic that lets you step into and out of view and take those strange shortcuts," Teboho says.

*Well, that's true, but that doesn't really feel like a spell to me,* I respond. *It's just kind of something I can do.*

"Hana shares a lot of properties with magical beasts, I've noticed," Sindri chimes in. "Not to call you a beast, Hana, it's just the term for a creature whose biology relies on a certain kind of magic, and therefore all living members of the species *have* that magic. No known magical beasts are sapient—except arguably you, if you count as one—so the terminology isn't really designed for people."

*It's fine,* I assure him.

"My point is," he continues, "I suspect Hana's Space affinity is a consequence of her species, whereas her Order and Transmutation affinities are the only ones demonstrating synergy with her personality and each other."

"Hmm. An interesting theory," Hagoro nods. "Here's mine: Hana's magic focuses on destroying things, then putting the pieces back together in a way that suits her."

I don't have a response for that, and neither, it seems, does anyone else. What the heck, guy? You know what, screw it. He's obviously got this secret society thing going on, and his secret society obviously doesn't like me, and he's either going to come clean on

515

that or he's going to be a threat. I have no reason to burn bridges with this man, and I'm not going to fall for the cliché of alienating the reasonable person who only ends up being a villain because the hero doesn't bother to talk to them. I scribble out a simple message, struggling to keep it short and to the point. I want to call him out on what a jerk he's being by phrasing my magic that way, to say that I understand the sort of nasty stuff he's implying by claiming that the spells which best fit my personality are a thinly-veiled narcissism metaphor, but that's unproductive and writing with my claws is a pain in my extradimensional butt. So... short and sweet it is.

**What am I?** I ask him, because he's certainly *acting* like he knows and that's a heck of a lot more than I can say.

He seems almost surprised, his eyebrows rising as he reads the words. We're almost to the edge of the bridge now, and he lapses into silence for the rest of the walk, all the way up the massive flight of stairs, and a good way down the road. It must be at least half a gosh dang hour before he finally speaks up, and it really startles me when he does. Was he spending that long considering his response? Kagiso, Teboho and I had long since devolved into our usual friendly banter, and all of us jolt when Hagoro finally clears his throat and answers my question with a question of his own.

"You are a girl from another world, are you not?"

Kagiso and Teboho don't know that, so they're extra confused. It's one of the cards I've been holding closest to my chest, and I'm not sure it's wise to play right now. But lying? Lying seems worse. So I write.

**Yes.**

"You're not the first," Hagoro says. "You won't be the last. And that's a problem, because your kind? They set the tree aflame. They pulled the roots from the Great Soil. Your kin engineer our destruction at every turn, and people like me exist to stop you."

Well. That's... okay. Okay! That's really good information, actually! I'm not the only isekai victim, and presumably not the only one that got stuck in a weird monster body, and the cultists hate me because the jerks who came before were apocalyptically terrible. I can work with that, maybe.

**I don't want to hurt anyone or anything,** I write.

"Really?" Hagoro says. "Then why are you accompanying a professional assassin on his job?"

I flinch, then start writing frantically.

**That's different!** I insist.

"Is it?"

I angrily tap the tablet in the place I've already written "yes."

"Why's that?"

I huff with annoyance.

**If you decide I'm going to hurt the world, will you kill me?** I write.

"Possibly," he admits, and it's still chilling even though I expected a yes.

**So sometimes you have to hurt someone to protect people.**

I finally had to accept that recently. Where did I... *no, doesn't matter.*

"I suppose that's true," Hagoro agrees. "So you want to protect people, then?"

**I don't know how I could cause any of the tragedies you're describing, but I want to see if there's anything I can do to fix them,** I write. **But if there isn't, I'm not arrogant enough to try something stupid that makes them worse. I don't want to be your enemy.**

It takes me frustratingly long to scribble that all out, my legwriting getting progressively worse as I rush to get the words on the slate, but I want to make this offering of peace clear. I want to cooperate, not oppose. Hagoro reads it all slowly, seeming to take the time to read it again as well, and then nods.

"I see," he says simply. "Well. You may certainly color me curious. Extradimensional invaders are not normally so reasonable. I can assure you of this, if nothing else: as of right now, we are allies. Chaos mages are extremely dangerous and it is important that we do not splinter with this task ahead of us. After we handle the situation, I would be open to speaking with you further."

**Okay,** I write, because there really isn't much else to say to that. My mind is reeling with all this new information and I'm not sure what to do about it. People like me are common enough—and dangerous enough—that a whole organization is dedicated to stopping us? That's crazy. Am I going to end up with the kind of strength that can uproot world trees? That seems... basically impossible. I know that I'm strong, but a foot of cut-anything spell is hardly apocalyptic. Will I just keep getting stronger, or something? I guess that's hardly uncommon for fictional characters in my position.

All these other apparent isekai victims are also concerning. Hagoro seems surprised that I'm willing to work with him, but more than that he seems *suspicious.* Why is that? Were they seriously that bad? No, wait, stupid question, they apparently caused actual apocalypses. But why is it unreasonable that some of us might want to help? If all these people come from Earth then yeah, you're gonna have some bad apples, but statistically you'll get someone who at least *wants* to be decent, even if they might not be good at it, and I feel like it would take a *very special* sort of sociopath to uproot the gobble-darn tree that everybody lives on! Something's not adding up here.

"So, ah, what's this about another world, Hana?" Teboho asks.

Oh. Oh, right. Now I'm going to have to explain things. Well... screw using the tablet to write this all out. If Hagoro wants to know where I come from, he can ask somebody else.

*Yeah, uh... so you may have already noticed I seem to know some weird things and not know some other things,* I say.

"Didn't seem weird," Kagiso shrugs.

"Er... no, it was definitely a little strange," Teboho says hesitantly. "I just... well. I thought you were like Kagiso."

Wait, what?

*The heck does that mean?* I ask

"Well... you know. I just figured you were a bit... strange."

...Does Teboho think I'm autistic?

"Not strange," Kagiso grumbles. "Just efficient."

*Yeah! Like, first of all, if I was 'like Kagiso,' then that'd be awesome, because Kagiso is great.*

"Hehe. Best hat."

*And second of all—*

"Okay, okay, never mind!" Teboho backpedals. "I didn't mean to touch a nerve."

It's not a nerve. There is no nerve! I'm very normal and I have always been very normal up until the point where I started mutating and waking up in other dimensions and having magic and stuff! I mean, other than my Pokémon obsession. And the fact that I don't even try to talk to most people. And the bit where I don't love my family for some reason. But those don't count! Normal people can have those traits!

*...Second of all, yeah, most of my memories are of another universe. When I go to sleep, I wake up there in a different body. When I sleep there, I wake up here. It's very disorienting and I don't know why it happens.*

And that just opens up the floodgates. Everyone starts talking at me all at once, and I suppose I can't really blame them. Question after question after question defines the hours of our journey to follow, every moment we spend closing in on the dangerous Chaos mage filled with stories of my home rather than anything more substantial. And honestly? I'm happy about that. Gladdened by it, really. I don't want to think about what we're going to do. Back on Earth, I'd been so freaked out over whether or not I should be killing Sindri (which was really silly of me, since he's a great friend) I forgot to panic about the *other* person I'll probably have to murder. After all, I'm the most Chaos-resistant person here, even counting the apparently-powerful Order-aligned paladin. I'm *also* the person who not only has a powerful killing stroke available to me, but I have a powerful killing stroke that *isn't easily stopped by Chaos.* The most common manifestations won't affect Space magic, whereas they'd fairly easily destroy anything created by, say, Matter magic. So we have pretty much every possible reason for the strategy to involve me doing this alone. I'm not looking forward to it.

*If you're lucky, it might not come to that,* Sindri says.

*Oh?* I ask. *Really?*

*Yes, I think there will be another tactic we'll try first,* he assures me. *You might not need to do anything other than be present.*

*Why's that?*

"Remember back before your eyes grew in, where I mentioned I was trying to devise a spell to allow us to share sensorums?"

*Oh yeah!* I say. *You were gonna do that! I thought you gave up!*

"Of course I didn't give up," he huffs. "I just didn't want to unveil it until it was ready. I'm somewhat of a perfectionist, you know. If we're going to make use of it, however, we'll need to practice on the way."

"A dangerous fight like this one seems like the worst possible place to test out a technique with less than a day's practice," Hagoro chides. "Especially if it messes with one's usual perceptions."

"Normally I'd agree with you," Sindri nods. "But the goal behind this strategy will be to take out the Chaos mage from well outside their field of vision, before we've revealed ourselves, without any risk on our ends. And if it fails, we can simply deactivate the spell and move to our second plan without issue."

"Hmm," Hagoro hums in consideration. "And you won't need to cast on me to make this plan work?"

"Not at all," Sindri assures him. "It's actually a plan that synergizes the skills of all four of us. But let's see if my spell even works as intended first, shall we? Teboho, I'm going to cast it on you as a final test before I speak the incantation."

Teboho nods, and Sindri just... doesn't appear to do anything until suddenly Teboho jolts in surprise, closes his eyes and clutches his head.

"Oh! Oh, goodness, this is odd," Teboho mumbles. "Oh, I'm seeing d... and hearing, Goddess, I'm also hearing double. Sindri, can you not...?"

"Ah... yes, I can adjust that," Sindri nods. "Apologies, I usually test this with my birds, and they're not hearing the same things I am. There we go, sight only."

"This... this will take some getting used to," Teboho mutters.

"But *can* you get used to it?" Sindri presses.

"Hmm... yes. I think so. But what's this plan of yours about?"

"I believe that, if I speak the spell aloud, it will be strong enough to link all four of us," Sindri answers. "And hypothetically, it *should* mean that Kagiso and Teboho will be able to see past barriers and walls in the way Hana does. The Chaos mage is currently holed up in a cave which digs into the flesh of the world tree, veers off to the side, and then doubles back on itself a few times. Given Hana's range, she should be able to see the back of the cave where the Chaos mage waits from fairly early inside the cave itself. If she shares this visual knowledge with Kagiso, it's hypothetically possible that Kagiso could ricochet a shot down the entire length of the cave and take out our enemy that way... and if there are any complications in plotting a course, Teboho should be able to summon barriers for Kagiso to bounce her attacks off of."

Kagiso grins.

"I like plan," she nods.

*Uh... my senses are pretty darn weird,* I warn them. *Are you sure it's safe for other people to see in four dimensions?*

*It's certainly a lot to take in,* Sindri agrees. *But it's more confusing than painful. I can't really understand what you're seeing all that well, but Kagiso has a talent for that sort of out of the box thinking, and as long as you're focusing mainly on three dimensions, that's also what we'll focus on.*

Huh. I guess he's already tested the spell on me. Really would have been nice if he told me, but it's okay I suppose.

*Go for it, then,* I allow.

"Alright," Sindri agrees. "Ready, everyone?"

He inhales, and She's here, beholding all of us with weighty, terrifying dullness. She gives me a cursory pat hello, scratches Kagiso behind an ear, flows around Teboho like water and smirks silently at Hagoro, but the ultimate focus of Her attention is, of course, the man who summoned Her. Sindri. She doesn't touch him like She normally does me, merely tasting the name for his new spell and rolling metaphorical, metaphysical eyes. A dull name, a boring name, an unexciting name, but one that, She supposes, does indeed qualify. It will do. It's *fine.* Almost begrudgingly, She speaks the words.

"**Share Senses**."

My world... does not explode into a cacophony of vision and sound, which I have to admit I didn't really expect. It certainly blooms outwards a bit, extra points of vision flowing into my mind, but I realize that this is pretty darn boring by the standards of my current sensorium. I already have three hundred and sixty degree vision, not to mention crazy higher-dimensional omnivision that I *still* haven't fully wrapped my head around. These... extra data points of 2D perception representing 3D space? They're barely a footnote compared to what I'm already seeing basically all the time.

Kagiso and Teboho, on the other hand, both collapse onto the ground and hiss in agony, prompting me to reluctantly dismount Kagiso's head. This is probably my fault. I guess I should narrow my focus. My spatial sense isn't technically ever seeing less than everything it's able to see, but I still pay more or less attention to different things, twisting how I mentally handle the concept of 'looking at things,' and the mentality of what I'm doing matters a lot when we're using a spell designed by a guy whose magic shares information between minds.

I narrow down what I'm looking at—which is surprisingly difficult, considering how I've been getting more and more used to the exact opposite—and try to take things back to the level I was barely handling when I was first consciously aware of these senses. Thankfully, there's not much around us. Just the forest, my friends, and the paladin guy who thinks I'm going to try to kill the world that one of my friends invited along for some Goddess-forsaken reason. I focus on that friend, lacking anything better to focus on, and move my attention around the inside of his body. Weak points, like the spine and major arteries. Sindri's lungs. Sindri's heart. Huh, it's beating extra fast. I hope he's okay.

Gradually, as I keep my mental eyes steady, Kagiso manages to get enough of a handle on herself to reach up and cover my physical eyes with her arms, blocking out most of my vision. Oh, right, that's *also* way more than I see as a human. Whoops. At least that seems to finally do the trick, and the team starts being able to function again.

"Well!" Teboho says, his voice strained. "I think we'll need to get Hana a blindfold to prevent this splitting headache, but this should be something we can work with."

*Aw, man! But I just got the ability to see back!*

"You'll still be able to see through our eyes, Hana," Sindri chuckles. "I think a blindfold is a good idea. Let's make you one."

"Hana sight pretty..." Kagiso coos, wiggling in place with her eyes closed. "Sindri body so soft! Squish, squish! Hehe! Hehehehe! Blood move!"

Well, she's certainly having a good day. Gosh, Kagiso is such a cute little weirdo. Personally I'm not particularly interested in or particularly grossed out by all the organs I'm constantly seeing on a daily basis. It's just kinda how people look to me now. I swap my attention over to the inside of Kagiso's body and she squeals in delight, poking at the muscles on her arm whenever I look at them and watching them squish around in response. Her laughter gets louder and more manic the whole time I look at her.

"Hana, I think you're going to give my sister a heart attack," Teboho comments dryly.

"No!" Kagiso insists. "Heart still beats! Look! Look!!!"

"I... I see it, Kagiso," Teboho sighs. "It does indeed still beat."

"You are certainly quite the colorful group, aren't you?" Hagoro comments, watching all this play out from a respectful distance.

"The important thing is, can you make ricochets using the information you see through Hana's senses, Kagiso?" Sindri presses.

Kagiso grumbles in irritation as I move my focus over to a set of trees, though that grumbling stops when I also include a random friend noodle in my range. Gosh, these fuzzy snake guys are everywhere. Kagiso hums to herself for a bit, then pulls out her bow and fires a shot, bouncing it off of three different trees before stabbing the friend noodle in the brain. Rest in peace, you cute little worm.

"Yes," Kagiso concludes. "Can do."

"Excellent," Sindri nods. "Then with luck, this won't even be a fight."

Yeah. I hope so. Unfortunately, I don't have luck. It takes most of the day for us to finally reach the cave with our quarry, but I'm completely exhausted by the time we get there and I've barely even done anything. We're here to kill. At the very least, I'll have to be a part of the attempt. And then, after that's all said and done with, I'll still have to deal with the gosh dang cultist. He's been watching me like a hawk the entire time, every interaction I have with everyone silently observed, judged with the absolute arrogant attitude needed to decide whether or not to kill an innocent teenage girl. ...Well, mostly innocent, I guess. But so far I've only killed in self-defense.

Guess it's time for that to change.

The cave is little more than a hole in the ground, likely dug by some oversized magical predator before being forcefully stolen by our current quarry. The upper part of the cave is stone—as one generally expects from caves—but as it burrows downwards it eventually swaps over to wood. It's unintuitive to my usual expectations, even if it makes perfect sense. My job for now is just to look for anyone currently in the cave, and from the mouth I can't sense far enough into it to tell. It's quite deep, though Sindri's right: it's a lot longer than it is deep, and it's got a lot of switchbacks. I should be able to see our target before anyone else gets a straight shot... most importantly including the Chaos mage.

"Well, this is it," Sindri nods. "Is everyone ready?"

*As I'll ever be,* I answer nervously.

"This is my job, after all," Hagoro smiles. "I came prepared."

"I'm ready to finally get justice," Teboho says.

"...To get vengeance," Kagiso whispers.

"Then here we go," Sindri nods. "Everyone stay quiet from here on out. Mental communication and hand signals only."

We all nod. I mean, I don't know any hand signals and I wouldn't be able to use them even if I did, but I figure Sindri and Hagoro might have fancy Chaos hunter code signs or something that he can just translate for us. We enter the cave, Bulupunu the lightning lizard tiger moron heading first. If there are any traps, well... as Sindri says, he works as a tamer because animals are comparatively expendable. Everyone (except, again, me) has their weapons at the ready: Teboho with a thick shield and a long spear, each wielded with two hands, Kagiso with her bow and a pair of rocks, even Sindri with his sword. Slowly and carefully, we descend. Slowly but surely, I see more and more of the cave. The layout is... odd, to say the least.

Though the hole is mostly a twisting cylinder, looking like it was bored out by some kind of giant worm twisting down into the guts of the World Tree's branch, at a certain depth that abruptly changes. The cave continues, but rather than being carved out evenly, it becomes... jagged. No, that's not quite right. I zoom my focus out a little and *then* I see it. The deepest part of the cave has been dug out not as a cylinder, but as a series of overlapping spheres. Like something just eliminated a spherical area of matter from existence, moved to the far side of that now-destroyed zone, and then did it again. That's... certainly got some terrifying implications about what this Chaos mage can do. I dictate this information to the team, just in case they aren't focusing on my senses at the moment. Both Kagiso and Teboho tense at the report, and I get the impression that they might be remembering a similar sight in what was once their village. Unexpectedly, though Teboho nudges his sister with an elbow and points ahead.

*...Kagiso,* he murmurs over the link. *On the wall, there. Does that look familiar to you?*

I'm still blindfolded, so I focus on the input I'm getting from Teboho's senses for a moment. To my surprise, there's a painting on the wall, of all things. I didn't see it with my spatial sense since the dye doesn't really have any noticeable thickness. The work is very abstract, almost nonsensical at first glance with a dozen colors mixing together in a wild mess of dense information, but it's possible to puzzle out meaning and pattern. I start to understand the painting section by section: a girl, first. Kneeling for some reason? No, she's sobbing. Sobbing and angry. I struggle at first to figure out what's around the girl, because it seems to be other people: I can make out arms, legs, torsos, but tend to lose track of where they connect to one another until I ultimately realize that they *don't* connect with one another. Body parts and corpses. The girl is surrounded by death. Is this... a depiction of the village? Is that what Teboho is pointing out?

"Very familiar," Kagiso whispers, her eyes going wide. "**Helen drew this."

Huh?

*Who's Helen?* I ask.

*Don't speak out loud!* Sindri admonishes.

*A human that lived in our village,* Teboho answers me. *Her name was Helen. She was an artist. There's no way this isn't her work!*

*Helen alive,* Kagiso agrees, a smile starting to form on her lips. *Someone alive!*

*The Chaos mage must have kidnapped her,* Teboho agrees. *But why? No, that doesn't matter. Sindri, I think we have a hostage situation.*

*That... no,* Sindri says, shaking his head. *Kagiso, Teboho, I've had the Chaos mage under observation this entire journey. They fled your village alone.*

*What? But... how's that possible?* Teboho asks. *You're not saying that Helen is the Chaos mage, are you?*

*I don't have the slightest idea,* Sindri answers tersely. *I don't know who this 'Helen' person even is. But the Chaos mage that destroyed your village—our target—is the only person in this cave other than us.*

*Well, what does the Chaos mage look like?* I ask.

*Human, straight long hair. Tattered, baggy clothes. I've been tracking them at a distance via birds, so I can't give you a better description than that.*

*Not even a hair color?* I ask.

*What? Black, obviously.*

Oh, right. I forgot that all humans in this world are black. ...Again.

*Anyway, we need to keep moving,* Sindri says, urging the party along. *We're in enemy territory. Let's get this over with as cleanly as possible.*

We start to move again... except for Kagiso, who continues to stare at the wall painting until Sindri grabs her elbow and yanks her forwards. We creep in deeper together, and wall paintings start to show up more frequently, each as confusing as they are gruesome. We don't waste any time trying to decipher them, and once we reach the second bend in the cave we're finally deep enough for me to see our target.

I didn't expect her to be so young.

Younger than me, probably, though not by much. The person at the end of the cave is a scruffy-looking girl, small and thin in the way that hints at a history of malnourishment, though as of right now she seems to not be starving. Her sunken eyes and blank expression indicate she's doing much less well mentally than she is physically, though. She sits in a large chamber, carved out in a similar fashion to the deeper parts of the tunnels: spheres of disintegration twisting open a cavern in the wood. Somewhat impressively, she's managed to start a campfire inside her wooden cave without burning the whole thing up or suffocating herself: a wide pile of rocks, stone, and dirt forms an elevated fire 'pit,' raising the flickering flames up above the flammable ground and leaving plenty of space on each side to catch falling embers. I guess she must have a history of hiding out in caves. In her hand she has a small block of wood, which she is using a knife to carve into a humanoid figurine.

Sindri, Kagiso, and Teboho see this as well, and the agitation in the latter two is so obvious it pours over the mental link in an anxious waterfall. My spatial sense isn't exactly easy to parse compared to normal sight, and that's the only hope Kagiso and Teboho have for a while as they obsess over the information I'm feeding them about the girl's face, over and over, until they can't lie to themselves any longer.

*...That's Helen,* Teboho realizes.

*Friend is alive,* Kagiso agrees quietly.

*So your village was unknowingly harboring a Chaos mage,* Sindri scowls. *How did she stay undetected?*

*Hmm. Small home. No Pneuma mages,* Kagiso answers.

*No,* Teboho snaps. *I can't accept this. This is absurd. That's Helen! She lived with us for nearly a year! She's a damn Art mage, not a monster!*

*The only human in your village,* Sindri sends flatly. *Alone. With no family. Settling in a place without a Pneuma mage to detect her. Take the shot, Kagiso.*

*Do NOT take the shot!* Teboho snaps, turning and starting to pace down the hallway ahead of us. *That is the last person in my fucking life who's still alive after... this has to be a mistake. This has to be. We had her over for dinner regularly! We hung one of her paintings on our wall! She was like family to all of us!*

*Teboho, stop!* Sindri orders. *Teboho! Listen to me! She's the Chaos mage! Kagiso, take the shot!*

Kagiso stands motionless, and Teboho keeps on walking. He's *furious* now, ranting angrily over the link.

*We did not come all the way here to kill one of the people I'm trying to avenge! One of the only people left that I actually care about! We did NOT!*

"Helen!" he shouts out loud, destroying any opportunity we had for surprise.

The Chaos mage jolts, looking up from her work with a terrified expression on her face.

"Teboho!?" she shrieks back. "Teboho, get away!"

"Helen, it's you, right? I'm here to help!"

"I don't fucking need your help!" she snaps back, lowering into an amateur's fighting stance with her carving knife in one hand and her little sculpture in the other. *"Go away!"*

"Helen, I'm not going to allow any... anything..."

Teboho slows down and stops, his eyes widening. I focus my attention through his senses, and find him staring at a much larger and more intricate painting made of a mosaic of smaller pictures. Different tints and hues of color form concentric rings, each made out of a smaller depiction of an emotion-filled face: rage, sadness, joy, disgust, and on and on and on. The faces change with each ring, beautiful on the outside but growing more and more hideous the closer they are to the center, at which point there is a stylized representation of Helen herself, curled up naked in the fetal position. Teboho stares at the picture, enraptured for only the barest moments necessary to see the piece in its entirety.

And then he dies.

It happens in an instant. The emotional and visual link cuts out first, and then I watch as a sphere of black nothing blooms. It starts inside the center of Teboho's brain, looking to my spatial sense as a near-perfect void as it balloons outwards, consuming the entirety of his head, then his neck, then his shoulders all the way down below his waist before finally stopping just above his knees. Then it recedes, leaving nothing in its place. Teboho's disembodied legs collapse to the stone. The Chaos mage shudders, her eyes squeezing shut when it happens.

*Kagiso! Now!* Sindri snaps. *You have to shoot her now!*

There's no response. I realize suddenly that I'm not getting sensory feedback from Kagiso at all. She, too, is staring at a wall, enraptured by a much smaller painting than the one that killed Teboho. Her mind feels like nothing but light static. Her emotions are strong over the link, but they're a mess, jumbled to the point of completely nonsensical. No will, no clarity, no awareness. Only Chaos.

*Fuck!* Sindri hisses, yanking Kagiso away from the wall and covering her eyes. *Hannah, you're up!*

530

I'm up. I leap off of Kagiso's head and into the fourth dimension, immediately meeting world tree wood and burrowing into it with ease. Sindri deactivates the sensory-sharing spell, which is probably what we should have done the moment we saw *any* art in the cave. The Chaos mage is obviously dual-element with Art, and their magic either doesn't transfer between the link, or it *does* and we were a fraction of a second away from being killed alongside Teboho in a chain reaction before his brain ceased existing. Which is something I'm just going to have to do my best to not think about, because if I spend any time at all on thinking about the fact that *Teboho is dead, holy shit my friend is dead he's dead he was so wonderful and kind and now he's fucking dead* then I'll just have a complete mental breakdown and be unable to prevent my friends from sharing the same fate. I have to fight, the adrenaline pumping through my veins demands it. Handle the threat, ignore the pain, and everything else can matter when I make it out alive.

So. The Chaos mage can make paintings that kill you when you look at them. It seems like they have to be pretty big paintings, though, as the one Kagiso was staring at was much smaller than the one that killed Teboho and it only seemed to disable her. Art magic encompassess the realm of emotion, and applying Chaos to emotion would be debilitating: *desire* would get randomized, any action one might take being rapidly swapped between good, bad, wanted, and unwanted to a paralyzing degree. But the larger and more elaborate the art, the more Chaos she can shove in it, and when the Chaos concentration hits critical mass, then *don't think about it don't think about it don't think about it.* I need to focus on moving my legs, on digging myself as quick a path as possible to the back of her murdering head. I have a lot of experience with digging, so it doesn't take long.

I am in position, watching my target as her heart thumps at a million miles an hour, stress and terror oozing through her features. Well, good. She should be scared. Her messy hair and ragged clothes make it obvious she's been on the run for quite a while, and it's all ending now. Time to strike. I cut myself a hole back into w=0 space, leap towards the back of her neck, and—and holy shit she's just a scared little girl *what am I doing!?*

My focus locks on the figurine in her hand and my spells wink out, leaving me as nothing but a confused, flailing mess of limbs. I bonk into her on the way down and she shrieks, a burst of all-consuming blackness flowing out of her body and washing over me... to little effect. It *does* sting a little, certainly more than lightning did, but I'm still largely unharmed when I collapse to the ground, my body twitching with confusion as the figurine fills my head with confusion. What's going on? Why do I feel so *weird?* Am I having a seizure? My body isn't reacting right, but I can still think normally, kind of. Where's Sindri? Holy motherfucking shit Sindri was mind controlling me aaagh that's right!!!

"Oh fuck, oh fuck, I'm sorry, I'm sorry, I'm sorry!" the Chaos mage whines, backing away from me.

I feel like the eye of a hurricane, with absolute insanity roaring on every side of me while I wait, oddly calm within it all. If I focus, I can feel Friends in the back of my mind, chastising me for thinking poorly of Sindri and demanding I do the right thing and kill the girl in front of me. And yeah, she... she killed Teboho. She's killed a lot of people... if Sindri is to be believed, I suppose. Is she crying?

If I do kill her, will I ever get a better shot at stopping Sindri?

I don't know what's happening to my head. Maybe it's because I resist Chaos so well but Sindri doesn't? But I can still barely control my body, the seizing twitches of my limbs nearly flopping me into the campfire. I focus as best I can, trying to control myself, to command even a single leg. The others are on the way. Kagiso, Hagoro... Sindri. When they get here, they'll kill her, even if they have to do it blind. Their eyes are closed as they stagger down the cavern path, hands against a wall to lead them where they need to go. I have to still my shaking, to *move.* I have to gamble on this. Even if it ends up being a mistake, it's a mistake I can't afford to not make. I manage to get Spacial Rend active on a single claw. I'm so sorry, Teboho.

**Help,** I write, my limbs shaky. The Chaos mage's—Helen's—eyes go wide.

"What?" she whispers. "What the fuck?"

**Kill human,** I write, and then my 'friends' finally make it into the chamber.

Hagoro steps in before anyone else, his weapon at the ready, but Kagiso makes the first attack. Firing an arrow directly at Helen, the Chaos mage lets out a burst of disintegration, obliterating the attack... only to get hit in the back of the head by a stone that just bounced off three walls. Helen cries out in pain, staggering forward into the range of Hagoro's spear.

Hagoro frowns, and does not attack. His eyes rove around the room, noting the campfire, the dropped carving, the blank walls, and my message to Helen.

"Hagoro, what the fuck are you doing!?" Sindri roars, pointing at Helen and sending Bulupunu to keep her off-balance, blasting her with lightning that she has to focus on obliterating with her magic or be fried. "You're the only one other than Hana that can break through her defenses!"

"Ah. Sorry, friend," Hagoro answers absentmindedly. "Just... getting a handle on the situation."

And then he strikes. A simple twist of his body and his polearm flashes through the air, dealing instant death.

"Fucking Pneuma mages," Hagoro grumbles quietly as Sindri's head rolls to the floor. "**Zone of Law: Ceasefire.**"

Bulupunu, Helen, and Kagiso all freeze as magic floods the area around us, the Goddess appearing in a flash to erect holy boundaries around the entire room. Even more terrifying, She *remains* in the room. Bulupunu, being a wild animal no longer bound to a man's control, does the sensible thing and immediately dashes for the exit. Unfortunately, he also does a less sensible thing and makes a swipe at Kagiso as he leaves. The Goddess smirks, making an eldritch facsimile of a tsking noise, wagging Her finger back and forth before sending agony through the poor animal's body, forcing it to abort its strike thanks to the violence of its convulsions. Silly little animal. The Goddess' law is absolute. Bulupunu gets the message that time, shakily getting to his feet and scampering off.

I feel my head start to clear and my body stop writhing as Kagiso collapses to the ground, dropping her weapons and clutching her head. She lets out a horrid wail, agony and fury and despair all mixing in a single, horrible sound as, with the dead man's magic no longer affecting us, she realizes the full scope of everything Sindri has done. ...No, actually, that's untrue. I'm not sure we'll ever *stop* seeing the ramifications of Sindri's casual disregard for our personhood. I don't know how much he did, but I do know it'll be a broken part of me until the day I die. But for now? I'm free. We're finally free. Goddess, I wish I could cry.

She rolls Her eyes at me, as if to say 'grow tear ducts then, idiot.'

"So then," Hagoro sighs, turning to the Chaos mage. "Hele, was it?"

She blinks, her whole body shaking in terror as she looks up from Sindri's corpse and stares at the dentron paladin.

"It's, um... Helen, actually," she manages.

"Helena," Hagoro corrects himself incorrectly. "You seem lucid enough. Now that we're all clear-headed, would you be interested in resolving all of this with a friendly conversation?"

She glances around nervously, her focus mainly on the chamber exit... and then on Hagoro, standing between her and that singular avenue of escape. He can't attack her while Zone of Law is up, so maybe it would be safe... unless he can deactivate the spell any time he wants to. Holy cannoli that would be so broken. I wouldn't put it past the Goddess to give someone magic that good, though.

"S-sure?" Helen manages, though at this point I'm struggling to care overmuch about whatever Hagoro and the Chaos mage are getting up to. The paladin saved me, so he's good in my book. I stagger to my feet, my muscles sore and strained from their recent

534

convulsions, and slowly I make my way over to Kagiso. Kagiso, who just lost her brother. Who was betrayed by a man she trusted with her life. Who has no one else left in this world, no family, no home, and no future. I crawl over to her, and she scoops me up in her arms, holding me close. Tears drop from her eyes and land on my carapace, flowing down over my smooth shell. It's the most emotion I've ever seen from her before. As the water from her face drips over my own eyes, we cry together, huddled up in a cave with her family's murderer and our minds' savior. We can't even muster up the will to care about them.

Right now, and perhaps for a long time coming, all we have is each other.

# 28

# BIG REVEAL

Kagiso hugs me tightly, almost cracking my chitin as the tears stream slowly down my carapace. The paladin and the Chaos mage talk in the background, exchanging little niceties, assurances that they don't intend to fight, hesitant and barely believed. It doesn't really go anywhere until the subject abruptly changes.

"How much was lie?" Kagiso asks quietly.

Helen and Hagoro both turn to look at her, because even a whisper from Kagiso demands attention right now. There's a horrid tension in her muscles, fury bubbling inside of her and demanding an outlet. She's grieving, yes, but Kagiso grieves like a force of nature.

"To answer that, I'd need to know what all he told you," Hagoro answers calmly. "What happened?"

For a moment, I think Kagiso is going to attack him. Not for any wrong he committed, but just *because.*

"Teboho come with me on hunt," she says quietly. "We return, village gone. Just... craters. Empty. Except for Sindri. He there. He ask if we want justice. We never even think of say no. No ask who, no ask how, no ask risks. Just go."

"I see," Hagoro answers softly.

"Trusted him on everything," Kagiso hisses, the words flowing out of her, far more than she usually bothers with all at once. "Now, head full of questions. Said all Chaos mages must die. But Helen was friend. Wouldn't have. Right? And you Chaos hunter. You sparing her. So was lie, yes? All was lie?"

Hagoro and Helen share a glance.

"...Did you destroy Kagiso's village?" he asks.

Helen turns away and stays silent, though the guilt on her face is answer enough.

"I see," Hagoro says. "Truthfully, Kagiso, I suspect Sindri lied about very little. Perhaps even not at all."

"What," Kagiso growls.

"Officially, it is the job of a Chaos hunter to kill anyone or anything aligned with the element, without exception," Hagoro confirms. "Most of our work involves hunting beasts with that particular alignment, since sapient Chaos-aligned individuals tend to be killed at birth. It's hardly unheard of for a mother to be unwilling to do so, of course, or for one to be born in a place that can't check on such things. It's under those conditions that we see the truth of things."

He glances at Helen again.

"...Chaos mages aren't inherently malicious," he says. "They're just people with a form of magic that's hard to control, but like all magic they still *want to use it.* Yet they can't, lest they be outed as a Chaos mage and killed. So their control gets worse with disuse, and tragedies start to happen. That is not how it has to be, however, and the Disciples of Unification defy this law. This is secret, for obvious reasons, as we would be banned from most nations if this became evident, but I work as a Chaos hunter to seek out people that can be saved and bring them somewhere they can live without fear."

Helen jolts with surprise at that, first staring at Hagoro in shock... but her eyes quickly narrow into deep suspicion. For my part, I just listen, watch, and do nothing, because I'm utterly out of willpower. I'm so exhausted, physically and mentally, that if someone told me that I was dead right now, I'd believe them.

"So you are criminal," Kagiso grunts, "and Sindri upstanding Chaos hunter. No lies. Then why get in head?"

"Well I don't know the man all that well," Hagoro says, nudging the headless corpse with his boot, "but I suspect he was just insecure. Anyone with a mind control spell is the type of person who would want to mind control people, that's how magic *works*. They want the certainty of trust rather than the actual presence of it, and so they violate others and think to themselves all the while that it's for a good cause. Chaos hunters fight what they see as unambiguous evils, people marked by the very Goddess as a monster from birth. From the very start, they're clearly not interested in thinking complexly about morality."

The Goddess herself chuckles at that, the non-sound thundering through my carapace as she continues hanging lazily in the room thanks to Hagoro's Zone of Law. I'm not quite sure how to interpret Her amusement, but it feels like the more salient issue is the implication behind Hagoro's claims on magic. If someone who would enjoy mind controlling people gets mind control spells, what sort of person gets *disintegration spells?* He's contradicting his own anti-typecasting rant about Chaos mages by typecasting Pneuma mages immediately afterwards, and I don't understand why. I guess I don't even know if I care why, since I'm not in much of a position to care about anything right now. It just strikes me as a red flag, I guess. Is he manipulating us by demonizing our abuser? Does it *count* as manipulation to demonize someone's abuser, considering that abusers are extremely justifiable targets of demonization? I wish I could just not think about these things, but I'm slowly starting to come back to myself and realize that I'm still in a room with two of the most dangerous people I've ever met, both of whom just killed someone and both of whom potentially have reason to want to kill *me.*

Despite how terrifying that is, though, my brain is mostly fixating on the claim that Sindri didn't have any ulterior motives. I'm not even really sure why. It makes a kind of sense, I suppose. His spell was subtle at first, weak and unspoken. It couldn't have covered up any fundamental contradictions with reality until a day ago. I really wonder what he was thinking that whole time. Did he really just want me for my power? To just use me to do his job? No ulterior motives, no grand lies, just a man seeing an opportunity to destroy a threat to society with fewer casualties and deciding to take it?

Did Sindri believe he was a good man? Knowing him he probably did, and something about that just makes everything that happened all the more chilling.

My chain of thought is finally broken when Kagiso stops holding me in a deathgrip, instead placing me gingerly on the ground before standing up and walking over to Sindri's corpse. Glowering down at it, she lifts a foot and I wish I could look away as she *stomps,* driving ribs into lungs and splattering gore up out the empty neck hole. I don't have the luxury of only seeing that, though, privy as my senses are to the snap of every rib, the way the heart squashes flat and unloads blood all across the inside of his chest. Then she lifts her foot right back up and slams it down again, then again and again and on and on, her growl evolving into a furious scream. When his torso is nothing more than a bloody pulp she releases the last of her anger with a roaring kick to his severed head, which bounces off of every wall in the room, picking up speed before eventually splattering against the ceiling like a watermelon shot out of a cannon. Mixed shards of bone and brain and guts and gore rain down from above, though Kagiso ignores it all and just stands still, her body heaving with heavy breaths.

Hesitantly, I scuttle up next to her and bump against her ankle. She relaxes, even if only slightly, and I take that as permission to crawl up her leg and onto her shoulder, using my cleaning magic to get the red stains out of her albino fur. As overwhelmed as I am, cleaning is the only thing my brain seems capable of.

"Good Hana," Kagiso mumbles quietly, and I move on to untangling her hair.

540

"I'm... surprised you could do all that inside the bounds of my spell," Hagoro comments absentmindedly, though he immediately seems embarrassed about addressing us. Kagiso just shrugs.

"Didn't attack anyone."

"Would you?" Helen asks suddenly. "If you could do that to me, would you?"

Kagiso turns her head to stare at the Chaos mage, giving her a long, slow blink.

"...You do it?" she asks.

"I... yes," Helen answers. "I killed everyone."

"Why?"

She seems taken back by the question, her face flashing a briefly haunted look before she turns away, nervously fiddling with the small sculpture she picked back up at some point.

"...It's not like it was on purpose," she mutters.

Kagiso shrugs.

"Okay. Believe you."

Helen *flinches,* a somewhat crazed look on her face as she stares at Kagiso in disbelief.

"...That's it?" she asks. "I... I killed your whole family. I killed Teboho!"

"He believe you too," Kagiso answers, turning away from her.

*"That's why he died!"* Helen shrieks.

Kagiso just glances up at where so much of Sindri's head is still stuck to the ceiling.

"...Disagree," she murmurs.

"To some extent, I also disagree," Hagoro butts in. "Chaos magic is inherently volatile, true, but you *can* learn to control it. The fact that circumstances conspire against you ever successfully doing so simply means—"

"I know how to fucking control it!" Helen snaps. "I have to use it. It builds up if I don't. I just made a mistake living with people, that's all."

"Well, Helena, I assure you that we can give you ample opportunity to—"

"Y-y-you know what, fuck you!" she suddenly snaps at him, jabbing a finger in his direction. "Shut up! Fuck you! I don't even know your name! I'm not going anywhere with you! All of you should just get the fuck out of here and leave me alone!"

Kagiso frowns at that, turning to face her.

"...But just found you," she complains.

"Kagiso I *fucking killed everyone!*" she snaps."Are you stupid? Why the fuck are you still standing here?"

"Didn't kill everyone," Kagiso answers, pointing at her. "One friend left."

Helen gapes at her for a moment, then slaps a hand over her face, breaking out into humorless, hysterical giggles.

"What the fuck is *wrong* with you?" she asks. "Fuck, no, don't answer that. You're *Kagiso.* You've always been completely nuts. We aren't friends, you stupid fuzzy bitch."

Kagiso wrinkles her nose.

"You make me nice picture."

"You asked me to draw you a bloody liver!" Helen laughs. "I made it as gross as I possibly could!"

"Yes," Kagiso nods. "Was nice. Hung in room."

"Ooooh, okay, I get it," Helen chuckles. "You're just insane. Did you ever even care about your family to begin with?"

I rub my legs together so fast I barely even know what I'm doing, a monstrous hiss filling the chamber with the sound of a threat. I don't know what's going on here, I don't know Helen the way Kagiso apparently does, but I am *not* okay with anyone making fun

542

of her like that. I hop off Kagiso's shoulder and land on the ground, quickly starting to scratch out a message with my legs.

**You don't get to say that,** I scribble out. **Apologize.**

"Apologize?" Helen drawls. "I killed a whole fucking town and you want me to apologize for being *mean* about it?"

**Well,** I write, **it would be nice if you apologized for the murder, too.**

"Oh, yeah, sure, *that'll* make things better," Helen mocks. "I'm so sowwy I killed everyone you ever knew and loved! Can we be fwends again?"

"Yes," Kagiso answers.

"Shut up!" Helen screeches. "Seriously, what the fuck is wrong with you!?"

Hagoro slams the butt of his polearm into the ground, and all of a sudden the feeling of being surrounded by the Goddess vanishes, the Zone of Law removed. It feels like being in a warm bath and suddenly having all the water disappear, the cold harshness of reality leaving me naked and bare.

"Ugh," Helen shudders. "Finally."

"I think we've reached a point where magical intervention is no longer required," Hagoro says. "I vote we exit this cave, and perhaps find somewhere to rest."

"I'm not going anywhere with any of you," Helen growls.

"Yes you are," Kagiso grunts, suddenly walking forwards and grabbing Helen by the wrist. She sputters in protest, but Kagiso just yanks her forward and starts heading towards the cave exit. "Traps off, Helen?"

"W-what?" she stutters. "No, they're not... they don't turn off. They just aren't all charged. Look, I can... you'll be fine."

"Okay," Kagiso nods, and continues dragging a staggering Helen out of the chamber. I tilt my body to get a better look at Hagoro with my eyes. He glances down at me and shrugs, then follows the two girls. I scuttle afterwards as well. This is… more than a little surreal. As we wind our way up the tunnel, we inevitably pass by Teboho's legs. Stress fills me as Kagiso approaches them. Is she really going to be okay? I'm pretty sure *I'm* not okay, and he was her brother.

Kagiso reaches down to grab both legs as she passes by, still keeping one hand around Helen's wrist. She picks up the disembodied limbs, looks them over a few times, and then offers one in my direction.

"Hana hungry?" she asks.

I trip, lose my footing on the wood and end up doing a full roll backwards before stopping myself. I stand back up and firmly shake my body no.

"Hmm. Okay," Kagiso says, frowning a little. She tosses both legs to the side. Everyone gapes at her, which she either ignores or straight up doesn't notice.

At a certain point after exiting the cave, Hagoro figures out that Kagiso doesn't actually have a specific location she's leading us to, so he steps ahead and finds us a decent camping spot. He, Kagiso, and Helen start working together to clear out the area and make a fire pit, though it's noticeably less organized than it was with Sindri and Teboho. Helen also spends the entire time complaining, though she does seem to have a lot of camping experience. Which… makes sense, I suppose.

"So," Helen grunts at me. "What the fuck are you, anyway?"

Valid question! Unfortunately…

**I have no idea,** I answer.

"Your legs are all funky," she continues. Well, what the heck do I say to that? I drum them in a wave pattern, noting how they wink in and out of my normal vision as I do so.

**Thank you for noticing?** I write.

She squats down next to me, poking me with a finger. I'm... not sure how to feel about this girl. On one hand, she killed Teboho, but also she seems to be Kagiso's friend, or something? I don't really understand their history and I'm too awkward to ask. I still just feel numb anyway.

"...For a monster that tried to assassinate me, you're weirdly polite."

**You saved me,** I write back.

She blinks.

"What?"

**Your magic counteracted the mind control I was under,** I explain. **You saved me. You deserve thanks for that, if nothing else.**

"If nothing else, huh?" she asks.

**You killed Teboho. He was a really good person.**

She snorts, but it doesn't come off as dismissive as she probably intends it.

"Yeah," she agrees seriously. "I know."

She walks off, and I stare at her with no better insight on my opinion of her than before. She's abrasive, sure, but it's in the sort of weirdly fragile way that I bet Ida could easily reduce to tears if she wanted to. She's killed a lot of people on accident. That's pretty bad, but is it worse than me? I've killed a few people on purpose.

"So. Hana," Hagoro says, being the next to approach me while Kagiso and Helen continue to work. "Let's talk about your future."

**Sure,** I write out numbly.

"You've mentioned that you want to work to help the world," he says. "That you want to put effort into solving the problems that plague us."

**Of course,** I agree.

"How far are you willing to go in pursuit of that?"

I drum my legs, not entirely sure how to answer that.

**I dunno,** I write. **Medium far?**

He looks confused for a moment, then chuckles good-naturedly.

"Ah-ha, I see. Could you elaborate on that?"

**Could you?** I counter. **I don't know enough about the world to understand what you're asking me to tell you. I've been here for… I dunno, less than twenty days, probably?**

His eyebrows rise.

"Really? So little?"

**Really. So like, I don't know what sorts of things I would be doing if I joined up with you guys.**

"You're interested in joining?"

What? Ugh, this guy.

**No, I just said I didn't understand what that would entail.**

"Oh, I see," Hagoro nods. "Well… hmm. That's somewhat of a tricky question to answer, considering that it delves into some of the secrets of our organization."

"So, what, do you expect it to just follow you blindly?" Helen grunts. "That's some shady shit right there."

**I'm a girl.** I quickly write at her, grumbling internally. **I'm not an 'it.'**

"Whatever."

I hiss at her, and she ignores me. Hagoro clears his throat.

"…I suppose, given the circumstances, I could elucidate you," he concedes. "In truth, Hana, you wouldn't be doing much. You're neither qualified nor capable of handling the underlying issues facing our world as it is."

He seems to hesitate, so I decide to encourage him.

**That makes perfect sense,** I write. **Please continue.**

"Of course, of course. You're largely important because you can help us acquire unique insight into your condition. If we successfully study the link between the two worlds you inhabit, then we can ideally gain insight on how to sever that link, and ultimately prevent any more of your kind from being created in the first place."

Woah. Okay. Pretty extreme, but the circumstances caused by people like me are all pretty darn extreme themselves. I can see the justification behind trying to just stop us from existing entirely, especially if most of us are genocidally unreasonable enough to cause apocalypses.

**With you so far,** I confirm. **What would that actually entail? Sitting around and being poked at by scientists?**

"Ah… essentially, yes," Hagoro answers in a very suspicious manner.

**So what's the catch, then?** I ask, since there obviously is one.

"Well, ah… you would be doing nothing else," he answers. "And, well, we haven't usually worked with cooperative individuals like yourself, so ideally this wouldn't be as much of an issue, but *historically,* the tests have always culminated in the subject's death."

Silence. Kagiso and Helen both stare at him, dumbfounded, as I find myself without any idea of what to say.

"It's for the sake of the world," Hagoro presses awkwardly.

"Wow, uh, yeah, I'm glad I already told you to fuck off," Helen supplies.

"Helen, I assure you that we're genuinely interested in keeping you safe," Hagoro answers her.

"I don't really like whatever the fuck your definition of 'keeping people safe' is!" Helen snaps back.

"Hana is a unique case," Hagoro insists, but Helen is already looking like she's tensed to bolt. And I don't even remotely blame her!

**This 'unique case' says no,** I quickly scribble. **You can't seriously expect me to agree with that.**

"Hana, please…" Hagoro presses.

**Please what? Submit myself to lifelong suffering and death because** *other people like me* **have done really bad things? That's a load of beans and you know it!**

"It's a load of what?" Hagoro mutters. "No, wait, it doesn't matter. I… I'm sorry, Hana, but I'm afraid I have to insist."

A chill flows through my body. Really? Already? Things are going badly *this soon?* Ugh. I guess I expected this. I tense myself for an attack, but Hagoro just keeps talking.

"I know… I *know* how unreasonable this sounds. Trust me, I'm aware, but… you must understand, the world is at stake! If not you, then the next one of you, or the next, or the next! Whatever it is that brings you will *keep* bringing you until we learn how to stop it."

"Holy shit I can't believe I almost thought you were being honest," Helen hisses, and a darkness even my spatial sense can see blooms around her palm. "You were just going to kill me too, weren't you?"

"No," Hagoro shakes his head, but he readies his spear as well. "I wasn't. But if I must, then—"

"**Velocity**," the Goddess says with Kagiso's voice, and in one fluid motion my fuzzy friend raises and fires her bow. The arrow screams towards Hagoro, catching him by surprise but only connecting with his magically-enhanced armor. I watch, almost in slow motion, as the arrow taps his chest plate and seems to stop instantly, not even so much as scratching the metal. For an instant I despair, wondering if we've just started a fight we can't win, but then Hagoro *rockets* backwards, suddenly launching hundreds of miles an hour in the same direction that the arrow once traveled and smashing into a tree.

548

"Won't hurt him," Kagiso grunts, and sure enough his organs barely jiggle from the hard impact. A limit to her spell? "We run."

I'm good with running anyway. I dash towards Kagiso and she scoops me up into her arms, yanking Helen's shoulder as she passes.

"Hey!" Helen snaps, apparently ready to fight, but she still follows along as Kagiso refuses to let go.

The Goddess, I notice, does not leave, even after Kagiso's spell is long over. She hovers all around us, suffusing the air and whispering silent chuckles. Licking her lips in anticipation, she watches as Hagoro inhales to speak.

"**Zone of Law: No Retreat**."

Kagiso screams, convulsing as her body is forced to a stop. She trips, faceplanting into the dirt and forcing us to face down Hagoro as he extracts himself from the ruins of a tree and promptly thunders towards us. I almost take a step into a nearby barren zone, but a sudden feeling of attention from the Goddess has me discarding that plan. I'm not resistant to Order *or* Barrier. Kagiso *is,* and she still got floored.

Even as Hagoro rushes towards us at a speed I never would have expected from a man so weighted down, my mind can't help but wander a little. It's funny, in a horrid sort of way. For all his evil, for all his violations, Sindri was right about one thing: I really do have to learn to kill if I want to survive in this world. I'd wondered back on Earth about all sorts of horrifying conspiracy theories. I'd thought maybe the bandits he had me kill weren't bandits at all, but more victims he prepared in some evil attempt to train me like a fucking Pokémon. But they weren't, were they? The Tree of Souls is just a lawless, dangerous place, ravaged by magic and the people who think the power it grants them allows them to force their will on others. I'd come here to kill someone on his behest. Now I stand beside her against his killer. The world really is absurd sometimes, isn't it?

Fuck it. I'm too tired to care anymore. There's only one rational response to this.

"**Spacial Rend**," I intone, and the Goddess pulls the breath from me with joyous laughter.

All at once, I feel a mental pressure leave me. My movement becomes a lot less restricted when I intend to *fight*. I don't try to find out if I can leave this dimension yet, though, instead leaping up on Helen's shoulder, causing her to yelp in surprise as I bring a claw up to intercept the glaive about to take her head. Hagoro aborts the strike, avoiding my Spacial Rend-enhanced claws and preventing me from destroying his weapon.

"Get off!" Helen shrieks, trying to grab me and throw me off of her despite the fact that I just saved her life. Crap, I can't accidentally cut her!

"**Ricochet**," Kagiso hisses, throwing a pair of rocks which Hagoro has to block to prevent them from striking weak points in his armor. She's in serious trouble, though, being a ranged fighter that can't step backwards, and Hagoro knows it. He quickly circles around us to take a swing at her, which is when Kagiso grabs *me* and winds up her arm for a throw.

Wait... no! No no no no no! I hiss as loudly as I can. Kagiso, don't do it!

"**Ricochet**!" she roars, and then yeets me directly at Hagoro.

If I had a stomach that actually existed in the third dimension, I'd be unloading its contents through the air. Kagiso didn't *just* throw me, she put some serious spin on it, turning me into a deadly pinwheel of sharp legs. I don't actually get dizzy or disoriented, perceiving my own body from the outside like I do, but that only allows me to realize how completely screwed I am in the split-second before Hagoro's expertly-swung blade carves me in half as I fly. It's a perfect overhead chop, I'm going to be completely bisected. I watch in utter horror as my body approaches and ultimately connects with that magical blade, my own empowered legs too strained by centrifugal force to make any sort of counterattack. This is how I die, huh? Being thrown like a baseball by a four-armed, four-breasted catgirl that's currently smiling like she just won the lottery. Huh. Wonder what that's about.

I bounce off of the blade.

The moment I make contact with the edge of the glaive, my momentum *shifts,* my speed multiplying dramatically and sending me on a high-velocity trip into the ground. But of course, I bounce off of *that* too, and the combined impacts seem to have halted my ridiculous spin. I hold a claw out as I ascend, and carve Hagoro's body from scrotum to sternum.

His armor's thick, but my 'blades' ignore it, passing through the magical plate without issue. I don't think I cut him deep enough to kill, but it's a *long* cut, and it's deep enough that blood blooms from it at startling speeds. Hanging in the air above him like a perfectly set volleyball, I watch as he staggers backwards from the blow, and then his *own* Zone of Law kicks in, wracking him with pain as the Goddess howls with laughter. Then she vanishes, Hagoro deactivating the spell and—judging by his rapidly-closing wounds—activating a healing spell in its place. Well, can't have that. Obeying my instincts, I take both of his right arms on the way down, severing them just below the shoulder. His weapon clatters to the ground next to them, and he falls to one knee.

"...I yield," Hagoro croaks.

"You think we're gonna fucking listen to you after that?" Helen growls, raising her arm towards him and taking an ominous breath. I hiss to try and stop her, jumping between her and the man that just surrendered, but it's already too late.

"**And So She Wept**," the Goddess says with a smile, "**Finding Beauty In Oblivion**."

I am struck by annihilation, and I wake up on Earth screaming from the pain.

My first instinct is to clamp down on the noise. The last time I woke up screaming my mom rushed into the room, and I don't need *that* making everything worse. Because like, beans on toast, did I just *die?* Ohhhhh Goddess I think I died! I mean, maybe. If I died and woke up here, does that mean it's over? That I won't go back when next I sleep? Or will it be worse somehow? It would totally figure if the Goddess runs Hell and decides to send me there whenever I sleep now.

But... hold on. I should calm down a little. I already had this scare once before when I was first being persistence hunted by Sindri. It's very possible I was just knocked unconscious. I resist Chaos, after all. Plus, like... I'm pretty sure I can check? When I use my shapeshifty spell I sort of feel both of my bodies. If I can still do that, logically my other body is still alive, right? Of course, that would necessitate accelerating my transformation, at least a little bit. Is that worth not being anxious all day over whether or not I'm literally dead?

Huh. Wait, I think it is. Am I really going to take action to reduce my anxiety? *Really?*

...

Wow! Okay then! Time to recklessly use magic with far-reaching long-term consequences to solve a short-term problem. Brendan is going to be so proud of me!

I sink into the headspace for my Transmutation spell without even bothering to figure my humanoid limbs out. I just close my eyes again and focus on that magic-filled thread spanning between worlds, reaching out across it and letting the power flow through enough to get a glimpse at my other self. It's barely more than a vague impression, but it's enough to know I'm alive, if heavily damaged. I let magic flow through the spell, trying to repair my other body like I repaired myself when I miscasted here on Earth. I feel it start to work a bit, and I figure that's all I need. Don't want to overdo things. I let myself come back to my body, releasing a deep breath before opening my eyes and immediately getting a massive headache.

Aw, lard. What did I do to myself this time? Cycling through my limbs, I get out of bed and check myself over in my room briefly, not seeing anything out of the ordinary. At least, not until I rub my temples and come back with a clump of hair in my hand. Oh, *no.* I can't go bald! I won't be able to hide *that!* I mean, I guess I could get a wig, but... aaaagh no no no no no!

I quickly rush to the bathroom, not bothering to cover myself up first since I can sense that there isn't anyone in the hallway. I strip down and take another look at my head, tugging lightly at my hair. To my utter horror, I come away with a few more small clumps... but that's it. I have a handful of hair, but most of it still seems to be firmly rooted in my scalp where it belongs. What the heck is... wait. What are those spots on my forehead? There are little dark spots under the skin, two on my forehead and one next to each temple. Am I going to grow horns or something? They're just a little smaller than my... eyes.

I'm growing eight more eyes, aren't I?

I pull my hair back, and sure enough there's a discolored spot of my scalp over every part of my head that went bald. Eight little patches form a ring around my head, each small enough to easily get covered by the hair I have left. Not the ones on my face, though. Sure, they're not all that visible *right now,* but the time bomb has officially started ticking. I guess I could wear a headband or something, but it's all just so *visible!* Right on my face! Gah! Imagine when the eyes actually grow in and I get a bunch of new holes in my skull and they all start bleeding at once when they emerge and it'll just... nope! Nope nope nope let's not imagine that actually, I changed my mind! I'm gonna just go shower and consider this as little as possible.

Honestly, there's a lot I don't want to be thinking about right now. I'm so sorry, Teboho.

I manage to keep my head blank all the way to the bus stop, my mind simply too exhausted and overwhelmed to put much effort into thinking about things in the first place. Makeup covers the discolored spots where eyes are growing in under my skin, and it'll just have to do. I follow Brendan's advice and face towards his house instead of the street, and therefore spot him long before he can somehow surprise me. I give him a dull wave.

"Did you figure out any spells last night?" I ask him.

"What?" he asks back, blinking in surprise.

I open my mouth, then close it. Oh holy carp I totally forgot to tell him he's an Art mage. I feel a blush start rising up my cheeks.

"Uh... you're a wizard, Harry," I tell him numbly. "Sorry, I should have said so last night but like... well, I had a bad day."

"Wait, like really?" Brendan gapes, his eyebrows rising. "Holy shit, Hannah. I think a Harry Potter quote is the absolute worst possible way you could have told me this."

"Look. I... I've been better, Brendan. Sorry."

"Oh. Right." Brendan stares at me, and with what must be absolutely herculean effort, he focuses on something other than the possibility that he has magic. "...What happened?"

"Well, two people died," I answer quietly, "but at least one of them was Sindri."

"...Was the other the Chaos mage?"

"No," I answer. "Teboho."

"...Fuck."

"Yeah," I nod. "I don't think I can talk about it right now. Your magic is Art magic. That's about all I know."

"I am not going to be able to focus on school today *at all*," Brendan sighs.

Our bus ride is quieter than usual, and I'm okay with that. My first class is with Ida, so naturally she approaches me right away, looking particularly cocky.

"Hey," I nod. "How are you doing?"

"I'm fucking awesome," Ida answers. "What about you?"

Eh, no sense lying. Won't work on her.

"I'm not great," I admit.

"Is there anything I can do to help?" she asks.

"Probably not," I shrug.

She steps forward and jabs me in the ribs with a finger.

"Fuck you!" she snaps. "I take that as a challenge. You don't know what I'm capable of."

...And then she walks back to her seat, leaving me feeling distinctly Ida'd. Well, whatever. I have... a lot to do, since I need to catch up on all of yesterday's classwork as well as today's. I mean, actually doing any of this is laughable since I probably won't even be passably human by the time any of it is due, but it's something *to* do and that's what my brain needs right now. My whole head feels like a giant bruise, physically and emotionally, and losing myself in routine is the only way I know how to cope. I make some decent progress in first period, but second period today is gym class. I'm... not looking forward to it.

I deliberately wait outside the locker room until after Autumn leaves, only then going inside and changing in a bathroom stall. I don't want to ogle her, *especially* after we've de facto confirmed we aren't dating, and I don't trust my self-control at the moment. Or in general, I guess. I'm late getting out of the locker room, but the extra laps I'm forced to run as a result don't even register to me. I run pretty much on autopilot, setting a pace without really thinking about it and moving without putting any real effort into it. I do my best not to think about Autumn as I approach her from behind and pass her, but unexpectedly she shoots a hand out and startles me out of my funk.

"Hey!" she hisses at me. "Slow the fuck down, you idiot!"

I blink dumbly at her.

"...Jet?" I guess.

"Yeah, it's me," she quickly dismisses. "Now don't use that name at school, and start acting like you're tired. You're moving at the pace of a competitive runner, a nerd like you should be dying by now."

Huh? Oh. She's protecting my secret identity or whatever. That makes sense.

"...Thanks," I nod, and slow down a little. "Sorry."

"Don't apologize to me," she grumbles. "Are you okay? You seem really out of it."

I turn away from her and don't respond. I'm not sure I can.

"...That's a no, then," Jet sighs. "Look, if it's about... *her,* I'm sorry. She hasn't told me shit, but I assume that means the two of you didn't talk yesterday?"

"Yeah," I confirm.

"Alright, then you probably shouldn't press her today, either. She'll get over it a day or two from now, probably."

"Okay."

She gives me another concerned look, which I don't have any way to prevent myself from knowing about with my spatial sense so focused on her. It feels weirdly intrusive to be *unable* to look away, at least for a certain definition of 'look.' My spatial sense still doesn't give me fully comprehensible sight like it does on the other side, but the impressions I get from it are often just as good. And the way Jet's body is moving underneath her outfit is... well, yet another thing that I'm actively trying not to think about.

Hmm. There is one thing I need to say, though.

"There's a chance you have magic now," I say. "I can't really check you to make sure when we're in public, but some other people I've casted around have souls, even though most people don't. So be careful."

Jet chuckles humorlessly.

"You think I might have a soul, huh? How touching. I guess there was no way I was getting out of that still normal. Hey, if all else fails, that'd be one way to convince you-know-who that I'm not crazy."

I nod, but don't answer. Jet frowns, but also seems content to be silent. The rest of gym passes without incident, and if the teacher notices my oddly high stamina he doesn't comment on it. The lunch they serve today doesn't smell like something I can actually eat, so I go without. Classes fly by one after the other, and I'm fairly certain that by the time I get back on the bus home I haven't said a single word to anyone since gym class.

"...Hannah?" Brendan asks as he sits down next to me.

"Hmm?" I mumble.

"Hey, Hannah. I'm here for you, alright?"

I turn my head and look up at him, blinking twice to try and push away the fog.

"...I'm tired of this," I mumble.

"I'm sorry," he says. "I... can I hug you?"

"Yeah," I allow, and he does, putting his arms around me in the middle of this stinky old school bus. That's all it takes for the dam to break and for me to start to cry.

There are no despairing wails, no loud laments at the unjustness of my situation. Just silent sobs, tears falling onto Brendan's hoodie and little shakes of my body to accompany them. It's not fair. Not fair that I should have to be a part of so much death. I'm just some girl. It's not fair. It's not.

I don't want to be a part of this twisted game the Goddess is playing. I don't know why she chose me, or even if she chose me, but I don't think I'm up to the task. I didn't have my life together before all this started, the combat trauma, mind rape, and general agony aren't exactly helping me out. I can't do this anymore. I just can't. Something has to change. This is too much, and all I have to weather it is my routine.

"You gonna watch the stream today?" I ask, sniffing up another tear as Brendan and I step off the bus.

He opens his mouth to say something, but he ends up shaking his head in exasperation instead.

"Wouldn't miss it for all the Art magic in the world," he answers, and we part ways.

I trudge upstairs, my legs feeling like lead… though not because of gym class today. I drop my backpack in my room and head to the bathroom to quickly fix my makeup with a spell. Along with my hair. And the rest of my appearance. I'm a lot more presentable after I sort the extra blood out of my eyes, removing any traces that I was just crying. Deep breath, fake smile. Even behind the facemask, it's important. They can see happiness in your eyes, just like they can see fear.

I double-check that my room is clean and everything is positioned right (it always is) and I sit down at my desk, taking in one last gulp of air before booting up Twitch.

"Hey everybody!" I announce happily. "Welcome back to the Nuzlocke!"

I immediately get a message informing me that I've received 30 subs from Lucarivor29.

What.

Lucarivor29 that's enough for the reveal right? :3

SwalotRancher holy shit the bit

PentUp It is time!!!

NougatKin Activate DD hand tier

ZirconCommando egirl mode engaged

"Uh. Wow," I manage to say, dumbfounded. "This is a surprise. Uh, thanks, Lucarivor."

I... did not expect this. I barely even expected it at *all*, let alone this soon.

PentUp give us the hand pics DD

BirbBirb yeah!!!

Well, you know what? Screw it. Sure. Why not! I don't even care anymore. I make a show of it, peeling the first glove off partway only to swap to the second glove before anything actually comes off. I can't believe I'm doing this. On camera, to the world! There's no going back from this, but for some reason it's so hard to care right now. I've done a lot of things I can't undo. What's one more?

The gloves come off. I flex my fingers, showing off the contrast between the bone-white chitin and the pitch-black joints. Then I shake my hair out, pull it back a little, and remove my mask, giving the chat a wide, wide grin.

"I am uncontrollably mutating into a horrifying abomination," I announce, "but that's a bit too terrifying for me to handle right now, so I'm going to distract myself with Pokémon."

The chat, predictably, goes ballistic, some people calling the bit lame but most seeming *super* into it. My heart is beating a million miles an hour as I adjust the camera to have a good view of my hands as I play, though it really seems to be the teeth that are getting the most attention. I get to show them off every time I talk, and for some reason it's exhilarating. Scary, certainly, but not in the way I was expecting. Not in the way that my life usually goes. Sure, they all think it's fake, but... they like how I look. People actually like who I am.

Predictably, it's my most successful stream to date. People really like a good gimmick.

# 29

# COMING OUT

NougatKin This is such a crazy fucking vtuber rig

Lucarivor29 It's obviously not a vtuber rig tho???

LavAbsol DD that's such awesome costume work! Did you make it yourself?

Zoroa!Queen Just joined stream and omg that gastly's name is an oof

SwalotRancher isn't it dangerous to switch train on rattata??? Pursuit is in this gen

PentUp i think the hands are a costume but the teeth are digital

Zoroa!Queen ya but they don't learn pursuit until level 13. safe until route 34

"Uh, did I make this myself?" I read aloud, since people have to know which question in the massive chat I'm actually answering. "I mean, technically yes, since I grew it. Like, I know none of you are going to believe this is anything but a bit, because that's what a reasonable person would believe, but this is super real and there's even more of it! I'd demonstrate but I promised to never show my feet on camera. I can stretch my other limbs though, I suppose."

I wiggle limbs five and six free of the bindings I put them in under my shirt and let them peek out a bit. Unfortunately, I'm sitting, so they don't really make it very far into frame. I briefly stand up,

561

wave at the camera with one of them, and then sit back down to get back to video games. Egh, maybe I shouldn't have. They kind of lift up my shirt a little bit.

LavAbsol Okay, that's super cool.

PentUp ...uhhhhh okay that looked like it was coming out of her skin wtf

SwalotRancher how do you know the exact route lol

Zoroa!Queen I play a lot of nuzlockes lol. Spearow also learns pursuit at 13 btw

Xenoversal oh shit the bit is today

ZirconCommando show us the FEET

"Thanks for the info, Zoroa. That's good to know," I encourage. "Also, I can and will ban you, Zircon."

ZirconCommando i can and will find a better streamer

"Uh, I mean, okay then. Have fun with that!"

I take a moment to boot the jerk, which my chat encourages with the vigor of spectators at a gladiatorial arena. It's certainly true that the internet can be horribly vile, but I honestly love my little corner of it. There will always be nasty people, but I don't have to just sit back and let them be nasty. So I remove them, and that encourages more nice people to stay. It's pretty neat.

I think it's especially funny how much of the stream just doesn't flick a single booger about my ongoing mutation and just keeps talking about Pokémon. Like, I love that, and it's honestly a huge mood, but it's still really funny. I'm genuinely unsure how much to encourage people to believe that this is real. On one hand, everyone assuming it's fake might keep me off the radar of whatever magic-suppressing organization probably exists. On the other hand, it prevents the strategy of 'become so well-known that the secret organization can't hide your disappearance' from working. People randomly disappear off of the internet all the time; it'd be disappointing if I randomly stopped streaming one day, but nobody would suspect foul play. I'm genuinely unsure of which path to take with this, so… I guess I'll just play it by ear.

I'll just keep telling the truth, I guess. Maybe I'll eat some raw eggs on stream or cut something up with Spacial Rend. No incantations, though. I don't know how the Goddess' voice reacts to being recorded and I'm not sure I want to find out. Somewhere along the line, though, when the time is right and I feel like people will take it seriously, I'll explain the situation in detail and ask people to make a big stink if I vanish. Hopefully that will be enough, and if not, well… hell, I'm kind of proud of myself for making it this far.

The stream is honestly a lot more comfortable now that I'm not wrapped up in a million layers of protective clothing, too. I might even be able to reach the keyboard with my extra limbs! It would be pretty funny to play with them, but… eh. Probably not comfortable yet. Hopefully they'll grow some more.

…Wow, did I really just think that? Geez, I totally did. You know what? Not going to think about it any more than that. The whole point of playing Pokémon is to *avoid* introspection.

All good things must come to an end, though. As I stream into the wee hours of the morning, I eventually feel the inevitable call of sleep. It was nice getting to de-stress like this, but I guess I have to face the music and deal with… I don't even know. I'm too tired to care, honestly. I should probably be ready for a fight, though. I close my eyes, and as usual the stress of those thoughts does nothing to keep me awake before soreness overtakes my sensorium.

Holy cannoli I hurt *all over.* I glance at myself and wince at the pockmarked holes in my chitin where the Chaos magic fought against my aura and managed to gain some ground. I was nearly dissolved to death! When I twitch all my legs in sequence, though, I learn that I'm probably not all that seriously injured. Everything seems to work right and my internal organs are fine. I either healed off any major damage I sustained from casting my spell the other morning, or I was never seriously damaged and just blacked out from the pain. Given how very little seems to have changed from then to now, I'm guessing it's the latter.

Kagiso is screaming at Helen, presumably because she just shot me with a murder blast, but I can't really make out what she's saying because it's mostly just incomprehensible anger noises. *Helen* is yelling back at her, pointing at me and blaming me for jumping in front of the blast in the first place, which to be fair *is* very stupid and something I absolutely did.

On the upside, it seems to have worked: Hagoro is alive. I guess I'm not sure if it's actually because of me or because of his armor, though, since that's been slagged even harder than my carapace and seems to have protected even the parts of him that weren't covered by it. I guess he did say it was Chaos-resistant at the start, though. Whatever, I want to take credit for it so I'm gonna. I take a deep breath and let out my loudest hiss, shutting up the two bickering women.

**I'm fine,** I write. **Let's decide what we're doing with Hagoro.**

"Hana!" Kagiso chirps, rushing over and scooping me up into a hug. Which *hurts like hell,* so I have to hiss at her and make her put me down again.

"We need to kill him," Helen says, ignoring our antics and jumping to the topic at hand. "And you need to not fucking jump in the way, even if you *are* a fucking bullshit Order mage with resistance and regeneration."

I hiss again, though softer this time, and write out my response.

**I won't let you execute someone who surrendered.**

I feel like this should be pretty darn straightforward. Even if you ignore all the really important moral reasons to not execute a surrendered opponent—and I'm not going to ignore them, they're important to me—from a practical perspective, respecting surrenders is advantageous because it encourages people to respect *you.* Not only is this dude far from the only apocalypse cultist that's likely to come after me, but he's a paladin that has literal law magic. I'm pretty sure we can trust him to respect his *own* surrender and not immediately betray us. And yeah, he'll probably escape and cause problems for us later, but... I dunno. I still don't want to kill him.

That's all a bit much to write out, though, so I just present it as an ultimatum. Helen seems important to Kagiso, so I'm willing to give her the benefit of the doubt, but if she's going to fight me over this I *will* throw down. I'll hate it, but I'll do it... and I'm pretty sure I'll win.

Helen scowls as Kagiso looks back and forth between us, not seeming to have an opinion of her own. Eventually, the Chaos mage lets out a long suffering sigh and throws her hands up into the air in exasperation.

"Well, you guys have fun with him, then. I don't know why I'm hanging around with you idiots in the first place. Fuck you, and goodbye."

"No!" Kagiso yelps, grabbing Helen's arm again. "Stay! Stay?"

*"Stop touching me!"* Helen snaps back, pulling free. "And stop trying to get me to come with you!"

Kagiso's ears droop, and she shrinks down a little.

"But... Helen is only one left," she says quietly. "Don't have anyone else."

The Chaos mage's eyes go wide, a whole host of emotions running over her face. She seems genuinely guilty about what she's done, blaming herself for the tragedy—perhaps justifiably so. And yet the only surviving victim of her actions is asking her to stay because *she has no one left other than the one who did it.* How must that feel? I can't even imagine what's going through her head. Helen grits her teeth and looks away, but she doesn't leave.

"Thank you... Hana."

I raise my body a little to look at Hagoro, who is apparently still conscious. His healing spell has long since scabbed over the amputations I gave him, but it doesn't seem to be regrowing his arms at all. There's probably some Order mage out there who can restore limbs, and I suppose he'll be all right until he finds them. Get it? Because I cut off both of his left arms. ...Dang, should I eat them? Agh, wait, what the heck, me!? You already said no to Teboho's, you can't eat *this* guy's arms with Kagiso around. ...No, wait, that's not why this is a bad idea, what the actual—

"I made myself your enemy," Hagoro continues, "but you still spared me... and protected me. You could have taken my head as easily as you took my arms."

What do I say to that? Writing a lot is a pain, but I'm not sure how to shorten 'I didn't grow up in a culture where executing an enemy would *ever* happen, let alone be considered normal, you guys are all just crazy.'

**I'm not a killer by choice,** I ultimately decide on.

"Is that so?" he says, making a noise that's somewhere between a chuckle and a cough. "Oh, Goddess. Why her?"

The Goddess, predictably, does not deign to answer.

**Honestly, I don't actually know what to do with you,** I admit.

"That is fair," Hagoro nods. "I can't reasonably expect you to guard me or provide for me. I am of little use for you, and of much danger. But I can say this: if you simply depart and leave me be, I will neither perish in the forest nor follow you. We will go our separate ways, and I will remember the gratitude you are owed for this."

**Is that gratitude actually worth anything?**

He sighs.

"I will still be allied with those who seek your capture, Hana. And I will still aid them in this task. The risk you pose is too great."

Well, that sucks. But I kind of figured that was the case. Uuuugh. Am I just creating my own recurring villain, here? The alternative is to murder him in cold blood, though, and I just can't do that! Still though, this guy's terrible. I hope all his pretzel sticks turn soggy.

566

**Maybe people like me only end up destroying the world because jerks like you won't leave them alone,** I silently grumble at him.

"Oh, Hana," Hagoro says sadly. "If my life could end this terrible cycle, I'd sacrifice it in a heartbeat. But it can't. Yours might."

Ugh. What is there to say? He's a religious zealot convinced that I have to suffer for the good of the world, just like the ones back home. I drum my legs in annoyance before quickly scribbling out my answer.

**Don't come back, Hagoro. Please?**

He smiles sadly, then turns to look up at Helen instead of answering me.

"It's possible to fool aura sight," he announces.

The Chaos mage jolts out of her funk and turns to glower at him.

"What?"

"If you refuse to accompany me, your safest bet is to stick with these two," Hagoro continues. "If you stand close enough to a powerful Order mage, their aura will subsume the Chaos energy given off by your soul, and you'll only read as an Art mage to any detection spells. As long as you aren't attacking anyone, no one will think to check twice."

Helen narrows her eyes, but doesn't answer.

"Hana can help you safely discharge your magic, as well, thanks to her resistance. I know it's just words, but that's the most help I can offer you now. Will you allow me to leave in peace?"

"Whatever," Helen grunts. "If the little freak doesn't want to do the smart thing and just get rid of you, I'll play along. But leave your weapon on the ground."

He nods, standing up unsteadily without touching his discarded polearm... or discarded actual arms.

"Thank you," he says. "I'm sorry it has to be this way."

**It really doesn't,** I write.

"No, the fuzzy bastard's right," Helen says, shaking her head. "It's always this way, no matter what."

Using a tree to support his first steps, Hagoro slowly walks around us and heads back towards the city we came from. The three of us silently wait as he departs, and only after he's well outside the range of my spatial sense do I scuttle over to the others and write.

**What now?**

Because that's the burning question, isn't it? We came here to kill a Chaos mage, but now she's a seemingly-unwilling teammate, half our prior teammates are dead, and the three of us have no families (in this universe), no homes (in this universe), and as far as I know, no objectives (in any universe). The only thing I could maybe consider a goal is trying to figure out how to solve the problems destroying the world tree, but those issues are so impossibly massive that I don't have the slightest idea where to begin. So what, then? Do I just wander around and wait for my Protagonist Energy to kick in and give me the infinite might necessary to do the sorts of horrors that my predecessors supposedly did, but in reverse? That's hardly a plan.

"Well, as novel as it is for someone other than me to be getting tracked," Helen drawls, "we can't stay here. I guess if you aren't going to leave me alone, I can at least help you drop the trail of your inevitable pursuers."

"I go where friends go," Kagiso nods.

**About that,** I write. **Sorry, I don't have an easy way to bring this up, but... what should we do about Teboho?**

Kagiso frowns.

"He dead?" she reminds me. "Nothing can do."

**I mean like, should we bury him or something?**

"No? That make it harder for animals eat, I think."

"Dentron tend to leave their dead out in the wilderness," Helen informs me. "And we're already in the wilderness. I know it's kind of morbid, but it makes sense to just... leave him."

Her expression is impressively even as she says that. That murder is already compartmentalized, huh? Mood, I guess. I just... I wish it hadn't been Teboho. I feel like I should be mad at her *because* it was Teboho, *because* it was that ever-positive bundle of joy that made my time here in this world so much more bearable. He was so kind, so steadfast. He taught me so much, and now he's just... gone. Why don't I feel worse about this? Why am I already looking ahead? Were my emotions just a consequence of Friends, now dispelled with Sindri's death? Or am I just so cold of a person that it simply doesn't affect me to lose a friend I haven't known for all that long? Kagiso also doesn't seem as affected as I might expect, either. She had her outburst against Sindri's corpse, but now she's latched onto her brother's killer like a starving remora. Did she love him before he died? Is she just good at hiding it? Or is she like me?

"Okay, so here's the plan I had before you idiots caught up with me and... well, all *this* happened," Helen announces, seeming to take our silence in stride. "Nychtava will ferry people between branches if you have the money, they don't tend to ask questions about your element, and they'll accept both electrum and amber. This branch has a colony of them nearby, and we can hire one to fly us to a lower branch without being tracked. I was hiding out here trying to find a way to sneak in, but if what that paladin asshole said is true, we could probably just go in the front gate together."

**Where will we go when we get to a lower branch?** I ask.

"Our separate ways, ideally," Helen grumbles.

"Slaying Stone," Kagiso suggests. "Hana want help world, yes? Problems start with Slaying Stone."

"...Is the Slaying Stone really a worse problem than the huge fire or the roots?" Helen asks.

"No? But fire is up and we go down. Roots even more down. Slaying Stone on way."

**Makes sense to me,** I scribble. Plus, seeing more of the world will be really important in regards to learning about the world, and I have to actually understand the problems people are facing before I can work out a plan to maybe fix them when I get really strong in the future, or however the heck this actually works.

"Alright, fine, whatever," Helen grumbles. "Follow me, I guess."

**Actually, one more question,** I write. **Do we have any money?**

"We didn't," Helen smirks before pulling a small pouch out of a grubby pocket. "But that Sindri guy did."

Woah. When did she loot... eh, whatever, not going to think about it.

**Lead the way, then,** I write, and scuttle up Kagiso's leg.

"Mmm. Hello Hana," Kagiso says, giving me a pat. "Not me, today."

She holds out an arm towards Helen, as if inviting me to swap over to her shoulders. Neither Helen nor I are enthused by this prospect.

"Uh, what? I'm not carrying your weird bug friend," Helen insists.

"But... need to get used to?" Kagiso frowns. "Hagoro say have to be close to disguise aura."

"'Close to' doesn't mean 'attached to!'" Helen protests. "You just carry her, and then you can walk... close to..."

She slowly trails off, staring at Kagiso for a moment before turning away.

"Y'know what, never mind, gimme the freaky spider."

She grabs me and yanks me off of Kagiso, so I hiss at her because of course I'm going to hiss at somebody who does that, especially if they're a jerk like Helen!

"Shut up!" Helen snaps at me. "You heard her. If you want me along I need your aura. Come on, let's go."

I never actually said I wanted her along, but I don't have anything to write on so I let that slide. She starts walking in a huff, Kagiso quickly falling into step beside her. The pair set a brisk pace, much faster than we traveled to the city in the first place, but I suppose there had been more of us and Teboho was injured. Kagiso and Helen both seem to prefer the increased speed, and while I occasionally dismount Helen to go grab a fuzzy little friend noodle to eat, I mostly just sit on her head.

It's surprisingly comfortable, all things considered. Helen is as dirty as one might expect from a girl that just spent weeks roughing it alone in an attempt to escape from her crimes, but it's nothing a little surreptitious cleaning magic can't fix. It's actually much harder than it usually is to cast on her—thanks to the whole Chaos mage thing, presumably—but I still manage it. She definitely notices what I'm doing at some point, grabbing some strands of her previously-gnarled hair and rubbing them between two unexpectedly clean fingers. She gives me a steady look for a moment but doesn't comment, so I take that as tacit permission to continue. Maybe she'll be less grumpy when she's not covered in five layers of filth. I know I will be.

Her clothes are a more difficult issue. Not cleaning them, since that's as easy as cleaning anything else, but their other problems. The light traveling garb is baggy on her in a way that suggests it was probably stolen from a noticeably larger man, and the many accumulated tears in the rough dun shirt and trousers can't simply be sorted back together. I'm not great at it, but I can do basic repairs with a sewing kit. Maybe I can improvise a... wait, no, I don't have hands. Right.

Well, the important thing is the body underneath the clothes, and while there's certainly a notable collection of cuts and bruises, they're all pretty superficial. I'm not a doctor or anything, but her organs all look about as good as I've seen organs look: i.e. none of them are leaking fluids they aren't supposed to be leaking. Her figure underneath her outfit isn't much to write home about, as much as I feel like a total creep for noting that. The nice way to put it would be 'boyish,' while the Ida way to put it would be 'flat as a pancake run over by a bus.' She doesn't have anything in the hip or butt department either; I'd almost think she was biologically male if not for the fact that she doesn't even have the upper body strength to pass for that. That and, uh, y'know. I can see all of her reproductive organs. Constantly.

A-anyway! Changing away from *that* train of thought! My point is that her body, while healthy, does seem pretty underdeveloped. Like, she's very much postpubescent, but somewhere along the line her body just decided to give up on anything more than the bare minimum effort required for that particular series of physiological changes. Combine that with the fact that her mother was legally required to kill her at birth and I'm starting to suspect that she didn't exactly grow up with a stable food supply. That changed later in life, as evidenced by her ability to set such a grueling pace for our journey, but I doubt her childhood was pleasant.

"I gotta say," Helen suddenly pipes up, "I was not looking forward to traveling with anyone, but I really appreciate that you two know how to shut up."

I mean, I'm mute, but thanks I guess.

"Why start talking then?" Kagiso asks, and I can't help but let out a short hiss of a laugh.

"I... fuck! Okay, fine, I won't say anything nice!" Helen snaps.

"Oh! Is nice? Good to say nice. Thank Helen!"

"Uuugh. Kagiso, you're going to give me a headache," Helen complains.

"No?" Kagiso says, tilting her head. "This not magic I can do."

Helen groans and puts her face in her hands.

"Are you *sure?*" she whines."Because it's totally happening."

"Maybe Helen need drink more water!" Kagiso declares happily. "Have some. You want? Probably not contain blood this time."

"No, Kagiso, I have plenty of... ugh. Look, are either of you getting hungry? I think it's about time to take a break."

"Okay," Kagiso shrugs. "I hunt something?"

"We don't... actually, sure. Yeah. Go hunt something, Kagiso."

"Hehe. Yay."

Helen and Kagiso find a fallen log to sit on and drop their packs by it before Kagiso grabs her weapons and runs off. Helen waits for Kagiso to be out of sight and then groans, collapsing onto the log in an exhausted huff. She then reaches down to the ground, grabs a stone, and clenches it in a fist. When she opens her hand, there's nothing there. She reaches down a second time and I take that opportunity to jump off her head, landing on the ground in front of her and shaking my sore body out.

"Enjoy the ride?" Helen asks sardonically, destroying another stone.

**It wasn't so bad once I tidied up the place,** I write back.

She lets out an amused snort.

"Yeah, you really fucking made yourself at home, didn't you?"

**Sorry,** I write. **I should have asked first, but I didn't think of it until we were already on the move.**

She blinks in surprise and glances away from me. That's... what she does when she's embarrassed, isn't it? Well, I guess she could avoid eye contact as a response to a bunch of different emotions, but judging by the way the blood vessels on her cheeks are widening I'm willing to bet on embarrassment.

"That's not... you don't have to say sorry," she mumbles. "Honestly, it was... I mean. Y'know. Thank you."

Huh! I got thanked! That's nice of her.

**You're welcome,** I write, because I have been trained from a young age to automatically respond to politeness with politeness. That just seems to make her more embarrassed, though. She annihilates another rock.

"...You really think it'll work?" she asks slowly. "The thing where we can fool aura checkers?"

Well, I guess there's an easy way to find out.

"**Aura Sight**," I beseech the Goddess to say on my behalf, opening up an extra sense to the world. Helen jolts a little when the words are spoken, almost bolting before she seems to realize I'm not attacking her.

From where I stand opposite to her, I can pretty easily see her aura's Chaos and Art elements. I also realize I can see my *own* aura's elements from my usual vantage point of looking at myself with my spatial sense. Neat! With that established, I crawl towards Helen, and sure enough the intensity of her Chaos flavor starts to diminish as I get closer. Hopping up into her lap, I find that it disappears completely. My own Order aura, likewise, gets a lot weaker, making the distinct taste of Transmutation a lot more noticeable by comparison. I hop off of her and increase the distance between us and approach again just to make sure it's consistent, but sure enough Hagoro seems to have been honest.

**Yep, it works,** I tell her. **As long as I'm on you at the time, you just look like a pure Art mage.**

"...Holy fucking shit," Helen sighs. "And you're not just like, tricking me with this? Leading me to a city where I'll get caught?"

Uh. Kind of a weird question. It's not like I would tell her if I was, but I doubt saying that would be helpful.

**Why would I do that?** I ask instead.

"Lots of fucking reasons, I don't know," Helen mutters, destroying another rock. "Too many to count. You came here with a Chaos hunter, for fuck's sake. Then you let that paladin go, that was fucking suspicious." She drums her fingers against her thigh, getting increasingly agitated. "If you're really a goodie-two-shoes that doesn't like killing people, but you wanted me dead, you'd take me somewhere I'd die on my own. Right?"

Where is this coming from? Is she paranoid?

**I don't like killing people, but I've done it,** I write to her. **If I wanted you dead, I wouldn't take you anywhere near a city**

574

**where other people might get hurt. I'd have just stabbed you through the head on the way here.**

Which would have been completely trivial. As much as I genuinely don't want to kill anyone, ever, I don't think I'd be able to live with myself if I thought Helen was going to cause another tragedy like she did with Kagiso's family and I just did nothing. I like to think I'd find the courage to stop her. I'm divinely chosen to travel between universes, for falafel's sake. I'd better be able to muster up *some* semblance of heroism.

"Right, yeah," Helen mutters. "That makes sense. I'm just stupid."

**I'm not going to pretend to like you,** I write, since I want to be clear about that. **But I don't hate you, either. I'm willing to give you a chance.**

"A chance, huh?" she scoffs.

**Yes. Because Kagiso obviously cares about you, and I care about Kagiso.**

"Why the fuck *does* she care about me?" Helen asks.

**You'd know better than I would. I just met you.**

She's quiet for a bit before answering.

"I guess we were kinda friends," she admits softly. "I didn't really belong in that village, and everybody knew it. They were all nice, but I was still the newcomer to a place where most people have lived with their family for generations, and I was the only human besides. At first it was just... somewhere to stay for a few nights before moving on, you know? But even though I was an outsider, everyone was so kind."

She looks up at the canopy above us, letting out a pained sigh.

"But to Kagiso, I never even was an outsider. I don't know if she understands what that means. The only part of me being human that she cared about was the fact that I could eat more meat than everyone else. The little freak really liked shooting stuff, cooking it up, and feeding it to me. Probably because it got her family off her back about killing wastefully. She's just... a total weirdo."

She says it all with a slight smile on her face, though. A fond smile, there for only a moment before it vanishes.

"...And then I went and destroyed it all. Ruined everything, like I always do. I should have known better than to stay."

**You said that in order to avoid that, you just have to use your magic more,** I write. **Is that true?**

"Huh?" she grunts. "Oh. I mean, yeah, but by 'use my magic more' I mean like *this.*"

She twists around, holding out a hand towards a patch of ground behind her. At first, nothing seems to happen, but before long a vibrating, spherical void appears as a tiny point in space. It expands outward, consuming air and earth alike before eventually vanishing, leaving a crater about three feet in diameter in its wake.

"I have to actually destroy stuff, you know? A lot of stuff. And that tends to leave a lot of evidence, especially in a small village that knows the surrounding area like they know a pimple on their nose. So I tried to get by with less, but... well, I was just fooling myself, and everyone paid for it."

She sighs, slumping over and grabbing another rock to destroy in her palm. If she has to do so much more than that, what's with the rocks? Is it just a habit? Was that how she was trying to hide and contain her powers while in Kagiso's village, and it just ended up not working?

"That's why we're going our separate ways once we make it to a lower branch. Okay?"

I don't answer, because I'm not entirely sure how to answer. As far as I'm concerned, it's not up to me whether or not the current group sticks together. Sure enough, Kagiso returns long before I would have finished scribbling out my sentences anyway. Helen orders me to move and then obliterates everything I've written before Kagiso can see it, which I guess is fair. She's entitled to a private conversation if she wants to keep it that way. Kagiso has slaughtered some kind of big snake thing that'll be more than enough food for all three of us, so at least that's taken care of. I wait for her to carve out a large portion for Helen and a smaller portion for herself before tearing into the rest of the corpse raw. The monster is longer than Kagiso is tall and noticeably thicker, but I am *exceptionally* hungry and have no qualms about devouring the entire thing, bones and all.

By the time Kagiso has finished cooking and the three of us have finished eating, the sun is already starting to go down. While burrowing my way into the carcass of a giant monster and eating my way back out like a chestburster *has* been extremely fun, it's also been a pretty inefficient method of consumption. Kagiso would clap every single time I emerged, though! I was basically required to keep going. Helen, on the other hand, glances between the two of us like she just figured out the solution to a curious mystery and doesn't like the answer one bit. It's not a big deal, though. We're not chasing anyone anymore, and while we might be *running* from someone, we have both a massive head start and the advantage of them not having any idea where we are. No birds tracking us, now that Sindri's dead. And speaking of Sindri, Helen must have nicked more than just his wallet, because she and Kagiso start setting up his tent, too.

The camp only has two tents now instead of three, but there's still something painfully familiar *about* watching the others set up camp. Whenever I started to apologize for not being able to help, it was Teboho that assured me things were okay and that everyone was simply doing what they can... and it was Sindri that ensured we'd never really argue with each other in the first place, whether we liked it or not.

Desperate to distract myself, I glance over to the pit Helen made with her Chaos magic. Perfectly round and perfectly smooth. There's something uniquely beautiful about it, really. On a whim I dash towards it at full speed, and right when my feet would drop across the edge I curl up into a ball, rolling along the rim. I make three quick rotations around the inside before finally rolling to a stop, feeling exhilarated and somewhat silly. That was pretty fun, though!

"Where did you even find that weird thing?" Helen mutters to Kagiso.

"Under rock," Kagiso shrugs.

Hey, that was a *burrow,* thank you very much. It's been a really long time since I've dug at all, come to think of it. I mean, unless my dinner today counts. I guess it kind of does. Still, though! Thinking about it, Helen mentioned that she couldn't make holes like this because it would get her found out, so doesn't that mean people might use these holes to track us? Like, if someone came across it, they'd probably go 'oh hey, a Chaos mage was here.' So I guess I'll just... dig around the area to hide it some? That'll probably help. It's sad to see such a perfect hole go, though.

"Hana!" Kagiso calls out. "Take first watch?"

I wriggle my way up out of the dirt and write a quick affirmative. Kagiso nods, she and Helen heading to their tents to sleep. With all the energy from my recent meal and my sudden burrowing compulsion I end up putting *way* too much effort into fixing the hole Helen made, but when I'm done with it the packed dirt looks pretty much the same as it did pre-destruction. Good job, me! Oh wait crap I think I've been doing this way past when I was supposed to wake up second watch.

Who is supposed to be second watch, anyway? Do I wake Helen or Kagiso? I'm hesitant about leaving our lives in Helen's hands, but only because I suspect she's not used to *taking* watches, since she's been traveling alone. I doubt she'll betray us in the middle of the night for no reason, and it's not like Kagiso and I are going to only get half a night's sleep every night from now on. We'll have to include Helen at some point. So I go wake her, since that means I'll get to snuggle into bed with Kagiso. My warm, fuzzy friend barely stirs after I manage to coax Helen out of her tent and crawl into my favorite sleeping bag. Snuggling into the crook of Kagiso's arm, I quickly pass into slumber.

...And then I wake up, because that's how my life works. Limbs, check. Body, check. New mutations... don't see any. I head into the shower like normal, and sure enough my newly-budding eyes don't look much different than yesterday. The skin is a little darker, maybe? Nothing makeup can't fix. I give myself a quick wash, eat the small patches of skin that come off of my legs, and head downstairs to swallow a few eggs. Something about this feels weird, but not in a bad way. It takes me until I make it to the bus stop and turn to face the direction Brendan will arrive from before I figure it out.

It's all become a routine. Everything I did this morning was more or less automatic, totally thoughtless from scrubbing the chitin on my extra limbs to using my spatial sense to ensure no one catches me swallowing raw eggs. None of that felt weird today. It was just... what I do now. I feel like that should be scary, but it's mostly just a relief. I wave at Brendan as he arrives, and he waves back.

"Still covering up?" he asks as he approaches. "You already revealed everything on stream yesterday. Which was awesome, by the way."

"That was online, though!" I whine. "Coming out online is *way* easier than doing it in real life! It basically doesn't even count."

"'Coming out?'" he repeats, raising an eyebrow.

"Eh. Coming out as gay, coming out as being a monster... it's honestly a coin toss on which my family will be more horrified by."

"I hate how that probably isn't a joke," Brendan sighs.

"If I'm being real they'll probably be way cooler about the monster stuff," I shrug. "At least all their favorite news channels aren't running political hit pieces against people with chitin."

"Well, at least you seem to be in good humor today," Brendan says, shaking his head. "Feels good to get it out there in part at least, doesn't it?"

"…Yeah," I admit after a moment of thought. "Yeah, I guess it does."

Brendan nods slowly, taking a deep breath and letting it out. I'm so happy to have him as a friend. Without his help I don't think I'd be doing even half this well. He's the one who gave me the courage to set that subscriber incentive in the first place!

"Thank you, Brendan," I tell him, because it needs to be said.

"I think I might be transgender," Brendan blurts.

…

Huh?

What?

"Transgender?" my dumb face asks.

"Y-yeah," Brendan says. "Y'know, like… the T in LGBT? I'm saying I might be a girl."

"Oh," I manage to say, which is a *stupid* thing to say, holy carp what is wrong with me? This is… this is huge! I need to be supportive!

"I-I'm not like, y'know, sure. It's just something I've been thinking about and I figured I'd mention it. Try to… well, get it out there. At least in part. Um, I mean, it's probably nothing, but…"

"No! Nono, it's… I'm sorry, it's good, that's good!" I stammer. "I was just surprised, is all! I just, I mean, I don't know very much about that sort of thing, but I am with you one hundred percent! It's good! Girl is good. You're good. Yep."

Oh my Goddess, Brendan would be *so cute* in a skirt. Man, none of my clothes are gonna fit him, though. Er, fit her? Maybe? Point is, that's criminal.

"…You're imagining me as a girl, aren't you?" Brendan says flatly.

"You will be *adorable,*" I confirm."I mean, not that you aren't adorable right now. Or, well, not in *that way,* but… um, I mean I guess maybe that way? Oh Goddess, is this why I used to want to date you so badly? Is that how it works? Is that *not* how it works? Am I being offensive!?"

"It's fine, Hannah," Brendan says, chuckling slightly. "I appreciate the support, but like I said I'm not sure yet."

"Oh, right! Right, yeah. Yep." Aaaaa girl Brendan, though! "I assume this is a Friend Code secret?"

"For now, yeah," he(!?!?!) nods. "Thanks."

"Of course! Of course, yeah. Wow."

I am going to have to do so much research I am very out of my depth.

The bus arrives, and that means this conversation is officially over until we're alone again, but my brain is still left reeling. I pretty much zone entirely out of the rest of the bus ride *and* all of English class, though as Biology approaches I realize I'm going to be seeing Autumn so I do my best to get my brain in working order.

Brendan's revelation is… a lot, and despite being gay as hell I feel pretty under-educated about trans people, but thinking about it logically I'm pretty sure my job as a friend is to just support whatever identity gets decided on. Maybe ask a few questions here and there. Oh gosh will Brendan stop being Brendan? Will he change his name!? I guess probably! Oh noooo I'm going to mess it up all the time and feel so bad. No! Bad Hannah brain! Focus on Autumn, and I guess Biology maybe, if you have room. Actually, wait, where *is* Autumn? Her seat is empty.

It's empty when class starts and it remains empty after class ends. Autumn… isn't at school today. That seems strange. Hopefully it's nothing? I wonder if I should text her. I feel like that'd be overstepping boundaries? Gosh, I don't know. This could be a horrific magical emergency, but it could also just be a cold! I worry about it all the way through third period and into lunch, where sure enough she's not in the library either. Definitely absent.

"Catch, weirdo," Ida says behind me, and I'm turning to intercept what she tosses at me before it even leaves her hand, my spatial sense telling me its trajectory instinctively. My hands clap around a huge bag of Kentucky Fried Chicken.

"I noticed you avoid the lunch room on days they don't serve meat," Ida smirks. "So I made sure to pick something up for you. Bam. Day improved."

"Um... th-thank you," I stutter, blinking in surprise. Golly gosh, this smells *good.* "What are you doing in the library, Ida?"

"Uh, looking for your nerdy ass, what else?" Ida fires back. "What's up? You seem a little freaked out."

"Oh, I'm just..." I start, instinctively going for a deflection before Ida steps forwards and karate chops me in the side of the throat. Ow!

"No bullshitting me. What's up, Hannah?"

"Uh..." I manage, wincing as I rub the spot she hit. I guess she *is* in the know for everything that matters here. "Autumn is absent today, which might be nothing but it might be... y'know. A very big something. She knows about me."

"Uh, woah. Going fast and hard on your crush, huh?" Ida smirks. "How bold of you, Hannah."

"I-It's not like that!" I sputter. "It was a total accident. She kind of knows and she kind of doesn't, it's complicated. I don't know if she has magic or not, but if she *does* and it's related..."

"Then that could be really bad, right," Ida sighs. "Well, do you have her number? Have you tried texting her?"

"I don't know if it's appropriate to do that when she's kind of avoiding—"

A conspicuous buzzing sound erupts from my phone, cutting off my sentence. My sense of dramatic timing compels me to check it, and sure enough...

"...It's a text from Autumn," I say despondently.

"Of *course* it is," Ida says, rolling her eyes. "What does it say?"

**What's happening??? Jet says you can help???**

"Aw, crapbaskets," I sigh.

Judging by those two sentences I'm going to guess 'magic things,' I text back. **Are you safe and alone?**

**Are you fucking with me right now?** she asks.

**No. I'm sorry.**

Those three dots that indicate she's typing appear and disappear over and over, a long period of stress where she's either writing an essay or repeatedly changing her mind on what to say. Judging by the length of her message, it's the latter.

**Jet says you can help. Can you help?**

**I can try**, I promise. **Don't investigate any weird feelings and try not to push any new mental buttons until I get there, okay?**

**Are you coming over???**

"Hey Ida, could I have a ride to Autumn's house?" I ask.

"Of course," she nods seriously.

"We might end up missing classes," I warn her.

She rolls her eyes.

"I'm *even more* down to give you a ride now, you chitinous baboon."

**Unless you don't want me to come over, yeah,** I text Autumn back. **It's probably for the best. It would be easier and safer than trying to explain all this over text.**

It takes a while for her to respond again, but it's a simple enough message.

**Okay.**

I nod to Ida and we both wordlessly sprint to her car while I quickly send a text to Brendan letting him know that Autumn needs magical aid and I might be late getting back from lunch. I just have to hope that the magic secret police either don't control the NSA or just think we're talking about a game or something. Surely they can't screen every text message with the word 'magic' in it? It's probably safe as long as we don't write down any details on how real magic actually works.

With how much Ida speeds, it doesn't take long for us to get to Autumn's house. Ida and I agree that she should stay in the car, since she and Autumn don't really know each other and Autumn seemed pretty freaked out. I really, really hope she's not in danger! Bursting out of the car, I rush up her sidewalk and ring the doorbell once before I remember that hers doesn't work and knock instead.

**Come in,** she texts me.

I do so and close the door behind me, calling out to her.

"Autumn! It's me!"

"Hannah!" she calls back, but I've already found her with my spatial sense and so make my way to a small bathroom, in which she sits on the floor looking completely shell-shocked. The first thing my stupid brain notices is that she's in her underwear, but the more relevant points of interest filter into my conscious thought soon enough. Her ears are different, in a subtle but noticeable way. Just a little too pointy, and a little too high up on her head for humans. They're moving, growing, changing shape too slowly to track with the human eye but no less inevitably.

I doubt her ears are the source of all the blood, though.

Her whole back is stained with dried, crusted brown-red, the back of her bra soaked through and probably ruined. She's no longer actively bleeding, but the source of the wound is all the more obvious because of it: two twitching proto-limbs emerge from between her shoulder blades, small and far from fully formed. They must have torn themselves free from the skin of her back this morning, the tiny, leathery wings far too small to function but doubtlessly still growing.

"Wh-what's happening to me?" Alma whispers, tears running down her face and dropping onto her knees as she rocks back and forth on the floor.

"Well, uh… remember when you told me you love urban fantasy?" I say hesitantly, taking off my glove and wiggling my fingers at her. "Congratulations. You live in it."

She faints, and I barely have time to catch her before she hits her head.

# 30

# ALMA'S HOUSE

Okay! Status report, brain: we're inside Autumn's house, she's mutating into a monster like I am, she is *in her underwear* and I am *touching her*, she is *very* soft, and oh gosh oh no oh beans she's unconscious she fell unconscious aaaaah that's really really bad!!!

Status confirmed: this problem is way too big for a stupid little Hannah to handle on her own. I whip out my phone and call Ida.

"Did you fuck it up already?" she says as soon as she answers.

"I showed her my fingers and she fainted and now she's unconscious and I don't know what to do!"

"Oh fuck, alright, I'll be there in a sec. She's breathing, right? Did she hit her head?"

Uhh oh geez that's a good question!? Wait, yeah, she's breathing, her diaphragm is moving, her heart is beating. I can't see those things yet but I still know them somehow.

"Yeah, she's breathing. And I caught her head before she could hit anything."

"Alright, save the panic then, she'll be fine. See you soon."

She hangs up on me, leaving me along with a cute girl under my arm. Goddess dangit I am blushing so hard. I need to be focusing, but all I can think about is the fact that I'm kneeling down here with her, my arm across her back, and *cut it out brain, do something useful!* Though I mean... I guess there's nothing I *can* do other than make sure she doesn't stop breathing, at least as far as I know. If she's not injured, she'll probably wake up on her own.

Just like that, her eyes flutter open. They bulge upon seeing me for a moment, but then suddenly narrow. Autumn glances around and frowns at me.

"...You two had better not been snogging or something," she grumbles.

"What?" I blink. Oh, right, this is probably Jet. "No! She fainted. I had to catch her."

"Alright, well, let go of me. I'm f—"

"I'm here," Ida grunts, peeking her head through the doorway and glancing up and down at Autumn's body. "Woah! Nice."

"Who the fuck is this?" Jet growls. "Did Alma invite you in?"

"I invited her in, Jet," I say. "Because again, you *fell unconscious.* I freaked out a little. She knows magic, too."

Jet opens her mouth to protest as she sits up on her own, scooting away from me, but then she sighs.

"Okay, fine. Thank you for doing whatever you thought you needed to do to help me. Fainting definitely isn't normal for us, but we have lost a *lot* of blood today. Also: this is your fault, isn't it? Fuck you."

Shakily, she gets to her feet, twisting to look at her back in the bathroom mirror. Oh beans and rice that pose does *wonderful* things to her muscles aaaah oh no Hannah stop looking. Jet's hand-sized, still-budding wings wiggle, and she grimaces. Crap, say something, say something!

"I mean... I dunno if it's my fault?" I hedge. "Though it's either my fault or the Goddess' fault, I guess."

"The same goddess that turned you into swiss cheese for wasting a few seconds of her time?" Jet asks.

"Uh, that one, yeah."

"I think I'll blame you, then," she grunts. "Safer that way. So what the fuck happened?"

"Uh… I mean, it looks like you're probably a Transmutation mage, like me," I tell her. "So… now you get to suffer. Sorry!"

"Oh my god, Hannah, what the fuck kind of encouragement is that?" Ida says, bursting into a series of giggles. "This is why she fainted, isn't it?"

"Goddess," I correct her. "And I've had weeks to get over this, sorry. Like, I know it's kind of inconsiderate, but it's hard to not be excited about having someone else who understands what I'm going through."

"I don't think I do," Jet grunts. "I only dealt with half of this. Alma had the… initial effects happen to her. I just cleaned up the blood."

"You want me to help with that?" I ask. "I have a cleaning spell."

"Of course you do," Jet grumbles.

"Sorry, I'm a little behind on the story here," Ida chimes in. "Who's Alma?"

"My headmate," Jet grimaces, glancing away. "I have DID."

"Oh. Cool," Ida shrugs.

"In my case it really isn't," Jet mutters, but she smirks a bit as she says so. "I'm Jet, by the way."

"Ida," Ida nods. "I'm Hannah's competent friend."

"Well good, because she sure fucking needs one."

Hey! Brendan's competent. …Otherwise, fair.

"I'm sorry, can we stop roasting me for a moment and deal with the magical transformation stuff?" I groan. "I feel like that might be a better use of our time."

"Deal with it how?" Jet challenges. "Judging by your entire fucking body, I assume you don't have a way to reverse this. The help I wanted from you is for you to talk to Alma and explain what's going on so she'll calm down, but *apparently* whatever you did just made her pass out and swap back to me again, and I sure as hell don't have a plan!"

"I don't know how to calm her down!" I yelp. "I don't know how to calm *me* down! I have like five panic attacks a week because of this crap! I can give you tips on how to cover up, but..."

"We don't *need* tips on how to cover up, we have plenty of experience with that," Jet snaps. "What we need is some idea of how to control this."

"I don't know *how* to control Transmutation magic!" I fire back. "Mine just... *goes!"*

"Wait," Ida says. "Both of you calm down. Let's back up on that, Hannah. You're not controlling your Transmutation magic?"

"No! You think I want to look like this?"

"Then are you certain Jet is a Transmutation mage?"

My mouth falls open, but no words come out of it. I... surely not, right? This couldn't be... no. Oh no, it could. Back when Jet found me out and I tried to channel my Transmutation spell to heal myself, nothing seemed to happen but I was definitely doing *something*. Jet even said that she felt tingly. I ended up figuring out that my self-changing spell wasn't only Transmutation magic, but that doesn't mean I wasn't casting anything. It just means I was casting something that I wasn't trying to cast. Is this my fault? Is this really my fault!?

"**Aura Sight**," I invoke, the Goddess licking her lips with anticipation as the knowledge floods into my mind: Light. Jet's aura feels like Light, Pneuma, and a background hint of Barrier. She absolutely has magic, but none of it is Transmutation. No. No, no, no no no no!

"I... I'm contagious," I whisper in horror. "I did this to you. Oh Goddess, Jet, I'm so sorry."

"*Please* warn us before you do the divine invoking thing," Ida shudders. "She always fucking touches me, ugh."

"Sorry!"

"Wait, stop apologizing for a second," Jet presses. "Just explain. What did you do?"

"I... I just used a spell to figure out what kind of magic you have," I tell her. "And you don't have Transmutation! This has to be because of the magic you got exposed to on Saturday!"

Jet groans, running one hand through her hair which kinda looks like she's lathering it with shampoo, which of course my brain automatically connects to shower and the concept of a naked Autumn and oh dear my mental image of naked Autumn is *concerningly* clear, spatial sense why are you doing this please stop now is *not* the time!

"Yeah, okay, I figured it was something like that," Jet grumbles. "I'd be real fucking pissed at you if you weren't my only lifeline here. I know I said I didn't want to be involved, but I guess I don't have a choice now, so... fuck it. Tell me everything. Then stick around and tell Alma everything when she swaps in, ideally *without* making her pass out this time."

"S-sure," I nod. "But, um, could you put some clothes on first?"

"I'm sorta covered in blood," Jet points out.

I quickly flex my Order magic, pull all the lingering stains off of her back and bra, and drop all the gathered flakes of dried blood into the toilet.

"There," I announce. "Clean."

Jet blinks, checks herself over, and then throws her arms up in exasperation before stomping past us to presumably go find something to put on.

"Shit, I want that spell," Ida whines.

"I can probably teach it to you," I shrug.

"For real?"

"Yeah, I've named it so I can share it," I confirm. "We should take it slow, though. Invoking magic can still kill you if you do it wrong."

"But it's a *cleaning* spell, Hannah! That's so useful! Totally worth it."

"I guess so," I agree. "I really want your repair spell, too. I can't repair things."

"Oh, about that," Ida says, smugly putting her hands on her hips. "It's also a healing spell."

"Seriously?" I ask. "Your magic is nuts. All the more reason to want it, now."

"I dunno..." Ida says, smirking mischievously. "I really like having these cool spells to myself. They get less special if other people have them, you know?"

"Well, rest assured, it's *your* spell," I tell her. "You will always be the most powerful user of it. I'll be casting a drastically weaker version if you do choose to share it."

"Oh, that's less lame then," Ida nods. "Still though, is that how this whole mage thing works? We just get free magic and then incestuously leak it all to every other mage we know like a sewage-borne infection until everyone's a god?"

"Uh... no," I tell her. "It takes most people a really long time to name a new spell, let alone learn someone else's, and you can't actually learn most people's spells. You need to have the same or complementary elements. Like, while you can learn my Order spell, you won't be able to learn my Space spell, and Brendan's an Art mage so we won't be able to learn his magic at all and vice-versa."

Wait, shoot, should I have said 'her?' I didn't even think about... oh no, Brendan told me to keep it a secret anyway. Stay the course, Hannah!

"Aw," Ida frowns. "So I kind of miss out because I'm pure Order, huh? What about Autumn, can we learn whatever spells she gets?"

"Well, one of her elements was Pneuma, so she can certainly learn..."

I trail off, my eyes going wide with horror. Oh *fuck*, I didn't even think about that before.

"Uh, you okay?" Ida asks.

"Autumn's a Pneuma mage!" I hiss, grabbing Ida by the shoulders in panic.

"Yeah, okay, cool. Why are you freaking out about that?"

"That's soul magic! Mind control stuff! We could be in serious danger!"

"As opposed to danger from literally anything else involving magic?" Ida asks. "Come on, I seriously doubt Autumn knows how to cast, and if she did, why would she want to cast on *us?* You're overreact—"

"Don't!" I snap at her furiously, and she goes still. "Don't say I'm overreacting. You've never been mind raped. You don't get to talk."

Ida stares up at me for a moment, then nods slowly, gently pushing my arms off her shoulders.

"Okay," she says. "Then here's what we do: I'll go out to the car and wait. When you're done in there, you come out *alone,* without her, and I'll heal you when you get to me. That should get rid of any mind control."

I hesitate, stepping away from her. I hadn't meant to raise my voice or snap at her like that. I guess out of anyone to lose my cool at, I'm glad it was Ida. She's not even fazed.

"...How would you know whether or not your healing spell gets rid of mind control?" I ask. "That seems like a pretty big stretch."

"Hannah, please," Ida dismisses. "You're friends with the best, remember? It'll work. Trust me."

I hesitate. I really, *really* don't like this plan.

"The alternative is for us to both scarper, right now, and leave Autumn to deal with this shit without an explanation," Ida reminds me.

Dang it, she's right. I've been burned by a Pneuma mage before, but... just *being* a Pneuma mage doesn't automatically mean you mind control people, right? Pneuma is soul magic. Maybe it helps her with her own soul or something. It could let her swap between her two selves more easily! Yeah, it's probably just that. ...Or is that what I would think if I was being mind controlled!?

...Ugh, it doesn't matter. I don't think I can bring myself to leave Autumn in the lurch. I either have to trust her to not be that sort of person or trust Ida to be strong enough to save me. I can do both. I hope.

"Okay," I agree. "See you later, Ida. I'll text you if I need you."

"If you ask me to come inside I'll assume you're compromised," Ida warns. "You *know* I'm not falling for anything stupid, so don't try it."

"Understood," I nod.

She nods back and departs. I take a deep breath and let it out slowly. It's fine. It'll all be fine.

"Already plotting without me, huh?" Jet asks behind me, causing me to let out a *very* undignified scream and scramble into some semblance of a fighting stance before remembering that we had that entire conversation in the middle of her house. She's returned from putting on a tank top and shorts because of course she has, dressing oneself doesn't take very long.

I take a deep breath, calming myself as best I can. Ida's right, Autumn probably knows nothing about the kinds of magic she can do. Should I hide it from her? ...No, wait, that's stupid, that always backfires. Honesty is the best policy, as always.

"Kinda, yeah," I admit. "You have a really, *really* scary kind of magic, a kind I've been heavily traumatized by. I needed to work something out with Ida so I don't just freak out and leave."

594

Her eyebrows raise.

"Oh. Huh. Alright. Something powerful?" she asks.

"Something subtle," I answer, shaking my head. "There are a bunch of types of magic, but the one you have that I'm afraid of is Pneuma. It's soul magic, and a guy used it to mind control me into being a slave once. I'm very much not over it."

"Uh, holy shit, I'd imagine not?" Jet says, her eyes going wide. "That sounds *super* fucked up. I never want to use that kind of power."

I let out a slow breath.

"Well… it's really reassuring to hear you say that," I admit. "But the thing about mind control is that I have to second-guess everything I think about anything, so…"

"So shit's fucked, I got you," Jet nods. "Look, I don't know anything about any of this stuff, but the last thing I wanna do is cause problems. The way I see it, you're in control here. You say jump, I'll say how high, because someone basically just threw me into a goddamned nuclear reactor room and I have nothing but your instructions to go by to prevent a complete meltdown."

"Alright," I nod. "I guess… I'll start with the basic warnings and work from there?"

"Sure," Jet nods back. "Use me as practice for explaining all this to Alma. You wanna sit down? Have you had lunch?"

Aw turds on toast I left the KFC Ida got me in her car.

"Um, yeah, food would be nice, thank you. Um, I'm a carnivore, though."

"Well I'm not a vegan so I can probably find something for you to eat," Jet smirks, and I swear I see her too-long ears wiggle a little bit.

Her home is a lot smaller than mine, with no second story and a pretty cramped kitchen-living room combo. It's also kind of messy, with rough carpet that clearly used to be a much lighter shade and a concerning amount of dust over everything. I can't help but magically sweep it up as I make my way over to an old couch and sit down after giving it an *extra* big blast of magic and shoving the huge clump of I-don't-want-to-guess-what-it-all-is out a nearby window. Jet frowns at the sight, but doesn't comment.

"Okay..." I say, gathering my thoughts. "I guess the best place to start is the Goddess. She gave you a soul at some point, and that soul lets you use magic. But the soul is ultimately part of Her power, and to use your spells at their strongest you have to invoke Her. That's what happens when I say a spell out loud, and as you saw... there are some pretty severe consequences for doing so incorrectly."

"Right," Jet nods. "Magic is super dangerous, check."

"Using your magic *without* invoking the Goddess' attention is both possible and pretty safe, though. I was told the magic you get is based on who you are, and while I can't really confirm that, I know people generally aren't ever hurt by their own spells, even if those spells are extremely destructive. Like, I know somebody who has *disintegration magic.* She can just remove matter from existence entirely, but she hasn't so much as lost a finger."

"Okay, with you so far," Jet says, grabbing a pan and setting it to heat up on the stove.

"There are a bunch of different magical elements, and you have three, which is apparently really rare. Pneuma, like I said, plus Light and a little bit of Barrier, though that one feels way weaker than your other two."

"Those are some weird names," Jet grunts. "Alma would know more about this shit than I would, but I've never heard of 'barrier magic' before. I've heard of Light, but that one's a huge surprise, frankly. Call me an edgelord but I'd have assumed I'd get Dark, if anything."

"Oh, um, I mean you might have?" I tell her. "Light magic encompasses anything you do with light. So making it, altering it, or removing it. Darkness as a concept is inherent to Light."

"Well fuck, I guess I'm an edgelord after all," she sighs, dropping some things into the pan and letting them sizzle. Whatever it is, it smells salty and delicious.

"Maybe!" I respond. "I have no idea, honestly. But the thing is, you probably will. The magic you get should resonate with you, and you'll be able to call it pretty instinctively. From my and Ida's experience, you'll be able to do it even without much practice. It just... feels right, y'know? And the more you use it, the better you'll understand it, and the stronger you'll be able to make it. At least, I think that's how it works. Some of that is conjecture, but I'm learning to trust my instincts when it comes to magic."

"And is that why my body's all fucked up now?" Jet asks. "Because you started using spells instinctively, without understanding or practice?"

She says it so mildly, like it's a comment on the weather rather than an accusation that I have permanently and fundamentally destroyed her life due to my carelessness. The words push an ache into my chest, sparking the eternal flame of guilt ever brighter.

"...Essentially, yes," I admit quietly. "I'm sorry."

She doesn't respond, focusing on whatever she's cooking for a while, the crackle of the skillet turning what would be an awkward silence into merely an awkward delay. After a few minutes the noise stops and with a clink of silverware she's heading my way with two plates. She hands me a greasy, sausage-filled omelet that sets my mouth immediately watering. Her own omelet seems to have a lot more ingredients: I see mushrooms, peppers, and onions at a glance, and it makes me long for them. But ultimately, while I can probably digest them, I know they wouldn't actually taste how they used to. Those flavors just don't register on my tongue anymore. I dig into my eggs and sausage, however, and it's beauty in my mouth. What the heck, how is this so good?

"This is delicious," I say, quickly swallowing another bite.

"Uh, thanks I guess," Jet shrugs. "I just made it because it's fast and easy."

"Well, I usually eat raw eggs for breakfast, so this is worlds better!"

Jet stares at me for a moment.

"You should stop eating raw eggs for breakfast," she says patiently.

I'm definitely not going to do that.

"You're probably right," I agree honestly.

Jet eats a lot slower than I do, using a knife and fork to carefully take apart the fluffy eggy goodness and eat it piece by piece. Out of sheer awkward energy, I purposefully try to slow down, but since I don't really chew things I instead have to stand up and ask where the glasses are so I can get us water. That and the occasional slow sip wastes enough time that I can keep pace with Jet's slow eating speed. I don't want to pressure her to go faster!

About halfway through her food, though, Jet seems to stop eating entirely, pausing mid-cut with a knife to blink a few times. She quickly glances around, though the confusion the action implies is expertly hidden from her face. When she finally glances up and looks at me, her eyes widen ever so slightly. She swallows, even though no food is currently in her mouth.

This isn't Jet anymore, is it?

"Autumn?" I hedge, since the last time I called her 'Alma' she kind of freaked out at me.

"Hannah," she nods, staring really obviously at my teeth. "Hey."

"Sorry for scaring you earlier," I blurt.

"I... yeah," she says dumbly. "Sorry for... getting scared. I mean, it's still you, right?"

"It's still me," I nod. "I've, uh, pretty much been like this the whole time."

"Yeah," she says, seemingly to herself. "That makes a lot of sense. The blood in the bathroom."

"Yeah, that... was my teeth falling out. Not a fun time."

"I bet," she agrees. I see the straps of her tanktop shift a little, and I know instinctively that she's wiggling her stubby wings. "I haven't had a fun morning, myself."

"You seem to be a lot calmer now," I point out.

She's quiet for a moment before answering.

"Jet was calm," she eventually says. "Jet... came to terms with stuff while we shifted over. I still kind of have that mood now that I'm me."

I nod, not really understanding but wanting to be supportive anyway. Something certainly feels different about her that I can't put my finger on. Beyond the fact that her personality is different, I mean. But it's nothing physical, I don't think, so what could... oh! I focus on her with my still-active Aura Sight, and sure enough her Barrier magic suddenly feels way stronger and her Light magic feels barely there. The taste of Pneuma feels the same, though. Interesting.

"Jet, uh, wanted me to explain some things to you," I say awkwardly. "Are you cool with that, or...?"

She nods, resuming her meal, so I take a breath and get started. Sure enough, having done it with Jet first really does help, and I know some of the important things to emphasize and the stupid things to not say. Alma seems genuinely fascinated, a lot of the nerdy love for this kind of stuff that Brendan has coming through in her expression, but it's tempered by hard-earned cynicism. Alma's taste in fiction is considerably darker than Brendan's, from what I've picked up, and she recently had her back explode in a fountain of blood this morning. She's frightened, but she's equally excited, and that gives me hope that things will be okay.

"So the *whole time* we were on our date, you had the freaky hands and teeth and stuff," Alma clarifies.

"That's why I had a smoothie for lunch," I confirm. "So I could just stick the straw up through my mask without taking it off."

"Ohhh my god, that makes so much sense. I was afraid you had an eating disorder!" she chuckles.

"*I* was afraid that you'd *think* I had an eating disorder!" I grin back moments before my brain ticks backwards and replays the conversation a little. "...Wait, did you say 'date?'"

"Uh..." Alma says, a blush forming on her face. "I mean... I had fun? Until the whole mugging thing, anyway. I'd be down to, y'know, do something like that again. Assuming the government doesn't find us and lock us up."

Wait, really? *Really!?* Oh my gosh oh my gosh.

"You're cool with the whole 'I'm turning you into a literal monster' thing?" I ask. "Because like, that's a hundred percent my fault."

"Well... yeah, but you didn't do it on purpose, right?" she hedges. "And, I mean, honestly I don't know if I can complain about having wings. It's scary as hell, but it's not like I have a life to get screwed up by it, you know? I've just sorta been... existing."

Is that a good reason to be okay with it? That doesn't seem like a good reason to be okay with it. She continues before I can comment though.

"Are *you* okay with it?" Alma presses. "Like, you know about Jet, and... y'know. I won't always be around."

"I mean, that's fine?" I say. "I like Jet. I don't think she wants to date me—"

"They don't wanna date *anybody,*" Alma grumbles.

"Uh, yeah, and that's her right I think? Or their right? I'm sorry, have I been using the wrong pronoun this whole time?"

"Oh, not really," Alma shrugs. "She or they. Last I checked Jet's fine with either."

"Right, okay, so um... Jet's neat. I like her. I also like you. And I know you two would have to work out anything in the dating sphere, and... well I mean, honestly, we should probably be talking about the whole magical transformation problem, not dating, but my *point* is that I'd be happy with whatever you guys work out. I *assume* I'd just be dating you but not Jet, and we'd have to work around that? That's fine with me."

"We should definitely be talking about the magical transformation problem," Alma agrees. "But that's scary so let's keep talking about dating."

Oh gosh oh no she's going to enable my bad habits why is that hot.

"I don't... like getting close to people," Alma continues. "People scare me. Part of it is because *Jet* scares me. I barely even know them, but they run half my life. They've made some things better, and I'm grateful for that, but they've made some things a lot worse. Like, they've gotten us arrested and stuff, you know? They say they just want to help, but... I don't know. It's scary, not being able to remember so much. I'm embarrassed about it and every time I *have* opened up about them it's gone horribly. Nobody seems to *get it.* But... you kinda do."

Huh?

"Uh, I assure you that I do *not,*" I tell her."I have no idea what you're going through, I just... y'know. Take what little I do understand and be polite about it. Jet explained how you two want to be treated and so I'm just rolling with that."

"Well, most people don't even do that much," Alma shrugs. "So thank you. It means more than you think just to hear stuff like being called 'you two.' To not be lumped in with them. I appreciate that a lot."

"Oh," I say dumbly. "Well, uh, no problem I guess."

"Anyway, that's... all I wanted to say," Alma shrugs, blushing slightly. "I really appreciate you reaching out to me over lunch and inviting me to do things and I'm really happy you turned out to be so nice and it feels maybe a little fast but I definitely find you attractive so if things work out with Jet then, um, yes. I'd very much like to date."

Aaaaaaaaaaaaaaaaaaaaaaaaaaaaaaaaaaaaaaaaaaaaaaaaaa!!!          Oh
Goddess oh Goddess oh Goddess oh Goddess *a cute girl thinks I'm
attractive and wants to date me!!!*

"I... even the monster bits?" I manage to ask.

She hesitates a bit at that, which causes me to briefly panic, but
then it passes and she gives me a shy smile.

"Well I mean I'm not going to say it isn't a little weird..." she admits
quietly. "But, um, it isn't like I'm not in the same boat now! We can
be weird together!"

She wiggles her ears at that, and I can't help but bust out into a
small chuckle.

"Well," I say, "that's amazing and I'd love to date you too! In fact, I'll
probably hyperventilate and die later just thinking about it. But
speaking of things we need to talk to Jet about, I *do* want to
mention some other details about your magic."

"Oh?" she asks, leaning back a bit. "I'm definitely excited to try it
out."

"Well, interestingly, I think it's likely you and Jet have different
spells," I say. "I don't know if you each have your own soul or if you
have a shared soul that manifests differently, but *you* have a really
strong Barrier aura and a really weak Light aura, while Jet has the
opposite. You both have an equally strong Pneuma aura."

"That's the scary mind control one, right?" she asks, leaning back in
her seat.

Yes. Yes, it is the scary mind control one. The one that had me
wrapped around a man's finger for weeks without ever knowing it.
The one where I have to constantly remind myself not to think
about the fact that Alma has it, and then just panic about whether
or not I'm being mind controlled into not thinking about it instead.
It's that kind of magic.

"That's... correct," I confirm, swallowing nervously. "Though it's
possible your Pneuma magic just manages your soul, or maybe it

manages the fact that you have two souls, or maybe it does something else entirely. There's supposedly a lot of things Pneuma mages can do that have nothing to do with mind control."

And I'll just have to keep telling myself that to stave off the panic attack. It'll be fine.

"Well, I can figure out my Barrier spells and ignore the Pneuma spells, right?"

"Uh... hypothetically maybe? But practically speaking, no. If you're anything like me you'll stumble into using all your spells in one way or another. Plus, there's always the chance that you don't have any pure-Barrier spells and all your magic is a combination of Pneuma *and* Barrier."

"What kind of magic would that even be?" Alma wonders.

"Well, I dunno, that's for you to find out," I shrug. "It's your magic."

"My magic," she repeats, awe filling her voice. "Wow. So Barrier is like... what? Walls and stuff?"

"Walls, zones, areas," I list, nodding. "It's the antithesis of Motion. It's about halting, preventing, defending, or doing something in a particular chunk of space. Why? Do you feel something? Magic *should* be pretty instinctive if you're looking for it."

"Kinda, yeah," Alma nods. "But uh, shouldn't I practice this alone? What if you get hurt?"

"Well first of all, fair's fair on the 'magical experimentation in public' thing. Second of all, I'd rather be here to help and share what I know than to just leave you to figure it out alone. And third of all, if things *do* go really badly, I have a healer on standby in your driveway."

"Wait, what?" Alma asks. "A healer?"

I blink. Did she... oh *right*, she wasn't around when Ida was inside!

"Another mage friend," I tell her. "Her name's Ida. She drove me here."

"Ida? Ida Kelly? Like the popular bitch?"

Geez, why does everybody hate Ida? I mean, I guess she *does* hang out with a bunch of bullies most of the time. And she's so arrogant she literally has magic based on that. And she insults people constantly in basically every conversation. Okay maybe that was a stupid question.

"Yeah, that Ida," I nod. "She's really not all that bad once you get to know her. Y'know, if she likes you. But she'll probably like you! She seemed to get along with Jet."

"Hannah, you are literally the only person I know who gets along with both me and Jet."

"Well, sure, but how many people do you know?" I ask. "Like, actually know."

"...Low blow," Alma pouts, and I chuckle.

"Hey, I have... four friends, counting you," I assure her. "And counting alternate universes. So, y'know, I'm throwing stones from a glass house over here."

"Wait, alternate universes?" Alma asks. "That sounds like a really really important thing that you just sort of skipped over there."

"Uh... yeah, I'm an extradimensional spider on a world tree sometimes," I shrug. "It's kind of a whole thing, I'm not sure I wanna get into it right now."

Her jaw drops open and she takes a moment to try and figure out words to say before closing her mouth again. Open, closed. Open, closed.

"...Okay I *really* want you to get into it though, that just sounds... what? What the fuck? Other *universes?*"

"Look, it's... it's a lot, and a really important friend died over there recently and I just really don't want to think about it while I'm having a nice time, okay? I promise I'll explain later."

She huffs out a sigh, but nods.

604

"Alright, I'm sorry," she says. "But now that I'm going monster mode with you, you should at least answer this: is that gonna happen to me?"

Uh. Huh. That is a very good question I should have thought of sooner.

"I don't... think so?" I hedge. "I mean, you're not a Space mage. But if you do, it should happen whenever you sleep, so we'll know by tomorrow I guess. In the meantime, are you gonna test out your magic or not?"

"Okay, okay," Alma grumbles leaning forward in her chair enough for me to see the cloth of her shirt wiggle as her wings stretch out from being squished. "God, this feels so weird."

"Goddess," I correct. "I dunno if She cares about being correctly addressed, but I say better safe than sorry, especially when we're about to test magic for the first time."

"Goddess, okay," Alma nods. "...Fuck, religion is real."

"Right!?" I exclaim.

Alma lets out a huff of air that basically says "I'm way too overwhelmed to think about that right now," (which is a huge mood) before getting up and heading towards the center of the room, away from the couch. Then she closes her eyes, focusing on whatever feeling she perceives as her newly-budded magic. I wait quietly, letting her focus. When she finally opens her eyes, they open *wide,* an awed breath escaping her lips as she glances around, slack-jawed like she just got teleported to the Grand Canyon. I, too, glance around, but only because as far as I can tell, nothing whatsoever has changed.

"Uh, you okay, Alma?" I ask.

"Hannah?" Alma calls out as if she doesn't know where I am. She is maybe five feet in front of me.

"Yep, I'm here," I say. "Everything looks exactly the same to me."

"Wait, really?" she asks. "Not to me! I hear you, but I don't see you!"

She steps towards my voice and puts her hand out, seeming to come into contact with something invisible like a gosh dang mime. I stand up and cautiously walk towards her, reaching out my own hand to touch hers.

"What *do* you see?" I ask, and then I run into something. My outstretched hand stops barely four inches away from hers, and a ripple in the air blooms outwards from my touch, the crest of the wave revealing a solid wall wherever it passes. The wall is white with red, blue, and pastel pink speckles, with stripes on the trim where it intersects the floor and ceiling.

To be clear, I'm talking about where it intersects with the floor and ceiling *of this new room,* because I realize suddenly that I'm walking on tile, not carpet like I was before, and the ceiling is some sort of giant painting, depicting what looks like part of a face. I can't make it out, though, because the ripple that emitted when I touched the wall has lost most of its coherency, vanishing before revealing much and leaving most of the ceiling as a ghostly, fading apparition. I take my hand away and the entire wall starts to fade, but even after it disappears entirely it seems to still be *there.* I reach forward and touch it again, the ripple revealing its appearance once more.

Notably, what I can see of the wall intersects with some of the chairs in the room, passing through them as if they weren't even there. I take my hand away and let it vanish again, allowing me to see Alma wandering around on the other side of it. I can only assume *she* sees the building in its entirety, and as she moves towards the table in the middle of the room I get the distinct impression that she's seeing the magical building *instead* of the real one. I almost call out to her to stop her from walking into the table, but I'm too slow and she literally walks *into* the table. As in she steps directly through it, not interacting with it in the slightest. I wave my hand at a nearby chair and smack directly into it, though. What the frizzle is going on?

"This is so cool," Alma breathes, looking up and then starting to walk up a set of *invisible stairs,* which is about my sanity limit regarding this whole thing. I punch the closest invisible wall, hard, causing a powerful ripple to emit outwards and reveal the entire room to me. The picture on the ceiling is of a sleeping face, half of it Autumn's and half of it a dark mess of broken mechanical parts barely in the shape of a face at all. More importantly, though, it also reveals the room's exits. I take the one that I *think* will lead me towards Alma, but I can't really tell. My spatial sense is just as confused as the rest of me.

"This is awesome!" she announces. "It's like a giant house that I made with my mind!"

"It's *super* freaky from my perspective!" I call back, thumping another wall as I step into an area I can no longer see. This room *does* have chairs, a table, and couches, but they aren't in any of the same spots as the actual chairs, table, and couches, which I can *also see.* "You walked through a table and now you're going up stairs that don't exist!"

"If they don't exist, then how am I walking on 'em?" she challenges, a huge grin on her face. "Ever think about that? Huh?"

The current magic room fades away from my view just in time for me to witness Alma start phasing straight through the ceiling as she ascends. Oh gosh, that's probably not good.

"Alma, stop!" I yell up at her. "You're going through the roof! People might be able to see you!"

"Woah, shit, really?" she asks, backing down a couple stairs. "But I'm like... indoors."

"Yeah, and you're darn lucky the *giant magical house* you've apparently created is invisible to other people, because otherwise they'd see *that.*"

"...Oh," she says, blinking in surprise. "Yeah, that's... a very good point. So you can't see all this, huh?"

"I can see a little of it at a time, if I touch something," I inform her. "But I can *also* still see and interact with the original room, whereas you just walk right through it."

607

I finally make my way to the base of the magical staircase and meet Alma on the way down. She waves at me, adorably excited about this entire thing, and out of curiosity I ascend the stairs myself after kicking one to make it all visible. I don't see the end of the stairwell, of course, because from my perspective it just eventually intersects with the real house's ceiling. Sure enough, I can only walk up a few stairs because the ceiling is still tangible to me.

"You can't see this, huh?" I ask, pressing on the ceiling with one hand.

"No, you just look like a mime," Alma shrugs, reaching up and passing her hand straight through. "I don't see anything here."

"See, that's what it looks like to me when I watch you go up the stairs or touch walls or whatever," I say.

"Weird," Alma says. "So you're affected by the real world, and you're *also* affected by anything my magic creates, but you can't *see* anything my magic creates unless you touch it or something near it, whereas I can't see or touch anything real. That about sum it up?"

"Yeah," I nod. "This is *wild.* How big is this place?"

"I have no idea!" Alma says.

"Well, you should probably get rid of it for now, then," I tell her. "If it's bigger than your house then other people might accidentally run into it."

"Oh, that makes sense," Alma agrees. "How do I do that?"

"What?" I ask automatically, since the question is a little too scary to process.

"How do I turn it off?" Alma asks.

"Um," I respond eloquently. "You just... turn it off. Aren't you sustaining it with your magic?"

"Uh... not really? I just kinda *used* it, and it's here now."

Oh dear. That's probably bad.

"...We should figure out how to leave," I suggest.

Alma nods rapidly and we walk off the staircase together, me mostly just following her in an attempt to not run into anything I can't see. At some point she just straight up walks through a wall, though, leaving me completely in the lurch.

"I can't go that way!" I yelp. "Not unless you want me to cause a lot of property damage!"

"Don't damage the real house!" she snaps back. "But you can try to damage the magic house if you want. It'd be useful to see what happens."

I nod and flick a Spacial Rend active on my fingers, earning me a quiet 'woah' from the other side of the wall as a true void of location caresses and extends from the tips of my fingers. I carve into the magical wall, my spell cutting through it like it isn't even there... a bit more literally than I expected, since it straight up just doesn't interact with the magical house, almost like it really *isn't* there. But... it definitely is. I can't cross this barrier.

I gulp. Something about Spacial Rend not being able to cut it makes me really uncomfortable, for some reason. Spacial Rend has always been inviolable, utterly overwhelming in its capacity to cut *anything.* Even as someone who hates violence and fighting, that's always been a comfort to me. When I *do* fight, I know I'm the one bringing the sharpest knife. My Space magic has been all I ever needed to come out on top, but against Alma I'm completely impotent.

There's probably a lot of magic that counters mine, now that I think about it. I've just been arrogant and lucky. I lean against the wall, soaking in that frightening revelation when suddenly the magical room disappears, leaving me supported by nothing and sprawling face-first into the floor.

"Figured it out!" Alma calls out, and I hear the back door of the house opening as she lets herself in. "I had to find the exit to the magic house and leave. It disappeared when I did. I don't think it can exist if I'm not inside it."

"You have an *insane* spell there, Alma," I say, getting up off the ground and walking back into the living room to meet up with her. She stiffens a bit when I call her that, but she quickly relaxes.

"Yeah," she agrees. "It's pretty nuts. I'm already getting a ton of cool ideas on how to use it. I just need to see how well I can control the size and shape..."

"Just try not to get caught, okay?" I warn her. "We still don't know what happens *if* we get caught, and your spell is pretty huge."

"Yeah, I get it. Don't break the masquerade. Ugh, it's going to be a pain trying to focus on school with all this happening."

Yeah, welcome to my life. Also: holy crap, school! I totally forgot about school! I grab my phone and check the time, feeling despair take me as I see fifth period has already started. I'm going to miss two entire classes! My perfect attendance record! Noooo! What if they call my mom? No, no, that's crazy, there's no way the school will call my house for just two absences, right? Besides, it'll be too awkward to go back now. I still need to head to work, though.

"Welp, um, I guess it seems like you're doing pretty well then?" I hedge. "I hope I helped."

"You did, really," Alma nods. "Thank you, Hannah. You have to get going?"

"Yeah," I confirm. "Sorry."

"It's fine. Really," she says, smiling. "This was a bit more traumatizing than the magical fantasy awakening I always dreamed about, but I'm feeling a lot better thanks to you."

"Good," I smile. "Great. Talk to you tomorrow?"

"Talk to you tonight, maybe?" she hedges. "Over text, I mean. If I have something cool to say."

"Okay, but plausible deniability is the name of the game over anything a particularly unscrupulous version of the NSA could monitor," I warn her.

"So just... the regular NSA?" Alma asks.

610

"Yeah."

She lets out a small chuckle and waves goodbye, so I wave back and turn to depart, blushing so hard I might burst. This was fun. A lot more fun than I expected a call for help to be. Also I maybe have a girlfriend now aaaaaaaaaa!

I exit Autumn's house and find Ida sitting in her car tapping away on her phone, so I walk up to greet her.

"Hey, Ida! I'm ba—"

"**No Less Than Perfect**," the Goddess says with Ida's lips, and then I feel Her power wash over me, into me, *through* me, flowing and caressing every inch of chitin and skin, soothing all my aches, checking each and every wrinkle in my brain for something out of place. It's a borderline orgasmic experience, and by the end of it I'm left feeling like I just got out of a two-week healing spa resort trip. No, better than that. *Nothing* hurts anymore, not even the slightest discomfort exists in my body, no matter how small. I feel energized, but in a *healthy* way, like I've just woken up from the best sleep of my life rather than just downed more than the recommended daily amount of Red Bull.

I am *stunned* by the experience. I can't move or speak, only bask in how... how *perfect* I feel right now. And the frightening part about it is that the feeling isn't going *away.* My body will hurt again later, I know this. I'll get injured, wear and tear will accumulate, things will go wrong. But I have actually, physically been changed in such a way that at least for now? I don't have those problems.

"Hey, Hannah," Ida greets me, still looking at her phone. "So did I just wipe a bunch of mind control, or were you clean?"

"H... how?" I manage to breathe. "I thought... Ida, you weren't supposed to—"

"You said I shouldn't name a spell until I fully, completely, one hundred percent understand it," Ida says, cutting me off. "But I don't do anything less than a hundred percent. Of course I'm gonna get that shit first try."

She finally looks up from her phone and smirks at me.

"So?" she asks. "How was it?"

"I... indescribable," I manage, opening the passenger door and getting into her car. "Was that your *repair* spell? It's... it's insane."

"There are some major limitations, but nothing all that annoying," Ida shrugs. "You need to focus, though. Mind control?"

"Huh? Oh! No, I don't think so," I tell her, running back through my memories of Alma and I talking. "Yeah, I think we're good. Nothing jumps out as suspicious to me."

"Cool," Ida says, starting the car. "Well, now that we have this taken care of, you wanna hang out with me for a while?"

"Uh... I would, but I need to go to work," I admit.

"You are a half-bug woman with a taste for raw meat and a magic spell that mutates people," Ida says. "You really, *really* don't."

"I-I can just not cast that spell!" I protest. "Look, if I break any more from my routine now my mom will find out and everything will go to hell from there. Let's just drive around until school ends and then you can take me home."

She sighs, but she backs out of the driveway anyway.

"One of these days I *will* figure out how to seduce your stupid, dense ass," she grumbles.

Wait. S-seduce!? Wait, she's still... oh gosh, oh geez.

"I-I'd prefer you didn't!" I sputter. "I think Alma and I might be dating now?"

Ida gives me a suspicious side-eye, which is all the more uncomfortable given how fast she's currently driving while not looking at the road.

"You're going to date *Alma*," she says like she's talking to a particularly stupid child."The girl with the magical element that you're so traumatized by you nearly had a breakdown in the middle of her house."

612

"She... she makes like, soul houses with it, or something!" I protest. "She's not that kind of person!"

"Uh-huh," Ida grunts. "Have fun telling that to your panic attacks."

No, it's not... it's not like that! It'll be fine! I just won't think about it. Not thinking about trauma has always been my most reliable response to trauma. My phone buzzes, taking me away from my thoughts. See? Distractions are always the answer.

It's a text from my mom. My heart skips a beat, utter terror filling me at the prospect that yes, she must have been informed of my absence by the school. My life is over. Shakingly, I read the words.

**Your therapy appointment is this Saturday at 9:30am.**

Oh. Well. That's *much* worse.

# ABOUT THE AUTHOR

Natalie Maher writes books (but you knew that, you're reading one) and gets extremely awkward whenever she has to talk about herself (like right now, because "about the author" blurbs are traditionally written in third person but she has to write her own). She thinks that life is messy and likes it when fiction is even messier. She can be fairly easily reached via her Discord server, and if you're interested in advance updates, in-progress stories, or just giving her more money (please give her more money) she has a Patreon. Thank you for reading!

Made in United States
Troutdale, OR
12/10/2024

26284743R00345